NIGHTFALL

Also by Shannon Messenger

KEEPER
L⊛ST CITIES
NIGHTFALL

SHANNON MESSENGER

Aladdin

New York   London   Toronto   Sydney   New Delhi

ALADDIN

An imprint of Simon & Schuster Children's Publishing Division
1230 Avenue of the Americas, New York, NY 10020
First Aladdin paperback edition October 2018
Text copyright © 2017 by Shannon Messenger
Cover illustration copyright © 2017 by Jason Chan
Also available in an Aladdin hardcover edition.
All rights reserved, including the right of reproduction in whole or in part in any form.
ALADDIN and related logo are registered trademarks of Simon & Schuster, Inc.
For information about special discounts for bulk purchases, please contact Simon & Schuster Special Sales at 1-866-506-1949 or business@simonandschuster.com.
The Simon & Schuster Speakers Bureau can bring authors to your live event.
For more information or to book an event contact the Simon & Schuster Speakers Bureau at 1-866-248-3049 or visit our website at www.simonspeakers.com.
Cover designed by Karin Paprocki
Interior designed by Mike Rosamilia
The text of this book was set in Scala.
0818 OFF
2 4 6 8 10 9 7 5 3 1
The Library of Congress has cataloged the hardcover edition as follows:
Names: Messenger, Shannon, author.
Title: Nightfall / Shannon Messenger.
Description: First Aladdin hardcover edition. | New York : Aladdin, 2017. | Series: Keeper of the lost cities ; 6 | Summary: "Sophie must uncover the truth about the Lost Cities' insidious past, before it repeats itself and changes reality" —Provided by publisher.
Identifiers: LCCN 2017043779 (print) | LCCN 2017057266 (eBook) | ISBN 9781481497428 (eBook) | ISBN 9781481497404 (hardcover : alk. paper)
Subjects: | CYAC: Psychic ability—Fiction. | Memory—Fiction. | Elves—Fiction. | Friendship—Fiction. | Sisters—Fiction. | Adventure and adventurers—Fiction. | Fantasy. | BISAC: JUVENILE FICTION / Fantasy & Magic. | JUVENILE FICTION / Action & Adventure / General. | JUVENILE FICTION / Social Issues / Friendship.
Classification: LCC PZ7.M5494 (eBook) | LCC PZ7.M5494 Nig 2017 (print) | DDC [Fic]—dc23
LC record available at https://lccn.loc.gov/2017043779
ISBN 9781481497411 (pbk)

For Nadia and Roland,
best niece and nephew an aunt could ask for
(and not *just* because you're the only ones—
though that does help)

;)

PREFACE

SOPHIE STARED AT THE GLEAMING
trail that wound down. And down. And down.

Disappearing into the misty shadows far below.

The path of ancient silver and gold stones
shouldn't exist—and yet it had been there all along.

Hidden in plain sight.

Buried under lies.

Wiped from memory.

But never truly gone.

She glanced at her friends as they braced themselves for
the dangerous journey ahead, and found their expressions
mirroring her own.

Reluctant. Rattled. But also: *Ready.*

Whatever waited in those murky depths was far more than a secret.

It was an answer.

A *truth*.

And it was time to uncover it.

Time to stop believing the pretty stories they'd been fed all their lives.

Time to see their world for what it really was.

Time to take something back.

So together—as one—they locked hands and started the long, slippery descent.

Into the past.

Into darkness.

ONE

"YOU REMEMBER ME?"

The question slipped from Sophie's lips before she could stop it, and the weighted words seemed to hit the floor of the messy bedroom with a thud.

The wide-eyed, trembling girl standing in front of her slowly nodded, and Sophie's heart swelled even as it plummeted into the sour pit of her stomach.

Her little sister *shouldn't* remember her.

Technically, she wasn't even her sister—at least not genetically. Sure, they'd grown up together in the same house in San Diego, California, both believing they had the same parents—despite the fact that Sophie's blond hair and brown eyes didn't match her family of light-eyed brunettes.

But that was *before.*

Now they were in the *after.*

A world where elves were real creatures—and nothing like the silly stories that humans had invented about them. They were beautiful. Powerful. Practically immortal. Living across the globe in hidden glittering cities. Ruling the earth from the shadows.

And Sophie was one of them.

Born from humans—but *not* human—as part of a rebel group's secret genetic experiment called Project Moonlark. Her DNA had been tweaked. Her abilities enhanced and manipulated. All to mold her into something special.

Something powerful.

Something she still didn't fully understand.

And after years of feeling out of place—even among the family she loved—the elves finally showed Sophie the truth about her life and brought her to the Lost Cities. They'd planned to fake her death to cover her disappearance, but she'd begged to be erased instead, to spare her parents the grief of losing a child. So her family's minds had been "washed" by specially trained Telepaths, to make them forget that Sophie had ever been born. And they'd been relocated to a new city and given new names, new jobs, even the fancy new Tudor-style house that Sophie now stood in, with its quaint windows and wood-paneled walls.

But erased memories were never *truly* gone. All it took was the right trigger and . . .

"I don't understand," her sister whispered, rubbing her eyes like it would change what she was seeing. "You . . . shouldn't be here."

Major understatement.

Sophie wasn't supposed to know her family's new names or where they lived—and she definitely hadn't been allowed to visit them—to ensure that something like this *never* happened. And yet, here she was, raising a mental shield to block her sister's chaotic thoughts as they pounded through her consciousness like stampeding mastodons. Human minds were more open than elvin minds, and they broadcast everything like a radio station on full blast.

"Listen, Amy—"

"That's not my name!"

Sophie kicked herself for the slip. "Right, I meant—"

"Wait." Her sister mouthed the name a few more times, as if her lips were remembering the feel of it. "It is, isn't it? I'm . . . Amy Foster?"

Sophie nodded.

"Then who's Natalie Freeman?"

"That's . . . also you."

Amy—Natalie—whatever Sophie was supposed to call her—groaned and pressed her fingers against her temples.

"I know how confusing this must be," Sophie told her. Triggered memories tended to flash back in scattered bits and pieces, leaving lots of holes. "I promise I'll explain, but—"

"Not right now," a crisply accented voice finished for her.

Sophie flinched. She'd almost forgotten they had an audience for the Most Stressful Family Reunion in the History of Family Reunions.

"Who are you?" her sister asked, backing away from the guys standing slightly behind Sophie.

"That's Fitz," Sophie said, pointing to a dark-haired boy whose teal eyes flashed as he offered a smile that would put any movie star to shame. "And that's Keefe."

Keefe gave her sister his famous smirk, reaching up to smooth his expertly tousled blond hair. "Don't worry—we're all in the Foster Fan Club."

"They're my friends," Sophie clarified when her sister shrank back another step. "You can trust them."

"I don't even know if I can trust *you*." Her eyes narrowed at Sophie's outfit: a fitted purple tunic with black leggings, boots, and wrist-length black gloves. Fitz and Keefe also wore tunics and pants, and while none of the outfits were *that* elf-y, they definitely stood out next to her sister's jeans and TARDIS T-shirt.

"You trusted us enough to stop hiding, right?" Keefe asked, pointing to the still-open closet door.

Sophie's sister turned toward the dark nook she'd emerged from, where most of the clothes had been heaped into a pile on the floor. "I only came out because I heard you guys say you'd get my parents back."

And there it was. The reason Sophie had broken all the rules and raced to the Forbidden Cities to check on her family. She'd spent months protecting her adoptive elvin parents, believing they were the ones that Keefe had warned her were in danger. But they'd both forgotten she had another family to worry about—a family without powerful abilities and bodyguards to keep them safe.

"Can you really find Mom and Dad?" her sister whispered, giving Sophie the cue to tell her, "Of course we will! Everything is going to be okay!"

Sophie wanted to. But . . . the Neverseen were behind this.

The same villains who'd kidnapped Sophie, tortured her, and killed people she dearly loved. And no matter how hard Sophie fought to stop them, they always seemed to be ten steps ahead.

Keefe reached for Sophie's shaky hand. "We'll get them back safe. I *promise*."

His tone was pure determination. But Sophie could see a shadow darkening his ice-blue eyes.

Guilt.

A few months earlier, Keefe had run away to join the Neverseen, planning to be a double agent and destroy the wicked organization from the inside out—but they'd played him the whole time, tricking him into leading Sophie and her friends down the wrong paths.

Part of Sophie wanted to shove Keefe away, let him shoulder the blame for every terrible thing that had happened. But deep down she knew he wasn't the only one who'd missed the warning signs. He'd also been working every day to make up for his mistakes. Plus, it was dangerous to let him feel guilty. The elvin conscience was too fragile for that kind of burden.

So Sophie squeezed his hand, twining their fingers together as she turned back to her sister. "It'll help if you tell us everything you can about the people who took Mom and Dad."

Her sister wrapped her arms around her stomach, which wasn't as plump as Sophie remembered. She looked taller now too. And her curly brown hair was cut shorter. In fact, everything about her seemed so much older than the hyper nine-year-old she'd been when Sophie had left—and it hadn't even been two full years.

"I don't remember much," her sister mumbled. "Dad was helping me with my homework when we heard strange voices downstairs. He told me to stay quiet while he went to see what was going on, but I snuck out to the landing and . . ." She swallowed hard. "I saw four people in the living room wearing long black cloaks with these creepy white eyes on their sleeves. Mom was passed out over one of their shoulders, and another had a cloth pressed over Dad's mouth. I wanted to run down and help—but there were so many of them. And Dad stopped moving a couple of seconds later. I tried to crawl to a phone to call the police, but then I heard them say something about searching the rest of the house, so I ducked into the nearest closet and buried myself in clothes."

Sophie shuddered as she imagined it, and her nose burned with a sweet scent, remembering the smell of the cloying drugs the Neverseen favored during their abductions. "Did you see any of their faces?"

"They had their hoods up the whole time. But one of them . . ."

"One of them what?" Sophie pressed.

"You're not going to believe me."

"Try us," Keefe said. "You'd be surprised what we can believe after hanging around this one."

He elbowed Sophie gently in the ribs, and Sophie knew he was trying to break the tension. Humor was Keefe's favorite coping mechanism.

But she didn't have the energy to joke around. Especially when her sister whispered, "One of the guys kept disappearing somehow. Like with quick flashes, fading in and out of sight."

Fitz muttered something under his breath. "That was Alvar."

"You know him?"

"He's done a lot of awful things," Sophie jumped in, shooting Fitz a please-don't-say-he's-your-brother look. She doubted it would help her sister trust them.

"How did he disappear like that?" her sister whispered. "It almost looked like . . ."

"Magic?" Sophie guessed with a sad smile. "I remember thinking that too, the first time I saw it. But he's what we call a Vanisher. All he's doing is manipulating light."

"What about the mind reading thing?" her sister asked.

"One of them said he was listening for nearby thoughts as he searched the house, so I thought about darkness and silence just in case."

"That was really smart," Sophie told her, stunned she had managed to pull that off.

Her sister shrugged. "I've seen a lot of movies. But . . . could he really do that?"

"If he was a Telepath," Fitz said. "Which means it was probably Gethen."

The name sent Sophie spiraling into nightmares of crumbling castle walls and jagged mazes of rubble. Screams echoed in her ears as the world turned red—partially with her rage, but mostly with the memory of a wound that cut too deep for her to stop the bleeding.

A slow breath cleared her head, and Sophie concentrated on her churning emotions, imagining her anger, fear, and grief as thick threads before tying them into a knot under her ribs. She'd learned the technique from her inflicting mentor, a way of storing the power as a reserve. Embracing the darkness to let it fuel her later.

"Are you okay?" Keefe asked, tightening his hold on her hand.

It took Sophie a second to realize he was *also* talking to her sister, who'd turned so pale her skin had a greenish sheen.

"None of this should be real," her sister whispered. "These things you're telling me. These weird names you keep saying. Mom and Dad being taken. And then you show up out of nowhere and it feels like . . . like you should've been here this whole time. And now my name feels wrong. And this house feels wrong. *Everything* feels wrong."

Sophie hesitated before moving to her sister's side and wrapping an arm around her shoulders. They hadn't been touchy-feely sisters back when they'd lived together. In fact, they'd spent most of their time bickering.

But after a second, her sister hugged her back.

"Where have you been, Sophie? And how do you know these scary people?"

Sophie sighed. "There's a really long, really complicated story I need to tell you. But right now, we need to stay focused on finding Mom and Dad, okay? Did you hear anything else that might be useful?"

"Just the part I already told you, about taking them to Nightfall. Do you know what that means?"

Sophie glanced at Fitz and Keefe.

They'd only seen the word once, in one of Keefe's recently recovered memories—an inscription carved in elvin runes across a mysterious silver door set into a mountain:

The star only rises at Nightfall.

They didn't know what the phrase meant, or where the door led, or even precisely where the door was. But they knew it unlocked with Keefe's blood, and that his mom—who'd been one of the leaders of the Neverseen before getting trapped in an ogre prison—had declared it to be his "legacy."

If that door leads to Nightfall, Sophie transmitted to Keefe, sending her thoughts directly into his head, *wouldn't the Neverseen need to have you with them in order to get inside?*

Keefe focused on the floor. *They would, if they didn't already have some of my blood.*

WHAT?

Yeah . . . not-so-funny story: I traded some for part of the secret I needed to steal the caches.

ARE YOU KIDDING ME?

Caches were marble-size gadgets the Councillors used to store Forgotten Secrets—information deemed too dangerous for anyone to keep in their memory. Councillor Kenric had given Sophie his when he died—and Keefe had stolen it from her to buy his way into the Neverseen. But he got it back before he fled—and he also took the cache that belonged to Fintan, their leader. Dex was now trying to use his ability as a Technopath to hack into the gadgets. But even if they learned something important, Sophie *never* would've told Keefe to trade his blood for the caches.

I know, Keefe told her. *It wasn't my most brilliant idea. I thought I was so close to taking the Neverseen down that it wasn't going to matter. So, when Fintan asked for my blood, I told him he needed to prove that I could trust him by answering one question. And once he did, I had to hold up my end of the deal.*

But I thought you were going to trade Tam's leaping crystal for that information, Sophie reminded him. *Wasn't that why you left me stranded in one of the Neverseen's hideouts?*

Keefe cringed.

Of all the mistakes he'd made during his time with the Neverseen, that one had been the hardest for Sophie to forgive.

That was my plan, Keefe admitted. *But Fintan interrogated me when I got back, and I had to use the crystal to convince him not to burn off my arm.*

Ice rippled through Sophie's veins. *You never told me that part.*

I know.

His shadowed eyes made her wonder what other nightmares he'd secretly endured. But she'd have to save those worries for another time. At the moment, they had much more complicated problems.

Do you really think Fintan would help you steal the caches if they're actually important?

Yeah, Foster. I do. Because he had no idea that he gave me the other piece of the code phrase weeks earlier, after he had too much fizzleberry wine. Trading my blood was a bad call. But I SWEAR the caches are still a score. And I should've told you—I was planning on it, and then everything happened in Lumenaria and I forgot.

Sophie closed her eyes, wishing she could stop her mind from flashing to crumbling walls. But the memories refused to be ignored.

In one night, the Neverseen had destroyed the elves' magnificent glowing castle while Sophie, the Council, and the leaders of all the intelligent species were inside for the ogre Peace Summit. Most of the leaders made it out with only minor injuries—and Lumenaria was already being rebuilt. But nothing could erase the message the Neverseen sent that day, or bring back the prisoner that had escaped from the dungeon, or the lives that had been stolen away.

I'll fix this, okay? Keefe promised. *I'm going to fix everything.*

You mean "we," Sophie corrected. *WE are going to fix this.*

If they'd learned one thing from all the disasters over the last few months, it was that none of them should be working alone. It was going to take *all* of their abilities, all of their ideas—and a scary amount of luck—to get through whatever this was.

Does that mean you don't hate me? Keefe asked. His mental tone sounded softer—almost timid.

I told you, I'm never going to hate you, Keefe.

But I keep giving you new reasons to change your mind.

Yeah, you really need to stop that. She offered him half a smile, and he gave her the same when she added, *But we're in this together.*

Team Foster-Keefe IS pretty awesome.

And Team Vacker-Foster-Keefe is even better, Fitz transmitted, making Sophie wonder how long he'd been eavesdropping.

Fitz was one of the only Telepaths who knew how to slip past Sophie's impenetrable mental blocking. Actually, he was the *only* one, now that Mr. Forkle was . . .

Sophie shut down the devastating thought, not ready to tear open the still-too-fresh wound.

Don't worry, she told Fitz. *We're going to need all the help we can get.*

Though we need a WAY cooler name, Keefe jumped in. *How about Team Foster-Keefe and the Wonderboy?*

Fitz rolled his eyes.

"Why are you guys staring at each other like that?" her sister asked, reminding them they had someone watching their rather lengthy mental exchange.

"We're just trying to figure out where Nightfall could be," Sophie told her.

She'd have to reveal her telepathy eventually—as well as her other special abilities—but she wanted to give her sister more time to adjust before she dropped the *I can read minds and teleport and inflict pain and speak any language and enhance other people's powers* bombshells. "Can you think of anything else that might be important?"

"Not really. After they said the thing about Nightfall, the house got super quiet. I waited another couple of minutes to make sure it was safe, and then I ran for Mom's phone and called 911. I was scared the police would take me if they knew I was here alone, so I said I was walking by the house and saw men dragging two people away. I hid in the trees when the cops showed up—but maybe that was a bad idea. I heard them say they thought my call was a prank, since there were no signs of robbery. One of them said something about following up in a few days, but so far, I haven't seen them."

"How long ago was that?" Fitz asked.

Her chin wobbled. "Five days."

Keefe looked like he was trying hard not to swear. Sophie felt like doing the same—or punching the walls and screaming as loud as she could.

"You don't think it's too late, do you?" her sister whispered. "You don't think they're . . . ?"

"No." Sophie let the word echo around her mind until she believed it. "The Neverseen need them alive."

"Who are the Neverseen?" her sister asked. "What do they want with Mom and Dad?"

"I wish I knew," Sophie admitted. "But they won't kill them."

At least not yet.

The Neverseen had been trying to control Sophie since they'd first learned she existed, so she was sure they'd use her parents as the worst sort of blackmail. But there had to be more to it. Otherwise they would've let her know the second they had their prisoners.

At least the Neverseen didn't know her sister heard them say they were going to Nightfall. All they had to do was find that door—and Sophie was pretty sure she knew how to do that.

She just wished it didn't involve trusting one of their enemies.

"I know what you're thinking," Keefe told her. "And I'm in. All the way."

"Let's not get ahead of ourselves," Fitz said, pointing toward the windows, where the sky was fading to twilight. "First, we need to get out of here. They probably have someone watching this place, waiting for us to show up."

Sophie nodded to her sister. "Go pack a bag as quick as you can. You're coming with me."

"Uh, that's *way* too dangerous," Fitz warned. "If the Council found out—"

"They *won't*," Sophie interrupted. "As soon as we get back, I'll hail the Collective."

The Black Swan—the rebel organization that created Sophie—had an extensive network of secret hideouts. And they'd always come through when Sophie needed their help.

Then again, that was before Mr. Forkle was . . .

This time, she couldn't stop her brain from finishing the sentence with "murdered."

She pressed her palm over her chest, feeling for the new locket under her tunic, which held the last task Mr. Forkle had entrusted her with before he took his final breaths.

When an elf passed away, they coiled their DNA around a Wanderling seed and planted it in a special forest. But Mr. Forkle had asked Sophie to hold on to his seed, claiming she'd somehow *know* when and where to do the planting. He'd also asked that his body be removed from the rubble before anyone saw it, which meant only a handful of people knew he'd been killed. But the rest of their world would find out soon enough. The Council had extended Foxfire's midterm break in light of the tragedy in Lumenaria—but school was scheduled to restart in less than two weeks. And one of Mr. Forkle's secret alter egos had been principal of the academy.

Keefe moved closer, leaning in to whisper, "I'll take care of your sister, Foster. The place I'm crashing in is small—and it smells like sasquatch breath mixed with rotting toenails. But I guarantee no one will find us."

Keefe had been living on the run ever since he'd fled the Neverseen—and his offer wasn't a horrible suggestion. But Sophie wasn't letting her sister out of her sight.

"She's coming with me to Havenfield. We'll figure out the rest once we get there."

"Uh, I'm not going anywhere with a bunch of strangers," her sister informed them.

The last word stung more than Sophie wanted to admit, but she did her best to shrug it off. "Do you really think you're safe here? Even if the Neverseen don't come back, the police might. Do you want to end up in foster care?"

Her sister bit her lip, leaving indentations in the soft flesh. "What about Marty and Watson? Who's going to feed them?"

Sophie's eyes prickled. "You still have Marty?"

The fluffy gray cat used to sleep on her pillow every night, and it had broken her heart to leave him behind. But she'd figured her family would need him. And Watson must've been the dog she'd heard barking when they'd first arrived. Sophie had asked the elves to move her family somewhere with a yard big enough to allow them to finally get the puppy her sister had always wanted.

"I guess we'll bring them with us," Sophie decided. "Get Watson on a leash and put Marty in his carrier."

"Okay, seriously, we can't do this," Fitz said, reaching for Sophie's hands to force her to listen to him. "You don't understand how dangerous this is."

"It'll be fine," Sophie insisted. "The Black Swan will keep her hidden."

"The Black Swan," her sister whispered. "Wait. I think . . . I think they said something about that. Everything was happening so fast, it's hard to remember. But I think one of them said, 'Let's figure out why the Black Swan chose them.'"

Sophie shared another look with her friends.

"I take it you guys know what that means?" her sister asked.

"It . . . might be about me," Sophie said. "It's part of that long story I have to tell you—but we should get out of here first."

She tried to reach for her home crystal, but Fitz wouldn't let go of her hands.

"You're not understanding what I'm saying," he told her. "Do you have any idea how risky it is to light leap with a human?"

He'd kept his voice low, but her sister still snapped, "What do you mean *a human?*"

"Exactly what you think he means," a slightly deeper, even crisper voice said from the doorway.

Everyone whipped around to find the three others who'd insisted on joining Sophie, Keefe, and Fitz on this hastily planned—and highly illegal—excursion to the Forbidden Cities. Fitz's father, Alden, who looked like an older, more regal version of his son. And Sandor and Grizel, who instantly triggered a massive amount of screaming.

"It's okay," Sophie promised. "They're our bodyguards."

That only seemed to make her sister scream louder.

To be fair, both Sandor and Grizel were seven feet tall and gray, with flat noses and massive amounts of rock-hard muscle—plus gigantic black swords strapped at their sides.

"Wh-what are th-they?" her sister stammered.

"Goblins," Sandor said in his unexpectedly high-pitched, squeaky voice.

"And we mean you no harm," Grizel added in her huskier tone.

A hysterical laugh burbled from her sister's lips. "Goblins. Like from the bank in Harry Potter?"

Fitz grinned. "She sounds like Sophie did when I first told her she was an elf."

The word triggered another round of hysterical laughter.

"Okay, so two things," Keefe jumped in. "One: How is she understanding us? I just realized we've all been speaking the Enlightened Language, and she has too."

"I gave her—and her parents—a basic understanding of our language before we relocated them," Alden explained. "In case something like this ever happened. Communication can be a powerful weapon, and an essential defense."

"What is he talking about?" her sister shouted. *"WHAT DID YOU DO TO MY BRAIN?"*

"That's the second thing," Keefe said, fanning his arm the way he always did when he was reading emotions through the air. "I'm betting your sister is about three minutes away from a meltdown of epic proportions."

"I'd wager it'll be sooner than that," Alden said through a sigh. "This is exactly the kind of worst-case scenario I hoped we'd never have to face. Fortunately, I came prepared."

"What are you doing?" Sophie asked, yanking her hands free from Fitz as Alden reached into the inner pocket of his long blue cape. She'd been afraid he'd pull out a vial of sedatives. But the round silver disk he tossed at her feet was much more terrifying.

Sophie had used the same gadget the day she'd drugged her family so the elves could erase her. And as the world spun to a blur, she realized she should've held her breath the second the disk hit the floor.

"Please," she begged when her sister collapsed. "She's going to need me. You can't erase me from her life again."

Keefe lunged to help Sophie, but only lasted a second before he went down. Fitz followed a second after that.

Sophie's knees gave out, but she crawled for her sister, pleading with Alden to change his plan. He'd always been so kind to her—a loyal, trustworthy advisor. Almost a father figure. But his face was sad and serious as he released the breath he'd been holding. "Don't fight the sedatives, Sophie. You can't beat them."

He said something else, but she couldn't understand him. Her ears were ringing, and the light kept dimming.

She hated this feeling—hated Alden for putting her through it. But she couldn't focus enough to rally any of her defenses.

"Please," she said again as her face sank against the carpet. "Please don't take my sister away from me. Not again."

Through her hazy eyes she saw Alden crouch beside her, his lips mouthing, *I'm sorry.*

Then darkness swallowed everything.

TWO

AKE UP, SOPHIE."

The words floated around her mind, starting out muffled and growing louder and louder. Sophie wanted to shove the voice away—wanted to curl up within herself and never be dragged back to face whatever reality was waiting for her. But then the voice added, "There's no reason to worry," and she rushed back to consciousness in a wave of fury.

She only knew one person who used that expression. The same person she wanted to punch as hard as she could—which was pretty darn hard, thanks to the Sucker Punch gadget clamped around her wrist.

A pale blue glow stung her corneas as she ripped open

her eyes and found herself in a dimly lit sitting room filled with fancy furniture that was so pristine, it looked like it had never been used. Alden sat across from her in a plush silver armchair, and his hair and clothes were uncharacteristically disheveled.

"Where's my sister?" Her head felt like a T. rex had been chewing on it, and her mouth might as well have been covered in fur.

"Sleeping peacefully in the next room," Alden promised. "Grizel brought Fitz and Keefe back to Everglen. And Sandor— of course—insisted on staying by your side."

Sandor nodded from the shadows in the corner.

"As for your sister's pets," Alden added, holding up his arms to show her the shredded sleeves of his tunic. "We brought them with us—though they were *not* happy about it."

"At least they could put up a fight," Sophie muttered.

"I thought that might be your response. So let me assure you that your sister's memories have not been altered."

She waited for him to say, *yet*. When he didn't, she relaxed her grip, realizing she'd been squeezing a velvet cushion from the long black sofa she lay stretched out on.

Alden handed her a bottle of Youth—the special water that elves drank for its unique enzymes. "You must be thirsty."

"Yeah, that happens when someone drugs you."

She was tempted to dump the bottle over his head. But her throat felt like it had been lined with crumpled paper, so she sat up and chugged a huge gulp, letting the cool sweetness clear her foggy mind.

"I know you're angry," Alden said, "and you have every right to be. But your sister was seconds away from a breakdown, and it would've been impossible to leap her in such a frantic state. Fitz wasn't exaggerating when he said that light leaping with humans is risky—even under ideal circumstances. Not only is their concentration weak, but they tend to panic as their bodies split apart and their instincts tell them to fight our assistance. So given her hysteria, the only way to move her safely was to render her unconscious."

"That doesn't explain why you drugged *me*," she argued.

Alden leaned back in his chair. "Tell me this: Do you think your sister would've ever willingly taken a sedative?"

"Probably not."

"I agree. And who do you think she'll be more likely to forgive after being sedated without her permission? A sister who was drugged right along with her? Or a sister who stood by and let it happen?"

Sophie *really* hated that he'd made a good point.

"And what happens now?" she asked, studying the dim room again. Most of the elvin houses she'd seen were bright and airy, with tons of windows and chandeliers. But the only light came from a single sconce set onto the crystal wall, flickering with a small flame of blue balefire.

"Now we wait for your sister to wake up—which should be

soon—and then you'll explain all the arrangements I've made. It took me most of the night to get everything settled."

"Wait—how long was I unconscious?"

"A little more than fourteen hours."

FOURTEEN HOURS?!

"Don't worry," Sandor said from the corner. "I let Grady and Edaline know you're safe and that I'll be bringing you home later."

"Thank you," Sophie told him, glad to hear her adoptive parents weren't worrying. "But why didn't someone wake me up sooner? I could've—"

"Done what, exactly?" Alden interrupted. "Contacted Keefe's mother?"

Sophie refused to flinch, even if she was surprised that he'd guessed her plan. "Lady Gisela's the only one who knows where Nightfall is."

"Indeed. And I believe she warned you that the next time you contacted her, you needed to use her son's blood."

Keefe's mom had altered his Imparter, adding a listening device and a special sensor that accessed a secret channel when smeared with Keefe's blood. Dex had bypassed the blood sensor once, but Keefe's mom had made it clear during their brief conversation that she wouldn't answer again unless they reached out the creepy way.

"I have no doubt that Keefe will do *anything* to help," Alden continued. "But that request does not bode well for what her assistance will cost. Let's also not forget that there's a good chance the abduction of your family was part of her original plan."

"I know," Sophie mumbled, choking down the sourness in her throat. "I'm still figuring out what to do about all of that. Maybe I would've made more progress if I'd been able to talk to my friends, instead of being drugged for the last *fourteen hours!*"

Alden fidgeted with his shredded sleeves. "I truly am sorry for the lost time. But I didn't want to wake you until I had your sister settled. I know you wanted to hide her with the Black Swan, since you've grown to rely on their order—"

"I'm *part* of their order," Sophie corrected, holding up the swan-neck monocle she'd earned when she swore fealty several months earlier. "So are your son and daughter. And your wife."

"Which makes me very proud of my family," Alden said. "But it doesn't change the fact that the Black Swan is in turmoil. After losing Mr. Forkle"—he paused, as if mentioning the name merited a moment of silence—"the remaining Collective members need time to put into practice whatever contingency plan he mentioned. I reached out to Tiergan tonight, and he assured me that the Black Swan will work tirelessly to help you find your human parents. But he also agreed that the order is currently incapable of providing any sort of stable home."

"If Tiergan doesn't think my sister should stay with the Black Swan, I wouldn't have argued."

"And what about when I tell you that the only reasonable alternative is to place her somewhere that will be very difficult for you to visit?"

He pointed to the crystal set into an etched silver loop in Sophie's choker-style necklace—an elvin registry pendant, which tracked and recorded her every move. "The Black Swan's Technopath has scrambled our signals for the next few hours. But we can only pull that trick so many times, and this apartment is an *incredibly* valuable secret. Tremendous lengths were taken to keep this fifty-first floor concealed—and how long do you think it would take before the Council came to investigate why you've been frequenting this building?"

"If you think I'm going to leave my sister alone—"

"Of course not," Alden interrupted. "I've arranged for her to live with guardians—*temporary* guardians," he clarified when Sophie cringed. "None of these arrangements are meant to be permanent. I'm simply trying to create a safe, stable environment for your sister until we reunite her with her parents."

"And then what happens?" Sophie had to ask. "Are you going to wash their minds again?"

"I haven't planned that far ahead. And neither should you." He reached for her hand. "I know how painful it was for you to let yourself be erased last time, so I understand why you don't want to live through that again. But—"

"This isn't just about me," she jumped in, pausing to chase down the words to explain what she was slowly realizing. "My family is a part of this—whether we want them to be or not. And I think they need to *know* that. Maybe they would've done something differently when they heard the Neverseen in their house if they'd known that someone might come after them. Think about it. My sister found a way to keep her thoughts quiet enough that Gethen couldn't find her—and the only reason she was able to do that is because you gave her a way to understand what they were saying."

"Yes, but allowing them to have a subconscious knowledge of our language is a very different thing than leaving them consciously aware of our world. Do you really think they could keep that kind of secret and go about life as normal? Or that they'd be okay with the fact that someone else has adopted their daughter?"

"I don't know," Sophie admitted, hating how complicated the whole mess was. "But erasing their minds doesn't feel like the right answer anymore."

Alden leaned back in his chair. "No. I suppose it doesn't. But this isn't the time for us to be figuring these things out. Right now there's an eleven-year-old girl in the next room who's just discovered that everything she knew about the world is wrong. You remember how that feels—and you didn't have the added trauma of watching your parents be abducted. She needs someone to help her understand what's happening. And I need you to convince her that this apartment is the perfect place for her to be—because it is. Tell her you'll visit when you can, but that you'll also be busy working to find her parents and bring them back to her safely."

"You really think she's going to agree to sit around while I hunt for my family?"

"She won't have a choice, given the limitations of her species. And do you honestly want her in that kind of danger?"

No.

Especially if Keefe's mom was involved.

"Perhaps if you help your sister to understand exactly how vicious the Neverseen can be, she'll be grateful for the safe hiding place," Alden suggested.

"Right, because hearing that the people you love are in danger *always* makes you want to do nothing."

Alden sighed. "I never said this would be easy. But I have the utmost confidence that you'll find a way to convince her. Please, Sophie," he added when she opened her mouth to argue. "I know you've gotten out of the habit of turning to me for help. But you used to trust me to handle things like this. I put a *lot* of thought into the best solution for both you and your sister. She cannot light leap safely. Cannot defend herself. Cannot even fully grasp the intricacies of our daily lives—not to mention that her very presence in our world is illegal. All she'll do is slow you down, limit where you can go and how you can travel, and give you one more—very vulnerable—person to protect. And your time is already going to be strained between school and—"

"School?" Sophie interrupted. "You think we won't have this settled before school starts?"

"I . . . think it's wise to prepare for the long term—just in case."

She wrapped her arms around her stomach to fight the rush of nausea. "I'm not going back to Foxfire while my family's missing."

"I think that would be a mistake. Your education has been interfered with enough, between your banishment and this midterm break extension—not to mention all the time you've missed in order to recover from your various injuries. And Foxfire is going to be on an accelerated curriculum when it resumes, so each day will be even more crucial. I promise, while you're at school, others—including myself—will be hard at work looking for your family, or doing whatever else needs to be done to resist the Neverseen. That's the advantage to being part of an order. Everyone in the Black Swan has other facets to their lives, and they trust others in the organization to take up the reins while they tend to them. You and your friends are no different. But let's not argue about it until we're to that point—*if* we get to that point, okay? Can we agree that in the meantime, the responsible thing to do is to keep your sister *here*, where she'll be safe, hidden, and cared for?"

Once again, he'd made a bunch of annoyingly valid points.

And there had to be ways to visit her sister more often than he was saying. Maybe she could—

"I see those mental wheels still spinning," Alden interrupted. "And if you find an alternative solution, I'm open to suggestions. But for now, our focus needs to be on convincing your sister that as long as she stays here, everything is going to be okay."

"But what if it isn't? What if my parents . . . ?"

She couldn't say the rest.

Alden leaned closer, tucking a strand of her hair behind her ear. "We both know I can't promise that there won't be challenges ahead. But I *can* promise that whatever happens, you're strong enough to handle it."

Sophie knew he meant the speech to reassure her. And it did help a little. Except . . .

"Sometimes I get sick of being strong."

"I don't blame you. You've endured more in these last few years than most of the Ancients have in their long lives. And it's forced you to grow up far too soon and shoulder responsibilities no one your age should ever need to bear. I can't tell you to keep fighting, but . . . the only alternative is giving up, and—"

"And then they win." Sophie finished for him.

She stared at the swan's neck curving around her monocle and reminded herself of the oath she'd sworn in order to earn it.

I will do everything in my power to help my world.

"Where exactly are we?" she asked, switching to a subject that didn't make breathing feel impossible.

"Of all the places you can think of, where would be the most naturally suited to house a human? Hint: It's also in a city that the Council rarely visits because it's such a tedious process to access."

"You brought us to Atlantis?"

"Yes—and the cat did *not* enjoy the journey."

Sophie had to smile at that, imagining Alden holding Marty's thrashing body while sliding down a gigantic whirlpool to the bottom of the ocean. No wonder his sleeves were shredded!

The elves had originally built Atlantis to serve as the union between the elvin and human worlds—a place where both species could live together and learn from one another. But several thousand years ago, the humans started planning a war to take over, and the Ancient elvin Council decided the smartest solution would be to disappear. So, they sank the city with a massive tidal wave and shielded it inside a dome of air, letting it thrive in secret under the water while humans forgot that elves were real.

"You really think it's a good idea to hide my sister in the middle of a city?" Sophie asked, remembering the crowded streets and bustling canals she'd seen during her visits.

"So long as she remains here, no one will be able to find her."

Sophie stared at the windowless walls again. They were

shimmery and smooth and actually quite pretty. But the room still felt like a prison.

"It's a big apartment," Alden promised. "And it's filled with all kinds of luxuries to keep her as comfortable as possible. I also took the liberty of packing some of her human things before I brought her here."

"But what is she going to do all day?"

"Whatever she wishes. She'll have her guardians. And her pets. And she'll have an Imparter, so that you can check in with each other whenever you want. I've also arranged to bring in a supply of books and games to entertain her. And Quinlin and Livvy have been working on a schedule to educate her about the complicated history between elves and humans."

Fun as *that* sounded . . .

Sophie was about to voice the complaint when she recognized one of the names.

"Quinlin Sonden? The Telepath you brought me to see in Atlantis the day I moved to the Lost Cities?"

Alden nodded. "This is technically his apartment, though his official address lists him as living on the fiftieth floor. He built this place—as well as the restricted level you might remember seeing at his office—so he could better assist me with projects that needed to be kept away from prying eyes. No one will protect your sister as faithfully as Quinlin will. And his role as Chief Mentalist will also allow him to watch the Council for signs that they might suspect something."

"But what if my sister feels weird living with some strange guy she's never met? Especially since I don't remember Quinlin being very . . . cuddly."

Gleeful laughter rang out behind her, and Sophie turned to find an elegant black female standing in the narrow arched doorway, clutching her sides as she cracked up. She needed several gasping breaths before her voice was working well enough to say, "No, that's definitely not a word I'd use to describe my husband."

"You mean *ex*-husband, don't you, Livvy?" a sharp voice corrected from the hall.

Livvy's smile faded as she stepped aside to let Quinlin stride into the room. He looked exactly as Sophie remembered him—dark skin, shoulder length black hair, and sharp features to match his expression. Still insanely handsome—as all elves were. But everything about him seemed *serious.*

"Actually, I never made the 'ex' official," Livvy retorted, tossing several of the tiny braids woven throughout her hair. "I didn't feel like dealing with the drama. So unless you decided to file the match-fail on your own, you're still legally stuck with me."

It sounded like they were talking about divorce—which Sophie didn't realize existed in the Lost Cities. The elves relied on an incredibly strict matchmaking system, where any couples that disobeyed were branded a "bad match" and faced scorn for the rest of their lives—and so did their children. It was one of the few ways that the elves were deeply prejudiced. They didn't care about wealth or skin color. But bad matches—and the Talentless—were considered a disgrace, despite how unfair and arbitrary the distinctions were.

Quinlin let out the kind of sigh that made his whole body droop as he turned to Alden. "I still think it's a mistake to involve Livvy. I can handle this—"

"Well now, what was that? Thirty seconds?" Livvy interrupted. "That's all it took to get to, *I can do everything myself?* And the mystery of why I left is *solved!*"

"And *you* barely made it thirty seconds before picking a fight," Quinlin snapped back. "Now you know why I never chased after you."

Livvy's eyes narrowed. "If I'd *wanted* to be chased, you can bet you'd be begging at my heels."

Alden cleared his throat. "Perhaps we should save this conversation for when you two are alone?"

"We *won't* be alone," Livvy informed him. "I'll be living up here and he'll be living downstairs and the only time we'll be together is when we're with the girl."

"She has a name," Sophie said, even though she wasn't sure if her sister wanted to be called Natalie or Amy. "And is this what it's going to be like for her? Being trapped in this apartment listening to you guys snipe at each other all the time?"

"No," Alden, Quinlin, and Livvy all promised as one.

"I'm sorry," Livvy added. "It's strange being back after so

many years. But Quinlin and I have lots of practice at pretending things between us are normal."

"And . . . I suppose Livvy will make your sister feel much more at home than I can," Quinlin said quietly. "She'll also be able to keep her company when I have to work."

"And vice versa," Livvy added. "Though I'll be doing most of my work here. I'm planning to do a full detox on your sister to rid her body of all those human chemicals. And I'll give her a thorough checkup as well."

"Are you a physician?" Sophie asked, remembering how Elwin had done similar things to her when she first moved to the Lost Cities. And something about Livvy's answering smile set her mind itching.

The connection finally clicked when Livvy tossed her braids again, revealing tiny blue jewels twinkling among the tight weave. Sophie sucked in a breath. "You're Physic!"

THREE

I'D WONDERED HOW LONG IT WOULD TAKE
you to put it together," Livvy—Physic—said as she patted
Sophie on the head. "Though, to be fair, my disguise was
pretty minimal."

Physic was known for wearing colorful Mardi Gras–style
masks that only covered the top of her face—way easier to
see past than the bizarre full-body camouflage the rest of the
Black Swan hid behind. And yet, as Sophie studied Livvy's
full lips and softly rounded nose, she doubted she would've
recognized her if it hadn't been for the way she kept tossing
her sparkly braided hair.

"Wait," Quinlin interrupted. "Who's Physic?"

"I believe she's the Physician who works with the Black

Swan," Alden said, studying Livvy from a different angle.

Quinlin went very still. "*You're* with the Black Swan?"

Sophie couldn't tell if Livvy looked nervous or proud as she told him, "Surprise?"

Silence followed, stretching so long that it went from uncomfortable to suffocating.

"Well, this is definitely a twist I hadn't anticipated," Alden eventually said. "But the Black Swan has proven time and again to be masterfully unpredictable. And . . . I owe you a tremendous debt, Livvy, for saving my son's life."

Fitz had been impaled by a giant bug's antennae during the Black Swan's less-than-perfect prison break into Exile. If Physic hadn't sealed the wound—and helped Fitz purge the venom from his system—he never would've survived.

"No debt at all," Livvy assured him. "I was just doing my job."

"And how long have you been doing that job for?" Quinlin demanded.

Livvy's smile faded, and she squared her shoulders. "Okay, if you really want to do this . . . I swore fealty about a year after you and I were married. And that bulging vein right there"— she pointed to his forehead—"is why I never told you."

"I have a right to be upset that I've been lied to for"—he counted on his fingers—"nearly eighteen years!" He sank into the nearest chair, covering his face with his shaky hands. *"Eighteen years."*

"I've always wondered if some part of you suspected," Livvy said quietly. "Apparently not."

Quinlin's laugh was so cold, it left goose bumps on Sophie's skin.

"Eighteen years," Alden repeated. "You must've been one of their founders."

"Actually, the Black Swan has been around far longer than anyone realizes," Livvy told him. "But Forkle brought me in to help with Project Moonlark and—"

"You were part of Project Moonlark?" both Alden and Quinlin interrupted.

"You knew that, right?" Livvy asked Sophie.

"I guess I should've assumed." Sophie had known that Physic had once been a member of the Black Swan's Collective. And she'd known that Physic had helped the Black Swan heal her abilities after she'd faded. Physic had even slipped once and revealed that she'd been involved with the mysterious allergic reaction that Sophie had when she was nine—but Sophie still didn't know exactly what happened that day. Mr. Forkle had erased the memory and never given it back.

"You were truly part of the project?" Quinlin murmured, staring at Livvy as if he'd never seen her before in his life.

"Forkle wanted my medical expertise," Livvy explained. "Not that I knew much about modifying genetics. But he did most of that with Calla."

Another name that punched Sophie right in the heart.

Calla had been one of the gnomes living in Alluveterre, and she'd chosen to sacrifice her life to save her people from the deadly plague the Neverseen and ogres unleashed. All that was left of Calla now was a beautiful tree—called a Panakes—growing in the Havenfield pastures, blooming with the same pinkish, purplish, bluish blossoms that Sophie had in her pockets. Ever since she'd lost Mr. Forkle, she'd kept a handful of the healing flowers with her at all times. It probably wouldn't have saved him, but she'd forever wish she'd had the chance to try.

"My role was preparing Sophie's embryo for implantation in her human mother," Livvy continued, "and making sure her mother's body would accept the baby as though it were her own."

Sophie squirmed. The way Livvy talked about the process made her feel like she was some sort of alien spawn.

"Why did you choose my parents?" she asked, remembering what her sister had heard the Neverseen say. "Was there something special about them?"

"Yes, and no. They were special because they *weren't* special, if that makes sense. We needed you to keep a low profile in the human world, so we searched for a family who didn't seem like the type to use your intelligence or beauty for their advantage. They also had to be kind, loving people who would provide a safe, healthy home. And Mr. Forkle especially liked your mother's mistrust of human medicine, since that meant she'd be less likely to ply you with those chemicals as you grew up."

"And that's it—there weren't any other reasons you picked them?" Sophie pressed.

"If there were, Forkle kept them to himself. Why?" Livvy asked.

"It might be important. Is there anyone else in the Collective who would know?"

". . . Maybe."

Sophie didn't miss Livvy's hesitation.

But Alden was focused on a much bigger revelation. "So . . . you knew Prentice was innocent when I arrested him?"

Livvy closed her eyes. "Yes."

The word was barely a breath, but it seemed to reverberate off the walls, shaking the room—the apartment—the entire world—to its very core.

Because Prentice's arrest had changed *everything*.

Prentice had been a Keeper for the Black Swan, in charge of protecting their most valuable secrets—the most important of which had been Sophie's existence. And back then, the few elves who knew about the Black Swan had believed that the shadowy organization was run by villains. So when Alden discovered Prentice's involvement, he had him arrested and brought before the Council. The Councillors ordered a memory break—a brutal method of extracting memories by telepathically shattering the person's sanity—and assigned Quinlin and Alden to perform the task. They both gave Prentice a final chance to cooperate, but Prentice held firm, letting them turn him into a babbling, drooling mess in order to keep Sophie hidden. And Quinlin and Alden had spent the next twelve years scouring the human world to find her, while Prentice spent the same years locked away in Exile as his wife was murdered and his son had to be adopted and raised by Tiergan.

"How could you not tell me?" Alden demanded. "How could you let me arrest him?"

"We didn't know you'd caught on to Prentice until it was too late," Livvy said quietly. "Even when he called swan song, I thought it had something to do with what he was investigating, not that he was about to be arrested."

"What was he investigating?" Sophie asked.

"Honestly? I have no idea," Livvy admitted. "We didn't share as much back then. It was safer to keep everything compartmentalized."

"Well, we know it had something to do with the Lodestar symbol," Sophie reminded her.

She'd recovered the asterisk-shaped map to the Neverseen's hideouts from the shambles of Prentice's mind—and only after she'd transmitted the words "swan song" to him. But that still didn't tell them how Prentice had found the symbol to begin with, or if he'd learned anything else when he made the discovery.

"What made you go after Prentice?" she asked Alden, regretting the question when his eyes clouded over.

He blinked several times to clear the regrets away. "Quinlin noticed discrepancies in Prentice's records. Times when his registry pendant claimed he was at his post as Beacon of the Gold Tower, but he wasn't actually there. So I started watching closer."

Livvy frowned at her husband. "You never told me you had anything to do with Prentice's arrest."

"And you never told me the Black Swan were on our side!" Quinlin snapped back. "Even when I admitted that I had reservations about performing the break!"

Alden flinched.

He and Quinlin used to be Cognates—the same rare telepathic relationship that Sophie shared with Fitz. But it required absolute trust and complete honesty, and when Quinlin hid his doubts from Alden about breaking Prentice's mind, it damaged their connection beyond repair.

"I did what I could," Livvy argued. "I warned you not to do anything you didn't believe in. And I fed you questions to ask when you met with Prentice—"

"You met with him?" Alden interrupted.

Quinlin looked away.

"The day before the break," Livvy answered for him.

Alden sank into the nearest armchair. "Why didn't you tell me?"

"Because . . . it didn't change anything," Quinlin mumbled. "It was obvious that Prentice was hiding something."

"That was the problem." Livvy rubbed the center of her

forehead. "Even if the two of you *had* refused to perform the memory break, the Council would've ordered another pair of Telepaths to do it. And Prentice couldn't reveal where Sophie was hidden—not when it was still so early in the project. The point of having her born from humans was to let her gain a unique perspective on the species—the kind of perspective she could *only* acquire by truly believing she was one of them during her formative years. If the Council dragged her back to the Lost Cities, everything we'd worked for would've been a waste. And Prentice knew that. He also had faith that Forkle's genetic modifications would give Sophie the ability to heal shattered minds someday—and he was right. She *will* fix him."

"As soon as you tell me it's time," Sophie agreed.

"I wish it were up to me," Livvy told her. "*I* think he's ready. But the Collective is afraid that since we still don't know why his consciousness disappeared, it could happen again."

"I thought he got buried under his shadowvapor," Sophie reminded her. "And that's why Tam was able to use his ability to bring him back."

"That was a symptom, not the cause," Livvy corrected. "Something had to push him that deep. And without knowing what it was, we can't guarantee it won't happen again. But I'm not convinced that's a good enough reason to leave him trapped in madness. He's suffered long enough."

"Years," Alden added. "And you knew it would be that long when you let us break him. You knew Sophie wouldn't be able to heal him until she was old enough to manifest—and that we'd likely learn the truth about the Black Swan long before she was ready. You *had* to know the toll that would take on us."

Livvy looked away. "I *did* watch to see how you were holding up after we rescued Sophie. But you did too good of a job of pretending to be okay—and when we realized you weren't . . ." Her voice hitched. "From the moment Tiergan told us you'd broken, all of us—every single one—worked tirelessly to get Sophie to a place where she'd be able to bring you back."

Alden swallowed hard. "And what about when our Cognate connection crumbled after the break? No remorse for that?"

"That was between you two. *You* chose to hide your concerns," she told Quinlin. "And *you* chose to let that shake your trust," she reminded Alden. "Neither had to be the giant, insurmountable things you let them become."

Quinlin snorted. "Clearly you don't know anything about Cognates."

"Maybe not," Livvy said. "But there was nothing I could do. You were different after the break, Quinlin. You retreated from everyone—even me. It was the beginning of our end."

"And yet you stayed with me for several more years," Quinlin noted. "Was it to spy on my search for Sophie—perhaps even to ensure I wasn't successful?"

"I suppose I deserve that question," Livvy told him. "But it still makes me want to punch you."

"*Punch* me?" Quinlin repeated.

"Yes! You really think I would do that?"

"I honestly don't know what to think anymore, Livvy. Clearly we never knew each other at all." Quinlin stalked to the wall, staring at the opaque crystal as if he could see through to the city beyond.

Livvy shook her head, curling and uncurling her fists. "I didn't come here to analyze our failed relationship, or to relive the Prentice nightmare. I came here because a little girl has been separated from her parents—parents who've been unknowingly wrapped up in a dangerous project for more than a decade. I helped bring this trouble into their lives. The least I can do is keep their daughter safe while we figure out how to rescue them. Can we please focus on that and leave the past in the past?"

Several beats passed before Alden nodded.

But Quinlin wasn't ready to concede. "You told us Forkle recruited you. But you didn't say why you agreed to join."

Livvy flicked her hair. "It was simple. Our glittering world is full of cracks, and I thought I was the only one who noticed them. When I met someone who shared my concerns, I decided to trust him."

"You can do better than that," Quinlin pushed, turning back to face her.

Livvy sighed, crossing to the opposite end of the room and settling into the shadows. "Fine. You want the whole story? It goes back to my Physician training. I spent years learning how each of our cures was developed, hoping I'd someday create my own. And I was stunned to discover that one remedy had its origins in the human vaccine for smallpox. The idea of using one virus to stop another was something no one would've attempted if the humans hadn't found proof that it worked. So I wanted to explore what else we might learn from them—and when I told my professor my plan, he laughed me out of the room. I ended up agreeing to drop the idea, but a few months after you and I were married, I was putting something away in your office, and I discovered that you had a pathfinder with a blue crystal."

Quinlin sucked in a breath.

Livvy's eyes dropped to her hands. "I'm sure you had your reasons for not mentioning to your wife that you were one of the few elves approved to visit the Forbidden Cities. But I figured . . . if you were using the pathfinder in secret, I could too. So, I waited until the Council sent you on an overnight assignment, spun the crystal to a random facet, and followed the path to a city near the ocean, with a long red bridge that stretched across the water."

"Sounds like San Francisco," Sophie noted.

"Maybe it was," Livvy said. "I was too distracted by the people sleeping on the street while others averted their eyes. It was almost enough to make me think my Instructor had been right to see no value in anything humans had to offer. But I'd come that far, so I tried to find one of their medical centers. And the longer I wandered, the more I started to see past the grime and disorder. I saw couples hand in hand. Parents caring for their children. Even their architecture, while primitive, had its own sort of beauty. But then I found a hospital."

Sophie shuddered, remembering her own hospital stays.

"It was horrifying," Livvy agreed. "Needles and blood and beeping machines leaking radiation. I even saw someone die." She wiped her eyes. "And the worst part was, I could've saved him with *one* elixir. In fact, I could've cured the whole hospital in a few hours. But I didn't have any medicine with me because I hadn't gone there to give. I'd gone there to *take*. I thought I couldn't be any more disgusted with myself. But as I was trying to leave, I stumbled into the children's wing, and . . . I'll spare you the nightmares."

"You couldn't have helped them," Quinlin said gently. "If you had, you would've created chaos."

"That's what I told myself when I got home. And I kept repeating it as I spun the crystal on the pathfinder so I'd never find the facet again. But I spent the next few hours vomiting anyway, thinking about what I'd discovered about myself—and about us as a species. We tell ourselves that we're the superior creatures on the planet. And yet, we'll scour the globe to preserve animals—we even had the dwarves hollow out an entire mountain range so we could build a Sanctuary for them. But we've stood back and let *billions* of humans die. Yes, their life spans are fleeting. And yes, they tried to betray us all those millennia ago—and I have no doubt that some of them would do it again if they knew we existed. But none of that—*none* of that—justifies letting innocent people suffer and die. Especially children. You should've seen them smiling at me, waving hands that were taped to plastic tubes and needles."

"You're talking about that time I went to help the dwarves, aren't you?" Quinlin whispered. "I came home, and you were so shaky."

"I thought about telling you what happened," she whispered. "But I didn't know how you'd feel about me taking your pathfinder. So I kept it to myself—until I met Forkle. And after he heard my story, he brought me to meet the rest of the Black Swan and showed me their idea to fix the problem between elves and humans—and asked for my assistance."

Sophie's stomach dropped when Livvy turned back to face her.

"How am *I* supposed to fix any of the things you're talking about?" she asked.

"That's up to you. It's one of my favorite things about Project Moonlark. We created you, yes. But your life is still *yours*. *You* get to decide what you want to do with it. That's why we've never told you our hopes or goals—why we didn't make a specific plan. We simply made you to the best of our abilities and let you find your own way. And now here you are, at this turning point in history, facing down enemies with unimaginably evil schemes. No one expects you to solve everything. And we certainly don't expect you to fight alone. But I personally can't wait to see what else you do with the gifts we gave you, whenever the time comes."

"I think we've gotten off track," Alden said, when all Sophie could do was stare and blink.

"Maybe I have," Livvy agreed. "Forkle was the master of notes and mysteries. I've always been better at laying it all out there. So I'll admit that we don't have a clue what the Neverseen wants with your human family. And I think we all know that whatever their plan is, it'll be huge, and intricate, and nothing we're expecting. I'm telling you that because I want you to know it's okay to be scared. And angry. And overwhelmed. Just trust yourself and your gifts—and your friends. And never doubt that wherever this is heading, we've done all we can to prepare you."

There was no possible coherent reply to any of that, so Sophie didn't bother trying.

"I should go check on my sister," she said, standing on wobbly legs.

Alden handed her a domed silver tray she hadn't noticed on the table next to him. "Mallowmelt always makes a difficult conversation better."

She gave him a small smile, remembering when she'd been introduced to the gooey, amazing cake.

"I'm not going to lie to her," she warned as she headed for the door. "If she wants me to tell her more about the Neverseen, I'm going to share everything I know."

Livvy smiled. "That's my girl."

FOUR

ETTING HER SISTER TO AGREE TO Alden's arrangements turned out to be an even bigger challenge than getting her to understand where they were, and why she'd forgotten that Sophie existed. But exhausting as both conversations were, Sophie also had to give her sister credit.

She'd always thought of her as kind of a crybaby—quick to tattle and whine and play for sympathy. But there was steel in her sister's posture. Ice in her eyes.

Her sister might've looked small in the giant canopy bed, and out of place in her wrinkled T-shirt among all the jeweled pillows and intricate crystal chandeliers. But she wasn't intimidated by her flashy surroundings. And she wasn't afraid of the things Sophie was describing, either—not that her determination would matter against villains like the Neverseen.

Involving her would be like bringing a snarling bunny into a den of hyenas.

The fifth time their argument circled back to the beginning, Sophie decided to try a visual demonstration. She held her half-empty bottle of Youth out in front of her and concentrated on the base, imagining her mental energy crawling inside the glass and buzzing around like a swarm of bees. The longer she let the force hum, the more the power swelled, until the bottle exploded into shimmering powder mixed with sprinkles of water that rained down on the bed.

"That," Sophie said over her sister's screech, "is called outward channeling. It's a skill that every elf has. And Gethen— the Telepath who took Mom and Dad—used it to destroy an entire castle full of people. And that's only the beginning. Fintan—the Neverseen's leader—is a Pyrokinetic. He can snap his fingers and call down unstoppable flames called Everblaze. And the Neverseen also have a Vanisher and a Guster and a Technopath and a Shade and a Psionipath and—"

"Am I supposed to know what any of that means?" her sister interrupted.

"No. But the fact that you don't proves my point. The things we're facing—you can't even imagine them, much less help fight them. I have *five* special abilities—I'm pretty sure that's more than any other elf has ever had—and the Neverseen have still almost killed me a bunch of times."

"Keeping your sister alive has been the greatest challenge of my career," Sandor added from the shadows. "And I say that as someone who has fought ogres, as well as a band of renegade trolls."

Her sister had no response to that.

Honestly, Sophie didn't either.

She grabbed one of the room's satin chairs and scooted it next to her sister, sinking down onto the squishy cushion. "I hate having to scare you—"

"I'm not scared."

The way her legs were trembling under the blankets suggested otherwise, but Sophie decided not to mention it.

"Okay, fine. I also know how it feels to be told to sit back while everyone else does all the important stuff," Sophie said quietly. "But this is something you *can't* help with. It's too big. Too complicated. And you're too . . . human."

The words hit her sister harder than Sophie expected.

"I'm not saying that's a bad thing," she promised.

"It sorta sounds like you are."

Shame prickled Sophie's cheeks as she realized her sister was right. All this time around elves had made her pick up some of their snobbery.

"I'm sorry. I just meant . . . these problems belong to *my* world. It's not your job to deal with them."

Her sister became very interested in dusting the specks of powdered glass off the bed.

"What?" Sophie asked.

"Don't you already know what I'm thinking?"

"I would if I weren't blocking you. Human thoughts are *loud*. Plus, Telepaths have to follow rules to respect people's privacy. Is that what's bothering you? You think I'm eavesdropping?"

"No." She looped her hair around her finger so tightly, the end of her finger turned purple. "I guess I just thought the one good thing I was going to get out of this nightmare was having my sister back. But . . . you're an elf. You have a goblin bodyguard, you live in a bunch of cities that are supposed to be myths, and you talk about humans like you think we're the biggest losers ever."

"I don't think you're the biggest losers ever—I swear. What I said before came out wrong." Sophie reached for her sister's hand, relieved when she didn't flinch away. "And you *did* get your sister back. Why do you think I'm trying so hard to protect you?"

"I don't need your protection!"

She definitely did.

But Sophie knew saying that wasn't going to help anything. So she went with a different kind of honesty.

"The thing is . . . you didn't remember me until today—and I know that wasn't your fault. But all of this time, I've still remembered you. I missed you guys so much that I had to stop myself from thinking about you. Maybe if I hadn't done that . . . maybe if I'd checked on you more often . . ."

She didn't finish the sentence, but her sister must've guessed.

"It's not your fault that Mom and Dad were taken," she told Sophie.

"It is and it isn't. If it weren't for me, the Neverseen wouldn't have known any of you existed. And I may not have asked the Black Swan to make me this way, but I've still made my own choices."

Sophie fidgeted with her monocle, her reminder that she'd accepted her role as the moonlark voluntarily.

"I can't let anything happen to you," she said quietly. "I could never live with that guilt. I promise I'll check in—and you can hail me anytime you want. Just please say you'll stay here in Atlantis, where it's safe. I finally have you back. I can't lose you again."

Her sister sighed. "You'll tell me *anything* I want to know?"

"Unless you ask something I don't have the answer to—but then I'll try to find out."

Her sister chewed her lip, leaving teeth marks so deep they looked ready to bleed. "Then I want the whole story—the one you promised you'd tell me earlier. I want to know what you've been doing all this time, and why you have a bodyguard, and why these Neverseen people keep coming after you."

"You realize that's a *really* long story, right?" Sophie asked.

Her sister shrugged and scooted over on the bed, patting the space she'd cleared beside her.

Sophie was pretty sure she'd never sat that close to her sister when they lived together, but as she settled under the blankets, her sister rested her head on her shoulder and it felt like the most natural thing in the world.

Sandor brought over the tray of mallowmelt for them, and Sophie handed her sister a slice of the chocolatey, butterscotch-y goodness.

"This isn't like fairy food, is it?" she asked, poking the cake with her fork. "I'll still be able to eat normal food afterward?"

Sophie laughed. "Of course. Though you might find other desserts disappointing."

Her sister poked it a few more times before taking a tiny bite—her eyes stretching huge. "Okay, this is the best thing I've ever put in my mouth."

"I know," Sophie said with a grin. "One slice is never enough."

"It won't be," her sister agreed, snatching the other plate.

"Um, that one's *mine*," Sophie reminded her.

She shrugged. "You won't have time to eat it anyway. You have a long story to tell."

"Ha. Fine." Sophie tugged on her eyelashes as she tried to figure out where to start.

Her sister tilted her head. "I remember you doing that when

you were nervous. It's so weird how the memories pop back. Is that going to keep happening?"

"Probably. Whenever you find the right trigger."

She nodded, going back to poking at her mallowmelt. "Were you the one who erased my mind?"

"No. I actually don't know who did—or how they do it. They call them the Washers. I guess they're specially trained for that."

"That's . . . creepy."

Sophie wished she could deny it.

"Are they going to do that to me again?" her sister whispered.

The best answer Sophie could give her was, "I hope not. That's why I'm telling you all of this. Maybe if you show them you can keep our secrets, it'll convince them you can handle it."

"Then get back to that story," her sister commanded, taking another bite of cake. "And start at the beginning. I want to know how you found out you're an elf in the first place. I'm betting that was a weird day."

Sophie nestled back against the pillows. "It was. And it all started with a field trip, a giant dinosaur model, and an especially noticeable pair of teal eyes."

FIVE

OPHIE HADN'T PLANNED ON SHARING
so much, but her sister kept asking questions. So,
they covered everything from her being adopted
by Grady and Edaline to the craziness of going to
Foxfire and living at Havenfield. Her sister couldn't believe
that dinosaurs weren't extinct, and she hadn't been able to stop
laughing when Sophie described the antics of her troublesome
pet imp named Iggy. But her favorite stories were the ones
about the incredibly rare alicorns, and how Silveny and Greyfell were going to have a baby.

Both slices of mallowmelt were gone by that point, and
Sophie told her sister about custard bursts and ripplefluffs and
cinnacreme and starkflower stew, and how the gnomes grew

all kinds of bizarrely colored vegetables that tasted like pizza and cheeseburgers and other delicious things.

"Gnomes," her sister repeated. "So . . . all the fantasy creatures are real?"

"Not *all* of them. But a lot. And they're not like the stories people tell."

"Like how your ears aren't pointy?" her sister asked, licking up every last crumb on her plate. "Or wait—are they?"

She tried to pull aside Sophie's hair, and Sophie swatted her hand.

"They're *not*. Though . . . I guess they will be, if I live long enough to be Ancient."

"How old is ancient?"

Her sister nearly choked when Sophie explained about the elves' indefinite life span.

"Gnomes live a really long time too," she added, trying to make it sound more normal. "They're like trees—they even have green thumbs and green teeth, and can sing to plants. And dwarves are kinda like kid-size moles, with pointed noses and shaggy fur and squinty eyes because they spend so much time underground."

"Wow. The world is . . . really strange."

"You have no idea. Trolls age in reverse. And Sandor has a secret girlfriend."

Sandor shot her a glare that could've withered flowers.

"What?" Sophie asked. "Who's she going to tell?"

Sandor muttered something about "respect for privacy."

"Anything else weird about you?" her sister asked.

Sophie snorted. "Where do I begin?"

She described each of her special abilities in detail: Telepath, Teleporter, Polyglot, Inflictor, Enhancer. And she showed her sister more of the skills every elf had, like levitating, and telekinesis, and channeling energy into her muscles to make her stronger or faster. When she was done stalling, she finally explained about Project Moonlark, and all the times she and her friends had nearly lost their lives.

Even though she glossed over the gory details and emphasized that the elves' medicines could treat pretty much anything, it still led to the question of whether anyone had actually died. And every name cut away another sliver of Sophie's heart.

Jolie.

Councillor Kenric.

Calla.

Mr. Forkle.

"I don't know how you made it through all of that," her sister whispered.

Sometimes Sophie didn't either. But she knew her sister needed hope. So she leaned her head against hers and whispered, "The same way we're both going to get through *this*. One day at a time. One problem at a time. Each tiny bit of progress slowly adds up to something big."

"But we're fighting an evil organization—and they have ogres!"

"You have *goblins*," Sandor reminded her, unsheathing his massive sword and slashing it so fast, the black blade was nothing more than a blur. "I can assure you—we're the better allies."

"The ogres also don't seem to be working with the Neverseen anymore," Sophie added. "King Dimitar signed a new treaty at the Peace Summit that basically said he'd leave us alone if we left him alone."

"Assuming he wasn't lying so he could carry on his warmongering without anyone watching him," Sandor grumbled, ignoring Sophie's that's-not-helping glare. "There are also the ogre-rebels to consider—assuming they truly are *rebels*, and not another of Dimitar's tricks."

"My adoptive parents were attacked a few weeks ago," Sophie reluctantly explained—while shooting Sandor a look that said *I will yell at you later.* "But it was only a small band of ogres, and most of them were taken down in the fight."

"How can you say that like it's not a huge deal?" her sister asked.

It was. Grady's goblin bodyguard had been killed in the skirmish. But Sophie was trying to keep her sister calm, so she said, "Because even if there are ogre rebels to worry about, they're working with the Neverseen, so that's what we need to focus on. It's like fighting a monster—no matter how many claws and fangs it has—if you chop off its head, you win."

"Unless it's a hydra," her sister argued.

"Those aren't real," Sophie told her. "At least, I don't think they are. I haven't heard anyone mention them—but I'm still trying to learn it all myself."

Her sister sighed. "I just wish I understood *why* this is happening. I still have no clue what these Neverseen people actually want."

That was probably because Sophie had no idea either. The Neverseen had started out following something that Keefe's mom had called the Lodestar Initiative—but Sophie had never been able to figure out exactly what the plan involved. And it might not even matter, because when Fintan took over, he shifted the Neverseen's focus to something he'd vaguely called his "vision," which seemed to have something to do with breaking an unidentified prisoner out of the dungeon at Lumenaria. He'd also brought Keefe to human cities and made him use his ability as an Empath to make a list of personality traits he'd called "criterion." But Sophie had no idea how any of that tied together, or what their ultimate goal was.

"All you need to know," she told her sister, "is that I'm going to stop them. I was made for this—which used to scare me. I used to wish I could be normal. But now I'm glad I have these abilities, because they help me fight. And I have a group of powerful friends who are always there to back me up—even when I tell them not to."

Her sister snorted. "You make it sound like you're Super Elves. All you're missing are the capes."

Sophie bit back a smile. "Actually . . . we do wear capes—but not because of that."

Her sister stared at her like Sophie had just admitted she had a detachable head.

"If you think that's bad, you should see the frilly, ridiculous gowns I have to wear to anything formal," Sophie added.

"The gloves are pretty weird too," her sister noted.

"They are. But I'm the only one who has to wear them. I can't turn my ability as an Enhancer off, so if I don't cover my fingers, I'd enhance everyone I touched—and we're trying to keep the ability secret. Dex said he's going to see if he can make some sort of gadget that would give me more control."

"Was Dex the one with the teal eyes?"

"No, that was Fitz."

"And Fitz is your boyfriend?"

Sophie nearly toppled off the bed. "No! Why would you think that?"

"Because you get all dreamy-eyed when you talk about him."

"I do not!"

"You're doing it right now!"

Sandor snickered from the corner, and Sophie flung a pillow at his head.

"Trust me," she told her sister. "Fitz and I are friends. That's it."

It was true, even if part of Sophie didn't want it to be. And even if there'd been that moment under Calla's Panakes tree that she still didn't totally understand.

Against her will, her mind flashed to the way his teasing smile had faded and he'd leaned in so close, it almost felt like he might—

"What about the other guy?" her sister asked, interrupting the memory almost exactly the same way Keefe had that day under the tree. "The one whose hand you kept holding."

"That doesn't mean what you think it means," Sophie insisted. "We have to hold hands for leaping and stuff, so it's not a big deal."

"Are you sure? He was looking at you pretty intense."

"Because he's worried," Sophie said as she searched for another pillow to fling at Sandor's newest round of snickers. "Keefe feels like he should've figured out what his mom was up to and stopped her—especially since she tricked him into helping her in small ways. She's horrible."

Sophie wasn't sure what scared her more: imagining what Lady Gisela was going to demand in exchange for information on finding Nightfall—or the fact that she'd probably be willing to give it to her.

"How's it going in here?" Livvy called through the door. "Ready for a tour of this place yet? I promise it won't be as boring as it sounds!"

Sophie glanced at her sister, noting the way she'd pulled the covers up to her nose. "Can we have a few more minutes?"

"Was that one of the people I'll be living with?" her sister whispered, after Livvy's footsteps retreated down the hall.

Sophie nodded. "She's really nice. And I just found out that she works with the Black Swan, so she'll probably tell you stuff before I even know about it."

"What's her ability?" her sister asked. "Anything I should be afraid of?"

"Actually, I'm not sure if she's ever told me—but you don't have to be afraid. It's safe here. They're going to take super good care of you."

Her sister twisted her fingers so tight, it had to hurt.

"It's okay to be nervous," Sophie told her. "I was terrified when Alden first brought me to Havenfield to meet Grady and Edaline. But that worked out awesome."

"But I don't want a new family."

"You aren't getting one. Quinlin and Livvy are only helping until everything is back to normal."

She braced for her sister to ask more questions about what "normal" meant—but sadly, she chose something even harder.

"Do you like them better than us? Your new family?"

Sophie sighed. "There isn't a *better*. I love them—but I'll always love you guys too."

"But you let them adopt you."

"Well . . . yeah. The thing is, all the years that I lived with you guys, I always knew something was off. I could *feel* it, even though I didn't understand what was wrong. And then Fitz brought me to the Lost Cities, and it felt like . . . taking a deep breath for the very first time."

Her sister nodded. "I guess I get that. But then . . . you're never coming home."

"Not to *live*," Sophie admitted. "I belong here. But I might be able to visit someday—if you guys wanted me to."

She couldn't really wrap her head around how that would work—how she'd blend her old life and her new without everything getting tangled up.

But there had to be a way.

If she could convince everyone to let her family keep their memories . . .

If they got her parents back safely . . .

"I know everything's a mess right now," she said. "And I don't know what's going to happen. But I promise we'll figure it all out, okay?"

She waited for her sister to agree before she reached for her hands. "In the meantime, I have a question. What am I supposed to call you? Amy? Natalie?"

"Oh." She scooted down under the covers. "Is it bad that I don't know?"

"Not after everything that's happened. But you *do* need a name—unless you want me to call you, 'hey you.' Or maybe you'd rather try a title, like The Doctor?" She pointed to her sister's T-shirt.

Her sister couldn't seem to smile. "It's just . . . neither name really feels like me anymore."

"Well . . . you could always choose something new."

Seconds crawled by.

"Amy's the name Mom and Dad chose for me, right?" she asked.

"Yeah. Mom even told me she picked it because it meant 'beloved.'"

Her sister's eyes turned watery. "Okay . . . Amy it is."

Sophie had no idea if that was the right or wrong choice—or if there even *was* a right or wrong in their situation. But it felt really good to call her sister by the familiar name again.

"So then, *Amy*—think you're ready to see where you'll be staying?"

"You'll come with me?"

"Of course. We're in this together."

She helped Amy up and kept an arm wrapped around her trembling shoulders as she led her to the sitting room, where the adults were waiting.

Quinlin looked just as nervous as Amy—he was wringing his hands so hard, Sophie could see his skin twisting.

But Livvy was all smiles, tossing her sparkly braids and declaring, "There's my new best friend!"

Amy's timid grin faded.

"You okay?" Sophie asked.

"I'm not sure." Her frown dug deeper into her cheeks as she took a longer look at Livvy and said, "I . . . know you."

SIX

OU *KNOW* HER?" SOPHIE ASKED. "How can you *know* her?"

Amy closed her eyes, massaging the sides of her forehead. "I think . . . she was my doctor. She came to the house one night and asked me a bunch of questions about how I was feeling. And she gave me this candy that kept changing flavors. I forgot about it until I saw the sparkles in her hair. Now I remember thinking they looked like real jewels."

"They are," Livvy said, examining a couple of her braids. "I guess I should've known they'd give me away."

"Does that mean you helped relocate my family?" Sophie asked.

"No, she did not," Alden said, with a look for Livvy that said, *care to explain?*

Livvy sighed. "What your sister's remembering happened a few years ago."

"Years?" Sophie repeated as Quinlin muttered something under his breath. "How many years?"

And then she knew. "I was nine, wasn't I?"

"By the human way of counting age . . . yes," Livvy said quietly.

"The human way?" Amy asked. "What's the *human* way? And what happened when you were nine?"

Sophie stuck with the question that wouldn't require a *long* conversation about birthdays versus inception dates. "Do you remember when I had that big allergic reaction and ended up in the hospital?"

"Sort of. I remember Mom freaking out at the doctors because they couldn't figure out what you were allergic to."

"What about before that?" Sophie asked. "Do you remember how I got sick?"

Amy's forehead got all scrunched. "Huh. I don't—but my head's still kind of a mess."

"I'm sure it is," Sophie told her, turning back to Livvy. "But I think it's funny how my sister and I have the same blank spot in our memories—the same time she also saw you. Did my allergy have to do with Amy?"

Livvy twisted her braids. "Right now isn't the time for this conversation. That memory was taken for a very specific reason. We can't give it back until you're ready."

"I'm ready," Sophie insisted.

"Me too," Amy added.

"I figured you might say that," Livvy glanced to Quinlin and Alden as if she was hoping they'd jump in with a subject change.

No such luck.

"The most I can tell you is that there was an accident that day." She seemed to choose each word carefully. "One that we feared would leave lasting trauma. So your memories were taken, to ensure that neither of you would be haunted by the experience."

"What kind of accident?" Sophie asked.

"I can't tell you that."

"But it was something you guys did?" Sophie pushed.

"Actually, it was something that just . . . happened. And when it did, I was called in to help. And then things got complicated."

"Because you gave me Limbium and I turned out to be deathly allergic to it?" Sophie guessed.

Livvy shuddered. "If I'd known it was possible for you to have such a severe reaction, I wouldn't have suggested trying it. But I'd never seen an allergy before. Luckily the human doctors were much more familiar with what was happening and were able to fix what I couldn't. And that's truly all I can say. Anything more might trigger the memory—and with all the emotional stress you're dealing with at the moment, that wouldn't be a good idea. Trust me."

"It's kinda hard to trust someone who's hiding things," Amy told her.

"I know. And I wish I had something better to offer than: Someday you'll understand."

"Ugh, I hate when adults say that," Sophie grumbled.

"Same here," Amy agreed. "Can't you use that mind-reading thing to find out what she's hiding?"

"Not without violating the rules of telepathy," Alden jumped in.

"But it's *not* against those rules to steal someone's memories?" Amy countered.

"It is," Quinlin said. "Though it can be allowed in certain instances."

"And this is one of those instances," Livvy assured them. "When the time is right, I promise all will be revealed. In the meantime, try to keep in mind that the missing moment has zero relevance to anything you're currently facing. I know the mystery of it all gives the moment a sense of importance, but what happened back then was . . . a blip. It was a problem that popped up and was dealt with, and has nothing to do with the Neverseen."

Amy glanced at Sophie. "Are you really okay with this?"

"No," Sophie told her. "But I've been trying to get them to give me this memory back for months, so . . ."

She closed her eyes, wishing all the new bits of information would sink in and trigger the memory on its own.

"Wow," Livvy said. "Those are some unhappy faces. And I get it. I really do. So let's try this. Amy? Think about the portion of the memory that you've managed to recover, and ask yourself: Were you afraid of me that day?"

"No," Amy said slowly. "I thought you were nice—but that was probably because you had candy. And sparkles."

"Sparkles do make everything better," Livvy agreed. "And mood candy is delicious—I wish I had some with me now because it would help me make my point. Most people don't realize that emotions can't be erased—even if the memory of what caused them is taken away. So if I'd done something to you that day, you'd still have all the feelings that went with it. Understand?"

"Sorta?" Amy said.

"It's murky, I know," Livvy told her. "But think about what you're feeling right now—and I don't mean all the stress of this conversation. I mean something deeper—is there anything that feels like a gut instinct, telling you to be afraid of me?"

Amy thought long and hard. "I guess not."

"Then can't we build on that? Yes, there's a secret between us. But it's not a harmful secret. It's one that's being kept for your protection. And Sophie—I know you're probably tired of hearing that—but does it help at all to remember that the person who decided to erase that memory was Mr. Forkle? He was adamant that we wait for the right circumstances before we gave it back. And now isn't the time."

"She's talking about our old neighbor, right?" Amy asked. "The guy who was always outside mumbling to his gnome statues? Didn't you tell me he was an elf and that the Neverseen killed him?"

Sophie nodded, her mind already back in Lumenaria, watching Mr. Forkle take his final breaths.

He'd promised her in that moment—even when he had so little energy left—that she *would* get the answers he owed her.

But he didn't say how or when.

So maybe she owed it to him to be patient.

She glanced at her sister. "Will you feel okay living here, knowing all of this?"

"Do I have a choice?" Amy asked.

"Yes," Alden assured her. "If you're not comfortable, I'll find an alternative situation. Same goes for if you decide to try it, and then feel it isn't working out."

"If I might add something," Quinlin jumped in. "I know you don't know my wife very well—or me for that matter. But everyone in this room is on your side. We have our flaws. And we come with strange baggage. But no one will fight harder to make this right and get your parents back."

Amy reached for her eyelashes, giving them a good, hard tug—then winced. "Ugh, Sophie, how can you stand that?"

Sophie smiled. "We all have our things."

"Well, yours is weird," Amy told her. "And your world is even weirder. But . . . I'll deal—if you guys promise me something."

She waited for all of the adults to nod before she said, "I want your word that no one is going to erase any memories again without my permission."

Amy would never be able to hold Alden to her demand—and Alden had to know that.

And yet, Sophie believed him when he said, "You have my word."

It was a dim, flickering hope—but Sophie clung to it as tightly as Amy clung to her hand.

Maybe something good would come from all of this panic and ugliness.

Maybe she really could have her family back in her life.

It would be confusing and complicated—and probably change a ton of things for everyone.

But it would be worth it.

And she wanted it. More than anything.

SEVEN

HE DOORS IN THIS WING ARE ALL decoys," Livvy explained as they continued with the tour. "That way if someone did manage to find their way up here, they'd only be able to see what we want them to see. The real paths are all camouflaged. See?"

She pressed her palm against the shimmering surface, and Amy gasped as Livvy's fingers sank deep into the crystal.

"It doesn't hurt," Sophie promised as Livvy shoved the rest of her body through the wall. "It's like walking through cold sand."

Amy needed a deep breath before she was willing to try— and she dragged Sophie with her. Together they pushed into the crystal, letting the tiny, shimmering grains brush their skin before they emerged into a library with floor-to-ceiling books and gleaming silver ladders.

"That's a lot of books," Amy noted.

"It is," Quinlin agreed as he joined them, followed by Alden and Sandor. "This is my research—recorded in code to ensure no unwanted eyes can access it without my permission."

"Even me," Alden noted with a tinge of sadness.

"I share anything important," Quinlin promised. But Alden didn't look convinced.

"The only book you need to know is this one," Livvy said, striding to one of the shelves and reaching for a red-and-gold spine. She waited until everyone had crowded close before she tilted the book to a thirty-degree angle.

A burst of air shot up from under their feet and launched their group like a cannon blast, straight through the crystal ceiling and into a small room lined with colorful shelves.

"Welcome to the pantry!" Livvy told them. "Arguably my favorite room in this whole apartment—especially when I've been the one doing the shopping."

"That's a *lot* of Prattles," Sophie said, pointing to a shelf that had to be holding at least a hundred boxes of the buttery, nutty candy known best for the collectible pins inside.

"Candy is essential," Livvy said, handing Amy a box of Prattles before she led them through an actual door this time, into a sleek silver kitchen. "Warning: This next passage takes a little trust."

She pointed to a wide fireplace flickering with blue and yellow flames.

Sophie could tell the fire was a hologram—but that didn't stop her from holding her breath as Livvy dropped to her knees and crawled straight into the blaze.

After all the infernos she'd survived, Sophie couldn't bring herself to look until Livvy called, "See? It's all an illusion!"

And when Sophie's vision focused again, she realized her sister was staring just as dazedly at the flames. "You okay?"

"Yeah," Amy mumbled. "I just haven't seen fire since the huge arson attack that happened a few months back. We had to evacuate our house and go to this overcrowded shelter—and then the winds changed and even the shelter was in danger. All the roads were closed, and there was another fire in the opposite direction, so there were a few hours where we thought we might be trapped."

Sophie's heart turned a whole lot heavier.

She knew exactly which arson attack her sister meant. In fact, she'd watched her family huddle together on the floor of the shelter through the unregistered Spyball the Black Swan had given her—right before she'd decided to break a bunch of elvin laws so that she could prove the fires were Everblaze and force the Council to step in and extinguish the flames.

She'd been kidnapped right after—and then her abilities had broken, and Alden's sanity collapsed, and Silveny was attacked, and Kenric was murdered, and the Council turned against her, and she was banished along with all of her friends, and the gnomish plague was unleashed, and Keefe ran off, and Lumenaria fell, and so many other devastating and distracting things had happened that Sophie had never stopped to wonder . . .

Had there been a larger purpose behind those fires?

And if there had been, were they already too late to stop it?

EIGHT

ID YOU MONITOR THE EVERBLAZE
fires like you did with the white fires in San
Diego?" Sophie asked Quinlin, sending a
silent plea into the void that there was still
time for her to be asking this question.

The white fires had been the Neverseen's attempt to
flush Sophie out of her human hiding place, because they
knew she'd been living somewhere in the area. They'd even
shaped the fire line into the sign of the swan to force the
Black Swan into action. So Sophie had assumed their goal
had been similar with the Everblaze—that the fires had
been the Neverseen's way of testing the moonlark, to see
what she'd do under that kind of pressure. Brant had even

implied as much after he kidnapped her, during his searing interrogation.

But what if there'd been more to it than that?

Sophie's whole focus had been on figuring out who sparked the flames, and stopping that person from burning anything again. But after seeing what happened with Lumenaria—how the Neverseen could play a long, intricate game to achieve their goals—that might've been a tremendous mistake.

"I kept an eye on them as much as I could," Quinlin said. "Why?"

Sophie ignored the question, asking him to send any notes he'd made to Havenfield, along with a map plotted with the location of every fire he knew of.

What if there'd been a pattern to the fires?

Or what if they'd been designed to destroy something important?

Or what if it had all been some giant distraction, while the Neverseen did something even more terrifying?

The possibilities whirled around her mind, making Sophie dizzy.

"Do you guys always watch things going on with humans?" Amy asked. "Or did that arson attack have to do with the Neverseen?"

"The answer is yes to both," Alden told her. "The Council's official policy is to leave humans to their own devices—for many complicated reasons. But Quinlin keeps an eye on things, just to be safe. As do I. As do the Black Swan. And in the case of those fires, we now know that they were set by Pyrokinetics. But the blazes were thoroughly investigated," he added, focusing on Sophie.

"So was Gethen," she reminded him. "The Black Swan held him prisoner for months, and questioned him multiple times before they handed him over to the Council, who *also* interrogated him. And still, none of us realized he'd let himself be arrested for a reason—even when he out-and-out told us he wanted to be in Lumenaria."

"I know," Alden said. "But the important thing to remember is, *he was still in our custody.* The Everblaze was extinguished months ago and the damage has been repaired and rebuilt. And it was all relatively minor. The fires mostly scorched empty land and small neighborhoods—which was still devastating for the humans, of course. But it's not the kind of damage that sends a larger message. If the Neverseen had been making a point, they would've taken out important human landmarks."

"Then why *did* they spark the fires?" Sophie asked, hating how little sense it made, now that she was finally questioning it. "They had to know that unleashing a storm of Everblaze would lead to Fintan's arrest, and then to his mind being shattered in a memory break—and yeah, I ended up healing him. But they didn't know I could do that back when they set the fires. *I* didn't even know I could do that. So it doesn't make sense that they would risk all of that just to get the Black Swan's attention—especially since I'm sure they could've done that another way. Do you really think they'd sacrifice so much without a very good reason?"

None of the adults wanted to answer.

"I hope I'm overreacting," she said, feeling like her stomach was turning inside out. "But in case I'm not, we need to reinvestigate and make sure the fires weren't the start of something—or a cover-up for something—and we missed it."

"I'm not saying you're wrong," Alden told her. "But I'd also hate to have this sidetrack you from the much more important search you should be spending your energy on."

Sophie had started to nod when realization punched her in the chest.

Was *that* why the Neverseen took her parents?

To keep her so frantic and distracted that she'd keep missing the other, much more dangerous plans already in action?

A scene took shape in her mind, straight out of the action movies she'd watched growing up:

The villain taunting the hero with an impossible choice—the people they loved in mortal danger on one side, and the rest of the world on the other.

And no way to save them both.

"You okay?" Amy asked, nudging Sophie's arm until Sophie looked at her. "You're shaking."

Was she?

Sophie forced air into her lungs.

She couldn't bring herself to voice her newest worries—couldn't risk having her sister think she wouldn't be giving 100 percent of herself to rescuing her parents.

But if she was right, then the one-problem-at-a-time approach she'd relied on in the past was never going to work—and maybe it never had.

Maybe *that* was why the Neverseen kept winning.

They were toying with everyone, keeping eyes trained on the wrong dangers, like evil magicians who'd perfected their illusions.

But if that was true—how could Sophie fight back when she was already so many steps behind?

The solution drifted to the surface of her mind after a few long seconds—sharp and sour, but also incredibly clear.

The Neverseen had tipped their hand several weeks back, giving a hint of what they needed.

They'd kidnapped Prentice's son, Wylie, and interrogated him about his mom's murder. But he'd managed to escape before they could learn anything. And now the Black Swan had him hidden away while he recovered from the trauma, under such heavy guard that the Neverseen would never be able to get to him again.

So, if Sophie could find out what they had been trying to learn, she'd have a bargaining chip of her own—and maybe a much better insight into what they were planning. And she was also pretty sure she could learn what she needed from the same person she'd already been planning to turn to.

Keefe's mom had to know more about why the Neverseen were looking into Cyrah's death.

After all, she'd been the one to murder her.

NINE

A
NYONE PLANNING ON JOINING
me over here?" Livvy called from the other
side of the fireplace.

Amy kept her eyes trained on Sophie. "What aren't you telling me?"

"Just some theories I need to think through," Sophie told her, tugging out an itchy eyelash. "I promise I'll tell you if I'm right about any of them."

"If it helps," Alden said when Amy's frown twisted into a scowl, "she often makes the same excuse with my children. And me, for that matter."

"It's not an excuse," Sophie argued. "I just don't like to freak people out until I've had time to look into things. Why worry everyone when there's a chance I'm wrong?"

"Fine," her sister said, turning to Quinlin, "then I'll look into it too. I want a copy of anything you're going to send to Sophie."

"But you don't even know what we're looking for," Sophie reminded her.

"I'm sure I can figure it out. Just because I don't have fancy powers doesn't mean I'm useless."

"Oh, I like her," Livvy called through the flames. "Tell you what, Feisty Girl—I'll make sure Quinlin gets you that info and we'll go through it together."

Amy smirked at Sophie.

"I never said you were useless," Sophie told her as Amy moved closer to the fire.

"You didn't have to," Amy said. "I know I'm not an elf—but this problem *isn't* just about your world. Those fires were in *my* world. So I might notice something you don't."

"She has a point," Alden agreed.

Amy flashed Sophie an especially smug smile, but it faded when she turned back to the flames.

"Problem?" Sophie asked as Amy shakily dropped to her knees.

"I know it's an illusion, but I . . . hate fire."

Sophie kneeled beside her and offered her hand.

Amy still needed a couple of long breaths before they both crawled into the flames together, each squeezing their eyes tight until Livvy told them, "You're clear."

Sophie dusted off her knees, noting that she was now inside an elegant dining hall with a massive table carved of solid gold that had to seat at least thirty people—which seemed like an odd choice for a secret room accessible only by fireplace in an apartment no one was supposed to know about.

"So, um, how rich are these people?" Amy whispered to Sophie as she squinted at the twinkling chandelier that shimmered with cascading crystals.

Sophie smiled. She'd gotten so used to the insane wealth of the elves that she'd forgotten how overwhelming it was at first. "Believe it or not, this is pretty normal around here."

Amy's jaw fell open as Sophie explained about the elvin birth fund.

"Are you saying you have millions of dollars?" she gasped.

"Actually, she's saying she has billions," Quinlin corrected. "Possibly even trillions—I haven't looked up the value of human money these days."

Amy blinked. "Yeah. Okay. I expect *lots* of presents."

"Liking this girl more and more," Livvy said as she twisted one of the platters in the gilded china cabinet, opening a circular doorway among all the goblets and plates. "And now comes the best part."

The path led them to a shimmering hallway lined with

five doors. "These are the main bedrooms," Livvy explained. "Pick any one you want—but I have a feeling you'll want the fourth one."

Amy's eyes stretched wider and wider with every room they toured—each huger and fancier than the last. But Livvy was right about the fourth bedroom. Painted in blues, grays, and purples, the room looked like it had been dipped in twilight, with a massive bed heaped with a mountain of fluffy pillows. And the view . . .

"Don't worry—it's one-way glass," Livvy explained as Amy made her way to the gigantic window that overlooked the silver-and-blue city.

"So this is Atlantis," she breathed.

The twisted skyscrapers gleamed in the pale glow of the balefire towers. Beyond them, the dark curve of the dome shielded the city from the watery depths beyond.

"We really are under the ocean," Amy murmured. "It's so weird not having any sky."

"It takes getting used to," Quinlin agreed. "The city lightens and darkens throughout each day to give some sense of the passing hours—and during the night cycle, the dome has a starlight effect that's quite breathtaking. But plan on your body needing some time to adjust to the new rhythms."

"Do you ever see, like, sharks swimming by?" Amy asked.

"I'm sure they're out there," Quinlin said, "but the dome absorbs any light, to keep the city better hidden."

Amy squinted at the darkness before turning her attention to the streets far below, where ant-size elves roamed the various sidewalks and squares and courtyards. Atlantis reminded Sophie of a futuristic Venice, with its intricate network of canals dividing up the city, bustling with fancy carriages floating along the water, being pulled by humongous sea scorpions.

"Humans really used to live here?" Amy asked, pressing her fingers against the glass.

"A very long time ago," Quinlin said quietly. "And a lot of things have changed since then. But you can still see remnants."

He pointed to something in the center of one of the more prominent squares. "It's hard to tell from up here, but that's called the Unity Fountain. It features two golden statues—one an elf, and one a human—standing side by side in a wide reflecting pool, with colored streams of water shooting around them to symbolize the ties binding our two species together."

"I'm always surprised the Council hasn't taken it down," Alden admitted. "Or at least removed the human figure. Especially after they terminated the Human Assistance Program."

"Human Assistance Program?" Amy repeated.

"It was our failed attempt to guide the human world without them realizing it," Quinlin explained. "Our brightest minds volunteered to live in the Forbidden Cities for a time, offering insights and innovation to those willing to learn. Many of your world's greatest advancements occurred—unbeknownst to them—because of the tutelage of elves."

"But not everything," Alden added. "Humans also have their own unique approach to research and discovery—that's why the Ancients built this city in the first place. A very long time ago, we wanted to bring our worlds together and benefit from each other's perspective. That's why even after the humans' treachery forced us to disappear, we couldn't keep away completely. And I've no doubt that those who worked in the Human Assistance Program gained much during their time there."

"Then why did they cancel the program?" Amy asked.

"Because the humans didn't always use our gifts for the purposes we intended," Quinlin explained. "Far too often, they took the knowledge we'd shared and created weapons, or pollutants, or other dangerous things. Eventually, we realized the program was deeply flawed and that we were doing both of our worlds more harm than good."

"How long ago was that?" Sophie asked.

"Not as far back as you might think," Livvy told her. "Your human schools probably taught you about the horrifying bombs that humans dropped to end their last 'world war.' But they don't realize that much of the early wisdom that led to their creation came from elvin scientists."

"Some argued that the knowledge they gave was generic enough that the humans likely would've discovered it on their own," Alden added. "But the Council couldn't ignore such a catastrophic loss of life—especially since the humans now had the potential to do it again."

"The ogres also didn't appreciate that humans posed a greater threat because of us," Quinlin added.

"Neither did the goblins," Sandor noted. "As I remember, my queen threatened to pull all military support if the program was not terminated."

"And *that* is why we can't let anyone know you're here," Livvy told Amy. "Contact with humans is now expressly forbidden—though our order felt that was a mistake, which is partly why we arranged for Sophie to be raised by a human family."

All Amy seemed able to say to that was "Huh"—and Sophie couldn't blame her. She'd been given bits of the story over her time in the Lost Cities, but she'd never had the pieces click together quite so clearly.

"Well," Livvy said, "that got . . . heavy."

"It did," Amy agreed, still staring at the silver-blue city.

"You okay?" Sophie asked her.

"Yeah. I was just trying to imagine what it would be like if you guys had never had to sink this place."

"I've often tried to picture the same thing," Livvy admitted, "but I never really know where to begin. Our species have been on separate paths for so long. . . ."

"I think it's safe to say that the world would be a very different place," Quinlin added.

"A better place?" Amy asked.

on her human family without telling them she was leaving.

"You don't have to explain," Edaline told her, pulling her into a hug. "Alden gave us plenty of updates. And we understand if you don't feel like talking."

"Thank you," Sophie grunted as Edaline's hug turned crushing.

Her adoptive mother might look like a fragile beauty with her wavy amber-toned hair, pink cheeks, and wide turquoise eyes. But she could also wrestle a mastodon and wrangle saber-toothed tigers. Edaline had even saved Sophie's life during the destruction of Lumenaria, using her ability as a Conjurer to send any falling debris into the void before it could crush them.

"Is there anything we can do?" Grady asked, shaking his tousled blond hair out of his bright blue eyes before he turned the mother-daughter hug into a group hug.

Sophie squeezed them tighter. "This helps."

Out of the corner of her eye, she checked the shadows for Cadoc—Edaline's goblin bodyguard—needing to remind herself that her parents were well protected. She found him right where he should be, with one hand by his sword and the other hand near a line of goblin throwing stars strapped to his leg—ready to shred the world at the first hint of a threat.

The Black Swan had also added new security features to Havenfield after the ogre attack. And Grady was a Mesmer—a rare special ability that allowed him a certain level of mind

The glee in her voice helped Sophie breathe a little easier.

Her sister would be happy here, even with everything else they were dealing with.

"That settles it, then," Livvy said, "We'll get your things moved in—though I saw those sad little satchels Alden packed, so I'm sure we'll also be making a list of things they forgot, and I'll make a shopping run."

"We only packed the necessities because I didn't want Amy to feel like we'd uprooted her whole life," Alden argued. "Plus, I was wrestling with an overly protective dog and a supremely mistrustful cat!"

"Where are they, by the way?" Amy asked.

"In the larger conservatory on the opposite end of the apartment," Quinlin told her. "And since I'd like to keep the skin on my face, I'll leave moving them here to you."

Wrangling a skittish cat and an exuberant beagle through the secret passages was definitely a process. But it helped that Marty remembered Sophie. He'd slunk right toward her, rubbing his big furry body against her legs and filling the air with the hum of his squeaky purr.

"You're leaving now, aren't you?" Amy whispered when Sophie set the fluffy cat among the pillows on Amy's new bed.

"I probably should get home. But keep this with you in your pocket." She grabbed the small silver square that Livvy had left on Amy's nightstand and explained how all she'd have to do is say, "Show me Sophie Foster," and the Imparter would hail her. "I don't care if it's the middle of the night—if you need me, call for me, okay?"

"Same goes for us," Livvy said, wrapping an arm around Amy's shoulders. "I know you might feel hesitant to rely on us. But we're here for *anything* you need. You don't have to put on a brave face or pretend like everything's okay. If you want to talk, cry, laugh, eat junk food till you're sick, or do all of the above, you just say the word. Or if you'd rather we leave you alone so you can snuggle with your fur-babies, that's fine too."

Amy gave a shaky nod. "And you're going to start searching for Mom and Dad?"

"As soon as I get home," Sophie promised.

"As soon as you get some sleep," Alden corrected. "And don't tell me you just slept fourteen hours from the sedatives—that kind of rest actually exhausts the body. It's also far later than you realize. So please go home and go to bed. Wait for the morning, when you can regroup with your friends, and the seven of you can start scheming together."

"Actually, you have something else to do tomorrow morning," Livvy interrupted, fussing with her braids. "Tomorrow, Tiergan will be collecting you and your friends from Havenfield and bringing you to one of our most heavily protected hideouts. The Black Swan is finally ready to move forward with their contingency plan. And trust me, it's going to change everything."

TEN

N O MATTER HOW HARD SOPHIE pressed for details about the contingency plan, the most Livvy would tell her is, "Prepare for an emotionally exhausting day."

But when Sophie finally gave up and agreed to let Alden take her home, Livvy did add, "You're going to be angry. And none of us will blame you for that. But *try* to remember that it was Mr. Forkle's request to have us wait."

With *that* cheerful thought fogging up her brain, Sophie barely registered the goodbye hug she gave her sister—and she endured the lengthy process of leaving Atlantis in a daze.

"Do *you* know what the contingency plan is?" she asked when they'd launched out of the ocean in a giant bubble and were drifting on the cold breeze. The night sky twinkled and the dark ocean churned far below, making her feel very small when Alden shook his head.

"Tiergan told me they wanted you to be the first to see," he said quietly.

"*See?*" she repeated. "So it's something they're going to show me?"

"I noticed the same word choice. And when I pressed him on it, he told me I would understand when the secret had been revealed. They definitely know how to be mysterious."

"More like annoying."

Sandor snorted his agreement.

"If it cheers you at all," Alden said as he fished his pathfinder out of his pocket, "I'm sure Fitz and Keefe have spent this time deciding how best to punish me for sedating you. I expect Biana and Della also assisted."

"Don't be surprised if Grizel ropes you into her dancing scheme, either," Sandor warned.

Grizel had turned a search of Keefe's bedroom into a contest to see who could discover the most secrets. And after their win, Sophie, Linh, and Grizel each got to call in a favor from one of the guys. Sandor would now be dancing in what sounded like an embarrassingly tight pair of silver pants—and Fitz would be joining him, as punishment for the time he snuck away with Sophie to meet up with Keefe. Linh would be making Tam buy her a pet of her choosing. And Sophie had foolishly waited too long to decide Fitz's punishment, and ended up losing the favor to him in a follow-up wager.

He hadn't called it in yet, and she was dreading what he would come up with.

"You should probably be careful with any hair products you use," she warned Alden. "Otherwise you might end up with blue spikes or red frizz."

"I probably deserve worse." His smile faded when he added, "I'm sorry again. For everything."

Sophie focused on the stars. "I know."

He didn't promise her that everything would be okay.

Or tell her she had no reason to worry.

He didn't even try to interrogate her about whatever she was planning.

All he said was, "I believe in you, Sophie Foster," as he raised his pathfinder up to the silvery glow of the moonlight.

And Sandor added, "We all do."

Then their bubble burst and the light carried them away.

Sophie wasn't surprised to find Grady and Edaline waiting up for her on the crisp white couch in Havenfield's elegant main room. Nor was she shocked to see shadows under their eyes and creases pressed into their foreheads. Her adoptive parents were champion worriers—and considering how many brushes with death Sophie had survived, she couldn't totally blame them. Plus, she'd rushed off to check on her human family without telling them she was leaving.

"You don't have to explain," Edaline told her, pulling her into a hug. "Alden gave us plenty of updates. And we understand if you don't feel like talking."

"Thank you," Sophie grunted as Edaline's hug turned crushing.

Her adoptive mother might look like a fragile beauty with her wavy amber-toned hair, pink cheeks, and wide turquoise eyes. But she could also wrestle a mastodon and wrangle saber-toothed tigers. Edaline had even saved Sophie's life during the destruction of Lumenaria, using her ability as a Conjurer to send any falling debris into the void before it could crush them.

"Is there anything we can do?" Grady asked, shaking his tousled blond hair out of his bright blue eyes before he turned the mother-daughter hug into a group hug.

Sophie squeezed them tighter. "This helps."

Out of the corner of her eye, she checked the shadows for Cadoc—Edaline's goblin bodyguard—needing to remind herself that her parents were well protected. She found him right where he should be, with one hand by his sword and the other hand near a line of goblin throwing-stars strapped to his leg—ready to shred the world at the first hint of a threat.

The Black Swan had also added new security features to Havenfield after the ogre attack. And Grady was a Mesmer—a rare special ability that allowed him a certain level of mind control. Hopefully all of that would be enough to protect her family from the Neverseen.

Still, Sophie felt the need to add, "Please promise me you'll be extra careful."

"Same goes to you, kiddo," Grady told her. "I have a feeling I don't want to know about all the dangerous things you're now planning to do, but I'm hoping you'll tell me anyway."

Sophie sighed. "Right now, the only plan is to get through whatever the Collective is going to reveal tomorrow."

Neither of her parents had any theories for what the Black Swan could possibly be arranging.

"Well," Edaline said, tracing her fingers gently down Sophie's back, "if you think of anything we can do, we're here."

Sophie kissed them each on the cheek and headed for the curved central staircase. Her bedroom took up the entire third floor, and she stood in her doorway while Sandor made his nightly security sweep. But as her eyes followed him around her enormous room, she couldn't help wondering what her sister would've thought if she'd come home with her.

The glass walls overlooked the ocean, the delicate flowers woven into the carpet were lovely, and the enormous canopied bed looked ready for a princess—and Iggy's purple poof of a body bouncing in his tiny cage added a unique sort of quirk. And yet, the room didn't necessarily say anything about Sophie's new life. She hadn't bothered to decorate—even after Keefe had pointed out that almost nothing in the room seemed to be *hers*—in large part because she'd spent most of her time in the Lost Cities either worrying that Grady and Edaline wouldn't adopt her, terrified that the Council would exile her, or banished and fighting to stay alive.

"All clear," Sandor said, striding to his usual post outside her door. "I'll give you one hour with lights on, in case you want to record anything in your memory log. But then I expect you to go to bed."

"We both know sleep is *so* not going to happen," she argued.

"That doesn't mean you shouldn't try. Please, Sophie. It sounds like you're going to need the rest."

Fighting would only waste her precious lights-on time, so Sophie showered and changed into her pajamas as fast as she could. And when she emerged from her bathroom, her eyes went straight to her wall of bookshelves, searching for her old scrapbook—which was coated in a thin film of dust.

She'd remembered to take the album with her when Fitz brought her to live in the Lost Cities, but she'd barely let herself look through the photos since. Now she climbed into bed and forced herself to study each picture, reliving the memories she'd buried away.

Trips to the beach, and the zoo, and Disneyland. Every first and last day of school. Plus all the smaller moments, like licking cookie dough off of wooden spoons with her sister, or the two of them proudly holding up Ella and Bun-Bun—their special stuffed animals—to the camera.

"You look so young," Edaline said over her shoulder, making Sophie nearly drop the scrapbook. "Sorry—I thought you heard me approaching."

She eyed the photo album with a burning sort of curiosity, and part of Sophie was tempted to cover the pictures and keep the two halves of her life separate. But if her human family really did get to keep their memories, she was going to have to let everything merge.

She patted the bed and flipped back to the beginning as Edaline scooted close, wrapping her arm around Sophie's shoulder.

"Look at those big brown eyes," Edaline whispered, studying the first layout of photos.

"Yeah, even as a baby I was weird," Sophie mumbled.

Blue eyes were standard among the elves, but Sophie's tweaked genetics had made hers an earthy tone with scattered flecks of gold. She'd been teased *and* praised for it, so the only thing she knew for sure was that she'd always be different.

"You were beautiful," Edaline insisted.

Sophie snorted. "Oh please—look at my giant head!"

"All babies have big heads. Besides, you needed space for that powerful brain."

"Riiiiiight. I'm sure that's it." Sophie squinted closer at the pictures. "I was also a very serious baby."

In every photo her face looked scrunched with concentration, like she was trying to make sense of the world.

Or maybe she'd been pooping. With babies, it was hard to tell.

"You were perfect." Edaline touched the edge of a picture where toddler Sophie had been dressed in so many ruffles she looked like a flower. "You *are* perfect."

The next page was full of family photos—just the three of them back then, though in the third one Sophie's mom had clearly been pregnant.

"Sometimes I forget that you had a whole life before you came here," Edaline whispered, and the wistfulness in her voice stirred up a whole new batch of worries.

Edaline turned to the next page, to a photo of Sophie sunken into a faded old couch with her baby sister propped in her lap. "You must miss them so much."

Sophie nodded.

But she couldn't bring herself to mention that she was hoping her human parents might be allowed to keep their memories. Because she hadn't really thought about how it could affect Grady and Edaline.

She'd known it would be messy and complicated, but she'd mostly considered how it might change things for her—and her human family.

What if Grady and Edaline didn't think it was good news?

What if it damaged the bond they'd worked so hard to build?

What if . . .

There were too many "what-ifs."

And she wasn't ready for any of them.

"You're sure you don't need to talk?" Edaline whispered as Sophie whipped the scrapbook closed.

"I don't really know what to say right now," Sophie admitted.

"Well . . . I'm here if you change your mind."

Edaline helped her put the photo album away before she snapped her fingers to lower the shades over the windows and left Sophie alone. Everything was quiet after that—except for Iggy's leaf-blower snoring.

But as soon as Sophie closed her eyes, each of those "what-ifs" took on vibrant, terrifying shapes.

She'd battled nightmares before—and she was no stranger to sleepless nights. But the hollow chill that settled into her heart felt different.

She lay there sweating and shivering, clutching her bright blue stuffed elephant and trying to talk herself through it. But when her chest started to constrict, she threw back her covers and rushed for the door.

"What's wrong?" Sandor asked as she sprinted for the stairs.

"I . . . need my family."

It felt like the silliest, most childish thing to admit—especially since she'd brought Ella along with her. But Sophie couldn't face that suffocating loneliness any longer.

She realized halfway to the second floor that she'd never actually been in Grady and Edaline's room. When she'd first moved in, she'd considered the space off-limits—though no one had ever told her that. And since then, the most she'd ever done was peek through a crack in the doorway while the room was mostly dark. If Sandor hadn't been right behind her, she might've turned back—but pride drove her forward, and even though her knock was barely audible, Grady answered immediately.

"Everything all right?"

Sophie cleared her throat. "I'm fine. I was just wondering if—are there T. rexes on your pajamas?"

Grady glanced down at his fuzzy pants covered in neon-green, feathered dinosaurs. The shirt was plain white, with a roaring dinosaur face in the center of the chest. "They were a gift from Elwin while you were living with the Black Swan."

Sophie smiled. Elwin—Foxfire's resident Physician—was known for his fondness for goofy, animal-covered clothes.

"I'm guessing you're not here to discuss sleepwear," Grady noted.

The temptation to wimp out surged again, but Sophie managed to mumble, "I was wondering if I could sleep in here. With you guys."

She'd expected Grady to ask why. Maybe even be a little annoyed that she'd be crowding up his bed.

Instead, his smile was a mix of touched and sad as he told her, "Of course," and stepped aside to let her in.

The room was already dark, but Sophie could make out wispy curtains and sleek silver furniture as she shuffled across the bunny-soft carpet to the enormous bed. Each of the posts reminded Sophie of a tree, stretching metal branches toward the ceiling to form an intricate canopy, with thin strands of gossamer fabric woven around twinkle lights, like faded starlight.

Edaline moved to the center of the bed, making room for Sophie to climb in.

"You don't mind?" Sophie asked as she crawled under the covers, which felt especially warm and soft against her skin.

"Of course not." Edaline adjusted her pillows as she settled next to Sophie, wrapping one arm around Sophie's waist and using the other to gently rub her back as Grady joined them on the other side of the bed.

"Here," he said, snapping his fingers and making a series of softly colored orbs glow around the room, casting delicate shadows across the walls. Each shadow made different shapes—soaring birds, majestic mountains, floating fish, graceful beasts. "Jolie was afraid of the dark when she was little," he explained. "So we added these."

"We wanted her to see that the shadows that scared her could be beautiful and powerful when we learn how to take control of them," Edaline added.

Taking control.

It sounded so simple.

And so impossible.

But Edaline was right—that was the only way to get through this.

Tomorrow Sophie would hear the Black Swan out, hoping they had a solid plan. And if they didn't, she'd have to figure out how to move forward with Keefe's mom—unless anyone had any better ideas.

In the meantime, she would focus on the good things she had. Leave all the "what-ifs" alone until they became "for sures."

"I love you guys," she whispered as she settled against Edaline, hugging Ella tight.

"We love you too," Grady whispered back.

It still took quite a while. But eventually sleep found her. And even though her dreams weren't pleasant, the steady warmth of her family chased away the worst of the nightmares.

ELEVEN

ON'T COME OUT UNTIL YOU'RE
dressed," Sandor called through Sophie's
bathroom door the next morning as she
stood in the dressing area of her closet,
tying the sash on her silky green tunic.

Despite the somewhat restful night of sleep, she'd still woken
around sunrise, her limbs itchy with nerves for the day ahead.

At least her sister had slept. Amy had been curled up in bed
with Watson and Marty when Sophie hailed her to see how she
was doing—and she had *not* been happy to be woken up.

Sophie stepped out into her room. "Why? Is something . . ."

Her voice trailed off when she spotted Keefe standing in her
bedroom doorway.

He was at least an hour early. And he looked . . . tired.

"Yeah, I know," he said, scratching at his hair—which was much less carefully styled than usual. "I look like I lost a fight with my pillow."

He did. His dark circles were *fierce.*

"Meanwhile, you look especially sparkly," he added with a slow smile.

Sophie fussed with her jeweled sleeves—which matched the emeralds lining the knee-high boots she'd slipped over her lacy gray leggings. Biana had frustratingly pointed out that elaborate clothes would do a better job of disguising her gloves, so Sophie was trying to force herself to get used to wearing glitter and frills.

Keefe's lips tilted into his famous smirk as he crossed the room to stand closer. "I meant that as a compliment, Foster. Sparkles look good on you. So does the new hairdo."

He reached up, his fingers skating gently along the edge of the intricate braid weaving through the front part of her hair. She'd been awake so long, she'd decided to listen to Vertina— the tiny face programmed into her spectral mirror, who loved to offer beauty advice, regardless of whether Sophie wanted to hear it.

"If you're trying to impress me, it's working," he told her, and she felt her cheeks warm—until he added, "But, you *always* impress me, so maybe you were thinking of someone else?"

Sophie took a step back.

She knew he was only teasing, but that didn't stop her face from experiencing an entirely different kind of burn.

Keefe cleared his throat. "Looks like we both had the same idea about wearing green."

He tossed back the sides of his pine-colored cape, revealing an intricately embroidered sage-toned jerkin with peridot buttons.

"It seemed fitting, since we haven't been able to do a planting," Sophie mumbled, clutching her locket with Mr. Forkle's Wanderling seed. The elves didn't wear black to their versions of funerals, preferring the color of life instead.

Keefe nodded. "I had to sneak into Candleshade to grab this from my closet—though honestly, I'm not sure if my dad's living there right now. The place felt way too dark and quiet."

Sophie frowned. "Where else would he be?"

"Maybe his 'secret apartment in Atlantis'? Or, his 'secret beach house'? They're his 'escapes' for when he needs a 'break,' because, you know, a two-hundred-story tower isn't big enough for the three of us to all live in. Or *wasn't*," he corrected.

He tried to shrug it off, but Sophie could see the hurt etched between his brows. Keefe's father had never physically hit him, but he'd done plenty of emotional damage with his insults, and unrealistic expectations, and the way he'd made Keefe feel like a constant bother.

"Did you grab Mrs. Stinkbottom while you were there?"

she asked, trying to lighten the mood. But she'd forgotten that she'd spotted the so-ugly-it's-cute plush gulon in Lord Cassius's bedroom in Candleshade, as if he'd been sleeping with it while Keefe was away.

"I did, actually," Keefe said. "Couldn't leave her behind again. I shouldn't have left her in the first place."

"You shouldn't have," Sophie agreed. "I bet you'll sleep better tonight."

"Probably." He smiled, shaking his head. "I never thought I'd need a stuffed animal to sleep. But . . . I never knew I needed a lot of things before I met you."

Somehow he'd moved closer, and Sophie's throat went dry as he reached up and touched her braid again. Their eyes locked, and when his lips parted they seemed to curve with a different word than the one he eventually said. "Anyway. We don't have a lot of time before the rest of the Foster Fan Club gets here, so I'm going to ask this fast—and I want a *real* answer, not that distract-and-avoid thing you're becoming a master at. You're planning to reach out to my mom, aren't you? To ask her to take us to Nightfall?"

"We might have to," Sophie admitted. "But not until we're more prepared."

"But every minute we waste—"

"I know." Sophie pressed her fist against her knotted emotions. "Believe me—I feel sick about every lost second. But I've thought a lot about it, and the thing is, your mom knows we'd never reach out to her unless we were desperate. And she'll use that to her advantage."

"How does waiting change that?" Keefe asked.

"It gives us a chance to make sure there isn't anything else we're missing."

"You really think we're going to come up with a better idea?"

"I don't know. Maybe the Black Swan's contingency plan will—"

"Uh, we're talking about the Black Swan," Keefe interrupted. "I'm betting they're going to tell us who they've elected to replace Forkle in the Collective and then order us to read some boring books and practice using our abilities—and while I'm sure you and the Fitzster won't mind the excuse to stare into each other's eyes—"

"It's called Cognate training," Sophie corrected. "And that's not what we do."

"Keep telling yourself that."

Sophie ignored him. "Physic warned me that the contingency plan is going to make me angry. That sounds like it has to be something big."

"Or maybe she knows you're going to hate whoever they're electing to fill his place in the Collective. Ugh—what if it's Timkin Heks?"

The idea of having the father of one of Foxfire's most outspoken mean girls bossing them around—even if Stina had been a *little* better lately—made Sophie want to fling things.

"It won't be Timkin," she tried to convince herself. "He's too new to the order."

"Then who do you think it'll be?" Keefe asked.

"No idea."

For her, Mr. Forkle *was* the Black Swan. She couldn't imagine it without him, even though she was going to have to.

"Well, even if they appoint someone we like—and the rest of the Collective has some other brilliant plan for what to do without Forkle—that still doesn't get us any closer to Nightfall. We need my mom for that."

"Maybe," Sophie admitted. "But you don't stick your hand in a viper's nest until you have a plan to avoid getting bitten."

"Okay, I'll give you points for the fancy metaphor. But I can handle my mom. She loves glory and attention—and Fintan took that away and left her to rot in an ogre prison. She's going to want payback. Especially when she finds out that Fintan has enough of my blood to get into Nightfall. She called that place my legacy—but we both know she really meant it was *her* legacy. And now the Neverseen are in there without her."

"Right, but you're forgetting that your mom still has her own agenda," Sophie reminded him. "And taking my parents could've been a part of her plan."

"I know. But she also needs me—and I'm not saying that because I think my mommy loves me and misses me. I haven't believed that lie in years."

He said it so matter-of-factly, it made Sophie reach for his hand.

He watched her gloved fingers wrap around his. "I'm just saying she wouldn't have left the note you guys found in my closet, or rigged my Imparter, or demanded you get me away from the Neverseen, if she didn't need me for something. So, let's find out what it is."

"We will. I'm sure we will. We just need to be prepared."

"I *am* prepared—and I know you're probably thinking about the epic fail I had with the Neverseen—"

"That's *exactly* what I'm thinking," Sophie agreed.

"But this won't be like that. I didn't know Fintan. I *know* my mom."

"Do you?" Sophie asked as gently as she could. "She lied to you most of your life, and manipulated you and erased your memories."

"Yeah, she's definitely not going to win any Mom of the Year awards," Keefe muttered. "And yeah, she's fooled me in the past. But I've had a lot of time to think about things, and I'm pretty sure I've figured her out."

"Pretty sure?" Sophie repeated. "You want to risk everything on *pretty sure?"*

"The only thing I'm risking is *me.*"

"Which is way more than I'm willing to lose." It came out mushier than she'd meant it to, so she added, "And I know the rest of our friends will agree with me."

114   NIGHTFALL

Keefe snorted. "I'm betting Bangs Boy won't."

"Well, maybe he would if you'd stop calling him Bangs Boy."

"Yeah, but that's never going to happen."

Keefe had invented the nickname because of Tam's long jagged bangs, which Tam had dipped in melted silver to annoy his selfish, domineering parents. The hairdo was actually awesome—and matched the silver tips his twin sister, Linh, had added to her long black hair for the same reason. But Keefe insisted on teasing him relentlessly about it. Probably because Keefe and Tam had disliked each other from the moment they'd met.

The funny thing was, neither of them realized how much they had in common. If they'd get over themselves, they'd probably be best friends.

"I appreciate the concern, Foster," Keefe said, slowly pulling his hand away. "But we both know that sooner or later we're going to *have* to reach out to my mom. So why not do it before we waste a bunch of time we can't afford to lose?"

"Because"—she took a deep breath—"there are bigger things to think about, beyond what's going on with my family. It *kills* me to say that. But . . . it's also true. Whatever's happening to them right now is just one small piece of the Neverseen's plan. And I think they're trying to keep me distracted—trying to keep all of us so focused on the rescue that we don't notice what they're actually up to. Just like they did with Lumenaria."

The color drained from Keefe's face. "Any idea what else they're working on?"

"Nope. But I'm starting to wonder if it goes back to that first attack with the Everblaze. We never really looked into *why* they set all those fires in the human world, and I think we need to figure that out. Did anyone ever bring the fires up when you were living with the Neverseen?"

He shook his head. "Fintan was always going on about the wonder of fire and how things need to burn so that something stronger can rise from the ashes—blah, blah, blah. But it was just his usual tirade about how the Council never should've banned Pyrokinetics."

"Well, I still think there had to be a bigger reason for the Everblaze," she said quietly. "But even if I'm wrong, we know this is about more than two abducted humans."

"That doesn't mean we should ignore a solid plan to help them either."

"But we don't *have* a plan. Believe me, I'm trying to put one together. But there are so many things we need to consider—like Wylie's mom. Fintan wouldn't have abducted Wylie if there wasn't something crucial he needed from him. So maybe if we figure that out, it'll give us some leverage, or at least tell us what Fintan's 'vision' is or . . . I don't know. It made a lot more sense in my head yesterday."

"Actually, that does make sense," Keefe said. "But there's only one person who can give us that information—and hey, it's the one I've been saying we need to reach out to!"

"She's not going to tell us for free. Same goes for any help finding Nightfall."

"So let's see what she demands."

"Do you honestly think your mom is going to ask for something we can actually give?"

"I do. I think she's that desperate—and if I'm wrong, all we wasted was a conversation. That's why I got here early. I promised I wouldn't do anything without you again, so . . ."

He reached into his pocket and pulled out something small, green, and shiny.

"Is that a Prattles pin?" Sophie asked, squinting at the tiny metal animal.

"A gulon," Keefe agreed with a wink.

"Okay, seriously, will you *please* tell me what happened during the Great Gulon Incident? I'm really getting sick of everyone avoiding the question."

"It's an *awesome* story. But now's not a good time." He pulled something else out of his pocket, and Sophie's whole body turned cold.

"Please tell me that's not . . ."

Keefe held it up over his head when she lunged to grab it. "It is. Dex gave it back to me a couple of weeks ago."

"He shouldn't have done that."

"I agree," Sandor said, stalking into the room. One of his large gray hands hovered menacingly near his sword as he held the other out to Keefe. "Give that to me, before you do something foolish."

For one endless second, they stared each other down.

Then Keefe jabbed his finger with the sharp end of the gulon pin and dragged it through his skin, cutting a deep red gash.

"Sorry, Gigantor," he said through gritted teeth as he scrambled to the other side of the room. "Foolish is my specialty."

"Don't!" Sophie shouted—but he'd already smeared his blood across the back of the silver screen.

"It's going to be okay," Keefe whispered as the small gadget flashed with a dull glow.

Sophie shook her head, her brain too clogged with words she wasn't supposed to say to come up with a response. But she still heard Lady Gisela's sharp, arrogant voice as it poured in through the still-blank Imparter.

"It's about time."

TWELVE

GLAD YOU'RE BOTH HERE," LADY
Gisela said as Keefe tapped on the blank
Imparter screen. "That makes everything so
much easier."

"You can see us?" Sophie asked, relieved her voice sounded
strong and steady.

"Of course. Just like I can see your goblin looming behind
you, looking ready to snatch the Imparter and crush it. I
wouldn't let him do that, by the way. Obviously you need my
help, otherwise you never would've decided to trust me."

"We don't *trust* you," Keefe said, his hands shaking so much,
he barely kept his hold on the blood-coated gadget.

Sophie wondered if he was in pain, since his cut was still streaming red. But then she realized . . .

This was the first time he'd spoken to his mom since he found out she might be dead. And the last time he'd seen her, she'd tried to kill him—and his friends.

"Do you expect us to believe you don't already know what's going on?" Keefe snapped.

"I have my theories," Lady Gisela told him. "But Fintan's proving to be simultaneously predictable *and* foolhardy, thinking he can shred my plan and choose which pieces to follow—as if it wasn't painstakingly constructed after years of unparalleled research, then fine-tuned until everything was perfected."

"Just so we're clear," Sophie said, "your plan was the Lode-star Initiative?"

"That's the name I eventually settled on, yes. And save your breath asking for specifics. Things may be salvageable yet, and neither of you are ready to accept that."

"And we never will be," Sophie told her. "Any plan that involves killing innocent people—"

"Who said anything about innocent?" Lady Gisela interrupted. "If you're talking about what happened to those goblins in Lumenaria—and Councillor Terik's leg, for that matter—I told you, that was Fintan's 'vision.' As was his moronic plan with the ogres and the gnomish plague. I could never conceive anything so inelegant."

"Then why did King Dimitar tell me at the Peace Summit that when Fintan first approached him about the plague, he called it the Lodestar Initiative?" Sophie asked.

"How would I know? Perhaps Fintan made his own amendment. If you don't believe me, consider this: That was the same conversation where Fintan convinced Dimitar to lock me away in his reeking prison."

Bile coated Sophie's tongue.

As much as she despised Keefe's mother, she'd never forget the memory she'd seen of Lady Gisela begging for her life as she was dragged toward the ogres' legendary prison. Her skin had been covered in strangely curved wounds, most so deep they probably left scars.

Maybe that was why Lady Gisela wasn't letting them see her.

"What about the abductions?" Keefe asked.

His mom sighed. "That whole ordeal was Brant's uninspired solution—bring in the moonlark, search her memories to find out what the Black Swan were planning, then wipe her mind to neutralize her and see if we couldn't reprogram her to work for us. I told him they would've been prepared for that scenario, but he lacked the patience to wait for a better alternative. *And* he was idiotic enough to kidnap an unnecessary child while he was at it."

Keefe wrapped his free arm around Sophie, holding both of them steady. "Those aren't the abductions I meant. And you know it."

"Do I? Then you'll need to be clearer. Unless . . ."

Her voice trailed off, and when she spoke again, the words shook with a barely bridled rage. "How many humans have they taken?"

"You don't know?" Sophie wished she could stretch out her consciousness and dive into Lady Gisela's mind—but without knowing where Keefe's mom was, or being more familiar with the feel of her thoughts, she wouldn't be able to make a strong enough connection.

When Lady Gisela stayed silent, Sophie decided she couldn't treat her family like pawns in a game. "They took my human parents."

Lady Gisela swore under her breath. "I suppose they do love to make things personal."

"To keep me distracted, right?" Sophie asked.

"Sounds like the moonlark is finally learning to ask the right questions."

"Does that mean I should also be asking if there was another reason behind the Everblaze attacks several months ago?" Sophie pressed.

She could hear the smile in Lady Gisela's voice when she said, "Definitely a question I was surprised no one asked before. Every action is . . . multifaceted."

"And I'm assuming you're not going to tell us what some of those other facets might be?" Sophie asked.

"For the fires? Is that really what you want my help with?

And keep in mind, I'm only going to help you with *one* thing."

The answer should've been yes. The fires could be more important than anything.

But even knowing that—even knowing the Neverseen were manipulating her into focusing on something personal— Sophie couldn't make herself say the word.

"We need to get Foster's family back," Keefe said, making the choice for her. "Why would the Neverseen take them? Is there something important about them?"

"I'm sure that's what they'd like to find out. Though for Brant, this is mostly about revenge. Your escape made him look bad, Sophie. And then you took great pleasure in spoiling some of his other plans—*and* you helped cost him his hand. He's determined to make you pay."

Sophie frowned at Keefe, wondering if he'd caught the same thing she did. "Don't you mean 'was'?"

"Was what?" his mother asked.

Sophie and Keefe shared another look.

"Didn't you hear that Brant was killed in Lumenaria?" Keefe asked.

Silence followed.

If it weren't for a few crackles of static, Sophie would've worried the connection had been severed.

"Was it an accident?" Lady Gisela whispered. "Or did they turn on him as well?"

"Neither," Sophie told her. "He died when he attacked Councillor Oralie."

Lady Gisela barked a laugh. "*She* took him out? Miss ringlets and rosy cheeks? I'm not sure I believe that."

"She had help." And no way was Sophie telling her about what happened to Mr. Forkle in the process.

"Well," Lady Gisela said after another stretch of silence, "that's certainly an interesting shift in the balance. Especially for Ruy."

"Why?" Keefe asked.

"Didn't you live with them?"

Keefe glanced at Sophie. "Ruy and Fintan *did* argue a lot."

"I'm sure they do even more now that Fintan has his new advisor," Lady Gisela added. "In fact, that explains this sudden acceleration."

It took Sophie a second to put together who she must be referring to. "You're talking about the prisoner they freed from the Lumenaria dungeon."

The prisoner who'd been held there for *thousands* of years.

The prisoner who was so dangerous, the Council had erased any knowledge of them from their memories—as if that could somehow make the problem disappear.

"She's quite the legend," Lady Gisela said. "But that's all I'm going to tell you, because she may yet be useful to me."

Keefe huffed a disgusted laugh. "I love how you keep acting like you still have any power in this mess. The Neverseen cut you up, locked you in prison, and left you for dead."

"If I'm so powerless, why are we having this conversation?"

Sophie hesitated before admitting, "Because they took my parents to Nightfall."

"Of course they did. That's what I designed it for."

"So . . . my family *is* part of your plan?" Sophie whispered.

"None of this is going the way I wanted it to" was the only answer Lady Gisela gave—which wasn't much of an answer at all.

But Keefe moved on to the more important question. "What is Nightfall? Some sort of prison?"

"It's the future—though Fintan has never truly understood the concept. And I won't ask how he got in, Keefe, since I'm sure I won't like the answer."

"You won't," Keefe agreed. "So why don't you tell us how to get there, and we'll clear them out for you?"

His mom sighed. "I expected you to be cleverer by now. Do you really need me to remind you that I already told you how to find it?"

"The starstone?" Sophie guessed.

In Keefe's only memory of Nightfall, his mom had used a smooth, softly glowing stone to leap her and Keefe to the doorway. The rare jewel was set into one of her hairpins—the same pin she'd used to draw Keefe's blood for the lock.

"Starstones always remember the last place they've been," Lady Gisela confirmed. "I told you that would be important someday."

"Funny, it'd be a lot easier to remember these things if you hadn't wiped them out of my head!" Keefe snapped. "And hey, while you were at it, you could've told me where you hid the stupid pin!"

"I didn't hide it. I lost it."

Keefe snorted. "You expect me to believe you lost your only way to get to Nightfall?"

"Of course not. But it's the only way *you'll* be able to find your way there. And it just so happens to be in the one place I need you to pay a visit to for me anyway."

"How convenient," Sophie grumbled.

"Yes, I love when things come together so neatly. Especially when we're pressed for time, so I won't have to deal with any whining or arguing."

"I wouldn't be so sure about that," Keefe warned her.

"Really? Should I describe some of the tests Sophie's parents are enduring while you snipe like a petulant child?"

"What kinds of tests?" Sophie asked, struggling to breathe.

"Hmm. Perhaps it's better to let you imagine."

"Don't listen to her," Keefe said. "I know this trick. She used it all the time on my dad—pretended there'd be some huge problem if he didn't give her exactly what she wanted. And then, once she was satisfied, it would turn out to be a 'misunderstanding.'"

"Are you willing to stake her family's lives on that?" Lady Gisela asked.

Sophie wasn't. "Where's the starstone?"

"Let's not get ahead of ourselves. First you need to agree to deliver a message for me—one that *must* arrive pristine and unopened. I'll know if you tamper with the seal, and you won't like what happens."

"And how am I supposed to get this mystery message?" Sophie asked.

"Leave that to me. If you agree, you'll find it waiting for you tomorrow, and even your goblin will be scratching his head, wondering how it got there."

The squeaky sound behind them was probably Sandor's growl, but Lady Gisela seemed unimpressed.

"Do we have a deal?"

"Not without more information," Sophie told her. "I'm not agreeing to deliver something that could be a kill order."

"Trust me, Sophie, if I wanted someone dead, they'd be dead already."

"Like Cyrah Endal?" Sophie countered.

"You brought Cyrah up the last time we talked too. What is your strange fixation with her?"

"Fintan's fixated on her too. And I'm assuming you know why."

"I do. But I've never agreed with it."

"Then why did you kill her?" Sophie demanded.

"What makes you so certain I did?"

"Don't!" Keefe interrupted before Sophie could answer.

"She's dodging the question, trying to get you to tell her everything we know."

"Which means there *is* something to know," Lady Gisela seemed to purr. "Fascinating. Fintan's scrambling everything up even worse than I'd imagined. We can use that."

"We're not a 'we,'" Sophie told her.

"Perhaps not yet. But we will be. Once you agree to deliver my message."

"I told you, I'm not agreeing to that without knowing where I'm going and who I'm giving it to," Sophie told her. "And how do I know you won't betray us afterward and never tell us where to find the starstone?"

"Because the starstone is where you'll be heading, and retrieving it will be entirely up to you. You and your friends are good at being *creative*. And the message is nothing to trouble yourself over. In fact, depending on the result, you may even be thanking me."

"You still haven't told me where I'm going," Sophie reminded her.

"And I won't, until you agree. I'm also withholding one crucial piece of information you'll need to get past Nightfall's security until I know the message has been delivered. It's your call. If you'd rather track down Nightfall on your own, be my guest. But I made sure it's a place no one can find unless they already know where it is—and much as my son may think he can figure it out on his own, he doesn't have enough information, even if he recovered every one of his erased memories."

"How many missing memories are there?" Keefe asked.

"Telling you would be playing fair."

Keefe gritted his teeth so hard, Sophie could hear them grinding against one another.

"This could be another one of her tricks," Sophie reminded him. "To make you second-guess yourself."

"I suppose that's a valid point," Lady Gisela said. "But you've recovered how many memories, Keefe? Two? Or was it three? Do you really think I would've made it that easy?"

Keefe rubbed his temples, and Sophie reached for his hand.

"It's fine, Foster," he told her. "I'm done obsessing about the past. All I care about is the future."

"And that future is growing increasingly bleak, the longer you delay your answer. Tell you what—I'll sweeten the deal. I'll share everything I know about Cyrah Endal—but not until after you deliver my message. That's my final offer. And it expires in thirty seconds, so think quickly—and keep in mind that if you come crawling back to me later, the price will increase *significantly*."

Sophie tugged on her eyelashes and tried to rush through a mental list of pros and cons.

Even without knowing where the message was going, she was sure its contents wouldn't be good. But would it be bad enough that it was worth ignoring this chance to help her family and learn about Wylie's mom?

"Your choice, Foster," Keefe told her, and the red streaming from his hand made it pretty clear how much he was willing to sacrifice.

"Twenty seconds," Lady Gisela warned.

Sophie glanced at Sandor.

The massive goblin sighed. "I think you can guess my opinion on the matter. But you'll have my protection either way."

"Ten seconds," Lady Gisela said.

Sophie closed her eyes, her mind like a pendulum swinging back and forth.

"Deal," she barely managed to whisper.

"Wise decision," Lady Gisela told her. "I hope this is proof that you're realizing I'm not your enemy."

"I guess we'll see once you tell me where you're forcing me to deliver a message."

Lady Gisela laughed. "I'm not *forcing* you to do anything. My help simply doesn't come free—something you should consider the next time the Black Swan expects your assistance. Take it from someone who had to learn the hard way—making sacrifices for an organization won't earn you their loyalty. *Demand* it."

"I'll keep that in mind," Sophie muttered. "Now tell me where I have to go."

"What's the hurry? You won't have the message until tomorrow—and judging by the green you're both wearing, I'm guessing you have *other* plans for today."

"Don't," Keefe warned. "*Don't* make jokes about that."

"So it's serious, then," Lady Gisela murmured. "I must say, this conversation has been far more enlightening than I'd imagined. Who could you have lost? Was it—"

"STOP!" Keefe shouted. "Or I swear, I'll give what I found in Candleshade over to the Neverseen."

Sophie's eyebrows shot up.

"Yeah," Keefe told her. "I did some digging while I was there this morning. And I found my mom's secret stash. It was pretty obvious, actually, once I really thought about it."

"Well," Lady Gisela said, her voice tighter than it had been. "Good to see you finally solved that puzzle—but there's no need to make threats, Keefe. Be ready bright and early tomorrow—you'll be heading to Ravagog to deliver my message to King Dimitar."

THIRTEEN

OU WANT US TO GO TO THE OGRE capital," Sophie clarified.

"And deliver a message to the guy who sliced you up and left you to die in his prison?" Keefe added.

Lady Gisela's voice sounded hollow when she said, "King Dimitar's loyalties have changed since then. He no longer supports the Neverseen."

"He doesn't support *anybody*," Sophie argued. "I was there at the Peace Summit. He agreed to every concession in the treaty, in exchange for a guarantee that the elves—and other species—would leave his people alone. I'm sure the city gates are locked—and the secret path we snuck through last time will be sealed up, if it wasn't destroyed in the flood."

"Well then, it's a good thing you and your friends have proven to be so resourceful. Because that's the deal you agreed to. And let's also not forget that the starstone you need is in King Dimitar's possession. I had it with me the day I was taken, and the guards stole everything. Even the clothes off my back."

The shiver in her voice matched Sophie's shudder.

"Are you sure the ogres wouldn't have thrown it out?" Keefe asked.

"I suppose I can't be certain of *anything*, given the unpredictability of the ogres," Lady Gisela said quietly. "But I do know Dimitar is fond of his trophies. He has a whole room in his palace where he keeps the treasures he's taken from those he's imprisoned or killed. And I was considered a prize, so I suspect mine will be prominently displayed."

"I don't understand why you want to reach out to him," Sophie mumbled. "Unless this is about revenge—"

"It's not," Lady Gisela interrupted. "I won't claim that some part of me hasn't loved watching Dimitar suffer for his alliance with Fintan. And I doubt I'll weep whenever his life ends. But for now, we have a common enemy, and that is too powerful of an asset to ignore—something I'm hoping you'll also see the wisdom of, eventually."

"I wouldn't hold my breath."

"Said the girl who already agreed to deliver my message."

"This is more than a message delivery!" Sandor growled.

"You barely made it out of Ravagog once, Sophie—and I won't be able to accompany you without embroiling my species in treaty violations."

"I know." Sophie tried to think of a plan, but everything ended in pain—or prison—or war.

"King Dimitar isn't exactly a big fan of me or my friends," she reminded Lady Gisela. "He's not going to read anything I bring him."

"Won't he?" she asked. "Dimitar may despise you and everything you represent. But he knows the weight of your role in our world, and that ignoring you could lead to consequences for his people. He'll open the scroll and memorize every word, if only to make sure he's informed and prepared."

"I'm not going to pretend the message is from me," Sophie warned.

"I didn't ask you to. You could tell him a sasquatch wrote it for all I care."

There was a joke there—but Sophie didn't make it.

Shockingly, neither did Keefe.

"Well," Lady Gisela said, sounding far too pleased with herself, "I'll leave you to figure out how you're going to make this happen. If it helps at all, I wouldn't make a demand I considered impossible. Stop panicking and *think*. And keep an eye out for the message tomorrow. Once it's delivered and you have the starstone, hail me again and I'll give you the last piece you need. Oh, and Keefe?"

She seemed to wait for him to look at the Imparter.

"Your father was wrong about you," she said quietly. "You're not a disappointment. *Yet.*"

The Imparter went dark without so much as a goodbye.

"Same old Mom," Keefe muttered, squeezing the gadget so hard, Sophie wondered if it would crack.

She hooked her arm through his and dragged him toward her bathroom. "Come on. We need to treat your wound."

The gash in his finger was still bleeding, dripping spots of red on his brown boots as she led him over to the sink.

"Ugh, you didn't need to cut this deep," she grumbled when the gentle stream of water separated the skin.

"Guess that's what I get for rushing."

"Yeah, we're going to talk about that in a minute. First let's see if we can stop the bleeding."

She took several deep breaths, trying not to think about all the red as she fished through the drawers of colorful vials—Edaline kept a *plentiful* supply of medicine around, thanks to Sophie's accident-prone tendencies. "I think this is the right one."

She could always hail Elwin if she was wrong—the friendly physician was kind enough to make house calls. But then they'd have to explain what happened, and she had enough challenging conversations ahead.

Grady and Edaline were *not* going to be pleased with this new bargain. Neither would the Black Swan. And she was sure Sandor wasn't done with his lectures.

"Does it sting?" she asked Keefe as she slathered on a cold turquoise balm.

"Nope. But I sure wish it smelled better."

So did Sophie—especially since some elvin remedies had lovely ingredients like yeti pee.

But Keefe's wound was clotting, so she let the treatment settle for a few more seconds, then wiped his hand clean with a damp towel and dotted the wound with a silver paste.

"Thanks," Keefe mumbled as she wrapped his finger in gauze.

"Need an elixir for the pain? I'm sure we have some."

He grabbed her hand to stop her fussing. "I'm all good now, Foster. Unless you want to try kissing it to make it better."

She rolled her eyes and pulled away.

"So . . . ," he said as she put the supplies carefully back into the drawer. "On a scale of one to ten zillion, how angry are you?"

Sophie was still deciding.

"It's okay," Keefe told her. "Unleash the lecture! Here, I'll even start it for you." His voice shifted up to an uncanny impersonation of hers. *"How dare you ambush me, Keefe? I don't care if you're the most gorgeous guy I've ever seen—WAY better looking than other guys with their dimples or weirdly teal eyes. You had no right to show up and surprise me like that!"*

Sophie pinched the bridge of her nose. "This isn't a joke."

"Aw, come on. Don't I at least get points for not hailing her by myself, making the deal alone, and running off to Ravagog without you?"

"No," Sandor growled from the doorway.

"He gets *some*," Sophie corrected. "This *is* an improvement. But you still can't spring something on me like that. That's not how teamwork goes."

"I know." Keefe fussed with his new bandage. "If it hadn't involved my mom, I never would've done it. I just . . . I know you get *protective* of me sometimes—especially when it has anything to do with my oh-so-awesome family. And I appreciate it. But I care way more about helping *your* family. I didn't want you hesitating because of me, so I thought I'd make the hard decision for you—but everything after that was up to you."

Sophie let out a slow breath.

"I'll make it up to you," he promised. "How about I let you demand a special favor? I won't even put a time limit on it and steal it back later like *some* greedy people. And anything's game! You want me to sing, I'll belt it out like a siren. You want me to dance, I'll treat you to my most epic shimmy. Here, I'll give you a free taste."

He wiggled his hips around the bathroom, and Sophie felt her traitorous lips smile.

"Or maybe you'd rather I put my incredible Empath talents to work and help you solve the complicated square you're always telling yourself is a triangle?"

She shook her head, refusing to admit she knew what he meant. "I already know what I want."

One of Keefe's eyebrows shot up. "Is that so?"

"Yep. Give me the Imparter."

Keefe's smile faded. But he obediently handed it over—only to have it snatched by Sandor.

"That doesn't count as your favor," Sandor informed them. "I was going to confiscate this anyway—and don't you dare go easy on him with what you demand, Sophie. I'm sure Grizel can help you come up with some humiliating ideas, if you need inspiration. And I expect *you*," he told Keefe, "to hand over whatever you found at Candleshade."

Keefe's lips quirked up again. "Funny story? I only said I found something to see how my mom would react—and she fell for it! So now we know there *is* something worth looking for. Come on, Foster, admit it—that was pretty clever."

"It was," Sophie reluctantly agreed. "But do you really think we're going to be able to find it? There must be a million different places she could've stashed it in that giant tower."

"Yeah, I'll have to see if I can trick a clue out of her after we deliver her message."

Sophie sighed. "I love how you make it sound like we just have to knock on the gates of Ravagog and King Dimitar will invite us in for a party."

"A parade in our honor seems more likely," Keefe teased.

Sophie wandered back to her room and stared at the bookshelf, as if the answer were sitting there waiting for her. "What do you think her message is going to say?"

"Probably some desperate plea for an alliance," Keefe said as he came to stand beside her. "But don't look so freaked out. No way is King Dimitar going to trust my mom again. You saw those cuts he made to her face. And didn't he call the Neverseen 'lunatics' in his speeches at the Peace Summit?"

"But your mom's not with them anymore. And we both know she's a master of manipulating people."

"Maybe, but . . . if King Dimitar is stupid enough to trust my mom, he's going to do that whether we're the one delivering the letter or not. That's the part you have to remember—if she wasn't using us, she'd find another way. She's annoyingly resourceful like that."

"She really is." She squared her shoulders and turned to face him. "So, the big question is—assuming we find a way to get into Ravagog—how on earth are we going to get the hairpin from Dimitar?"

"Maybe he'll give it to us," Keefe suggested.

It was hard to tell who scoffed louder—Sophie or Sandor.

"No, really. I'm serious!" Keefe insisted. "I'm not saying he's going to be our new BFF. But didn't he turn down the Neverseen's latest offer after he talked to Lady Cadence? So maybe we should ask her for some pointers on how to get through to him. In fact, she might be our ticket into Ravagog. Didn't the treaty say she'd be granted access whenever she wants?"

"She probably *is* our best chance," Sophie admitted. Lady Cadence had lived with the ogres for years and was one of their most supportive allies.

"What was that?" Keefe asked. "Did the Mysterious Miss F. just agree that I'm a genius? Because that's what I heard! And it's filled my heart with all the warmest, softest fuzzies."

Sophie shook her head. "You really are the most ridiculous person I've ever met."

"And that's why you adore me. That, and my awesome hair." His smile faded. "All kidding aside, though? We're getting that starstone tomorrow—and then my mom's telling us about what happened to Wylie's mom, before we head to Nightfall and get your parents back. And I know you're going to tell me it won't be that simple—and it probably won't be. But whatever it takes, it's going to happen. Do you know why?"

When she didn't answer, he took both of her hands, and she couldn't ignore the rush of warmth that tingled through her when she met his eyes.

There was no teasing glint to be found. Just pure determination when he told her, "Because Team Foster-Keefe is going to win."

FOURTEEN

OMEONE CLEARED THEIR THROAT, and Sophie dropped Keefe's hands and jumped back, expecting to find Grady scowling at them. He'd been ramping up the protective-dad vibe for a while—especially when it came to Keefe. Half the time he wouldn't even call Keefe by his name. He was simply "That Boy."

But when she glanced at her doorway, she found the rest of her friends, all dressed in solemn shades of green, along with Grizel—and Biana's and Dex's bodyguards, Lovise and Woltzer.

It was impossible to tell from her friends' expressions which one of them had done the throat clearing. Fitz's jaw looked clenched, Tam was glaring through his silver-tipped bangs, Dex's periwinkle eyes were narrowed and his dimples were nowhere to be seen, and Biana had popped one hand on her hip to match her raised eyebrows. The only one Sophie could rule out was Linh, who always had an aura of sweetness around her pink-cheeked face—even when she was unleashing tidal waves to wash away half of an ogre city.

"Are we interrupting something?" Fitz asked.

"Just the usual," Keefe told him. "Foster's going on and on and *on* about how she can't live without me. It's really quite exhausting."

"Actually, we're trying to come up with a plan," Sophie corrected, before relating the details of their conversation with Lady Gisela, as well as outlining the deal they'd made.

Grizel whistled, sauntering over to Sandor with a grace that matched her lithe frame. Her black bodysuit shimmered like snakeskin, and Sophie didn't miss the way Sandor's eyes tracked Grizel's every movement.

"These kinds of problems never happen on *my* watch," Grizel told him, her husky voice lilting with the tease.

"That's because you're stuck trailing the Wonderboy," Keefe jumped in. "His idea of excitement is when he changes the way he parts his hair."

"Excuse me, I've almost died just as many times as you have," Fitz reminded him. "Maybe more."

"So have I," Dex jumped in.

"We all have," Biana corrected.

Tam elbowed Linh. "You sure you don't want to get some less dangerous friends?"

"Uh, are you forgetting that I'm the Girl of Many Floods?" Linh reminded him.

"Exactly," Tam said, flicking his bangs out of his silver-toned eyes. "I have enough problems already."

Linh responded by gathering the moisture in the air into a golf ball–size sphere and splashing her brother in the face—receiving "Wows" from Fitz and Dex for her efforts.

Sophie would never cease to be amazed at how the twins could resemble each other so closely and still have completely opposite temperaments. Even if he wasn't a Shade, Sophie suspected Tam would be just as surly. Meanwhile Linh managed to be serene *and* feisty with each of her pink-lipped smiles.

"So what's the plan for tomorrow?" Dex asked, patting the sides of his strawberry blond hair, which—Sophie noticed—he'd styled the way Biana had shown him during her makeover.

"We're still working on it," Sophie admitted. "I'm hoping Lady Cadence will agree to help. And, um . . . don't freak out, but I think only Keefe and I should go."

Naturally, there was a whole lot of freaking out.

"I'm not saying that because I'm trying to protect you," she told them when the shouting had quieted. "I'm saying it because we can't focus on only one thing."

She rehashed her theory about her family's abduction being

a distraction from bigger, more important schemes, like the fires and Wylie's abduction.

"So if all of us go to Ravagog to get the starstone, we're doing exactly what the Neverseen want. We need to divide and conquer." She turned to Dex. "Have you made any progress on hacking into the caches?"

"Not as much as I'd like," he admitted. "The good news is, the cache that belonged to Fintan feels weaker than Kenric's—and that's the one that'll probably tell us who they broke out of the dungeon."

"Then I think you should make that your focus," Sophie told him. "We need to learn as much as we can about the prisoner from Lumenaria. Keefe's mom called her Fintan's 'advisor.' If you work on the cache nonstop, how long do you think it'll take you to crack it?"

Dex chewed his lip. "Honestly? I have no idea. It doesn't communicate with me the way other gadgets do."

"Do you think it would help if Sophie enhanced you?" Tam asked. "Wasn't that how you figured out how to hack into the Imparter?"

"That's right!" Dex was practically bouncing as he pulled a small satchel out of his pocket and dumped the two marble-size caches into his hand. Both were made of smooth clear crystal, with smaller rainbow-toned crystals set inside—seven in Kenric's and nine in Fintan's, each colorful speck holding one Forgotten Secret.

"You carry the caches around?" Sophie squeaked, glancing over her shoulder as if a thief might appear from the shadows. "Don't you realize how dangerous that is?"

"It's way riskier leaving them unguarded around the triplets," Dex promised—which was a fair point. Dex's siblings brought new meaning to the word "handful." "Besides, it's a good thing I have them with me. Now we don't have to wait to see if enhancing helps."

He looked so adorably excited as he tucked Kenric's cache away and held on to only Fintan's that it was hard not to feel at least some of the same thrill as Sophie peeled off one of her gloves.

"Wait," Fitz said, scooting closer and wrapping his arm around Sophie's waist.

"I'll be fine," she told him. "I barely feel anything when I do this."

"Still, it's better to be prepared, right?" His smile did all kinds of fluttery things to her heart.

And maybe she was imagining it, but he smelled better than normal—a little spicy and crisp, like he'd started wearing some sort of fancy elvin cologne. It took all of her willpower not to lean closer and take a long breath.

Dex rolled his eyes. "If anything, *I'm* the one who's going to fall over."

"Awww. I got you, Dexy," Keefe said, wrapping his arms around Dex's waist. "What? Was that not what you were hoping for?"

Tam snorted. "Pretty sure the last thing he wants is an Empath holding on to him when he goes anywhere near Sophie's hand."

"You guys are the worst," Biana told them.

"We try," Keefe said. "And by the way, dude," he told Dex, "have you invented some new elixir I don't know about? When did you get so tall?"

Sophie tilted her head. "He's right."

When she'd first met Dex, he'd been a little shorter than she was. And now he and Keefe were basically the same height.

Dex shrugged, blushing all the way to his ears. "I don't know. Must be a growth spurt."

It probably was. But Sophie had also been so distracted, she hadn't been paying attention. Which probably made her a terrible friend.

"You ready?" Dex asked.

She reached out her gloveless hand. And as soon as her fingers connected with his, Dex's knees buckled.

Keefe grinned. "Typical Foster, always knocking guys off their feet."

Sophie sighed. "Should I—"

"Don't let go," Dex told her, tightening his grip. "I'm fine. It's just . . . intense."

Keefe and Tam both snickered.

"Here," Linh said, dragging Sophie's desk chair over so Keefe could lower Dex down. "Better?"

Dex nodded. But his eyes seemed to roll back in his head as the warm tingles in Sophie's fingers grew stronger and stronger.

"I think this might be too much," she told him.

"No," Dex insisted. "A little longer."

He kept his grip for another endless stretch before he slumped over. The cache slipped from his grip, and Keefe barely managed to catch it.

"You okay there, dude?" Keefe asked. "Need us to call Elwin?"

Dex shook his head, staring blankly at the floor. "That thing is the strangest gadget I've ever felt. *Nothing* I do will make it speak to me."

Sophie's heart deflated as she pulled her glove back on. "Does that mean you won't be able to hack in?"

"I . . . can't tell. Do you have any paper?"

Sophie rushed over to her desk and grabbed a notebook and pencil, and Dex scribbled a bunch of numbers and symbols—then scratched out everything and turned to a new page.

He scratched out everything he wrote there, too.

"Who has the cache?" he asked.

Keefe handed it over, and Dex squinted at the tiny inner crystals.

"The mechanisms are too simple," he said, mostly to himself. "It must need . . ."

He flipped to a fresh page, drawing a circle and a series of intersecting lines. Sophie thought he must be crossing out his work again, but after a few more dashes he set down his pencil and held the cache up to the sunlight.

"I know what it needs!" He squinted at the tiny crystals and nodded a few times before he told them, "A password!"

FIFTEEN

A PASSWORD?" SOPHIE REPEATED, wishing she could feel as excited as Dex looked. The odds of them guessing something like that didn't seem good.

Especially when Dex told her, "Yep. Each of the inner crystals needs one to open."

"Just so I'm clear—you're saying we need to figure out *nine* different passwords?" Tam asked.

Dex nodded. "But only if we want to access every single secret."

"Right, but there isn't a way to know exactly which crystal is the one we need, is there?" Linh asked, biting her lip when

Dex shook his head. "So, we're probably going to have to open at least a few of them to find the right secret."

"Maybe *all* of them," Fitz said.

"Can you hack around the passwords?" Biana asked. "Like you did with Keefe's Imparter?"

"I actually didn't hack that. Sophie guessed the right word. And with the crazy security I'm feeling on this . . . nope."

"You're sure?" Sophie pushed. "Human hackers find ways to break through passwords all the time."

"Yeah, but that's human technology," Dex said with a slight smirk. "Trust me, there's no algorithm that's going to solve this."

"So where does that leave us?" Sophie asked.

Dex mussed his hair. "I honestly don't know."

The confession seemed to bounce around the room, feeling heavier each time it hit.

Biana shook her head. "No way—no underestimating yourself like that. You're Dex Dizznee. You built the Twiggler. You translated the Lodestar symbol. You built this." She held up her hand and pointed to the pretty pink panic-switch ring he'd given her.

Fitz held his up too. So did Tam and Linh. And Sophie pointed to the bump under her glove.

"Dude, what's a guy gotta do to join the ring club?" Keefe asked, wiggling his bare fingers.

"Maybe not run off and join the enemy?" Fitz suggested.

The words were like a record scratch, screeching everyone into awkward silence.

This was the first time they'd all been together since Keefe's betrayal.

Keefe cleared his throat. "Yeah . . . so . . . about that."

"It's okay," Sophie told him. "You don't have to—"

"No," Keefe interrupted. "I do."

He forced himself to face each of his friends, lingering longest on Fitz. "I'm sorry. I know you think I'm an idiot for running off. And . . . I guess I am. I thought the fact that my mom had built something she called my 'legacy' meant that I was valuable enough to the Neverseen that they'd bring me in on all their plans and I could find a way to stop them. But it turns out I'm worthless."

"No, you're not."

Surprisingly, the words came from Tam.

"Having a family like yours messes with your head," he added, tugging his bangs over his eyes. "I know how that goes. You still made a bad call—or *lots* of bad calls, actually. But . . . if you don't do it again, we're cool."

One side of Keefe's mouth quirked as he nodded.

Sophie let out a breath she hadn't noticed she'd been holding.

"Anyway, back to my pep talk," Biana said, turning to Dex. "I *know* you can figure this out."

"Biana's right," Sophie agreed. "Even if it takes time, you'll get it. You always do."

Dimples sank into Dex's flushed cheeks as he grinned at both of them.

"Well, at least I know what I'm aiming for now," he said, scribbling a few more notes before he held up Sophie's notebook. "Can I borrow this?"

"Keep it," Sophie told him. "And if you need me to enhance you again, just let me know."

He nodded, tucking the notebook into his cape pocket and returning the cache to his satchel. "I'll work on it every chance I get."

"And in the meantime," Tam added, "what if we talked to the guards who took care of the prisoner? I know all the Peace Summit's goblins were killed in the collapse"—he paused as the four bodyguards bowed their heads—"but didn't the Council bring in a whole new security team just for the Summit? So what about the guards who were working in Lumenaria before that? Wouldn't they have to know at least a few things about who they were guarding to be prepared in case anything happened?"

"I can ask Councillor Oralie for their names," Fitz offered. "She rigged my Imparter so I can reach her directly—but I left it at home."

"Can you hail her as soon as we're done with the Black Swan?" Sophie asked. "Hopefully by then, Quinlin will have sent your dad the information on the fires and you can start sorting through that, too. And I think Biana and Tam should go to Candleshade and try to find whatever Lady Gisela hid there. Dex can keep working on the passwords. And maybe Linh should go visit Wylie, since you guys have been spending so much time together. Make sure he's prepared for whatever we're going to find out about his mom's death. Then we'll all regroup once Keefe and I have the starstone."

"Most of that sounds great," Fitz said. "But there's one part we need to change. I should be going with you to Ravagog."

"Wait for it," Keefe jumped in, right before Fitz added, "We're Cognates."

"Aaaaaaaand, there it is!" Keefe said. "He's adorably consistent, isn't he? Don't forget to show her the rings, too."

Fitz rolled his eyes. "She doesn't need me to."

But he *did* tilt his hands so the verdigris bands on his thumbs were much more prominently displayed.

Sophie wore a matching set under her gloves, each ring stamped with one set of their initials. The special metal had a magnetic kind of draw, keeping their hands connected whenever they worked telepathically.

"You know we're stronger together," Fitz told her, and the intensity in his eyes made her mouth go dry. "You never would've gotten past Dimitar's blocking last time without me."

"But I'm not going there to read his mind," Sophie reminded him. "I'm going to deliver a message and hopefully convince him to give me the hairpin. We need to get through this without causing another interspeciesial incident."

"And you think bringing Keefe along is going to do that?" Fitz asked. "He's the one who caused the big distraction last time. Dimitar probably hates him more than all of us."

"Eh, I'm pretty sure King Dimitar hates us all equally," Keefe said.

"Which is another reason I think we should keep the group as small as possible," Sophie jumped in. "The less this visit reminds him of our last one, the better. The only reason I'm including Keefe is because his mom seems to want him involved. Why else would she insist we contact her with his blood?"

"Plus, y'know, Foster can't live without me," Keefe added.

"Don't make me smack you," Sophie warned.

Keefe smirked. "I'd like to see you try."

"So would I," Tam informed them.

"Obnoxious boys aside," Biana interrupted, "you're assuming Dimitar is going to just hand over the starstone. I doubt he will. And if he doesn't, you're going to need my help." She tossed her silky dark hair and blinked out of sight, reappearing seconds later on the other side of the room. "And Tam should be there too, in case we need his shadows. We'd still be a smaller, less suspicious group, but we'd also have a backup plan in case things go wrong. And let's face it: Something usually goes wrong."

She had a point.

"Okay, so Keefe, Tam, Biana, and I will figure out how to deliver up before she trips?" Keefe asked. "I say she'll lose it on the sixth step."

"Nah, she'll make it at least ten," Fitz countered.

Sophie glared at both of them—but didn't argue. The Black Swan had given her many gifts, but they'd completely neglected the grace department.

"I won't let you fall," Sandor promised.

"Actually, you, Grizel, Woltzer, and Lovise should stay here," Tiergan told him. "This staircase is the only way in or out of Brumevale, so if you keep a steady guard, you'll be able to ensure that no danger reaches us."

"Is there a reason you don't want us in your little hideout?" Grizel asked as she played rather menacingly with a goblin throwing star.

"It's simple logic," Tiergan assured her. "Where can you best engage a threat? On solid, steady ground where you can see them coming *and* block them from reaching the only path? Or hundreds of feet in the air, on narrow steps?"

The four goblins exchanged a look.

"And what of any dangers above?" Lovise asked. "How do you know there isn't an ambush waiting for you at the top?"

Tiergan smiled. "No one has set so much as a toe in Brumevale without our permission for millennia."

"Besides, if someone was waiting for us up there, with all this moisture in the air, all I'd need to do is take off my glove, grab Linh's hand, and let her go wild," Sophie added.

felt a tiny pang when Fitz agreed, especially when he flashed his most adorable smile.

She tried to tell herself it was nerves—and it probably was. After all, she had a lot of scary things to deal with.

It definitely *didn't* have to do with the pretty way Linh was blushing.

"Okay," she said. "So, we all have a plan! Unless whatever the Black Swan shows us today changes something."

"Do you think it will?" Biana asked, biting one of her perfectly glossed lips.

"No clue," Sophie admitted.

She shared what little Livvy had told her in order to prepare.

"I still can't believe she's Physic," Biana confessed. "Do you know she used to come over all the time when I was little? Quinlin, Dad, and Fitz would disappear into Dad's office, and Livvy would hang out with me and Mom—and sometimes Alvar."

"She was probably making sure we weren't getting too close to finding Sophie," Fitz said—which made sense, but felt strange, imagining her spying on them.

Even stranger was realizing Alvar was doing the same thing.

"So now we know who Granite, Physic, and Squall are," Biana said, glancing at Dex during the last code name. He'd been understandably shocked when it turned out his mom, Juline—who also happened to be Edaline's sister—was the Froster in the Collective who disguised her identity by crusting her body with ice. "That means we need to figure out Wraith and Blur. Maybe if we think of all the Vanishers and Phasers we know, we can narrow it down."

"You won't be able to guess," a voice said behind them, and everyone turned to find Tiergan climbing the last few stairs.

"You're not in your rock-dude disguise," Keefe noted. "Did you get sick of getting pebbles stuck in uncomfortable places?"

"And you're not wearing green," Sophie added.

"I'm not." Tiergan fidgeted with his long blond hair, which he'd pulled into a loose ponytail at the nape of his neck. "Today is not a day for disguises, or mourning—though you were all very generous to honor our loss with your wardrobe choices."

"What is today a day for?" Fitz asked.

"Truth."

Tiergan's olive skin seemed paler than usual as his dark blue eyes drifted to Sophie. "What I'm about to reveal is a secret that only a handful of others know—and you will not be allowed to share it with *anyone*, except the select group we've chosen."

"That better include her parents," Grady called from downstairs, making Sophie wonder how long he'd been eavesdropping.

"Yes, you and Edaline are on the list," Tiergan shouted back. "But we'll go over that later. Right now, we have a lengthy journey ahead."

"Of course we do," Keefe said through a sigh. "What are

you putting us through this time? More eckodons blasting us through water vortexes?"

"Sadly, there won't be any animal friends assisting us," Tiergan told him. "The hideout I'm bringing you to is a bit more straightforward. Shall we?"

He pulled a pathfinder out of his pocket, and Sophie noticed the crystal was iridescent pink—a color she'd seen Mr. Forkle use before—as he adjusted to a specific facet and offered her his free hand.

She took it, and her friends quickly formed a chain, with Keefe claiming Sophie's other hand before Dex or Fitz could grab it.

"You okay?" Keefe leaned in to ask. "Because you kinda feel like you want to barf."

"I'll be fine," she insisted.

"It's okay to be nervous," Tiergan told them as he raised the crystal to the light and cast a shimmering beam across the floor. "Part of me never believed it would come to this. But . . . here we go."

SIXTEEN

THEY REAPPEARED SOMEWHERE HOT, with thick swirls of white fog fuzzing out any glimmer of sky. If it weren't for the solid feeling under her feet, Sophie would've thought they'd leaped into the center of a cloud.

"The water is so alive here," Linh whispered. "It almost feels playful."

She waved her hands and the fog shifted, curling into a flock of birds that fluttered around them—earning another "wow" from Dex and Fitz.

"Yeah, well, I'm not a fan," Keefe told Tiergan, shaking his drooping hair out of his eyes. "This place feels like we've been stuffed inside a verminion's cheeks."

Biana crinkled her nose. "Ew."

"Don't worry, we won't be staying long," Tiergan told them. "This is the access point to Brumevale, much like the island we use to reach Atlantis."

He pulled a tiny glass vial from his pocket and showed them the label:

ONE WHIRLWIND—RELEASE WITH CAUTION.

"Please tell me you're not launching us out of a tornado," Sophie begged.

Tiergan smiled. "No. The wind is to give us clarity for the climb."

He hurled the vial toward his feet, and the sound of shattering glass was quickly drowned out by the roar of wind as a cold breeze whipped around them, growing faster with each rotation.

Sophie's hair swatted her cheeks, but otherwise the wind was gentle, whisking away the worst of the heat as it swelled into a wide funnel and stretched skyward. The centrifugal force drew all of the mist to the edge, clearing the air inside the vortex to reveal . . .

. . . The kind of staircase that screamed *This will be the death of everyone.*

The narrow blue stones hovered in the sky with nothing to anchor them. No railing to hold on to. Just open air, and plenty of space to fall.

"Should we take bets on how many stairs Foster makes it

standing. A satisfying *CRACK!* filled the air when the crystal shattered against the ground.

"WHAT WAS THAT?" Sandor demanded.

"Sorry!" Sophie called down as the bodyguards shouted battle preparations. "Don't worry—everything's fine!"

Grizel shouted something back, and Sophie was glad she couldn't make out the words.

Fitz laughed. "I'm going to pay for that later. But how'd it feel?"

"*Really* good. Thank you."

"Ugh, score one for Fitzphie," Keefe mumbled. "Shouldn't we be climbing?"

"Yes," Tiergan called from above. "You've all made this climb far more interesting than it usually is. But it's time to focus. We're about to step through the shroud."

Linh paled as she nodded.

She'd practically shoved Sophie away when she'd first heard that Sophie had manifested as an Enhancer, terrified of what might happen if she turned even more powerful.

"I have no doubt the seven of you could find all kinds of impressive ways to create havoc should you need to defend yourselves," Tiergan assured them. "So, is everyone agreed?"

The goblins shared another look before Sandor begrudgingly instructed them to move to sentinel positions along the edge of the funnel.

"When should we expect you back?" Woltzer asked.

Tiergan glanced at the sky, smoothing the strands of his hair that had broken free from his ponytail. "I suspect they'll need several hours—so we should get moving."

He headed for the first floating step, and Sophie half expected the stone to crumble under his weight. But it held steady, somehow not even shifting.

"Aren't you coming?" he asked when none of them followed.

Everyone looked to Sophie to go first—the wimps.

"Right behind you," Fitz told her as she carefully climbed onto the bottom stair. "I'll make sure you don't fall."

He placed a hand on the small of her back, probably to steady her—but the soft contact gave Sophie another rush of flutters.

"I think this is a two-person job," Keefe said, nudging Fitz over so he could place a hand on her opposite side. "This is Foster, after all."

Sophie sighed. But on the sixth step, her ankle wobbled, and she would've toppled to the left if Keefe hadn't been ready to nudge her back to the right.

"Not a word," she told him, realizing his prediction about when she'd trip had come true.

He snickered. "At least this proves I know you better than the Fitzster."

"No, it's that I have more faith in her," Fitz corrected. "That's what being Cognates means."

"And yet, I seem to remember Foster hiding some sort of important secret from you during your trust exercises. Did something change while I was gone, or . . . ?"

Sophie glanced over her shoulder to glare at him.

The fact that she was holding something back was a touchy subject with Fitz—especially since she couldn't tell him *why*. Cognates were supposed to share everything. But there was absolutely no way she was going to tell Fitz she'd had a major crush on him since the day they met—even after their sort-of "moment" under the Panakes tree.

Fitz could've meant dozens of things when he'd leaned in and suggested they "skip the talking."

Keefe raised one eyebrow. "You okay there, Foster? Your mood seems to be making some sudden shifts."

"Yeah, because I'm trying to decide if I can shove you off the stairs without knocking Biana down."

"I can jump out of the way," Biana offered.

"And I can give him an extra shove as he tumbles by," Tam added. "I'd come up there and do it myself, but I'm *trying* to be a good brother and wait for my slothlike sister."

"I'd like to see you try climbing in heels," Linh told him.

"Here," Dex said, placing his hands on her shoulders to help her keep her balance.

"Are you getting handsy with my sister, Dizznee?" Tam asked, cracking up when Dex jerked his arms away. "Only kidding, dude."

"Anyone want to trade brothers?" Linh asked.

"You can have both of mine," Dex offered, "but you have to take my sister too. And keep in mind that last week they snuck into my closet and cut out the backsides of all of my pants."

Keefe snickered. "I think the triplets just became my new heroes."

"So here's a question," Tam said as the climb stretched on. "Wouldn't it be easier to levitate to the top?"

"I doubt even the Exillium Coaches could navigate air this thin," Tiergan warned.

Dex huffed a weary breath. "Maybe we should try it anyway."

"I'd be game for that," Biana agreed.

"My goodness—clearly we need to have the lot of you get more exercise if you'd rather risk your safety than climb a few stairs," Tiergan scolded—though he was huffing as hard as any of them.

The stairs were *steep*.

And the air was definitely getting thinner.

Sophie had to force herself to breathe slower to keep her head from getting woozy.

"I'm sure I speak for everyone," Keefe grunted, "when I say: Are we there yet?"

"Almost," Tiergan promised. "Everyone dig deep—and don't look down."

"Steaming sasquatch poop—that's a long way to fall!" Keefe announced.

Fitz moved closer to Sophie, his new cologne tickling her nose as he whispered, "I almost forgot. I brought you a present."

Her heart skipped at least five beats when he slipped an orange velvet satchel into her palm. He'd been bringing her lots of tiny gifts lately—and she'd been trying hard not to read too much into it.

"Ugh, anyone else ready to vomit from the Fitzphie?" Keefe asked.

"I am," Dex said, as Linh asked, "Did Fitzphie become an actual thing?"

"I don't even know what 'Fitzphie' is supposed to mean," Tiergan noted.

"Want me to explain it?" Tam offered.

"No," Sophie said, opening the satchel and pulling out a fist-size crystal prism. It was heavy like a paperweight, and when she held it up to the light, rainbow sparkles flashed across her fingers, highlighting words carved across the base, along with the Foxfire seal.

"That's called a Radiant," Fitz explained. "It's the highest honor any prodigy can receive when they complete the basic levels at Foxfire. Alvar was so disgustingly smug about earning one that he told my mom she should keep it on the mantel in our main sitting room, so it could inspire Biana and me to work harder."

"Ugh, I forgot about that," Biana grumbled. "I can't believe Mom did it."

"I know. So I think it's time to destroy it. And considering where we are, maybe it'd be fun to let it take a really nasty fall."

"Gotta give you credit," Tam told Fitz. "That's pretty much a perfect gift."

It was. Though Sophie felt bad taking it.

"Shouldn't you or Biana do the honors?"

"Nope. Alvar was there when they took your parents," Biana argued. "And when you were kidnapped."

"Just throw it extra hard, for us," Fitz added.

Sophie glanced at Dex. "Alvar helped kidnap you, too."

"So boost your throw with the Sucker Punch I made you," he suggested.

They seemed pretty sure, so Sophie gathered whatever mental energy she could muster and channeled it into her arm muscles. A burst of force from the Sucker Punch gave her throw extra oomph as she hurled the Radiant down the center of the curving stairs, where none of the bodyguards would be standing. A satisfying *CRACK!* filled the air with when the crystal shattered against the ground.

"WHAT WAS THAT?" Sandor demanded.

"Sorry!" Sophie called down as the bodyguards shouted battle preparations. "Don't worry—everything's fine!"

Grizel shouted something back, and Sophie was glad she couldn't make out the words.

Fitz laughed. "I'm going to pay for that later. But how'd it feel?"

"*Really* good. Thank you."

"Ugh, score one for Fitzphie," Keefe mumbled. "Shouldn't we be climbing?"

"Yes," Tiergan called from above. "You've all made this climb far more interesting than it usually is. But it's time to focus. We're about to step through the shroud."

SEVENTEEN

OLD AIR MADE SOPHIE SHIVER AS she passed through a thick veil of moisture, and as soon as her head was clear, she sucked in a shallow breath.

A narrow white lighthouse sprouted straight out of the clouds, standing alone in a silent pocket of sky. And even though Sophie couldn't see any water, her ears prickled with the faint swish of waves slapping against a shore.

She waited for a beam of light to flash, but the tower stayed dark, as if it were a remnant from another time, long since forgotten.

"Welcome to Brumevale," Tiergan said, his voice hushed as he took Sophie's hand to help her navigate some sort of platform before descending down a few steps onto solid ground.

The swirling white mist climbed to her waist, obscuring whatever terrain lay under her feet, and goose bumps pebbled Sophie's skin as their group moved toward the lighthouse. A deep, soulful hum, almost like a melody, seemed to radiate from the structure, but Sophie couldn't find the source.

"How old is this place?" she whispered.

"Ancient," Tiergan told her. "The Black Swan didn't build this tower. We simply reclaimed it."

"Did the lighthouse ever work?" Dex asked.

"*Long* ago. This area has a rather complicated history. But I shouldn't be the one to tell you that story."

"Who should?" Biana asked.

"The person who was affected." Tiergan led them around to the other side of the lighthouse, where a narrow silver door had been nestled into the stones.

"What do you guys use this place for?" Fitz asked as Tiergan uncovered a hidden DNA panel.

"It's always been a place for reflection," Tiergan told him. "Project Moonlark was actually conceived here—though most of the genetic work was done at our High Seas facility. That's the hideout where we healed your abilities, in case you were wondering," he added for Sophie, "which has since been abandoned, thanks to the Neverseen's assault."

"Why was only 'most' of the work done there?" Dex asked.

"To ensure that the two elves who donated their DNA for the project never met. Anonymity was essential to protect their identities."

"But *you* know who they are?" Sophie had to ask.

"Actually, Mr. Forkle kept your genetic father's and mother's identities entirely to himself—though that information hasn't been lost."

"Because of that gadget he gave me before he died?" Sophie guessed. "Does that mean you haven't gone through it?"

"It wasn't intended for me. You'll see why soon enough." He licked the DNA panel, triggering a creaky click as the door unlocked. "I'm afraid our group must split for the moment. Mr. Forkle's instructions were explicit that Sophie be brought in alone."

"Do you really want to go up there by yourself?" Keefe asked.

"No," Sophie admitted. "But . . . it's what Mr. Forkle wanted." And she owed him that much.

Call me telepathically, if you need to, Fitz transmitted. *I'll keep my mind clear.*

She gave him as much of a smile as she could. *Thanks.*

Tiergan offered her his arm. "Ready?"

He wasn't a touchy-feely kind of guy, so the gesture felt especially unnerving as he pulled her closer to his side.

"I'll see you soon," she told her friends before he pushed on the door, making the hinges creak as the door slowly swung inward to reveal . . .

"Oh good—more stairs," she grumbled.

Keefe snorted. "Stay snarky, Foster. It'll help."

She stole one last glance at her friends and let Tiergan lead her into the lighthouse. The door clicked closed behind them, and the silence of the tower was nearly overwhelming. She hadn't realized how loud the wind was—or that strange, soulful humming—until the heavy stones sealed away the noise.

"On a scale of one to ten," she whispered as they started up the corkscrew staircase, "how bad is this going to be?"

"Quite honestly, Sophie, I have no idea how you're going to react. But I'm here for whatever you need, whether it's a shoulder to cry on or someone to scream at."

If she hadn't been verging on panic before, the words definitely pushed her closer to the edge. But she focused on counting her steps, making it to three hundred and eighty-seven before they reached another weathered door, this time carved from a rich, cherry-colored wood.

The round chamber beyond was small, and decorated with shabby armchairs and faded rugs. But that gave the room a lived-in feel that had Sophie's shoulders relaxing. It was a room where she could imagine people sipping mugs of tea as they gazed out the huge, curved windows at the calm, endless blue.

But her worries rushed back when the ceiling creaked with a series of soft thuds.

Footsteps.

She noticed the narrow staircase tucked in the shadows the

same moment she realized the footsteps were heading toward it—and she tried to prepare herself for whoever would be coming down those stairs. If Keefe was right—if Timkin Heks was about to stride into the room and declare himself her leader—she was going to have to find a way to deal with it.

But that wasn't who appeared.

She screamed and stumbled back, shaking her head so hard it felt like her brain was slamming against her skull—because the bloated, wrinkly figure standing in front of her couldn't possibly be there.

He *couldn't*.

And yet, Mr. Forkle offered a nervous smile as he took the last steps into the room and filled the air with the dirty-feet stench of ruckleberries.

His piercing blue eyes locked with hers, flickering with a dozen unreadable emotions as he mumbled, "You kids are going to have a very hard time understanding this."

EIGHTEEN

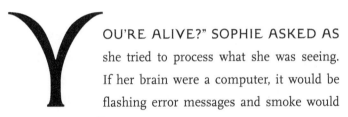OU'RE ALIVE?" SOPHIE ASKED AS
she tried to process what she was seeing.
If her brain were a computer, it would be
flashing error messages and smoke would
be coming out of her ears.

"Perhaps we should sit down for this conversation?" Mr.
Forkle suggested, taking a careful step toward her.

"No!" Sophie backed farther away, nearly toppling down
the stairs.

She should be happy to see him alive—and part of her was.

But a vicious rage was crystallizing under her skin.

"You lied to me!"

Actually, it was much crueler than that.

"I watched you die! I was covered in your blood!" She'd never, ever forget how warm and sticky it felt. Or the choking iron smell that didn't wash off for days. "And now you just walk in here and ask me to sit and talk about it, like that's not a big deal?"

Tears welled in her eyes and she blinked them back. He didn't deserve them. Not anymore.

"Quite the contrary, Miss Foster. This is a *very* big deal. Why do you think I insisted you be brought in alone? I wanted to give you the time to process this privately. But I also knew you wouldn't want to be the one to explain any of this to your friends. So, I had Tiergan bring them along so I can tell them—and I will. As soon as you're ready for me to have that conversation."

"And that's supposed to make up for the fact that you let me believe you were dead for *weeks*?" She reeled on Tiergan. "You knew?"

"Don't blame him," Mr. Forkle told her. "I was the one who insisted the rest of the Collective wait to tell you."

"What kind of sick game—"

"No games," Mr. Forkle interrupted. "Only a desperate, half-formed plan. I thought I was prepared for this, but it's been . . . incredibly difficult."

"Am I supposed to feel sorry for you? Poor Mr. Forkle—faking your death must've been *so hard*."

More pieces fell into place, each more disgusting than the last.

"Is this why you asked Oralie to take your body away and make sure no one saw it? And why you told me not to plant your stupid Wanderling?" She ripped the locket off her neck. "Is this even a real seed?"

"Please," he whispered, holding out his arms like someone facing down a feral animal. "Please be careful with that."

"Why should I?"

"Because it's all I have left." His voice choked as he added, "That seed is not fake, Miss Foster. Nor was what happened in Lumenaria."

He needed several deep breaths before he added, "What you hold in your hands is all that remains of my brother."

The words moved like sludge through Sophie's brain.

"Your . . . brother."

Mr. Forkle nodded, looking away to wipe his eyes. "My twin brother. *Identical* twin."

Okay. *Now* Sophie needed to sit.

Everything was wobbling and shaking—or maybe that was her. She didn't know anymore.

She didn't know anything.

Tiergan wrapped an arm around her shoulders and guided her to one of the armchairs.

"You knew about this?" she asked, tempted to shove Tiergan away. But she didn't have the strength.

He nodded as he lowered her onto the lumpy cushion.

"For how long?" Sophie demanded. "Before Lumenaria?"

"Yes," Tiergan admitted. "But they still kept the truth from us for *many* years. It wasn't until Project Moonlark, when we were trying to figure out how to keep an eye on you while you lived in the Forbidden Cities. We'd often joked that Forkle seemed to be able to be two places at once. We never realized that he really could be."

"It was the secret that was never meant to be shared," Mr. Forkle added quietly—though Sophie realized then that it wasn't Mr. Forkle.

Not really.

She swallowed hard as a fresh swell of grief hit hard. She hadn't noticed how much hope had filled her until it washed away.

"So, your brother," she said. "He was the one who . . ."

Her words trailed off as she struggled to find a way to describe their relationship.

Mr. Forkle hadn't necessarily been a father figure. But he'd often taken care of her. And sometimes, he'd even made her believe he cared.

"He was the one who lived next door to me?" she finished lamely.

"That's the part that's going to be especially confusing." He lumbered closer, looking and moving so familiarly, it broke her heart. "There was never any division between us. I was him and he was me. We only ever had one life, that we shared equally."

Sophie frowned. "Does that mean . . . sometimes I was with you?"

"In a way it was *always* me. We shared every thought. Every feeling. Every memory. Nothing was ever separate—except for our bodies. *Physically*, our time had to be divided, which was why we created a rigid schedule, and never deviated, even when it was inconvenient. But I beg you not to try to guess it. Our existence was seamless. Anything we ever said or did came from both of us, even though only one of us was present in that moment."

"That . . . doesn't make sense."

"I know. But for us, it was a perfectly natural way of being." He sank into the chair across from her, staring out the window. "Wherever either of us went, whatever we witnessed or accomplished individually, it was simply a part of our collective whole. We always considered each other before we made decisions—and we updated each other on *everything*. Before we manifested as Telepaths, we made it a habit of staying up late, rehashing every detail of our days. And once we could connect our minds, we started swapping memories fully—holding nothing back. So, when you were with him, it was no different than if you were with me."

"But why?" Sophie had to ask. "Why lie to everyone and live like that?"

"Because it was either share a life, or face the scorn of identical twins. And back when we were born, our world was even more restrictive than what you see now. We never would've been allowed to attend Foxfire, or been invited to join the nobility—and that would've only been the beginning of the limitations. But regardless of any of that, the decision was also out of our hands. When I made my surprise appearance—two minutes and twelve seconds after my brother made his—my parents had to make a choice. And they chose this."

"They didn't know they were having twins?" Sophie asked, finding that hard to believe. Even humans knew how to find that out ahead of time.

"They claim they did not—and you must keep in mind that this was a long time ago. They didn't do as many tests back then. Though I do think my parents *suspected*. I find it rather suspicious that my mother chose to give birth somewhere private, instead of going to the birthing center. My father was a physician, and insists that my mother's pregnancy had been so healthy that they saw no reason to make her leave the comforts of home for delivery. But that also made it incredibly easy for them to falsify the paperwork and erase any trace of my existence."

He lifted the swollen folds around his neck, revealing a registry pendant set onto a strained silver chain. "Technically, the feed this crystal generates isn't mine, and never has been. But it's the only life I've ever known. My mother told me once that if we'd been fraternal twins, she would've simply tucked me away and faked a second pregnancy. But we were identical. They could never register me without my DNA giving us away.

So my father came up with this much more complicated solution. He gave us one name. One inception date. One registered strand of DNA. And from that moment on, we were raised to see ourselves as two halves of a single whole. Only one of us ever left the house at any given time. And we were never allowed to mention the existence of the other—to anyone."

"That sounds horrible," Sophie mumbled.

"Perhaps. But it was the only life either of us knew, so we never resisted. It took us more than a decade to realize that others didn't share their lives with anyone else. We'd always assumed everyone had another like them, hidden at home."

"And you weren't furious when you figured out they'd lied to you?" Sophie asked.

"Of course we were. But had we come forward, our parents would've been exiled for falsifying registry records—and my brother and I would've become the ultimate pariahs. The only logical path was the one we were already on. So, we decided to see it as an advantage. And in many ways, it was. Only *we* had a built-in backup system. Only *we* could do the work of a single person in half the time. As Tiergan said, we could be two places at once. And eventually, we realized that it was a phenomenal waste to hide one of us away while the other was out in the world. So we mastered the art of disguise. But every role was played by both of us. We also began to study genetics, trying to determine if there was a reason for our world's prejudices against multiple births. Nowhere could we ever find any proof of the feared 'inferiority' in our genetic circumstance. But the more we studied, the more we began to realize that there were ways to adjust DNA to affect someone's abilities. And when we thought about how slowly our society was crumbling—so slowly that very few realized it—a plan started to form. But we needed help, so we reached out to the Black Swan."

Sophie sat up straighter. "I always assumed you were the one who founded the order."

"Many have assumed that. But the seeds were in place long before our inception. This tower is proof of that. All we did was help shape the existing members into a true organization. And yes, as Tiergan said, we kept the nature of our dual existence a secret. The Black Swan had enough to hide. But as Project Moonlark took form, we realized that some would need to know the truth to understand the depth of our plan. So we revealed ourselves to a very select group, as I am now doing again."

"I still remember when they walked in," Tiergan said with a deeply sad smile. "They didn't give us any sort of warning. Just called a meeting, and when we showed up, there were two of them. Pretty sure I screamed."

"You did. That was a much happier reveal than this one."

Mr. Forkle wiped his eyes again.

Sophie tried to think of something to say, but even with him sitting right in front of her, it was still so hard to believe.

"And you and your brother really shared *everything*?" she asked. "You never kept any secrets?"

"We couldn't. Our life would've collapsed. That's why even with his final breaths, my brother made sure there would be no gaps in my memories."

He reached into his pocket and removed the round gadget that Mr. Forkle had pressed into Sophie's hand as he lay dying.

Sophie glanced at Tiergan. "That's why you said it wasn't intended for you."

He nodded. "Not that I wasn't tempted to take a peek, but . . . they weren't my memories."

"They were mine," Mr. Forkle rasped. "My brother recorded everything he saw at the Peace Summit, as well as his showdown with Gethen and Brant to protect Councillor Oralie. Even his farewell to you is there, to make sure I knew everything. Right up to the end."

A shuddery sob slipped out with the words, and Sophie watched his shoulders shake as she fought back her own emotions. Her eyes stung and her nose ran, but she swallowed away the tears. She wasn't ready for them.

"He also reminded me of our agreement," Mr. Forkle added as he stood and paced to the window. "The one we'd worked out in case something like this ever happened—though it wasn't much of a plan. Mostly it involves me learning to do less, since I'll have to shoulder the burden alone now. I don't think either of us truly believed this would be our reality, but . . . here we are."

He offered a weak smile, but Sophie shook her head. "I don't understand why you waited this long to tell me."

He sighed. "You probably won't like this answer, Miss Foster—and you're welcome to think me cruel if you wish. But I decided that my brother deserved to be mourned. He deserved to have his loss *felt*—and if I'd made an appearance right away, it would've been too natural for everyone to act like he was still with us. I'm him, after all. But also not completely. So I asked the Collective to hold off. I'd actually planned to go another week, until we were closer to when I'd need to return to work at Foxfire. But when Tiergan told me about your family, I knew you would need me. So here I am."

Warmth swelled with the words and Sophie fought it back.

Everything felt too fragile.

Her heart was breaking all over again—both for him and the brother they'd lost.

"Things will have to change," he added quietly. "I'm still deciding what will and won't be sacrificed. But I know I won't be able to sneak away as often as I used to—especially once I return to my responsibilities as principal. Fortunately, no one will be suspicious of you or your friends paying regular visits to my office, thanks to your propensity for trouble." He offered a weak smile. "And I'll probably need to pare down my total number of identities. I'm just struggling to decide the best way to do that without drawing too much attention. And then, of course, there's simply the challenge of being me. My brother was my balance—and I was his. I'm not sure how I'll get anything done without having him question everything

I'm thinking. It feels like I've been left with a hollow body and only half a brain, and . . ."

Sophie met his watery eyes—so familiar, but somehow so wrong. "I . . . don't know what to feel," she whispered.

He snorted a thick laugh. "That makes two of us."

"Three of us," Tiergan agreed. "And I'm sure your friends will feel the same."

Sophie sank back against her chair and tried to imagine how they were going to react. All she could picture were blank stares.

"Are you ready for me to tell them?" Mr. Forkle asked.

She shook her head. She needed to sort out her own thoughts before she could face any more chaos.

"What am I supposed to call you?" she asked.

"The same things you always have, Miss Foster. I'm still him. I always have been. And I will be, until it's my turn to draw my last breath, should that day happen."

The words were equal parts reassuring and devastating.

This had to be what Mr. Forkle meant when he'd promised her that his death wouldn't be as bad as she thought it would be. And she could see why he might think that.

But . . . he was still dead.

His blood had still stained her hands. His last rattling breath had really been the end.

Somehow it felt like losing him all over again.

She focused on the locket still clutched in her fist, trying to fight off a surge of tears. "Am I supposed to give his seed to you? Do you know where to plant it?"

Mr. Forkle nodded. "We chose a spot long ago. Neither of us wanted to be in the Wanderling Woods. We wanted to commemorate our shared life the same way we lived it—together, and just outside the bounds of our world."

It took more strength than Sophie would've expected to stand and offer the locket to him.

"Actually, he wanted you to be with me when I plant it. I was hoping we could go there together later today. Hopefully it'll give us that elusive bit of closure we'll need as we try to regroup from here. We'll also bring your friends, of course. And the few others who'll soon be in on the secret. Everyone who heard about my death will have to know the truth about my brother, otherwise they'll wonder why Magnate Leto is still at Foxfire, and why Sir Astin will sometimes appear in the Lost Cities, and why this bloated body will still be an active part of the Collective. But the rest of the world will continue on as though nothing has changed, and I'll need you to act accordingly. I'll do my best to make it seem as if that really were the case."

Everything he said made sense.

But it also didn't.

And the idea of saying goodbye—with him right beside her . . .

It hurt her brain.

And her heart.

And something even deeper inside.

Everything was slowly unraveling. And even though Sophie knew he'd asked her not to, she couldn't stop her mind from sorting through her memories, trying to find a pattern to which Forkle had been which.

What if the better brother was gone, and all that was left was the cranky guy who wrote confusing notes and grumbled about "you kids"?

"I'll do all of that," she whispered. "If you'll tell me one thing—one memory that was *you*. I promise I won't ask for more than that. But I need something to help me figure out how to feel about this."

Mr. Forkle's sigh felt endless, and she flinched as he reached for her free hand, bracing for a stern lecture. But all he did was gently pull the glove off, careful not to touch her skin as he pointed to the small star-shaped mark on the back of her hand. "I'm the one who gave you this."

Her breath caught. "You were the one who healed my abilities?"

"I was. And I wish I'd managed the process better."

He'd made her drink an entire ounce of Limbium to reset her brain, and then injected her with a human remedy to stop her allergy from killing her. He probably should've stabbed the needle in her leg—maybe then she wouldn't have gotten the scar. But he'd gone with her hand, leaving the small star as a permanent souvenir of the trauma.

But that wasn't the part of the memory that Sophie's mind focused on.

Mr. Forkle had given her a choice about the risk she'd be taking, making it clear she could go on just as she was if she didn't want to face the danger. He'd also taken the time to answer one very important question to set her mind at ease. And afterward, when the Neverseen dropped out of the sky to steal Silveny, it was Mr. Forkle who'd charged in to protect her, along with several dwarves.

It wasn't a happy memory.

But she also remembered trusting him completely—with her life, and Keefe's life and Silveny's.

"Okay," she whispered, pulling her glove back on.

"You'll do the planting?" Mr. Forkle asked quietly. "And then we'll try to move forward?"

Sophie didn't know how. But the only answer she could give was, "We'll try."

And with those words, the tears she'd been choking back since the moment he came down those stairs finally broke free.

For several seconds she cried alone. Then warm, pudgy arms pulled her into a ruckleberry-scented embrace, and she clung to Mr. Forkle as her tears soaked his wrinkled tunic and he whispered the only two words that made her feel any better.

"I'm here."

NINETEEN

ATCHING HER FRIENDS COME
face-to-face with the gone-but-*not-*
gone Mr. Forkle was even more
emotionally exhausting than Sophie
had imagined. And it felt like the cramped tower might burst
from all the pressure.

Fitz was furious—which wasn't surprising. Sophie had seen
his grief-torn rage before, during the days they'd temporarily
lost Alden to a guilt-broken mind. But thankfully, this time
Fitz's shouts were saved entirely for Mr. Forkle. And Mr. Forkle
bore it well, enduring the tirade until Fitz settled into one of
the armchairs in a daze.

Biana cried—huge, shaking sobs that twisted her flawless

features into something red and puffy. Some were tears of fury. Others dripped with joy and relief. And the overwhelming combination would've made Biana collapse if Dex hadn't let her soak his shoulder with snot and tears until her cries faded to hiccup-y whimpers.

Dex's reaction, meanwhile, was much more analytical. He pummeled Mr. Forkle with question after question, and demanded to know a specific time when he'd interacted with *this* Forkle. Sophie was sure he'd probably been hoping the elf in front of them was the one who pulled them away from their kidnappers in Paris, but that seemed to have been the other brother. But the Forkle still with them *was* the one who'd been there—as Magnate Leto—the day the Council forced Sophie to wear the ability restrictor that Dex had been tricked into designing. It was another far-from-happy memory, but still one where Mr. Forkle had done everything in his power to get them through. And for Dex, that seemed to be enough.

Tam only had one nonnegotiable demand: that Mr. Forkle let him take another reading of his shadowvapor—and the amount he found was the same as what he'd sensed before. Mr. Forkle seemed so genuinely surprised by the discovery that Sophie wondered if Tam had taken a reading of the other brother the last time. But Tam didn't ask. He just moved to a dark corner and settled into the shadows.

Linh endured the whole scene in silence, her silver-blue eyes focused on something in the distance. She only spoke once, and the question wasn't one Sophie would've guessed—though she probably should have. Linh wanted to know if either of the Forkles had ever regretted hiding that they were twins. And Mr. Forkle had taken her hands and reminded her that his choice hadn't really been a *choice*. But he also went on and on about how proud he was of Linh and Tam for standing up to their parents. And he told her that hopefully someday, all the powerful, brilliant multiple-birth children would force their world to set aside its ridiculous prejudices. With those words, Linh had gone to stand next to Tam, the two of them sharing a look that seemed to communicate something privately between them.

And then there was Keefe, who simultaneously endured the entire range of emotions—fists curled with fury, eyes watery, skin pale from shock, hands shaking with a nervous, almost hopeful energy. But when it was his turn to speak, he chose to move to where Sophie sat curled up in one of the armchairs and crouched down to her eye level to ask how *she* was doing.

"Keeping your promise, I see," Mr. Forkle said, smiling sadly at Keefe. "Not that I ever doubted it."

During his final moments, the other Mr. Forkle had made Keefe promise that he wouldn't let the tragedy break Sophie.

"I'm fine," Sophie assured Keefe. "This is all really weird. But . . . better than we thought it was, don't you think?"

Keefe sighed. "I think . . . I'm getting tired of finding out everyone's been lying to us and hiding things." He turned to

Tiergan. "Any life-changing pieces of information you've been holding back?"

Tiergan shuffled his feet. "No one ever reveals *everything*."

"I take it that's a yes?" Fitz pressed.

"How did this become about me?" Tiergan waved his arms toward Mr. Forkle. "If it helps, I can assure you that *I* don't have a secret identical twin."

"Very few do," Mr. Forkle said, staring out the windows again. "In fact, I might very well be the only one. Or, I should probably say I *was* the only one—though I suppose I technically still have a mostly secret twin, whether he walks the earth or rests underneath it." He sighed. "I'm not sure I have the right words for the complexity of my new situation."

Tiergan moved closer, placing a steadying hand on Mr. Forkle's shoulder. "We'll figure it out as we go."

Mr. Forkle nodded, reaching up to rub his eyes before he turned back to the group. "Going back to Mr. Sencen's complaint, the simple truth is, we *all* have things we hold back. Maybe we have no choice. Or maybe they're small things that we feel aren't anyone else's business. Whatever the reasoning, secrets are simply a part of life."

"Isn't it better without them, though?" Fitz asked. "Don't you think it's going to be easier to trust each other now that we know the truth?"

He didn't look at Sophie as he said it, but she couldn't help wondering if he meant the questions for her.

And while her secret was downright trivial compared to the day's revelations . . . maybe he had a point. She was risking their Cognate training—something that would make them more powerful and give them a better chance against the Neverseen—because she was too embarrassed to admit to her silly crush.

Sharing it would be humiliating. And it would probably end in rejection.

But . . . then it would be over, and they could move forward.

After we get my parents back, she transmitted to Fitz, *I think we should work through some more trust exercises. And this time . . . no holding back.*

Fitz's eyebrows shot up. *You're sure?*

No.

She already wanted to wimp out.

It'll be good for us, she told him, trying to believe it.

Fitz's answering smile was so bright, it made all her insides flip—and then flip again when he said, *Might be even better than you think.*

Keefe cleared his throat. "Everything okay? I'm picking up some *strange* mood swings."

"Yep," Sophie said, turning away to hide her flushing cheeks.

"I hope that's true," Mr. Forkle said. "Because the last thing I want is to distract any of you from our greater cause. We're trudging through the depths of a long, tumultuous battle, and I sincerely hope that today's revelation proves to all of you that the Neverseen haven't achieved as large of a victory as was once believed. I stand here before you ready to work, ready to fight, ready to do whatever needs to be done to win this battle. The question is, are you still with me?"

The seven friends shared a look.

Even though their faces were still pale, Sophie saw zero doubt in their eyes.

"We are," they said together.

Mr. Forkle nodded, then turned away, clearing the thickness from his throat. "You kids are going to make me cry."

And with the oh-so-familiar first words—words that had long been Mr. Forkle's trademark—everyone else found themselves fighting back tears too.

But somehow, they all seemed to decide that it wasn't the time for crying.

It was time to get back to work.

"Well," Mr. Forkle said, "we still have to endure a few more of these difficult conversations—as well as my brother's planting. But before we do that, I'd like to show you the reason I had Tiergan bring you to Brumevale."

He snapped his fingers, and the glass windows slowly lowered, letting a rush of cold, fresh air surge through the stuffy room.

At first, Sophie thought the wind was giving her goose bumps, but as her senses settled, she picked up the same haunting melody she'd heard earlier—only so much louder and clearer. The song was rich and soulful, and somehow felt both fiercely hopeful and achingly sad.

"Moonlarks," Mr. Forkle explained. "I don't know if you realize how rare it is to find their nests in the wild, but this is the only one I've found, in all my years. And they return to it time and again, generation after generation. It took my brother and me years to understand why. The waves you hear in the distance are where they leave their eggs to fight the currents, knowing only the strongest will reach the shore to hatch and survive. I once thought the creatures cruel for abandoning their young that way, leaving them without any guidance or protection."

His eyes focused on Sophie, and she nodded. She'd actually wrestled with trusting the Black Swan at first, knowing they'd similarly left her to struggle among humans.

"But the songs you're hearing," Mr. Forkle whispered, "are sung by both the mothers and fathers, calling the eggs toward the shore. And even when the babies hatch, their parents continue singing night and day, either for comfort or instruction— I'm not sure. What I *am* sure of is that while they leave the fledglings to fend for themselves, they're also always there, just out of sight, urging them on. *That's* why I agreed to name our plan Project Moonlark when Calla suggested it—*not* because you would be alone, Miss Foster. But because I intended to make sure you never truly would be. I would always be somewhere close by, guiding you however I could. And that goal holds, even now, when there's only half of me left—and not just for you. Everyone in this room is under my care. So, before we leave, I want you to close your eyes and *feel* the power of that assurance."

Sophie should've felt silly, standing there with her friends, tearing up while listening to wind-whipped birdsong. But the strength and courage carried in the melody nestled deep into her heart. And the harder she concentrated, the more her mind filled with scattered images—scenes of tiny chicks covered in silver fluff skittering over white sand with their scrawny legs.

She wasn't sure if the images were part of her imagination, or if her uniquely enhanced telepathy had connected her with the adult moonlarks' thoughts.

But she transmitted back, *It's going to be okay.*

"Looks like we're ready to head out," Mr. Forkle said, snapping his fingers to raise the glass windows, shutting out the moonlarks' songs and settling the tower back into silence.

"I don't expect to return here for quite some time," he explained, tracing his palm almost wistfully across the back of an armchair. "I think it's best if you go back to Havenfield to wait for me. I still need to make myself known to your bodyguards, and I'm sure you'd rather skip that particular conversation. It's likely to involve an impressive amount of threatening."

"Who here thinks Grizel will slap Forkle?" Keefe asked.

"I'm glad your sense of humor is still intact, Mr. Sencen. But keep in mind that my patience has now been reduced by half."

"Do you want me to tell my parents about . . . all of this?" Sophie asked, feeling queasy even imagining it.

"No. I want you to go to Everglen and tell Alden and Della to head to your house for an announcement. And then leap to Eternalia and tell Councillor Oralie the same. Your mother already knows to bring your father over," he told Dex.

"That's right," Dex said with a sigh. "My mom already knew. That's why she looked so nervous when I left. Ugh, just when I thought she was done lying to me."

"Don't blame her for her silence, Mr. Dizznee. Blame me. And for the record, your mother struggled with her knowledge of my shared life more than the others. She told me once that she finds herself looking at her triplets and imagining how miserable they would be if she'd forced them to lie and hide the way I've had to. And yes, they were fraternal—but even if they were identical, your parents never would've chosen the path my father took. Your parents are some of the boldest, bravest people I've ever met. And everything your mother has done—and continues to do—has been in the hopes of creating a better world for her children. Please don't hold that against her."

Dex kicked his shoe, but didn't argue.

"Anyway," Mr. Forkle said, "hopefully by the time everyone has gathered, I'll be done with the goblins. But if I'm delayed, none of you are under any obligation to answer their questions. And in case you're wondering, this group should be the last of those allowed to know the truth. The Black Swan have done an excellent job of covering the absence of my various identities while I've taken time to mourn. Everyone else has no idea there's been any change."

"What about the Neverseen?" Sophie asked. "Gethen had to know he dealt a lethal blow with that sword."

"I'm sure he did. And should any of us have any contact with them—"

"I love how you make that sound like an 'if,'" Fitz interrupted.

"Very well, Mr. Vacker. *When* any of us have any contact with them, I think it's important we let them continue with their false assumption. They have no knowledge of my other identities—or at least, that's what I'm assuming. You would know better than I would, Mr. Sencen."

"I didn't tell them anything about you," Keefe promised. "The story I stuck with was that I secretly suspected you were Councillor Alina—and *please, please, please* let me be there when Fintan finds out you're still around. I want to see him pee his pants!"

"I'm sure you do," Mr. Forkle said as Tiergan retrieved his pathfinder and created a beam to take them to Everglen. "But the longer the Neverseen stay in the dark, the better. Let them bask in their perceived victory as long as we can."

Part of Sophie wanted to argue that it *had* been a victory, since the Neverseen still took someone from them. But as she watched Mr. Forkle prepare his own pathfinder, she realized they'd won as well.

The Neverseen may think themselves brilliant schemers, full of plans no one would ever suspect.

But when it came to game-changing secrets, the Black Swan would always be the best.

TWENTY

R. FORKLE ARRIVED AT HAVEN-
field with a handprint-shaped blotch
on his left cheek, and Grizel seemed
mighty pleased with herself when she
strolled in behind him.

Sandor, meanwhile, was a walking storm, and his thunderous focus went immediately to Sophie and lightened only when
he was back at her side, muttering under his breath about the
duality of elves.

Woltzer and Lovise looked mostly puzzled—but that was probably because they hadn't had many interactions with Mr. Forkle,
or his various identities. Neither had Cadoc, and the three of
them stood together while everyone else struggled to process.

And struggle they did—though the adults were shockingly consistent with their reactions to the Great Forkle Reappearance, as Keefe had dubbed it. There was gasping. And shouting. And rushing to hug their children to make sure they were okay with the news—or, in Juline's case, making sure that Dex was still speaking to her. All of which was followed by *lots* of questions. And while the conversation was mostly a rehash of things Mr. Forkle had already gone over with Sophie and her friends, two new questions did catch Sophie's attention.

Dex's father, Kesler, somewhat morbidly wanted to know what happened to the other Forkle's body after Oralie hid it.

Apparently, the late Mr. Forkle had told Oralie how to contact the Black Swan, and Wraith had snuck into the ruins and brought the body back to one of the Black Swan's hideouts, where Physic made sure it was given a proper burial.

The other question came from Councillor Oralie, who stood on the far side of Havenfield's enormous living room in her blush-toned gown. Her jeweled circlet was noticeably absent from her ringletted blond hair as she whispered, "Can you ever forgive me?"

Mr. Forkle moved to her side and reached for her fragile, shaking hand. "There's nothing to forgive, Oralie. I would've made the same choice my brother did in that moment. And you're an Empath, so you know I'm telling the truth."

Empaths often served as living lie detectors, using their

ability to read the shifts in emotions to gauge the honesty of the speaker.

Oralie's shadowed blue eyes shimmered with tears. "But if I'd—"

"One thing I've had to learn," Mr. Forkle interrupted, "and I suspect you know this better than most—is that it's far too easy to analyze a tragedy after the fact and feel like you should've been able to prevent it."

"Yes," Oralie whispered. "It is."

Sophie had a feeling Oralie was *also* thinking about the day Councillor Kenric was taken from them. She'd long suspected that Kenric and Oralie had been in love, but never acted on it.

"For the record, the only person truly responsible for my brother's death is the person who stabbed him," Mr. Forkle added. "And for all the other 'what-ifs' that led him to that moment . . . there's nothing we can do about them. The past is the only finite thing in this uncertain world, and in a way, that's somewhat comforting."

"How?" Tam wanted to know.

"Because it gives us a fixed point to learn from. For better or worse, this loss—and any others we've suffered—makes us stronger, smarter, more determined than ever to fight back with everything we have. But in order for that to happen, we have to let go of our regrets." His voice hitched and he turned away, smearing tears with the back of his hand. "Part of me will always lament that I didn't listen to Miss Foster and focus harder on interrogating Gethen. But . . . I'm choosing to channel those feelings into our cause. I hope you'll do the same, Oralie. We could use a Councillor on our side, now more than ever."

"I'm already on your side," Oralie whispered, reaching up to trace the part of her forehead where her circlet usually rested. "And if any of you are worrying about my presence here"—her focus lingered on Kesler and Juline the longest—"you have my word that none of what I've seen or heard today will ever be repeated. You should also know that the balance in the Council is shifting. Those who mistrust your order are finding their voices overruled. I suspect Councillor Emery will be contacting your Collective soon about *truly* joining forces. We're just trying to get things settled with the other world leaders first. The attack in Lumenaria has created a diplomatic nightmare."

"I can imagine," Mr. Forkle said quietly. "And we're ready to help with whatever the Council requires. In the meantime, know that we'll be working behind the scenes to the fullest extent of our abilities. In fact, it seems Miss Foster has some rather interesting plans taking shape."

Sophie's eyes widened. "Did you read my mind?"

She covered her ears when he nodded. The gesture wouldn't block him, but somehow it made her feel better.

"I don't remember giving you permission," she noted.

"Would you have, if I'd asked?"

"Yes. But that doesn't make sneaking in okay!"

"No, I suppose not. For what it's worth, I was mainly trying to see if I *could* still slip past your blocking, or if your point of trust had been altered by everything that's happened. And once I was through, I caught a glimpse of what was on your mind, and—it's no excuse—but curiosity got the better of me. So I have to ask . . . are you really intending to go to Ravagog?"

The word was a match hurled into a box of fireworks.

"I guess I should've clarified," Mr. Forkle shouted over the din. "Their current plan is uncharacteristically reasonable."

That quieted everyone enough for Sophie to explain her charming conversation with Lady Gisela, and how she was planning to bring Keefe, Biana, and Tam with her to ask Lady Cadence for help arranging a meeting with King Dimitar. And while she was at it, she told them Fitz would be looking into the fires and searching Candleshade for whatever they now knew was hidden there, while Dex would keep working on Fintan's cache, and Linh would check on Wylie. The only part she left out was any mention of her sister.

"I feel the need to emphasize exactly how dangerous the information in those caches could be," Oralie said when she'd finished. "And if you *do* manage to access it, I hope you'll notify me."

Sophie nodded. "Dex thinks we need passwords to get past the caches' security. Is that true?"

Oralie frowned. "All I've ever been told is that there *is* a way to recover the secrets. But the specifics of how have never been explained. Accessing a cache is supposed to require a unanimous vote, so I've always assumed we'd be given instructions then. I could try asking another Councillor, but the person most likely to know would be Bronte, and I'm not sure if you want him to suspect what you're up to."

"Let me play with it a little more on my own, first," Dex told her.

"If you want to help," Fitz jumped in, "I was planning to ask you for the names of any goblins who worked at Lumenaria and might've tended to the prisoner before she escaped. To see if they know anything about her."

"How do you know it's a female?" Oralie asked.

"My mom told us," Keefe told her. "And I don't know why she'd lie about that."

"I suppose," Oralie said. "Though it's strange that I'm not feeling even the slightest sense that I've ever heard of an Ancient female criminal. Whoever she is, they did a very good job of erasing her. I'll put together a list of guards. You might also want to ask Fallon Vacker."

The name sent a strange ripple through the room.

Sophie didn't know much about him, only that he was Fitz's great-great-great-great-great-great-great-great-great-great-great-great-great-great-great-great-great-great-great-grandfather and one of the first members of the Council.

"He . . . rarely accepts company," Alden said quietly.

"Is that why we've never met him?" Biana asked.

"You have lots of relatives you've never met," Alden reminded her.

"Really?" Sophie asked. Her brain still struggled with the indefinite elvin life span. But she'd always assumed they kept in touch with their numerous relatives—especially a legendary family like the Vackers.

"Most of the Ancients live very solitary lives," Alden explained. "All that time and experience makes it hard for them to relate."

The explanation made sense—but something about the way his jaw had tightened had Sophie wondering if there was more to the story. Especially when she considered what Alvar claimed when he'd revealed himself as one of the Neverseen.

You'll understand, someday, when you see the Vacker legacy for what it is.

"Can't you at least *ask* Fallon for a visit?" Biana pressed.

Alden sighed. "I suppose I can try. But I wouldn't get my hopes up."

Oralie promised to send the list of goblin guards to Fitz that night, and Sandor offered to coordinate with his queen if any of the goblins had returned to Gildingham.

"And while we're adjusting plans," Della said, blinking in and out of sight as she crossed the room, "I want to go with you to Ravagog." She might've looked like a Disney princess with her wavy dark hair, perfect features, and green mermaid-cut gown. But Sophie had seen her drop Mr. Forkle without breaking a sweat—while wearing heels.

"I think that'll be up to Lady Cadence," Sophie warned. "*If* she agrees to help, I'm sure she'll have a *lot* to say about who does and doesn't get to go."

Della nodded. "Then I want to go with you when you talk to her today."

"So do I," Mr. Forkle jumped in. "I also expect a thorough update when you next contact Lady Gisela."

"And I want to know everything she has to say about what happened to Cyrah *before* you tell Wylie," Tiergan added. "I know my son has asked you to keep him updated. But he's still recovering from his abduction. I need to make sure nothing sets him back."

"Of course," Sophie promised.

"Well then," Mr. Forkle said, "it sounds like we have quite a lot to do. So I suppose we should move on to my brother's planting."

"Only if you're feeling ready," Tiergan told him.

"I'm as ready as I'll ever be."

"Then I'll let Blur and Wraith know to meet us at the planting site," Dex's mom offered. "And I brought this." She fished a delicate green bottle out of the pocket of her cape.

Kesler side-eyed his wife. "Did you steal that from Slurps and Burps?"

Juline's cheeks flushed, but her posture stayed tall and proud. "The store is half mine, so it's hardly stealing."

Kesler grumbled something about never-ending secrets, but he wrapped his arm around his wife and pulled her close, tucking her amber-colored hair behind her ear.

Sophie wasn't sure exactly what was in the bottle, but she'd seen others like it used during the plantings she'd attended. And it made her heart feel prickly.

"You're welcome to join us," Mr. Forkle told Councillor Oralie.

"I wish I could. But my absence would be noticed. Councillor Terik is meeting with Elwin this afternoon—as well as a team of Technopaths—to make some adjustments to his new leg, and the rest of the Council is expected to be there for moral support."

Sophie glanced at Dex. "I thought you were helping with the prosthesis."

"I *was*. But he wanted me to design something that could be permanently attached, and that's too . . . complicated."

"It's absurd is what it is," Kesler corrected, then quickly apologized to Oralie.

"Actually, I agree," Oralie told him. "I think Terik's hoping they'll be able to build something that will function *exactly* the way he was able to before Lumenaria—and I can't blame him for the inclination. But technology is not flesh. He'll be much happier if he allows his body to adapt."

"It can't be easy, though," Grady said quietly. "Especially since so few understand what he's enduring."

"I wonder if it would help him to speak to the Redek family,"

Alden suggested. "I know Caprise's injuries were vastly different, and her struggle is mostly emotional. Still, they can at least relate to the challenge of having a drastic change in physical circumstance."

Oralie seemed intrigued by the idea, but Sophie couldn't follow the rest of the conversation. Her failing friendship with Marella Redek was one of her bigger regrets—especially since the last time she saw her, Marella had begged Mr. Forkle to try triggering her special ability, hoping she'd become an Empath and be able to help her mom.

"Did any of you guys ever find out if Marella manifested?" Sophie whispered to her friends, feeling both better *and* worse when they all shook their heads.

Oralie moved to leave then, holding a shimmering pendant up to the light. "It's incredibly good to see you," she told Mr. Forkle, choking slightly on the words.

He cleared his throat. "It's good to be seen."

As soon as Oralie glittered away, he removed a blue pathfinder from his pocket and reached for Sophie's hand. "Let's go say goodbye to my brother."

TWENTY-ONE

ARE WE IN NORWAY?" SOPHIE asked, wishing she'd added a cape to her outfit when the blisteringly cold wind hit her.

They'd leaped to a sharply angled slope in the middle of a green-gray valley, with snow-crowned mountains surrounding an ice blue lake—or was it a fjord?

"That's what the humans call it, yes," Mr. Forkle agreed, his deep breaths clouding the air. "And that"—he pointed to the massive rock jutting horizontally out of the mountain far above them—"they call Trolltunga."

"Troll Tongue?" Sophie asked when her Polyglot sense translated the Norwegian term.

Mr. Forkle smiled. "My brother and I gave the humans the

nickname, and it's stuck all these years—along with so many of the stories we invented. I suppose we had a touch too much fun ensuring that the legends about us stayed as convoluted as possible."

He turned away to wipe his eyes and Sophie hugged herself, trying to think warm thoughts. Even with the body temperature regulation tricks she'd learned at Exillium, she couldn't stop her teeth from chattering.

"Here," Keefe said, wrapping his cape around her and fastening it under her chin. "Can't have you turning blue on us."

He shook his head when she tried to protest. "You didn't refuse the Fitzster's gift, did you?"

She wanted to point out that Fitz's gift didn't require him to be stuck freezing for who knew how long. But she had a better solution.

She unfastened the pin and scooted closer, wrapping one arm—and part of the cape—around him so they could share.

Tam snorted. "Guess we have to score one for Keephie."

Grady's sigh had a whole lot of groan mixed in.

"Wait." Kesler glanced at Dex, who was shaking his head at his dad—hard. "Does that mean—"

Juline elbowed him before he could finish the question.

"My brother just likes to make trouble," Linh said through the silence that followed.

"And for once I don't mind." Keefe scooted even closer, resting his head on Sophie's shoulder.

She shoved him away, taking the cape with her. "And now you can freeze."

"Worth it!" Keefe decided.

"Are we waiting for something?" Fitz asked, squinting at the blue-white sky.

"Blur and Wraith should be here momentarily," Mr. Forkle promised, counting his paces across the ice-crusted ground until he reached a small patch of muddy grass. "This is it."

"Really?" Kesler asked. "I mean, the view is nice, but . . . there are lots of amazing views on this planet."

"There are," Mr. Forkle agreed. "Though the sky here is spectacular. And this region holds many of our fondest memories. But honestly, we chose this place for the challenge. Everything on this slope has to fight for its spot on the earth, through wind and snow and rain."

"You wouldn't rather give yourselves a tiny bit of peace at the end?" Biana asked.

"I'm not sure our Wanderlings would know how to survive without struggle," he said. "Plant them somewhere easy and they'd wilt from sheer boredom. *This* is the life we know— beauty and treachery in equal measure. And think of the stories we'll inspire! Humans hike up this way a few months out of the year, when the conditions allow. I look forward to hearing how they explain the sudden appearance of a tree unlike any others, standing tall in Trolltunga's shadow. I wouldn't be surprised if they blame it on magic. Or elves. And I may have to—"

The rest of his sentence was cut short by a flash of light as three figures leaped onto the slope.

"I thought today wasn't a day for disguises," Tam said, pointing to Wraith's headless floating silver cloak, and the smudges and swirls of color and shadow that made up Blur.

"But it's also not a day for distractions," Livvy corrected—though she was noticeably mask-free.

Wraith's cloak rippled when he moved closer, his voice eerily disembodied as he said, "Revealing who we are would sidetrack everyone."

"And in my case, it requires a loooooooooooong story," Blur added.

"A boring one at that," Livvy said. "Mine was way better."

"How's my sister?" Sophie asked her.

"Doing well. She's helping Quinlin organize the paperwork he'll be sending over about the fires. And she's officially addicted to Prattles. She already devoured *six* boxes, and asked me to bring you this."

She handed Sophie a grayish-brown pin of a creature that looked like a messed-up combination of a saber-toothed tiger, a hippo, and a giant rat.

"A gorgonops?" Biana jumped in. "I've been trying to find one of those for years!"

"They are rather rare," Livvy agreed. "That's why your sister said she wanted you to have it—though I suspect she may have also thought the pin was . . . less than pretty."

Sophie smiled. "That sounds like the Amy I remember."

Her sister used to love trying to trade the things she didn't like, pretending she was doing Sophie a favor. And the gorgonops definitely wasn't a creature that was going to win any beauty contests.

"Do they keep these things at the Sanctuary?" Sophie asked.

"In a restricted area," Grady said. "We had one at Havenfield for a while and his fangs were bigger than my head."

"He dug his way into the mastodon pasture once," Edaline said quietly. Her shudder said the rest.

"Some creatures do not mix well with others," Mr. Forkle agreed. "But they still need our protection."

The elves believed that every species existed on the planet for a reason, and to allow any to go extinct could have tremendous consequences for the delicate balance of the earth's environment.

Sophie tucked the pin into her pocket and asked Livvy to tell her sister that she'd hail her before she went to bed.

"Well," Mr. Forkle said, "I suppose I've stalled long enough. My brother deserves to rest."

He dropped to his knees, taking a slow, deep breath before clawing at the cold mud with his swollen fingers. It seemed strange he hadn't brought a shovel—especially when Sophie noticed his nails cracking—but maybe that had been deliberate. Maybe he wanted the planting to hurt a little.

When he'd scraped out a fist-size hole, he wiped the mud on

the sides of his cape and turned to Sophie. Her hand shook as she dug the locket from her cape.

Soft sniffles rippled through their group when he let the tiny seed drop into his palm. Sophie had never actually seen a Wanderling seed before, so she hadn't known what to expect, but somehow she'd imagined something more . . . exciting.

The seed had no real color—just a faint milky tone—and was shaped like dried-out, already-been-chewed gum. But coiled carefully across it was a strand of thick black hair, and Sophie's already prickly heart plummeted into her stomach.

"Goodbye, my brother," Mr. Forkle murmured, bringing the seed to his lips. He whispered something only the seed could hear before he placed it carefully in the hole and covered it with soil.

Juline moved to his side and poured the clear serum from the green bottle over the mound, then shattered the glass against her knuckles and scattered the shimmering remains like confetti. The glinting shards sank into the ground and everyone stepped back, holding their breath.

It took much longer than the other plantings Sophie had been to, but eventually a tiny green shoot peeked out of the ground. And as soon as the light hit it, the sprout surged with a rush of energy, stretching higher, growing thicker, and spreading out branches until the sapling was taller than all of them.

The trunk was narrow, but the bark was thicker than other trees, and coarser too, with a swirled pattern of brown and gold and red and black and even a few threads of green. The leaves were equally varied—some wide and flat, some thin and curled, some shiny, and others covered in a cottony fuzz. Berries sprouted among them, the exact blue as Mr. Forkle's eyes—the only part of his appearance that Sophie could recognize. The rest was such a hodgepodge of colors and textures, it almost felt like the Wanderling was trying to reflect all of Mr. Forkle's identities at once. And it seemed to lean, as if it was angling itself, waiting for someone else.

Mr. Forkle wiped his eyes and ran a shaky hand down the trunk, whispering more words that only he and the tree could hear.

Sophie decided to transmit a few of her own—the one thing she'd forgotten to say in Lumenaria.

Thank you for everything you did for me.

"Rest well, my brother," Mr. Forkle said, stepping back to join his small band of supporters. "I'll take it from here."

TWENTY-TWO

I THOUGHT WE WERE GOING TO LADY Cadence's house," Sophie said as the scenery glittered into focus.

Mr. Forkle had leaped the eight of them—Sophie, Biana, Tam, Keefe, Della, Sandor, Woltzer, and himself—to a river so wide, it looked more like a lake. White swells crashed against the dark rocks, and the roar of water tickled Sophie's ears.

"The best anyone can do when visiting Riverdrift is find the general area," Mr. Forkle explained, pointing south, to where the water cut through a tangle of unruly woods. "The rest we'll have to do on foot."

"Aw, not another epic journey, Forkle," Keefe whined,

slumping against Sophie's shoulder. "My feet are still recovering from the eight thousand stairs you already made us climb."

So were Sophie's.

They'd also lost time going home to change. Mr. Forkle hadn't wanted Lady Cadence to see them all in green—which was probably smart. But now the sun was setting and all she could think was that her parents had been missing for another whole day.

"There's a curve in the river about half a mile up ahead," Mr. Forkle called over his shoulder. "She usually lays anchor somewhere near there."

"Wait—we're getting on a boat?" Tam asked.

"A houseboat," Mr. Forkle clarified. "King Dimitar refused to let Lady Cadence establish any sort of permanent home in Ravagog. But he did agree that she could set up something temporary. So, Riverdrift was her solution. She designed the vessel herself and kept it docked along the Eventide—until the Council made her sail back to the Lost Cities to mentor Sophie."

"Well, it's probably smart we didn't bring Linh, then," Tam said. "She might sink the place."

"Aw, she has awesome control," Biana argued.

"Not lately. She's started calling water in her sleep. I've been waking up to giant water-beasts prowling around the room. She's even made a few life-size water elves—two of which looked so much like my parents I actually screamed."

Mr. Forkle frowned. "Sounds like she could do with formal training. I can arrange for her to have a Hydrokinetic Mentor—and a Shade Mentor for you as well—if you transfer to Foxfire."

Tam pulled on his bangs. "Ugh. That would make my parents *way* too happy."

"I'm sure it would," Mr. Forkle agreed. "But had life not thrown you such a complicated detour, you'd be attending the academy already—which isn't to imply that your education through Exillium has been a waste. I wish every prodigy could achieve such mastery of their skills as the two of you have."

"But if you guys come to Foxfire we could have lunch together every day," Biana jumped in. "And hang out in study hall. And team up in PE. It would be epic!"

"It would," Sophie agreed, even if it was hard to imagine life ever being that simple again.

"At least talk to your sister about it," Mr. Forkle encouraged Tam. "She's worked so hard to master her talent, I'd hate to see her lose that hard-won hold."

Tam nodded. "Would we have to move back home?"

"I see no reason why. Foxfire has no requirement about prodigies living specifically with their families. And it would make no difference to Tiergan."

"You guys are living with Tiergan?" Sophie asked. "I thought Blur was going to be your guardian when you moved back to the Lost Cities."

"That was our original plan," Mr. Forkle said. "But Blur's

living situation has grown slightly complicated. And Tiergan realized that Wylie wouldn't be needing his room now that he's settled into the cabin with Prentice."

"I didn't have high hopes for living with a guy who spends half his time looking like a giant half-carved statue," Tam admitted. "But Wylie's room is more like three rooms, so we still have our own space. And Linh loves digging through his music."

"Music?" Sophie repeated. The Lost Cities hadn't seemed to be very musically oriented.

"The songs probably aren't what you're imagining," Mr. Forkle told her. "Elvin composers tend to focus on 'natural melodies.' Elegant tapestries of natural sounds."

"They're very soothing," Della said. "And Tam's mother has composed some of my favorites. As has his grandmother."

Biana stopped walking. "I don't know why I never put it together that you guys are *those* Songs."

"Wait—your last name is Song and your family makes . . . songs?" Sophie had to ask.

"Ugh, don't even get me started," Tam grumbled. "Our *real* family name is supposed to be Tong. But my great-great-great-great-great-great-great-great-great-grandmother started calling herself Lady Song, and when she registered her daughter, she put that as the surname—and it's been passed down ever since. Stupid, right?"

"Eh, at least the name comes from your mom's side," Keefe

told him. "Sencen comes from my dad. Can't *wait* to ditch that one someday."

"So then how do people decide which last name gets used?" Sophie asked.

"It's up to each couple," Della told her. "In my case, Vacker was such a legendary name that it was only natural for me to take Alden's. But the Heks name is from Vika's side of the family. It generally comes down to which name holds more distinction."

"Or what message the couple is trying to send," Mr. Forkle added. "I suspect Juline went with Dizznee because she wanted people to know she wasn't ashamed of her husband, even if the matchmakers didn't approve their marriage."

All Sophie could say to that was "Huh."

It never ceased to amaze her how much she still had to learn about elvin culture—and it was cool that they didn't just pass down names arbitrarily. But she wondered how they'd feel if she kept her *human* last name. She couldn't imagine letting the name go—assuming she ever got married, of course. For that, she'd have to go through the whole terrifying matchmaking process with its endless questionnaires, and lists of matches, and Winnowing Galas. It was enough to make her want to move back to the human world. Or stay fourteen forever.

Or wait—was she fifteen now?

The elves tracked age by something they called an Inception Date—a fact Sophie had only discovered a few months earlier, when she'd also learned she was nine months older than she'd once believed.

She was in the middle of counting how many weeks had passed since then when the river curved again, and the strangest contraption she'd ever seen came into view. It was as big as any of the other elvin mansions, resting on a huge silver barge with two giant steel paddlewheels mounted to the back. The house itself reminded her of Howl's Moving Castle, with all the different metal structures smashed together and piled on top of each other. Some were gold and round, with porthole-size windows dotting the sides. Others were copper and square, with riveted metal shutters. A central pyramid-shaped tower was made of cut glass, surrounded by three chimneys spewing some sort of multicolored mist.

"I take it this isn't what you were expecting?" Mr. Forkle asked.

They all shook their heads.

"One of the great follies of the elves," Lady Cadence said, stepping out of a copse of trees. "We always want everything to be pretty."

"There's nothing wrong with favoring beauty," Della argued.

"I'd agree if you'd used the word 'enjoying,'" Lady Cadence told her, smoothing the strand of long raven hair that had broken free from her tight braid. Paired with her buttoned-up-to-the-neck black shirt and starched black pants, she almost looked like she was wearing a military uniform. "But *favoring*

"I had a feeling it wasn't." Mr. Forkle reached up to rub his temples. "Am I to assume you're suggesting an ogre–Black Swan alliance?"

"A temporary one, yes. Dimitar still has his heart set on his new course of isolation—and in some ways, it's not a bad plan. The ogres have made some unfortunate mistakes. It will be better for them to keep to themselves while their capital is rebuilt, and the other species they've harmed take time to cool off."

"Those of us who've had our loved ones aurified in our Hall of Heroes will never *cool off*!" Sandor snapped.

"And Dimitar's actions weren't *mistakes*. They were acts of war!" Woltzer added.

"Mostly they were *wrong*—which Dimitar is beginning to see." Lady Cadence poured herself a second cup, and refilled Mr. Forkle's. "I don't expect any of you to be friends. But like it or not, we share this planet. If we want to achieve real peace, we're going to need to work together."

"Ogres don't want peace," Sandor argued.

"Some might say the same of goblins. Tell me this, if the ogres were to vanish, would I no longer see a sword at your side and pockets full of throwing stars?"

"Ogres aren't the only threat," Woltzer reminded her.

"Some of them aren't a threat at all. Which is why an alliance could be to our advantage."

"And Dimitar's on board with this?" Mr. Forkle asked. "He

said, with a bigger smile than Sophie had ever seen her have. "Though you've also proven my point. What some admire, others may not—and neither side is *wrong*. We should all be challenging ourselves to keep an open mind."

"Is it okay if we have a closed nose?" Keefe asked. "Because I'm picking up a pretty strong stink of curdleroots—or are we supposed to find the value in that too?"

"No," Lady Cadence told him, motioning for everyone to follow her. "The plants are useful for my research. But the aroma is universally odious."

She led them up a rickety ramp and onto the gently rocking deck of Riverdrift, heading for the glass pyramid portion of the houseboat, which turned out to be . . . empty.

"It's best to sit when bartering, don't you think?" Lady Cadence asked, snapping her fingers and making an enormous table and nine throne-size chairs appear in the center of the room. A second snap conjured up a fancy porcelain tea service with nine fragile teacups. Whatever was in the teapot smelled warm and citrusy—but when she poured, the liquid was sludgy and green.

"Don't be fooled by your eyes," Lady Cadence said, handing the first slime-filled cup to Sophie. "This is one of my favorite ogre treats."

"I'll pass," Sandor and Woltzer said in unison.

"Your loss." She made two of the cups disappear.

Mr. Forkle sipped bravely from the cup she handed him,

and nodded his approval. "Hopefully your barter will be equally appealing."

Lady Cadence took a long draw of her tea. "I think you'll find my terms more than fair, considering what you're asking."

"But we haven't even told you what we need," Biana pointed out. She sniffed her cup before taking a sip. "Oh, it's actually good, guys—you should try it."

Sophie, Keefe, and Tam reluctantly took her advice. And Biana was right. It tasted kind of like a warm strawberry-lemonade milkshake—a little weird, but not unpleasant. Even Della didn't seem to mind it.

"There can only be one reason you would come to me for help," Lady Cadence told them. "You want something from the ogres—either a meeting with King Dimitar, or for me to ask him to give you something."

"Or both," Mr. Forkle said, taking another sip.

One of Lady Cadence's eyebrows shot up. "*That* is a very large order."

"It gets larger." Mr. Forkle explained about the message they had to deliver from Lady Gisela, and the starstone they needed to recover, and how time was of the absolute essence to rescue Sophie's human parents.

"Dude, I don't think you know how to negotiate," Keefe told him, spinning his cup on the table and somehow managing not to spill it. "You're supposed to undersell."

"This won't be a negotiation," Mr. Forkle corrected. "I've

no doubt Lady Cadence decided what she wanted before she agreed to meet."

"How very astute of you," Lady Cadence said, downing the rest of her tea. "Though the things I want shouldn't pose too much of a challenge."

Mr. Forkle leaned back in his chair. "I'm listening."

"Okay, first: I want you to let me mentor a session on ogres at Foxfire—one that *all* prodigies are required to attend in order to come to a proper understanding of their ways."

"And what makes you think I have the power to grant that?" Mr. Forkle asked.

She stood and paced to the farthest corner of the pyramid. "It's funny—everyone still calls me *Lady* Cadence. Have you noticed that? It's honestly how I still think of myself. But technically my title is *Master* Cadence. I was appointed as the Beacon of the Silver Tower to replace Master Leto when he was appointed as principal of Foxfire. And the funny thing about being Beacon is that there's actually very little for me to do. So I've taken to exploring the tower, and I found something rather interesting on the roof. Do you know what's up there?"

"Isn't it a greenhouse?" Biana asked.

"Mostly, yes. There's a huge glass bubble where the prodigies grow their splendors for the Opening Ceremonies. But off to the side, tucked behind all the gardening tools is a rickety shed that looked forgotten. I climbed through all the clutter to investigate, and it seems someone used it as another greenhouse. The soil in the troughs looked freshly churned, so I dredged it, to make sure my prodigies hadn't been harvesting anything dangerous." Her eyes locked with Mr. Forkle's. "*Someone* was growing ruckleberries."

Sophie barely managed not to squeak.

Mr. Forkle merely smiled. "If you have something to say, Cadence, say it."

"In front of everyone?"

"Why not? They already know I'm sometimes Magnate Leto."

"Well then," she said, smoothing her shirt and trying to recover, "I suppose that makes things simpler. I hope the fact that I haven't shared my discovery makes it easier for you to see the value of my other demand. If you want my help with King Dimitar, I want to know that we're truly on the same side. So, you have to let me join the Black Swan."

TWENTY-THREE

I WAS UNDER THE IMPRESSION THAT YOU weren't a fan of our order," Mr. Forkle said, finishing the last of his sludgy tea.

Lady Cadence sauntered back to the table and snapped her fingers, making a glowing silver orb appear in the center. Sophie hadn't noticed how dark it had gotten until her eyes squinted at the sudden brightness.

"I could be a very big fan," Lady Cadence said, "if you widened your vision to ensure it wasn't limited to the elves."

"Fixing the problems in our world will benefit *all* species," Mr. Forkle assured her. "Just as *all* are currently struggling because of the Neverseen's divisiveness."

"That's not what I meant."

"My guess would be Sophie. You've made it abundantly clear that she holds a certain value to our world. Most likely he'll want her to prove that she deserves his generosity."

"Why do I not like the sound of that?" Keefe asked.

Sophie didn't either.

And Sandor looked ready to unsheathe his sword and start hacking at things.

But . . . if that was the only way to get the starstone to take them to Nightfall, she'd do it. Whatever it took to get her parents out of there.

"Let me be clear," Mr. Forkle said. "If I entrust Miss Foster to your care for this meeting, you *must* assure me of her safety. And Mr. Sencen's as well."

"Won't you be joining us?" Lady Cadence asked.

"I . . . have other matters to attend to."

He probably did—but Sophie wondered if he also didn't want Dimitar seeing him alive, in case he was in contact with Fintan.

Lady Cadence's eyes narrowed at Sophie and Keefe. "And you two will do whatever I tell you without causing any trouble?"

Keefe batted his eyelashes. "We would *never* dream of causing you any trouble."

"We *won't*," Sophie emphasized, kicking Keefe under the table, "because my family's lives are on the line."

Lady Cadence nodded, turning back to Mr. Forkle. "Then yes, I can assure they'll leave Ravagog in one piece."

made it unmistakably clear at the Summit that he wanted zero contact with our kind."

"But he does trust me," Lady Cadence reminded him. "Following my advice spared his people further tragedy. It also nearly cost me my life—something Dimitar does not take lightly. The ogre rebels who attacked Havenfield were there for *me*."

"How can you be so sure?" Sophie asked. Dimitar had implied the same thing when she saw him at the Peace Summit—but he didn't have any proof.

"I can be sure," Lady Cadence said, setting down her tea, "because Dimitar's soldiers caught the ogre who got away."

Chairs crashed to the floor as Sandor and Woltzer jumped to their feet.

"You're sure it was him?" Sandor asked.

"Yes. He had the scar across his chest from Brielle's final attack. And he tried to fall on his sword to spare himself the punishment for treason."

"Then why hasn't he been handed over to our queen?" Woltzer demanded.

Lady Cadence swallowed hard, her complexion turning as green as her sludgy beverage. "Because . . . he did not survive Dimitar's interrogation."

Several cups spilled as Sandor's fist pounded against the table. "That vengeance belonged to my people!"

"Vengeance is a fool's mission." Lady Cadence conjured a

napkin and mopped up the sticky mess. "It does nothing to right any of the wrongs."

"And yet Dimitar had no problem claiming the vengeance for himself," Woltzer reminded her.

"Vengeance was not his goal. He was attempting to send a message to his people about the consequences of rebellion—and while I find his method grotesque, I can understand why he was impelled to take the matter so seriously. Before the prisoner succumbed, he confessed that at least a dozen ogres have left Ravagog and sworn fealty to the Neverseen. They saw our mighty castle fall by Fintan's hand and see it as proof that he'll deliver on his grandiose plans."

"And I'm assuming the prisoner didn't mention what any of those plans are?" Della asked.

"Just the same ramblings about letting the ogres take back the resources that are currently being squandered on humans, and granting them the freedom to expand their territories. But now the rebels think Dimitar has lost the nerve to fight for his people—and they blame *me* for weakening his mind with my elvin reasoning."

"But . . . the Neverseen are elves too," Biana reminded her.

"Exactly. That's the treachery of greed. Everything stops being about logic and becomes a simple matter of who tells you what you most want to hear. And Fintan is a master at pouring sugar in people's ears—though he doesn't deserve all the credit. This rebellion is rooted in mistakes that our society has made for centuries."

"How can you be certain that all of this isn't a ploy to cover the fact that the ogres are violating their new treaty?" Sandor asked. "These rebels might not be *rebels* at all."

"That could even be why Dimitar refused to hand over Brielle's killer," Woltzer added, "knowing my queen would drag the truth out of him."

"I realize that such reasoning fits neatly within the box you choose to place the ogres in. But the only truths to be gleaned from the prisoner were the facts I've already shared—and I can swear to that because I was *there*." Her arms trembled slightly, and she pulled her hands into her lap. "Dimitar offered me a chance to face my intended murderer before he was condemned, promising that if I found any proof of the ogre's innocence, his life would be spared. So . . . I went. And Dimitar made it clear to the warrior that I was his only hope of salvation. And yet . . ."

She cleared her throat, reaching up to fiddle with her Markchain pendant.

"I lived with the ogres for years. I've seen them at their very best and their absolute worst. And I've never seen anything like him. The things he shouted—the horrors he *chose* to suffer . . . no one could fake that level of pure, poisonous hatred. Doubt me if you want. But keep in mind that the mark of most extremists is that they resist change, claiming they're trying to protect something they fear they're about to lose. Sound like anyone in this room?"

"Now we're *extremists?*" Woltzer asked.

"Good intentions can be just as extreme as bad ones," Lady Cadence told him. "Don't let yourselves make that mistake. We *need* Dimitar as our ally. Neither the Black Swan, nor the Council, nor even the goblins are prepared for a threat of this magnitude. And before you go claiming otherwise," she told Sandor, "let's not forget that you've recently recovered from numerous serious injuries caused by *one* ogre working with the Neverseen."

"He threw me off a mountain," Sandor protested, "while I was weakened by the lack of oxygen."

"I'm not doubting your abilities as a warrior. I guarantee Fintan chose that mountain because he knew the conditions would leave you at a disadvantage."

"Actually, *we* chose it," Biana corrected. "We were planning to ambush *them*, and they found out and turned everything around on us."

"That may be," Lady Cadence told her, "but they still knew you would be caught off guard. They don't fight fair—and they always have a strategy. Don't you think it's time we start doing the same?"

"Are you suggesting we ask Dimitar to give us a battalion of ogre warriors?" Mr. Forkle asked, holding out his hands to silence Woltzer's and Sandor's protests. "I can't imagine him agreeing to that—and even if he surprises me, the Council will never allow an army of ogres to dwell within the Lost Cities, even under the banner of allies. And the Black Swan has no means to hide them. Nor the desire, I might add. I'm a risk-taker, Cadence, but you've found my limit."

Her lips twisted into a smile. "Quite honestly, I'm not sure what I'm suggesting, nor am I certain what Dimitar will be willing to offer. All I'm asking for is the chance to find out, and the support of the Black Swan for whatever I can arrange. This rebellion has affected both ogres and elves alike. It's time we figure out how to fight it together. And what better opportunity than when we're already journeying to his city and asking him to hand over one of his prized spoils?"

"Does that mean you'll take us to Ravagog?" Sophie asked.

"Not all of you. I can't bring the goblins, of course. And *you*"—she pointed to Tam, Biana, and Della—"can only have one purpose for tagging along for this meeting, and I'm not bringing thieves into a friend's palace."

"We'd only steal if he won't give us the hairpin," Tam argued.

"That doesn't make it right. Dimitar is not so unreasonable as you may believe—especially if you let me take the lead. He'll likely give you a challenge to convince him he should hand over what you seek."

"What kind of challenge?" Sophie asked.

"Any number of things. Dimitar likes to consider his allies worthy, so I wouldn't be surprised if he chose to test you in some way."

"Test who, exactly?" Mr. Forkle asked.

"My guess would be Sophie. You've made it abundantly clear that she holds a certain value to our world. Most likely he'll want to her to prove that she deserves his generosity."

"Why do I not like the sound of that?" Keefe asked.

Sophie didn't either.

And Sandor looked ready to unsheathe his sword and start hacking at things.

But . . . if that was the only way to get the starstone to take them to Nightfall, she'd do it. Whatever it took to get her parents out of there.

"Let me be clear," Mr. Forkle said. "If I entrust Miss Foster to your care for this meeting, you *must* assure me of her safety. And Mr. Sencen's as well."

"Won't you be joining us?" Lady Cadence asked.

"I . . . have other matters to attend to."

He probably did—but Sophie wondered if he also didn't want Dimitar seeing him alive, in case he was in contact with Fintan.

Lady Cadence's eyes narrowed at Sophie and Keefe. "And you two will do whatever I tell you without causing any trouble?"

Keefe batted his eyelashes. "We would *never* dream of causing you any trouble."

"We *won't*," Sophie emphasized, kicking Keefe under the table, "because my family's lives are on the line."

Lady Cadence nodded, turning back to Mr. Forkle. "Then yes, I can assure they'll leave Ravagog in one piece."

Somehow that didn't sound the same as *safe*.

"But King Dimitar will need some assurance that I have the Black Swan's permission to broker an alliance," she added.

"I'll arrange for a member of our Collective to join you—assuming we have a deal, of course," Mr. Forkle told her.

"Are you agreeing to my terms?" she asked.

Mr. Forkle reached for his neck, tracing his fingers along the chain of his registry pendant. "I can't grant you the Foxfire session until the next school year, since the prodigies' schedules will already be overloaded to make up for lost time. And I can't speak for the entire Collective, so this is still pending an official vote. But . . . welcome to the Black Swan."

TWENTY-FOUR

HOW WORRIED DO I NEED TO BE?"
Grady asked when Sophie, Keefe, and Sandor
leaped back to Havenfield and found him out
in the pastures, clinging to a thick black rope
that rose high into the inky sky.

The most enormous silver-blue bird Sophie had ever seen
was tethered to the end, circling among the winking stars.

"I don't know," Sophie told him. "That thing *does* look like it
could carry you off and eat you."

Grady gave the gleaming bird some extra slack. "Nice try.
This big guy is our new argentavis. He only eats carrion—at
least until I can show him the glory of gnomish vegetables.
And I think you and Keefe have been spending too much

time together. You're starting to sound like each other."

"I know! Our little girl is growing up and getting so snarky!" Keefe pretended to wipe his teary eyes. "I've never been so proud."

Grady shared a look with Sandor before he let out an endless sigh. "*Anyway.* How'd it go with Lady Cadence?"

"Better than I expected," Sophie admitted. "She said she'd bring us to King Dimitar tomorrow, and she even thinks she can convince him to hand over the starstone."

She decided not to mention that she might face some sort of "challenge" in order for that to happen. Instead she filled him in on Lady Cadence's demands to Mr. Forkle.

Grady tightened his hold on the rope. "A few years ago I would've laughed at the idea of an ogre-elvin alliance. And a few months ago, I would've called it treason. But . . . Lady Cadence may have a point. The way those ogres fought—I've never seen anything like it. And my power was useless against them, thanks to those thinking caps."

"But you haven't been trained for battle," Sandor argued.

"Cadoc and Brielle had," Grady reminded him. "And they were taken down in minutes. If Verdi hadn't busted out of her enclosure, I doubt I'd be standing here right now—and poor Verdi has a permanent limp because of it."

Keefe reached for Sophie's hand, but the extra support didn't stop her bloodstained flashbacks. The pasture they were standing in had been strewn with bodies when she and Sandor had finally gotten there. And for a few harrowing minutes, Sophie had been sure she was going to find Grady and Edaline among them.

"My people have protected the elves for *centuries*," Sandor said quietly. "Are you ready to discount us after one close call?"

"Of course not," Grady told him. "But I never want to attend another aurification—especially yours."

Sophie nodded, trying not to imagine Sandor's gilded, lifeless body standing among all the others in the goblins' Hall of Heroes.

"So, if the ogres are willing to clean up their own mess for us, why not let them?" Grady asked.

"Because trusting ogres has never ended well," Sandor told him. "A fact I doubt Lady Cadence is planning to cover in her new *session*. I may speak with my queen and see if we should demand a chance to teach *our* side of things. I've endured enough of Sophie's multispeciesial studies lectures to know that your curriculum has been incredibly sanitized. I've never been able to decide if it's the result of arrogance or ignorance."

"You're forgetting that Sophie is only a Level Three," Grady said as he attempted to rein in the argentavis—earning a piercing screech and a whole lot of flapping wings. "Certain truths are reserved until our prodigies are mature enough to process them. And some are restricted to the elite levels, for those preparing to enter the nobility."

"Does that mean anyone who doesn't qualify for the elite levels won't learn the whole truth about our world?" Sophie asked.

"There's no such thing as a 'whole truth' when it comes to history," Grady told her. "There will always be classified information only given to those who need to know. Even the Council divides up their secrets."

"And then erases a ton of stuff from their minds," Sophie added.

She'd always found the concept strange. But she'd never thought through what it *really* meant.

"So then . . . even the Councillors don't know our complete history, do they?" she asked.

"They know everything they need to know," Grady assured her.

"How can you be so sure? I mean . . . we have an escaped prisoner running around, plotting creepy stuff with the Neverseen—and, according to Oralie, the Councillors don't even know who she is. And I know they never meant for her to get out of Lumenaria, but she *did*. Am I really the only one who thinks the whole Forgotten Secrets thing seems . . ."

"Dangerous?" Sandor finished for her.

The word in her mind had been "stupid." But his was probably better.

"I just remember in my human schools," Sophie said quietly, "sometimes everyone would whine that studying history was boring—"

"Because it is," Keefe jumped in. "I get more sleep in elvin history than any other session."

Sophie often shared his struggle. As did Sandor.

"But," she added, "the teachers were always telling us that if we didn't know our history, it might repeat itself."

"Which would be a valid point if the humans truly were learning and improving," Grady said gently. "But even with all that knowledge—all that *history*—don't they still live with war and crime? Don't they still cling to their same prejudices? The Councillors believe that the truer lessons don't come from the facts or details. They come from the emotions triggered by the experiences—and those never get erased. If something inspires caution or reserve—or outrage and indignation—the Councillors still carry those feelings with them, even after the memories are wiped away."

"Yeah, but emotions can be warped," Keefe said quietly. "Every horrible thing my dad ever said to me came from his twisted idea of love. He was a jerk *because* he cared—or thought he did. We all know the only person he *actually* cares about is himself."

The words felt too raw to touch.

Keefe cleared his throat. "I just overshared, didn't I?"

Sophie shook her head, a dozen different responses warring in her mind.

"No, it clearly was," Keefe said. "You all have that head-tilted-with-sympathy thing going on now. So hey, how about a subject change? Grady, did you know Sandor and Grizel have been sneaking off for snuggle time?"

Grady wheeled toward Sandor. "I'd wondered if there was something going on with you two. Glad to hear it!"

Sandor flushed pink from head to toe. "I . . . should start preparing for tomorrow. I'll be setting traps for when Lady Gisela attempts to deliver her message. She may think she can slip past me—"

"She will," Keefe interrupted. "Don't ask me how. But believe me, if I thought there was even the slightest chance we could catch her, Foster and I would be having a slumber party tonight."

"No you wouldn't," Grady informed him.

Keefe smirked. "Worried I'll prank you?"

"Definitely not what I'm worried about."

And on *that* note, Sophie decided it was time for another subject change.

"Are you going to start staying at Candleshade?" she asked Keefe. "Since your dad isn't there?"

"Nah. With my luck, he'd come back. Plus, the Neverseen might be watching the place."

"Your father isn't at Candleshade?" Grady asked, frowning when Keefe nodded. "He hasn't made an appearance in Eternalia in a while, either."

"Probably hiding from my mom."

"Or . . . could they be working together?" Sophie had to ask.

Fitz had wondered several weeks earlier if Keefe's dad could've been the one to help Lady Gisela escape. The theory was a *little* hard to believe—Lord Cassius was more of a fancy clothes guy than a busting-people-out-of-an-ogre-prison guy. But Mr. Forkle and Dex had both planned to look into it, and Sophie couldn't remember if she'd ever followed up.

"Nah, my dad cares way too much about his precious reputation to get dragged down with my mom's mess," Keefe assured her. "If anything, he's trying to find her so he can redeem himself with her arrest."

"Maybe."

Still, Sophie made a mental note to ask Dex about it the next time she saw him. He'd offered to hack into Keefe's dad's registry records to track his recent movements. Might be a good idea to see if they could get a current location.

"So where *are* you going, then?" she asked Keefe. "You've never told me where you're hiding out."

"I know." He fussed with his cape.

"Why don't you want me knowing where you're living?"

"Because it's my turn to be the mysterious one."

The joke felt like a cover.

"Don't go tilting your head with sympathy again," he told her. "It's not a big deal. If it was, would I have offered to let your sister stay with me? Speaking of which, didn't you promise you'd be hailing her with an update on the search for your parents tonight? She's probably sitting in her room, staring at her Imparter, wondering if you forgot her. She might even be crying."

"Wow, that's how you're going to get out of answering my question?" Sophie asked.

"It worked, didn't it?"

She sighed. "You're off the hook—for now."

"Then I better take my cue," Keefe said, tipping his fingers toward Grady in a salute as he pulled a scuffed-up crystal from his pocket—a clear one, Sophie noted, so he had to be leaping somewhere within the Lost Cities.

Right before he stepped into the narrow path, he told Sophie, "See you bright and early, Foster. Tomorrow we start fixing this mess."

TWENTY-FIVE

THIS HOPEFULLY GOES WITHOUT saying," Grady told Sophie as Keefe glittered away, "but I expect you to come straight home after you're done in Ravagog. And I *will* be going with you when you head to Nightfall to rescue your parents. We need a plan that the Neverseen can't predict."

"But they know you're a Mesmer," Sophie reminded him. "They're probably more prepared for you than anyone else."

"Yes, but they *don't* know that you're an Enhancer. And who knows what I'll be able to do if you use your ability to enhance mine?"

His voice quivered with the suggestion, and Sophie felt the same rattle deep in her bones.

Grady's ability was already scarily intense. She wasn't sure she wanted to find out what he'd be able to do if she boosted that power.

"But if she enhances you in front of them, they'll know what's happening," Sandor pointed out, "and they'll realize she has a new weakness for them to exploit."

"Being an Enhancer isn't a weakness," Grady argued.

"Fine, let's call it a *vulnerability*," Sandor conceded. "Isn't that the reason she's wearing gloves and keeping it secret?"

"We'd want to save it for an emergency," Grady agreed. "But I should still be there in case it comes to that."

It wasn't a horrible suggestion, but . . .

"Can we wait to decide until we have the starstone, and Lady Gisela tells us whatever important security thing she held back?" Sophie asked, still only half sure if she believed both of those things would actually happen. "I'm sure that's going to change everything anyway."

"Fine. But I'll be holding on to Keefe's Imparter in the meantime," Sandor told her, "that way you can't contact his mom without me."

Sophie gritted her teeth. "I know I've run off in the past, but I'm not stupid enough to do that with this—just like I'm not stupid enough to think we're actually going to fix anything tomorrow."

Her voice wobbled with the confession, and Grady gave the argentavis's rope more slack so he could reach for her hand.

"No one would *ever* call you stupid, Sophie. We just want to help."

"I'm going to need it," she whispered. "I don't know how to fix this."

It was the truth she'd been trying to bury under all the shaky plans they'd been cobbling together, hoping everything would somehow mesh into something solid and whole. But so far, all they'd *really* done was make a deal with Keefe's conniving mother and agree to meet with a cruel king who'd already tried to kill her—twice. All of which would cost them precious time and put more people she cared about in danger.

"I don't know how to fix this either," Grady said, gently pulling her into a hug. "But I *do* know we're not going to stop until we get your parents back—and deal with whatever else the Neverseen are planning."

"Which is why you should try to rest while you can," Sandor told her. "Want me to ask the gnomes if they can bring a late dinner up to your room?"

"That's right!" Grady said, nearly losing his balance when the argentavis fought to fly higher. "Dex is up there, waiting for you."

Sophie blinked. "You're telling me this *now*?"

"Sorry. I was waiting until Keefe went home, and then I got sidetracked."

"Why were you waiting for Keefe to leave?"

"Dex said he had something important to give you—oh, but

he told me to tell you it doesn't have anything to do with the cache because he didn't want you getting your hopes up."

Unfortunately, her mind had already made that leap.

"Besides," Grady added, "I thought it might be nice for you and Dex to have some one-on-one time. Remember how often you guys used to hang out?"

"We still do," Sophie argued. "We just have a lot going on."

"And yet I sure seem to see a lot of Keefe these days. . . ."

Sophie scowled.

Sandor coughed.

Grady shrugged.

"I just don't want you to forget how many great guys you have in your life," he told her. "Especially Dex."

"I haven't. Dex is my best friend, remember? And thanks to you, he's been stuck in my room all alone, waiting for me all this time."

"Don't worry, I warned him it might be a while," Grady told her. "He said he'd play with Iggy while he waited."

Dex's idea of *playing with Iggy* usually ended with an imp makeover. So Sophie wasn't surprised when she found Dex sitting among all the flowers in her carpet, holding a tiny creature that was no longer a purple poof.

"He looks awesome, doesn't he?" Dex asked, flashing his dimpled grin as Iggy flitted his batlike wings and flew over to Sophie's palm. His fur was now a bright Kelly green and hung in long wispy layers that flipped out like feathers.

"He feels so soft," Sophie said, rubbing Iggy's tummy and triggering his squeaky purr.

"That's because I mixed the Greenleaf elixir with some Floof," Dex told her. "I picked the color for Forkle—or I guess I should say it's for the Forkle we lost. Hope you don't mind. I had time to kill."

"Yeah, sorry about that. Grady *just* told me you were up here."

Before Dex could answer, Iggy unleashed a ground-shaking fart that filled the whole room with the choking stench of rotting grass.

"Ugh, it's a good thing he's cute," Sophie grumbled.

"I could bottle that smell and make the ultimate stink bomb," Dex agreed. "But I'm a little afraid of what would happen if Keefe got ahold of it."

"Probably better if we don't unleash that havoc upon the world. Oh! But that kinda reminds me—did you ever hack into Keefe's dad's registry file and see if he could've helped Keefe's mom escape?"

Dex frowned. "I did, but his feed looked normal. Just lots of trips to Atlantis. He definitely didn't go anywhere near the prison. Why?"

Sophie sighed. "Well . . . I guess that's not surprising. But can you check his feed again? Keefe said it looks like his dad's not staying at Candleshade, and I want to know where he is."

It also seemed like a good idea to add *find out how Lady Gisela escaped* to their never-ending list. If Keefe's mom had someone helping her, they needed to know who.

"I'll hack into his records again tomorrow," Dex promised. "Might as well do *something* useful."

Sophie rolled her eyes and plopped down next to him on the carpet. "Do you really need me to give the 'you have the most important job' speech again?"

"I dunno. It *is* one of my favorites. And I *am* working on the cache, by the way. It's just insanely complicated."

"I know. If it makes you feel any better, Lady Cadence only agreed to take me, Keefe, and someone from the Collective to Ravagog tomorrow. She booted out Tam, Biana, and Della—something about not bringing thieves into her friend's castle. According to her, Dimitar will give us the starstone if I prove my value in some sort of challenge."

"Uh . . . is it me, or does that *not* sound good?"

"I'm sure it won't be," Sophie admitted. "But if it helps us find Nightfall, it'll be worth it."

"I guess. Is Sandor freaking out?" Dex glanced toward her open door, where her bodyguard's usual post was empty.

"Actually, he didn't put up that big of a fight. I think he's more focused on setting traps to catch Lady Gisela tomorrow. Or maybe he figures the challenge can't be more dangerous than trying to steal the starstone?"

Dex fussed with the flowers on the carpet. "I can't believe

I'm saying this, but . . . you don't think Fitz should go with you, so you guys could go all *Cognate—RAWR?*"

"*Cognate—RAWR?* Is that the technical term?"

"I mean, I can talk about the 'staring into each other's eyes' thing if you *really* want me to."

Sophie held Iggy close and whispered, "Feel free to go fart on him."

Instead, Iggy blinked his watery green eyes and unleashed a belly-shaking burp.

"I guess I brought that on myself," she muttered, carrying the stinky imp over to his cage. "Besides, I doubt Dimitar would ever assign a challenge where my abilities gave me an advantage."

"Probably true." Dex stood, stretching his legs. "Well . . . if it gets ugly, you'll have your panic switch. Though I'm not sure how I'd get to Ravagog to help."

"We'll be fine. We're doing things Lady Cadence's way, and she always seems to handle King Dimitar without a massive disaster."

"Let's hope. But just in case, I made you something—and I know it's probably going to seem a little weird at first, so hear me out."

He reached into his cape pocket and handed her two thick black wristbands made of soft fabric, with silver snaps and big silver embroidered words—which made Sophie choke.

"Um . . . Why do these say 'Sophie Foster + Dex Dizznee'?"

Dex's grin was enormous. "Because crush cuffs make the best camouflage."

TWENTY-SIX

UCH," DEX MUMBLED, "YOU DON'T
have to look *that* horrified."

"I'm not *horrified*," Sophie promised,
barely stopping herself from dropping the
crush cuffs. "I just . . ."

How on earth was she supposed to explain this?

There'd been times when Dex had made her wonder if
maybe . . .

But she'd always shrugged it off, or pretended not to notice.
And lately he'd been better—*way* less pouty and pushy—which
had been a relief, because Dex was sweet and hilarious and
brilliant and a million other awesome things.

But, he was *just* a friend.

"Relax," Dex told her. "Like I said, the cuffs are only for camouflage. Remember when I told you I'd build a gadget to block your enhancing? I figured that might be a good thing for you to have in Ravagog, in case Dimitar makes you take off your gloves."

He clicked a hidden latch on one of the snaps, flipping back the top to show a ton of intricate circuitry.

"See? I designed these microtransmitters to put a force field around your hands so that anyone touching your skin isn't *actually* making contact—and it's a nonreactive force field, so you won't zap anyone if you touch them. But we should probably test it, to make sure everything's working."

Sophie peeled off her gloves in a daze and snapped on the cuffs, which fit snug, resting right where her wrists ended and her hands began.

"They aren't too tight, right?" he asked, tugging on the fabric. "I didn't want them sliding down your arm, in case that weakened the force field, but I don't want them cutting off your circulation either. And I went with snaps because you can pull them off way faster than a button or a clasp."

She tried to focus on the practical points he was making, which truly did make a lot of sense. But all she could think about was how anyone who saw her wearing them would assume that she and Dex were . . . well, something they *weren't*.

"Ready to test them?" he asked.

When she nodded, he grabbed both of her hands, and

Sophie pressed her fingertips against his skin, half hoping she'd feel the familiar warm tingle and be able to call the whole thing a fail.

But Dex pumped his fist. "Woo! I don't feel anything!"

Why—WHY—did he have to be such a talented Technopath?

He held on a few seconds longer, then checked the snaps again. "Everything looks okay. But it's probably a good idea to wear gloves tomorrow too, since I threw all of this together a couple of hours ago and there might still be some glitches. I'll make something more permanent now that I know the concept works."

"OH!" Sophie let loose a breath she hadn't noticed she was holding. "So these are only temporary?"

She could live with temporary.

Maybe she could even turn them inside out in the meantime.

"And you'll make the permanent ones with normal bracelets, right?" she added.

"Why? They'd be way more noticeable. Crush cuffs are one of the only things people never take off."

"They also never take off nexuses," Sophie reminded him. "Wasn't that what you said you'd use to make these?"

"That was the plan. But nexuses have complicated clasps—and even when I simplified the latches as much as I could, they were still *way* harder to take off than these. Isn't it smarter to have something you can snap off super quick in case you need to enhance someone in a hurry—and put back on really easily when you're done?"

Unfortunately, he had a point.

"Well . . . what if we went with a *plain* cloth bracelet, then?" she asked.

"I don't think anyone makes those. Cloth bracelets are always crush cuffs. If they don't have names on them, it'll look super weird."

She shrugged. "I have brown eyes and grew up with humans. Everyone expects me to be weird."

"Right, but I thought you also didn't want to have people asking questions about your hands. Isn't that why you're dressing all fancy now, so the gloves won't stand out?"

She really wished he'd stop making such well-reasoned arguments! It meant she only had one option left, and it was the extra, extra, extra, extra, *extra* awkward one.

She stared at her wrist, tracing her finger over the giant silver letters—which felt like they were somehow getting bigger. "If people see me wearing these, won't they think we're . . ."

She couldn't make herself say it.

He shrugged. "I guess some might think I'm your *hopeful*—but that's just a matchmaking thing. People give out the cuffs before they register, like they're trying to tell the matchmakers, 'Pair me with them!' It's not like the matchmakers listen. All they care about are genetics and abilities."

Dex had admitted once that he wasn't sure if he'd be

registering for the match, or if he'd refuse, to protest the way they'd treated his parents—and Sophie honestly hadn't decided if she'd be doing the same. She wasn't thrilled with the idea of being told who she was allowed to love.

"It's just people's way of feeling like they have a little control over their lists, even though they don't," Dex added. "The cuffs don't *actually* mean anything."

And yet, Fitz hadn't worn any of the cuffs he'd been given as midterm gifts.

And Biana didn't wear any.

Or Keefe.

Or Tam and Linh.

Or Jensi.

Even Marella, with all of her flirtiness, didn't have a pair.

"It's going to start a bunch of rumors, Dex," she said carefully.

"So? They already say all kinds of stuff about both of us."

"Right, but . . ." She grasped for something—anything—that would be gentler than *we're not hopefuls*—feeling her heart lighten when she realized there was one last, desperate protest.

"We're cousins," she finished.

Dex blinked.

Then he cracked up.

"*That's* what's bothering you? We're not *actually* cousins, Sophie. Everyone knows you're adopted."

"I know. But technically your mom is my mom's sister. Won't that freak people out?"

"Nah. We're not genetically related—and honestly, do you *ever* think of me as Cousin Dex?"

"No," she begrudgingly admitted. "But—"

"You're *way* overthinking this," he told her. "Did you freak out this much when Fitz gave you rings with *his* initials on them?"

"Those are a Cognate thing."

"Maybe. But not all Cognates have them. And I've heard people gossip about you guys because of them."

Really?

That definitely did not help her queasiness.

"So if you're fine with *that*," Dex continued, "why—"

"I never said I was," Sophie interrupted.

"Okay, but if I ordered new crush cuffs with Fitz's name on them and used *them* for the next batch . . ."

"It would still feel super weird," Sophie finished.

And it would.

For different reasons—but he didn't need to know that.

"Would it feel weird if Fitz was the one to give them to you?" Dex pressed.

She hated herself for blushing at the thought. "We're not talking about a hypothetical. We're talking about *this*." She pointed to the names on her cuffs again—which seriously had to be getting bigger.

Astronauts could probably read them from space.

"Is it really so bad to have people think you want the *option* of dating me?" Dex asked without looking at her. "That's all a hopeful really means. It's just a possibility—that's it."

When he put it that way, it didn't sound *as* scary.

But . . . giving him the answer he needed still felt like agreeing to a whole lot more.

She stared at the intricate embroidery, trying to think of anything she could say to dig her way out of this mess, but her mind kept circling back to something Dex had already said—something she probably shouldn't keep poking at, but . . . she had to know.

"So. Crush cuffs have to be ordered in advance?"

"Yeah. It takes a few days for them to customize the names. Why?"

Because he'd said he threw the gadgets together for her that day . . .

Somehow Dex managed to pale *and* flush. "I've, uh . . . I've been planning to use crush cuffs for this for a while. And . . . I put my name because . . . I thought it'd be funny—that's it."

She wanted to believe him.

It would've been *so* much easier if she could.

But he was too fidgety. And he wouldn't look at her. And she could see sweat trickling down his forehead as he backed a few steps away.

"Dex," she said gently. "I—"

"It's fine, okay?" He pulled so hard at the bottom button on his jerkin that it popped off in his hand. "Just drop it."

She wished she could. Every alarm siren in her head was screaming, *DANGER! DANGER! DANGER!*

But deep down, she could feel that this time was different.

They'd torn something open—exposed something raw and deep. And if she tried to pretend they hadn't—let him walk out of this room without patching it up—their friendship would never be the same.

And Dex was worth fighting for—worth wading neck deep into the terrifying, embarrassing muck, if it gave her a shot at saving what really mattered.

She just didn't know *how*.

Words would only hurt. But what else was there?

"Maybe . . . it's time for a trust exercise," she decided after what felt like an eternity.

"I'm not a Telepath," he mumbled miserably.

"No," Sophie said, "but you're my best friend. And this is important."

Nerves tangled up in her throat as an idea took shape—one of those all-in kinds of plans that could far too easily backfire into a nightmare of unparalleled proportions.

"I think," she said slowly, "that there's a really easy way to settle this—once and for all."

"Settle what?" Dex asked.

"That's where the trust comes in," she said. "Close your eyes."

"Why?"

She put her hands on her hips, tapping one foot until he obeyed.

"Fine, my eyes are closed now, happy?"

"Terrified" was a better description.

But one final look at the crush cuffs had Sophie taking a slow step forward. Then another.

She could do this. She just had to think of it as . . . an experiment.

And maybe she was a *little* curious.

"What are you doing?" Dex asked as she closed the last of the distance between them.

"Just testing something."

She found herself marveling again at how much taller he was than the boy she'd first met, and took one deep breath for courage—then another to steady her nerves.

When she couldn't stall any longer, she tilted up on her toes and leaned in, lingering a hairsbreadth away, so he'd have the option of pushing her back if he wanted.

He didn't.

So she closed her eyes and pressed her lips against his.

TWENTY-SEVEN

I T WASN'T A MOVIE-WORTHY KISS—THAT was for sure.

Their noses bumped. Sophie's lips felt too dry. And Dex started out with a startled squeak.

Then for one truly horrifying moment, it almost felt like he wasn't going to kiss her back.

But he *did* kiss her back.

And that made it . . .

So much worse.

He reached for her face, but his fingers somehow ended up tangled in her hair. And his knees crashed into hers, nearly knocking them both over.

The whole thing couldn't have lasted more than five seconds, but all Sophie could think was, *Is it over yet?*

And then it was.

And they stood there, staring at each other.

And it was so, *so* awkward.

Dex's eyes were stretched wide and his breathing was way too fast and Sophie couldn't decide if she wanted to cry or burst into nervous giggles. She settled for covering her mouth with her hand.

"You kissed me," Dex eventually whispered.

All she could do was nod.

He reached for his lips, brushing his fingers across them. "I . . . always imagined it different than that."

"Different how?"

He stumbled over to her bed and sank onto the edge. "I don't know."

Seconds crawled by.

"Don't hate me," he mumbled, "but . . . didn't it feel weird?"

Relief flared, even as the words gave Sophie's pride a good hard smack.

"I'm not saying it was *bad*," he added quickly. "It's just . . ."

"There was no spark," Sophie finished for him.

"Yeah." His relief faded to a wince. "Does that mean I'm a terrible kisser?"

"I don't think it's you."

"Well, it wasn't *you.*" The conviction in his voice made her blush.

He brushed his finger across his lips again, staring blankly at the wall. "I just couldn't stop thinking the whole time, you know? I kept worrying my breath was bad or trying to figure out what I was supposed to do with my hands. And, I mean, I always knew it'd be awkward at first, but I'd figured at some point all of that would drop away and I'd just sorta . . . *feel.*"

"I think that's how it *should* be."

She forced her shaky legs to move her close enough to sit beside him—but not *too* close.

Space was good right now.

They needed a cushion of air to hold all the angst swirling between them.

"I think it's *us,*" she added gently. "I think neither of us could relax because deep down we know we're better as friends."

His eyes shifted to the dark sky outside her windows. "That's why you did it, huh? You already knew you didn't like me that way."

"It's more than just me, Dex. Otherwise you would've felt something during the kiss."

"But I've liked you for *years!*" His face turned redder than she'd ever seen it when he realized what he'd just admitted. "Ugh—could this get any more embarrassing?"

"Sandor could be here," Sophie reminded him. "Or my parents could've walked in."

Dex groaned, and they both glanced at the door, needing to make sure they didn't have an audience.

"How long have you known I liked you?" he asked without looking at her.

"Honestly? I'm not sure."

She'd spent so long pretending not to notice, it was hard to pin it down. But it *might* have also been part of the reason they'd been spending a little less time together—and why they mostly hung out in bigger groups.

Dex buried his face in his hands. "And you never felt . . . ? Actually, never mind, I don't want to know."

"Hey now, don't forget—kissing me did *nothing* for you." She was trying her best not to let that sting. "So your head may have been telling you one thing, but deep down, the rest of you wants something else."

He didn't look convinced.

And the silence that followed felt like it had eyes, staring at both of them, daring them to be the one brave enough to end it.

Sophie stepped up first. "Thanks, by the way."

"For what?"

"For . . . caring about me like that. For thinking I'm special enough."

He snorted.

"No, Dex. I mean it. I've never had anyone think about me that way."

He snorted louder.

She shook her head. "You weren't there when I was growing up. You didn't see how hated I was."

"Yeah, but that was around humans. Around here . . ."

"What?"

He tilted his head. "We both know I'm not the only one who—"

She held up her hand. "Let's not go there."

She could only stomach one brutally uncomfortable subject at a time. Especially since she was pretty sure she knew what he was going to say—and she had no idea if it was true.

"All I'm trying to say," she told Dex, "is that I'm honored you thought of me that way. And your friendship seriously means everything. *Please* tell me this hasn't ruined that."

He looked away again, fussing with the button he'd torn off. "It's probably going to be weird for a while. So I guess it's good you want me to stay home and work on the caches."

Her eyes and nose burned as she nodded. "Just . . . let me know when you're ready, and I'll try to give you space until then."

"I don't need *space*. I need . . . I don't know what I need," he mumbled.

The only thing Sophie could think to say was, "I'm sorry."

"Don't be," he told her. "You could've been way meaner about this. You could've thrown the crush cuffs in my face."

"I would never do that, Dex. I *do* care about you. Just not . . ."

"Yeah." He went back to fiddling with the torn-off button. "I promise I'll find something else to use for the replacements. I don't know what I was thinking."

"Hey—you had some pretty solid points about the camouflage," Sophie reminded him.

"Yeah. But . . . I think deep down, part of me wanted to know if you'd be willing to wear them—which was stupid. You already have a ton of stuff to worry about with your human family and going to Ravagog tomorrow. You didn't need *this*. It's just been like . . . a giant *maybe* in the back of my mind for so long that when I thought I'd found a sneaky way to finally get an answer, I couldn't resist."

"How long have you had the cuffs?" Sophie had to ask.

He ducked his chin to hide his face. "I got them for you for midterm. And then I wimped out and gave you your iPod instead."

"Wait. You ordered these when we were Level Twos?"

That was more than a year ago.

"Pathetic, right?"

Sophie shook her head. "Very, *very* sweet."

"You don't have to say that."

"But I mean it. And if you don't believe me, think about this. You're my first kiss."

A slow smile spread across his lips, and he sat up a little taller. "You're my first kiss too."

Sophie grinned back at him. "See? We'll always have that. And I couldn't think of a better person to share that memory with."

She hadn't expected the words to feel true. But they really did.

It felt like she was standing on the edge of a terrifying sea of *new*. And who better to dip her toe in with than a friend?

"The next time you kiss someone," she added quietly, "it's going to be perfect. And I'm going to want to hear all about it."

"Am I a jerk if I admit I do *not* want to hear about your next kiss?"

Sophie laughed. "No, I think that's fair. But don't worry, it won't be happening for a *long* time."

"Sure it won't."

She could argue, but it was probably better to let that conversation die.

"Well," Dex said, scruffing his fingers through his hair until he looked like he'd just wandered through a tornado. "It's been . . . a strange day. First Forkle's back. Now this."

"Yeah, definitely not the way I expected it to go," Sophie admitted. "And tomorrow's going to be a whole lot more complicated."

"Ugh, I just realized you'll be hanging around Keefe. How long do you think it's going to take him to drag this story out of you?"

Sophie groaned.

Keefe was going to *slay* her over this—and there was no way she'd be able to hide it. Her emotions were way too strong.

"Maybe you shouldn't wear the cuffs," Dex suggested.

She shook her head. "It'll be fine. It's way more important to protect the ability. I can handle Keefe. Or, if he gets too annoying, I'll throw him into the river."

Dex cracked half a smile, but it faded pretty quick. "How much are you going to tell him?"

"It depends on how much he guesses."

"Um, this is Keefe. He's going to guess everything."

"Probably," Sophie agreed, silently cursing all Empaths.

"And he'll tell everyone," Dex added through a sigh.

"Not if you don't want him to," Sophie promised. "I know Keefe is the master of teasing, but he's your friend too. If I tell him to keep it quiet, he will."

"Let's hope."

"Does that mean you don't want the rest of our friends knowing?"

"I don't know. What am I supposed to say? *Hey guys, pretty sure you all knew I used to like Sophie, but she shot me down so let's move on, okay?*"

The "used to" hurt more than Sophie had expected. So did the "shot me down."

"You don't have to tell them anything you don't want to," she promised. "But, if it would help, you're welcome to tell them I got all weak in the knees after the kiss. It's technically true."

His dimples made a slight appearance, but faded just as fast. "It's going to be so humiliating."

She couldn't blame him for feeling that way. After all, wasn't that why she'd put off confessing her crush to Fitz?

Her insides tangled when she remembered the promise she'd made to finally come clean—*what had she been thinking?*

Maybe she could figure out a different confession.

Or avoid any form of Cognate training indefinitely . . .

"I'm sorry," she told Dex, feeling the need to say it again.

"It's not your fault."

It was and it wasn't. Either way, there was nothing either of them could do.

She started to reach for his hand, then stopped herself. Dex noticed, but didn't say anything.

Instead, he stood on his still-shaky legs and pulled out his home crystal pendant. "Guess I'll see you later."

Sophie nodded.

Her heart felt like it was dropping out as he held the crystal up to the light.

But before he leaped away he asked, "Still best friends, right?"

A soft smile curled her lips, and her heart pulled back into place. "Forever."

TWENTY-EIGHT

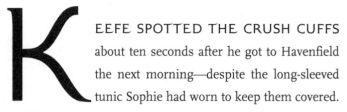EEFE SPOTTED THE CRUSH CUFFS about ten seconds after he got to Havenfield the next morning—despite the long-sleeved tunic Sophie had worn to keep them covered. And he dragged out the rest of the story with a relentless bombardment of questions.

But the epic teasing Sophie had been bracing for never happened.

Instead, he lowered his voice and asked, "How's Dex?"

"Hopefully okay." She peeked around the pristine living room, glad to see they were still alone.

Keefe's mom had indeed managed to slip past all of Sandor's traps and security during the night, leaving behind nothing but the faint scent of ash, a sealed black scroll in the center of Havenfield's kitchen table, and a tray of caramel-drizzled pastries—which of course no one was willing to eat. Sandor and Cadoc had been scouring the grounds ever since, trying to figure out how Lady Gisela had pulled off the trick. And Grady and Edaline were upstairs in Grady's office, inspecting the scroll to make sure it wasn't hiding anything dangerous— and probably trying to see if they could find a way to read the message.

"What about you?" Keefe asked, pointing to the dark circles rimming Sophie's eyes. "Couldn't sleep after crushing Dex's fragile heart?"

"I didn't crush it," she said, kicking the side of her sturdy black boot.

At least, she hoped she hadn't.

Keefe must've sensed her doubt, because he moved a little closer. "I'm just kidding. All you did was prove my dad's theory."

It took Sophie a second to realize he was talking about Lord Cassius's book—*The Heart of the Matter*—where he'd claimed the heart and the head held two different sets of emotions.

"Since when did you start agreeing with him on that?" Sophie asked.

"Since Lumenaria, when you enhanced me."

Her eyebrows shot up.

Keefe smoothed the front of his navy blue jerkin, which

looked snug in the shoulders, as if whatever training he'd done with the Neverseen had added some muscle. "I'd assumed that the enhancing made everything feel more intense than normal. But I realized later that some of what I picked up didn't match the usual Foster Feelings you're always flinging my way."

"Empaths," she grumbled, pulling her cape closed, as if that could keep her emotions away from him. She'd gone with a black pants-and-tunic ensemble that morning, hoping it would make Dimitar take her more seriously.

"Hey, it's not my fault you hurl your emotions at me like we're in a big old splotching match of feels," Keefe told her. "I'd ignore you if I could."

"And I'd block you if *I* could."

Keefe laughed. "Then it looks like we're stuck with each other. But if it makes you feel any better, it turns out you're only giving me a *tiny* piece of the Foster Puzzle. I got a glimpse of the bigger picture and . . . well . . . let's just say it was very enlightening."

Sophie stared at the rainbow sparkles reflected on the marble floor from the chandelier. "How so?"

"Nope. Not gonna tell you."

"Uh—they're *my* feelings."

"Yeah, but once you know about them, it . . . changes things. That's the part that's missing from my dad's theory. He never explained *why* the emotions in the heart and the head are different. But I figured it out. It's because we're aware of what goes on up here"—he tapped the side of his head—"so we control those feelings in subtle ways. We'll encourage any emotions we're comfortable with, and fight the ones we aren't. But here"—he pressed his hands against his chest—"everything is beyond our control. And once you become aware of it . . ."

He flicked his hands, like he was holding something that went *poof!*

"Think about what happened with Dex," he added. "In his head, he wanted the Dexphie ship to set sail so badly that he kept fighting for it, even when he got some pretty clear signals that he was bound for a crash. But deep, deep down, he knew you were better off as friends, and you kissing him finally brought that feeling out. And now that he knows it, he'll never look at you the same ever again."

The words shouldn't have hurt quite so much.

"Hmm," Keefe said. "Please tell me you haven't decided you want what you can't have."

"No!"

Though maybe she did—just not the way he meant.

"Don't you miss when crushes were only silly, secret things?" she asked quietly. "Suddenly it's all getting so . . . *real*—and not just because of this. I mean . . . Fitz already finished filling out his matchmaking packet. And you probably need to go pick up yours—if you haven't already."

Keefe smirked. "So *that's* what kept you up tossing and turning? Wondering if I've registered for the match?"

"Ugh, that's *so* not what I was saying."

"Suuuuuuurrrrre it wasn't."

She tried to roll her eyes and turn away, but he grabbed her hands to stop her. "I don't want you losing sleep, Foster. So let me set that powerful little mind of yours at ease. I have *not* registered for the match, and I won't be for a while."

"Why not?"

He shrugged. "Waiting to see how a few things shake out."

Sophie had no idea what that meant, but no way would she give him the satisfaction of asking. "Well, FYI, these dark circles are because of my sister. I hailed her to check in after Dex left, and she made me stay up super late updating her on everything."

"Everything?" Keefe asked. "Even . . ."

He made an obnoxiously loud kissing sound.

Sophie shoved him away.

She actually *had* told her sister what happened with Dex, and it had been surprisingly helpful. Turned out, Amy was an excellent listener—but Keefe didn't need to know that.

He jumped back in front of her. "Okay, fine, you want me to be serious again. I don't like it. But I will. Because I *do* get what you're saying, Foster. All of this . . . *stuff.* It makes everything way more complicated."

Sophie nodded. "I just don't want to lose anything that matters, you know?"

"You haven't *lost* Dex," Keefe promised. "Trust the Empath!"

When she didn't smile, he leaned in and whispered, "And here's another thing you can count on. You'll never lose *me*. No matter how any of this *stuff* goes down."

There was a softness to his voice. Maybe even a sweetness. And for a second, Sophie's breath seemed to catch.

But then he leaned back and added, "I have way too much fun annoying you."

Sophie sighed. "That does seem to be one of your talents."

"And you adore me for it. In fact, maybe we should find out if we're meant to be."

He puckered his lips and Sophie shoved him a little harder that time.

"Hey—how come the Dexinator gets the smooch test and I don't? Do you realize that thanks to you, sweet, innocent little Dex has now kissed someone before I have? And you too?"

"Really?" Sophie blurted. "Never?"

"I realize it's hard to believe, considering . . ." He waved his arm in front of himself, like his looks said it all. "Don't get me wrong—I've had plenty of offers, but . . ."

He shrugged.

"What about Biana?" Sophie had to ask. "You told me you kissed her mostly on the cheek."

He'd been loopy on pain medicine when he admitted it, but she could tell he hadn't been lying.

"Eh. That doesn't count. She dared me to do it, for one thing. And the only reason I caught a tiny corner of her mouth was because she turned her head on me at the last second. Thank goodness I had my eyes open, or it would've been a disaster."

He let out a long, weary sigh.

"You know what, Foster? You're way braver than I am. I guess we already knew that, considering your number of near-death experiences. But . . . I've never had the guts to be honest the way you were with Dex. I keep telling myself, 'If I don't encourage it, it'll fade.' And it's helped a little, but . . ."

Sophie had to fight the urge to ask if he meant what she thought he did. She'd already strained one friendship—and she had *no* doubt Biana would consider that a violation.

Plus, Biana had been a little less flirty with Keefe lately. Maybe her crush *was* fading.

Still, Sophie couldn't stop herself from saying, "Please don't lead her on."

"Never. Why do you think I don't flirt with her? I even go out of my way to flirt with everyone else around her so that it'll be more obvious, you know?"

"Yeah," Sophie said, fighting a strange, prickly feeling.

Finally—a solid explanation for why she was always subjected to so much Keefe-teasing.

She'd known there had to be one.

But for some reason . . . it stung.

Two big blows to her pride in two days.

She might as well come clean to Fitz and get the trifecta of humiliation over with.

"Hey," Keefe said. "I—"

Grady strode down the stairs and shot Keefe a look that had him backing even farther away.

Edaline trailed behind, offering a smile that looked mostly like an apology.

"Everything check out with the scroll?" Sophie asked, trying to force her face into an expression that said *nothing to see here—we definitely weren't talking about kissing!*

"It seems safe," Edaline assured her.

"Only if we ignore the fact that we have no idea what this thing says," Grady argued, holding up the scroll and shaking it. "I think everyone's forgetting that there's a reason humans say 'don't shoot the messenger.'"

"They'll have Lady Cadence to keep them safe," Edaline reminded him. "Dimitar was seconds away from dragging Sophie off to one of his work camps after he caught her trying to read his mind—and Lady Cadence talked him out of it."

"Yeah, that makes me feel *much* better about this plan," Grady grumbled.

"I know. But we *have* to do this." Sophie repeated all the reasons she'd agreed to Lady Gisela's deal in the first place—and she wasn't just saying it for him.

She couldn't let the whole rejecting-Dex thing—or any of her boy-related worries—distract her from the much more important problems they were tackling. And not *just* rescuing her parents.

When she'd talked with her sister, Amy told her that she and Quinlin had been going through human newspaper articles about the fires, and they'd found that twenty of the burned areas were experiencing an unprecedented regrowth of rare wildflowers—which seemed way too perfect of a number to be a natural occurrence. Even the humans were calling it the Extraordinary Efflorescence.

Sophie had no idea why the Neverseen would plant a bunch of flowers in the human world—and only at certain fire sites. But she'd seen enough over the last few years to be skeptical of coincidences.

That was the kind of detail she needed to stay focused on—not all of this other drama.

"Are we ready?" she asked, holding out her hand for Lady Gisela's scroll.

"I thought you were waiting for someone from the Collective," Grady reminded her.

They were. And Sophie had assumed it would be Granite, since he was usually the one who stepped in for Mr. Forkle.

But a few minutes later, a smudge of shadows and color phased through Havenfield's front door.

"The Collective thought I'd be the best one for this assignment," Blur explained. "That way if Lady Cadence is overestimating King Dimitar's generosity, we have a way to make sure we don't leave without the starstone." He phased through the wall again to illustrate. "But I'm just the backup plan," he promised Grady. "Everyone ready to head to Spateswale?"

"We're not going to Riverdrift?" Keefe asked.

"We are. Lady Cadence moved it to a new river after she finished swearing fealty last night. I guess Spateswale is the most direct path to Ravagog."

"So she's officially part of the Black Swan now?" Sophie asked.

"She is. And she's already given us three separate lectures on the ogres."

A loud sigh sounded behind them, and everyone turned to find Sandor in the entrance to the kitchen. His hard eyes focused on Keefe. "If Sophie returns with so much as a scratch, I'll let Grizel determine your punishment—and I think you'll find it to be creative *and* memorable."

"Live in fear of the scary girlfriend," Keefe mumbled. "Got it."

"And the terrifying father," Grady added. "I can make King Dimitar look cuddly."

"Um, excuse me—if anything happens to me, the only one responsible is *me*," Sophie informed them.

"Well said," Edaline agreed as she strangled Sophie with a hug. "But everyone work together to make sure nothing happens to *any* of you, okay?"

She pulled Grady into the embrace, and he reluctantly stretched an arm around Keefe.

"Awww, it's like I'm already part of the family," Keefe said, earning a grumble.

Blur laughed. "Well, if nothing else, this should be entertaining. Come on, guys. Let's go see if you two can annoy King Dimitar into giving us what we need."

TWENTY-NINE

**HAT ARE THOSE THINGS?"**
Sophie shouted, keeping her back
against one of Riverdrift's metal
towers as she watched the giant
water beasts swarming through the dark, choppy water.

The bluish-gray creatures looked like the oversize spawn of
a shark, an alligator, and an eel—with beady eyes and extra-
long snouts and about twenty million needle-sharp teeth.

And there were *five* of them.

"Pannoniasaurus," Lady Cadence said, rolling up the
sleeves of her stiff gray jacket. "They're a rare freshwater type
of mosasaur. Don't worry, I've worked with this particular pod
for years."

That would've been a lot more reassuring if one of the beasts hadn't chosen that moment to leap out of the water and whip its massive tail at Lady Cadence, nearly knocking her into the river.

"They're just trying to get me to swim with them," Lady Cadence explained. "That's how we usually spend our morning."

"Anyone else *not* surprised that Lady Cadence has seriously scary pets?" Keefe asked.

"They're more than pets," Lady Cadence said, swinging a long copper lasso and catching the beast who'd just tried to knock her into the water.

Her muscles flexed as she cinched the rope and dragged the end over to a wide steel post in the center of the prow, which had two bars jutting from either side and a large loop in the center. "How else did you think we were going to get a structure this massive to sail upriver?" she asked as she tied the end of the rope through the loop with an incredibly complicated knot.

Blur pointed his smudge of an arm toward the two huge paddle wheels at the back of the boat. "I thought that's what those were for."

"Those are only for downriver." Lady Cadence swung another lasso toward the remaining four pannoniasaurs—and caught nothing but air as they dove under the water. "Every current will be raging against us today. Ravagog is one of the most inaccessible places on this planet. That's why the ogres chose the location."

"You mean *stole* the location," Sophie corrected.

Ravagog had originally been the gnomes' homeland—called Serenvale—until the ogres ran them out, chopped down the trees, and poisoned the water with toxic enzymes.

"I expect you to keep comments like that to yourself when we face King Dimitar," Lady Cadence told her, tossing the lasso again—and catching her target that time. "He may not be *your* king, but his title demands respect. And like him or hate him, you need his help to free your human family."

Unfortunately, she was right—which was probably why Sophie's stomach felt like she'd been swallowing shards of ice as Lady Cadence dragged the thrashing mosasaur closer to the steel pole and knotted the end of the lasso through the loop again.

She repeated the process with the next beast, and the next, until all five were secured, then gripped the two bars, almost like she was holding the handles of a bicycle.

"Everyone ready?" she asked, not bothering to wait for their answer before she stomped down a lever, raising a massive silver anchor out of the water. Her whole body strained as she locked her legs and cranked the handles toward the center of the river, making the houseboat lurch as the beasts dragged them the same direction.

Keefe would've face-planted onto the deck if Sophie hadn't grabbed his arm before he hit. "Whoa, *you're* catching *me?*" he asked.

"I know—what's happening to the universe?" Sophie caught him again as Lady Cadence jerked the handles the opposite way.

"Better hold on to the rails," Blur advised, pointing to the rapids ahead.

"This part will be bumpy," Lady Cadence agreed.

The houseboat was too wide to go around the rocks, so they sailed straight over, launching the craft airborne before it crashed back to the water's surface—up-down-up-down-up-down. Water sprayed the deck every time they landed, and the wind was punishing on every rise, making Sophie wish she'd worn her hair in a tight bun like Lady Cadence had. Drenched strands kept whipping her cheeks, and she scooted closer to Keefe, partially to shield herself behind him, but mostly because he was slumped against the rail like a piece of soggy laundry.

"You okay?"

"Oh yeah, never better." He looked as gray-green as the river.

"He needs some of this," Lady Cadence said, tossing Keefe a vial with something milky inside. "It helps with seasickness."

Blur took one as well. "Whew, that stuff is strong!"

"Bring it on," Keefe said, downing his in one gulp—and then nearly gagging it back up. "Ugh. It's like drinking liquefied hair!"

Sophie declined the vial Lady Cadence offered her. Her stomach wasn't *happy*, but she didn't feel all that different than when she'd ridden roller coasters with her human family. And strangely, her balance wasn't thrown off. If anything, it was improved. Her feet seemed to instinctively know how to move, making tiny adjustments to keep her legs steady.

"Is this what normal people feel like when they walk on regular ground?" Sophie asked, crossing the main deck and back without losing her footing once.

"It's a little drier," Blur said. His outline was becoming clearer as the cold spray spritzed him again and again. He was skinnier than Sophie had imagined, and shorter too, but he kept his face turned away, hiding his features.

"I'm ninety-nine-point-nine percent sure that I'm dying," Keefe croaked.

"Aw, is the elixir not helping?" Sophie asked.

"If it was supposed to make me feel like sludgers are swimming around my stomach, then it's doing a great job!"

"Try this," Lady Cadence told him, tossing Keefe something that looked like a gray walnut. When he cracked the shell, it was filled with a reddish-brown goop that smelled like burnt garlic.

Keefe gagged. "Yeah, that's a big nope."

He held the remedy as far away from his nose as he could. "I don't know if I'm going to make it, Foster. And in case I don't, there's something I need you to know."

He motioned for her to lean closer—so close she could feel his breath on her cheek, and a fresh wave of goose bumps streaked across her skin.

"You need to know," he whispered, "that—"

"Oh, stop being so melodramatic!" Lady Cadence interrupted, cranking the handles left, to change the boat's direction again. "Either slurp down that bilepod, or quit whining."

"Does that mean I can whine all I want if I eat this thing?" Keefe asked. "Because *that* might be worth it."

"This is going to be a very long day," Lady Cadence muttered.

"Wait—what were you going to say?" Sophie asked when Keefe closed his eyes and curled up tighter.

His lips were half grimace, half smirk as he said, "I'll tell you later. Right now I'm focusing too hard on not throwing up on you."

Sophie scrambled away.

"Everybody, brace yourselves," Lady Cadence called. "We're coming up on the first fork, and the river changes can be a little jarring."

"Jarring" didn't begin to describe it. It felt like they were tipping over as Lady Cadence cranked the handles all the way to the right, and the boat jackknifed onto the narrower tributary.

"Anyone see my stomach back there?" Keefe moaned, forcing himself to suck down the bilepod like an oyster.

"How many more river changes do we have?" Sophie asked.

"Three," Lady Cadence said.

Keefe whimpered. "Someone hold me."

He was so pale and soaked and shaky that Sophie had a

feeling he wasn't kidding. And since she couldn't stop shivering herself, she moved behind him, wrapping her arms around his shoulders and pulling them both down so they were sitting on the slick deck, leaning against each other.

"If you need to throw up, do *not* turn around," she warned as she wrapped her cape around both of them to keep in whatever warmth she could.

"Actually, this is helping," Keefe said. "Your cape smells way better than this miserable boat."

"Thanks . . . I think?"

His breathing seemed to calm, and his trembling eased. But a rough patch of waves had him tensing up again.

"Drink this," Lady Cadence said, tossing him a yellow vial. "And plug your nose before you open it."

Keefe squinted at the liquid. "Why does it look like pee?"

"Kelpie urine is the absolute best way to regain your equilibrium."

Keefe tossed the vial into the river. "Not even if I really was dying."

"You're going to regret that when we make the next change," Lady Cadence warned.

"Yeah, I don't think I will."

But he didn't look good when the houseboat turned onto the choppiest river yet.

"I think you need to take your mind off of it," Sophie told him. "Try going to your happy place."

"I have no idea what that sentence is supposed to mean—unless you're offering to teleport us out of here."

"I wish." Sophie could only teleport when she was free-falling. Plus, the ogres had force fields protecting their city, and there was no way to know what would happen if she tried teleporting through. "But seriously, it's a visualization technique. You imagine yourself in your favorite place to take your mind off everything going on around you."

"What's your happy place?" he asked.

"Probably flying with Silveny."

There was nothing quite like racing through the sky, surrounded by fluffy white clouds.

"That's a good one," Keefe said. "I'm going to picture myself there too. Just you, me, and Glitter Butt."

"Glitter Butt?" Lady Cadence asked.

"That's Keefe's nickname for Silveny," Sophie explained. "Because her fur is so shimmery."

Keefe elbowed Sophie. "Tell her the real reason."

Sophie rolled her eyes. "Alicorn poop also tends to be sparkly."

"It's one of the greatest things in the whole world," Keefe added. "And Glitter Butt loves her nickname, by the way. Almost as much as she loves me. Foster tries to deny it, but I'm totally her favorite."

"It's a tie," Sophie corrected.

"Keep telling yourself that." Keefe closed his eyes and rested his head against the rail. The color was slowly returning to his cheeks and his features were beginning to relax. "Remember that flight we made to the High Seas hideout?"

Sophie smiled. "Yeah, I think you whined the entire way."

"We all have our gifts. And speaking of whining—"

"No whining in the happy place! Seriously, Keefe, try to concentrate."

Everyone got quiet after that, and Sophie watched the smooth green hills race by, trying to spot anything familiar. Ravagog was tucked among dark, jagged mountains and hidden behind a massive iron gate—though Linh's tidal wave had smashed the barrier to pieces.

It hit her then—she would have to *see* the destruction they'd caused.

Even if the bridge and gate had been rebuilt, there would surely be remnants of the ruin.

Washed-out buildings.

Flooded sections of the playa.

Graves.

"Hey," Keefe said. "You know what I remember most about that flight with Silveny? That was the first time I felt you trust me. Like, *really* trust me."

It was also the first time that Keefe had peeled back his joking, teasing mask and given her a glimpse of the deeper, serious side he hid away to keep anyone from getting too close to him.

"I like it when you trust me," he said quietly.

"So do I."

He scooted ever so slightly closer. "You still do, right? Even after . . ."

She had a feeling that if she snuck into his mind, he'd be remembering the moment he stole her cache and handed it over to Fintan to prove his commitment to the Neverseen. But Sophie was remembering the moment she woke up on a cold, rocky beach and found herself in a newer, darker version of her world, surrounded by the crumbled ruin of everything that used to be. She hadn't known at that point just how devastating Lumenaria's collapse would end up being. But she knew that things would never be the same—and that Keefe was right there with her.

He'd escaped the Neverseen the night before and camped nearby in a dark, freezing cave in case she needed him.

"Of course I trust you," she promised.

He seemed to let out a breath he'd been holding. "One of these days—"

The rest of his sentence morphed into a moan as Lady Cadence steered the boat through what Sophie hoped was the final turn.

"Not gonna make it," Keefe groaned.

"Go back to the happy place. You're not here, you're flying with Silveny—and she's filling my head with way too many KEEFE, KEEFE, KEEFEs."

Keefe's smile looked completely miserable.

"Have you checked on Silveny lately?" Blur asked.

"Not as often as I should be." Sophie was supposed to check on the pregnant alicorn at least once a day to make sure Silveny and Greyfell were safe, and that there were no complications with Silveny's pregnancy. But she'd been so overwhelmed, she kept forgetting.

She closed her eyes, trying to stretch out her consciousness and feel for her connection to the alicorns. But no matter how hard she pushed, her mind stayed silent.

Maybe she was too close to the strange force fields of Ravagog.

Or maybe Silveny was sleeping.

Or maybe she should be worried . . .

She tried to stuff the niggling doubt away—tried to remind herself that Silveny could call for help if she needed it.

But sourness still sloshed inside her like the tossing waves.

She vowed to try again as soon as they were back in the Lost Cities. And if Silveny still didn't respond . . .

"Okay there, Foster?" Keefe asked.

She nodded.

"Not sure I believe you. So how about we brainstorm that favor I owe you? Are you leaning toward humiliation, punishment, or servitude?"

"Go for servitude," Blur told her, right before a huge wave hit the prow and drenched him head to toe. For the briefest moment, his features were outlined by the water—and while Sophie didn't recognize him, his full lips and round cheeks felt strangely familiar.

"How about I steal the Fitzster's match packet for you?" Keefe suggested.

"How about no?" Sophie told him, not even wanting to *imagine* what might be in there.

"Okay, then what if—"

"Just so you know," Lady Cadence interrupted, "from here on out, you shouldn't say anything unless you're comfortable with Dimitar's soldiers hearing it."

"Are we in Ravagog?" Sophie asked.

None of the scenery looked familiar. The Ravagog she'd known had been a series of swampy caverns, along with elaborate structures carved into the side of a mountain. But all she could see was stark, barren earth stretching into striated badlands.

"This is called the King's Path," Lady Cadence explained. "It brings us to the restricted portion of the city, where Dimitar keeps his private palace. He showed me the route when he realized this boat was too wide to fit through the main gate. If I wasn't wearing this"—she pulled her Markchain out from under her cape—"the battalions stationed in these foothills would've blasted us to splinters by now."

Cold sweat trickled down Sophie's spine as she scanned the hills again. No matter how carefully she searched, she couldn't spot a single ogre. But she had no doubt they were out there, weapons trained and ready to fire.

"Prepare to dock," Lady Cadence said, and every nerve in Sophie's body sprang to life.

The mosasaurs pulled them toward a flat rock that jutted out into the water, and Lady Cadence cranked the lever to drop the anchor.

"How far is it from here to the palace?" Sophie asked as she helped Keefe to his feet.

"See that gap in the badlands up ahead?" Lady Cadence pointed to an especially deep crevice barely a hundred yards away. "That's where we're headed."

The shadowy crack looked neither grand nor palatial.

It looked dark.

And dusty.

And miserable.

Lady Cadence hopped onto the dock and secured the house-boat to a deadly-looking hook, before lowering a short platform for them to disembark.

"SOLID GROUND!" Keefe shouted, dragging Sophie to a nearby boulder and bending down to kiss the rock's edge. "I don't care if this place smells like morning breath—I'm never leaving."

"That can be arranged."

The scratchy, all-too-familiar voice came from the shadowy crevice, and Sophie's legs stopped wanting to cooperate.

"What's the matter?" King Dimitar asked as his gorilla-shaped body emerged from the darkness, moving with a regal grace that didn't match his hunched posture or especially long arms. "Not happy to see me?"

King Dimitar camouflaged perfectly with the mottled rocks around him, right down to the lumpy features of his face. The only parts that stood out were the glinting yellow stones set into his ears and the polished metal of the diaperlike armor he wore.

"The fifteen minutes we agreed upon begin now," he told Lady Cadence, scratching the swirling black tattoos that crowned his bald head. "Go ahead and convince me why I shouldn't kill all of you."

THIRTY

LADY CADENCE LAUGHED—WHICH definitely wasn't the reaction Sophie had expected her to have to King Dimitar's time-limited death threat. Especially since his hand was hovering uncomfortably close to the hilt of his spiked sword.

"Don't take him too seriously," Lady Cadence told Sophie, smoothing her somehow-still-immaculate bun as she turned to face the ogre king. "Dimitar greets me the same way every time I visit. And he has yet to make good on his threat."

Dimitar cracked his knuckles. "There's a first time for everything."

Lady Cadence sauntered closer—close enough to be within sword swiping range—before lowering herself to one knee and dipping her head in a bow. "Good to see you again, my friend. Thank you for conceding to this meeting."

Dimitar's only response was a grunt.

His eyes shifted to Sophie, and she hastily dropped to one knee, her dark clothes still dripping water as she did her best to copy Lady Cadence's posture—from a much safer distance. Blur did the same at her side, though it was hard to tell, now that he'd smudged his form again.

Keefe stayed standing tall.

His hair was droopy and his clothes were soggy and he still looked a little green. But his shoulders were square and his gaze was intent on the ogre king.

"Am I supposed to see this as bravery?" Dimitar asked him. "The arrogant young elf lord who dares to taunt me?"

"Psh, like the Council would ever make *me* a lord," Keefe snorted. "Though, Lord Keefe does have a nice ring to it."

"What are you doing?" Sophie whisper-hissed. "We need this meeting to go smoothly."

"I know," Keefe said. "But I'm the Mercadir for our group. And Mercadirs don't bow. They salute."

"Am I supposed to know what a Mercadir is?" Sophie asked as Keefe raised his left arm toward his nose in a zigzag motion.

"Actually, the salute looks like this," Lady Cadence corrected, sweeping her arm from her nose to her chest and making a similar zigzag as she stood. "And no, Sophie, I wouldn't expect you to know the term. I'm surprised Keefe does. A Mercadir is an ogre military designation. Dimitar's army has no ranks—all soldiers answer directly to him—but he holds a small group accountable for ensuring his orders are carried out, and those soldiers are his Mercadirs."

"Which gives them no power," King Dimitar added, narrowing his gaze at Keefe. "If that's what you're after."

"Yeah, not in it for that," Keefe told him, copying the salute Lady Cadence had shown him. "All I care about is that you hold *me* accountable if something goes wrong today—and not her."

He pointed to Sophie.

"That's *not* what we agreed on!" Sophie snapped.

"Maybe not. But I'm not going to let you face any consequences for *this.*" Keefe slipped his mom's scroll from his pocket and Sophie felt her jaw fall, wondering when he'd stolen it from her.

Had he played up the whole seasick thing so she'd be close enough for him to pick her pocket?

"I believe that's mine," Dimitar said, holding out his hand.

Keefe tucked the scroll away again. "You can have it as soon as you confirm that I'm the Mercadir."

Dimitar scratched his pointed gray teeth with a long black fingernail. "It almost seems as though you *want* things to go poorly today."

"No, I *want* you to give us the starstone and show us a way home that doesn't involve a boat—and maybe commission a few statues in our honor to celebrate. But I've learned to prepare for the worst when it comes to my mom, so in case something in that scroll gets your metal diaper in a bunch, I want to make sure you keep Foster out of it. Take it out on me—which shouldn't be too big of a sacrifice. I can already tell you want to punch me."

"I would tread carefully, Mr. Sencen," Lady Cadence warned. "The punishment for a Mercadir is far more severe than a punch. How do you even know the title?"

"From you. I found the reports on ogre culture that you sent the Council while you were living in Ravagog. Looks like Alvar was stashing them so no one would read them."

Lady Cadence sighed. "I knew I shouldn't have trusted that arrogant child."

Sophie regretted the same mistake. She'd even asked Alvar to serve as their guide when they'd infiltrated the ogre capital—and he'd probably planned to betray them while they were there. If she hadn't changed their strategy halfway through the excursion, who knew what could've happened?

Which made her wonder . . .

"How long have you had an alliance with the Neverseen?" she asked Dimitar.

"That's none of your concern."

Lady Cadence frowned. "Was I still living in Ravagog?"

The king's silence said it all.

"Is *that* why you canceled our weekly meetings those final months?" she asked. "I'd assumed it was because I sent the Council the update on the soporidine."

"It was both. The boy revealed himself to me after you and I had our rather vocal disagreement on the matter. And he assured me that he would 'take care of it.'"

"*That's* why you agreed to ally yourself with their order?" Lady Cadence gasped.

"What's soporidine?" Blur asked, beating Sophie to the question.

"I think it's some sort of protein," Keefe jumped in. "She wrote up a whole report on it—but it was long and boring, with all these science-y words, so I mostly skimmed."

"It's an amino acid," Lady Cadence corrected, narrowing her eyes at the ogre king, "secreted by a hybridized bacterium called *Bucollosisia*, which the ogres cultivated during one of their experiments."

"See?" Keefe said, making a snoring sound.

"Trust me, that discovery was anything but boring," Lady Cadence assured him. "The bacteria themselves are harmless— but the soporidine they secrete is the most potent sedative I've ever experienced. A single drop accidentally touched my skin and I was gone for three days. No thoughts. No dreams. Even my vitals changed. And there was no way to awaken me. The only reason I regained function is because the soporidine eventually wore off. Had I been exposed to a larger quantity, I might never have woken again."

"Just from touching it?" Sophie asked, her breath turning sharp when Lady Cadence nodded. "So it could be used as a weapon?"

"Such dramatics," Dimitar said, a snarl creeping into his tone. "Cadence knows as well as I do that the unsustainability of the bacterium makes it nearly impossible for us to mass-produce soporidine."

"*Nearly* impossible isn't the same as *impossible*," Sophie hated to point out.

"Spoken like someone who has no knowledge of microbiology," Dimitar told her. "There is no food source for the microbes, so they perish within a few seconds of their creation—most before they ever secrete any soporidine."

That still meant someone could cultivate the scary sedative—if they were really determined.

Lady Cadence must've agreed, because she stalked closer. "If the soporidine wasn't important, I wonder why you allied with the Neverseen to keep the Council in the dark about it?"

"I allied with the Neverseen because they agreed that I had the *right* to keep the Council in the dark," Dimitar snapped back. "You elves love to police the world, thinking you're doing some brilliant service. But most of the time your rules do nothing more than hinder progress."

"And what progress have you made with soporidine?" Lady Cadence demanded.

Dimitar gritted his teeth. "As it turns out, that substance had troubling effects on our species as well—which is why I'd asked you to hold off on notifying the Council until my researchers had a better idea of what we were dealing with.

And after so many years working together, I'd counted on your support. But you chose to be as small-minded as the rest of your kind."

"So you formed ties with murderous lunatics and decided to threaten an innocent species," Lady Cadence spit back. "Excellent decision."

"Aaaaaaand you wondered why I thought this meeting might need a Mercadir!" Keefe said as Dimitar gripped his sword.

"Don't," Sophie told him, but Dimitar was already circling Keefe with an expression that said Keefe had just been sized up and found . . . lacking.

"I do not give that title to elves."

"Then why'd you give it to my mom?" Keefe asked. "I saw her wounds. They were curved, like they'd been carved by—not sure how I'm supposed to pronounce this one: a shamkniv?"

"The 'k' is silent," Lady Cadence told him, still glaring at Dimitar. *"Sham-niv."*

"Fine, a shamkniv," Keefe repeated. "And according to her report, shamknivs are only used to punish a Mercadir who failed their assignment."

"You mean *this*?" King Dimitar drew a dagger-size weapon from a hidden compartment in his diaperlike armor. The blade was short and heavy, made of black metal that curved like a crescent moon, and Sophie felt dizzy when she glimpsed the dried blood on the handle.

"Yep, that's the one," Keefe said.

Dimitar moved the blade much too close to Keefe's face. "No one realizes the edge of a shamkniv is serrated until it's tearing their skin. The jaggedness ensures that each cut leaves a scar. And when a Mercadir has seriously disappointed me, I dip the end in flesh-eating bacteria."

Keefe swallowed hard. "Good thing I don't plan on disappointing you."

"*All* elves disappoint me."

"I'm feeling the same way about ogres at the moment," Lady Cadence told him.

For a second Sophie wondered if Dimitar was going to carve a few gashes into Lady Cadence's face—and Lady Cadence must've come to the same conclusion because she strode closer, placing her hand on Dimitar's arm. "But you and I have always managed to find a common ground. Even under difficult circumstances."

"Like when two of the children who destroyed my city come begging for my help while bearing a message from an elf who failed her assignment?" Dimitar asked.

"Well, when you put it like *that*," Keefe said.

The joke hit the ground with a thud.

"*Did* Lady Gisela fail?" Sophie had to ask. "I thought Gethen getting captured was actually part of their plan."

"That was not the source of my disappointment."

"What was?" Blur asked.

"And why was her punishment so much more severe than

others?" Lady Cadence added. "You know I've always disapproved of your use of the shamkniv. But you've at least limited the cuts to one or two for a first offense."

Dimitar tucked his shamkniv back into its hidden sheath. "You assume I was the one delivering the blows. Or that I was even involved with that part of her sentencing."

"Who was?" Sophie asked.

"It's none of your concern. But it was an elf—which exemplifies why I find little reason to put faith in your kind. For all your talk of peace, you allow any manner of atrocity to occur. And for all your power, you hold no actual control—even over your own people." He turned back to Keefe. "Give me *one* reason you deserve the title of Mercadir."

"Easy." Keefe held up the finger he'd sliced open the day before, which was no longer covered by a bandage. "I spilled my blood to get us here."

The gash was blackened with scabs, and Sophie wondered if she should've used a different balm—or called for Elwin. But in the grand scheme of wounds, it still looked like a paper cut pretending to be a battle scar.

And yet, King Dimitar said, "An elf willing to spill blood— even his own—is a rarity."

"For good reason," Blur told him.

"Ah yes, how can I forget your delicate sensibilities? Your poor, weak minds cannot bear the violence and gore."

"Embracing violence doesn't make you strong," Blur argued.

"True strength comes from finding a peaceful alternative."

"Yes, I've heard that excuse before. And I give it even less credence coming from someone cowering behind a disguise."

"Fear has nothing to do with it. This disguise is a statement—much like how you wear that"—Blur waved a smudged arm toward Dimitar's metal diaper—"to show your people that their king needs no armor to protect him on the battlefield. I appear like this to show *my* people that I will push through any boundary if it's in the best interests of our world."

"Still sounds like a coward's excuse to avoid being held responsible. Even this ridiculous boy has the guts to face me as himself."

"Does that mean you're accepting me as the Mercadir?" Keefe asked.

Dimitar studied Keefe again, before he turned to head toward the crevice he'd emerged from. "The title is yours. We'll see if you lose more blood before this day is over."

THIRTY-ONE

*T*HAT WAS AN INCREDIBLY DANGER-
ous move," Lady Cadence told Keefe, blocking
him from following the ogre king.

"Oh, you want to talk about dangerous?" he
asked. "How about the part when you almost started a brawl
with King Dimitar? You were supposed to be the person at this
meeting that he actually likes—that's why we brought you!"

"*I* brought *you*," Lady Cadence corrected.

"Technically true—though Keefe does have a point," Blur
said. "The Black Swan is counting on you to keep things peaceful today."

"And I did. But I will not hold back from telling Dimitar when
he's been a fool—especially when I find out he partnered with

the Neverseen *while I was still living here.* I'd always assumed the alliance formed when I was no longer around to be a positive influence. But apparently, he spent my final months lying to my face."

"Do you really think the ogres aren't planning something with the soporidine?" Sophie asked, trying not to imagine the horrifying possibilities.

Could they sedate a whole city if they misted the air?

Lady Cadence sighed. "I don't know. It's tricky. No food source naturally produces the amount of nitrogen the *Bucollosisia* require—and even if someone were to hybridize one, the bacteria also didn't produce any enzymes to digest it. But I don't like that the Neverseen are aware of it—especially since I was never able to conduct any of my own research on the bacteria. Things had turned so tense with King Dimitar— and the Council hadn't expressed any concern. But I had no idea they weren't getting my reports. Do you still have access to them?" she asked Keefe. "I'd love to take another look at my notes."

"I can get them," he told her.

"How?" Sophie wanted to know.

"I don't have to go anywhere near the Neverseen, if that's what you're worried about" was Keefe's only answer—which wasn't good enough.

"Excellent," Lady Cadence told him. "Bring all the scrolls to me when we're done here."

"I want a copy too," Sophie added. "And I want to know where you found those reports, Keefe. You can't keep—"

"*SHOULD I ASSUME THIS MEETING IS FINISHED?*" Dimitar called from the shadows. "*BECAUSE MY PATIENCE IS ABOUT TO BE!*"

"He's right," Lady Cadence whispered. "We'll circle back to these conversations later. Right now we need to focus. You need that starstone to find your parents, don't you?"

Sophie let out a breath as she nodded.

"Then we'd best get moving," Lady Cadence said, heading toward the crevice.

Blur turned to follow—but Sophie grabbed Keefe's arm to stop him from doing the same.

"Yeah, I know," he said, before she could launch into the tirade she'd been planning. "I feel that cloud of Foster Fury loud and clear. And you can hate me if you want. But I made a promise when I found out my mom was with the Neverseen—she only gets to hurt *me*. It's the only way I can live with myself."

His voice was raw—his arm trembling in hers—and Sophie realized he'd just let another mask slip.

She knew the funny, teasing Keefe.

And she'd seen glimpses of the scared, angry boy he hid underneath.

But beyond all of that was this new boy, broken into sharp, painful pieces. And the only thing holding him together was his determination to fix this mess they were caught up in.

"Keefe—"

"Sophie! Keefe! Get over here right now!" Lady Cadence commanded.

"We're not done," Sophie told Keefe, letting go of his arm as she turned to head toward the crevice.

His voice sounded especially small as he mumbled, "I hope not."

By the time they reached the rest of their group, the tension between King Dimitar and Lady Cadence seemed far less palpable. Sophie hoped that meant the king would be feeling more cooperative as he led them into the ominous gap in the mountain.

All other thoughts dropped away as the darkness melted into the vibrancy of the palace.

The main cavern was massive, with a ceiling so high, Sophie wondered if it stretched all the way to the mountaintop—though the height was broken up by long, needle-thin stalactites tipped with tiny glowing orbs. Each of the stone pillars supporting the cavern had been carved differently—some tall and twisted, others squat and robust—and they all glowed with colors unlike anything Sophie had ever seen. There were no names for the shades and tones—no comparison she could make to anything that existed. It felt as if they'd stepped into a new universe, walking on a sleek floor that brightened wherever their feet stepped down.

"Is this Foxfire?" she asked, squinting at the tiny illuminated specks glowing across an especially wide pillar.

Dimitar snorted. "You elves and your glowing fungus. You've always been so dazzled by glitter and light, you never think to see what's lurking in the dark—not that you can find these microorganisms anywhere but here."

"So this is bacteria, then?" Blur asked, scooting away from the pillars when Lady Cadence nodded.

"Also amoebas," King Dimitar added. "And protozoa. We utilize all manner of microorganism."

"Is that why it smells so . . . special?" Keefe asked.

The air was somehow both disgustingly sour and cloyingly sweet, like curdled milk stirred with extra-sugary frosting. And it felt thicker, like Sophie could chew her breath—which was *not* a pleasant sensation.

Dimitar sighed. "This air is some of the healthiest air you'll ever breathe, and yet you turn up your noses at it."

"I never found any evidence that these enzymes brought any improvement for elves," Lady Cadence reminded him.

"And I suppose if something doesn't benefit you, you assign it no value?" Dimitar countered.

Lady Cadence shrugged. "Don't pretend you don't do the same."

King Dimitar didn't argue her point, instead leading their group down the narrowest and darkest of all the hallways branching off the main square—a path lit only by a single strand of dangling orbs, each radiating the same otherworldly colors. As they walked, Lady Cadence explained that the palace was designed to fool intruders, so the important paths intentionally looked neglected and unimpressive. Any routes that reeked of opulence led only to traps.

The hall wound back and forth, the floor sloping down as they walked, until Sophie was certain they were heading for the dungeons. But when the long corridor ended, they found themselves in an even more spectacular cavern, where smoothed stalagmites stretched out of the ground in sharp angles and met in the middle, forming a path lined with sloped arches that glowed with a light that almost felt alive—probably because it was. Millions of tiny pricks of color were in constant motion, swirling and shifting and casting soft illumination on the two enormous thrones stationed on a raised dais in the center of the room.

"Two?" Sophie asked, not necessarily meaning to say it out loud.

"Yes," King Dimitar said, his expression almost amused. "Did you not expect me to have a queen?"

The thought definitely hadn't crossed Sophie's mind. Maybe she'd spent too long around the forever-unwed Councillors.

"You've never mentioned her," she said in her defense.

"I've never mentioned many things. Especially when it comes to my private life. The more your enemies know, the more they can exploit."

"We're not your enemies," Lady Cadence assured him.

"Is that so?" Dimitar turned his attention back to Sophie.

"Tell me, is my palace how you imagined it? Or were you picturing bloodstained walls and halls littered with bones?"

"You can't judge her for biases that you yourself have perpetrated," Lady Cadence interceded. "There's a reason you keep this palace private—even from the majority of your own people. Just as there's a reason that Queen Gundula doesn't sit at your side in the Triad when you render judgment, or accompany you on diplomatic missions. You've chosen exactly how you wish to present yourself as leader."

Dimitar's jaw tightened. "You know nothing of what I wish."

"I'm open to being enlightened."

"I'm sure you are," Dimitar said, stalking over to the wider throne, which seemed to be carved from a single massive boulder. Whatever microorganisms were on the stone reacted to his presence, blaring with a pure white glow as he plopped into the seat. "But that's not why you came here today," he added, turning to Keefe. "Let's not waste each other's time pretending you're not going to give that message."

"None of us know what it says," Keefe warned as he handed over the tiny black scroll. "So don't blame us if it's annoying."

"Knowing your mother I fully expect it to be."

The seals made a strange sort of buzz when King Dimitar broke through, and thin wisps of smoke swirled around the paper, which was shorter than Sophie had imagined—scarcely longer than one of Dimitar's fingers.

She couldn't breathe while Dimitar read, trying not to

imagine him pulling out his shamkniv and carving gashes into all of them.

But the king didn't so much as blink before he rolled the scroll back up and stuffed it into the waistband of his diaper.

"Am I to assume you won't tell us what she requests?" Lady Cadence asked.

"Who said it's a request?"

"Because it's my mom," Keefe said, "and she always wants something."

"I'm well aware of her greed." His fists tightened on the arms of his throne. "If you must know, she's offering information on which of my guards helped her escape my prison. Now that she no longer needs their assistance, she has no problem betraying them."

"Sounds about right," Keefe muttered.

Dimitar shrugged one shoulder. "She's a survivor. Some part of me can appreciate that."

"But the other part has to know she's going to want something in exchange for the information," Sophie told him.

"She made that abundantly clear—and I'm still deciding whether or not I'll give it."

"Don't do it," Keefe warned. "There's always a trick."

"Strange advice coming from the boy who shed his own blood and dragged his friends to this meeting on her word—and her word alone—that I have a certain item in my possession. What makes you so sure she was telling the truth?"

"Are you saying you don't have it?" Sophie asked, barely able to scrape together enough voice for the words.

If he didn't . . .

If they couldn't get to Nightfall . . .

"He has it," Lady Cadence assured her.

"Do I?"

Lady Cadence nodded, dipping a brief curtsy before approaching the throne. She slid her fingers along the edge of the arm until a soft click opened a secret latch in the stone.

Dimitar crossed his arms. "I don't remember telling you about that compartment."

"You didn't."

The king's eyes narrowed, but he said nothing as he reached in and pulled out a palm-length silver stick with a white stone tucked into a nest of intricate silver swirls at the end.

"I'll admit, I hardly see the value of such a trinket," he told Sophie. "But I suppose you elves do love shiny things."

Sophie could barely focus.

There.

Right there was the first piece she needed to find her parents.

All she'd have to do is reach out and grab it—or snatch it with her mind, using telekinesis.

But King Dimitar kept a tight grip—and his other hand lay ready by his sword.

"What do you want?" Sophie asked.

"Things you cannot give."

"Try me," she told him. "I'm up for any challenge you want me to face."

"I see Cadence has prepared you well—though I wonder if she gave you an accurate picture of what to expect?"

"It doesn't matter," Sophie told him. "I'll do whatever it takes."

"Or we could form an alliance," Lady Cadence jumped in, "and skip this drastic waste of time."

Dimitar raised one eyebrow. "You honestly think that ogres and elves could side together?"

"For the right cause, yes. And with the right leaders to guide them."

"Funny, I don't see any members of your Council here. So either you don't consider them to be valuable leaders, or that's who's hiding under there." He pointed to Blur's smudged form.

Blur laughed. "Definitely not."

"And I never said a *valuable* leader," Lady Cadence added. "I said the *right* leaders. The Black Swan has its own brand of authority—a kind of power that can act much quicker, and keep a more open mind."

"Yes, I relied on a similar authority when I made my ties with the Neverseen."

"We're stronger than they are," Blur told him. "But I think you already know that. Otherwise your city wouldn't be undergoing repairs."

Dimitar unsheathed his blade. "Do not speak of those losses so casually!"

"You realize you can't kill me with that, right?" Blur leaped forward, slamming his smudged chest into the spiked blade—which slipped through his indistinct form without drawing a single drop of blood. "Bet you wish your soldiers could do this, huh?"

"Actually, I prefer they learn to fight, instead of relying on gimmicks that breed overconfidence," Dimitar told him.

"Our abilities are not *gimmicks*," Blur snapped back.

"And yet, if I wanted you dead, it would be the work of only a moment to make it happen," Dimitar warned.

"Let's not focus on our differences," Lady Cadence stepped in, forcing Blur to back up. Dimitar reluctantly resheathed his sword. "I realize we may all find the idea uncomfortable—but we need each other. The Black Swan has proven to be a resourceful organization, but time and again, its efforts to stop the Neverseen have failed. And you're a good king, Dimitar. Someday I hope you'll become a great one. But your authority is slipping. If you're not careful, your world will dissolve into full-fledged rebellion."

"And how is uniting with an organization that you've just admitted is failing going to change any of that?" Dimitar wanted to know.

"Because we'll be each other's balance. I'm not saying it will be easy. But together, we *will* be stronger."

"And if your Council disagrees?"

"If we start small, they'll go along."

"Small," Dimitar repeated, reaching up and twirling the stone set into his earlobe. "And what *small* thing would you expect from this so-called *alliance*?"

"Whatever you're willing to give. We'll treat it as a trial run, to see how things come together. And if it works, we'll look into building on it."

"A trial," Dimitar said, holding up the starstone, letting it flash blue in the cavern's eerie light. "Isn't that what we were already discussing?"

"I'm looking for more than a hairpin," Lady Cadence countered, and Sophie had to force herself not to argue.

She had to remember that finding her parents was only one of their current problems, and likely one of the smaller ones.

"I suppose it will depend on how well you fare in the challenge," Dimitar said, his pointed teeth gleaming. "Feeling brave, little girl?"

"If it gets us the starstone." Sophie's voice cracked more than she wanted, but she at least managed not to flinch—even when Dimitar rose from his throne and whipped out his sword.

"I believe you," he said, slashing the spiked end under Sophie's nose. "So, I challenge you to a sparring match."

"Sparring?" Lady Cadence, Keefe, and Blur all seemed to ask on top of each other.

King Dimitar grinned. "First to draw blood three times wins."

"Sophie's not a warr—"

"She's *not*," King Dimitar interrupted. "But she doesn't need to be. After all, we have a Mercadir to handle these things for her, remember?"

He pointed his blade toward Keefe. "You spilled your own blood to get here—now show me you can spill mine. And if you can't, pain will be the least of your worries."

THIRTY-TWO

I GOT THIS," KEEFE SAID, FOR WHAT HAD TO be the tenth time as they followed King Dimitar through another palace tunnel. It seemed even darker than the last one—or maybe that was Sophie's mood.

"You don't," she told him before she turned to Lady Cadence. "You can stop this, can't you?"

Lady Cadence shook her head. "Dimitar has named his terms."

"Then let Blur steal the starstone and—"

"I can hear you," Dimitar warned, even though she'd been whispering and he was far ahead. "And you'd never get out of my palace, much less down the river past all of my guards."

"You might be surprised," Blur told him.

"No, *you'd* be surprised by how much security this palace has," Lady Cadence corrected. "Beneath our feet is an entire barracks of soldiers ready to spring into action. Besides—we didn't come here to steal."

"We didn't come here to *die*, either," Sophie snapped back.

"It's a sparring match," Keefe told her. "He's not going to kill me."

He glanced at Dimitar, who gave a pointed-tooth smile that knocked the grin off Keefe's lips.

"The bloodshed will be kept to a minimum," Lady Cadence reassured them.

"I don't know about a *minimum*," Dimitar corrected. "But . . . if he's smart, he should be able to walk out of the ring after he loses. And if he's foolish, he should be able to crawl to one of your medics."

"Even if I *am* crawling," Keefe said, his voice strong, despite how pale he was turning, "I won't be losing."

They'd reached their destination by then—another enormous cavern lit by four glowing obelisks in the corners. The walls were adorned with an abundance of metal items that would've looked perfectly at home in a museum—or a torture chamber: blades of all shapes and sizes, some gleaming, others disturbingly splattered with brown and red. Clubs. Axes. Spears. Metal orbs covered in spikes. All manner of terrifying hooks.

The rest of the space was empty, save for a large circle in the center filled with a glistening layer of—

"Salt," Dimitar said, following Sophie's stare. "Gives the same traction as sand—with the added bonus that if you knock your opponent down, you can press it into their wounds. Ample motivation to stay on your feet, don't you think?"

Bile rose in Sophie's throat.

"Elves are not warriors," Lady Cadence told him. "As you well know."

"And yet for years I've been led to believe that you make up for your lack of military training with your other advantages," Dimitar countered. "Aren't those abilities of yours supposed to be important?"

"Keefe's an Empath," Sophie jumped in. "All he can do is tell you what you're feeling."

Dimitar grinned again. "How unfortunate for him. Though that does improve my mood."

"It'll be fine," Keefe told Sophie. "I'm basically undefeated at tackle bramble."

"This isn't a game, Keefe—and you can't cheat."

"I *never* cheat." His wink said otherwise.

"It won't help," Dimitar warned. "Once we step into the ring, we do not leave until the match has a winner. Step one toe outside the salt and I get a free strike. First to draw blood three times is the champion. And I'm not completely unreasonable," he added to Lady Cadence. "Usually we spar with swords, but I doubt his skinny arms could support the weight—"

"My arms aren't skinny," Keefe argued, pulling back his

sleeve and flexing what looked like a well-defined bicep—until King Dimitar did the same, revealing muscles bigger than watermelons.

"I also won't use the *grusom-daj*," Dimitar said, referring to an ogre mind trick that seemed to cause as much pain as an Inflictor. "And I'll allow him to keep his pants."

"Um . . . what was that last one?" Keefe asked.

"Sparrers generally expose the same amount of skin, to ensure they have equal targets," Lady Cadence explained. "So you *should* have to wear what he's wearing."

"I'll settle for you removing everything from the waist up," King Dimitar added.

"Phew," Keefe said, unfastening his cape. "That diaper looks like it would cause some *serious* chafing."

"Stop treating this like a joke," Sophie snapped, grabbing his hands. "You realize the best-case scenario here is that you get seriously wounded, right?"

Keefe grinned. "You really are adorable when you worry. But you don't need to. I wouldn't have agreed if I didn't *know* I can handle it. See?"

He pulled his hands free and showed her how steady they were.

Then he gave her his cape and set to work unbuttoning his jerkin.

"There has to be another way to settle this," she tried, turning to the king. "How about a game of riddles? Or—"

"This is the way I have chosen," Dimitar interrupted, snatching a silver dagger from a long row of knives mounted on the wall. The blade was at least a foot long, with hooked barbs on the hilt, as if the weapon were designed to stab deep into an organ and tear it out.

"Please don't do this," Sophie begged Keefe as he unbuttoned his undershirt.

Any other time Sophie might've noticed how Keefe's lean build showed a rather impressive amount of muscle tone when he added the shirt to the pile draped over her arm. But when he moved next to the ape-size king, it was hard to think anything other than *RUN!*

"Let's see, which one looks good for stabbing," Keefe said, grabbing a wide black blade from the wall of weapons and testing a few swipes. His motions were somehow both sluggish and erratic, and when he tried to pivot, the weapon slipped from his grasp.

"The grip on that one's faulty," Keefe mumbled, kicking the weapon aside and snatching a dagger with a palm-length blade. "This one looks perfect for sneak attacks."

"You can't sneak up on him in an open ring," Sophie argued.

"That's what you think." He offered a smirk, but Sophie didn't buy the act.

King Dimitar studied him again, noting the way Keefe kept adjusting his grip on his miniscule dagger. "You display an uncommon amount of bravery for your species. Good to know there's a shred of fight hidden underneath the elvin pomp and circumstance."

"Just because we don't fight with blades doesn't mean we're afraid of battle," Blur told him.

Dimitar pointed his dagger toward the ring and glanced at Keefe. "Perhaps. But blades measure what truly matters."

"Do they?" Sophie said, reaching out with her telekinesis and floating a dozen swords toward Dimitar, each pointed at his chest.

"Do. Not. Threaten. The. King!" Lady Cadence snapped.

"I'm not *threatening*," Sophie argued, floating another sword toward him. "I'm showing him there's no need for this match."

"You think you can wield those weapons simply because you can lift them?" Dimitar asked, studying the blade he'd chosen.

One second his eyes were on his dagger—the next he'd leaped in a sweeping spin, swinging his arm and sending each of her weapons clattering to the floor.

"It's as simple as this," he said, stalking so close that Sophie was forced to take a step back. "I named the challenge. The boy accepted. Now, he must fight, or forfeit."

"*Don't* forfeit," Lady Cadence warned. "Whatever pains Keefe will experience in that ring are nothing compared to the punishment for that level of cowardice."

"She's right," Dimitar said, striding into the circle of salt and holding his blade toward Keefe. *"Shall we?"*

Sophie grabbed Keefe's arm. "I have a super bad feeling about this."

He covered her hand with his. "I know. But I'm not going to lose. And when I win," he added, turning to Dimitar, "you *will* give us the starstone?"

"You have no chance of winning," Dimitar told him. "But if you manage to make it through this match without sniveling or groveling, I'll allow you to take your trinket and go—after I make one strike against each of your companions. Consider their blood the price for traveling with a boy who thinks he deserves to be a Mercadir."

"I told you—Sophie stays out of this," Keefe argued.

"And I never agreed." Dimitar stomped his foot, and four holes opened up in the floor, followed by four enormous ogres in full body armor who crawled out and blocked the only exit.

"Like I said," Lady Cadence mumbled, "a whole battalion is underneath us."

"In case anyone was getting any ideas about running," Dimitar said. "You're all here to witness the battle. And you're all here to pay for the loss."

"The only loss will be yours!" Keefe sidestepped Sophie and charged into the ring, dagger raised, eyes wild, leaping for the ogre king.

Dimitar grabbed him by his shoulders and threw him to the ground, placing one giant foot on Keefe's neck, closing off his windpipe.

"Two other things we should be clear on," he said, as Keefe turned a purple-sort-of-red. "Number one: I will limit your wounds to treatable injuries, so long as you extend me the same courtesy. Come at me with a fatal attack—however flawed it may be—and you'll be dead before you swing your blade. And number two: Your friends are not allowed to assist."

"If you're going to take his loss out on us, we should be allowed to help him win," Sophie argued.

"That definitely would be fairer. But I don't play fair," Dimitar said, removing his foot from Keefe's throat. "Which is why the sparring begins *now*."

THIRTY-THREE

EFORE KEEFE CAUGHT HIS BREATH,
Dimitar had dragged his blade across Keefe's
shoulder with a sickening squish.

"That's one," he called over Keefe's guttural cry.

Sophie's vision blurred as red streamed down Keefe's
chest.

"I can't decide what I'm enjoying more, beating the boy—
or having the girl watch me do it," Dimitar said with a cold
smile. "Be glad I'm not kicking salt into his wound."

"I'm fine," Keefe promised, stumbling to his feet.

He didn't look fine. He looked pale and wobbly, and Sophie
had to press her fist under her ribs to keep her stored emotions under control. Every fiber of her being wanted to let her

darkness rain on the ogre king. But if she let that happen, she'd unleash the pain on *everyone*.

Keefe shrugged his shoulder, testing the motion. "It's really not that deep."

"It's not," Dimitar agreed. "But the next two will be."

He lunged again, fast and deadly—but that time Keefe managed to launch his body into the air, hovering out of the king's reach.

"Stay up there as long as you can!" Blur advised.

"Uh, duh," Keefe told him. His levitation was shaky, but he managed to keep himself afloat and pull his body to the opposite end of the room. "You said I couldn't *step* outside the salt, but you didn't say I couldn't hover above it."

"I suppose I didn't," Dimitar said as he moved as close to Keefe as the salt ring allowed. "Keep in mind, though, that for every minute you drag out this match, my next blow gets stronger— and I aim for a *far* more inconvenient place."

"You have to catch me first," Keefe told him.

"I intend to." Dimitar leaped in an arc, slicing for Keefe's feet before he twisted his body around, landing on the very edge of the ring—and it almost worked.

The blade shredded the sole of Keefe's shoe, but didn't hit skin.

"Good thing I wore the thick boots," Keefe said, tucking his legs up against his chest.

But his concentration was fading, his form bobbing unevenly through the air.

"Get back over the ring," Blur warned. "In case you lose your hold."

Keefe took his advice, dragging himself to the far end of the circle—and just in time. He plummeted, and Dimitar leaped toward him, blade slashing.

Sophie closed her eyes, bracing for Keefe's scream. But the only sounds were an angry grunt and a chorus of startled gasps.

"That's one," Keefe said, and when Sophie opened her eyes he was levitating again, while King Dimitar stared at the maroon blood streaming down his ribs.

It wasn't a large strike—barely more than a nick, just below the king's clavicle. But Dimitar's eyes were wide. His barrel chest heaving.

Which was probably why Keefe wasn't ready when Dimitar launched toward him with a mighty leap, dragging him down by his ankles and slamming Keefe into the ring with a bone-crunching thud. He slashed his blade under Keefe's ribs, a long, deep stroke that sent red spraying before he flipped Keefe over and shoved him into the salt.

"That's two," he snarled over Keefe's agonized groan.

"Let him up!" Sophie screamed.

"He'll get up on his own, or I'll finish this now."

Red was soaking the salt all around Keefe's torso, but somehow he managed to twist and kick Dimitar back, giving himself the seconds he needed to rise to his feet.

"I'm still fine," he promised. But Sophie noticed he kept

his left arm pressed under his ribs to keep pressure on the wound—not that it did much to stop the bleeding.

"You need to get to a physician," Sophie told him, checking her pockets to find the Panakes blossoms she'd remembered to bring, wondering if she should make him eat them or press the petals into the wound. Probably both.

"I've got time," Keefe promised.

"And we're almost done," Dimitar added with an asplike strike.

Keefe managed to retreat to the air.

"Back to hiding like a coward?" the king called.

"Why not? It smells better up here."

Red rained from Keefe's wound, and Sophie had to fight back a gag. She kept herself in control by tearing Keefe's cape into strips, ready to use for bandages.

"Keep wasting my time and I'll slice something off," Dimitar shouted at him. "You don't need all of your fingers."

"Tempting, but I'm really kind of attached to them," Keefe said. "See what I did there?"

He smiled, but his words were slurred, probably from the blood loss. And as Dimitar rolled his eyes, Keefe seemed to collapse, toppling toward the ring with flailing arms.

Sophie gasped, sure he'd lost control—but he flipped around when he neared the king, a primal roar blasting from his lips as he crashed into Dimitar, knocking him over and pinning the king's shoulders with his knees.

Salt flew.

Limbs thrashed.

And there were so many growls and snarls it sounded like feral beasts had entered the room.

Dimitar's guards pressed closer, their movements cautious, as if they weren't sure whether or not to aid their king. But Dimitar managed to fling Keefe off and send him skidding across the salt.

He swung his blade for Keefe's face, but his arm froze mid-swipe.

"Ah-ah-ah," Keefe told him, sweat dripping down his brow.

It took Sophie a second to realize he was using telekinesis to stay the king's hand.

"That was three." Keefe pointed to the maroon streaming from a small cut near the top of the king's metal diaper.

"Two," Dimitar corrected. "And you'll regret that miscount."

"No," Lady Cadence said, her eyes wide as she pointed to the side of Dimitar's face.

One of the yellow stones was now missing from his earlobe. And small drips of maroon trickled down the king's neck.

Keefe released Dimitar's arm so he could reach up and feel the wound. "Like I said. That's three."

"You did this with your bare hand," Dimitar said quietly.

Keefe nodded, holding up the splattered yellow stone with a shaky grip. "You never said the strikes had to be from the blade. Just that they had to draw blood."

Silence followed.

Then slow clapping filled the cavern, and Sophie turned to see Blur's solidified hands creating the applause. Lady Cadence cautiously joined him, but Sophie couldn't bring herself to celebrate—or even look in the king's direction—as she sprinted to Keefe's side, bandages at the ready.

She shoved a Panakes blossom into Keefe's mouth and ordered him to swallow it.

"It looks worse than it is," he told her, choking on the colorful petals.

But he wouldn't let her peel back the arm he held under his ribs.

"Come on, Keefe, I need to press the blossoms into the wound."

"Nah, I'm good. And hey, I got you a souvenir!"

He offered her the bloody yellow stone.

She shook her head, not realizing her eyes were blurry with tears until the wetness spilled over.

"Seriously," Keefe said, when she tried to move his arm. "No need to get blood on your gloves—or Dex's *very* special cuffs."

She sighed. "Show me."

"If you wanted to check out my abs—"

"Show me."

Keefe cringed and slowly pulled back his arm, revealing a deep gash that ran from one side of his stomach clear to the other.

"Told you he'd be crawling to the Physician." Dimitar flashed a particularly vicious smile, and whatever bond had been holding Sophie's knotted emotions in check finally snapped.

Cold darkness unraveled inside her, mixing with burning rage, the two like catalysts, blasting the searing ice through her veins.

A tiny voice in the back of her mind warned she was losing control, and that if she didn't stop, everyone in the room would suffer. But that voice was drowned out by the thunderous fury.

Red rimmed her vision. Her body shook—though it didn't feel like it was *hers* anymore. It was as if she'd been shoved far away, buried under the thick black hate that kept bubbling and churning, ready to drown the world—until a cool rush breezed through her.

Calm, it seemed to say.

Steady.

Relax.

And Sophie's mind obeyed.

Black and red faded to gray. Then to a dusky blue that grew brighter and brighter as the shaking eased and her mind cleared and she found herself staring into a pair of eyes the exact same icy shade.

"There you are," Keefe whispered, his breath warm on her cheeks. "You're good now, right?"

Pressure tightened on her hands and she glanced down to see his fingers twined with hers.

Her gloveless fingers.

Dex's crush cuffs were gone too.

"I took them off," he whispered, glancing down to where they were piled in his lap. "Didn't think it'd be a good idea to let you rage out on King Dimitar. And I didn't know how else to get through."

"I'm assuming you're not going to explain what you two are doing?" King Dimitar asked.

Sophie wasn't sure herself. It felt like Keefe had *controlled* her emotions—but he couldn't do that, could he?

Keefe must've thought so. He told the king, "Let's just say I'm saving you from one beast of a headache."

"And now we need to get you to Elwin," Lady Cadence added as she crouched next to Keefe and tried to wrap his arm around her shoulder.

"Not yet," Keefe said. "Starstone first."

Dimitar was still stroking his wounded ear, and his fisted hand made Sophie wonder if he would betray their bargain. But he lumbered to his throne, retrieved the hairpin, and handed it to Keefe—who slipped it into one of the pockets of his trousers.

"It pains me to admit that your mother was correct," Dimitar told him.

"What are you talking about?" Sophie asked.

He retrieved the black scroll from the waistband of his diaper. "She told me to challenge her son and let him prove that he's not worthless like the others."

"Awesome," Keefe grumbled, sucking air through his teeth as Lady Cadence gently pulled him upright. "My mom's love notes are the sweetest, aren't they?"

"You may find them lacking sentiment, but she's done you a great service. She requested a specific favor—which I've now decided to grant."

Dimitar slipped two fingers between his lips and made a screechy sort of whistle that left Sophie's whole head ringing.

The other four ogres dropped to their knees as the floor rumbled and a fifth ogre crawled out of a narrow opening in the center of the salt pit.

The young female warrior had a leaner build than the other ogres, but her body was pure muscle, accentuated by the metal breastplate she wore paired with a metal diaper of her own—which was studded with spikes. She looked almost stylish with her chin-length ashy hair, the thick black lines painted across her silver eyes, and the blue stone set into one of her nostrils. And yet, something about the fluid way she moved made Sophie suspect she was the most dangerous ogre in the room—aside from Dimitar.

Sophie had just noticed the thin tattoos circling the girl's forehead when Lady Cadence dropped to one knee, bowed her head, and said, "Good to see you again, Princess."

"Yes," Dimitar said, his gaze on Sophie. "I have a daughter—who happens to be one of my most powerful soldiers. Romhilda has—"

"Ro," his daughter corrected, twisting her blue nose piercing. "Romhilda is Grandma's name—and it's gross."

Dimitar gritted his teeth. "Fine. *Ro* has been training for battle since she was one month old."

Ro crossed her muscled arms as she turned to study Sophie and Keefe, her nose crinkling with distaste. "These scrawny kids are seriously the elves who flooded the city?"

"The water girl isn't with them," Dimitar told her, a growl creeping into his voice. "But yes, they are. And I need you to let that go, because they were not the ones who truly betrayed us that day. The real blame belongs to those cloak-wearing liars. Which is why I have an assignment for you."

He stalked toward his daughter, murmuring something Sophie couldn't hear—but she was too worried about how much blood Keefe was losing to care why Ro was there. "What's the fastest way to get him home?" she asked Lady Cadence.

"You should take him to Foxfire," Lady Cadence told her. "Elwin's already working in the Healing Center, prepping for when sessions resume. And you'll be able to leap there as soon as we're clear of the King's Path. I can sail Riverdrift home myself."

"Hmm, a boat ride and my first light leap," Ro said. "At least this is going to be entertaining!"

She grabbed Keefe from Lady Cadence, scooping him up like a baby.

"You're coming with us?" Lady Cadence asked.

"Pretty sure that's the plan—unless I missed something." Ro glanced at her father.

"I'm starting to think *I* missed something," Lady Cadence said when Dimitar nodded.

"Weren't you the one who suggested a trial run?" the king asked. "It's a bonus, really, that this also satisfies Gisela's request."

"And what request is that?" Blur wanted to know.

Dimitar's eyes drifted to Keefe. "A bodyguard for her only son. Apparently he's made some powerful enemies. And we need to keep him alive, so he can fulfill his legacy."

THIRTY-FOUR

THINK YOU'VE OFFICIALLY BROKEN SOPHIE'S record for most Healing Center visits," Elwin said as he straightened his enormous iridescent spectacles and helped Keefe sit up on the narrow cot. He'd already cleaned and dressed Keefe's wounds and made him drink at least two dozen elixirs. "Or maybe you've tied her record—it's so hard to keep up with you two. Either way, I'm going to add your photo next to hers."

He pointed to the wall behind them, where a picture of Sophie in her humiliating mastodon costume from the Level Three Opening Ceremonies hung in all its glory.

"I've never been so proud of us!" Keefe said, holding up his hand for a high five.

Sophie left him hanging.

She didn't feel like celebrating when Keefe had a thick bandage covering his shoulder and a wide band of gauze wrapping completely around his torso, starting just below his armpits and stretching to the middle of his stomach.

Keefe winced as he lowered his arm.

"Still tender?" Elwin asked, shaking his messy dark hair out of his eyes as he pressed gently along Keefe's bandages.

Keefe sucked air between his teeth. "Yeah. Just a little, though."

"Is that bad?" Sophie asked.

"Not necessarily," Elwin said. "It's honestly what I'd expect with wounds this deep."

"Deep" was understating things.

"Dimitar practically gutted him," she grumbled, standing to pace again.

"At least he missed anything vital," Elwin said as he snapped his fingers and made a purple orb glow around Keefe's torso. "I think the Panakes blossoms you gave him made a difference too."

"And I stole his earring," Keefe added. "His head will always be lopsided now. You're welcome, world!"

He tossed the yellow stone up and caught it—then winced from the motion.

"Hmm," Elwin said, snapping his fingers again and changing the orb from purple to green. As a Flasher, Elwin used light to affect what his strange glasses allowed him to see.

"What's wrong?" Sophie asked.

"Probably nothing." But he frowned when he changed the orb from green to blue.

"You found something serious, didn't you?" Sophie asked when Elwin rifled through the satchel of medicines he kept slung across his shoulders.

She'd been trying to console herself with the fact that Bullhorn—Elwin's pet banshee—was still sleeping on Elwin's desk in the private-office section of the Healing Center, instead of screeching or curling up at Keefe's side, like he would be if Keefe was in mortal danger.

But Keefe looked so pale. . . .

"I'm starting to think you're doubting my abilities," Elwin told her, handing Keefe three more elixirs in various shades of pink.

"It's not *you*," Sophie promised. "I just wouldn't be surprised if Dimitar laced his weapon with toxic bacteria."

"If my father was going to do that, your boy would already be dead," Ro called from where she'd stationed herself near the main door to the Healing Center.

"Oh good, I was wondering when we were going to acknowledge the armed ogre in the room." Elwin padded over and offered a hand to shake. "And you are?"

"Ro," she said, side-eyeing Elwin's outfit, which was covered in tiny golden flareadons.

"She's my new babysitter," Keefe explained, wiping his

mouth after chugging his medicine. "Wasn't it sweet of my mom to get me my very own ogre?"

"Mommy issues alert!" Ro said. "Though I get it. I met your mom once, and after about five minutes I was begging my dad to let me stomp her. But like it or not, she did you a solid by getting me assigned as your bodyguard. Those little tricks you did during the sparring match aren't going to save you in a real battle. I trained with some of the idiots who've defected, and if they come after you, you'll be dead in one slash."

"And your father is . . . King Dimitar," Elwin clarified.

She pointed to her forehead tattoos. "He's going to owe me big-time for this. He didn't tell me how lame it is here in elf land—though I guess I should've known."

She crinkled her nose as she glanced through the doorway at the shimmering hallway. "No offense, but what's with all the crystal? It's sorta desperate, don't you think? Like *oh, look at us—we're elves, and we like light, so we make everything sparkly!*"

Elwin laughed. "It's always fascinating to see our world from another perspective."

"Well, if you like honesty," Ro said, following him over to Keefe, "it stinks here, too. Everything smells like . . ."

"Fresh air?" Sophie guessed.

"Awww, my girl keeps getting snarkier and snarkier," Keefe said proudly.

"I'm not your girl," Sophie snapped back. "And don't think I'm done being mad at you!"

"Ohhh, a lovers' quarrel!" Ro clapped her hands. "Those are my favorite. Anyone have snacks? I feel like we should have snacks for this."

"That's not what this is," Sophie told her. "We're not . . . never mind."

Ro grinned, flashing pointed teeth. "If you say so."

"Foster's not ready to face her feelings," Keefe stage-whispered.

"I'm ready to strangle you," Sophie countered.

"You should!" Ro said. "Or wait—am I supposed to tell you not to? I'm still not clear on how this bodyguard thing works. Like, if he's annoying me, can I smack him around a bit as long as I don't do permanent damage?"

"Be my guest," Sophie told her.

"But not until he's recovered," Elwin added. "Then, by all means. Maybe you'll finally knock some sense into him."

"I doubt it." Keefe winked, but Sophie looked away.

"By the way," Elwin said, "am I supposed to keep Ro's presence here a secret? Or is the Council aware that Keefe has an ogre princess protecting him now?"

"I think Blur went to tell them," Sophie said. "Or maybe he went to tell the Black Swan, and Lady Cadence went to tell the Council? I can't remember."

She'd been so desperate to get Keefe to the Healing Center that she hadn't paid much attention to what Blur and Lady Cadence had worked out. But there was no way they'd be able to keep Ro hidden from the Council—not if the ogre princess would be following Keefe everywhere he went.

And not if Ro was supposed to be a trial run for a larger alliance.

Sophie had been keeping an eye on the door, expecting twelve angry Councillors—and possibly the rest of the Collective—to come barging in for an endless shouting match. But so far, things had stayed mercifully quiet.

"Well," Elwin said, "just make sure Magnate Leto does an announcement before school starts, so the other prodigies are prepared to have an ogre on campus. Otherwise there's going to be major panic. No offense to you, your Highness—"

"Ugh, call me Ro," she interrupted. "Titles make me itchy. And wait—I have to go to *school*? Gross. If I have to sit through a bunch of lectures on how brilliant you elves think you are, I might start smashing your crystal walls."

"Don't worry, I spend most of my time ditching or in detention," Keefe assured her.

Ro grinned. "Sounds like you and I are going to get along just fine."

Elwin laughed. "I'm not sure I want to know what havoc you two are going to cause together. Just promise me you'll save the shenanigans until you're stronger, okay, Keefe?"

He flashed another orb around Keefe's middle—a deep red this time—and gave his biggest frown yet.

"There really is something wrong, isn't there?" Sophie asked.

"It isn't *wrong*," Elwin assured her, heading for the wall of shelves and scanning the pots and vials. "But it looks like I need to get the tissue regenerator deeper into his muscle. And to do that, I have to reopen the wound. It's not a big deal," he added quickly. "The seal I made is fresh, so a few drops of piquatine should do the trick."

"And by 'piquatine,' you mean . . . the stuff that melts off skin," Sophie confirmed.

"Cooooooooooooooooool," Ro breathed when Elwin nodded. "Can I watch?"

"If you want to. But I think Sophie should step out to the hall. This isn't going to hurt, but it will be . . . messy."

The word alone made Sophie's head woozy.

"Don't look so freaked," Keefe told her, offering a smile that didn't match the green-gray pallor of his skin. "I was just thinking this morning—you know what would be awesome? Having my skin melted off today!"

"How can you joke about this?" she asked.

He shrugged—then winced—and ended with his serious eyes. "Elwin says it's going to be fine, right?"

"It *is*," Elwin assured them. "Just give us five minutes, okay, Sophie? Use the time to hail Grady and Edaline and let them know you made it back safe."

Sophie *wanted* to argue, but then she remembered something she could use the time for. "Fine. Five minutes."

"Woo-hoo!" Ro said as Sophie headed for the door. "Bring

on the skin melting! Things are finally getting interesting here in Sparkle Town!"

"How about I let you hold the bowl to catch the liquefied skin?" Elwin offered, which was enough to make Sophie hurry out to the hall.

Once the door was safely shut, she closed her eyes and stretched out her mind, calling for Silveny with all the energy she could muster.

Seconds ticked by, and Sophie was on the brink of seriously worrying when Silveny's energetic voice filled her mind.

SOPHIE! FRIEND! HI!

Hi! Sophie transmitted back. *Thank goodness! I'm SO sorry I haven't checked on you in a little while. Are you and Greyfell okay? And how's the baby?*

GOOD! GOOD! GOOD!

Sophie let out the breath she'd been holding. *Where are you? Somewhere safe?*

SAFE! Silveny agreed, filling her mind with a picturesque scene of sweeping green hills and a trickling river with large mossy stones. It looked lush and empty—a perfect place for a pregnant alicorn to graze.

So you guys really are okay? Sophie asked.

OKAY! OKAY! OKAY!

Glad to hear it. But you should probably visit soon. I'm sure Vika wants to check on you and the baby.

There was a long pause. And then Silveny told her, *NO!*

No? Sophie repeated, sure she must've misunderstood.

NO! VISIT! NO!

Aw, come on. I know you're not a fan of Vika—and I don't blame you. But she's the one who knows the most about this stuff. And I'll be there the whole time!

The Heks family were experts on unicorn breeding, which was the closest the Lost Cities had to alicorn-breeding expertise.

But Silveny kept filling her head with a never-ending chant of *NO! VISIT! NO!*

Sophie puffed out a breath, not sure what to do. Silveny usually begged for a visit, and appeared the second Sophie suggested it.

Don't you want to see me? she asked.

MISS! Silveny agreed.

I miss you too. So why don't you want to visit?

LATER! LATER! LATER!

How much later?

Silveny just kept repeating, *LATER!*

Sophie rubbed her head. *You're sure everything's okay?*

OKAY! OKAY! OKAY!

Before Sophie could ask anything else, she told her, *BUSY! TALK! SOON!*

Then Silveny severed their connection.

THIRTY-FIVE

UNBELIEVABLE," SOPHIE GRUMBLED as she stretched out her concentration again, trying to reconnect with Silveny.

Her head stayed frustratingly silent.

Silveny was clearly ignoring her—but why would she do that?

Dozens of theories bubbled up, each more troubling than the last—until Sophie reminded herself that Silveny had assured her that she, Greyfell, and the baby were all okay. She must really be "busy"—though what a sparkly winged horse would be "busy" with, Sophie wasn't sure.

The most she could do at the moment was stay calm, trust Silveny's instincts, and be *much* more regular about checking on the pregnant alicorn.

The door to the Healing Center burst open then, and Elwin peeked his scruffy head out. "We're all set. Come back in whenever you're ready."

Sophie tried one more time to reconnect with Silveny before she gave up and headed inside, where she found Keefe propped against a pillow with his torso wrapped in an even thicker bandage.

"You missed all the fun," Ro told her. "There was ooze everywhere!"

Sophie tried very hard not to picture it.

"Did it fix the problem?" she asked Elwin.

"Yes, and no," he admitted. "This is one of those injuries that's going to take some good old-fashioned bed rest before he's truly back on his feet."

"How long?" Sophie asked.

"I'm guessing at least a week. Maybe more."

"Yeah, that's not happening," Keefe told him.

"You'll regret it if you don't," Elwin warned. "Play this smart and the most you'll have is a thin scar. But if you're not careful, you could end up with nerve damage."

None of that sentence was good—but the scar part hit Sophie the hardest.

Dex had a burn mark from their kidnapping. Fitz probably had some small remnant from the giant bug-impaling in Exile. And now Keefe?

How long would it be before all her friends had some sort of permanent mark?

"Easy, Foster," Keefe said as Sophie's hands curled into fists. "It's not a big deal. It'll make me look tough and soldier-y."

"He's right," Ro jumped in. "Scars are marks of honor. See this?" She pointed to a thick line curving down her back from the base of her neck to the dip of her breastplate, with thinner lines running along each side. "My dad gave me that the day I completed my training. It's a scar only his sword leaves."

"Wow, I thought *my* dad was harsh," Keefe mumbled.

"It wasn't harsh—it was a gift. Yeah, it didn't feel good when he slashed me—and I totally kicked him in the teeth to make it even. But that scar tells any soldiers marching behind me that I've held my own against the king. It's the mark of a leader, and it's earned me respect I never would've had without it."

"Maybe so—but he didn't slice up Keefe for *respect*," Sophie argued. "He wanted to hurt him—and he *enjoyed* it."

"Hey," Keefe said, grabbing her arm as she paced past him. "Need me to calm you down again? Because I can."

"Is that really what happened?" Sophie asked, remembering the blue breeze that blew through her mind and shut down her inflicting.

Keefe nodded. "You were losing it, so I tried to figure out which emotion was doing the triggering. And as soon as I took your gloves and cuffs off, I synced right into your emotional center. Somehow once I was in, I knew exactly how to shift your emotions a different way."

"That's . . . weird."

She stared at her hands, which were back in her gloves again.

"I put them back on when you'd calmed down," Keefe whispered. "And the cuffs are in your pocket. Wasn't sure if you were supposed to wear them outside of Ravagog."

"What do the gloves and cuffs have to do with anything?" Ro asked, narrowing her eyes when they both flinched. "Looks like I caught my first elf-y secret!"

"You didn't catch anything," Sophie told her.

"Riiiiiiiiiiiiight. That's why your pulses just doubled—yeah, I can hear them. I can smell your sweat too. And I get it. I'm an ogre. My dad's the king. And you guys have some . . . *issues*. But right now, I'm here to keep your boy there alive, and I can't do that if you're hiding things from me."

"Ugh, you sound like Sandor," Sophie muttered.

Keefe snorted. "Oh man, he is going to haaaaaaaaaaaate Ro."

"If he's a goblin, I'm sure the feeling will be mutual," Ro told them. "But nice try distracting me. What's the secret with the gloves and cuffs?"

"It's just a privacy thing," Keefe said. "Foster doesn't want me reading her feelings, because then I'd know how irresistible she finds me."

Ro raised one eyebrow. "That's the best story you've got? Ugh. Fine. But don't blame me if that secret costs you your life. Or a limb or two."

Elwin cleared his throat. "Regardless of that, you look a little pale, Sophie. So I want you to take one of these."

He handed her a vial filled with a deep violet liquid, and Sophie chugged it, only half-noticing that it tasted like milky rose petals.

"Does that mean we're done?" Keefe asked, swinging his legs around to the edge of the cot.

"Easy," Elwin said, blocking him from getting up. "You shouldn't be walking."

"On it," Ro said, reaching to scoop Keefe up.

He blocked her with his elbow and stood on his own. "I'm fine. See?"

It would've been a lot more convincing without the sharp breath he sucked through his teeth.

"Go *straight* home," Elwin told him. "And get in bed immediately. I'll check on you in the morning. Where are you staying?"

"I'd . . . rather not say."

Sophie shook her head. "Of course not."

"Hey, I wouldn't need an ogre shadow if everyone wasn't convinced that there are people coming after me," he reminded her. "I'm just trying to keep you guys safe. I promise, I'll come here for a checkup as soon as I can," he told Elwin.

"You'll come here first thing in the morning," Elwin corrected.

"That depends on what my mom tells us," Keefe argued. "If we're heading straight to Nightfall—"

"*You're* not going to Nightfall," Sophie interrupted. "You're doing bed rest until Elwin says you're better."

Keefe smirked. "It's cute that you think that."

"I mean it, Keefe."

Ro cracked up. "Wow, she just stamped her foot—that's adorable! Are they always like this?"

Elwin nodded.

Keefe wrapped his arm around Sophie. "Foster gets all worked up when she's trying to protect me."

"That's not what this is about!" Sophie snapped, pulling away. "Though would it kill you to do the smart thing, just once, and actually listen to someone when they're giving you good advice, instead of thinking you know everything and doing whatever you want?"

Keefe considered that for a second. "Yeah, that might actually kill me."

"Ohhhh," Ro breathed, "that eye roll she gave you was amazing!" She backed up a step when Sophie reeled on her. "Wow, and I thought my dad was the master of the death stare."

Elwin coughed to cover his laugh.

"Hey," Keefe said, grabbing Sophie's arm as she tried to stomp away. "I get it. You're mad at me—"

"No, you *don't* get it," Sophie interrupted. "You claim we're a team, and then you change the rules the first chance you get and drag me into whatever insane plan you've come up with and expect me to just be okay with it. Well, I'm *not* okay with it."

"Yeah. I'm sensing that. But—"

"There's no 'but' with this. Either you swear that you'll be honest with me from now on—and I mean *actually* honest. No more surprises. Or . . . I can't trust you anymore."

"You *can* trust me," he promised. "You heard Dimitar. My mom's message *told* him to challenge me. So he would've done it whether I took the title of Mercadir or not, and things would've ended up exactly the same way."

"Maybe," Sophie agreed quietly. "But you didn't know that when you demanded the title, so it doesn't count."

Keefe sighed. "I'm just trying to keep you safe. Is that really such a horrible thing?"

"I'm not some damsel in distress who needs you to swoop in—"

"I know that, Foster. Believe me, I'm *super* aware of how powerful you are. And brilliant. And special. And—"

"The sucking up's getting a bit desperate," Ro warned him.

"I'm just saying she's *important*," Keefe insisted, before turning back to Sophie. "You're the one who matters—I'm just some pawn in my mom's creepy game. So if I see a way to take the hit and make sure you're not the one covered in bandages, I'm going to do it. And I thought you of all people would understand that, considering how many times you've put yourself at risk, trying to protect your friends."

"There's protecting and there's steamrolling, Keefe. You're *pre*planning ways to betray me. You went there today knowing exactly what you were going to say. You'd done research—which you didn't bother sharing with me. That's not teamwork.

That's the Keefe Show, and we've already seen how that ends."

He flinched like she'd struck him.

But that still didn't stop her from adding, "I can't do it again."

"What does that mean?"

"I don't know. I . . . need some time to think. And it seems like you do too. So I guess it's a good thing you have a week of bed rest ahead of you."

"Right. So I'm just supposed to lie around doing nothing while you contact my mom and head to Nightfall without me?"

"No. You're supposed to get your strength back so you don't do permanent damage."

"I don't care about permanent damage."

"Yeah, I can tell."

"Pretty sure she's not just talking about your wound—in case you didn't catch that," Ro told him.

She shrugged when Sophie glanced at her. "What? He's a clueless guy. Figured I should help him out."

"Okay," Keefe mumbled. "I hear what you're saying, Foster. You're right, I've been taking over everything. I'll try to stop. And I'll send you that scroll about the soporidine when I send it to Lady Cadence—and anything else you want to read."

"Soporidine?" Elwin asked. "Should I know what that is?"

"Probably. I'll get a copy for you too. See?" He turned back to Sophie. "I'm sharing. Don't shut me out, Foster. You need me—and not just because I have this."

He reached for his pocket, frowning when he found it empty.

"You mean this?" Sophie asked, holding up the starstone hairpin. "It's not cool when someone steals from you, is it?"

"Whoa, I did not see that coming!" Ro said. "Gotta tell ya, I'm liking this girl more and more."

Keefe didn't look like he agreed when he told Sophie, "Okay. You've made your point. I'm sorry. I shouldn't have stolen my mom's scroll from you. I shouldn't have done a lot of things."

"Maybe if you say that enough times," Sophie told him, "you'll actually believe it."

"I *do* believe it, Foster. But I think you're forgetting that you *can't* do this without me. You need my blood to hail my mom—and to get into Nightfall."

"I know," Sophie said, pulling a clear satchel from her pocket, filled with some of his blood-soaked bandages. "But you spilled enough of it already. So I'm all set."

"Wow," Ro said. "If I'd known you elves were this intense, I would've visited way sooner."

Sophie couldn't look at Keefe after that. She didn't want to see the hurt in his eyes as she dug out her home crystal.

"You'll make sure he gets home safe?" she asked Elwin.

"If he won't tell me where he's staying, I'll take him to my place," Elwin promised.

"And I'll make sure he stays there," Ro added. "Sorry, dude," she told Keefe. "You called me your babysitter. Now you get your wish. Besides, I'm pretty sure she'll clobber you if you don't listen."

Sophie nodded, holding her crystal up to the light and keeping her eyes focused on the shimmering beam.

"Take care of yourself, Keefe," she whispered. "I'll see you in a week."

THIRTY-SIX

I WAS EXPECTING TO HEAR FROM YOU *yesterday*," Lady Gisela snapped through the Imparter. "And I'd expected to see you with my son—not a Vacker."

Fitz scowled at the silver screen, which once again remained blank for the conversation.

Sophie had reached out to Fitz telepathically as soon as she'd gotten home from the Healing Center, and she'd ended up telling him everything—the bloody battle with Dimitar *and* her fight with Keefe. He'd rushed straight over with another present to cheer her up—and because he didn't want her hailing Lady Gisela alone. But Sandor sent him home as soon as he'd given her the gift, refusing to hand over the Imparter until Sophie had gotten some rest.

She'd fought Sandor at the time, but in the early light of morning Sophie was glad she'd had time to mentally prepare for the conversation. And she was even more grateful that her parents had agreed to let her and Fitz speak to Lady Gisela alone—with their bodyguards supervising, of course. She'd had to promise a full update afterward, but at least she'd have time to process whatever they learned before anyone started arguing about how dangerous the next step would be.

"Well then," she told Lady Gisela, leaning back against the side of her bed in a way she hoped looked calm and casual, "you shouldn't have told King Dimitar to challenge Keefe to a sparring match."

She waited to see if Keefe's mom would ask if her son was okay—or at least worry about how Sophie managed to have some of Keefe's blood to activate the Imparter.

Instead Lady Gisela said, "Sounds like Dimitar accepted my bargain. Who did he assign as Keefe's bodyguard?"

"Why don't you ask King Dimitar?" Sophie countered. "Don't you two have an alliance now?"

"Far from it. All this means is that I showed him we have a mutual interest in keeping Fintan and his allies away from my son. But who he assigned is an excellent way of judging exactly how committed Dimitar is to the cause."

Sophie shrugged, keeping her expression neutral. She'd already held up her end of their deal. Now it was time for

Keefe's mom to come through with hers—and she wasn't giving her anything else in the meantime.

"It's his daughter, isn't it?" Lady Gisela asked. "Actually, wait. I bet it was his son."

"He has a son?" Sophie asked.

"No. But obviously you know he has a daughter. So that must be who he assigned—exactly as I'd been hoping. Thank you. You almost make it too easy."

Sophie gritted her teeth.

Lady Gisela laughed. "Now now, no need for sulking. The more you work with me, the better off you'll be. I assume you got the starstone?"

Sophie glanced at Fitz before she held the hairpin in front of the Imparter, letting the stone flash blue in the soft glow streaming through her windows.

Her feet itched to jump into the beam and go charging into Nightfall. But she knew they had to wait until they had a solid plan.

"So tell us what other security thing we're missing," Sophie demanded, "and everything you know about Cyrah Endal."

Lady Gisela clicked her tongue. "If you're in such a hurry, you shouldn't have waited all night to hail me. First things first—does the Council know there's an ogre princess serving as an elvin bodyguard?"

"What do you think?" Fitz asked.

"I'll take that as a yes. And I'm assuming the fact that you have two goblins standing beside you means that they've agreed to accept the new arrangement with the ogres as well?"

"'Accept' isn't the right word," Grizel said as she stalked out of the shadows. "But the elves have always had alliances with the ogres, so it changes nothing."

"Those sound like the words of your queen," Lady Gisela noted.

They actually were. Sophie had overheard most of Sandor's rather boisterous conversation with Queen Hylda after he'd gotten word that the Council was going to allow Ro to stay. And the queen's final verdict had been that Ro's presence in the Lost Cities didn't violate any treaties. Unless Ro did something to prove herself an enemy to the elves—or to the goblins living among them—no action should be taken.

"Well," Lady Gisela said, "it seems my plan is coming together quite nicely."

Sophie rolled her eyes. "Glad to hear it."

"You should be. It's going to fix everything."

"You can keep telling yourself that, but you couldn't even get a message to King Dimitar without my help," Sophie reminded her.

"And you did it, didn't you?" Lady Gisela countered. "Delegating doesn't make me weak. It makes me smart. Clearly you need to learn that."

"She's delegating to *me*," Fitz reminded her.

"Yes. And you're a poor substitute for my son."

"Don't worry, I'm sure you'll find plenty of other ways to manipulate Keefe into ruining his life," Sophie snapped back.

"His life isn't being *ruined*. I've given him a purpose—I'd think the moonlark, of all people, could understand the difference."

Sophie stopped herself from asking what purpose Keefe was being prepared for. She'd never get an honest answer.

But she couldn't resist making a different plea.

"Leave Keefe out of this. He's your *son*, not some genetic experiment, and—"

"What makes you so sure?" Lady Gisela interrupted.

Sophie's throat went dry.

There'd been a time when she'd feared that the Lodestar Initiative was the Neverseen's version of Project Moonlark, and that Keefe had run off to join them because he'd realized he'd been created as Sophie's nemesis—but she never found any proof to validate the theory.

And Keefe had cracked up when he found out that's what she'd been fearing, so she'd set the worry aside.

"You look pale, Sophie," Lady Gisela noted. "Does that mean it would change things for you?"

"If you designed him to destroy me?" Sophie asked, before she could stop herself.

Lady Gisela laughed. "I love how you assume it would have anything to do with you. Do the math, Sophie—when my son was born, you didn't exist. But the problems in our world did. And like it or not, my son is part of my solution."

Silence followed, until Fitz shook his head. "I don't buy it. Keefe doesn't have any crazy powerful abilities like Sophie does."

"He's exactly the way he needs to be—or he will be, when he starts listening to me."

"Well then, there's your mistake," Sophie told her. "Keefe doesn't listen to anyone."

"He listens to you."

"Trust me, he doesn't."

"Ah. So that's why he's not there. Interesting. I suppose excluding him *is* the best punishment. Especially given your choice of replacement."

"He's not here," Sophie corrected, "because these games you keep playing are slowly breaking him. And if you don't stop, he's going to shatter completely."

"The thing you need to understand, Sophie, is that sometimes we have to break so we can rebuild ourselves into something stronger. Look at me. Fintan thought sending me to prison would destroy me. But I got myself out. And now I know I can survive anything. There's a special kind of power in that."

"The same power you're using to betray the guards who helped you?" Sophie asked.

"I know you're young and blissfully idealistic. But sooner or later you're going to realize that there's no such thing as loyalty."

"Maybe for you," Sophie argued. "I know plenty of loyal people."

"Do you, now? I suppose you think the Vacker boy is one of them?"

"I am," Fitz said, scooting closer to Sophie.

"As am I," Sandor added, moving to Sophie's other side. Grizel stood next to Fitz.

"All that means is that someone hasn't found your weakness yet," Lady Gisela told them. "Or perhaps *Sophie* is your weakness. Either way, all it takes is for someone to figure out where you're vulnerable—and hit you there—and that loyalty will crumble. So you can either be the one exploiting people to your advantage, or risk that they'll exploit you."

"Is that what happened with Cyrah?" Sophie asked. "You used her weakness to force her to make the starstones you needed, and then killed her so she couldn't tell anyone?"

"I'm sure you'd love that to be true. You're so determined to assign me the role of villain in this story. Sadly, reality is rarely so one-sided. But we'll get to that later."

"That wasn't our deal."

"Actually, I very intentionally never gave a timeline for when our Cyrah conversation would happen. But you can unclench that jaw. I'm not going to stall the discussion endlessly. I'm just keeping the proper priorities. Right now I need a better idea of what the Neverseen are up to. And you need to find your family. So let's focus on Nightfall for the moment, shall we?"

Sophie nodded, even though she hated herself for it.

Once again, she was allowing herself to be distracted from the bigger picture. But . . . she was so close to getting her parents back.

"Good," Lady Gisela said. "Now, where should we start?"

"How about you tell us what Nightfall actually is?" Fitz suggested.

"I already have."

"Saying it's 'the future' doesn't mean anything," Sophie argued.

"It means everything. Nightfall is more than a place. It's an idea—though I can't take credit for it. At least not originally."

"Who can?" Sophie asked.

"The oldest records I've found link it to Fintan's new advisor. It was her focus—but she got herself arrested before she could make it a reality. And without her to spearhead it, the plan was forgotten—until I discovered her notes and realized the potential of her dream. It took me years—and some rather brutal sacrifices—but eventually I did what she couldn't and carved the facility into the mountain. But I also made some amendments to turn Nightfall into what it *needs* to be. And when I was done, I realized that the world wasn't ready for the change I'd be bringing. So I locked the door and sealed it away—I believe you saw that memory. Over time, I realized that something so crucial should have regular guards. And since the Neverseen were stretched far too thin, I had to invent an alternative."

"Please tell me there isn't some sort of robot army in there," Sophie begged.

"Of course not. The creatures I designed are far more elegant."

Sophie and Fitz shared a look.

"Are you saying you made some sort of . . . genetically engineered guard dog?" Sophie asked slowly.

"Don't be silly. These beasts could swallow a dog whole. And I didn't make *one*. I made three."

THIRTY-SEVEN

FOR A GIRL CREATED IN A LAB, I DIDN'T expect you to be so shocked by this revelation," Lady Gisela said, breaking the silence that had settled over Sophie's bedroom. "Especially since I never would've had the idea if it weren't for your creators. Mind you, I'm not a fan of altering the genetics of *our* species—but I could see the advantage of designing a lesser creature to fit my security needs."

Sophie was still trying to wrap her head around the idea when Fitz came to another realization.

"So you're admitting you didn't do any genetic experimenting on Keefe?"

Lady Gisela laughed. "Of course I didn't manipulate the

DNA of my *son*. Clearly you two have been spending far too much time with an order that disrespects elvin genetics. They may have given you some uniquely powerful talents, Sophie, but I'm not convinced you won't later discover that their alterations have unanticipated consequences."

Sophie shared the same worry—but that wasn't what she needed to be focusing on at the moment.

"What kind of beast did you make?" she asked. "Or *beasts*, I guess I should say."

Lady Gisela's voice sounded almost dreamy when she said, "I call them my gorgodons. Part flareadon, for their flame resistance. Part gorgonops for their fangs. Part argentavis for their wingspan. And part eurypterid, for their stinging tails. Equally at home on land, in the sea, or in the sky—"

"Wouldn't that be a gorgentaveridon?" Fitz interrupted. "It seems like the argentavis and eurypterid should be in the name."

Lady Gisela sighed. "Clearly this is why you get along so well with my son."

Fitz shrugged. "Hey, it's not my fault you chose a stupid name—which also sounds too much like a gorgonops, by the way."

"Can we focus?" Sophie jumped in. "You're telling me you grew three mutant creatures—"

"Hatched," Lady Gisela corrected. "From fire. Weren't you wondering if the Everblaze had served some larger purpose? You don't get much larger than these."

"*That's* how you made the creatures?" Of all the theories Sophie had come up with, *mutant beast creation* definitely hadn't been one of them.

"That's how I *hatched* them," Lady Gisela corrected. "I'd started making batches of eggs years earlier, but could never find a powerful enough heat source to incubate them. I'd actually given up on the project, until Fintan suggested using Everblaze. We tried a controlled burn first, but the eggs needed the kind of heat that only comes from a true, out-of-control wildfire. And since Brant had already been planning a firestorm, we arranged ten of the blazes specifically for incubating and hatching."

"Ten," Sophie repeated. "I thought you said there were *three*."

"The process didn't go exactly the way I'd expected," Lady Gisela admitted. "Genetics are . . . complicated. Despite my careful research, the gorgodons are covered in argentavis feathers instead of flareadon fur. So once the eggs finally cracked, most of the hatchlings were consumed by the flames. Fintan and Brant were able to steer the fire away—and Ruy was able to encase his in a force field until the fires moved along. But the rest of us could only stand by as life was given—and then taken away. Honestly, though, that turned out to be an advantage. The gorgodons are *much* deadlier than I anticipated. They have venomous fangs, venomous talons, *and* venomous spikes on their tails—as well as the ability to fly, breathe underwater, scale walls, and camouflage themselves."

Grizel breathed a word Sophie didn't understand. But she did catch when Sandor mumbled, "Abomination."

"And yet you willingly put your life on the line to protect something just as unnatural," Lady Gisela told him.

Sophie should've been insulted, but she was too busy trying to picture what the gorgodons must look like. No matter which way her mind combined the various creatures, the end result was huge and horrifying.

Fitz—thankfully—seemed to be thinking more clearly.

"Hang on," he said. "The Everblaze attack happened way after Keefe's memory of you bringing him to Nightfall and using his blood to lock the facility."

"Yes, and I already told you, my gorgodons are a security measure I added later."

"But how did you get in without Keefe?" Sophie asked. "Or is that another memory you stole from him?"

"No. By the time the hatchlings were strong enough to be moved to Nightfall, Keefe had grown far too *uncooperative* to assist me—unless it was unwittingly. But all I needed was his blood. And he was so distraught after attending your planting, Sophie, that I didn't even have to convince him to take the sedatives."

Sophie's heart seemed to still. "You drugged him and stole his blood after my funeral?"

"No. I offered him what little comfort I could—a night of dreamless oblivion. And he took it. Gratefully. And begged for more the next day. And the day after that. Poor boy was *devastated*."

"We all were!" Fitz snapped.

"And that whole time, you knew we were alive!" Sophie added.

"Well, yes, but I couldn't exactly tell anyone that, now could I? Besides, your final fates were still very much undetermined."

Fitz wrapped his arm around her as Sophie's mind replayed the sickening moment when Brant had ordered both her and Dex's deaths.

"You're even more heartless than I thought," Sophie said, rubbing the knot of emotions in her chest, trying to keep them bound together.

"Said the girl who used my son's blood to hail me today."

"I'm not the one who spilled that blood!" Sophie snapped back.

"But you still took it. And used it. How very ruthless of you. No need to look ashamed. It's good to see there's hope for you yet."

"Hope for what?" Sophie asked, not sure why she was bothering.

Of course Lady Gisela told her, "Things you're still not ready to accept."

"We're getting off track," Fitz said, pulling Sophie closer. "If these beasts are running loose in Nightfall, how did the Neverseen get past them?"

"The gorgodons have one weakness—the same weakness that destroyed the other seven we hatched. Which was why Fintan and I had agreed that when Nightfall was ready for use, he would contain them behind walls of balefire at the only access point to the facility to ensure that no one could get in or out unless we wanted them to. I see no reason why he would deviate from that plan—especially since he has to be preparing for you to come after your family."

"And there's no other way to get in?" Fitz asked.

"No. The dwarves who helped me construct the facility took measures to ensure that no one would be able to tunnel in. You'll have to go in the usual way and sneak past the gorgodons."

"Or, let me go first and I'll go hunting," Grizel offered.

Sophie's stomach soured.

The gorgodons might sound terrifying, but killing them didn't seem right—especially since the creatures were only doing what they'd been bred to do.

The nausea grew when Lady Gisela told Grizel, "You'd be dead long before you ever swiped your blade. Sneaking past them is the only way to get through—and it's not as difficult as you're imagining. The trick is to hide your scent the same way I snuck into Havenfield to deliver my message."

"Ash?" Sandor guessed.

"From *Everblaze*," Lady Gisela clarified. "The flames leave behind different elements than regular flames, which gives the ash a quality that blocks other scents. Cover yourself from head to toe—don't miss an inch. You'll look ridiculous, and you'll be washing ash out of your hair for hours, but the gorgodons can't smell you as long as the ash is there. And make sure you bring extra to cover your family once you find them, otherwise they'll give you away when you try to sneak out. You'll also want to go in with as small of a group as possible. I'd advise against more than four—and I wouldn't recommend including a goblin. Their scent is much stronger than ours."

"You're not going without me," Sandor informed them.

"If you care about your charge," Lady Gisela told him, "you'll listen to me. I know you want to believe you can come up with some simpler way to do this, but I was *very* thorough when I designed this security."

"Assuming you're right," Grizel said in a tone that made it clear she was not happy about that assumption, "won't they be trapped in the same cage of flames holding the gorgodons?"

"Look for the flame that rises higher than the others—that one's always an illusion. It will be too narrow for the creatures to pass, but your group will have no problem fitting if you go one at a time."

"You expect us to walk through fire just because you're telling us it's safe?" Fitz asked.

"Yes. Because I need you alive. And if I wanted to kill you, why would I bother warning you about the gorgodons?"

"Fair enough," Sophie decided. "Once we're free of the corral, where do we go? Can you give us a map of the facility?"

"There's only one place Fintan would have your family. On the fourth level, I designed a special observation room."

Sophie had to remind herself to breathe. "Why are they being observed?"

"Any number of reasons. And worrying about them won't change anything. If you want to help your family, get into Nightfall and take them back. You'll be entering on the second level, so you'll only need to make your way up two floors. You'll reach the main staircase if you keep right in all the forks off the main corridor. Don't try to open any of the doors you pass—you'll trigger alarms. And never go to the left—you'll get hopelessly lost. None of this is a trick, by the way. I know how you think, and I know you don't want to trust me. But I need your family out of Nightfall just as much as you do. So stay on the main path, keep right, and once you take the stairs to the fourth floor, *then* go left. You'll know the observation room once you see it. It'll probably be locked, but Keefe's blood is a master key."

"What if we run into the Neverseen?" Fitz asked.

"I'm assuming you can handle them, given the havoc I've seen you cause. Besides, if I know Fintan, he'll assign Ruy to keep an eye on things in Nightfall and have everyone else out working on other pieces of his vision. Surely you can handle one Psionipath."

Fitz leaned closer to Sophie. "We should probably bring Tam."

Sophie nodded.

Tam's shadows could break through Ruy's force fields.

"So it'll be you, me, Tam, and Grizel?" she whispered back.

"Bad idea," a high-pitched voice said behind them, and they all flinched as Biana appeared in the corner. "If stealth is key, don't you think you should bring someone who can disappear?"

"Have you been eavesdropping this whole time?" Fitz asked.

Biana didn't look the least bit sorry.

Sandor sighed. "Where's your bodyguard?"

"Don't blame Woltzer. None of you would've been able to stop me from sneaking out either. Just like none of you could tell I was here, could you?"

"It's hard to smell anything beyond your brother's cologne," Sandor grumbled.

Biana grinned. "I keep telling him it's overkill."

"Hey, I like it," Sophie argued—cheeks flushing with the confession.

"I'll leave that one alone," Biana told her. "But you have to admit it makes way more sense for me to go with you to Night-fall than Fitz. I know he's going to use the 'we're Cognates' line, but what's more important? Mind tricks you're probably not going to need? Or someone who can do this?"

She vanished again, reappearing on the other side of the room.

"Can you even disappear when you're covered in ash?" Fitz asked.

"I can make my clothes vanish. Why would ash be any different?"

"You should test it before you go," Lady Gisela warned. "As I said, ash from the Everblaze is different."

"And where, exactly, are we supposed to get this ash?" Sophie asked.

"There's hardly a shortage. Just go to any of the firestorm sites that aren't buried in flowers at the moment."

Sophie sat up straighter. "Why not the ones with flowers?"

"Because I hear they're quite crowded with humans admiring nature's splendor, and I'm assuming you're going for discretion."

The explanation made sense—but Lady Gisela had hesitated half a second before she'd given it.

"What's the real reason you don't want us going there?" Sophie pressed.

"I'm not telling you to stay away. I'm telling you that if you need ash, that's the wrong place to look. There isn't any ash left."

"You expect me to believe you've removed all the ash from *twenty* burn sites?" Sophie argued.

"I never said I was the one who gathered it."

"So the Neverseen did?"

Silence was the only answer, which told Sophie enough.

"Do you know what flowers they're talking about?" Biana whispered to her brother.

"Quinlin found articles," Sophie explained, "talking about

a phenomenon the humans are calling the Extraordinary Efflorescence. A bunch of the fire sites are covered in rare wildflowers right now, and no one knows why."

"Why would you plant a bunch of flowers?" Fitz asked Lady Gisela.

"That information isn't part of our bargain," she told him. "And I hope you won't be foolish enough to let this distract you from getting yourself to Nightfall."

"Why?" Fitz asked. "What's in it for you?"

"I already told you—I need more information on what the Neverseen are doing there. Especially which doors—if any—have the runes illuminated."

"That's not part of our bargain either," Sophie reminded her. "And don't even think about threatening to withhold information on Cyrah for this."

"There's no need. Once you collect your parents, you'll be desperate to cut another bargain with me."

"How can you be so sure?" Fitz asked.

"Because if I'm right about what Fintan's been doing to them in Nightfall, you're going to need my help restoring their sanity."

THIRTY-EIGHT

RESTORING THEIR SANITY.

The words were too sharp—too heavy—too much.

They pressed in from every direction, squeezing and choking until everything inside Sophie seemed to shut down.

She was vaguely aware of Lady Gisela ending their conversation, and of following Fitz and Biana downstairs. Just like she knew she was now sitting on the living room sofa with warm arms wrapped around her shoulders.

But she couldn't focus on who was next to her or what anyone was saying. And the more her imagination ran wild, the more her mind wrestled with one heartbreaking question.

What was she going to tell her sister?

"Nothing," a familiar voice told her, and it took her eyes a second to focus on Mr. Forkle, who was standing in front of her, along with Fitz. "You say nothing about any of this until you're certain of what we're dealing with. And I apologize for violating the rules of telepathy again—but you've been staring at the same spot on the wall for more than an hour and I needed to reassure myself that you weren't having a mental breakdown."

"I feel like I might be," Sophie mumbled.

"How can I help?" Fitz asked, a deep crease settling between his eyebrows as he crouched down to her level.

Sophie shook her head.

She couldn't stop what was happening to her human parents until she found them—and even then, she couldn't change what had already been done.

The arms holding her hugged her tighter and she glanced over her shoulder to find Edaline there, with Grady beside her.

"I know how easy it is to slip into despair," Edaline whispered, "but try not to lose hope."

"We're going to fix this," Grady added.

Sophie closed her eyes, wishing she could feel even a drop of confidence.

"Want me to give you something to calm your nerves?" another voice offered, and Sophie followed the sound to where Livvy stood by the wall of windows.

"Is Amy here?" she asked, pulling away from Edaline to scan the room.

"No," Livvy assured her. "She's with Quinlin, wading through more articles about the efflorescence—and I agree with Forkle. Right now she's happy, and proud of herself for catching the details Quinlin misses. There's no need to worry her about any of this until we've made sure it isn't another of Lady Gisela's games."

"But Keefe's mom has been honest about everything else," Sophie reminded her.

"Has she?" Tam asked from where he hid in the shadows below the curved staircase. "Because it sounds to me like she's really only been honest enough to manipulate you."

"Mr. Tam is very wise," Mr. Forkle agreed. "And before you argue, I want you to consider this: Gisela is not an Empath. Nor is she a Telepath. Or a Physician. Which means she has nothing to offer when it comes to 'restoring your parents' sanity.' So I find it rather suspicious that she would make such a claim—especially since she knows that the mere mention of it will trigger this level of panic."

"But what if—"

"No," Mr. Forkle interrupted. "No 'what-ifs.' Try to wait until we have *facts*. And remember, our medicine can fix nearly any physical malady."

"Nearly," Sophie mumbled.

The word was just as unsettling as when King Dimitar used it about the soporidine.

So was the word "physical."

"She said 'sanity,'" Sophie whispered. "Physicians can't fix that."

"A Washer can," Mr. Forkle said gently. "Whatever trauma your human parents have suffered will be linked to their memories. So if we wipe those moments away, it'll be as if it never happened."

"But what about their emotions?" Sophie had to ask. "Those can't be erased, right? So all the fear they're feeling—"

"Will be dulled when we tie those emotions to replacement memories," Mr. Forkle interrupted. "We would craft stories that echo the same sentiments in far less traumatic ways. Like a memory of a minor accident in those dangerous vehicles humans love to drive. The process would be complicated, of course. But effective, too."

"Unless something triggers the real memories," Sophie reminded him.

"That would be a concern. We'd likely have to do what we call a 'reset' and erase every single memory your parents have made since the day of their abduction. We try to avoid those because it'll leave a blank spot in their past, and that can make their minds fixate and seek out the triggers. But as long as we're careful to ensure their new identities feel seamless with their previous stream of memories, they'll learn to skip over the gap. And I know how confusing and impossible this all sounds—but I've actually done it before. Twice. And I have no doubt I can do it again."

Sophie nodded, telling herself to be glad they had a way to wipe away anything painful from her parents' minds. But . . .

"This only works if you erase me again," she whispered.

"You were thinking we wouldn't," Mr. Forkle said. It wasn't a question—but somehow, it felt like an answer, snuffing out that tiny hope she'd been carrying.

"I thought they'd be safer if they knew they were in danger," Sophie admitted. "And I figured, if they knew that . . . then maybe they could also know me—not to live with them," she added, glancing at her adoptive parents. "Just . . . to visit, occasionally. I knew it'd be super complicated, but . . ."

Grady and Edaline tightened their hug.

"We'd love for you to have that," they both assured her, and Sophie's eyes burned.

But it didn't matter.

She'd do whatever it took to spare her parents from trauma.

"Hey," Edaline said, wiping tears off Sophie's cheeks. "Let's not get ahead of ourselves, okay? We don't know how any of this is going to work out."

"Exactly," Livvy told her. "I wouldn't be surprised if Gisela said that to distract you from the slip she made, mentioning the efflorescence."

"Me too," Biana agreed. "Didn't you hear how nervous she sounded after she said it?"

"She should be," Mr. Forkle added. "She all but admitted the Neverseen planted those flowers. So now we need to figure out why. Just as we need to learn more about this soporidine. Mr. Sencen sent over the report you requested a little while ago"—he held up a crunched-looking scroll—"and I'll admit, it feels like we're missing something."

He was right, both of those were probably related to much bigger problems they should be tackling.

And yet, she found herself asking, "Shouldn't we be planning our raid of Nightfall?"

"We have been," Mr. Forkle assured her. "A group will be heading to the facility late tonight, while anyone there is hopefully asleep, and you'll have the best chance of sneaking in and out without detection."

"I still think we should try to capture anyone from the Neverseen while we're there," Fitz muttered.

"I know. And I understand the inclination," Mr. Forkle told him. "It's the same difficult decision I faced when I rescued Miss Foster and Mr. Dizznee. But the more you complicate a mission, the more it reduces your chances of success. And the most important goal is to recover Sophie's parents."

Sophie wasn't sure if that was true—but she couldn't bring herself to argue. Even if it was selfish. Even if it was playing into the Neverseen's game.

After Lady Gisela's warning, she had to get her parents out of there.

"When do we leave?" she asked.

"We're aiming for midnight," Mr. Forkle said, "assuming we can gather the ash you'll need."

"And finalize who's going," Edaline added.

"I am!" Fitz, Biana, Grady, Grizel, and Sandor all said at the same time.

"In case you were wondering," Tam told Sophie, "they've been fighting over this pretty much the whole time you've been sitting there. The only things they agree on are that Forkle can't go because the Neverseen would find out he's still alive, and that I should be there. I guess we're taking on mutant beasts?"

"Which is why *I* should be going," Grady jumped in. "I've tamed all of these creatures in our pastures."

"It sounds like these beasts can't be tamed," Sandor argued. "Which is why you need someone trained to hunt."

"But that person also needs to be stealthy," Grizel corrected.

"This is the part where Biana reminds everyone that she can turn invisible," Tam added. "And then Fitz will snap back that vanishing only protects *her*, and that he can give you extra mental energy if you need it. And then Grady jumps in saying that if he's there, he can mesmerize any threat, in case Keefe's mom is lying. And Sandor reminds everyone that you're *his* charge and *his* responsibility and round and round they go."

"Not this time," Biana said, turning to Sophie. "I think I can prove why I'm the best choice—but only if Sophie feels up to enhancing me."

Sophie wasn't sure where Biana was going with that, but she pulled off one of her gloves and offered her hand.

"Wow," Biana breathed, disappearing the second their fingers touched. "I forgot how liquid the light feels. I don't even have to *try* to let it pour through me."

"Okay, but how does this make you so important?" Fitz asked.

"I'm getting to that." Biana's grip tightened on Sophie's hand.

Seconds crawled by—enough for Sophie's palm to turn clammy. Then Biana's vanishing spread across Sophie like invisible paint.

"Careful," Biana said as Sophie jumped to her feet—which she could no longer see. Her whole body was just . . . gone. "It's super easy to trip or bump into stuff, since you can't see where you are."

Tam snorted. "Good thing Sophie's not clumsy *at all*."

"I'll keep her steady," Biana promised. "And hang on—I want to try one more thing."

She must've grabbed Fitz's hand, because he faded out of sight a few seconds later.

"See?" Biana said. "I can hide two of us—plus myself. And Tam can hide in the shadows. So once we dull our scent with ash, our whole group will be totally undetectable."

"Can you really maintain the effect the whole time?" Edaline asked.

"I think so. Now that I know how to do it, it almost feels automatic."

"But you still don't know if the ash is going to affect your ability," Fitz's disembodied voice reminded her.

"Okay, so let's get the ash we need for tonight and test it," Biana countered, letting go and making both him and Sophie reappear.

"A wise idea," Mr. Forkle agreed, removing a blue-crystalled pathfinder from his pocket. "Think you're up to visiting a fire site, Miss Foster?"

"I'm sure she is," Livvy jumped in. "But you're not. And neither are you." She pointed to Sandor and Grizel before pulling out a blue pathfinder of her own. "We need a group that's more discreet—and Grady's ability should more than cover us. Everyone take off your capes. It's not going to take us all day to gather some ash, so I'm sending us on a detour. Let's see if we can figure out why the Neverseen have taken up gardening."

THIRTY-NINE

THIS IS AMAZING," BIANA BREATHED as their group trekked toward the rolling hills of color. It looked like someone had taken buckets of paint and splattered them across the narrow valley—and huge crowds had turned up to take pictures of the spectacle.

But gorgeous as the scenery was, it was all familiar flowers—nothing that stood out as special.

"Maybe they did something to the soil," Livvy said as she dug several vials from her satchel and filled them with the dusty earth. "I'm taking samples for the gnomes. And I think we should walk around a bit, make sure we're not missing anything."

"I wish the gnomes could come here," Grady murmured. "But there are *way* too many humans."

"Seriously. I've never seen so many camera flashes. Speaking of which, I don't suppose there's any way you guys can be less attractive for the next few minutes?" Livvy asked. "You're drawing almost as much attention as the efflorescence."

Fitz grinned—and a girl who'd been watching him tripped over her own feet.

"You guys have plenty of admirers too," Sophie had to point out, nudging her chin toward several adults who were snapping pictures of Grady and Livvy as if they thought they were celebrities.

"I think Tam's causing the biggest stir," Biana said, tilting her head toward an entire busload of schoolgirls who were shamelessly gawking.

"Great," Tam grumbled, pulling his bangs lower over his eyes—which only seemed to make the group swoon more.

"Be glad Keefe's not here," Fitz told him as they strode deeper into the field. "He'd be calling them over and making you pose for photos."

"Why *isn't* Keefe here?" Grady jumped in.

"I've been wondering the same thing, especially since he sent over that scroll," Tam said.

Sophie turned away, examining a patch of poppies as she whispered enough gruesome details about Keefe's injuries to hopefully end the subject.

"Okay," Tam said, "but this is Keefe. I can't see him actually sticking with bed rest. Especially when his mom's sending us off to play with her freaky pets."

"He doesn't know about the gorgodons," Sophie admitted, very aware of how closely Grady was listening. "And nobody's going to tell him, okay? Elwin said he'd have permanent nerve damage if he doesn't give himself time to recover."

"But Keefe knows you contacted his mom, right?" Tam pressed. "Or does he think you're waiting for him?"

"He knows I don't need him right now."

She kept her eyes on the vivid blue butterfly fluttering by, wondering if the flowers were meant to draw some sort of special insect, like how the splendors attracted the flitterwings.

But if that was the case, wouldn't all the flowers be the same?

And wouldn't there be a whole lot more bugs buzzing around?

"There's more to that story than what you're giving us," Tam pressed.

Fitz shrugged. "With Keefe there's *always* more to the story."

"Seems like you got the full-length version," Tam noted.

"That's because Fitz rushed over to Havenfield last night after Sophie got home," Biana told him. "And I didn't sneak along, in case you guys were wondering. I saw him packing up another special present and figured I could skip the mushiness."

Sophie's cheeks burned and she tried to blame it on the

scorching sun. But Fitz's gift *had* been especially sweet. He'd brought her a box of something he'd called pudding puffs—fudgey squares that tasted like warm apple pie mixed with melted vanilla ice cream.

And he'd baked them himself.

If her life wasn't such a mess, she probably would've been up all night replaying the look in his eyes when he'd given it to her—a mix of pride and concern and something she couldn't quite put her finger on that had made it very hard to breathe.

But now wasn't the time to be thinking about things like that.

"Where's Dex, by the way?" Grady asked.

"I don't know. He's being weird," Biana admitted. "I tried hailing him yesterday, to see if he wanted to come over and work on the caches without the triplets around, but he said he wanted to be alone. Has anyone else talked to him?"

"Not since Forkle's planting," Fitz said.

Tam nodded.

Sophie became very interested in another butterfly.

"Iggy's green now," Biana said slowly. "I remember noticing that while you were talking to Lady Gisela."

"Dex did that when he came over the other night, didn't he?" Grady asked.

Sophie nodded, and tried to get them all back to talking about the flowers. But Biana didn't take the bait.

"Why did Dex come over?"

"He . . . brought something for me."

"I'm not an Empath," Tam said. "But I'm pretty sure there are some weird feelings going on right now."

"Me too." Biana leaned in to whisper to Sophie. "Did you and Dex get into a fight? He said he probably won't be around until school starts."

"Did he?" Sophie asked, fighting the urge to tug on her eyelashes.

Biana glanced at Fitz. "Am I the only one who feels like I missed something?"

"Nope," Fitz, Tam, and Grady all said in unison.

"It's nothing," Sophie promised, picking up her pace. "Dex is just working through some stuff. He asked me not to say more than that. Sorry."

Livvy came to her rescue. "Linh's missing today too. Is she with Wylie?"

"Again?" Fitz asked when Tam nodded. "She spent the whole day with him yesterday."

"Does that mean you guys didn't meet up to search Candleshade?" Sophie had to ask.

"Nope—they dumped that on us," Biana told her, pointing to herself and Tam. "Not that we found anything."

"Except proof that Keefe's dad is even more ridiculous than my father," Tam added. "Do you know he has an entire room dedicated to himself, complete with a life-size statue made of lumenite? It *glows*, guys. I'm going to have nightmares about it."

"So did Keefe." He'd told Sophie he used to dream it was going to come alive and eat him. "Did Linh say how Wylie's doing?"

"Much better," Tam said. "I guess he was actually making jokes, and adding light tricks to her water tricks. And she said it looked like his dad was watching them."

"Prentice has seemed almost lucid," Livvy agreed. "If he holds this way for a few more weeks, I'll hopefully be able to convince the rest of the Collective to approve the healing."

"Weeks?" Sophie whined. "I thought you said *soon*."

"I know it doesn't feel like it," Livvy told her, "but that *is* soon considering how long Prentice has been waiting."

Sophie sighed.

"So what did you do yesterday?" Tam asked Fitz.

"Besides bake for Sophie?" he asked with a far-too-adorable smile that made it hard to focus on the more important part of his answer. "Oralie sent over the names of the goblins who used to work at Lumenaria, and two of them are still stationed in the Lost Cities. So my dad took me to meet with them, but all they could tell us is that they were given permission to use lethal force—which was never allowed with any other prisoners. My dad was going to head to Gildingham today to see if he could track down the others. I'll let you know what he finds out."

"Thanks," Sophie mumbled, wondering how they could be working on so many projects and somehow not making progress on any of them.

Maybe that was what happened when they didn't focus on one thing.

Or maybe the Neverseen were too far ahead.

"Is something wrong?" Grady asked, and it took Sophie a moment to realize he was talking to Livvy, who was studying a scorched bush.

Livvy pointed to the bright purple berries dotted among the blackened leaves. They were shriveled like raisins and didn't seem familiar until Livvy said, "These are slumberberries."

FORTY

T HESE ARE WHAT YOU USE TO MAKE slumberberry tea?" Sophie asked, plucking one of the berries and giving it a tentative sniff.

Livvy nodded, tearing off a branch and adding it to her satchel. "This bush must've been planted several months before the fires to grow this large."

"And humans don't grow them?" Biana asked.

"No. The gnomes hybridized them," Livvy said, glancing at the sun to check the time. "So we should search a few more efflorescence sites to see if we find any."

She led them deeper into the valley, until they had enough privacy to leap to the next site, which was less crowded—probably because it was *much* colder.

The icy soil crunched under their feet and a biting wind nipped at their ears as they searched the plains of vibrant flowers for slumberberries.

No one found any—but Sophie did discover the charred remnants of thick vines with singed, spiky teal flowers.

"These look like dreamlilies," she said, careful not to touch the petals. The caretaker at the Sanctuary had used them to sedate Silveny, and he'd warned her that the slightest touch of their pollen could knock her out.

"They *are* dreamlilies," Livvy said, plucking some of the blackened blossoms by the stem and adding them to her samples. "And they're another gnomish plant that shouldn't be here."

The next leap brought them to a forest of towering evergreens, with hilly meadows of flowers trailing into the trees. And tucked among the blackened trunks, Livvy found the remnants of dark red flowers she called aethrials. It took Sophie a second to realize she'd heard of the plant from Calla, when she'd explained how she'd cross-pollinated several plants to make a special vine for Sophie's bedroom, to give Sophie better dreams.

Calla had used dreamlilies for that too.

And they found the third flower Calla had used—lacy pink blossoms called sweetshades—at the final efflorescence site they checked, in a marshy area that made their feet squish with every step.

"So . . . they grew different plants in different environments and then burned them," Tam said as Livvy collected more samples. "And they all have something to do with sleep."

"It almost feels like an experiment," Fitz added. "Doesn't it?"

"But for what?" Biana asked. "To make a more powerful sedative?"

"I've made a lot of sedatives in my day," Livvy told them, "and fire has never played a role. And it doesn't explain why all these other flowers have popped up."

"Unless what they really did was change the soil," Grady said. "Or maybe it was about the ash, since that's what they gathered."

"Maybe. Or they could've been trying to get rid of any evidence." Livvy checked the sky. "I wish we had time to search more sites. But we still need to gather the Everblaze ash for tonight."

"Right," Sophie said, dragging out the word. "Tonight."

"You focus on Nightfall," Livvy told her. "I'll focus on this. I'll even let your sister help me test some of the samples to keep her involved with everything."

"Why does that pathfinder have paths to all of the fire sites?" Tam asked as Livvy adjusted the crystal again.

"Because my husband has investigated far more than I ever realized." Livvy's eyes looked sad as she held the blue crystal up to the light, revealing *thousands* of glinting facets.

Fitz whistled. "Pretty sure even my dad's blue pathfinder isn't that complicated."

"I doubt it is. But your father was often limited in his assignments, because he had a family to consider. Quinlin only had me—and I was never a concern. Not that it matters." She cleared her throat. "Is everyone ready?"

They locked hands, letting the warm tingly light whisk them away to a stark, empty field.

"That's a lot of ash," Biana noted.

Definite understatement.

Every inch of ground was white and powdery, and the hills in the distance were black and gray—as if the fire had leeched the world of all its color.

"Recognize it?" Livvy asked Sophie as she handed out sacks for them to gather the ash. "Or is it too hard to spot without the flames?"

Sophie's eyes widened. "Is this where you guys sent me with Gildie?"

Livvy nodded. "It was one of the steadiest fires, so it felt the safest—though we knew it was still a tremendous risk."

"This is where you bottled the sample of the Everblaze?" Grady asked, pulling Sophie close as she glanced at the sky, almost expecting to see a golden flareadon circling through thick smoke with a bottle clutched in her talons.

"This is where Sophie proved that she was willing to do what's right," Livvy corrected. "Even when it's hard, and scary, and sure to have serious consequences."

Sophie still had nightmares about that day—the way the smoke had choked off her lungs and the heat had singed her skin, and the wind had shifted, putting her directly in the line of fire.

The flames were gone now.

As was the smoke and the searing heat.

And yet, Sophie could feel the same paralyzing terror.

Because she may have stopped the fires. But she'd clearly missed something big.

And it was only a matter of time before the Neverseen would make them pay for that mistake.

FORTY-ONE

"SEE?" BIANA SAID, SHOWING EVERY-
one at Havenfield how easily her ash-covered arm
disappeared. "I can still vanish. Though, ugh, this
stuff is gross. It feels almost wet, doesn't it?"

"I think that's because it's cold," Fitz said, dipping his hand
into one of the sacks and frowning at the thick whitish-gray
powder that crusted his fingers. "It feels like it's made of ice."

"That might be the leftover Quintessence from the frissyn
they used to snuff out the fire," Grady told them, offering towels
to wipe off the ash. "Or maybe the nitrogen from the flames
themselves? They may even be reacting with each other."

"Could that be why the Neverseen wanted the ash?" Sophie
asked.

"I suppose," Livvy told her. "But it wouldn't explain why we found those gnomish plants growing there. Is Flori still living here? I'd love her to test some of these samples, since Calla was so familiar with these blossoms."

"Check the Panakes," Grady told her. "She's usually out there, singing to her aunt."

"You'll let us know if you find anything?" Sophie asked as Livvy headed for the door.

"Of course. Just like I expect a detailed update on Nightfall. See how I'm assuming you'll be back safe? Make sure you prove me right."

She ducked outside, and the epic battle of Who's Heading to Nightfall resumed with a vengeance. They agreed Biana should go, but Sandor, Grizel, Fitz, and Grady were determined to claim the final spot—and without Mr. Forkle there to moderate, the debate showed no sign of resolving.

Apparently, he'd leaped away not long after their group left for the efflorescence, and hadn't told anyone where he was going.

"I can't believe you're all fighting so hard to be a part of this," Sophie mumbled, removing her glove and testing the freezing ash. "You realize this is going to be miserable, right?"

"Probably," Fitz agreed. "But you'd do it for us, wouldn't you?"

"And protecting you is my job," Sandor added. "So everyone needs to let me do it. If Sophie will be enhancing Biana, she's going to need someone guarding her even more vigilantly, since she'll be without her gloves."

Unease sloshed in Sophie's stomach as she stared at her exposed hand.

"You're not the only one who can wield a sword," Grizel reminded Sandor. "And *I* don't have lumbering feet."

"*Or* we go with a stronger weapon," Grady countered, "and have Sophie enhance *me* if anyone comes near her."

"But Sophie might need extra mental energy to enhance Biana for that long," Fitz argued.

"Pretty sure they're going to keep this up until the moment we have to leave," Biana told Sophie, "and I just realized we're going to need to change." She waved her arms, and her flouncy sleeves made a loud rustling swish. "Do you have anything more fitted?"

"No idea," Sophie admitted. Both Della and Edaline had gifted her with a *lot* of clothes, but she'd barely had time to go through even half of them.

"We should check," Biana told her, "otherwise I can leap home and get us something."

"What about Tam?" Sophie asked.

Biana studied his outfit. "He should be fine if he ditches his shirt."

"Um, what was that?" Tam asked, crossing his arms across his chest when Biana explained her noisy-fabric concern.

"How about I wear my jerkin without the undershirt?" he asked. "If I go shirtless I'll freeze."

"I guess that would work," Biana agreed, heading upstairs to Sophie's closet and flipping through one of the *many* racks of tunics. "We should probably put our hair in buns so it's easier to cover our heads with ash. And I might as well wash my makeup off."

"Are you *sure* you want to do this?" Sophie had to ask.

"Why wouldn't I?"

"Uh, because it's super dangerous. And it's going to be miserable. And it's not like you even know my human family."

"I don't have to know them to want to help. Besides, I hate to break it to you, but just because the Neverseen came after your family this time doesn't mean they won't come after mine next—or any of the other people we care about. Look at what happened with Wylie. We're all targets."

She was right—but the reality of it felt like a huge stone being dropped on Sophie's back.

"Don't you wish we could build some sort of protective bubble and put everyone we care about in it?" she asked.

"I'd rather lock the bad guys up and keep our freedom. Here, try this." Biana handed Sophie a sleeveless black tunic made out of the kind of slinky, skin-hugging fabric that Sophie usually avoided. When she tried it on, it was even tighter than she'd been imagining.

"Oh, that's perfect!" Biana told her. "And stop crossing your arms over your stomach—you look fierce!"

Biana found a similar tunic in a dark gray and changed

into it before heading into the bathroom to pull back her hair. Sophie did the same, and the end result made them look like something out of a human action movie—though Sophie wished she had the muscles to complete the effect.

"Ugh, I'm going to miss my eyeliner," Biana whined as she splashed water on her face. "My eyes look so boring without it."

"You have *teal* eyes," Sophie reminded her.

Biana reached for a towel. "Said the girl with the eyes everyone's always talking about—and don't you dare roll them. When are you going to realize that brown eyes are amazing? It's—" She frowned at the counter. "What are *those*?"

Sophie lunged to snatch the crush cuffs she'd forgotten about—but Biana was much too fast.

"Those, um . . . they're to block my ability," Sophie mumbled. "The snaps put a force field around my hands to prevent anyone from actually touching my skin."

"Okay," Biana said slowly. "But that doesn't explain why they say *this*."

She pointed to the giant *Sophie Foster + Dex Dizznee*, and if Sophie could've jumped out her window and teleported away, she would've.

"That was camouflage," she tried. "Dex thought crush cuffs would be the least suspicious, since they're one of those things people wear all the time. And he thought they'd be easier to take off than nexuses."

"I guess that does make sense," Biana agreed. "But, then, why aren't you wearing them?"

Sophie had really been hoping she wouldn't think to ask that.

"I . . . told Dex I was worried it might cause . . . confusion."

Biana blinked. "Wow. I bet *that* was a fun conversation."

"It was pretty much the worst."

"So *this* is why Dex seemed weird when I hailed him, huh? Poor guy. I mean, I knew something like this was going to happen eventually, but—"

"You knew he—"

"*Everyone* knows, Sophie. You were the only one I used to wonder about. You can be kinda oblivious when it comes to this stuff."

"I'm not *oblivious*," Sophie argued.

Biana raised one eyebrow.

Sophie sighed. "I don't know why we're talking about this. We're supposed to be getting ready to risk our lives again."

Biana gestured to their outfits. "We're ready. And, I can still hear them arguing downstairs. Besides, this seems like . . . kind of a big deal. You okay?"

"I'm fine."

Biana didn't look convinced. "What about Dex? You guys are still going to be friends, right?"

"I hope so. He said we would. He just . . . needs a little space."

"I'm sure he does." Biana set the crush cuffs down and moved closer, wrapping an arm around Sophie's shoulder. "Well, if you ever need to talk, I'm here, okay? I can't believe you didn't tell me sooner."

"Dex asked me not to. And I figured I owed him that, even though I told him he had no reason to be embarrassed."

"He doesn't. But I get why he would be. It's not fun having to admit that what you want just . . . isn't going to happen."

She said it like she'd been through it, and Sophie couldn't help wondering if she was talking about Keefe.

She thought about asking—but if she was wrong . . .

"I guess this is just the process," Biana said, leaning against the counter and fidgeting with the crush cuffs. "There's a reason we get hundreds of matches to choose from, you know?"

She tilted her head to study Sophie. "Do you realize you always cringe when anyone mentions matchmaking?"

"Do I?"

"Yep. I know it's different than how you grew up, but it's really not as awkward as you're imagining. You'll see."

Sophie forced herself to nod.

"You *are* going to register, aren't you?"

"I don't know," Sophie admitted. "Is that bad?"

"Of course not," Edaline called from Sophie's bedroom. "It's your decision. And you have plenty of time to figure it out before you have to make it."

Sophie was pretty sure everything inside her shriveled and

died of humiliation—especially when Edaline peeked her head into the bathroom with a sheepish grin.

"I know I probably shouldn't have admitted I was eavesdropping—but I figured you would've come out and found me anyway. And I swear I didn't mean to. I came up here to see if you guys were putting on the ash—and if you needed help—and by the time I'd figured out what you were talking about, I'd already heard the most embarrassing part. Don't worry, I'm not going to make you tell me more about it. I'll always respect your privacy, Sophie. *But*, if you do want my advice—or just want me to listen . . . please don't be embarrassed, okay? I know talking about crushes with your mom sounds as fun as being chewed on by a verminion, but you might be surprised by how much I can help."

The only response Sophie was willing to commit to was "Maybe."

She also had to ask, "Are you going to tell Grady?"

"How about I leave it up to you?" Edaline offered. "If you want him in the dark, he can be—but don't blame me if he keeps trying to nudge you toward Dex. I've already told him not to do that and he still takes any chance he can get."

"Aw, that's kind of sweet if you think about it," Biana said.

"You wouldn't be saying that if it was your dad doing it to you," Sophie argued. "And I guess Grady should know—otherwise he'll make it a thousand times more awkward."

"Probably," Edaline admitted. "But just so you know, all

we want is for you to be happy, and choose someone who gets how amazing you are. I think that's why Grady was trying to encourage Dex, because he could tell how much Dex adored you."

"Ugh, even *Grady* knew?" Sophie asked, burying her face in her hands when Biana giggled.

Edaline wrapped an arm around her. "So do Kesler and Juline. Dex hasn't exactly been subtle. But I also think most of us suspected he was fighting a losing battle."

"This is getting worse and worse," Sophie groaned. "I have to go into hiding now, right?"

Edaline kissed her cheek. "Believe it or not, this will get easier. Someday, you'll be so sure of what you want that you won't care who knows."

"You sure about that?" Biana jumped in. "This *is* Sophie."

"I'm sure," Edaline promised. "And I'm betting Sophie's had about all she can stand of this conversation—and we should probably get downstairs and get you covered in ash. It's getting close to midnight."

Edaline sounded as nervous as Sophie felt, but they both kept their heads high as they made their way back to the living room.

"Are they seriously *still* arguing?" Biana whispered to Tam.

"Yup. You're going to have to settle this, Sophie," he said.

"How?" Sophie asked.

Biana clapped her hands and shouted for everyone to be quiet.

"Who here thinks that Sophie should be the one to pick who fills the last slot, since it's her family and she's the moonlark?"

"Hey, don't dump this on *me*!" Sophie whisper-hissed.

"Sorry, Miss Foster, but I agree," Mr. Forkle called from the doorway. "But before you choose, I have one other option you should consider. I kept asking myself if there was any particular special ability that would provide an advantage on this mission—and yes, Mr. Ruewen and Mr. Vacker, I know what your answers will be. But I came to a different conclusion—one I resisted at first, as I suspect you will as well. All I ask is that you hear me out before you make your decision. And can we all agree that whatever Sophie decides, we will respect it without further debate?"

It took a few seconds before Sandor, Grizel, Fitz, and Grady nodded.

Mr. Forkle strode into the room, pacing the length twice. "Looking at your group, you have stealth covered quite nicely. But you're lacking in the area of defense. And I realize that slot is usually filled by bodyguards, but in this case, that's not an ideal option. You need something unexpected, in case Lady Gisela conveniently forgot to mention something. Or in case the Neverseen are prepared."

He paused to clear his throat.

Then cleared it again before he added, "And since you'll be facing creatures that are only vulnerable to fire, your best defense is to bring a Pyrokinetic."

FORTY-TWO

A PYROKINETIC," SOPHIE REPEATED, certain she must have misunderstood.

But Mr. Forkle nodded—and the gravity of what he was proposing seemed to suck all the air out of the room.

"If you're suggesting that you trigger the ability in Sophie—" Grady started, but Mr. Forkle held up his hand.

"No, Mr. Ruewen. My team and I were extremely careful to ensure that Miss Foster could *never* manifest as a Pyrokinetic. We knew her life would be challenging enough without a forbidden ability. Pyrokinesis is also far too volatile to risk combining with anything else."

Sophie couldn't help a small sigh of relief.

"Does she still have more abilities you could trigger?" Fitz asked.

"*That* is a subject for another time," Mr. Forkle told him. "Right now, we need to decide if you're bringing a Pyrokinetic on this mission."

"Which Pyrokinetic?" Grady asked. "Aren't they all a little . . ."

"Unstable?" Mr. Forkle guessed.

"I was thinking more along the lines of 'out of practice,' since they haven't been able to use their ability in thousands of years," Grady told him.

"They're definitely that as well. And denying their natural talent has been far more of a struggle for them than most people realize. Brant and Fintan aren't the only ones who lost part of themselves to their constant craving for flame. So I would never recommend any of the Pyrokinetics in the registry."

"Then who—" Sophie started, before his words clicked. "Are you saying there's another unregistered Pyrokinetic?"

Mr. Forkle nodded. "Someone manifested recently, and I've been doing what I can to ensure their ability remains undiscovered. But they've agreed to reveal themselves and help with this mission, provided that all of you swear not to tell anyone. Not even Mr. Dizznee or Miss Linh can be let in on this secret without express permission from the Pyrokinetic. Is that clear?"

"Does the Collective know about it?" Sophie had to ask.

"No. Given the recent havoc wrought by Fintan and Brant,

people distrust Pyrokinetics more than they ever have before—even many of us in the Black Swan. And I know it's with good reason"—his eyes focused on Grady and Edaline before drifting back to Sophie—"and I echo many of your concerns. But I do struggle with the idea of any ability being completely denied. If we're willing to accept that every creature exists on this planet for a purpose, it seems only logical to assume that every ability does as well. They come straight from our genetics, after all. And any harm or heartache that pyrokinesis has caused in the past does not feel like proof that the ability is unredeemable—only that we need better training and systems to manage it. Think of Miss Linh, and the floods she caused before she learned to properly harness her hydrokinesis. Would any of us argue that she should've been forbidden from calling for water ever again?"

"Fintan wasn't a newly manifested, untrained prodigy when his craving for Everblaze led to the death of five of his fellow Pyrokinetics," Grady reminded him. "Nor was Brant when he murdered Jolie."

Edaline rested her hand on his shoulder. "But those losses might not have happened if Brant or Fintan had been taught proper restraint."

"Are you *defending* them?" Grady snapped.

Edaline took a slow, steadying breath. "Jolie did. I've read the journal she left. Twice. And it's clear she saw the best in Brant, right up until the end. She went there that day hoping to make him realize he needed help. And she understood the impossible situation he'd been in."

"And that mistake cost Jolie her life!" Grady practically shouted.

"I know." Edaline blinked her watery eyes. "But haven't you ever thought about how much it would've changed things if Brant had been afforded the same privileges that others receive when they manifest? If he'd had training and education from a stable, reliable Mentor? If he hadn't been told to deny who he was and forced to live with the brand of Talentless? Think of your own struggles as a Mesmer. Where would you be if Bronte hadn't shown you the treacherous path you were on—and spared you the consequences that you technically deserved for wrongly mesmerizing him?"

"The truth," Mr. Forkle added when Grady stayed silent, "is that many of our abilities have the potential for harm. And while some of us have rules and restrictions to keep us better in check, none—besides Pyrokinetics—are forbidden from using their talent. Our Ancient Councillors let their fear and grief lead them to be unduly harsh—and it has resulted in all manner of catastrophes. I don't know how to ensure that this new child will not be led astray by the power. But I do know that forbidding the ability *will* lead to ruin."

"Even if you're right," Sandor said—and it didn't sound like he believed that to be the case, "you're seriously suggesting we allow a brand-new, untrained Pyrokinetic into an enclosed fortress with what sounds like very few exits?"

"I'm suggesting we bring the person who offers us the best advantage. I've worked with this child personally. I've seen them demonstrate both impressive power and tremendous restraint. And if we know the gorgodons submit only to fire, it seems wise to have flames in our own arsenal—especially since there's a chance Fintan might be there."

"Pretty sure a newbie is no match for Fintan," Fitz pointed out.

"I don't expect them to be—though should the need arise, let's not forget that Sophie could choose to enhance the Pyrokinetic's ability. But Fintan would never expect us to have a Pyrokinetic on our side, so the first sight of flames would throw off his guard and give you a chance to subdue him by other means."

"And we're sure we can trust this person?" Sophie asked.

"Yes," Mr. Forkle promised. "You should also keep in mind that this Pyrokinetic has far more to risk by revealing themselves than you do for accepting them."

Sophie glanced at Tam, Biana, and Fitz. "What do you guys think?"

"I wish I knew who we're taking about," Fitz told her.

"Yeah, if it's someone like Stina Heks, that's a *whole* other thing than if it's someone like . . . I don't know—Jensi," Biana added. "And yeah, Stina already manifested as an Empath, but you know what I mean."

Tam nodded. "I never trust anyone until I read their shadow-vapor, so . . ."

Sophie turned back to Mr. Forkle, "Is there a way to meet the person before we decide if we should include them in the mission?"

He stroked his chin. "I suppose—but if I bring her in, I need your word that you'll protect her secret."

"Her?" they all asked at the same time.

He waited for them to promise before turning to address someone who must've been standing just outside the doorway. "I'm assuming you heard all of that? Up to you if you'd like to come in and join us."

Sophie ran through a list of names, trying to guess who might be about to walk through the door. But never in a million years would she have expected to see a pixielike girl with huge ice-blue eyes, nervously twisting one of the tiny braids scattered throughout her straight blond hair as she made her way into the living room.

In unison, Sophie, Fitz, and Biana gasped, "Marella?"

FORTY-THREE

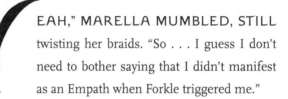EAH," MARELLA MUMBLED, STILL twisting her braids. "So . . . I guess I don't need to bother saying that I didn't manifest as an Empath when Forkle triggered me."

Sadness dripped off every word—and Sophie's eyes welled up. She knew how desperately Marella had wanted an ability that would help her mom battle her mood swings—and then to manifest *this* instead?

"You're really a Pyrokinetic?" she whispered.

Marella snapped her fingers, and a small tongue of flame appeared in her palm, dancing across her skin with flashes of red, orange, and yellow.

Everyone scrambled back.

Marella's lips twisted into something that was half smirk, half grimace. "Don't worry, I know how to keep it under control. But yeah, this is what I can do now. And apparently it's not going away."

"It's not," Mr. Forkle agreed. "Once an ability manifests, it cannot be switched off."

"That's the part that gets me," Marella admitted quietly. "If I hadn't forced him to trigger me—"

"I wouldn't be so sure," Mr. Forkle interrupted. "I may have given you a more powerful surge of mental energy than any of your Ability Detecting Mentors would have, but your pyrokinesis is *strong*. I can't imagine it would've stayed dormant."

Marella went back to twisting her braids. "I guess it doesn't matter. This is me now—in secret, at least. Officially . . . I'll have to be Talentless. No Elite Levels for me—but hey, who wants two extra years of boring sessions, right?"

Mr. Forkle rested a hand on her shoulder. "Change will not happen overnight. But you have a long life ahead of you, and it is my sincerest hope that the stigma will be lifted someday."

"Yeah, well . . . I'm not going to hold my breath," Marella told him.

"What was it like when you manifested?" Sophie asked to break the silence. "Did you know right away, or . . . ?"

"I thought I had a fever. So I took a few elixirs and went to sleep, hoping I'd feel better in the morning. Instead, I woke up in the middle of the night surrounded by flames. I bolted out of bed, thinking the house was burning down and I had to get my parents out. But after a few seconds, I realized the fire was only on *me*. And no matter how much I rolled around, it wouldn't snuff out."

"Did it hurt?" Biana whispered.

"No. But my brain kept telling me it *should*. Even now, when I look at this"—she held up her burning hand, letting the flames curl around her fingers—"I have to remind myself that my ability protects me. I wish I could say the same for my house. I scorched my room and part of the hall before my dad got to it with quicksnuff. And it was a good thing my mom was having one of her more clear-headed days and thought to tell the Emissaries that the fire was her fault. Of course they believed her, since it was 'Crazy Caprise Redek.'"

Her hand curled into a fist, snuffing out the flame.

"I'm sorry," Sophie told her, not sure if they were the right words. "And I'm sorry you had to go through that alone."

"I wasn't alone. Both of my parents have been way cooler about this than I ever would've expected. My mom stayed by my side the whole first day, in case I lost control again. And my dad went to the library in Eternalia to get any books he could find on pyrokinesis—not that any of them were helpful. The third night I woke up in flames, I decided to reach out to Forkle."

"I'd left her a way to contact me after I tried triggering

her," Mr. Forkle explained. "In case she ran into anything unexpected—though I never prepared for this."

"Me neither," Marella mumbled.

"Why didn't you tell any of us?" Biana asked her. "I know we don't hang out as much as we used to—"

"Uh, we *never* hang out," Marella corrected. "You all pretty much forgot I existed—until you realized my mom knew something about what happened to Cyrah. Then suddenly we were BFFs again."

"That wasn't the only reason," Biana argued.

"If you say so." Flames sparked to life across both of Marella's palms, and it took several slow deep breaths to snuff them out. "Sometimes my mood affects the ability," she admitted. "But Forkle's been giving me daily lessons for the last couple of weeks—"

"He has?" Sophie interrupted. "So, while we thought you were dead, you were—"

"Yes," Mr. Forkle told her. "The necessary secrecy of Miss Redek's lessons meant I could continue them, even before I felt ready to fully reveal myself to you and others. I realize my actions were far from ideal—but you already know why I delayed coming forward. Would you rather I abandoned Miss Redek during a time of dramatic adjustment?"

"No," Sophie begrudgingly admitted. But that didn't calm the anger bubbling in the pit of her stomach.

"Did you know we thought he was dead?" Fitz asked Marella.

"I had no reason to tell her," Mr. Forkle interceded. "But I filled her in before I brought her here tonight, since I fully expected this reaction."

"And I'm still not totally sure I get it," Marella added. "So . . . you were dead, but not dead, but still dead, and somehow also alive?"

Mr. Forkle winced, looking smaller somehow as he said, "Yes, I suppose that does sum up the situation. It's all very complicated."

"Most things are," Edaline agreed quietly.

"But how are *you* training her in pyrokinesis?" Grady asked. "I don't see what fire has to do with telepathy—unless having a twin brother wasn't your only secret."

"I have many secrets, Mr. Ruewen. But being a Pyrokinetic isn't one of them. And it's a good thing, because I would never be able to maintain the level of restraint that Miss Redek manages to hold. Nevertheless, you might be surprised by how many similarities there are between our abilities. Both require us to put barriers around ourselves in order to limit the power. And both can happen consciously *and* unconsciously. It's not a perfect fit, but it gives us a starting point to build on—and I'm hoping to eventually have her work with either a Guster or a Hydrokinetic, since there are stronger correlations between abilities that affect the elements."

"If you want a Hydrokinetic to help," Tam said, "why did you make me promise not to tell my sister?"

"I only made you promise not to tell her without Miss Redek's *permission*."

"I don't care if Linh knows," Marella said. "And I'll tell Dex at some point. But please don't tell anyone else. I can't end up on the Council's watch list. If they start monitoring me all the time, I'll never be able to practice—"

"That's starting to sound an awful lot like what Brant did," Grady interrupted. "I assume you know how that turned out?"

Marella paled. "Forkle's told me the story, yeah. But *that's* why I'm training. Denying the ability only seems to make it worse."

"And you're sure you can keep it under control in Nightfall?" Grizel asked. "Fear and adrenaline are powerful things, and you already lost your cool during this discussion."

"Only for a second," Marella argued.

"That's all it takes," Sandor snapped back. "One spark in the wrong place."

"That's why Forkle has me carry this." She pulled a fist-size pouch from under her shirt and loosened the strings to show them a green-toned powder. "It's a super-concentrated form of quicksnuff."

"A small sprinkle goes a *very* long way," Mr. Forkle assured everyone. "Kesler Dizznee made it, and we all know how brilliant his alchemy can be."

"I still think sending her to Nightfall is like lighting a fuse and tossing it into a room full of kindling," Grady warned.

"Then I suppose it's a good thing you won't be making the decision." Mr. Forkle turned to Sophie. "It's your call."

Sophie glanced at Tam and Biana. "What do you guys think?"

Biana chewed her lip. "Will you be able to hold my hand without burning me?" she asked Marella. "Because I can't turn you invisible without contact."

"Can you hold on to my wrist instead?" Marella asked. "My wrists rarely light up."

"Wrists work," Biana said.

"And her shadowvapor seems to be at a normal level," Tam added.

Marella glared at Tam's shadow. "Uh, I don't remember giving permission for a reading."

"You heard me say it was a deal breaker before you came in here," he reminded her.

"Fine—but don't push it, or I'll burn the bangs right off your forehead."

"Oh good," Sandor grumbled. "They haven't even left yet and she's already making threats."

Marella shrugged. "Now he knows not to mess with me."

Tam's answering smile seemed to say he was up for the challenge.

"So do we have a decision, then?" Mr. Forkle asked. "Because it's getting quite late."

"I have one last question," Sophie said, waiting for Marella to turn to her. "Are you *sure* you want to be involved in all of this? I know you got mad at us for leaving you out a while back—but I also remember you telling me that you didn't think you were cut out for dangerous things. And you won't get anything more dangerous than this. Especially since, if you use your ability around the Neverseen, Fintan may come after you."

Marella struggled to swallow. "Forkle gave me those warnings when he asked me to come here. And at first I was thinking, 'Uh . . . hard pass.' But then I thought about how I'd feel if my parents were trapped like yours are. And I knew you'd probably be willing to do anything to help me get them back."

"I would," Sophie promised.

Marella nodded. "So . . . might as well find out if the whole 'almost dying' thing is as miserable as you guys make it look, or if you're just being babies about it. Besides, what good is being able to shoot fireballs if you can't fling them at freaky beasts every once in a while?"

"To be clear," Mr. Forkle jumped in, "adding Miss Redek to the group will not change our original plan of using ash to sneak past the creatures, nor our aim to evade the Neverseen and focus on the most crucial victory."

"And you're not to create a single spark unless you're in immediate and inescapable danger," Sandor told Marella. "Understood?"

Marella's "Fine. Whatever" didn't exactly fill anyone with confidence—and Sophie could tell Sandor, Grady, Fitz, and

Grizel were all ready to go back to arguing that they should go instead.

But weren't people always saying you had to fight fire with fire?

She dipped her hand in the sticky, freezing ash and swiped a gray-white streak down Marella's arm. "Time to get ready. We're going to Nightfall!"

FORTY-FOUR

O I WANT TO KNOW WHY YOU have a blood-soaked piece of Keefe's cape? Or is that, like, a normal thing for you guys to have?" Marella whispered as their small ash-covered group shivered outside the massive silver door that Sophie had previously only seen in Keefe's memory.

Howling winds whipped through the night air, making the gray-white powder on their skin zing as if they'd been drenched in ice water. Sophie could barely distinguish their forms from the shadows and snow. The only thing that stood out was the faint blue flash of the starstone hairpin that she'd retucked into her bun after the leap—and the red-stained fabric in her hands.

The iron smell made her gag, but she sucked in a freezing lungful and reminded herself that Keefe was safe—which was more than she could say for herself at the moment.

"My theory is that Keefe made one too many jokes about Fitzphie, and Sophie finally threw him off a cliff," Tam told Marella, careful to keep his voice low.

"I could see that," Marella agreed. "By the way, how long has Fitzphie been official?"

Sophie choked on her next breath. "It's not."

"Seriously?" Marella asked. "Then what was with that hug?"

"That was just . . ." Sophie wasn't totally sure how to finish that sentence.

If she was honest, Fitz's goodbye hug had been a pretty big surprise—especially since she was already covered in ash, so he'd totally ruined his clothes.

He'd hugged Biana too, of course.

But . . . not for as long.

And he hadn't leaned down and whispered anything in Biana's ear—though all he'd said was that he wanted Sophie to be careful, and Biana didn't end up in the Healing Center as often as she did, so that was probably why.

Still, every time she thought about it . . .

Marella giggled softly. "Aww, I can see you blushing, even with the ash."

"I am not!" Sophie whisper-hissed.

"Careful," Tam warned Marella. "She might toss you off this ledge."

"I might toss both of you," Sophie told them.

Marella rolled her eyes—which looked especially huge now that her hair was swept back into a tight bun. "Are you afraid Biana's going to go all megabrat on you again because she's weirdly possessive of her brother?"

"I'm not *possessive*," Biana corrected, lowering her voice before she added, "I just don't like when people use me to get closer to him. I'm sure Linh knows how annoying that is."

Tam snorted. "Trust me, she doesn't."

"Doubtful," Marella whispered. "Have you seen you?"

Tam pulled his bangs over his eyes. "Yeah. I'm a twin. And a Shade. And a Wayward. And up until a couple of months ago, I was banished—sorta."

Marella shrugged. "You're talking to a Pyrokinetic, so . . ."

"Okay, can we focus?" Sophie asked, pointing to the door, which seemed to glint in the moonlight. "There are gorgodons waiting to shred us on the other side. And who knows what other fun surprises?"

She bent and patted the melder tucked into the top of her other boot, making sure it was still concealed. Sandor had insisted they each carry one—and he'd had Tam carry an obscurer as well. None of the gadgets could match the power of their abilities, but it felt good having a layer of technological backup. Just like it felt good knowing she had a flat packet of ash strapped to her stomach. They'd all worn them, to make sure they'd have enough for her parents.

Her parents.

Her brain wasn't totally ready to accept the fact that her family was somewhere beyond the massive door.

"Tam, can you start gathering your shadows?" she whispered. "And, Biana, can you turn us invisible? And, Marella—can you . . . do whatever you do to have some flames ready?"

"I *always* have flames ready," Marella told her. "Heat calls to me, whether I want it to or not. Why do you think I'm the only one not shivering right now?"

"Sounds intense," Sophie mumbled.

"It is. And just so you know, we're looping back to the why-do-you-have-Keefe's-blood conversation later—assuming we don't get eaten or something."

Sophie sighed. "First let's work on not getting eaten."

"Probably a good plan." Biana reached for Sophie's left hand, making them both vanish.

I'm going to open my mind to yours, Sophie transmitted to the group as Biana made Marella disappear and Tam shrouded himself with shadows. *And I promise I won't listen to any secrets you don't want me hearing. This is just so I can pass along any questions you guys have, so we're all able to stay in communication without talking and giving ourselves away.*

Does that mean we're ready to go in? Biana asked.

I am if you are.

Their responding *yeps* sounded as shaky as Sophie felt, but she moved toward the door anyway, tracing her fingers across the runes carved into the sleek metal.

The star only rises at Nightfall.

Maybe they were about to learn what the words meant.

Okay, she transmitted, taking a deep breath and reaching toward the sensor with the bloody scrap. *No sudden movements. And try to keep your breathing shallow. If all goes according to plan the Neverseen won't realize we're here until we're already gone.*

She didn't let herself imagine the million things that could go wrong—or think about Lady Gisela's warning about her parents' sanity. She grabbed on to her hope with everything she had and swiped Keefe's blood across the sensor.

No lights flashed.

No sirens blared.

And no snarling beast slammed against the door.

All Sophie was rewarded with was a soft click and the faintest whir of metal.

But when her fingers grasped the handle, she was able to gently turn the mechanism.

And slowly, painstakingly, she pulled open the enormous door.

FORTY-FIVE

*HERE ARE THEY?*

Tam was the first to ask the question—though Sophie could hear it forming in everyone's minds as dangling silver lanterns sparked to life one by one along the vaulted ceiling, revealing intricately carved white-stone walls lining a wide corridor that disappeared around a curve.

Nothing more.

No sign of the balefire cage Lady Gisela had promised.

Definitely no gigantic mutant beasts ready to devour them.

The elegant hall didn't even have the damp, musky scent that usually suggested animals were nearby. The air smelled dry, sterile, and ever-so-slightly smoky—but that might've been the ash coating Sophie's nose.

Do you think Keefe's mom lied about the gorgodons? Marella asked.

Why would she do that? Biana wondered after Sophie passed along the question. *She wants Sophie to tell her which doors have glowing runes.*

I don't see any doors so far, though, Sophie noted. The arched walls were nothing but solid stone, and the glittering white floor was perfectly smooth.

She glanced behind her, checking the door they'd entered through—which seemed to have sealed itself shut.

You don't think this is a trap, do you? she asked. *What if Lady Gisela's planning an ambush and made up the whole gorgodon story to make sure we'd come in a small group with no goblins to defend us?*

That's what I'm here for, Marella reminded her. *And if she made us crust ourselves with this disgusting ash for no reason, I'm going burn off all of her hair.*

Uh, guys? Biana chimed in. *I don't think she was lying.*

She dragged Sophie and Marella over to a section of the wall where three evenly spaced gashes marred the ornamentation. *Anyone else think these look like claw marks?*

Sophie traced her fingers along the jagged edge, realizing there were similar marks scratched into the floor a few feet ahead. And more on the ceiling.

Why does this not feel like good news? Tam thought.

Because it means they're still loose in the halls, Sophie told him.

She turned toward the shadows, searching for glowing eyes, or any other sign that they were about to become a midnight snack. She couldn't find anything—but Lady Gisela had warned them that the gorgodons could blend with the scenery.

So . . . what do we do now? Biana asked.

All of Sophie's instincts were screaming, *RUN FAR AWAY!*

But she reached down and checked to ensure that her melder was easily within reach in her boot before she transmitted, *I guess we head as quietly as we can toward the fourth floor and hope my parents are where Lady Gisela said they'd be.*

Preferably before the gorgodons find us, Tam added.

With that settled, they tiptoed down the hall, fighting back their screams every time a new lantern flicked on.

There must be motion sensors, Sophie transmitted.

Think there's any way to shut them off? Marella asked. *It's killing our stealth.*

The best solution they could come up with was to have Tam wrap the lanterns in shadows to mute all but the faintest hint of their glow—but it also meant they could barely see where they were going.

Every tiny sound blared through the facility, like Marella's slight "oof" when she tripped over another gouge in the floor, and when Tam scraped his arm on a jagged section of the wall. It felt like hours before they passed the first fork in the corridor—though it had probably only been a few minutes. And the hall split twice before they found the doors Lady Gisela had told them to watch for.

Side-by-side white double doors with runes carved into the top.

None of the runes were glowing.

And all of the doors were open.

Some were only cracked a sliver, but most had been pushed wide, revealing dark, dusty spaces.

Those runes mean "courage," Biana told Sophie, knowing her mind had only been trained to read the Black Swan's cipher runes. *And the door over there says "ingenuity."*

Think this has anything to do with the "criterion"? Sophie transmitted. *Keefe said Fintan was making him list qualities in people he'd want to save, and I bet they were things like this.*

But wouldn't Lady Gisela have labeled these doors long before that? Biana asked.

Good point, Sophie admitted. *Unless the criterion was part of her Lodestar Initiative.*

You know what's weird? Tam asked, thinning the shadows past one of the doors so they could see better. *These rooms are empty.*

They weren't always, though, Sophie noted. *Look at the dust patterns on the floor.*

Dark shapes on the marble formed the outlines of . . .

Furniture?

Equipment?

It was impossible to tell—but they found the same shapes in every room they checked.

Something feels wrong, doesn't it? Sophie asked when the hall split again, revealing more dark, open doors. It was like they'd stepped into one of those human movies where the rescue party shows up to a place that's far too quiet, and they slowly realize they've walked into a death trap.

It kinda feels like the Neverseen are moving out of this hideout, doesn't it? Tam asked.

Why would they do that? Sophie wondered. *They just lost a ton of hideouts. Plus, Keefe's mom spent forever building this place.*

Yeah, but they know she can find them here, Tam reminded her. *Or maybe they don't like having to rely on Keefe's blood to get in and out.*

Or the gorgodons got out of control, Marella suggested when Sophie shared what they'd been discussing. *Look at those gouged places in the arch. These things can chew through stone, guys. STONE.*

But it could just as easily be that the Neverseen are rearranging the facility, Sophie reminded them, forcing herself to cling to a more reasonable explanation. *Lady Gisela told us she made changes to the original plans for Nightfall. So maybe Fintan's advisor wants it back the way she designed it?*

That makes sense, Biana agreed. *Besides—who cares about these doors? That's not what we came here for.*

It's not. But Sophie still memorized each of the runes, hoping the translations would give them a better idea of what Lady Gisela had been planning. And when they rounded the next corner, they finally reached a flight of stark white steps jutting out of the floor at a steep angle.

Iron railings lined the edges, but they were bent and mangled, with gaps missing.

Looks like the gorgodons can chew through metal too, Marella noted. *Awesome.*

Still no sign of them, Biana said, and Sophie passed along her observation. *So the ash must be working. Or they're far away in another section of the facility.*

Or we're heading straight for them, Marella countered.

Sophie tried to share Biana's positivity as they began their climb, but the suffocating silence still felt too much like a warning. And the stairs were even steeper than they looked, leaving them huffing and puffing.

Remind me to get in better shape if I'm going to do stuff like this with you guys, Marella grumbled as they stopped on the third floor to catch their breath. *And let's hope all the sweat dripping down my back isn't washing off the ash.*

Sophie had been worrying about the same thing—and wishing they could just levitate to the next floor. But it would be too hard to keep themselves invisible while concentrating on a skill like that.

Looks like they cleared out this place too, Tam thought, thinning the shadows around them to reveal a wide room with a tall ceiling and lots of dust shapes on the floor.

Doesn't it kinda look like this was a storage space? Biana asked. *Look at how uniform the dust patterns are. They're all round. And all about the same size. And all in neat rows.*

Sorted into groups, Sophie added. *Looks like twenty different clumps.*

She worked the math in her head. Each group had twenty circles, so four hundred of . . . whatever.

Food for the gorgodons? Marella guessed.

Or ash, Biana suggested. *It could've been barrels full of everything they gathered at the efflorescence sites. Weren't there twenty?*

There were, Sophie agreed.

They should probably take a closer look, see if the floor had any sort of ashy residue. But straying off the path could lead to a trap, or get them lost. And once again, Sophie couldn't bring herself to lose focus on her parents.

We should keep moving, she said, starting up the next flight of stairs.

It felt even steeper than before—but that wasn't why her legs were shaking.

Any minute they'd find out if Lady Gisela had been bluffing about her parents' sanity.

Hey, Biana thought, tightening her grip on Sophie's hand. *Whatever's up there, we'll deal with it, okay?*

Sophie squeezed her hand back and counted her breaths, trying to keep them steady.

We're supposed to go left, she reminded her friends when they reached the fourth floor. And as soon as they stepped off the stairs, more lanterns flickered to life, illuminating a curved corridor that was narrower than the others, with walls, floor, and ceiling all made of cracked glass.

Anyone else think it smells funny up here? Tam asked. *It's . . . smoky.*

Sophie had been trying not to notice the same thing. *Maybe you guys should wait here.*

No way, Biana told her, dragging her forward.

At least this is the first corridor without any claw marks, Marella said.

She was right—until they passed the first curve. Then the whole hall was gouged and rutted, and parts of the glass were scorched and blackened with soot. The doors had even been torn off their hinges and left in jagged scraps littering the floor.

Not sure I want to know what happened here, Tam thought as they picked their way through the rubble, the broken glass crunching under their shoes. *But I'm guessing that's where the smell came from.*

Hopefully the fact that we're making all of this noise and nothing's trying to eat us means the gorgodons decided they didn't like hanging around here, Biana added.

Or they're on their way, Marella countered. *How much farther do we need to go?*

No idea, Sophie admitted. *Keefe's mom said we'd know it when we see it.*

And they did.

The path curved again and a new lantern flickered on, leaving them facing a huge glass bubble—a much larger version of the Exile cell Sophie had helped rescue Prentice from. It would've been the perfect cage for the Neverseen to hold and observe her parents. But the air in the bubble was cloudy, and the space inside was empty, except for something black-and-white piled on the floor—something Sophie's eyes recognized but her brain refused to accept.

She dropped Biana's hand, no longer caring about staying invisible as she sprinted for the bubble, desperate for a closer look.

"Never mind," Tam whispered. "That's where the smell is coming from."

From the pile of charred bones.

FORTY-SIX

I T'S NOT YOUR PARENTS," BIANA WHIS-
pered, pointing to the gruesome pile. "The bones are way
too big. See that curved thing in the middle of the pile?
That's a rib."

Sophie's eyes were too blurred with tears to make out much
of anything, but she managed to blink them into focus enough
to find what Biana was referring to.

"It's not them," Biana repeated. "I . . . think it might be
what's left of the gorgodons."

"So do I," Tam agreed quietly. "Fintan must've gotten rid of
them—which would explain why we haven't seen any—and
why it smells like barbeque."

"And why everything was so trashed out in the hallway,"

Marella added. "I bet the gorgodons wouldn't go down without a fight."

Sophie could feel the logic in their words, but she couldn't make her mind accept it. Not until she'd dug the piece of Keefe's cape out of the airtight pack and swiped more blood across the glass bubble's sensor.

Gears whirred to life where the bubble met the arched ceiling, making a noisy hum like a cheap fan as the glass separated down the middle and slid apart, releasing a plume of smoky air that smelled so strongly of cooked meat and rotting flesh that the stench left them coughing and gagging.

Sophie pressed her ashy arm over her nose and mouth and stumbled into the bubble to sort through the bones, which were even bigger up close—and many didn't match human anatomy.

Still, she kept digging all the way to the bottom, making sure there weren't any smaller bones buried underneath.

"Okay," she said, collapsing to her knees. "Okay, it's not them."

She'd needed to say the words out loud. Needed to have them slide across her tongue to believe them.

But that led to a terrifying new question.

Where are they?

She hadn't realized she'd opened her mind and transmitted the words until Biana whispered, "I'm sure they're somewhere else in the facility. Otherwise why would your sister have heard the Neverseen say they were taking your parents to Nightfall? It's probably like you said, the Neverseen are moving things around, making it match their original plans. If we keep looking, I know we'll find them—and now we don't even have to worry about the gorgodons."

"Yeah. We just have to worry about the Pyrokinetic who decided to burn them alive," Marella mumbled, backing away from the bones.

Biana pulled Sophie back to her feet. "We should get away from here in case opening the bubble alerted the Neverseen."

She dragged Sophie back into the hallway, and Sophie leaned against the gouged wall, sucking in huge gulps of the fresher air and trying to think.

"If we're going to search this place, we have to be smart about it," Tam whispered. "We can't afford to get lost."

"Can you do that Telepath trick?" Biana asked Sophie. "The one you do when we play base quest, where you track people's thoughts to home in on their location?"

Sophie's head cleared with a fresh rush of hope. "I can try—but I won't be able to enhance you while I do it."

"That's fine—we're visible now and it's not setting off any alarms," Biana reminded her.

"I can shroud us in shadows," Tam added. "And we have the obscurer."

With that settled, Sophie rushed to the stairs, needing a better view of the facility to get a feel for the layout.

She sank onto the first step, pressing her fingers against her temples and closing her eyes as she stretched out her consciousness, pushing it in every direction at once and feeling for any sign of life. It helped to imagine her mind as a veil, slowly draping over every inch.

But everything was cold, quiet, and empty, and the longer she worked, the more a headache flared.

"You okay?" Biana asked.

"I think the enhancing drained me more than I realized," she admitted, sucking in air to stop her head from spinning, spinning, spinning.

"Here," Tam said, and she cracked open her eyes to see his shadow falling over her face. "Does that help?"

"Wow," Sophie breathed as cold darkness flooded her mind, making everything hum.

It was a new kind of energy, heavier than she was used to, sinking down, down, down, dragging her consciousness with it as it spread like ink until—

"I feel something," she whispered. "It's weak. And I can't pick up any thoughts. Just a pulse of life. But it's definitely *there*."

"Where?" Tam asked, helping her back to her feet.

"Somewhere below us. That's as much as I can tell—but I might be able to keep the connection if you guys guide me, so I can keep my eyes closed and concentrate."

"On it," Biana said, wrapping Sophie's arm around her shoulder and leading her down the first step.

"Are we sure this is a good idea?" Marella asked when they nearly toppled over.

"It's fine," Biana said. "We just need to find a rhythm—see?"

The next step went a little smoother. And the one after that.

"No, that's not what I meant," Marella argued. "Couldn't we be tracking the Neverseen right now?"

"It's possible," Sophie admitted. "All I know is that there's someone there. But I have no idea who or how many."

"Or maybe it's *what*," Marella reminded her. "It could be one of the gorgodons. It was hard to tell how many were part of that pile of bones."

Sophie hadn't thought of that.

"Well . . . either way, we have to check," Biana said, guiding Sophie down another stair. "If it's a gorgodon, we're already prepared for that. And if it's the Neverseen, we'll find a way to deal with them. But hopefully it's Sophie's parents and we can grab them and get out."

They moved in silence, step by step, until they made it back to the level they'd entered on.

"But it's still farther down," Sophie whispered.

Marella whimpered. "It looks really dark down there."

"Hopefully some lanterns will kick on," Biana told her.

It didn't sound like they did—though Sophie couldn't tell with her eyes closed.

She was so focused on following the pulsing energy that she nearly lost her balance when the next step was flat ground instead of another stair.

There has to be a way." Sophie repeated the words in her head until they drowned out her other needling doubts.

She turned to Tam. "Can you break through the force field so we can get to him?"

Tam nodded, letting his shadow stretch toward the wall of flashing energy. The darkness sank into the milky light, fanning out in thin threads that crawled through the brightness like ink in water. And bit by bit, the force field unraveled.

Sophie froze, waiting to see if Alvar would react, but he stayed silent and still—even when she got close enough to nudge him with her toe. She tried to open her mind to his thoughts, but all she found was sludgy black. So she pulled her gloves on and tried to lift him by his shoulders.

"Someone take his legs. We need to get him back to the exit."

They couldn't light leap through solid stone—at least not with normal light.

"You Foxfire people always forget the obvious," Tam told her, floating Alvar's body off the ground. "Remember telekinesis?"

Sophie's cheeks burned. "Right. I guess that's smarter."

Then again, watching Alvar's bleeding, unconscious body float down the hall would surely become a recurring feature of her nightmares.

"Where are we taking him after this?" Tam asked as they followed him through the maze of corridors.

"Not Everglen," Biana told him. "Or anywhere near my family."

"The rune says 'rejected,'" Tam whispered.

The four of them exchanged a look.

"I'll go check it out," Biana told them. "That way Tam can keep you guys covered with shadows."

Sophie wanted to protest, but Biana had already turned invisible and started down the hall.

Scream if you need help, she transmitted.

Uh, if you hear me scream—run! Biana countered.

"I don't know how you guys do this kind of stuff all the time," Marella mumbled, leaning against the wall. "I feel like I've sweated out a year of my life."

So did Sophie.

Especially as she watched the door creep open, pulled by Biana's invisible hands.

A sharp gasp shattered the silence, and Biana blinked back into substance, shaking her head and stumbling back.

"What?" Sophie asked, already charging through the doorway, into a room divided by a glowing white force field that stretched from the ceiling to the floor.

A bound, unconscious figure lay trapped on the other side, dripping blood on the stones.

His face was swollen and bruised, his eyes were closed, and his chest was slashed and gouged.

But Sophie still recognized him.

Alvar.

FORTY-SEVEN

I S HE . . . DEAD?" MARELLA WHISPERED, squinting to get a better look at Alvar's still form.

"I wouldn't have been able to feel him if he was," Sophie reminded her.

She'd lost the connection now, which made her wonder if the strange shadowy energy Tam had given her was the only way her telepathy could pass through the force field.

"He's breathing," she added, watching Alvar's wounded chest make the shallowest of dips.

Biana turned away, covering her mouth like she was about to be ill, and Sophie wrapped her arm around her, struggling to figure out what to say.

Alvar had betrayed them—but he was still Biana's brother.

And he'd clearly gotten himself in *serious* trouble.

"We were supposed to find your parents," Biana whispered.

"I know." The tears Sophie was fighting choked off her voice. "But your brother—"

"I don't care about him," Biana interrupted. "Are you sure your parents aren't somewhere else in the facility? I think you should check."

"I mean it," she added when Sophie hesitated. "He helped capture them, remember? So just forget about him and let's see if we can still fix this."

"Biana," Sophie tried.

"Please," Biana begged. "I can't deal with him until we find your family."

Sophie had a horrible, sickening feeling they wouldn't have a choice. But she sank down on the rough floor and closed her eyes, letting her mind go blank before she pushed out her consciousness and made it drift through the facility like a soft breeze.

Sweat licked down the back of her neck, and her head throbbed from the strain—and all she found was cold, silent emptiness. She even asked Tam to boost her with shadows again, in case that really was the trick to sensing past Ruy's force fields.

"They're not here," Sophie finally had to admit, reaching up to rub her pulsing forehead, glad she had something to do with her hands. It eased the urge to punch the floor. "The Neverseen must've packed up what they wanted, killed the gorgodons, and ditched this place."

"Why would they do that?" Marella asked.

"No idea," Sophie admitted.

What if her parents were . . .

She clamped down on the thought, crushing it like the cruel little bug that it was.

Her parents had to be alive. The Neverseen would never destroy such a powerful bargaining chip.

She needed to focus on smarter questions, like: *How were they going to find them?*

They could ask Lady Gisela, but her help wouldn't come free. And Keefe's mom probably didn't know anything useful. Nightfall was her legacy—and the Neverseen had stripped it bare and slaughtered her precious creatures.

But what other leads did they have?

Her eyes strayed to Alvar, watching him take another shallow breath. Bonds tore into his wrists and ankles, and his body was covered in bruises. But the deep, curved gashes were what held her attention.

"They cut Alvar with a shamkniv," she said, explaining what she knew about the weapon.

"So they must've kicked him out of their order," Tam noted.

"Or that's what they want us to think," Biana warned. "They had to know we'd come here—so maybe they left him like this to trick us into taking him. They could be setting the same trap they used with Gethen."

"I dunno," Marella told her. "He doesn't look like he can last much longer. Maybe they thought he'd be dead by the time we got here?"

"Or they knew we'd be extra suspicious after Lumenaria, so they left him this battered to make us feel sorry for him," Biana countered.

Both were viable explanations.

But it didn't matter.

"Even if it's a trick, we can't leave him here," Sophie decided. "He might know something about where they took my parents, or what the Neverseen are up to with the ash and the efflorescence. I know it's a huge risk—but it's still our best option at this point. And he can't fool us if we're on to the game, right?"

"Unless there's more than one game," Biana reminded her.

"So we take the player off the field, or . . . I'm losing track of this metaphor." Sophie rubbed her pulsing temples. "All I'm saying is, we can make sure that Alvar has no access to anyone or anything that's even remotely important. Then it won't matter if the Neverseen have plans for him. Okay?"

Biana stared at her brother. "As long as you don't expect me to trust him."

"None of us are going to trust him," Sophie assured her. "We're just going to get him strong enough so I can search his memories and see what he knows."

"What if they wiped his mind, to make sure he couldn't help us?" Marella asked.

"Then I'll ask Mr. Forkle how to trigger the erased memories.

There has to be a way." Sophie repeated the words in her head until they drowned out her other needling doubts.

She turned to Tam. "Can you break through the force field so we can get to him?"

Tam nodded, letting his shadow stretch toward the wall of flashing energy. The darkness sank into the milky light, fanning out in thin threads that crawled through the brightness like ink in water. And bit by bit, the force field unraveled.

Sophie froze, waiting to see if Alvar would react, but he stayed silent and still—even when she got close enough to nudge him with her toe. She tried to open her mind to his thoughts, but all she found was sludgy black. So she pulled her gloves on and tried to lift him by his shoulders.

"Someone take his legs. We need get him back to the exit."

They couldn't light leap through solid stone—at least not with normal light.

"You Foxfire people always forget the obvious," Tam told her, floating Alvar's body off the ground. "Remember telekinesis?"

Sophie's cheeks burned. "Right. I guess that's smarter."

Then again, watching Alvar's bleeding, unconscious body float down the hall would surely become a recurring feature of her nightmares.

"Where are we taking him after this?" Tam asked as they followed him through the maze of corridors.

"Not Everglen," Biana told him. "Or anywhere near my family."

"Same goes for Havenfield and my parents," Sophie added. "And Dex's house. And the Councillors' castles in Eternalia. And we don't want him anywhere near my sister, so Atlantis is out— and we have to keep him away from Wylie and Prentice, too."

"I don't think we should lock him away in Exile, either," Tam said. "In case they're planning a prison break. And they could be hoping we'll take him to one of the Black Swan's hideouts, so those are all off-limits."

"Which leaves us with where?" Marella asked.

Sophie bit her lip. "Well . . . what about bringing him to your house? They have no idea you're working with us now, so there's no way that would be part of their plan."

"I guess that's true." Marella dragged out the last syllable. "But . . . his injuries would freak out my mom. Sorry, I know—"

"It's fine," Sophie assured her. "You're right. Bad idea. I was just thinking out loud."

They'd reached the stairs by that point, and Sophie noticed Tam gritting his teeth as he floated Alvar up.

"Here," Biana said, letting her mind take control—and smacking Alvar's body against the metal railing in the process.

"That was an accident," she insisted.

But a few minutes later she banged his shoulder.

Then his head.

"What about Foxfire?" Marella suggested, getting back to the bigger question. "Maybe keep him in the Healing Center and let Elwin treat his wounds?"

"And risk that Alvar does something to the school?" Sophie countered. "No way."

"I think the real answer is that we need to hide him somewhere new," Tam said as they turned down the final hall. "We should set up a cell in the middle of nowhere. I'm sure the Black Swan would help."

"But what do we do with him while they build it?" Sophie asked.

Tam mumbled his reply, and Sophie had to ask him to repeat it.

"I said my house would work."

Sophie shook her head. "We can't have him around Tiergan— especially with Tiergan's connections to Wylie."

"I didn't mean where I'm staying now," Tam corrected. "I meant . . . Choralmere."

Biana stopped walking. "You want to bring him to your parents' house?"

"Not *want*," Tam corrected. "But . . . the Neverseen wouldn't expect it."

He had a point.

"Do you even have a way to get there?" Biana asked.

Tam squatted and peeled back the thick sole of his boot, removing a small round pendant from the heel. "I stole my home crystal when I left with Linh, in case either of us ever got seriously hurt and we needed a way to get back to the Lost Cities for help."

"I can't believe you had to think about stuff like that," Sophie said quietly.

When she'd been banished, she'd headed straight for the Black Swan and let them take care of her.

"You're really sure you want to do this?" she had to ask as Tam stomped down the sole of his shoe and stood.

Tam nodded. "Why not? Time to give my parents a little payback."

FORTY-EIGHT

CHORALMERE SAT NESTLED BETWEEN the edge of a rainforest and a pristine cove, where turquoise waves lapped against the silvery shore. A gray stone path lined with glowing golden orbs stretched across the smooth sand to the main entrance of the massive house, which was even more elegant and auspicious than Sophie had been imagining.

Tiers of golden roofs crowned the square towers that formed the four corners of the outer wall—all of which had been built with blocks of crystal and garnet and amber. And three massive inner towers jutted from the center of the interior courtyard, made from the same sparkly bricks, but also decorated with gilded moldings and balconies around every window. Strings of gleaming golden lanterns tied all of the structures together, and lacy treetops peeked out of the center, hinting at a lush inner atrium.

But what truly stood out were the sounds drifting through the warm night air. Hundreds of wind chimes rang from somewhere within the courtyard, blending with a cacophony of soft whistles created by the long metal tubes lining the eaves. Paired with the crashing surf and the rustling palm trees, it felt like they were surrounded by an ever-changing symphony.

"Yeah, I know," Tam said when he noticed Sophie's and Biana's wide-eyed stares. "Now you see why my parents refused to leave this place."

"What do you mean?" Biana asked, unpinning her bun and unraveling her ashy hair.

Sophie did the same, noticing for the first time how hard her hands were shaking. She tried to channel that anxious energy into her legs, keeping them moving forward. That was the goal right now—don't stop, don't think, don't panic.

She'd given Marella the starstone hairpin and sent her back to Havenfield so that Tam's parents wouldn't know she was connected to the Black Swan—and so Marella could have the Collective send Livvy to help with Alvar's injuries.

Tam kicked the edge of one of the path's stones. "Well, a beachfront house isn't exactly an ideal location for a newly manifested Hydrokinetic. So when Linh started having problems, some of the Councillors suggested my parents move somewhere drier. But my mom said she'd be lost without the sounds of the sea. Apparently that was more important than her daughter—though of course she claimed it was Linh's fault for not trying harder to control her ability."

Sophie shook her head, not sure how she would face his parents without shouting at them.

Biana tugged at the tangled strands of her hair. "Sometimes I hate myself for not realizing our world can be so unfair."

"You aren't the only one," Tam reminded her. "And it's not like you had anything to do with what happened. The Council made the choice—and my parents didn't resist."

"I guess. But . . . my family's a part of it. 'The Vacker legacy'?" She made air quotes with the words. "I don't know what Alvar meant by that—but it's made me really think about what it means to be related to one of the founding members of the Council. All these decisions we keep questioning, like the prejudice against multiple births and the ban on Pyrokinesis? Those are all things Fallon probably decided."

"Even if you're right, he didn't make those decisions alone," Tam reminded her. "There were other members of the Council who had to agree—and there've been lots of other Councillors since then who haven't felt the need to change anything."

"I know," Biana mumbled. "But . . . some of them were part of my family too, along with tons of the nobility. And all my life, I've had everyone treat me like I'm special because of it— because I'm a *Vacker*. But maybe the Vackers aren't as awesome as everyone thinks. Maybe we've messed up the world."

She pointed to her unconscious brother, who looked so pale as he hovered between them that Sophie almost wondered if they hadn't shielded him well enough during the light leap.

"You can't change who you are, or who your family is," Tam told her. "Believe me—if I could, I would. All you can do is make sure you're living by what you believe in."

"I guess." Biana looked away. "Sorry. I didn't mean to make this about me. Is Linh going to be mad at you for bringing us here?"

"Not *mad*," Tam said. "But I need to hail her as soon as we get Alvar settled and let her know what's going on."

"You're sure you're okay with this?" Sophie had to ask. "We can find somewhere else."

"It'll be fine," Tam promised, taking a long look at the house before he started moving forward again. "Besides, I'm pretty sure we're about to give my parents a panic attack, so that'll be fun."

His smile looked forced as he led them to the gilded front door and started pounding hard enough to rattle the wall. He didn't stop, even when the windows blared with sudden light.

"All right!" Tam's father shouted. "I'm coming! What kind of—"

The rest of his outburst morphed into a gasp as he threw open the door. His black hair was sticking out on one side of his head and smashed down on the other, and his silver-blue eyes were puffy with sleep.

"Try not to look so happy to see me," Tam said as he shoved his dad aside and marched into the house.

"What's the meaning of this?" his dad barked, tripping over his silky black robe as he scrambled to get away from Alvar's floating body. "What have you done?"

"Nothing," Tam told him, motioning for Sophie and Biana to follow him. "But thanks for assuming the best of me."

"You show up at my door in the middle of the night with a floating body, while you and your friends are covered in silver paint—"

"Ash," Tam corrected, shaking his arms and sending silver-white flecks flying all over the spotless gold floor.

"Well, congratulations," his father told him, slamming the door so hard the chandelier trembled. "You found something that looks more idiotic than your bangs."

"Quan?" a female voice called from down the hall. "Who are you talking to?"

"It's nothing, Mai," Tam's father called back to her. "Go back to bed, my love. No need to trouble yourself with this."

"Trouble myself with what?" Mai asked, her voice much closer.

Tam went rigid when his mother peeked into the room.

Her ebony hair hung in two loose plaits, and her cheeks were flushed pink, like her daughter's—until she spotted her son. Then all color drained away.

"Tam?" she whispered, clutching the ends of her blue flowery robe as she stepped closer. "Where's Linh? And why are you filthy? And why—"

She screamed when she noticed Alvar behind him.

Lots of shouting followed, with both of the Songs demanding different answers. But Tam told them nothing as he floated Alvar down the mirror-lined hall. All Sophie and Biana could do was follow.

They passed a series of gilded fountains filling the air with rippling gurgles, until they reached the house's inner courtyard, where thousands of glowing wind chimes cast a soft light as they swayed from the branches of flowering trees. Beneath the canopy, urns of lacy plants lined a series of reflecting pools filled with colorful fish and crowned with wide, flat lily pads. It was breathtaking and peaceful, the kind of space Sophie would normally want to spend hours in. But all she could think about was how the extra water must've amplified Linh's struggles.

"So where exactly are we going?" Biana asked as Tam tossed open the arched doors to one of the towers and started up a flight of jeweled steps.

"To my mom's favorite room, because when I annoy—I annoy *hard*."

"Stay out of your mother's studio!" his dad yelled behind them.

"Can't stop me!" Tam shouted back.

"It's fine," his mom said as she ran to catch up to her son. "Use whatever room you need. Just tell me what's going on."

Tam ignored her, climbing all the way to the top floor, which was so high up, the air had turned mostly silent. The only thing waiting for them was a pair of stained-glass doors.

Mai grabbed Tam's arm as he reached for the handles. "This"—

she shuddered as she took a glance at Alvar—"is the Vacker boy, right? The one I hear has been working with those awful people?"

"Yeah," Tam admitted as Biana slouched lower. "And no one can know where he is, okay? We needed to stash him somewhere unexpected, and everyone knows this is the *last* place I'd go, so . . ."

Mai flinched.

Tam pretended not to notice as he yanked open the doors and snapped his fingers to turn on the thin strands of twinkling lights that stretched across the enormous, hexagonal room. Sophie had been expecting the "studio" to be for recording music, but it turned out to be an artist's dreamland. Each angled wall was dedicated to a different medium—watercolor, sculpture, ink, charcoal, colored pencils, and something that involved tiny glass pieces. Floor-to-ceiling windows divided each "station," and twinkling moonlight streamed through the square skylights.

"Is that Linh?" Biana asked, frowning at a painting-in-progress of a smiling teenage girl with black hair and silver eyes. The resemblance was there, but certain details were off—the lips were too thin and the cheeks were slightly too wide, and the silver touches were noticeably absent from the ends of her hair.

"It's my best attempt," Mai said quietly. "The only way I get to see her."

Tam snorted. "I notice there isn't one of me."

"No?" Mai flicked her wrist and used telekinesis to spin the canvas around. "It's hard to capture your intensity," she admitted. "But I did my best."

She looked so small—so sad. It almost made Sophie feel sorry for her—until she remembered the scraggly tents that Tam and Linh had been forced to squat in for *years*. She also noted that Mai had conveniently left Tam's silver bangs off the portrait. And she'd painted it in a way where she'd only see one of her twins at a time.

"Here," Mai said, rushing over to the round table in the center and sweeping the rolls of canvas and pots of paint hastily to the floor. "Set him down here. It'll make it easier for your Physician to examine him."

Tam did as she requested, gaping at the mess—vivid splotches of thick paint staining the floor.

"I spilled ink on your sleeve once, remember?" he said quietly. "Dad made me stay in my room for two days."

Mai looked away. "Things change."

For a second, Tam's eyes seemed to brighten. Then the shadows crawled back and he shook his head. "Not enough."

Mai fussed with one of her braids. "Can I get you anything else?"

"Towels," Sophie told her. "And bowls for water, so we can try to clean Alvar up."

Mai nodded. "I'll be right back. There's a bathroom at the end of the hall, if any of you feel like washing your faces. I can get you spare clothes, too."

"We're fine," Sophie said—then realized she shouldn't speak for her friends.

Biana's eyes were on her brother as she said, "I'm staying right here."

"Think his bonds are enough?" Tam asked, giving them a good hard tug as his mother left.

"I don't think he'll be waking up any time soon," Sophie reminded him.

Biana wandered over to Tam's portrait, pretending to study it closer—though she mostly seemed to be wiping her eyes.

"Will you be okay without me for a second?" Tam asked. "I really need to talk to Linh."

"Of course," Sophie told him. "Take as long as you need."

"Should I assume your sister is out taking similar risks tonight?" Tam's father asked from the doorway.

Tam shrugged. "You don't get to care if she is."

Quan blocked Tam from pushing past him. "You brought your troubles to us, Tam. You *chose* to involve us."

"Then how about you don't ruin it?" Tam snapped back. "How about you take this chance to do *one* nice thing for us without making your own selfish demands?"

Quan opened his mouth to argue, then closed it and stepped aside.

"Everything okay?" Mai asked as Tam stalked out of the studio.

No one answered.

She made her way to the center table, managing to avoid stepping in the paint as she set down the golden tray she'd been carrying, laden with towels and bowls and a steaming pitcher of water. "Should I . . . ?"

"Here," Sophie said, taking the cloth from her—not that she had any idea where to begin.

Under the bright lights of the studio Alvar looked even paler, and his wounds were so dark and jagged. She tried dabbing at a few, but that only seemed to break the scabs. So she settled for making a warm compress for his forehead, and another for his neck and hands.

"How long do you think it'll be before your Physician arrives?" Mai whispered.

A knock rang through the house in answer.

Quan stalked off to get the door, and Sophie's breath caught when she heard more than Livvy's voice greet him.

The next seconds were a blur, and then Livvy was dashing to treat her patient—her face covered behind a mask again—as Fitz ran to his sister and Grady crushed Sophie with a hug.

"I think I'll go check on my son," Mai said quietly as she watched Sophie sink into Grady's arms.

Sophie buried her face against Grady's chest, letting a few of the tears she'd been fighting slip free.

"I know you already know this," Grady whispered, stroking his hands gently down her back, "but we *will* find them."

We will, Fitz added, transmitting the words directly into her head. *Whatever it takes.*

Sophie peeked out from Grady's embrace and locked with

Fitz's beautiful eyes, feeling fresh tears when she noted his grief.

This is NOT your fault, she told him, before he could voice the apology forming in his mind.

Maybe not. But I'm still so, so sorry. His gaze strayed to his brother, and the rage in his mind turned into a storm. *I'll break his consciousness apart if that's what it takes to find them.*

She could tell he meant every word.

But memory breaks weren't the kind of thing that should be decided out of anger. And they always took a toll.

I'm hoping it won't come to that, she told him. *If you and I could find our way through Dimitar's mind, I'm sure we can poke around Alvar's head and find what we need.*

But if we don't . . . , Fitz pressed.

Then we'll figure it out.

"You guys might want to wait outside for a minute," Livvy warned—though Sophie realized she needed to call her Physic—removing a pair of shears from the black case she'd brought that looked like a tackle box. "I need to cut off the rest of his clothes to check for wounds."

"I'll need the clothes when you're done," Grady told her. "To check them for trackers."

Sophie froze. "I didn't even think about that. What if—"

"Relax," Grady said, gently guiding Sophie, Biana, and Fitz to the small space outside of the studio and closing the door. "Sandor's already setting up security perimeters outside to make sure we're prepared."

"Sandor's here?" Sophie asked.

Grady nodded. "So are Grizel and Woltzer, and at least a dozen dwarves. We have this covered."

"But still—I should've—"

"You had a *lot* to think about, Sophie," Grady interrupted. "And you did the right thing. You got yourself and your friends out of there unharmed, you chose the safest place you could think of, and then you got help. It's okay to let us take over from here."

Physic pulled open the doors and handed him a satchel of bloody scraps. "It's safe to come back in now. He's under a blanket."

"Will you be okay here for a few minutes?" Grady asked Sophie. "Sandor should take a look at these. And I should make sure Grizel hasn't slapped Tam's father. When I left, Quan was spouting off *lots* of instructions to make sure they didn't destroy Choralmere's ambiance."

"Sounds about right," Tam said, coming up the stairs behind them. "And feel free to let Grizel smack him around."

"How did Linh take the news?" Sophie asked as she watched Grady head back down.

Tam's smile faded. "Pretty much what I expected. She wanted to come over, but I talked her out of it."

"I wish you hadn't," his mom called from somewhere below them. Eavesdropping from the shadows.

"I know," Tam shouted down to her. "That's why I told her not to come. We have enough to deal with right now, without you using this as your chance to convince us to come home."

"But—"

"Don't," Tam cut her off. "If you really want to be a part of our lives, you need to wait until we're ready."

He stalked back into the studio without waiting for her to reply.

Sophie, Fitz, and Biana followed.

Sophie hadn't worked up the courage to look at Alvar when Biana gasped, "You removed his bonds?"

"It's my job to treat his wounds," Physic told her. "Even the ones under the cords. Besides, he's not going anywhere. Whatever sedative they gave him is crazy strong."

She picked up one of Alvar's arms and let it drop limply against his bare chest. A black blanket covered the rest of him from the waist down.

"But you *can* wake him up, right?" Sophie asked, remembering how Gethen had hidden his consciousness in the darkest depths of his mind to avoid interrogations.

"As soon as I figure out what he's on." Physic reached into her tackle box and pulled out seven slender candles, a jewel-encrusted lighter, and a pair of spectacles that looked like the ones Elwin was always using. "This is when I envy Flashers. Must make the process so much easier—especially since I'm stuck with this thing again."

She pointed to the bright blue mask, lined with gold beads and flecked with gold glitter. Fitting the glasses over it was a struggle, and the end result looked noticeably crooked. But she made it work as she used the lighter to spark the first of the candles.

The flame was brighter than normal fire, casting a deep shade of green across Alvar's face as she studied him.

Mr. Forkle didn't want to come? Sophie transmitted to Fitz.

He didn't think he should be around when Alvar wakes up. Plus, he wanted to bring Blur and Wraith the starstone—and a piece of Keefe's cape—so they could do another search of Nightfall with some dwarves. Juline was going to work with the gnomes to set up a cell for Alvar. And Tiergan went to update my parents.

Sophie's heart ached for Alden and Della. *You don't think you should be there for that?*

I probably should be, but . . . I need to be here.

He reached for her hand, and the way he clung to her made heat bloom across her cheeks.

Neither of them seemed to know what to say after that, so they watched in silence as Physic switched to an orange-flamed candle. Then yellow. Then blue.

"What's wrong?" Sophie asked when Physic finished working through the spectrum.

She removed her iridescent spectacles. "I'm not sure. Physically, he's stable—or as stable as you can be after that much blood loss. But I can't figure out what sedatives they gave him, and he's not responding to any of my elixirs."

"Wait," Biana said, and Sophie turned to find her holding several pots of paint. "Weren't we wondering if the Neverseen were making their own special sedatives?"

"I thought of that already," Physic said. "But all of those plants we found at the efflorescence sites—slumberberries and dreamlilies and aethrials and sweetshades—they all leave telltale markers in the cells. And I can't find traces of any of them."

She peeled back Alvar's eyelids and flashed the light of the red candle across them.

"Does that mean it's a mental thing?" Fitz asked.

"You guys would be able to tell that better than I can," Physic told him.

"Should we check?" Fitz asked, and Sophie was already on her way to Alvar's side.

"Maybe you should rest first," Physic told her. "You look pretty dead on your feet."

"I'm fine," Sophie promised.

"Then let me give you a mental boost," Fitz offered as he came up beside her.

He reached for her face, and Sophie closed her eyes and leaned in, letting him press his fingers against her temples. The second their skin touched, a rush of warmth flooded her mind—the energy softer than it had felt in the past. Smoother, somehow. Coating her thoughts like melted butter.

"Wow," she breathed. "Did you do something different?"

"You looked really tense," Fitz said. "So I tried sending energy from my emotional center."

"Well, it's amazing." She stretched her neck and channeled

a tiny bit of the warmth into her weary muscles. "I'm going to want you to do that every day."

Tam snorted. "Be glad Keefe wasn't here to hear you say that."

"I just meant—"

"I know what you meant," Fitz assured her. "And I'm here *any-time*."

She glanced at Alvar, feeling some of the warmth fade. "You ready?"

Fitz struggled to swallow as he offered her his hand and reached for Alvar's temples with the other.

"Think the gloves will affect this?" she asked as his palm pressed against hers.

Their thumb rings didn't snap together.

"Hmm. I forgot we haven't worked together like this since"—he glanced toward the door, lowering his voice in case anyone was eavesdropping—"you manifested."

"It's probably better to start with them on," Physic told them. "If it doesn't work, you can try it without them."

Sophie nodded. *You're really sure you're up for this?* she asked Fitz. *Alvar's memories are going to be rough.*

He stared at his eerily still brother. *Will you think I'm a coward if I admit I'm a little scared?*

If that makes you a coward, then I'm one too.

He tightened his hold on her hand. *Let's do this.*

She took a slow breath and nodded. *We go in three . . . two . . . one . . .*

FORTY-NINE

SOPHIE HAD PLANNED FOR DARKNESS. But she'd expected it to have an end—a barrier they could push past and find Alvar's consciousness hidden underneath.

But no matter which way they navigated, or how far they dove, they couldn't escape the emptiness. And the harder they pushed, the more the darkness seemed to tighten around them, caging them in, smothering them in the sheer nothingness.

Do you think it's because of your gloves? Fitz asked.

Sophie barely caught the words before they were swallowed up by the vacuumlike pull of the silence.

It's possible. But if I take them off, I'm going to enhance you—and probably Alvar too.

She'd never tested whether the ability only worked with hand-to-hand contact. But the energy came from her touch, so she was pretty sure it wouldn't matter where she placed her fingers.

I think we have to try, Fitz thought.

Yeah, give me one second. Sophie severed their connection and pulled her mind free to clear her head.

"I take it you're not having much luck," Physic said when she noticed Sophie peeling off her gloves.

"I've never felt anything like that," Fitz told her, rubbing his forehead.

The scary thing was, Sophie actually had—but she was trying really, *really* hard not to think about that.

"Ready for plan B?" she asked, wiggling her now exposed fingers to hide how much they were shaking.

"Wait," Biana said, moving behind Sophie and wrapping her arms around her waist. "Someone should hold you steady in case this gets too intense."

Physic did the same for Fitz, and the four of them held their breath as Sophie grabbed Fitz's hand the same moment they each pressed their fingers against Alvar's temples.

WHOA.

The thought came from both of them as Fitz's mind glowed with the rush of pulsing energy.

Is this what it always feels like when I enhance you? she asked.

Pretty crazy, right?

Suddenly he was ten steps ahead of her, his brain anticipating everything before her thoughts could even form.

And the *strength*.

The tiniest shove of his mind was like a wrecking ball, smashing against the never-ending black.

But it was like crashing into a wall of smoke. The darkness swirled around each hit without any impact.

Enhancing Alvar didn't have any effect either. Sophie could feel the tingling warmth leaving her fingers, but the energy was immediately swallowed by the darkness.

Got any other ideas? Fitz asked.

Sophie had one—but it wasn't so much an idea as it was a realization.

What? Fitz asked as he boosted her strength to drag their minds out of the mental mire. *I can feel you holding something back.*

I know—I just . . . need to think.

Ten seconds slipped by.

Then twenty.

Thirty.

Whatever it is, you can tell me, Fitz promised. *I won't freak out. If Alvar's broken—*

It's not that.

"I think I know what you're going to say," Physic told her. "And if it helps, I noticed the same similarity in his vitals. I checked twice, to make sure I wasn't making a mistake. But other than a couple of changes that would stem from the blood loss, everything else is the same."

"The same as what?" Grady asked from the doorway, making Sophie whip around.

"Is everything okay with Sandor and Grizel?" she asked. "Did they find any trackers?"

"None so far," he told her. "What about you guys?"

Sophie turned back to Alvar, searching his features for any sign of life—any clue that her theory might be wrong.

His deep gashes were now sealed, leaving angry red lines on his clammy skin. And there were purple bruises around his mouth. But mostly he looked . . . distant.

Unreachable.

"What were you and Physic talking about?" Fitz asked. "What does Alvar remind you of?"

"It's not *what*," Physic corrected. "It's *who*."

Neither Sophie nor Physic seemed to want to be the one to say it. So they did it in unison.

"Prentice."

FIFTY

THOUGHT YOU SAID ALVAR'S MIND WASN'T broken." Fitz's face didn't betray any emotion, but there was a hoarseness to his voice that he couldn't clear away.

"It isn't," Sophie promised. "Though . . . I guess there's a tiny chance it could be. His mind is too empty right now to be able to tell. But *that's* what I mean. That's exactly how Prentice's mind felt after we brought him out of Exile."

"You mean when his consciousness was *gone?*" Grady clarified.

Sophie forced herself to nod. "I'll never forget the way the darkness didn't have a shape to it. It just stretched on and on with endless nothing."

"His vitals match that too," Physic added quietly. "They're

almost identical to what Prentice's were when I started treating him at the Stone House. I've even ended up giving Alvar the same elixirs, and they've all been about as effective."

"So then . . . we need to lift a veil of shadowvapor, don't we?" Fitz asked, turning to Tam. "That's how you brought Prentice out of it, isn't it?"

"I can try," Tam told him. "But if it's as heavy as Prentice's was, I'll probably need to rest before I'll be strong enough to lift it."

Sophie offered her gloveless hand. "If you need me to help . . ."

"Let's see how it goes," Tam said, squaring his shoulders and letting his shadow crawl toward Alvar's face and sink slowly into his skin.

Sophie braced for bone-shaking screams, like Prentice made when his veils were lifted. But Alvar stayed silent.

Seconds dragged by—two hundred and seventeen of them—before Tam's shadow slunk back to its rightful place.

"I can't do it," he said, grabbing one of the towels and wiping the sweat off his forehead.

"Do you need more energy?" Fitz asked. "I might be able to give you a boost."

Tam shook his head. "It's not that. His shadowvapor isn't heavy. It's . . . gooey."

"Gooey," Biana repeated, a shaky edge of humor in her voice, as if she wanted to laugh and scream at the same time.

"I know, it's not a great description," Tam mumbled. "But it's the only way I can think to explain it. There's nothing solid enough to grab ahold of. No individual layers. And when I push it around, it floods in on itself and bunches up, like when you stir something thick and sticky."

"Then he's not like Prentice," Fitz said, turning to Sophie. "Right?"

"Or maybe the differences have to do with the fact that Prentice had a broken mind, and Alvar likely doesn't," Physic suggested. "Or because we're attempting this so much earlier for him. Judging by Alvar's wounds, I'd say he's been like this for barely longer than a day. And we didn't try lifting a veil in Prentice's mind for weeks."

"So . . . we can't wake him up?" Biana asked.

"For the moment, no." Physic's face twisted, as if the words felt sour as she said them.

"I'm not sure I understand how they could be the same," Grady admitted. "Are you saying the Council gave Prentice the same sedative?"

"It's a possibility," Physic told him.

Sophie frowned. "But I thought Prentice didn't even respond to the sedatives the Council gave him."

"So did I," Physic agreed. "Broken minds usually don't."

"That's right—my dad didn't," Fitz added, and Sophie noticed his hands were white-knuckled, probably reliving those harrowing days.

She let her mind drift to a different heartbreaking memory, and could practically feel the cold ocean wind on her skin from when she'd stood outside Lumenaria's towering gates, waiting with the rest of the Collective to exchange Gethen for Prentice's freedom.

"Bronte told us that Councillor Alina had to go to Exile and use her ability as a Beguiler to calm Prentice down before transport," she said quietly. "I remember wondering if she might've done something to Prentice that caused him to slip away. Do you think the Neverseen have a Beguiler working for them and did the same thing to Alvar?"

"Nothing a Beguiler could do would have this effect," Physic assured her. "They only *add* to the mind, amplifying existing thoughts and feelings to manipulate people. They can't take anything away—especially an entire consciousness."

"So . . . how can Alvar and Prentice be the same, then?" Tam asked.

"I'm honestly not sure," Physic admitted. "But I don't like coincidences—especially since we've never figured out what caused Prentice's downturn."

"I think it's definitely worth talking to the Councillors," Grady said.

"Are you sure we can trust them?" Biana asked. "It sounds like they might've done something to him."

"I've wrestled with that idea ever since they returned Prentice to us in such a confusing state," Physic told her. "But I've never been able to come up with a reason why they would harm him."

Neither had Sophie, when the same worry had reared up in her mind in the past. Anyone who damaged Prentice so severely would affect their own sanity with the guilt of it, and she couldn't imagine any of the Councillors taking such a personal risk—even Alina.

"But it is possible they did something unintentionally," Physic added. "So I think we need to ask them exactly what happened."

"Oralie would know, wouldn't she?" Fitz asked.

"She might not," Sophie warned. "She wasn't at Lumenaria for the exchange—only Bronte and Emery. And Alina and Terik were the ones who went to Exile to bring Prentice to us."

Physic checked Alvar's pulse. "I still think we should start with her, see what she knows and if she thinks we should let her investigate further, or ask the other Councillors ourselves."

"I can head to Eternalia at dawn, see if I can set up a meeting," Grady offered.

"That's right," Sophie mumbled, staring up through the skylights at the stars shining over them. "I forgot it's the middle of the night."

A deep, almost painful weariness dragged down her bones at the reminder.

"Maybe you guys should go home and get a little rest," Physic suggested.

"I'm not leaving my brother," Biana told her.

"Me either," Fitz agreed.

"It's not like any of us are going to be able to sleep," Sophie added.

"Well then, you might want to go back out to the hall," Physic told them. "Now that Alvar's wounds have sealed, I need to coat his skin with reveldust to make sure he's not covered in any ogre tracking enzymes."

They were halfway to the door when Tam froze.

"Did you do that?" he asked Biana, pointing to his mom's portrait of him, which now had jagged bangs slashed across the forehead.

Biana nodded. "I'm going to fix Linh's portrait too—unless you don't want me to."

Tam's grin was enormous as he stepped closer to admire her work. The brushstrokes were hasty, and the silver tips were too gray—but the painting finally looked like him. "Are you kidding? That's the best thing I've seen in a long time!"

"Um, not to spoil this moment, but you guys need to see this," Physic said behind them.

They all spun around to find a splotch of glowing purple on the bottom of Alvar's heel.

"I thought I'd start with his feet since you were still in here," she said, crouching to get a better look at the mark. "I think it's some sort of brand. The shape is very specific, and the mark looks pressed into his skin."

Sophie stepped closer, squinting at the twisted lines that

curved around each other before flaring out in spirals. It reminded her of a falling star.

"What does it mean when reveldust glows purple?" she asked.

"No idea," Physic said. "I've only seen red or green. But I'm not much of an expert on ogre enzymes. We'll have to ask Lady Cadence in the morning."

"Why not hail her now?" Sophie countered. "She's part of the Black Swan, right? We're all up dealing with this. Why can't she be too?"

"I suppose that *is* fair," Physic said, removing an Imparter from her pocket. "But I'm calling 'not it' for facing the wrath of a sleep-deprived Lady Cadence."

"I'll do it," Sophie offered, taking the Imparter and giving the command before she could wimp out.

"This better be important!" Lady Cadence snapped, her voice thick with sleep as her puffy-eyed face filled the small screen. "And I mean life-changingly important."

"It might be," Sophie told her. "What does glowing purple mean?"

Lady Cadence yawned. "Am I supposed to know what you're talking about?"

"Reveldust," Sophie told her. "What does glowing purple mean when you coat something with reveldust?"

"I've never seen anything turn purple before," she said. "You're sure it's not blue?"

"You tell me." Sophie held the Imparter up to Alvar's heel. "We captured a member of the Neverseen tonight, and we found this mark on his heel while we were searching for any way they might be tracking him."

"Well, I've never seen reveldust turn that color before, so I'm not sure—wait. Can you turn off the lights in the room?"

Tam snapped his fingers, leaving them with nothing but the pale moonlight and the purple glow, which had turned much brighter, and had a slight shimmer to it, with hints of opalescence.

Lady Cadence sucked in a gasp. "Is the prisoner unresponsive?"

"Yes," Physic told her. "Both to mental stimuli and all of my remedies. Do you know what they gave him?"

An agonizingly long pause followed before Lady Cadence said, "That mark is glowing with the residue of soporidine."

FIFTY-ONE

THE NEVERSEEN MUST'VE FOUND A food source for the *Bucollosisia*," Lady Cadence murmured, "otherwise they never would've had access to such a massive quantity of soporidine."

"*This* is massive?" Physic asked, pointing to the glowing mark on Alvar's heel, which was barely larger than an inch.

"It is," Lady Cadence assured her. "That mark is at least ten times bigger than the drop that spilled on me, and *that* had been a significant quantity."

"Soporidine—is that what the scroll Keefe sent over was talking about?" Biana asked.

"Yes," Lady Cadence said, launching into a brief explanation about the rare amino acid. "I honestly don't see how the

Neverseen could've pulled this off. I read through my notes again, and the *Bucollosisia* were a deeply flawed creation. I can't imagine what would sustain them."

Sophie stared at the flaky powder coating her skin, feeling the pieces click together. "It has to be the ash."

"Is that what's currently smeared all over you?" Lady Cadence asked.

Sophie nodded. "This has to be why the Neverseen gathered the ash from the efflorescence."

"Anyone care to explain what that means?" Lady Cadence requested.

Fitz gave her a quick rundown of the twenty Everblaze sites now covered in flowers, and how they'd found dreamlilies and slumberberries and aethrials and sweetshades growing there.

"Ash," Lady Cadence said slowly. "I'm trying to imagine how that would work."

"Well, didn't you say the *Bucollosisia* needed nitrogen?" Sophie asked, turning to Grady. "And didn't you say the ash from the Everblaze has nitrogen in it, and that's why it's so cold?"

"I'm nowhere near an alchemy expert," he admitted. "So that was partially a guess. But Everblaze is a solar flame, called down from the sky. And I'm pretty sure it absorbs nitrogen as it passes through the atmosphere."

"It does," Physic agreed.

"And frissyn has nitrogen in it too, I think." Sophie closed her eyes, trying to picture the formula for the only substance that extinguished Everblaze.

She couldn't understand most of the symbols, but she recognized nitrogen among them.

And the Council would've given the fires a generous dusting to halt the infernos.

"But the bacteria needed more than nitrogen," Lady Cadence reminded her. "The *Bucollosisia* also lacked the ability to break the element down."

"Maybe that's where the gnomish plants come in," Sophie suggested. "Or maybe the Quintessence in the frissyn is part of the process too. Or the Everblaze might change the nitrogen somehow. Or . . . I don't know—I'm horrible at this stuff. But didn't you say it seemed like an experiment when we were at the efflorescence sites?" she asked Fitz. "What if they burned the different plants with Everblaze and waited for the Council to extinguish the fires with frissyn—maybe they even did something else to the soil too, which would explain why there are so many flowers growing there now. And then they gathered it all up and tested it on the *Bucollosisia* in Nightfall until they found something that worked."

"All of that does sound feasible," Physic admitted.

"Can you turn off the lights and show me the mark again?" Lady Cadence asked, and Sophie moved the Imparter back to Alvar's heel as the room went dark. "That's *definitely* soporidine," she whispered, as if she'd needed to convince herself. "And with the amount he's been exposed to, it's amazing he's still breathing."

"His vitals are extremely weak," Physic said. "But they're holding steady."

"How long do you think it's going to take for the soporidine to wear off?" Sophie asked, already dreading the answer.

"I lost three days on a fraction of what he's been exposed to," Lady Cadence told her. "And with how much I'm seeing on his skin, I'm sure he'll be out for weeks. Maybe months."

"Months?" Fresh tears pricked Sophie's eyes, and she was glad the darkness could hide them.

Months before their only lead to find her family would actually be useful.

"I'm assuming that means there's no antidote?" Physic asked as Tam turned the lights on again.

"The ogres tried everything in their arsenal on me," Lady Cadence said through a sigh. "Nothing helped."

The word echoed in Sophie's head—*nothing, nothing, nothing.*

Which was probably why Biana was the one to ask the question Sophie *should've* been focusing on.

"Why would the Neverseen make a bunch of soporidine?"

"I'm guessing the obvious answer is: *to drug a lot of people,*" Physic said, tilting her head to study Alvar's pale face. "But there has to be more to it than that, or they would've used it already. They must be waiting for something."

Grady tore a hand through his hair. "We need to figure out what it is."

"And we'd better find a way to counteract the soporidine's effects, in case we don't stop them in time," Lady Cadence warned.

"Do you really think you can make something like that?" Sophie asked.

"I don't see why not," Physic told her. "If the Neverseen can figure out how to sustain the *Bucollosisia*, surely we can find a cure."

"Especially if we team up with the ogres," Lady Cadence added. "Soporidine is a threat to them as well, so I'm sure Dimitar would be willing to send some of his best microbiologists— but they'll need access to Alvar to run tests. As will I. Perhaps I can convert one of the rooms in Riverdrift into a cell."

Sophie froze. "What if that's what the Neverseen wants? The ogre rebels want you dead, remember? So what if Alvar's not as drugged as they're making us think he is, and they're counting on us to bring him to you so he can kill you?"

"I never thought I'd say this," Lady Cadence said, "but I think you might be overestimating my importance."

"Maybe I am," Sophie said. "All I know is that the Neverseen don't do anything without a reason. And they just tipped us off to the fact that they know how to mass-produce soporidine— *and* abandoned their Nightfall facility *and* got rid of Alvar. They wouldn't have done any of that if they weren't planning something *big*."

She latched onto the terrifying thought, clinging to each thread of fear that it triggered—because *this* had to be what the Neverseen were trying to distract her from.

This was why they'd moved her parents from Nightfall. To keep her too busy panicking and searching to investigate any of this.

She couldn't let herself make that mistake.

But she couldn't abandon her human parents either.

She'd have to stay on top of everything, even if her brain felt like it was stretching so thin it might tear.

"Okay," Physic said, clapping her hands. "I'll make sure the Collective sets up Alvar somewhere we can all reach him for testing. And you need to talk to Dimitar, Cadence. Will you be able to house any ogres he sends at Riverdrift?"

"Of course," Lady Cadence said. "But someone will need to alert the Council of their presence."

"I can handle that," Grady offered.

Lady Cadence nodded, clicking away and letting the Imparter go blank.

"What about us?" Fitz asked. "What should we be doing?"

"And don't even think about telling us to go home and go to bed," Biana added.

"Why not?" Grady asked. "You guys look exhausted. And filthy. And freezing. You need to get cleaned up and give yourselves a little rest. Anything important can wait a few hours."

Sophie reached for her eyelashes. "I . . . I have to talk to my sister." She turned to Physic. "Does she know you're with me?"

"I snuck out while she was sleeping. And she didn't know you were going into Nightfall tonight. She seemed to guess that something big was happening, but I kept her distracted with the efflorescence samples. So you can share as much or as little as you think she can handle—and it can definitely wait until morning."

Sophie nodded, deciding to give her sister a few more hours of peace.

"Okay, I hate to say this, but aren't we forgetting something?" Tam asked. "I mean . . . didn't you guys say that Alvar's mind felt like Prentice's?"

Sophie's heart stopped.

She could barely find enough voice to say, "Does this mean the Council gave *Prentice* soporidine?"

"I . . . don't know," Physic admitted. "The vitals match—but how would they have had any to use?"

"No clue," Sophie said. "But if they did . . ."

She didn't know how to finish that sentence. The implications were too huge.

"We need to find out," Tam said. "Do you think there could still be residue on Prentice's skin, so we could test him?"

"I doubt it. But it won't hurt to sprinkle some reveldust on him anyway. I can't do it until morning, though," Physic warned.

"Waking him up in the middle of the night would stress him out too much. But I'll go there first thing, I promise."

"So in the meantime, you four"—Grady pointed to Sophie, Fitz, Tam, and Biana—"should go home and rest up as much as you can."

"And I know you're going to argue that sleep will be impossible," Physic jumped in. "But it won't be if you take these." She offered them four hot-pink vials. "Yes, these are sleeping elixirs. Extremely mild ones that will only last a few hours. And yes, I realize you're not fans of sedatives. But take it from someone who's served nearly two decades with the Black Swan. Sometimes we have to remember that we are not machines. We may not like it, but we need food and sleep—even if we have to force it. Otherwise we'll run ourselves into the ground."

Sophie stared at the pink vials. "Who's going to stay here with Alvar?"

"Sandor will," Grady promised. "And Grizel. Havenfield and Everglen have enough security that we can spare one night without them."

"And I'll make the Songs set me up a bed in here," Physic added. "I also promise I'll be especially annoying," she told Tam with a wink. "If *anything* happens, I'll wake all of you up. Just take the elixirs and go home. Give your bodies the break they need and come back stronger. We have a lot of work ahead."

FIFTY-TWO

SOPHIE HADN'T ASKED PHYSIC WHAT was in the sugary pink sedative, knowing the answer would probably make her not want to take it. So she wasn't prepared for the *interesting* dreams.

The second she crawled under her covers, she floated off to rainbow-glitterland, complete with kittens in tiaras and cartwheeling puppies and candy islands surrounded by twirling dolphins in tutus. Everything was so happy and sparkly and bright—it made her head spin and her stomach woozy. But maybe that was the point. To make her grateful to return to reality—even if it wasn't nearly so cute. And to be glad to wake up and find *people* in her room, instead of dancing anthropomorphic animals.

"What's going on?" she asked, pulling her covers around her chest as she sat up to face Edaline and Lady Cadence.

"You woke me up earlier," Lady Cadence told her, frowning as she watched Sophie slip on her gloves. "So I figured it was only fair that I get to return the favor. Especially since you insisted on sleeping until noon."

"Noon?" Panic wedged in Sophie's throat when she glanced out her windows at the bright afternoon sunlight. "I thought the sedative was only supposed to last a few hours!"

"It did," Edaline promised. "But your body must've been so exhausted that once you were out, you were *out*. And we let you sleep because you needed it."

"*And* because it was time to let the grown-ups tackle some of these challenges," Lady Cadence added. "Oh, don't scowl at me like that—there's nothing wrong with admitting that certain things need a bit more wisdom and maturity to manage."

"It had nothing to do with that," Edaline insisted. "We just wanted to give you a chance to recover after an incredibly draining day. And don't worry, Mr. Forkle is here to update you on everything that's been happening—"

Edaline was still finishing the sentence when Sophie sprinted for the stairs. Which was unfortunately why she didn't realize she was still in her ruffly nightgown—with bed hair and morning breath—until she got to the living room.

Even more unfortunate was the fact that Mr. Forkle wasn't the only one waiting for her.

The other four members of the Collective were there, back in their bizarre disguises. And Livvy was Physic again, this time wearing a silver mask decorated with black feathers.

Grady was there too.

And Alden and Della.

And Fitz, Dex, Biana, Tam, and Linh.

And Sandor, Grizel, Woltzer, Lovise, and Cadoc.

And an imposing figure in a jeweled circlet and cape, with features as sharp as the points of his ancient ears—which was probably the reason the Black Swan had chosen to hide their identities.

"Good to see you, Miss Foster," Councillor Bronte told her as she fumbled through a curtsy while attempting to tuck as much of her messy hair behind her ears as she could. "I see you were eager to get this meeting started."

Her face burned.

And even though she'd been on better terms with Bronte for the last several months, her queasy stomach couldn't forget all the time he'd spent threatening to send her to Exile.

"Sorry," she mumbled, slipping into the robe Edaline had thankfully thought to grab before she and Lady Cadence joined them.

"No need to apologize," Mr. Forkle told her. "I, for one, am relieved to see you've gotten some rest. I would've let you sleep the entire day, but I feared you might not be too happy with me if I did."

"I wouldn't have been," Sophie agreed. "Where's Alvar?"

"Somewhere safe," Squall promised. The ice crusting her features made it impossible to recognize her as Dex's mom.

"It's been a very busy night, and an even busier morning," Mr. Forkle added. "We have *lots* of answers for you—but before we get into them, I need you and your friends to promise to hold your questions until we've finished explaining. Otherwise we'll never get through this."

When they nodded, he asked the six of them to take a seat on the couch—which didn't feel like a good sign for where the conversation would be heading.

"Don't worry," Biana whispered as she sat next to Sophie, followed by Linh, Tam, and Fitz. Dex squeezed in on the opposite side, sitting as far away from Sophie as he possibly could. "We all only woke up a little while ago."

That would've been a lot more comforting if the rest of her friends hadn't looked so well-dressed and showered. Biana had even braided her hair with jewels throughout the intricate weave.

Sophie felt even more uncomfortable when she noticed that Keefe wasn't there. She'd told him to stay away, but . . . it seemed wrong to have everyone gathered without him.

"Let's see, where to start?" Mr. Forkle asked as he turned to pace the length of the bright room. After three back-and-forths, he settled on the subject of Alvar, explaining that the eldest Vacker had been moved to a cell that the gnomes and dwarves had constructed early that morning—far enough away from everything to ensure that Alvar would pose no threat. But still readily accessible for Lady Cadence and the ogre researchers who had arrived from Ravagog that morning to begin work on an antidote for the soporidine.

"Are you guys okay?" Sophie asked Alden and Della when she noticed the bruiselike shadows rimming their eyes—not caring that she was breaking Mr. Forkle's no-questions rule.

"We have mixed emotions," Alden said, fussing with his slate-colored cape. "But we've known something like this was inevitable ever since we found out the truth about our son."

"In some ways, it's a relief to know he's no longer out there helping with the Neverseen's horrible projects," Della added. "I'm just sorry we can't learn anything from him right now—especially about where to find your human family."

"Which is still a priority," Grady assured her. "I know you're worrying that the Neverseen are using your parents as a distraction. But look at how many of us are here right now." He waved his arms around the crowded room. "And this is still only a fraction of the resources available. So we're more than capable of dividing our focus between projects. And we *will* find them."

"But . . . we don't have any leads," Sophie argued.

"Actually, we do," Granite told her. His voice was as crackly as his rocky disguise—which gave him the look of a half-carved statue come to life.

"Like what?" Tam asked.

Mr. Forkle smiled. "You kids are doing about as well with the no-questions rule as I expected."

"But since you asked," Bronte jumped in, "*I* am one of those leads." His sharp eyes homed in on Dex, who scooted deeper into the couch cushions. "It's come to my attention that you possess Fintan's cache—and no need to look so terrified. I'm glad your group managed to steal it—though I do hope you're taking every precaution to protect it."

Whatever you do, don't tell him you carry it around with you, Sophie transmitted to Dex. *And don't mention that you have Kenric's cache, either.*

Dex gave her the briefest of nods, his eyes darting quickly away as he told Bronte, "No one's getting anywhere near the cache unless I want them to."

"Excellent," Bronte said. "You and I will be working to access the secrets together to see what we can uncover about this prisoner he's working with. Fintan and I have a long history, so if anyone can figure out the passwords protecting his secrets, it's me."

"Does that mean he chose the passwords?" Sophie asked.

Bronte shook his head. "They're generated by the cache itself. It's a security feature, both to keep the secrets protected, and to provide a way for us to recover the information, should it become crucial. Each password is something that should inherently be instinctive to us, if we push our minds to trigger it—and I have several theories for what Fintan's might be. So plan on coming to my office in Eternalia every day," he told Dex, "until we gain access."

Dex definitely did *not* look excited when he said, "Yeah, sure."

Sophie tried to offer him a sympathetic smile, but he didn't look her way.

"We've also spoken to Lady Gisela," Granite said, making Sophie sit up straighter. "Sandor gave me Keefe's Imparter last night, as well as a piece of his soiled cape. And she was so shocked to hear about the state of Nightfall that she agreed to meet me there to see for herself."

"You *met* with Lady Gisela?" Sophie clarified.

Granite nodded.

"Please tell me you arrested her," Biana begged.

"I said the same thing," Bronte grumbled.

"We considered it," Mr. Forkle told them. "But Gisela is too cautious not to be prepared for that. And at the moment, she is of far more use to us when she has the freedom to investigate certain things on her own. Apparently the Neverseen stole something rather important of hers when they cleaned out her facility—something she called the Archetype."

"Did she say what it was?" Fitz asked.

"Only in the vaguest possible terms," Granite said. "Gisela is smart. She knows we have no alliance—though she kept claiming we were fools not to offer one. And she's clearly well trained at hiding secrets from Telepaths. I tried invading her mind while we were together, and I was only able to hear her most bland observations."

"Sophie and I could've gotten past whatever blocking she was using," Fitz argued. "You should've brought us with you."

"I wish we could have," Granite told him. "But Gisela demanded that the meeting be strictly between her and me. As I said, she's smart. She didn't even let me see her face."

Sophie wondered if that had to do with her scars from the shamkniv—not that it mattered. "Did she say anything about what Nightfall was supposed to be?"

"She said it's a testing facility, designed to measure worthiness. But she refused to say who she'd been planning to test or what would happen to those 'worthy' and 'unworthy,' or how those determinations were made—even when I suggested that the Black Swan might be open to a bargain. The only other information she gave me was to confirm that the third level in Nightfall was used for their soporidine experiment—and she only confessed to that when I revealed we had Alvar in our custody."

"Why would you tell her that?" Fitz snapped.

"Because I had to let her think she'd forced me into revealing a crucial secret. Also because I wanted to see her reaction. She was genuinely shocked. In fact, it's why she was willing to explain a few details about the soporidine. She didn't give any clues as to the drug's ultimate purpose, of course, or how much of the scheme was Fintan's plan instead of hers—but she did reveal that each of the twenty fire sites had different variables to alter the protein's effect and potency. And she thinks Alvar was exposed to the strongest variation."

"Of course," Sophie mumbled.

"Which is why Mr. Dizznee and I should get started on that cache," Bronte noted.

"Wait," Sophie said as he removed a pathfinder from his cape. "What about Prentice?"

Mr. Forkle shifted his weight. "Before I answer that, I need to remind each of you of your promise to hold questions until the end. Can you try actually sticking to that for this next part?"

He waited for all of them to agree before he nodded to Physic.

She stepped forward, adjusting the tilt of her mask as she told them, "I tested Prentice this morning. And I didn't find any marks like what's on Alvar's heel."

Sophie was trying to decide if she was relieved, when Physic added, "But there was a small glowing dot in the center of his palm. So he was definitely exposed to soporidine."

FIFTY-THREE

HOW COULD YOU DO THAT?" SOPHIE shouted at Bronte. "Do you have any idea how close we came to losing Prentice for good?"

She regretted the words when Alden's face went from pale to gray.

Della must've noticed the change as well, because she wrapped her arms around her husband, holding him close and whispering in his ear.

"*I* didn't do anything to Prentice," Bronte said calmly. "And for the record, neither did Emery or Alina. Or Terik—though I'd think his injury in Lumenaria would be proof enough that he's not involved with the Neverseen, without my needing to say so."

"He's not lying," Mr. Forkle added before Sophie could make that very accusation. "I spent the majority of the morning in Eternalia personally questioning all twelve Councillors, and I kept my mind open to their thoughts to ensure their honesty."

"And I made him bring me to Prentice to see this mark for myself," Bronte told her. "Even now, I still find it hard to believe that such an insignificant glowing speck on his palm could have harmed him so thoroughly."

"It looked like he was exposed to the same amount as I was," Lady Cadence said quietly. "Believe me, it's more than enough—especially with a broken mind amplifying the reaction."

"Why do you think I voted to allow more ogres into the Lost Cities?" Bronte told her. "I'm counting on you and your team to find a remedy to this substance, before the Neverseen unleash whatever they're planning."

"I still wonder if shadowvapor manipulation could draw Alvar from his trance," Physic jumped in. "If you're willing, Tam, I'd love to test a few theories out."

"Whatever you need," Tam promised.

"How did Wylie take this news?" Linh asked. "Did anyone explain what soporidine is?"

"I did," Lady Cadence told her. "I answered all of his questions."

"And *I* made it clear that the Council had nothing to do with his father's exposure," Bronte added.

Sophie couldn't make herself believe him.

You're sure *the Councillors weren't involved?* she transmitted to Mr. Forkle.

Yes, Miss Foster, he transmitted back. *I am. I bent the rules of telepathy a bit during my interrogations and combed through all of their minds much more carefully than they realized. And I was able to dredge up each of their memories of that day—and none of them gave me any reason to doubt their integrity.*

"So who drugged Prentice, then?" Sophie asked out loud.

Bronte turned to stare into the pastures, watching the argentavis fly loops around his aviary. "Most likely it was one of the dwarves working in Exile. We've known for a while now that some of their species have joined forces with the Neverseen. And Terik said he had several dwarves helping him retrieve Prentice from his cell and administer the sedatives. Any of them would've had ample opportunity to apply the soporidine to Prentice's palm without anyone noticing."

"Councillor Emery already went through the guard records." Mr. Forkle added. "Two different dwarves transferred into Exile not long before Prentice's scheduled departure, and have since resigned. We gave their names to King Enki, and he has confirmed that they're missing from the dwarven world. Oralie will be heading to Exile today to interview the current guards and see if any of them noticed anything that day—or could be traitors as well."

"I can't imagine the Neverseen would keep traitors there full-time," Bronte insisted. "It seems much more likely that they were brought in specifically for Prentice."

"But why?" Tam asked. "Why go to so much trouble to drug someone who already had a broken mind?"

"Probably because they knew we were getting ready to heal him," Physic told him, "and they didn't want us to find out what made him call swan song."

"I thought he called swan song because he knew he was about to be arrested," Dex reminded them.

Alden flinched, and Della pulled him close again.

"We once thought the same," Mr. Forkle admitted. "But as I'm sure you recall, Prentice knew about the Lodestar symbol. And he dredged up the final pieces of it when Miss Foster transmitted the words 'swan song.' Combine that with the tremendous efforts the Neverseen took to keep him shattered, and it seems fairly telling."

"Okay, but here's what I don't understand," Tam said. "It's actually been bugging me since Prentice showed us the symbol, but I didn't say anything because I figured I was new to the group, so I'd probably missed something. But . . . if Prentice knew the symbol was super important—which it seems like he did because of the swan song connection—why didn't he tell anyone about it before his mind was broken? Even if he was trying to protect the Black Swan's secrets, he knew the Lodestar symbol had nothing to do with you guys. So, why didn't he say, 'Uh, here's this big thing you need to look into since I won't be able to'? Wouldn't you have investigated the symbol if he'd shown it to you?" he asked Alden.

"Of course." Alden's voice sounded hoarse as he turned to Physic. "But it wouldn't have spared Prentice any of this pain. In fact, it only would've served as further proof that the memory break was necessary."

"Okay," Tam said, "but since Prentice knew the break was inevitable, wouldn't he at least pass along anything important while he still could, to make sure the secret didn't get buried after his mind was broken?"

"That does sound like Prentice," Granite murmured.

"And he didn't say anything to Quinlin during their private meeting, did he?" Alden asked Physic.

She shrugged. "I'm sure if he had, Quinlin would've investigated."

"So . . . you guys think it's weird too, then?" Tam confirmed.

Sophie definitely did, now that he'd mentioned it.

And no one had a good explanation.

"Well," Physic said, clearing her throat. "This makes our good news even more significant. Soon enough, we'll be able to ask Prentice these questions ourselves."

Sophie was on her feet without thinking. "Does that mean . . . ?"

"Yes," Mr. Forkle said when she couldn't finish the question, in case she was getting her hopes up for nothing. "Now that we finally understand why Prentice took such a drastic downturn and know we can prevent it from happening again, we're ready to try having you heal him."

FIFTY-FOUR

N OW?" SOPHIE ASKED, NO LONGER caring that she was in her robe. If the Black Swan was ready for the healing, she'd head straight to Prentice, morning breath and all.

"I thought that might be your reaction," Mr. Forkle said, a smile tugging at his lips. "But unfortunately we aren't planning anything *that* immediate. Prentice still has a tremendous amount of heartbreaking news to wake up to, and—"

"He's always going to have that," Sophie interrupted.

"He will," Granite agreed. "But I think I've come up with a way of easing him through the process. The last time you were in Prentice's mind, weren't you able to communicate with him?"

"Sorta." Sophie had actually spoken with a mental projection of Jolie, because Prentice told her he didn't know how to be himself anymore.

"Well, he's much more stable than he was before," Mr. Forkle told her. "So hopefully that will make it even easier for you to communicate. We think it's best if you explain the tragedies that have happened *before* you draw what's left of his consciousness back from whatever safe space he's tucked the shreds away. If he can handle it in there, he'll likely be able to face it once he's back in reality. And if he struggles, he won't shatter as hard as he would if he'd been healed completely."

It wasn't a horrible plan—though Sophie wasn't thrilled that she'd get to be the bearer of *all* the bad news.

I'll be right there with you, Fitz promised. *I know I can't go into a broken mind, but I can boost you like I did last time.*

He reached for her hand, and Sophie held on tight—until she caught Dex staring at their twined fingers.

She pulled back the same second Dex turned away, and Sophie decided not to look at either boy as she took a deep breath and said, "If that's how you want me to do it, I will."

"Excellent. But we're still not heading there now," Mr. Forkle warned. "And no, I'm not saying that because I'm trying to stall. You're forgetting that Lady Gisela still hasn't told you what she knows about Cyrah's death. And it's crucial that we give him *all* the bad news."

"Then give me the Imparter," Sophie said, holding out her

"Even though all those memories will have to be erased?" Sophie had to ask, her voice wobbling on the last word.

Now that it was going to take them even longer to save her parents from whatever they were enduring, she couldn't imagine their minds wouldn't have to be reset.

And so would Amy's.

"Is a day any less worth living simply because you're not going to remember it?" Bronte asked. "The joy she'll feel will still be real in the moment. Why not let her experience it?"

It definitely wasn't a horrible idea. Except . . .

"Is it too dangerous to leap her here?" Sophie asked. "Especially since she's coming from . . ."

She stopped herself in the nick of time.

Bronte smirked. "I love how you think I don't know that she's staying somewhere in Atlantis. And relax. How many times do you need me to assure you that the girl is safe?"

Alden cleared his throat. "It's . . . unlike you."

"Or perhaps you don't know me as well as you think," Bronte countered, before turning back to Sophie. "And to answer your concern, leaping her here should be no problem, so long as the person who brings her is prepared to shield her with their concentration. I'm assuming she's with Quinlin Sonden? His mental skills are excellent. And if she wears elvin clothes for the journey through the city, no one will suspect her."

Sophie had no idea how he'd pieced so many details together, but clearly she'd been underestimating the strict Councillor.

make sure she knows she's welcome to stay as long as she needs. She's actually starting to like it here. I taught her how to make ripplefluffs and she's been inventing all kinds of crazy flavor combinations."

Sophie couldn't smile.

She could barely think.

Which was probably why it took her much too long to realize Physic's mistake.

Bronte was still in the room, listening to every word they were saying.

And Physic had just revealed that her sister was illegally in the Lost Cities.

FIFTY-FIVE

I T'S ALL RIGHT," SOMEONE TOLD HER.

Sophie couldn't figure out who.

White-hot panic had clouded out everything but the searing tightness in her chest and the throbbing pulse in her ears.

"Breathe," the same voice commanded.

When she didn't respond, a prickle of cold scraped across her mind, as if something dark was crawling along her impenetrable mental shield.

Her eyes snapped into focus and she found Bronte crouched in front of her, his hands clutching her shoulders.

"Thought that might get your attention," he said without any hint of a smile.

"Please," she gasped. "Please—you can't—"

"Technically, I can do whatever the Council wills," he interrupted, rising from his crouch.

The dark jewels in his circlet glinted as he loomed over her.

"Fortunately," he added, dragging out the word for emphasis, "in this case, the Council's will is in harmony with yours. We have no desire to see any harm come to your sister—and it's a shame that you'd so easily assume we would. Oh, and for the record, I already knew she was here in the Lost Cities."

"You did?" Sophie asked.

"I told the whole Council this morning," Grady admitted. "I wanted them to understand why finding your parents needed to remain just as high of a priority as developing a cure for the soporidine. But I didn't tell them where she's staying, so there's no way they can get near her."

Bronte shook his head. "Even if you *had* told us where to find her, we have no plans to interfere with whatever the Black Swan has arranged. We would never abandon a child in need of our assistance."

Sophie had to clamp her lips shut to stop herself from reminding him how many times he'd threatened to do exactly that to her after she'd first been brought to the elvin world—or how the Council had no problem banishing Tam and Linh.

"You have my word," Bronte assured her, "that no harm will come to your sister as long as she's in the Lost Cities—and that she can stay as long as she needs. The Council already voted—and the decision was unanimous. I only ask one thing."

"You never said there were conditions," Grady argued.

"This is a *request*," Bronte corrected. "A personal one, I might add—which I very much hope you'll be willing to grant, Miss Foster."

The hairs on Sophie's neck bristled as she waited to hear what he'd ask—but she still wasn't prepared for him to say, "I'd like to meet her."

"My *sister*," Sophie clarified.

He nodded. "Today, if at all possible."

"Why?"

The question seemed to come from everyone in the room at once, with varying degrees of suspicion.

Bronte rolled his eyes at all of them. "Are you really surprised that I'm curious? This young girl is the first human to experience any part of our world for many millennia. Can you blame me for wanting to know what she thinks of it?"

"But she hasn't seen much," Sophie told him. "Only the place she's staying."

"Exactly why I'm hoping you'll bring her here this afternoon. I'm assuming you wouldn't want to take me to wherever you've tucked her away. Besides . . . to witness her reaction to this place—to both the estate and the creatures. Even to these."

He flicked the ends of his ears with an uncharacteristically wide smile, and Sophie tried to understand how he could be the same elf who'd scowled at her with the rage of a thousand suns when Fitz first brought her to Everglen and she'd gaped at the same pointed protrusions.

"I assure you, I have no ulterior motive," Bronte promised, turning back to the wall of windows. "I'm just an old fool longing for the past."

Sophie glanced at her friends, glad to see shock in their expressions, as if they were all thinking, *Who is this stranger and what has he done with Councillor Bronte?*

"You forget that Atlantis was not built as an obligation," he said when he noticed their gawking. "It was a dream. A future where these human creatures that looked so much like us—and yet lived such very different lives—might inspire us as much as we could inspire them. It was all for nothing, of course. Their greed destroyed everything. But forgive me for craving this small glimpse of what could've been."

"And you really think today is a wise day for such nostalgia?" Mr. Forkle asked.

"Why not?" Bronte countered. "You can't help Cadence or her team of ogres with their soporidine research. And it seems like an excellent way to ease your sister into the difficult conversations you still need to have. Bring her here, give her this glorious glimpse of our world, and then break the harder news she'll be forced to live with. Once she's seen more of the majesty of the Lost Cities, she may feel more ready to put her trust in us as a species."

"Even though all those memories will have to be erased?" Sophie had to ask, her voice wobbling on the last word.

Now that it was going to take them even longer to save her parents from whatever they were enduring, she couldn't imagine their minds wouldn't have to be reset.

And so would Amy's.

"Is a day any less worth living simply because you're not going to remember it?" Bronte asked. "The joy she'll feel will still be real in the moment. Why not let her experience it?"

It definitely wasn't a horrible idea. Except . . .

"Is it too dangerous to leap her here?" Sophie asked. "Especially since she's coming from . . ."

She stopped herself in the nick of time.

Bronte smirked. "I love how you think I don't know that she's staying somewhere in Atlantis. And relax. How many times do you need me to assure you that the girl is safe?"

Alden cleared his throat. "It's . . . unlike you."

"Or perhaps you don't know me as well as you think," Bronte countered, before turning back to Sophie. "And to answer your concern, leaping her here should be no problem, so long as the person who brings her is prepared to shield her with their concentration. I'm assuming she's with Quinlin Sondon? His mental skills are excellent. And if she wears elvin clothes for the journey through the city, no one will suspect her."

Sophie had no idea how he'd pieced so many details together, but clearly she'd been underestimating the strict Councillor.

"I suppose I can get rid of this too, then," Physic said, untying her mask and pulling it away to reveal her face.

Bronte's eyebrows arched. "Actually, Livvy, I hadn't made the connection. You and Quinlin have always been so . . . separate. I assume he knows?"

"As of a few days ago," she agreed.

He opened his mouth to ask her something, then closed it and turned to the members of the Collective. "Any of you prepared to dispense with the disguises?"

"Not quite yet," Mr. Forkle told him. "But perhaps someday. Should the Council continue to make the right decisions."

A bit of the infamous Bronte scowl returned, but he said nothing as he returned his focus to Sophie. "I believe we've gotten sidetracked. We were waiting for you to decide whether your sister will be paying us a visit."

"For what it's worth," Edaline said when Sophie hesitated, "I'd *love* to meet her."

The fragile hope in Edaline's voice settled it for Sophie, as did the happy crinkles around Grady's eyes when she nodded.

She couldn't pass up this unexpected chance to introduce her sister to her new family and give her a glimpse of her new life.

"Just give me a few minutes to change," she told Physic. "Then tell Quinlin to bring her."

FIFTY-SIX

W HOA."

It seemed to be the only word Amy could think to say—not that Sophie blamed her. She still remembered the wonder she'd felt the first day Alden brought her to Havenfield—and at that point, she'd already seen Everglen to help prepare her for the beauty of elvin homes.

The light leap with Quinlin had brought on the first "whoa," which wasn't surprising, since Amy had been unconscious when Alden took her to Atlantis. The house itself earned another, probably because it was almost a castle by human standards. And each part of the tour continued to elicit them, from seeing Fitz again to meeting Dex, Biana, Tam, and

Linh—which had earned a jaw drop along with the "whoa." To the bizarre disguises of the Collective. To watching the squat brown-and-green gnomes tending to Calla's Panakes tree. To the incredible spread Edaline conjured up with a snap of her fingers, composed of every delicious baked good the Lost Cities had to offer.

As a group, they'd feasted on the sugary, buttery treats until they were all leaning back in their chairs, convinced they might burst if they stuffed themselves with any more pastry—even Bronte. In fact, the generally surly Councillor had smiled so much throughout the course of the afternoon that Sophie wondered if his cheek muscles would be sore the next day.

Amy had been nervous around him at first, intimidated by his jewels and regal attire—but it hadn't stopped her from asking if she could feel the points of his ears, and causing everyone else to breathe their own "whoas" when Bronte let her.

He'd used the moment to assure Amy that the Council would keep her safe in the Lost Cities as long as she needed to stay. After that, he'd primarily been a silent observer.

Amy had been quiet as well, especially around Sophie's adoptive parents—though they'd still gotten their own "whoa," paired with a whispered "It's like you're being raised by movie stars." But Grady and Edaline had happily filled the silence, sharing hilarious stories about Sophie's adventures since she'd moved to the Lost Cities—with Alden and Della jumping in to give extra details. Amy seemed to hang on every word, and kept stealing glances at Sophie, as if she couldn't believe she was the girl they were talking about.

Sophie, meanwhile, was having just as hard of a time adjusting to the sight of her sister in elvin attire. Livvy had given Amy the dark blue tunic studded with sapphires and diamonds she now wore paired with silver leggings and knee-high boots—which had subtle wedge heels. But it was the cape that did Sophie in. Long, gray, and silky, and fastened around Amy's neck with a crest that Sophie had never seen before—round, with three hands reaching for each other.

Livvy had whispered in Sophie's ear that she'd had the pin made to represent Amy's family, and Sophie's eyes welled up at the gesture. But they spilled over when she studied the design again.

Three hands.

No fourth for her.

It was how it should be. How it would *have* to be.

And Sophie could live with that. She could let them go again, to spare them that pain.

But it would still hurt.

It would *always* hurt.

"I get it now," Amy mumbled as they stood outside Verdi's enclosure, watching the neon-green T. rex gobble up her dinner. The rest of their group had stepped back, giving Sophie and Amy some time alone together.

"Get what?" Sophie asked.

"Why you like living here. I mean, look at this place!"

She giggled as Verdi tried to use her too-short arms to wipe a bit of food off her fluffy snout.

"It's honestly the most beautiful place I've ever been," Amy whispered, "and I'm saying that after coming from Atlantis."

"That's right, what'd you think of your first ride in a eurypterid carriage?" Sophie asked.

"Not nearly as terrifying as the bubble-geyser thing. Can't elves ever do anything normal?"

Sophie smiled. "I'm pretty sure they can't."

Amy raised an eyebrow. "You realize you're one of them, right?"

"Yeah, I know. I'm still . . . getting used to the language."

"I guess that makes sense. And by the way—your friends?" Amy glanced over her shoulder to take another peek at them. "Are they in a contest to see who can be the most gorgeous or something?"

Sophie had to laugh. "They might be."

"It's ridiculous," Amy told her. "Especially Fitz's family. I mean, seriously, who looks like that?"

"Only the Vackers," Sophie assured her.

"Though those silver-haired twins? *Dude.*" Her sister leaned closer. "And the reddish-haired guy is the one you kissed, right?"

"Ugh, keep your voice down!"

"I did." She stole another glance at Dex. "Don't worry, he's talking to Quinlin and that guy with the pointy ears, anyway."

That was good to know—though Sophie wasn't surprised. Dex had done his best to stay a safe distance away from her all afternoon. But he wasn't the only one who could be eavesdropping.

"Not that you care what I think," Amy whispered, "but you totally made the right choice. The other guys seem more your type."

"And how, exactly, do you know my type?" Sophie had to ask.

"I guess I don't," her sister admitted. "You didn't have a lot of friends when you lived with us."

Sophie's cheeks flushed. "Yeah, well, no one wanted to hang out with the freaky twelve-year-old know-it-all who'd skipped a zillion grades."

"Probably true." Amy turned back to the munching T. rex. "I think I get that now too. How it must've felt growing up around humans. Because as much as I love it here? I can feel it—deep down—that I don't belong. You're all so powerful and pretty and I'm—"

"You're pretty," Sophie interrupted. Not that beauty mattered, but . . . she hated the idea of her sister feeling inadequate, even in a small, silly way.

Amy rolled her eyes. "I wasn't asking for a compliment. I just meant . . . this *really* is a whole other world. You live in mansions and sew diamonds onto your clothes like it's no big deal." She twisted one of the larger stones stitched along her tunic's hem, and Sophie wondered how many thousands of dollars the same diamond would sell for in the human world. "And while part of me keeps wondering how I'm ever going to go back to reality after being here, the other part of me . . . really wants to go home."

She choked on the last word and turned her face away.

Sophie scooted closer, wrapping an arm around her sister's shoulders, trying to think of something to say.

"I'm guessing it didn't go well yesterday," Amy whispered. "Otherwise Mom and Dad would be here. So just . . . give me the bad news, okay?"

Sophie bit her lip. "You're sure you don't want to wait until you're ready to go back to Atlantis? It might ruin the day."

"Just tell me," her sister begged. "I keep imagining the most horrible things."

Sophie nodded, trying her best to sugarcoat anything she could as she told the story of their time in Nightfall and how they didn't currently have a clear plan for where to search next. And she left out Lady Gisela's warning about her parents' sanity.

She also definitely didn't mention anything about having to erase their memories.

But her sister was still trembling by the end, and her eyes were red and puffy.

"I know this isn't going to make any of it better," Sophie said, holding her sister tighter. "But I've done this before. The part where it all feels hopeless, and like it's never going to come together. And you know what? Somehow, it *does*. It's never perfect. But it's usually better than I'd been fearing. And if you don't believe me, look at Mr. Forkle."

They both turned toward the heavyset figure watching them from the shadows of Calla's Panakes, trying his best to pretend he wasn't listening to their conversation.

"So that *is* our old neighbor?" Amy asked. "I thought I must be remembering him wrong when I saw him, since you'd told me he was . . ."

"Yeah, sorry—I should've warned you." She explained Mr. Forkle's dead-but-not-dead situation.

"Uh, that might be the weirdest thing ever," Amy told her when she'd finished. "And I'm saying that while staring at a fluffy dinosaur."

"Believe me, I *know*," Sophie said. "But it also proves that things aren't always as bad as they seem, right?"

"I guess."

"I know it still hurts. And I can't change that. But just . . . know that whatever happens, it's going to be survivable—and never stop hoping for the happy ending. Sometimes you get one you don't expect. I'll definitely be fighting for it with everything I have."

Amy wiped a fresh swell of tears as she leaned against Sophie's shoulder, the two of them clinging to each other, watching the sun make its slow descent toward the ocean.

"So where are those flying unicorn things you told me

about?" Amy eventually asked. "What are they called again?"

"Alicorns," Sophie told her. "And they don't live here. We set them free because it's safer if the Neverseen can't find them."

"Aw, it would've been cool to see them."

Sophie wished she could show her sister the sparkly flying horses and bring back all the "whoas" and smiles from earlier. But after her last conversation with Silveny, she doubted she'd be able to convince the pregnant alicorn to teleport over.

Still, it might be worth a try. . . .

"No promises," Sophie told her. "But I'm going to see if I can reach them."

"You can do that? Just . . . shout with your mind and talk to someone anywhere?"

"Depends on who I'm trying to reach. But, yeah."

Sophie shot her sister a slightly smug grin before she pushed out her consciousness, calling Silveny's name over and over as her mental energy spread and spread and spread.

It took longer than normal again, but Silveny's voice at least sounded chipper as she transmitted, *SOPHIE! FRIEND! HI!*

Hi! Sophie transmitted back. *How are you and Greyfell and the baby?*

GOOD! GOOD! GOOD!

Silveny flooded Sophie's head with images of the secluded meadow Greyfell had found for them.

That looks perfect, Sophie told her. *I'm so glad you guys are safe.*

SAFE! Silveny promised.

Sophie chewed her lip, trying to choose how to broach the idea of a visit without starting another alicorn tantrum.

Did I ever tell you I have a sister? she asked.

NO! The shout was especially loud. *SISTER! SISTER! SISTER!*

But despite the boisterous response, loneliness clung to Silveny's words, and Sophie wondered if Silveny had once had an extended family.

She sent Silveny a mental picture of her sister standing next to her. *This is Amy.*

AMY! AMY! AMY!

And you know what? Sophie asked. *She'd love to be your friend.*

FRIEND! FRIEND! FRIEND!

Does that mean you'll come meet her?

Silveny's thoughts went silent for a second, before she told Sophie, *LATER!*

But "later" means you won't get to meet her. She has to go back to Atlantis tonight. And I'm not sure if I'll ever be able to bring her to Havenfield again. Amy's also been going through some really scary stuff, and I was hoping you'd be able to cheer her up. But I'll tell her you don't want to meet her—

WANT! Silveny interrupted. *WANT! SISTER! FRIEND!*

Then come see us, Sophie challenged. *Please?*

A hint of the sadness and worry and desperation she'd been carrying must've clung to the plea, because Silveny's attention got a whole lot clearer.

SOPHIE OKAY? Silveny asked, her mind sifting through Sophie's mess of conflicted emotions.

I'm fine. It's just . . . been a rough week. And without meaning to, she shared a few of the harder memories.

Silveny studied each image, and a surge of something that could only be described as motherly worry flooded Sophie's mind.

HOLD ON! Silveny transmitted. *VISIT! VISIT! VISIT!*

The transmission was followed by a boom of thunder as a black line split through the sky—a tiny tear in reality, opening to the void beyond.

And out of the darkness, two shimmering winged horses appeared.

SOPHIE! FRIEND! HI!

FIFTY-SEVEN

I'M ASSUMING YOU INVITED THEM HERE?"
Bronte called as he craned his neck to watch the alicorns
circle overhead, their silver fur shimmering in the late
afternoon sunlight.

"Amy wanted to meet them," Sophie called back, grinning
as Silveny flew circles around Greyfell. It was easy to tell them
apart, thanks to Silveny's slightly smaller size and Greyfell's
blue-tipped wings.

"They're amazing," Amy whispered. "How did they crack
the sky like that?"

"Teleporting."

That earned another "whoa." Followed by several more when
both alicorns tucked their glittering wings and dove—streaking

toward the ground and barely stopping their freefall in time to land in the long grass a few feet away.

SOPHIE! SOPHIE! SOPHIE!

"Hi," Sophie said, stepping closer to check every inch of the alicorns for any clue to why Silveny had resisted the visit earlier.

Silveny's belly had a slight bulge to it, but that seemed normal considering the pregnancy. And everything else looked fine—her fur was sleek and shiny, her gold-flecked brown eyes were sparkling and clear as she studied Sophie every bit as closely as Sophie was studying her. And she looked far more concerned with the results.

SOPHIE OKAY?

Better now that you're here, Sophie told her, stroking the velvety fur along Silveny's nose. *I've really missed you.*

Silveny nuzzled into Sophie's shoulder.

Ready to meet my sister? Sophie asked.

SISTER! SISTER! SISTER!

Sophie turned to where Amy stood in jaw-dropped awe. "Amy, this is Silveny."

AMY! AMY! AMY!

"And that's Greyfell," Sophie added, gesturing to the much more reserved male alicorn, who stamped his gleaming hooves and whinnied.

Amy offered the most adorably shy wave.

"Here," Grady said as he rushed over with a huge armful of

twisted stalks. "Give them some swizzlespice and they'll love you forever."

TREATS! TREATS! TREATS! Silveny chanted.

Amy took two bunches of the stalks and held them out the way Grady showed her, grinning from ear to ear as the alicorns gobbled them straight from her hands.

When they'd devoured the whole batch, Silveny turned to the rest of the group that was watching them—and realized someone was missing.

KEEFE?

He's not here, Sophie told her. *But he's fine, don't worry.*

Silveny must've sensed the doubt in her answer, because she blasted Sophie with chants of *KEEFE! KEEFE! KEEFE!*

"You okay?" Amy asked as Sophie rubbed her temples.

"Yeah. Silveny's just *very loud.*"

KEEFE! KEEFE! KEEFE! KEEFE! KEEFE!

You're here to see my sister, Sophie reminded her. *She needs you to cheer her up.*

Silveny glanced back at Amy. *SISTER SAD?*

She's trying not to be, Sophie told her, feeling Silveny digging through her memories to understand what was happening.

SOPHIE SCARED? she asked.

A little, Sophie admitted.

Silveny nudged her with her nose, filling Sophie's mind with a rush of tender, reassuring warmth—along with an unexpected question.

FLY?

Do you mean fly with my sister?

YES! SOPHIE! SISTER! FLY!

Sophie bit her lip, glancing at Amy. "How scared are you of heights?"

Amy's eyes stretched huge. "We can fly with them?"

"Only if you want to."

"Are you kidding? Let's go! Let's go! Let's go!"

"Oh man—this is going to be a very loud flight," Sophie mumbled as Silveny transmitted, *FLY! FLY! FLY!*

"I have to admit, I'm a little jealous," Bronte said, coming over to watch as Silveny knelt to let them climb onto her back.

Sophie gave Amy the front spot and settled in behind her, wrapping her arms around Amy's waist to hold her steady.

"You've never flown with the alicorns?" Amy asked him.

Bronte shook his head. "Maybe someday."

Sophie tried to imagine a giddy Silveny looping through the sky with Bronte on her back—but she couldn't picture it.

"Why not today?" Amy asked. "Couldn't he ride Greyfell?"

All eyes shifted to the male alicorn, who seemed to understand what they were discussing—and did not seem happy about it.

It's up to you, Sophie transmitted to him. *You don't have to.*

Greyfell flicked his tail.

"Awww, you should let him," Amy told the grumpy alicorn. "You'd make his day. And I bet he'd give you a bunch more of those spicy sticks as a thank-you."

Greyfell gave her sister the alicorn equivalent of side-eye, and Sophie assumed the snuffle that followed was a no. But Greyfell slowly dipped his head and bent his knees, inviting Bronte to climb onto his back.

"Well, I'll be," Bronte whispered. His hands trembled as he hauled himself up, and Sophie could've sworn his eyes looked misty.

"Ready?" she asked, tightening her grip on her sister.

"Yes!" Bronte and Amy said in unison.

The word morphed into gasps and screams as the alicorns flapped their wings and launched into the sky. But the shouts quickly shifted to delighted squeals, then pleas to go faster and higher and spin and flip and more more more—for Amy at least. Bronte and Greyfell kept things much simpler.

Silveny offered to teleport them anywhere they wanted to go, but Sophie wasn't sure if that would be safe for a human. So they stayed soaring over Havenfield, sometimes stretching out over the ocean, and Sophie couldn't decide if she should marvel at her sister's fearlessness or worry about motion sickness.

Mostly, though, she loved hearing Amy laugh.

With all the bad news and stress, it was nice to give her this unforgettable experience.

Even if Amy wouldn't get to remember it for very long.

Sadness crept in with the realization, but Sophie fought it back, trying to savor the moment. They both deserved to lose themselves in this brief, happy escape before they'd have to return to reality.

So they flew for hours and hours, until the sun was long gone and the blue-black sky twinkled with the flickers of early stars. Most of the group had gone home by the time Silveny and Greyfell touched down again in Havenfield's pastures. Only Quinlin remained.

"I need my own alicorn," Amy decided, stretching her stiff legs after she dismounted. "Want to give me one as a present?"

Bronte snorted. "Sorry, these are the only two left on the planet, so they're not up for grabs. Even with a third one on the way."

Amy pouted. "Fine. I'll just have to visit them all the time, then."

"You will," Sophie said, wondering if her sister could hear the lie in her tone.

If she did, Amy didn't call her on it—and Sophie avoided Bronte's gaze as she turned back to Silveny, patting her side to thank her.

She realized then how heavily the pregnant alicorn was breathing. *Was all of that flying too much for you and the baby?*

NO! Silveny promised. *FUN! FUN! FUN!*

But the transmission sounded strained. And Silveny's eyes were heavy-lidded with exhaustion.

Maybe Edaline should check on you before you leave, Sophie suggested.

Silveny trotted backward. *NO! NO! NO!*

Why not? You like Edaline.

NO! NO! NO!

Don't you want to make sure you and the baby are okay?

SAFE! Silveny insisted. *SAFE! SAFE! SAFE!*

Sophie sighed. *You know you're going to have to let people check on you, right?*

LATER! Silveny told her, launching off the ground.

"Everything okay?" Bronte asked as Greyfell followed Silveny into the sky, both alicorns circling higher and higher.

The last thing Sophie wanted to do was worry the Council— especially since they could decide to take away Silveny and Greyfell's freedom.

"Everything's great," she told him, while transmitting to Silveny, *LATER better be SOON.*

Neither alicorn agreed before they teleported away.

"Huh," Amy said. "They left without the treats you owed them."

Bronte frowned. "They did, indeed."

"So did you have fun?" Sophie asked her sister, eager for a subject change.

"Uh, *yeah*—today has seriously been the best. Day. Ever!"

"I'm glad to hear you enjoyed it," Bronte told her.

"Did you think I wouldn't?"

"Honestly, I didn't know what to expect," he said, his eyes shifting to the stars. "Letting you experience our world so fully, as if there were no divide between our species . . . part of me had wondered if your mind could truly process it all. And I can't decide if this means any human could, or if you're simply special. Either way . . . there was such joy today. It seems we truly are missing out, keeping ourselves separate."

"You can change that, can't you?" Amy told him, gesturing to his jeweled circlet.

"If only it were that simple." His smile looked equally wistful and sad as he squeezed Amy's shoulder and told her he hoped they'd meet again, then raised a pathfinder and leaped away.

"I guess that means it's time for me to head back to Atlantis," Amy mumbled when she noticed Quinlin crossing the pastures toward her.

"Will you be okay?" Sophie asked.

Amy's voice sounded a little thick, but Sophie still believed her when she said, "Yeah."

"What about you?" Amy asked.

Sophie reached for her eyelashes—then stopped herself. "I'll be fine."

"And you'll keep me updated?" Amy pressed.

"As much as I can."

Amy nodded.

There was so much more they both could—should—say.

But they chose to save it for later. Just like they both avoided saying goodbye, as if they were afraid the word would be too permanent.

But before Amy stepped into the light, she told Sophie, "Thank you. For today. And for all the scary things you've been doing. I don't know how it's all going to work out, but . . . I'll be fighting for the happy ending too."

FIFTY-EIGHT

THE NEXT FEW DAYS MANAGED TO be both busy *and* uneventful as everyone scrambled to regroup after the revelations from Nightfall.

Grady worked with the Collective, trying to figure out what the Neverseen might be planning, and where they'd moved Sophie's parents.

Tam worked with Livvy, testing her shadowvapor theories on Alvar.

Dex worked with Bronte, trying to access the secrets in Fintan's cache—or Sophie assumed he did. Dex still seemed to be avoiding her.

Fitz worked with Alden, trying to meet with the remaining guards from Lumenaria to see if they knew anything about the escaped prisoner.

Lady Cadence worked with her team of ogres on the soporidine antidote.

Linh worked with Marella, learning to control their abilities.

And Sophie and Biana *tried* to work with Sandor, but no matter what they did, they couldn't convince him to give them the Imparter so they could hail Lady Gisela about what happened to Cyrah. He kept insisting that they weren't ready and needed a stronger plan.

Sophie didn't think she could get any more frustrated—and then Mr. Forkle reminded her that Foxfire resumed session on Monday, and that everyone was expected to attend. Even Tam and Linh had agreed to switch to the prestigious academy.

Others in our order will remain on top of all of your projects, he'd assured her, *and I'll call you to my office if there's ever anything important going on while you're in your sessions.*

Somehow that didn't feel like enough.

Then again, *none* of it felt like enough.

Probably because none of it was helping.

Every update was always a long stream of failures and dead ends. And no matter how many times Sophie tried to remind herself that this was part of the process—that they always hit these kinds of walls in their investigations—she couldn't help feeling like this time was worse.

"How are you holding up?" Fitz asked when he found her gathering fallen blossoms under Calla's Panakes tree during an especially vivid sunset. He'd been coming by every evening to check on her, even though her mood was getting sulkier and sulkier.

She shrugged and he plopped down on the grass beside her, setting a small box tied with teal ribbon in her lap before leaning against the wide trunk.

"You don't have to keep bringing me gifts," she told him. "Or putting up with me when I'm super grumpy."

"I know." His smile chipped away some of the edge of her bad mood. "Aren't you going to open it?"

Warmth tingled her cheeks as she untied the ribbon and found . . .

"Custard bursts?"

"That's what they're supposed to be—but I'm not sure if I pulled it off," Fitz admitted. "Who knew they were so hard to bake?"

The puffed squares definitely were more lopsided than the batches Edaline made—but somehow that made the gesture even sweeter.

And they still tasted *amazing*.

"Is this caramel?"

Fitz nodded. "My mom had me add a little bit of salt. She said that brings out the sweetness."

"It does." She shoved the rest into her mouth and tried to wipe the bit that dribbled down her chin.

"You missed a spot," Fitz said, reaching out to brush the corner of her mouth.

His fingers didn't touch her lips, but they were so close her face turned nuclear—especially since her mind kept drifting back to the last time they'd been alone together under the Panakes tree. The moment that had almost felt like a *moment*, but had probably been a whole lot of nothing.

"You're not sleeping, are you?" Fitz asked, and it took her a second to follow the rapid topic change.

"I'm sleeping enough."

"Liar." He pointed to the shadows under her eyes. "Nightmares or tossing and turning?"

She sighed. "Both."

"That's what I thought. And that's why I'm here. I think you need something to distract you from everything you're worrying about, so you can actually relax tonight."

"Okaaaaaay," she said, not sure where he was going with this, but her heart had shifted to a fast, fluttery rhythm.

It shifted again when he said, "So how about we finally settle that favor you owe me?"

Red Alert sirens went off in her mind.

He laughed. "Don't panic. I've decided to go super easy on you. All I want is something you'll have to tell me anyway, the next time we do Cognate training."

"That doesn't actually sound easy." Her palms were sweating, and she leaned back, knowing she was going to need space for whatever was coming.

"Wow, could you look any more terrified?" Fitz asked. "I promise, it's nothing bad. I just want to know what happened with you and Dex."

"Oh."

Somehow that was both better and worse than what she'd been expecting.

She turned away, fussing with the ends of the teal ribbon. "He asked me not to tell anyone."

"Okay, but you already told Biana," he argued.

"How do you know that?"

"I just do."

She cleared her throat. "Well . . . I didn't tell her. She saw something and figured it out."

"Then show me what she saw."

No *way* was that happening.

"You know, technically you're not supposed to be able to say no," he reminded her. "It's my favor. You owe me."

"I know, but what you're asking for isn't really *my* secret, you know?" she countered.

Fitz tilted his head, considering that. "Okay, fine, new

favor—and no cheating your way out of this one."

He waited for her reluctant nod before he said, "I want to know if you're really thinking about not registering for the match."

Aaaaaaaaaaaand, now her whole body was sweating.

"Did Biana tell you that?"

"Don't get mad—I sorta tricked it out of her when I was trying to find out what happened with you and Dex."

It felt like there was probably some sort of clue tucked into that sentence, but Sophie's brain was too overloaded to process it—especially with the way he was staring at her.

So she gave him the truth. "I'm still deciding."

He nodded slowly.

"Is that bad?"

She hadn't meant to ask the question, but it somehow shoved its way out of her mouth.

"Not *bad*," Fitz said carefully. "I do actually get why you might be intimidated by the whole process."

"It's more than that."

"I know—it's not a perfect system. I really do see how unfair it can be now."

"But?" she prompted, wondering why she was pushing him. This was *such* dangerous territory.

"But," Fitz said, sweeping his hair off his forehead, "aren't you curious to see who would be on your lists? Even if you decide later not to follow them?"

"Yes."

She hadn't meant to say that.

But it was true.

She *was* curious.

Also terrified.

And it would always feel wrong.

It was all so miserably complicated.

"Well," Fitz said, "you still have some time to think about it. I was just curious. And see? Favor settled. Was that as scary as you thought?"

It actually wasn't.

And somehow that was . . . disappointing.

Neither of them seemed to know what to say after that, so Sophie became very interested in gathering more blossoms, arranging them into a neat ring on the grass.

"For what it's worth," Fitz whispered, "I'll be hoping you decide to register."

It was hard to tell in the fading light, but she almost swore he was blushing. And with that, she pretty much melted into a pile of goo—which was stupid.

He could be worried about her facing the scorn of a bad match.

Or he could be trying to protect her.

Or—

He took her hand, tracing his finger over the bump of her cognate ring under her glove. "Just promise me you'll think about it, okay?"

Words.

She needed words.

She still hadn't found any when a painfully loud throat-clearing had her yanking her hand free and scooting back, ready to shout, *We were just talking!*

But it wasn't Grady standing behind her in protective dad mode.

It was Sandor, and he looked . . . pale.

"Sorry to interrupt," he said, "but I wasn't able to ignore this."

He held out Keefe's Imparter, and before Sophie could ask why he was giving it to her, Lady Gisela's voice trilled, "Hello, Sophie. We need to talk."

FIFTY-NINE

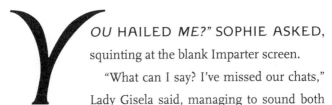**OU** HAILED *ME?*" SOPHIE ASKED, squinting at the blank Imparter screen.

"What can I say? I've missed our chats," Lady Gisela said, managing to sound both bored *and* superior. "Mind you, I'd hoped to find you with my son, and not the Vacker boy again. But you can correct that error in judgment later."

Fitz rolled his eyes and leaned back against the Panakes. "What do you want?"

"I want you to stop wasting time."

"We're *not*," Sophie said, even if it kinda felt like they had been.

"If that's true, tell me this: What exactly have you accomplished since you left my facility?" Lady Gisela asked.

"That's what I thought," she added when Sophie and Fitz didn't say anything. "And I've grown tired of waiting for you to realize that you need me. So here we are."

"We *don't* need you," Sophie insisted. "Everything you've had us do has turned out to be pointless."

"Has it? So you don't have a member of the Neverseen in your custody, and information about Nightfall and soporidine, and an alliance with the ogres?"

"You didn't have anything to do with any of that," Fitz argued.

"If it makes you feel better to tell yourself that, go ahead. I'll admit, some of my plans have changed—but all of those changes have turned out to be for the better. I'm actually quite amazed at how well everything is coming together. I just need the final piece. And I need you to get it for me."

"And why would we do that?" Fitz asked.

"Because it will be well worth your while."

"Yeah . . . I'm done risking my life—and my friends' lives—for your stupid errands," Sophie told her. "Especially since you haven't even come through with everything we already agreed on."

Lady Gisela sighed. "I can only assume you're referring to your obsession with what happened to Cyrah Endal."

"It's not an obsession."

Though Sophie decided then and there that she wasn't letting Gisela end their conversation until she had what she needed to heal Prentice—not after losing so many days trying to get Sandor to give her the Imparter.

"The fact that it's on your mind at all is proof of your foolish priorities," Lady Gisela insisted. "Especially when you should be focused on finding your fam—"

"I *am* focused on finding my family!" Sophie interrupted. "But I'm not going to let the Neverseen distract me from their bigger plans."

"And what exactly are those plans?" She huffed when Sophie didn't have an answer. "You have no clue what's going on— and you never will unless you accept my help."

"You only want to help yourself," Fitz argued.

"Trust me, this bargain will benefit all of us."

"Yeah, well, I'm not making a deal with someone who's already proven they don't hold up their end," Sophie told her.

"Does that mean you'd agree if I tell you about Cyrah?"

"It means I'll hear you out, instead of hanging up on you." Sophie counted to ten in her head, then handed the Imparter to Sandor. "You can take this back. I think we're done."

"Wait," Lady Gisela commanded. "If you insist on sidetracking us, fine. I'll give you your precious Cyrah story. But you're not going to like it—because *I'm* not the villain."

"Somehow I doubt that," Fitz told her.

"That doesn't make you any less wrong."

Sophie could hear fabric rustling, as if Lady Gisela had decided to sit for the next part of the conversation.

"All I wanted from Cyrah was the starstones," she said quietly. "I'd discovered that the Ancients used them for leaping before the pathfinder was invented. And since I needed a way to access certain facilities that weren't on the Lodestar map—"

"Facilities," Sophie interrupted, emphasizing the plural. "As in 'more than Nightfall.'"

"One secret at a time, Sophie. Surely you know that. Anyway, I figured no one would suspect starstones the way they might question an unfamiliar crystal. So I needed a Flasher who could make them for me. The skill had mostly become a lost art, but I knew Cyrah was talented enough to figure it out. And with Prentice in Exile, I also knew I'd be able to manipulate her into cooperating. In that sense, I suppose I do share some blame for what happened—but she was the one who demanded to know what I needed the starstones for. If she'd kept her questions to herself, she'd still be alive."

"Are you seriously blaming Cyrah for her own murder?" Sophie asked.

"Why not? We all share *some* responsibility for our actions."

"Uh, asking questions doesn't give anyone the right to murder you. Just when I thought you couldn't get any worse."

"I can get *much* worse, Sophie. You should be grateful for my restraint."

"Is that a threat?" Fitz asked.

"It's a reminder to think long and hard about who's truly your enemy, and who has spared you time and again. But we're getting off track. Going back to the story you've been so desperate for me to share, I tried to convince Cyrah that I was a member of the Black Swan and would be using the starstones to protect the newest hideouts—but Prentice must've coached her somehow. She asked too many specific questions, and my answers gave away that I was with the Neverseen—not that she knew the name of our order back then. But she knew I was on the other side, and she threatened to turn me in to the Council. I had to silence her."

"You mean kill her," Sophie clarified.

"Why would I kill her? I needed the starstones. I also much prefer keeping my sanity. I simply made a threat of my own. I knew the Black Swan had created a child, and that she was supposed to be this all-powerful *thing*, tucked away somewhere until the timing was right. I'd also heard rumors that Cyrah believed her husband would recover by some mysterious means. So, I put two and two together and told her that the Neverseen were close to finding the girl, and that once we did, she would be terminated—but that if Cyrah made me the starstones I needed, I'd make sure the girl had a chance to help Prentice before her untimely demise."

"How nice of you," Fitz muttered, scooting closer to Sophie and wrapping an arm around her.

"I thought it was particularly generous," Lady Gisela agreed. "And Cyrah became much more cooperative. But it took her several weeks to figure out how to achieve the blue flash I needed. And in that time, Fintan discovered what I was up to. He didn't like that Cyrah knew about my connection to the order, even after I'd assured him that she understood that both her husband's life—and her son's—were on the line if she betrayed our agreement. Evidently that wasn't good enough for him, so *he* was the one who got rid of her—without telling me. If you don't believe me, consider this: He didn't even wait until she'd delivered all of the starstones. She'd messed one up, and still owed me a replacement, which I never got, thanks to him."

Sophie wondered if that was the stone Marella's mom had found.

But Fitz went for the bigger question. "How did Fintan kill her?"

"He left that to Gethen. Fintan demanded I bring Gethen with me when I went to pick up the starstones in Mysterium. I've never worked out exactly what happened, but I saw Cyrah's expression shift as she stepped into the light. One second all was well. The next she looked pained and panicked. And when I turned to Gethen, he was sweaty and shaking. I confronted Fintan about it later, and all he told me was that I'd gotten sloppy—and I suppose I should've seen it for the warning it was. At the time, all I could think was that I *had* been sloppy— and it cost Cyrah her life."

There was a crackle in her voice, but Sophie couldn't decide if it was remorse or resentment.

Or maybe the whole story was a ploy to misdirect the blame on Fintan.

"If what you're saying is true," Sophie said, trying to fit the new details with everything she already knew, "why did Fintan abduct Wylie and interrogate him about his mom?"

"Because Fintan's convinced that Cyrah took so long to make the starstones—and messed up that final stone—for a reason. He believes that people who are forced to do things under duress always find a means to rebel. And since Cyrah would've known that she'd be putting her son in danger by doing so, he thinks she must've warned Wylie somehow— maybe even clued him in to what was happening, or gave him the missing starstone, or . . . who knows? You're the one who's friends with him—you tell me."

Sophie pressed her lips together.

"Fine, keep your secrets. It doesn't matter right now. That's what I keep trying to tell you. There's only one goal we should be focusing on—and yes, I do mean *we*. Like it or not, you need to work with me if you want to find your family."

"Why should I believe you?" Sophie demanded. "You're scrambling just as much as we are."

"So you admit you're scrambling?"

Sophie could've kicked herself for the slip. "I—"

"I know your instinct is to shut me out," Lady Gisela interrupted. "But our goals truly are connected. Find my Archetype and I'll show you. It's a book secured with a very special lock, to ensure no one can open it except me. Fintan stole it and I need you to get it back. The good news is, he'll have it in the same place he's keeping your human family."

"And where's that?" Sophie asked, wishing she didn't sound quite so desperate.

Gisela clicked her tongue. "Not until you agree."

"Agree to what?" Sandor demanded, resting his hand on Sophie's shoulder to remind her that she wouldn't be making any deals without consulting him. "It sounds to me like you want Sophie to take all the risks while you sit back and do nothing."

"Oh, I assure you, I will be *very* busy. But my primary contribution will be sharing what I know, so you can find the facility. You'll still have to figure out some things on your own—but without the information I have, you wouldn't even know where to start. And all I ask in return is that you recover the Archetype for me. Oh, and that you destroy the facility—but I'm sure you won't mind that part when you see what they're doing in there."

"What *are* they doing?" Sophie asked, bracing herself for the worst possible answer.

"It's hard to say for certain. But if it's anything like what was done there in the past, it's not going to be pretty. Especially for your family."

Panic mixed with dread, forming something thick and choking in Sophie's throat.

But she reminded herself over and over that the Wash-ers could erase every second of whatever her parents were enduring.

"Why not just raid the facility yourself?" Fitz asked Gisela.

"Because there's only one of me and a whole lot more of you. I'm also a fugitive, so I can't exactly go traipsing around Atlantis trying to find the entrance."

"Atlantis?" Sophie, Fitz, and Sandor all said at the same time.

"Sounds like I have your attention."

Sophie nodded, already wondering if she needed to get her sister out of the city. "What makes you so sure that's where they are?"

"Because I know what the mark on Alvar's heel means. It's stamped on every page of the journals that loosely inspired my own plans. I'd thought the writings were theoretical, but I've spent these last few days poring through them again, and now I can see the clues I missed."

"You're talking about the notes that inspired Nightfall," Sophie guessed.

"I am," Lady Gisela agreed. "Fintan *did* take your family to Nightfall. But not to my facility. He's keeping them in the origi-nal Nightfall. Where everything began."

SIXTY

TWO NIGHTFALLS?" MR. FORKLE asked as he stared at the stack of weathered blue journals Sophie was carrying. She'd found the books waiting for her at the bottom of the stairs when she emerged from her bedroom the next morning—exactly as Lady Gisela had promised they would be. "I'll admit, that's a twist I didn't see coming."

"Neither did I," Sophie said, setting the pile down on the table in front of the sofa. "But Keefe's mom claimed the proof is in these."

She'd tried reading the ancient yellowed pages, but they were filled with runes her brain couldn't translate. The only thing she recognized were the swirling lines of the falling-star symbol stamped in the corner of every page and pressed onto the covers with gold foil.

"And we don't know where this other Nightfall is," Tiergan noted.

"Only that it's somewhere in Atlantis," Sophie agreed.

"Oh good, because that's not a huge city or anything," Tam said, flopping onto the couch between Biana and Linh.

Their group was smaller that morning, thanks to all the projects they were juggling. Only Tam, Linh, Fitz, Biana, Grady, Alden, Mr. Forkle, and Tiergan were there—along with Sandor, Grizel, and Woltzer, of course, who were outside with Cadoc, trying to figure out how Lady Gisela had managed to sneak past their security *again*.

"Lady Gisela said the entrance will be marked with the Nightfall symbol," Fitz added.

Mr. Forkle grabbed one of the journals and traced his fingers over the swirling gold lines on the cover. "In all my visits to the city, I've never seen anything like this."

"Neither have I," Tiergan said.

"Same," Grady agreed.

"Quinlin's the best person to ask," Alden suggested. "He knows that city better than anybody."

Sadly, a quick hail to Quinlin confirmed that he'd never noticed the symbol either.

"Well . . . now that we know what to look for, I'm sure we'll be able to find it," Fitz said, deciding to be the optimistic one.

"Is that seriously our plan?" Tam asked. "We're just going to wander around Atlantis and hope we spot it?"

"No," Mr. Forkle said. "The Neverseen likely have eyes in the city, and we don't want them to know we're searching for them. Better to scour these notebooks first, see if there are any other clues to help us narrow down a more precise location. I'm sure there's at least one that Lady Gisela missed—or chose not to tell us so we'd have to work for it."

He turned to the first page and frowned at the tiny writing. "Wow, these runes are *ancient*."

"I thought all runes were ancient," Sophie said, glancing at Alden. "Isn't that what you told me?"

"Probably—and it's true in the sense that we've long relied on a more modern alphabet," Alden explained. "But our runes also evolved over time. So I believe what Mr. Forkle is saying is that these journals were written with letters that predate the runes we use more commonly."

"See these extra curves?" Mr. Forkle pointed to several marks in the journal. "Those flourishes were only used in our most ancient alphabet, before the characters were simplified to make them easier to write."

"So does that mean you can't read the journals?" Sophie asked.

"I can pick out some of the words, since many only have a few unfamiliar letters. But others are gibberish."

Grady grabbed one of the other journals and flipped through, seeming to have the same problem. Tiergan and Alden struggled as well.

"Would Bronte be able to read it?" Fitz asked.

"Probably. But I'm not sure we want to hand these over to the Council," Mr. Forkle warned. "Not until we know exactly what they say. Besides, if Lady Gisela can figure it out, I certainly can. I just need to get my hands on one of the ancient Lexicons."

"Quinlin has several," Alden noted.

"Perfect. Can you let him know that Sir Astin will be paying him a visit at his office later today to borrow them?"

"Should I tell him why?" Alden asked.

Mr. Forkle considered. "At this point, he's involved enough that it's probably better for him to know one of my identities. Perhaps we can translate the journals together. I'll have your sister help as well," he told Sophie. "It'll be good for her to stay involved."

"Shouldn't we be getting her out of the city?" Sophie asked. "Now that we know the Neverseen are targeting Atlantis?"

"Having a hideout there and targeting the city are two very different things," Mr. Forkle reminded her. "If anything, they're more likely to protect the city to prevent any harm from coming to their facility. It's also important to keep in mind that this Nightfall has apparently existed for thousands of years without causing any harm."

"But the person who built it was in prison," Sophie countered. "She's free now. And we all saw what the Neverseen did to Eternalia and Lumenaria."

"If it would make you feel better, Sophie, Amy's welcome to stay here," Grady offered.

Mr. Forkle shook his head. "I don't think that would be wise. Gisela has no problem breaching security here."

He patted the stack of journals as proof.

"What about Everglen?" Biana suggested.

"She would be more than welcome," Alden told her. "Though I'm not sure our home could guarantee her safety either. More than that, I think we need to consider the fact that this could be a ploy to flush Sophie's sister out of hiding. The Neverseen used a similar fear tactic to find Sophie, when they sparked those white fires around her city to inspire you to relocate her—and Gisela was in charge at that point."

"I was thinking the same thing," Tiergan admitted. "And if that's the case, it's far safer to leave Amy where she is. Gisela wouldn't resort to this kind of trick if she already knew how to find her."

"You think she's after my sister?" Sophie asked.

"I think we have to at least consider it," Mr. Forkle said gently. "The fact is, we don't know *what* Gisela's truly planning with any of this, so it's best to resist changing anything that's currently working. Look at what happened with Lumenaria. Had we left Gethen where we'd originally been holding him, he wouldn't have been anywhere near the

Peace Summit. It was only when we altered our plans that we fell in line with theirs."

"He has a point," Grady admitted.

"We'll monitor the city," Tiergan added. "I'll even alert the Council to see if they want to make adjustments to the security."

"And I'll give Quinlin a thorough update," Alden promised. "To ensure he knows to be extra vigilant."

"I'll also check the apartment myself when I'm there later today," Mr. Forkle assured her. "To see that every precaution has been taken."

Sophie couldn't argue with any of their reasoning. But every nerve in her body still itched to grab her sister and run.

"I wish she wasn't somewhere that's so hard to get to," she mumbled. "I know in some ways that's an advantage, but if something happens, it's a huge process to get there. Same goes for if they have to evacuate."

"If it would make you feel better, I can give you a small bottle of starlight from Candesia, and a magsidian charm that leads to the city, as well as to other crucial locations, like Havenfield and the Physician's office at Foxfire," Mr. Forkle offered. "But you know how illegal that is, so you'd have to let Edaline hide it in the void—and only use it in an emergency."

"Of course," Sophie promised, grateful for the backup plan—even if leaping with light from the unmapped stars was a complete misery.

Mr. Forkle set his journal back on the pile. "If that's settled, we still need to discuss the deal you've made with Lady Gisela. I'm assuming she didn't give you this information out of the goodness of her heart?"

Sophie fussed with her gloves. "She wants us to steal back her Archetype. I guess it's a book that no one can read without a special key."

"And that was her only demand?" Grady asked.

Fitz glanced at Sophie. "She also wants us to destroy the facility," he admitted.

Tam whistled. "I mean, normally I'm all for smashing things that belong to the Neverseen. But it kinda sounds like she's putting you in the middle of her revenge on Fintan."

"I'm already in the middle," Sophie reminded him. "Fintan has my parents."

Biana sucked in a breath. "Has anyone considered that this whole thing might actually be the Neverseen's trap? I'm sure they know we're in touch with Keefe's mom, since we couldn't have gotten into the first Nightfall without her. So maybe *this* is why they left Alvar there, knowing the symbol would lead us to this other facility."

"It's possible," Mr. Forkle admitted.

"I still have to check it," Sophie said quietly. "It's not like we have any other leads right now—and not just for finding my parents. This facility could also be where they're keeping their supplies of soporidine, or could at least have some clues to what they're planning. But if you guys don't want to go with me—"

"I'm in," Fitz interrupted, reaching for her hand and holding on tight.

"So am I," Biana promised. "That's not what I was saying. I just meant that we might want to be prepared for them to be expecting us—that's all."

"We need a plan," Tam agreed. "A good one."

"Do you think there's information about the facility in the cache?" Linh asked. "It could be the reason Fintan's new advisor was arrested."

"I'm sure it was," Alden said through a sigh. "Or at least part of the reason. I'll be sure to tell Dex and Bronte, in case it changes their strategy for the passwords. I need to head to Eternalia anyway. I'm meeting with another former guard from Lumenaria today. And I'm still trying to convince Fallon to meet with me. Maybe I'll just show up and force the issue. At this point, we need to exhaust every option."

"I agree," Mr. Forkle jumped in as Alden pulled out his pathfinder. "Which is why it would be wise for the rest of you to spend whatever time you can researching Atlantis to see if there's anything in our history that references the facility. I realize that kind of work is far from your favorite—but there may very well be subtle records that could help us narrow down the precise location. Or, more importantly, the time period it was constructed."

"Why is that more important than the location?" Sophie asked.

He sighed, running a swollen hand down his face. "Because one of the words I do recognize in this journal is 'human.' Over and over. And given how things deteriorated between our species, it's unsettling to know our side has a secret that's managed to stay buried for millennia—a secret connected to a prisoner so horrible, the Council erased her from their memories."

"Sounds like you think Nightfall had something to do with the sinking of Atlantis," Grady noted.

"I think it's crucial we find out. The best place to look would be the archives in Eternalia's main library. Perhaps you could take everyone there, Mr. Ruewen?"

Tam groaned. "You realize how huge that place is, right?"

"The search likely will be daunting," Mr. Forkle told him. "But we're all enduring tedious forms of information gathering." He tapped the pile of journals he'd be stuck translating. "I know it can feel slow and exhausting, but this is a vital step—especially when we're so frighteningly behind the curve."

Everything he said made sense—miserable and boring as it sounded.

But they were also forgetting something.

"What about Prentice?" Sophie asked. "I have the story about what happened to Cyrah now. Doesn't that mean I should start working toward healing him?"

"Absolutely," Mr. Forkle told her. "But that doesn't mean you should be heading there today. I understand how frustrating it is to hear me say that. But are you really prepared to share these heartbreaking revelations with him? Because every single word you say will either help him or harm him. It's a tremendous responsibility—one I would gladly take on myself, if I could. But I can't."

"I can help," Fitz offered, tightening his hold on her hand when he noticed the way Sophie had started shaking. "We all can. We'll write it up like a script that you just have to memorize and deliver. I'm sure it'll only take us a couple of days to get it all worked out."

"That's an excellent suggestion," Mr. Forkle told him. "But . . . I'd like to ask a favor. I want to be there for every stage of Prentice's healing—especially the first one, when he'll be the most vulnerable. And with Foxfire resuming session, I have too many responsibilities as Magnate Leto for me to be anywhere other than my office for at least the next week. I can still work on these," he promised, tapping the journals. "But I can't be sneaking away to where Prentice is staying. I'm sorry—I know it's an incredibly selfish request. If I could still be two places at once . . ."

His voice cracked and he turned away, shaking his head.

Tiergan moved closer, wrapping an arm around his shoulders. "It's not selfish. We *all* want to be there for this. And I'm sure the more time Sophie has to prepare for the conversation, the better. So how about we wait until everyone survives the first week of Foxfire? And in the meantime, we'll focus hard on these other projects."

Everyone nodded.

"But I think we need to tell Wylie today," Linh added quietly. "He should know what we've learned about his mom—and that we're scheduling his father's healing—in case he wants us to wait."

"I was thinking the same thing," Tiergan agreed.

"Do you think Cyrah told him anything about the starstones, or gave him the missing one?" Sophie had to ask.

"I feel like he would've mentioned it," Tiergan told her. "Especially after the Neverseen interrogated him. But I still intend to double-check. I was planning to head there now."

"I'll go with you," Linh offered. "In case he needs cheering up."

Tam glared at his sister. "Oh sure. Leave us in research torment while you go hang out with your friend."

"Uh, hello," Biana told him, pointing to herself and Fitz and Sophie, "you're hanging out with *us*."

"Yeah, but . . . in a *library*."

Biana laughed. "It's too bad Keefe isn't here—you two could have a contest to see who whines the most."

"I'd win," Keefe said from the doorway.

Time seemed to stop—or maybe it was Sophie's heart as she watched him stride into the room.

Keefe managed not to look at her as he folded his arms and flashed his famous smirk, telling everyone, "That's right— I'm back!"

SIXTY-ONE

HAT ARE YOU DOING HERE?"
Sophie asked.

Keefe's smirk widened as his eyes
finally found their way to hers. "It's
good to see you too, Foster—though yowza, that's a lot of emotions to hit a guy with all at once. In case you need help deciding, I'd go with the part of you that wants to run over here for
an epic Team Foster-Keefe hugfest, and *not* the part that wants
to rip off my arms and smack me with them."

She looked away, blinking hard, trying to figure out how
to respond.

Keefe closed the distance between them, but still stood a few careful feet away as he added, "In case you're wondering, I'm all healed."

He stretched out his arms and waved them around in a weird little dance without even the slightest wince.

"Elwin took me off bed rest last night. And you can barely see the scar. I'd show you to prove it, but it'd probably be weird to take my shirt off right now."

"It would," Grady agreed.

Keefe nodded. "I've also been eavesdropping outside—plus, Forkle hailed me this morning and caught me up on everything that's been happening. So I already know about the giant beast things my mom made, and how we have a drugged Alvar in custody, and how all that boring stuff from Lady Cadence's report about bacteria turned out to have something to do with flowers, and how there's apparently another Nightfall in Atlantis that's *not* part of my legacy, and that's where we need to go to get your parents. Oh, and my mom wants us to steal from it and destroy it—which totally kills the fun, but I'm still game for blowing a Neverseen hideout off the planet."

"When Elwin let me know that Keefe was back on his feet," Mr. Forkle explained, "I figured it'd be easiest if I got him up to speed, so that he wouldn't slow us down today with a ton of questions."

"Oh, I still have questions," Keefe said. "*Lots* of them. But I'm only going to ask one—for now."

His eyes shifted back to Sophie, and he struggled to swallow before he asked, "How much groveling am I going to have to do before you trust me again?"

"Hopefully a lot," Tam jumped in.

"I second that," Biana added. "And I don't even know exactly what happened."

Keefe's focus didn't shift from Sophie. "Your call, Foster. I totally get why you ousted me. I was being—"

"An idiot?" Fitz suggested.

Keefe shrugged. "I was going to go with 'a sparkly poop head.'"

Sophie's lips twitched at that. "I should get you a T-shirt that says that."

"I'd wear it." Keefe leaned slightly closer. "I'm sorry, Sophie. *Really*. And I'll do whatever it takes to make it up to you. That's why I stayed in bed, even though I knew my mom had to be dragging you into a million dangerous things. I wanted to prove that I could do the right thing. Well, that and Ro threatened to tie me down and cover me in flesh-eating bacteria if I didn't, and I could tell she meant it."

"That's right," Sophie said, standing on her tiptoes to scan the room. "Where's Ro?"

"Outside, messing with Sandor. Who knew she could do a killer impersonation of his bunny voice?"

That time Sophie's smile broke through.

"She also figured out how my mom snuck past all the security here within about three seconds," Keefe added. "And she spent the entire time I've been eavesdropping pointing out a ton of other things the goblins are doing wrong—so I'm pretty sure there's going to be an ogre-goblin rumble any minute now."

"Nah, I don't feel like messing up my hair," Ro said, sauntering into the house, patting her tiny pigtails.

Sandor, Woltzer, Grizel, and Cadoc scrambled in after her, taking up defensive positions around the room.

Ro flashed a smile that emphasized the points of her teeth. "You guys are hilarious. I told you, I'm here under a bunch of boring 'don't kill anyone' orders. Plus, I just painted my nails."

She held up her hands to show off her claws, which were a deep, shiny blue.

Sandor gripped the hilt of his sword.

Ro didn't seem to notice. "Now here's a shock—another elvin house decorated with sparkles! But at least this place has dinosaurs. And it's not as ridiculous as that towering monstrosity he grew up in." She pointed a blue claw at Keefe. "That place screams 'overcompensating.'"

"You've been to Candleshade?" Sophie asked.

"Only because he told me I could break stuff." Ro swung her arms, as if she were mentally bashing things with a baseball bat.

"I sent Ro to search for whatever my mom left behind," Keefe explained. "That way at least something was getting accomplished while I was stuck in bed."

"Uh, we accomplished a ton of stuff without you," Fitz reminded him.

"Yeah. I know." Keefe's smile faded and his eyes lowered to Sophie's hand—which she realized was still entwined with Fitz's.

"I found it, by the way," Ro said. "The thing his mom hid. It looks like junk to me—but it shut him up, so that's all that matters. Plus, it was awesome shattering that ugly crystal desk to get to it. If any of you guys need stuff smashed, let me know."

"I'll keep it in mind," Sophie told her, turning back to Keefe. "What did she find?"

He pulled four pieces of metal out of his pocket, two silver and two gold—each with variations in their curved edges.

"Okay . . . ," Sophie said. "What are they?"

Keefe held up one finger—an order to wait—before he selected one of the gold pieces, checked the edges a couple of times, and slipped it into the curve of one of the silver parts.

"He's going to show off now," Ro told them, "and pretend like he's a genius. But this took him *days* to figure out."

Keefe shrugged. "*Or* I had time to kill, and I knew you hated the noise."

He knocked the loose pieces together with his other hand, creating a surprisingly loud *Plink! Plink! Plink!*

Ro snarled.

Keefe smirked and went back to flipping the connected

pieces, twisting them a few times before he slid the other silver piece into the arrangement and twisted again.

"Okay, this is the part that's tricky." He rotated one of the pieces, and then adjusted them to three different heights before he tilted the final gold piece and tried slipping it in.

No go.

It took several back-and-forths—and a whole lot of muttering—but eventually the piece slid in. And once it did, the other pieces snapped together, creating a two-tone square about the size of an Imparter, but twice as thick.

"Ta-da!"

"Told you they wouldn't applaud," Ro said when everyone stared at the square, waiting for it to do something.

"Is it a gadget?" Sophie asked.

Keefe tapped it a few times. "It doesn't seem to be. Honestly, I have no idea what it is—but at least I figured out how to piece it together, right?"

Their murmured agreement was halfhearted at best.

Keefe sighed. "Tough crowd. I must've made it look too easy."

"I'm sure it *is* easy," Tam said, snatching the square from Keefe and snapping the pieces apart. But when he went to pop them back together . . .

"How's that working out for you, Bangs Boy?" Keefe asked.

Tam scowled.

No amount of twisting, flipping, or rotating the pieces could get any of them to connect, and Ro cringed at all the *plink, plink, plink*ing.

"Oh man, this is the greatest present you could've ever given me," Keefe told him.

"Whatever. It's stupid," Tam muttered.

"Can I try?" Biana asked.

She managed to fit two pieces together, but the last two refused to snap in.

No one could do any better. Not Fitz. Not Linh. Not Mr. Forkle, or Grady, or Alden. Even the goblins tried, and Grizel looked ready to crush the pieces into dust—which made Ro laugh so hard she snorted.

"Think you can do better?" Keefe asked Sophie. "Or are you afraid you'll have to admit I'm the real talent in this group?"

When he put it like that . . .

Sophie snatched the bits of metal and set to work. "So you really don't have any theories about what this is?"

"Nope. But remember how my mom said something like 'You finally solved that puzzle' when I told her I'd found something? This *has* to be what she meant. You're doing that wrong, by the way. You have to end with a gold piece."

Sophie held up the three pieces she'd fitted together—both gold and one silver. "Then how come I've gotten farther than everyone else?"

"Because you can be wrong and still smarter than these guys," Keefe told her with a grin.

"Or, I could ignore you and . . ." She tilted the last silver piece one way—then another—and finally twisted it around and *click!*

"Now *that* deserves applause," Ro said. "I love this girl so hard."

Keefe snatched the puzzle from Sophie, turning it around in his hands. "I don't get it. The way I do it has the silver splotches curving out and the gold circling in."

"So maybe *you* do it wrong," Tam suggested.

"It's a puzzle," Keefe argued. "The pieces should only fit together one way."

"Not if that's part of the challenge," Sophie countered. "Maybe it's not just about solving it, but solving it a specific way?"

"If that's true," Fitz said, "how will we know which way is right?"

Sophie had no idea, but she took back the puzzle, examining it from every angle before she pulled the pieces apart and tried solving it again. Keefe moved in to help—and while there was a whole lot of bickering, they managed to get three out of four clicked into place in another new arrangement.

"You have to twist the last one the other way," Keefe said as she wrestled with the gold piece.

"No, if I tilt it . . ." She angled the piece—then twisted the others and *plink!*

"Uhhhh, anyone else think it looks exactly the same?" Ro asked.

"It's pretty similar, but now the gold bits are all connected," Tam noted.

"Is that better?" Ro asked.

Biana sucked in a breath. "Yes! Don't you guys see it?"

Everyone squinted at the square.

Fitz caught it first. "There's a rune."

"And not just any rune," Biana said, tracing her finger across the golden shape. "It means 'Archetype.'"

SIXTY-TWO

O . . . THIS MUST BE THE KEY," SOPHIE
said, cradling the metal square so, so carefully
to make sure the pieces stayed together. "Lady
Gisela said the Archetype is locked—and I
guess it makes sense that she'd keep the key and the book
separate."

"But how is a metal square a key?" Tam asked.

"I don't know," Sophie admitted. "But I'm assuming it'll
make more sense once we have the Archetype."

"Perhaps I should hang on to that in the meantime," Mr.
Forkle suggested, "and have our Technopath check it for trackers or listening devices."

"Wait," Fitz said as Sophie helped Mr. Forkle wrap the

puzzle into a handkerchief. "Lady Gisela knows we have this, right? Keefe told her he found it?"

"So?" Keefe asked.

"*So* . . . then she has to know we're going to use it as soon as we get our hands on the Archetype, doesn't she? Which doesn't make sense. I'd figured the reason she didn't give us some big threat about what would happen if we refused to turn the book over was because she knew we couldn't open it."

"So did I," Sophie admitted.

"Well, but this is my mom we're talking about," Keefe reminded them. "She probably thinks I'm too dumb to put the key together the right way."

"Actually, she doesn't underestimate you the way your dad does," Sophie told him. "Every time I've talked with her, she's been frustrated that you weren't there."

"Only because she can't mess with my head," Keefe mumbled.

"Or maybe she doesn't care if we read the Archetype," Biana suggested. "Maybe she thinks it'll make us want to work with her."

"She did say something like that," Sophie admitted.

But Keefe's mom *had* to know their truce was only temporary, and that they were never going to trust her.

Which meant she *had* to have a plan for when it fell apart.

"What's especially strange is that she already handed over the journals," Mr. Forkle added. "Mind you, she's still leaving the bulk of the work of finding Nightfall to us. But that doesn't change the fact that we currently have no reason to return the Archetype or the key to her. So either she's become an incredibly poor negotiator—or we're missing her next trick."

"Unless she's still counting on what she said to me before we went into the first Nightfall," Sophie said, hating the reminder. "About how I'd be desperate to cut another deal because I'd need her to restore my parents' sanity. She made it sound like this new Nightfall is super creepy."

Keefe glared at Mr. Forkle. "Why didn't you tell me about that?"

"Because I'm not convinced it's a valid threat—and even if it is, we can fix any damage done to Sophie's family by altering their memories."

"You still should've told me!" Keefe took Sophie by the shoulders. "Don't let her get in your head, Foster. Remember, this is all just a game for her. And she'll say or do *anything* to win."

Sophie's mouth still tasted sour.

"All I know is that my parents have been gone for . . ." She stopped, deciding she didn't want to count how many days had passed. "We have to get them out of there."

"We will," Keefe promised. "Soon."

"Only if we get to work," Mr. Forkle said, gathering up the journals. "I'll start translating these, while the rest of you head to Eternalia, and then we'll exchange notes tonight."

Keefe sighed. "Come on, Forkle—you *have* to know I'm not going to waste time reading boring books."

"It's *not* a waste," Mr. Forkle argued. "We need—"

"Yeah, I caught your speech about why we need more information," Keefe interrupted. "And I'm not saying you're wrong. But do you really think it's smart to have *five* of us"— he pointed to himself, Fitz, Tam, Biana, and Sophie—"cooped up in a library looking for the same thing—especially since there's a good chance it's not even there?"

"Don't forget about me," Linh added. "I can start helping tomorrow—or maybe even tonight, depending on how long it takes with Wylie."

"Okay, so now we're up to *six*," Keefe corrected. "*Six* of us sitting in a stuffy archive flipping through ancient scrolls. You *really* think that's the best way to go about this?"

"I'm assuming you have another suggestion," Tiergan said.

"Yeah. We split up—some of us stuck in Boringville, and some of us in Atlantis searching street by street. I know it's a lot of ground to cover, but at least we know it's *there*, instead of just hoping we'll find something in a dusty old book. And I know you're worried about the Neverseen seeing us, but if we keep the group small, and make sure we do something normal while we're there—like buying stuff for Foxfire—it should throw them off."

"And I'm assuming you expect Sophie to come with you?" Grady asked.

"I don't *expect* Sophie to do anything," Keefe said, turning back to her. "I'm not trying to take control again, Foster—I promise. If you want to hit the books, go ahead. But I'm heading to Atlantis, okay? I'll go stir-crazy in the library. I won't be able to concentrate."

Neither would she.

"I want to go to Atlantis," Sophie admitted. "I'm not sure I can handle sitting around right now. I'm too antsy."

Keefe's smile was enormous. "Woo! Team Foster-Keefe is *back*!"

"I'm in too," Fitz said.

"And me," Biana added.

"Dude, I'm not gonna be the only one stuck on library duty," Tam told them. "But we're changing the team's name."

"We can't all be in," Keefe reminded them. "That's the point of splitting up."

"The only way this will work," Mr. Forkle said, "is if you make a schedule and coordinate who's going and who's staying for each shift. You're free to divvy it up however you want—so long as there's always at least one goblin with whoever's in Atlantis."

"I'd point out that you'd be way better off making sure they had an *ogre* with them," Ro jumped in, "but your paranoid Councillors told me I'm not allowed to be seen in your cities. Which means"—she turned to Keefe—"*you're* stuck in library land—assuming I can sneak into the building unnoticed. If not, you'll just have to catch up with everyone later. Believe me, I'm not happy about it either, but I'm not supposed to let you out of my sight, so . . ."

"You left me when you went to Candleshade," he reminded her.

"That was different. You were on bed rest. And I rigged traps around your room when I left."

Keefe's eyebrows shot up. "Wow, good thing I didn't get up to pee."

Ro's grin said it definitely was.

"Well, I don't need a babysitter," he told her.

"It's so precious that you think that. Look at him, guys—thinking he's all tough."

"I *like* her," Tam said.

Keefe shot him a glare that turned even colder when he directed it at Ro. "I'm going to Atlantis—and if you try to stop me, I'll make sure you take the blame for a very unfortunate incident in Councillor Alina's castle and get banned from the Lost Cities."

Ro studied her claws. "Do that, and *I'll* make sure my dad retaliates."

"Really? That's the best you can do? Run to Daddy?" Keefe asked.

"Just because you have daddy issues doesn't mean we all do."

"Okay," Mr. Forkle said, stepping between them, "in the interest of avoiding an interspeciesial incident, how about we provide extra security for Mr. Sencen, and you can blame us if anything happens, Ro?"

"What kind of security?" Ro asked.

"Me," Grady said before Mr. Forkle could answer.

Sophie was going to be touched by Grady's offer, until he added, "I'm sure Keefe's going to talk his way into all of Sophie's shifts, and I want to keep an eye on them. And if you doubt my abilities, keep in mind that I've made someone burn off their own hand."

Ro looked mildly impressed.

But she didn't agree until she looked at Keefe. "Fine—but only because he seems super bitter about this plan. What am I supposed to do while he's gone?"

"I can bring you to Riverdrift," Tiergan offered. "Lady Cadence has several of your father's best microbiologists working with her on the soporidine antidote right now."

"An ogre party boat?" Ro asked.

"I believe they're calling it a research vessel," Tiergan noted.

"Not once I get there." She wrapped her arm around Keefe's shoulder and messed up his hair. "Have fun with your chaperone."

On *that* note, Tiergan, Linh, and Ro left—and Mr. Forkle and Alden followed—leaving Grady with the less-than-happy task of arbitrating while Sophie, Keefe, Fitz, Biana, and Tam fought over the Atlantis schedule. Sandor, Grizel, and Woltzer added plenty of their own bickering, debating which one of them would cover security for each shift. And while Tam managed to force Keefe into a few of the research time slots, he gave most of them to Linh, not wanting her spending too much time underwater—no matter how many times Biana swore he was underestimating his sister.

From there, they took time to map out the city, arranging each shift so that it would cover mostly new ground—but with enough overlap to keep the visits from looking systematic if anyone was watching.

And thus began a string of endless, exhausting days where Sophie's feet throbbed from all the walking, and her eyes went blurry from all the reading, and she stumbled from shift to shift in a daze.

She didn't hear the jokes Keefe cracked.

Or taste the treats Fitz bought her.

Or resist Biana's attempts to give her a makeover every time they pretended to shop.

Or weigh in when Tam and Linh spent an entire Atlantis trip debating which pet Linh should adopt for the favor Tam owed her.

Because every street that showed no trace of the symbol, every lengthy account of Atlantis's history with no mention of the facility, every update from Mr. Forkle confessing that he'd found nothing useful in the journals—it all felt like a ticking clock growing louder and louder and louder.

Dex and Bronte had yet to access a single secret on the

caches. Lady Cadence hadn't made any progress on the soporidine—and they still didn't have any clue what the Neverseen were planning to do with it. And no matter what Livvy tried, Alvar wouldn't wake up.

Sophie forced a brave face every night when she checked on her sister, but all the things they didn't say piled up between them, making the conversation feel as tense as their smiles.

And before Sophie knew it, Foxfire was starting—and the panic hit hard.

She spent her last research shift—just her, Keefe, Sandor, Grady, and Ro—gathering the biggest stack of books she could carry so she could at least do *something* after school.

"Hey," Keefe said, blocking her as she tried to scoot past where he'd been sitting at the long obsidian table. "Did you seriously think you could hide these from me?"

He reached up and wiped one of the tears trickling down her cheeks.

She shrugged and looked away, hating that he'd caught her.

She wasn't crying about the things she should be worrying about—the huge, unsolvable problems that would surely affect everybody.

She was being selfish and crying about the family she wouldn't even get to keep.

"Okay, two choices," Keefe told her, standing up and tilting her chin toward him. "You can tell me what's wrong. Or I can put my Empath powers to work—but keep in mind,

Option B will likely pick up on all kinds of *other* feelings."

Sophie gave him her surliest scowl, but he didn't back down.

She looked away again, her eyes tracing the swirling facets in the dark ruby walls, which made the library look like it was made of jeweled mahogany. The room was probably supposed to feel cozy and opulent. But all Sophie saw was red.

And still, Keefe waited, so she told him, "It's just . . . we're getting *nowhere*. And if we can't figure it out when we're all working on it around the clock, how is anything going to get done when we're all back at Foxfire and we have to let the adults take over?"

Grady snorted. "You know, most people consider adults to be *better* at these kinds of things than teenagers."

Sophie and Keefe shared a look—and had to laugh.

Grady sighed. "You two are definitely spending too much time together."

"I take it that means you haven't joined Team Foster-Keefe?" Ro asked. "Because I have to admit, they're pretty cute together. Especially when she gets that look in her eye like she's going to tear off his head."

"All I meant," Sophie said, doing her best to ignore Ro, "is that there's so much going on right now, we can't afford to lose seven people—eleven, if you count Bronte and Lady Cadence and Tiergan and Mr. For . . ."

She caught her slip just in time.

"Darn, almost got one of the juicy secrets," Ro said. "Though

I'm pretty sure that means your wrinkly leader teaches at Foxfire."

"It's called mentoring," Sophie corrected, "and you can believe whatever you want."

"I will."

Sophie hoped that meant Ro would stick with her Forkle-is-a-Mentor theory and not look too closely at the principal.

"Anyway," Keefe said, "if it feels like the grown-ups aren't pulling their weight, we can always dit—"

"No ditching," Sandor and Grady interrupted in unison.

"Figured you guys would say that," Keefe told them, "even though you can't *really* stop us." He winked at Sophie. "But I think you're also forgetting, Foster, that we've managed to get a lot done when school is in session. We stopped the gnomish plague while going to Exillium—and you managed to look into the Everblaze while juggling midterms. You even got your abilities fixed—and healed Alden—during the first term this year."

The word "healed" unleashed a whole other storm of panic.

Her friends had been coming over every night to work on the script for Prentice, but everything they'd come up with either felt too mushy or too cruel. Finding the right balance was starting to feel impossible.

"Would it help if I'm there for the healing?" Keefe offered. "I could keep track of Prentice's feelings. Or I could . . ." He glanced at Ro and his mouth shifted to a different word. "I could . . . do what I did to calm you down while we were in Ravagog."

Ro rolled her eyes. "Could you guys be any worse at hiding stuff?"

Sophie ignored her, remembering that soothing blue breeze that had eased her panic. "That actually might be a good idea."

"Wow, you must really be scared if you're accepting my help that easily." Keefe felt her forehead, as if checking for a fever. "I don't need to take you to Elwin, right?"

Sophie sighed.

But . . . the joke did help.

The whole conversation helped.

Her eyes had dried, and that *tick-tick-tick*ing in her ears quieted.

And Keefe knew it. His smile was adorably smug as he grabbed half of her books to help her carry them home.

Grady, meanwhile, was studying Keefe like he'd never seen him before in his life.

"I'm glad you're back," Sophie told him, keeping her voice low—just for the two of them.

Keefe's smile turned unbearably sweet. "Me too, Foster. Me too."

SIXTY-THREE

RETURNING TO FOXFIRE FELT EVERY
bit as wrong as Sophie had expected.

But in small ways, it also felt right.

Even with the worries ticking away in her
head—and even with the pressure of finals already looming—
there was something comforting about wearing her amber-
brown uniform again, and watching Mr. Forkle appear as the
sharp-featured, dark-haired Magnate Leto, and wandering the
colorful halls, surrounded by laughter and gossip.

It felt like proof that someday things truly would return to
the way they'd been when she'd first moved to the Lost Cities
and had no idea the Neverseen existed.

Still, there were definitely challenges.

Homework was a big one. In the past, Sophie had always been able to finish her assignments in study hall. But study hall had been cut in half, to add extra lecture time to each session. Her mentors had also doubled the workload to keep up with the accelerated curriculum. So every day, Sophie and her friends found themselves dragging home a thick stack of work that left almost no time for anything else. And while the adults did their best to pick up the slack—and gave Sophie lengthy updates every night to ease her mind—their reports were always filled with stories of failed attempts and false leads, with little actual progress.

Ro's presence on campus was another problem—despite the stern lectures Magnate Leto kept giving at orientation every morning on how Ro was a distinguished guest and should be treated with honor and respect. The ogre princess didn't seem to mind the glares and whispers and screams—she even flashed claws and teeth to encourage them. But watching the other prodigies' reactions made Sophie uneasy. After spending time with Ro and seeing her intelligence and humor—obnoxious as both could sometimes be—Sophie finally understood why Lady Cadence was always defending the ogres. And it turned her stomach to see how deeply the elves' prejudice truly ran.

Lunchtime was another complication. Jensi chose not to sit with them—and Sophie couldn't totally blame him, thanks to how crowded their table had gotten, now that Tam, Linh, and Marella were regulars. But it still made her sad every time he passed them by to head over to the Drooly Boys. And she wished Maruca would stop claiming the seat next to her. As Wylie's cousin, Maruca knew all about Prentice's upcoming healing, and spent the hour asking so many questions that it turned the healing into its own kind of stressful countdown.

Four days.

Three days.

Two days.

One.

Then Sophie was stumbling on shaky legs into the cozy mountain cabin that Prentice and Wylie were sharing, not sure if she was going to throw up or pass out—especially when she saw how many people were waiting for her. Sandor, Grizel, and Ro chose to wait outside in order to patrol the surrounding forest. And the rest of the group had been limited only to those directly affected by Prentice's sacrifice, or those who could provide Sophie with help or assistance. But the small wood-paneled room was still crammed with all five members of the Collective—though Tiergan had left behind his rocky disguise for the day. Quinlin and Livvy had also arranged to leave Amy with Grady and Edaline in order to join them. And Alden, Della, Fitz, Keefe, Tam, and Linh had all clumped together, their expressions as mixed as Sophie's tangled emotions.

Wylie stood in the center of it all, next to a figure propped on a narrow bed, staring out the round window overlooking the snowcapped mountains—and Sophie could spot the changes in Prentice immediately. His usually dull, sweaty skin was now a rich, smooth umber, his blue eyes were clear, his tangled hair had been twisted neatly into smooth dreadlocks, and his full lips were miraculously drool free. He looked calm. Handsome, even. No sign of the twitching or thrashing Sophie had gotten so used to seeing.

Still, Sophie had to work up the courage to hold Wylie's piercing stare. She started with his arms, relieved to find no trace of the blisters that had marred his dark skin after the Neverseen's interrogation. Then she moved her gaze to shoulders that looked even broader than she remembered, and finally to his face. His nose and lips were sharper than his father's, and his smile—the rare times she'd seen it—came from his mother.

But his eyes were 100 percent Prentice's.

And Sophie saw terror in those piercing blue depths.

And uncertainty.

And sorrow.

But there was also hope and peace and gratitude.

Sophie didn't feel worthy of the last emotion. After all Prentice had done to protect her—and all Wylie had endured because of that sacrifice—she owed them this.

Had owed them for a very, very long time.

"Remember," Mr. Forkle said as he led Sophie to a carved wooden chair that had been set up next to Prentice, "your goal is simply to catch Prentice up as much as you can and prepare him for what he'll find when he wakes. We trust you to judge how much he can handle."

"And tell him I love him, okay?" Wylie added quietly. "Tell him . . . I don't care how long it's been, I just want him back."

"I will," she promised.

"I'm right behind you," Fitz said, reaching for her hand. They'd decided to have her keep her gloves on, afraid enhancing would be too much for Prentice. "Squeeze my fingers if you need me to give you a boost."

"I'm also happy to help any way I can," Mr. Forkle promised.

"As am I," Tiergan said, moving to stand beside Wylie.

"Same goes for me," Alden added, clearing the tremble from his throat.

He glanced at Quinlin, as if he expected his former Cognate to make the same offer. But Quinlin was too busy staring at Prentice with a glazed, unreadable expression.

"Wow, there are a *lot* of Telepaths in this room," Keefe said as he took his place on Sophie's other side. "Good thing you were smart enough to *also* bring an Empath. Deep breaths, Foster—you've got this. And I've got your back. If I feel Prentice's emotions getting too intense, I'll do this." He clutched her shoulder—not tight enough to hurt, but enough to demand her attention. "So if you *don't* feel me doing that, you don't have to worry, okay? And if I feel either of you losing control, I'll pull off your glove and calm you both down. So just relax and do your Moonlark mind-healing thing."

"Not healing," Mr. Forkle corrected. "*Just* communicating. And if you need Mr. Tam to lift a veil of shadowvapor for any reason, all you have to do is say the word."

"Or if Prentice needs to be sedated, I'm ready," Livvy assured her, holding up a clear elixir.

"Don't be afraid to abort if it's not going well," Tiergan added. "Even if it means putting things off another day—or week—or month. We'll wait."

Sophie nodded blankly.

Fitz leaned closer. "Just stick to the script, Sophie. It's a good one. You're ready."

Sophie blew out a breath. "Okay."

Her eyes trailed back to Wylie—seeking that final assurance. And his shaky nod settled it.

"All right, Prentice," she said as she closed her eyes and dove into his mental darkness. "Let's start bringing you back."

SIXTY-FOUR

UM . . . HI, SOPHIE TRANSMITTED, too startled to think of anything more articulate as she studied the lovely red-haired female who stood in front of her in a gauzy pink dress.

Sophie had been prepared for another surreal projection as she'd pushed past the sharper bits of Prentice's shattered consciousness. But this was . . . *unexpected.*

The redhead waited for her on the shore of a glassy lake, surrounded by swaying grassy plants that looked like glittery cattails. And Sophie recognized her even before she smiled her achingly familiar smile.

Cyrah?

Wylie's mom nodded. "Hello, Sophie."

Her voice added a melodic curl to the words and Sophie marveled at the detail Prentice had managed to pull together for the vision. He'd rendered each curve of her face perfectly. Added each fleck of violet into Cyrah's eyes. And when she tossed her long straight hair, the sun turned the strands every possible shade of red.

"I had a feeling you might be coming to see me soon," Cyrah told her. "And I tried so hard to be prepared. I wanted to be me this time—the real me."

You mean Prentice, Sophie clarified.

Cyrah nodded. "I wanted to show you I was ready. But . . . I couldn't figure out who I am. So this was the best I could do."

This works, Sophie promised, even if it meant she was going to have to break the news of Cyrah's death to the woman herself—sort of. And the script she'd carefully practiced seemed to unravel.

"She's one of the few things I've been able to hold on to," Cyrah added, each word pounding a nail into Sophie's heart. "Though I guess I'm not saying that right. I'm supposed to think of me as her right now, aren't I? This is always so confusing."

It was.

You're doing the best you can, Sophie told her.

They both were.

Distantly—in another world—she felt soft pressure on each

of her hands and a thread of warmth trickling through her brain. Tiny reminders that she wasn't in this alone.

"Are you looking for another memory?" Cyrah asked, adjusting one of the jeweled combs tucked into her hair. "If so, I should warn you. They're not in much better shape than the last time you were here. I keep trying to pull things together. But it's such a mess."

I know. That's why I'm here.

Cyrah sucked in a breath. "Is it time to . . . ?"

We're working toward it, Sophie promised. *But we have to do this in steps, to make sure we don't overwhelm you.*

"That sounds . . . slow." The sky flooded with storm clouds.

It won't be, Sophie said, hoping that was true. *And no matter what, it WILL happen.*

The clouds receded, but the sky stayed dimmer than it had been, the air colder, with a sharp wind that rippled the smooth surface of the lake.

"You told me not to think about how many years have passed," Cyrah whispered. "And I've tried not to. But . . . I need to know."

Are you sure?

Some small, wimpy part of Sophie couldn't help hoping the answer would be no.

But Cyrah told her, "I think it'll help me start piecing things together."

Sophie nodded.

She realized Cyrah couldn't actually see her, so she gathered her consciousness, shaping it into something more focused and solid, until she had a body of sorts—a mental avatar that appeared in the scene. The soft fabric of the teal tunic she'd dreamed up brushed her imagined skin as she reached for Cyrah's trembling hand and led her over to a cluster of boulders nestled among the sparkly plants, then took a seat on the uneven stones.

If this gets to be too much, Sophie transmitted, *you have to tell me, okay?*

Cyrah chewed her lower lip. "Give me a second."

Blinding flashes erupted across the lake, and dozens of graceful black swans emerged from the sparks, tucking their dusky wings as they glided along the glassy water.

"Swans help me focus," Cyrah explained. "Especially black ones."

I remember you telling me that.

Sophie jumped when more swans appeared at their feet, bobbing their noble heads and filling the air with their slightly mournful squeaks.

Does that mean you remember the Black Swan?

Cyrah reached out to stroke the nearest swan's neck. "The words feel familiar. And there are flickers. A sense of urgency, and . . . something like a warning. But not enough to wrap my mind around."

That's still good, Sophie told her. *It gives us somewhere to start.*

"I thought we were going to start with how long it's been."

You're sure you can handle that?

"I'm not sure of anything. But . . . is it the worst thing you're going to share?"

No, Sophie admitted, deciding to be honest.

The swans flapped their wings, and their squeaks turned to groans, making it hard to hear Cyrah mumble, "Then tell me."

A fresh thread of warmth boosted Sophie's mental strength, giving her the courage to say, *It's been about thirteen years.*

Icy rain erupted around them, matching Cyrah's tears. "That's . . . a very long time."

It is, Sophie told her. *And . . . it's my fault. You put yourself through all of this—gave up all those years—to protect me.*

The confession shredded something inside Sophie. But Cyrah's rain turned warmer, until it was mostly a mist hovering around them.

"I had to protect the moonlark," she whispered, reaching out to brush Sophie's cheek. "And I knew the risks. I may barely remember what I look like—or what it feels like to be *awake*. But I've always known this was my choice. And . . . that I had to trust."

Prentice had used a similar phrase once before—the first time that Sophie had tried searching his memories.

We have to trust.

He'd trusted *her*.

Counted on her to fix him. Taken that unimaginable risk.

And she'd failed him all this time.

But not anymore.

Wylie wanted me to tell you he doesn't care how long it's been, she transmitted. *And that he loves you.*

"Wylie."

The name brought back the sun, melting the mist and casting glints of gold across the black swan's feathers.

But the clouds slowly returned. "He must be all grown up."

He's a Level Eight at Foxfire, Sophie admitted. *And he's missed you every single day. But he never gave up hope that you'd come back. And Tiergan's taken amazing care of him.*

"Tiergan?"

Sophie's heart stopped with the slip.

"Why has Tiergan been taking care of him?"

It . . . doesn't matter.

Thunder cracked all around them, sending the swans scattering. "Why has Tiergan been taking care of him. Did I—did Cyrah . . . are they together?"

No! Sophie promised. *It wasn't like that.*

"Then what was it like?"

It's . . . hard to explain.

"Try."

Not now.

"Why?"

Far, far away Sophie could feel pressure on her right shoulder—Keefe's warning.

Because this is getting to be too much for you.

"I'll decide when it's too much! Is this what you meant when you said there would be worse things to tell me? Is it something with Cyrah?"

Sophie tried to pull her mind back—tried to melt into a blip of thought and ghost away—but Cyrah snatched her wrist with an iron grip, chaining her to Prentice's consciousness.

"Tell me!"

I will, Sophie promised. *But not until your emotions are under control.*

"I don't care about my emotions!"

You will if this sets you back months and months.

"You think I can just forget this? You think the question won't be trapped in here with me, rattling around my head while I wait and wait and wait for you to come back?"

Cyrah's features widened with each word, and her red hair turned black and twisted into dreadlocks as her skin darkened and her body stretched taller.

The new form was smudgy and indistinct—like a crayon drawing by a small child.

Still, Sophie knew who she was looking at. *Prentice?*

He struggled through a nod, and a fresh crack of thunder shook the scenery, sending the last of the swans flapping away.

Warmth crashed into Sophie's mind, paired with a soft, blue breeze. But neither stopped the lake from cresting into a wave and crashing over her, dragging her to a bubble of inky black.

"Just tell me," Prentice begged. His form looked even sloppier in the shadowy pocket. And his voice sounded as brittle as the jagged memories that swarmed around them, slashing and shredding and clawing closer.

He repeated the plea again.

And again.

And again.

The shards broke through, aiming for Sophie's skin. And when they couldn't break past her mental shields, they turned on Prentice, smudging his weary form like jagged erasers.

"This is how it's going to be for me," he told her. "Just this, endlessly."

The shards kept blurring and smearing.

Until there was very little of him left.

So when he repeated his plea a final time, Sophie told him everything.

Every heartbreaking, ugly detail.

Until the shards of memory stilled.

And the lasts wisps of Prentice vanished.

SIXTY-FIVE

*O!"*

Sophie wasn't sure if she was transmitting the plea or screaming it.

But she could feel bursts of warm tingles blasting through her consciousness as the blue breeze swirled faster and faster.

Prentice, please!

PLEASE.

You have to come back.

She repeated the cry as she dove into the jagged memories—not caring what chaos she might find on the other side.

Dark nothingness awaited—the space so black and empty, it

felt like dropping into a void—leaving her falling, falling, falling, so fast and so far, she might as well have dropped through the center of the universe.

The blue wind chased her down—raced ahead—managed to catch her.

And the jolt forced her to stop.

Think.

As if there was a distant voice chanting, *"You've got this! You've got this! You've got this!"*

The confidence mixed with the next rush of warmth, and she slowly remembered that Prentice couldn't be *gone*.

He'd simply hidden himself away. And she could find him. If she didn't give up.

With that resolve fueling her, she grabbed the blue wind and tugged, shaping it into feathers—gorgeous cerulean wings that fluttered at the slightest wisp of thought and shimmered in the darkness.

Please, Prentice, she transmitted. *If you won't come back for me, do it for Wylie. He loves you. He needs you.*

She repeated the plea again and again, until the darkness seemed to tighten—until there were edges behind the blackness. Barriers that held in her sounds, filling the space with soft, looping echoes.

Some small part of her mind found the effect familiar, but she was too focused on adding images to wonder why. She didn't have nearly as many memories of Wylie as she'd like—and too many of them were heartbreaking. But maybe Prentice needed to see that.

Maybe he needed proof of just how much his son missed him to find the strength to return.

So she showed him the heated arguments she'd had with Wylie about healing his father, and Wylie's hopeless visits when they'd feared that Prentice had been lost forever. She even showed him a glimpse of the injuries Wylie sustained during the Neverseen's interrogation. And she finished with the last image she'd seen, of Wylie clinging to Prentice's hand, asking her to tell him that he loved him.

He's waiting for you, she told Prentice.

Come back.

Come back.

Come back.

Far away there was pain in her shoulder—Keefe warning her that Prentice's emotions were crashing—and a fresh blast of blue wind surged to lift her wings and make her lighter.

But other than her echoes, Prentice's mind stayed silent—and there were no warm trails to follow. No sign of recognition.

Please, Prentice, she begged. *So many people need you here.*

She showed him glimpses of Alden's guilt and devastation, and the Collective's frustration and impatience, and Tiergan's grief and loyalty—as well as glimmers of his love for Wylie.

When that didn't make a difference, she added her own

struggles to the mix—every tear she'd shed over her role in his current situation. Every nightmare. Every wasted day.

Don't you see how much you matter? she asked. *How deeply you're loved?*

Maybe he needed proof.

So she scraped together every ounce of love she could find within herself and poured it into the darkness in a white hot rush.

The light swirled with the black, mixing into a hazy shade of gray.

When it still wasn't enough, she dug deeper, reaching into her heart and tapping into that raw emotional well, where everything burned with a new kind of heat. It seared every thought as she gathered up the force of it, erupting into sparks as she blasted it into Prentice's consciousness—and the blue wind fanned the sparks into flames.

Harmless flames.

Helpful flames.

Flames that danced and crackled and gobbled up the murk.

Warmth followed, swelling from within that time—growing and growing and growing until it melted each of the jagged shards of memory and welded them into some sort of mass as the rising energy launched Sophie up, up, up—so fast, so sudden, it knocked her back into her body, leaving her blinking and trembling and gasping for breath, her now-bare hands held fast by clammy, shaking palms.

People called her name, pummeled her with questions—each voice stomping on the next until their words were a mush of *noise.*

Except one.

One voice that silenced everyone.

All eyes turned to Prentice as he blinked eyes that were clearer and more focused than they'd been in over a decade, and moved lips that had done nothing but mumble and groan and drool but now formed hoarse, crackly words.

"I think . . . I'm back."

SIXTY-SIX

*P*RENTICE WAS HEALED.

Sophie hadn't meant to do it. Hadn't recognized that she was unconsciously going through the steps of a healing.

But . . . Prentice seemed okay.

He was disoriented, and overwhelmed, and heartbroken.

But he hadn't shattered.

He'd simply clung to his son, and they'd both cried together, until his weak body collapsed into sleep—*real* sleep, Livvy assured them. She'd quadruple-checked.

She'd also had Keefe read Prentice's emotions to make sure they were holding steady. And had Tam take a quick reading of his shadowvapor to ensure it was within a normal range.

Mr. Forkle also chose to monitor Prentice's dreams.

He could do that now, without risking his sanity.

Because Prentice was healed.

But he wasn't back to normal, either.

His memories were a mess—the splintered fragments mashed together so haphazardly that there was no rhyme or reason to anything. And no matter how hard any of them tried to help him make sense of it, his mind remained chaos.

"It's up to Prentice now," Mr. Forkle said as he took the seat next to Sophie on one of the benches lining the cabin's wraparound porch. "He's the only one who can sort out his past."

Blur and Wraith had left already. As had Della. And the rest of the group had ducked outside to give Wylie, Prentice, and Tiergan some privacy to discuss what happened to Cyrah.

"But he *will* get back to normal?" Sophie asked.

"'Normal' is a relative term," Alden reminded her, his eyes on the forest beyond, where a smoky mist seemed to be thickening as the day stretched on.

He didn't look as peaceful as Sophie would've expected. Mostly thoughtful.

Fitz went over and wrapped him in a hug.

"From this point on, Prentice will have his health," Mr. Forkle told them. "And his son. And the chance to make new memories. The rest? Only time will tell. The consciousness continues to shatter after the initial break, so after all of these years, his memories have all but dissolved. Imagine a piece of glass that you smash with a stone. One hit and it's easy enough to see how to fit the shards back together. But smash it again? And again? And again, and again, and again?"

It shouldn't have been a surprise. But the reality of it flattened Sophie's heart. "There's really nothing we can do?"

"If you're hoping for a quick fix, no," Mr. Forkle admitted. "But I do think it would be wise for all of us to make memory logs of everything we remember about Prentice, or things we've glimpsed in his mind, or—"

"I disagree," Quinlin interrupted. "He's already lost more than a decade of his life—why waste another second of it trying to scrape together the past? He should be focusing on rebuilding and moving forward."

"Why can't he do both?" Linh countered.

"Because nothing good can come from looking too deeply into the tragedies that can't be changed." Quinlin paced to the farthest corner of the porch, tracing his hand along the railing. "We all watched Grady and Edaline fall apart after Jolie—are we really wishing the same for Prentice?"

"I think it's too early to know how he'll respond—long term—to Cyrah's loss," Alden said quietly. "But I can't imagine he'll want to forget her."

"I never said forget her," Quinlin argued. "But he already remembers enough. Any more will only add to his pain— which is why we should treat this memory loss as the gift that it is."

No one seemed to know what to say to that—not even Sophie. And it killed her that Quinlin might be right—that it might be better to leave Prentice with fragments and mysteries than put him through additional grief.

She couldn't figure out why it hurt so much—or wouldn't let herself admit it—until she was away from Keefe's prying Empath senses, alone in her bed later that night with nothing but Iggy's snoring and her own miserable thoughts for company.

Some tiny, desperate part of her had been clinging to the hope that whatever secrets had caused Prentice to call swan song—whatever had helped him to know about the Lodestar symbol—would somehow lead them to Nightfall.

It was a silly, illogical idea. But now that it was gone, the only choice left was to go back to their needle-in-a-haystack ways.

Back to endless piles of schoolwork, and discouraging nightly reports and nothing, nothing, nothing.

No answers.

No plan.

Each day dragging her further from her human parents and leading the Neverseen to their surely inevitable victory.

"I saw this human movie one time," Dex said to her on the fourth day back at Foxfire after the healing, making her drop the book she'd been pulling from her locker.

She hadn't noticed him beside her.

Had barely noticed anything. For days.

"It was about this plague that turned everyone into zombies," Dex continued, retrieving her book and handing it over. "There were all these people shuffling around with glassy eyes and rotting flesh. It was super gross—but also kind of hilarious to see what humans are afraid of."

"Okay," Sophie said as she closed her locker. "You're telling me this . . . why?"

"Because that's what you're starting to remind me of—without the bloody sores. I mean, Fitz gave you another box of pudding puffs at lunch and you didn't even blush. And you've been walking around with this stuck to your shoulder all day."

He peeled off a bold-lettered sign that said, ALL HAIL TEAM FOSTER-KEEFE!

She blinked.

He lowered his voice, making sure no one nearby was listening before he asked, "You're worrying about your parents, right?"

A lump caught in her throat. "I shouldn't be."

"Why not?"

"Because there are so many huger problems—like the soporidine and—"

"Hey," he said, waiting until she looked at him. "You're allowed to care about your family."

Tears welled in her eyes. "We've lost almost another week.

And I know the Washers can erase their memories—but that doesn't help them right now, with whatever misery they're suffering."

"I know. But . . . I bet they don't even know how long it's been, or where they are, or what's happening. You and I didn't, remember? They kept us drugged."

"Not the *whole* ti—"

"Don't," Dex interrupted. "If you're going to find them—and fix all these other problems—you need to stay focused. And there's a *really* good chance I'm right about them being sedated—you have to admit that. So can't you try to believe it, and use it to shut the nightmares down before they get too distracting? Just tell yourself, *They're sleeping, they're sleeping, they're sleeping.*"

Her logical side wanted to poke a million holes in his theory.

But . . . he had a point.

She had no idea what her parents were dealing with—so why not hope for the best instead of assuming the worst?

"I'll try," she promised.

"Try it now," he pushed. "Close your eyes and think it until you mean it."

It took so many repetitions that Sophie lost count. But by the end, her nerves had settled and her nausea had faded, and everything felt a little bit clearer.

"Keep that up—every time the panic comes back, okay?" Dex pleaded. "And if you need to talk, hail me. Anytime."

She nodded and he reached for her hand, giving her gloved fingers a gentle squeeze before realizing he was going to be late for his technopathy session and racing away.

It wasn't until Sophie was halfway to her own session that she realized . . .

That was the first time Dex had talked to her—*really* talked to her—since their infamous kiss.

It was a small victory compared to the massive battles they were still waging. But she was still grateful for it.

And later that night, she actually slept.

SIXTY-SEVEN

EX'S SUGGESTION KEPT SOPHIE out of zombie mode for another week—though it required a lot of mentally chanting, *They're asleep, they're asleep, they're asleep.*

But it also dredged up a whole other kind of worry.

If the Neverseen *were* keeping her parents sedated . . . could they be using soporidine?

And much as she tried to tell herself that being in a deep, comalike trance was better than them being conscious prisoners, she couldn't help wondering what kind of a toll a drug like that would take—especially since Lady Cadence and the ogres still seemed no closer to a cure.

So when Friday rolled around *again*—and there hadn't

been the slightest bit of news or progress—Sophie found herself ignoring Sandor and climbing to the top level of Foxfire's glass pyramid instead of heading to her afternoon session. And when the door to Magnate Leto's office was locked, she plopped down on the floor to wait for him.

"Whoa—is the Mysterious Miss F. *ditching*?" Keefe asked several minutes later as he strode up the stairs, followed by Ro and Magnate Leto. "Or did you get sent here? Either way, you clearly deserve the highest of high fives."

"Why are *you* here?" Sophie asked, ignoring his raised hand as she stumbled to her feet.

"Tiny incident in the Level Five wing—but don't look at me. This one was all on her." He hooked a thumb toward Ro.

"Why does that not surprise me?" Sandor grumbled.

Ro batted her eyelashes. "Hey, it's not *my* fault if someone gets their foot broken while trying to trip me."

"It is if you stomp on them as hard as you can," Magnate Leto argued.

His usually sleek hair looked much more disheveled than usual as he led the way into his triangular office.

"You should've heard the crunch," Keefe whispered when Sophie followed him in.

"And the squealing," Ro added. "You elves are such melodramatic babies. The bone barely even poked through her skin."

Sophie shuddered. "Who was it?"

"I don't think you know Shayda," Keefe said, collapsing into one of the tweed armchairs across from Magnate Leto's gilded, antique-style desk. "I barely know her either—except that she always gives me *lots* of presents at midterms and finals." He winked. "By the way, love what you've done with the place, Leto."

"I'm sure you do." Magnate Leto sank into his own chair, which was more of an upholstered throne now.

"You're welcome for making it so you don't have to stare at ten thousand reflections of yourself every day," Keefe told him.

Sophie elbowed Keefe as she sat beside him. "You don't get to brag about leaving me covered in shattered glass."

"Wait—did you wreck this place?" Ro asked, studying the sloped glass walls and pointed ceiling with new appreciation.

"He did." And Sandor's glare made it very clear that Keefe hadn't been forgiven. "He's lucky the floor didn't shatter with the walls."

"I knew it was thicker," Keefe mumbled, "just like I knew the cloak would keep Sophie covered."

Ro whistled. "You know, when you're trying to impress a girl, it's probably better if you don't almost kill her."

"Eh, this is Foster. She loves the thrill."

"Moving back to the much more pressing matter," Magnate Leto interceded, "Shayda Adel happens to be the daughter of two important Emissaries."

"So? I'm a *princess*." Ro pointed to the tattoos on her forehead.

"I'm aware. But royalty or not, you'll still have to face consequences for your actions—and not just the detention I'm going to make you both serve through the end of the school year. The Adels will insist the Council issue their own punishment."

"What about the punishment for *her* assault on *me*?" Ro countered. "She was trying to knock me into that ugly jeweled dragon statue in the atrium—and if you think I'm going to let some scrawny elf make a fool out of me—"

"Miss Adel's punishment will be the days of bed rest she now requires while her bones heal," Magnate Leto interrupted. "And yours will likely involve some sort of apology during orientation next week—which I recommend you attempt to sound sincere for. I understand that some of my prodigies have been far from welcoming—and I'm working to correct that. But in the meantime . . . play nice. And if anything like this happens again, try defending yourself in a way that Elwin can quickly heal with an elixir."

Ro crossed her arms. "Fine. But I'm going to need a list of exactly what kinds of injuries that leaves available—ranked in order of how painful they are."

"Can I get a copy of that list too?" Keefe asked.

Magnate Leto rubbed his temples. "Some days I miss being Beacon."

"Hey, if you ever need a day off principal duty, I'd be *happy* to fill in," Keefe offered.

"Me too! Me too!" Ro said.

"And what about you?" Magnate Leto said, ignoring them and shifting his attention to Sophie. "To what do I owe this visit?"

Sophie glanced at Ro. "Um . . . I need to talk to you alone."

"Wow, subtlety is *not* your thing," Ro told her. "So let's end the misery—I already know this guy is the Forklenater. Took me about two seconds to figure it out after I met him. The berries might mask his scent for your noses—or his." She grinned at Sandor. "But one whiff and I was like, come on, who are we kidding?"

"Interesting," Magnate Leto said, leaning back in his chair. "Have you shared this knowledge with your father?"

"Nope. He'll respect you more if you tell him yourself. And I never thought I'd say this, but . . . I want you guys to keep working together—even after he tracks down the jerks who defected. Your Councillors are too stuffy—and the Neverseen are backstabbers. But the Black Swan might actually be useful."

Magnate Leto's lips twitched into a smile. "I appreciate your discretion."

He turned back to Sophie. "I'm assuming you're here about the journals?"

Sophie nodded. "Please tell me you've finally learned something that might help?"

"As a matter of fact, I have. I'd been planning to call a meeting once we finished the school week and I could take a break from this identity. But since you're here . . ."

He reached into his desk and held up a rough sketch of the Nightfall symbol, tracing a finger along one of the lines. "What does this look like to you?"

"I'm guessing the correct answer isn't 'a line'?" Sophie said.

Keefe leaned closer, squinting at it. "I think it's a rune."

"It is. As is this." Magnate Leto traced his finger over another line in the design. "And this. And this. And this. And this. And this. Seven runes in all, which means this isn't just a symbol. It's a signature."

Now he had Sophie's attention. "You know the name of the escaped prisoner."

"I do." He ran his finger over each of the runes again. "Vespera."

SIXTY-EIGHT

ESPERA."

The name gave Sophie goose bumps— and not just because they finally had a piece of concrete information about the new villain they were chasing.

"Do you think that's the password?" she asked. "For one of the Forgotten Secrets in Fintan's cache?"

"It's seems worth testing," Magnate Leto said.

He promised to make sure that Bronte and Dex met at Havenfield the next morning—then ordered Sophie and Keefe to return to their sessions while he cleaned up Ro's foot-smashing mess.

Sophie did as he asked, but the whole rest of the day her

brain was a constant loop of *Vespera, Vespera, Vespera*. And the more the name repeated, the more certain she was that they'd found their breakthrough.

This had to be the big *AHA!* that would make everything come together and finally help them get ahead of the Neverseen's plans.

It felt like morning would never get there—but then it did. And Dex was already waiting for her when she made her way downstairs. So was Bronte. And Mr. Forkle. And Alden and Della. And Grady and Edaline. And Tam, Linh, Biana, Fitz, Keefe, Grizel, Woltzer, Lovise, and Ro.

Bronte insisted on giving all of them a lecture about the risks of learning a Forgotten Secret—and made the goblins and Ro wait outside—and Sophie was going to explode with impatience until Dex brought out the cache, and they all held their breath as he whispered "Vespera" to the tiny crystal orb, and . . .

. . . absolutely nothing happened.

Bronte tried saying it louder, with more authority, but it didn't make a difference. Just like it didn't matter when Keefe tried saying it with an unsettlingly accurate mimic of Fintan's voice. Nor when Dex closed his eyes and tried to say the name through the strange language of Technopaths—even when Sophie enhanced him.

"How can that not be the password?" she groaned, sitting on her hands so she wouldn't do something stupid, like grab the cache, run outside, and hurl it off the cliffs.

"Honestly, I'm not surprised," Bronte admitted, and she switched to wanting to throw the cache at his head. "The passwords are supposed to be personal to the cache's owner, so Vespera's name is too generic. *But*, I can run it through the registry and see if it turns up any records. And I'll share it with the rest of the Council in case it dredges up a rare memory."

"I can also run it by the former Lumenaria guards," Alden offered. "And Fallon as well. He wouldn't let me in the last time I visited, but he did respond a few times when I shouted through the door."

Every plan sounded awfully similar to the things they'd already been wasting time on.

But . . . they knew the prisoner's name now. That *had* to make a difference.

And yet, when they regrouped at Havenfield the next day, no one had any good news.

"Maybe 'Vespera' is an alias," Biana suggested as she squished into the space on the couch between Dex and her brother. "Or . . . maybe we arranged the runes wrong."

"I guess it could be Evespar," Linh said. "Or Apreves, or Pravese, or . . . are those actually names?"

"We could play with ugly anagrams all night," Keefe told her. "Or we could solve this the faster way. Who has my old Imparter?"

"I do," Sandor said from his post in the corner. "But I don't see why we need to involve your mother again."

"Because she's the only one who's helped us so far," Sophie reminded him.

"Ohhhh, does this mean I get to stab Keefe?" Ro asked when Sandor handed over the silver gadget and Sophie took a seat on the bottom step of the staircase.

Keefe sat beside Sophie. "Just my finger—and keep in mind that I have an elixir that will turn you sparkly pink if you cut me too hard."

Ro's grin was downright wicked as she drew a dagger from the back of her breastplate. "I bet I'd look good in sparkles."

"Wait," Sophie said, before Ro could draw any blood. "Mr. Forkle can't be here when we hail her. And I doubt Lady Gisela will talk with Bronte around either."

"If I know my mom," Keefe said, "she'll be way more helpful if we don't have any adults listening in. She thinks we're easier to fool without them."

"You *are*," Bronte said, earning groans from all of Sophie's friends. "What? It's a fact. Adults have more experience."

"Yeah, well, go be experienced in the kitchen," Keefe told him. "Feel free to make us some snacks while you're there. And OW!" He yanked his hand away from Ro. "Did I say you could stab me yet?"

"You would've been way flinchier if I'd warned you first. Besides, I barely nicked you—but if you want me to kiss it and make it better when you're done . . ." She puckered her lips—which she'd painted blue that morning—and made a loud smooch. "Or were you going to offer that job to Sophie?"

"Don't hate me for saying this," Grizel whispered to Sandor, "but I'm starting to like this ogre."

Sandor let out a squeaky sigh.

Keefe, meanwhile, waited for the adults to file into the kitchen before he smeared his blood across the Imparter and held it up to face him, angling it to show as little of the room as possible.

"Looks like the reckless son has finally returned to fight for his legacy," Lady Gisela said through the blank screen. "And with his loyal bodyguard, no less. Hello, Princess—it's *so* good to see you. Are you enjoying your time in the Lost Cities?"

Ro shrugged. "It's not so bad when I get to smash things. I had a *lot* of fun in your old house. You didn't care about that desk, did you?"

Sophie could hear the scowl in Lady Gisela's voice when she said, "No, my son already retrieved what I needed from there."

"I did," Keefe agreed. "So now you can tell us all about Vespera."

"And here I thought you were hailing me to say you'd finally gotten your hands on the Archetype."

"Nope. If you want your stupid book back, you have to tell us where to find it," Keefe told her.

"I already gave you my journals. And if you've figured out the signature, you've no doubt spotted the other clues. *Your* job is to find where it all leads."

"Maybe you should tell us what clues you found," Fitz jumped in, "so we can make sure we caught them all."

"Ah. The Vacker boy *is* around," Lady Gisela said. "And still contributing very little, it seems. But if you need me to spell it out, there are several entries that talk about steps—and I'd once thought Vespera meant a list of tasks. But now I believe she means literal stairs. I can't tell if they identify the facility or are simply a part of it, but either way it gives you a landmark to watch for. There's also a part where she goes on and on about rebuilding after the sinking—and I'd thought she meant rebuilding her *plans*. But I think she meant the facility itself—or part of it, at least—which is why it has to be in Atlantis. And the part about leaving her mark on Nightfall implies the facility is branded with her symbol."

"So . . . you're not actually sure about any of this," Sophie said through gritted teeth. "These are all just theories."

"No, Sophie, these are facts. You've read the journals. You saw how she described it. Or wait—have you?"

"I didn't have time to translate thousands of ancient runes," Sophie admitted.

"Ugh. What a horrible time to delegate. That explains why this is taking so much longer than I'd expected. I've been wondering how you could stand to let so much time pass."

"We haven't been *letting time pass*," Keefe snapped. "We've been working on it every day."

"Not hard enough. Read the journals—you'll find a whole

other kind of motivation. Or, if you'd rather keep trusting the Black Swan, I'd recommend demanding they share what they clearly haven't bothered mentioning. I'm sure they're around there somewhere. Probably eavesdropping right now. And once you have a proper understanding of exactly what's at stake, I'd recommend you start using your brains and track down Nightfall. Don't hail me again until you do."

The Imparter went silent.

"Gotta love my mom's pep talks," Keefe muttered, wiping his bloody finger on his dark cape.

"I'm assuming you heard that," Sophie called to Mr. Forkle. "Care to explain?"

"Any details I haven't shared have been to spare you unnecessary worry," he called back, then shuffled slowly into the room.

The others followed, and Sophie was glad to see that Grady and Edaline looked as confused as she felt. So did Alden and Della.

Even Bronte.

"I don't need you *sparing* me—"

"Yes, Miss Foster. You do. We all know this threat is deeply personal to you—and that every day it's a struggle for you not to give in to your panic. There's no reason to add to this extra burden."

"Keefe's mom sure made it sound like there is," Linh noted.

"Lady Gisela is simply casting the doubt on me so you won't focus on how supremely unhelpful she's being," Mr. Forkle insisted.

"Or you're both just super annoying," Tam countered.

"If you won't tell me, give me the journals," Sophie added.

Mr. Forkle folded his hands. "I don't have them with me."

"Then go get them," Biana told him. "We'll wait."

Sophie stood. "Or I could push into your mind and find it myself."

"I'll help," Fitz offered, moving to stand next to her. "Remember how well that worked during our Cognate training?"

"See? That's why I heart these kids," Ro said. "They don't just make threats—they *mean* them."

Mr. Forkle reached up to rub his temples. "You're not going to let this go, are you?"

Everyone shook their heads.

He raised his eyes to the ceiling, muttering something none of them could catch before he told them, "Then I'm going to need to sit. We're *all* going to need to sit."

He made his way over to one of the empty chairs, taking longer than normal to get himself situated.

"Done stalling?" Sophie asked.

"Not quite." His voice filled her mind. *This is an elvin secret. The only way I can share it is if you all promise not to repeat it to the other species.*

"Whoa, why did every elf in the room just flinch?" Ro asked.

"Pretty sure they're communicating telepathically," Grizel told her. "And I take it that means we don't get to hear this mysterious secret?"

"Not until we verify that the journals are accurate," Mr. Forkle told her. "And even then . . . this one is tricky."

"See, it's things like this that are why my dad doesn't trust the elves," Ro noted.

"If he'd like to share everything he's keeping from us about your people, tell him to set up a meeting," Bronte countered.

Ro responded with a gesture that probably wasn't meant to be polite.

"Secrets hinder our ability to protect you," Sandor added.

"And yet, sometimes they're necessary," Mr. Forkle said. "I still maintain that it would be best if none of you burden yourselves with this information. But . . . it seems your minds are made up."

"They are." Sophie sank back onto the stair, and Keefe and Fitz took the spots on either side of her, each grabbing one of her gloved hands.

Mr. Forkle closed his eyes.

The thing you need to understand, he transmitted, *is that Vespera had a very specific vision for Nightfall—one that's every bit as shameful as it is disturbing. And we don't know the extent to which she carried it out—nor whether she's still holding to the same plan at the moment. So what you're insisting I tell you will sound horrifying—but that doesn't mean all of it happened, or that it's happening again.*

Sophie tightened her grip on Fitz's and Keefe's hands. *That's fine. I can handle it.*

I truly hope you can, Miss Foster. Because Nightfall was built for . . .

She could feel his mind struggling to find some way of softening what he was about to say.

Eventually, he simply told her. *Human experimentation.*

SIXTY-NINE

OPHIE WAS GOING TO VOMIT. RIGHT in the middle of her living room.

Her mouth watered and her stomach heaved—but before she lost it completely, a pure white breeze whisked across her consciousness. She hadn't felt Keefe remove her glove, but she was grateful for the bright, soothing tendrils that swept away the mounting darkness.

It gave her the courage to ask, *What kind of experiments was Vespera doing?*

Most of the details weren't provided, Mr. Forkle told her. *And the few that I've found are nothing like the horrors you're currently imagining.*

If that's true, why didn't you tell me about this sooner? Sophie argued.

Because I know how hard you've struggled with thoughts of what your parents might be enduring, and I feared you would see this as confirmation.

Isn't it?

No. The word was adamant—almost an order, commanding her to accept it.

And she tried to.

But she couldn't.

Why was Vespera experimenting on humans? Fitz asked, tightening his hold on her other hand.

Mr. Forkle rubbed his temples again—harder that time. *According to her journals, she was striving to understand how humans could commit such terrible atrocities without shattering their sanity. She believed that if we—as a species—didn't find a way to harness that same level of ruthlessness, that it was only a matter of time before humans would take over as the dominant species on our planet.*

A collective shudder rippled through their group.

Did the experiments have anything to do with sedatives? Alden asked.

You're wondering if the soporidine could be related? Mr. Forkle guessed. *I wondered the same thing, but the research seemed to involve studying her subjects' active choices.*

A fresh wave of nausea hit Sophie hard. *So . . . my parents are definitely awake for what they're going through.*

Not necessarily, Mr. Forkle insisted. *We don't know anything for certain.*

And that's the problem, isn't it? Sophie snapped back. *We don't know anything.*

They still had no idea what the Neverseen were planning with the soporidine, or where to find her family, or—

"Breathe, Foster," Keefe whispered. "You have to keep breathing."

She hadn't realized she'd stopped.

"Yeah, I'm not loving how pale you're all getting," Ro noted.

"Me either," Sandor agreed.

"Have you told us everything?" Bronte asked.

Mr. Forkle shook his head. And all the bodyguards grumbled when he closed his eyes and switched back to transmitting.

There's the timeline to consider, he informed them silently. *The runic alphabet used in these journals—as well as subtle references in numerous passages—suggests that all of this was occurring before the sinking of Atlantis. And over the last few weeks, I've been conducting my own research. And I've found a number of missing persons reports long buried in our ancient archives—filed by humans living in Atlantis.*

The color drained from Bronte's face.

Alden didn't look much better when he asked, *Any record of how the Council responded?*

I suspect the majority of the information exists only in Fintan's cache, Mr. Forkle told him. *But . . . from what I can tell, the Councillors wrote everything off as a misunderstanding.*

Sounds familiar, Alden said, his teal eyes colder than usual as they flicked to Bronte.

Bronte looked away.

Were any of the missing humans found? Fitz asked.

Mr. Forkle ran a hand down his face. *If they were, there's no record of it. But . . . I can't imagine Vespera would've let them go. Even if she wiped their minds, their sudden reappearance would be evidence of her crimes.*

So she killed them, Sophie said.

Something black and cold churned inside her, and Keefe scooted closer, sending new tendrils of that soft glowing breeze to push the darkness back.

It's possible the deaths were natural occurrences, Mr. Forkle reminded all of them. *Human life spans are fleeting. Vespera might've simply kept them imprisoned until their days ended.*

How is that better? Sophie asked.

No one had an answer.

How many humans went missing? Fitz asked.

The records I found were vague. But it seems safe to assume there were hundreds.

Bronte swore under his breath.

"Oh good," Ro said. "Now the Councillor is swearing. Totally seems like something your bodyguards should be kept in the dark about."

Bronte shook his head, his voice a hoarse whisper as he told her, "This can *never* be shared."

So you see the connection too, then? Mr. Forkle asked.

All of the adults nodded.

I don't, Sophie hated to admit.

Alden moved to the windows, staring into the distance. *It's the timing.*

Are we supposed to know what that means? Fitz asked.

Consider what we teach about Atlantis in elvin history, Mr. Forkle told them. *How the greedy, spiteful humans planned a war against our innocent ancestors because they feared the elves' natural abilities and craved more power.*

But if Vespera was capturing humans and experimenting on them—and the Council refused to investigate what was happening, Alden added, *the humans would've had good reason to want to overthrow that authority.*

"Still breathing there, Foster?" Keefe asked.

She tried.

But all of this was too hard—too *huge.* And it wasn't just about Atlantis.

The elves didn't simply sink their shimmering city under the ocean. They terminated all of their treaties.

From that point on, humans were no longer counted as an "intelligent species"—no longer allowed to know the true realities of the world around them.

And all of this time, it was the elves' crimes that had caused it.

And the monster who'd committed those crimes was free—and she had Sophie's parents . . .

She pulled away from Fitz and Keefe, curling her arms around herself, trying to hold it together.

"This is why I didn't want to tell you," Mr. Forkle mumbled.

"Secrets are why we're in this mess!" Sophie snapped. "If the Council hadn't erased Vespera from their minds and locked everything away in a cache, we could've found Nightfall by now!"

"She's not wrong," Ro noted.

"Even if she isn't," Bronte told her, "we can't change what's been done."

Sophie knew he was talking about the past, but she couldn't help wondering if the words also applied to her parents.

What if everything they were enduring was too much—even for the Washers?

Arms wrapped around her—so many that she wondered if everyone in the room was trying to hug her at once.

But even with that support—even with a windstorm of Keefe's mental breezes—nothing could stop the gaping hole from tearing open inside her.

She'd fought so long, so hard to keep control—to keep perspective—to resist falling into the Neverseen's schemes.

But she couldn't stop imagining her parents in that ancient, wicked place.

"Tell me we have a plan to find them," she begged.

Each silent second that followed widened that guttural hole, and Sophie sank into it—felt part of herself disappear into that dark void.

She sank further still when they started talking about searching Atlantis, and doing research, and hacking caches, and creating a cure for the soporidine in Alvar, and meeting with Fallon Vacker and the Lumenaria guards.

She wasn't sure what she'd expected to hear, but she couldn't listen to the same worthless assurances—couldn't pretend that they stood a chance of working.

"I'm sorry," she rasped, pulling free of the smothering embrace and fleeing upstairs.

Shouts followed her, but she slammed the door—shut them out—burrowed under the covers, clutching Ella.

She waited for the tears to come. But she was too numb. Too lost in that hollow emptiness that now lived inside her, swallowing up everything else.

Sleep wouldn't find her either—but she couldn't get up. Couldn't open her eyes. Couldn't respond when her parents came in to check on her.

"I shouldn't have told you," a familiar voice whispered sometime later, and the pain in the words finally got to her.

She peeled back her covers and found daylight—and Magnate Leto—and realized . . .

School.

She'd missed school.

"If my brother had been here," Magnate Leto said, sinking onto the farthest corner of her bed, "I suspect he would've talked me out of sharing. He was always better at knowing your limits. But now there's only me and . . . I made the wrong choice."

Sophie focused on the crystal stars dangling over her bed. "Hiding it from me doesn't change anything."

"It changes *you*," he said. "It keeps you fighting. Keeps you steady. Keeps you from becoming *this*."

She could see it then—the worry in his eyes mixed with the utter doubt in himself. And she knew if she didn't fix it, things would go back to the way they used to be, when the Black Swan tried to shelter her with riddles and vague notes.

So she dragged herself out of bed, heading for her stack of untouched homework.

"I'm better now," she told him. "I just need to stay busy."

He didn't look convinced.

Neither did Grady or Edaline, who were lurking in the doorway, watching her as if she were some spooked animal.

She asked for breakfast to ease their worries—or was it lunch? It could've even been dinner for all she knew—and when Edaline conjured up plates of food, she forced herself to eat every bite.

Fitz dropped by to check on her that night, and she tried to give him a real smile—tried to blush for his newest gift. But her heart didn't even flutter when he hugged her and promised everything would be all right.

Going back to school was absolute misery, but she made herself do it—made herself go through the motions. She had to convince all the nervous eyes watching her that she was okay, so they'd keep including her in their nightly updates—even if there was never any good news.

So she endured the endless pattern: sessions, homework, research, checking on her sister, bedtime, repeat. Even though it felt like she was drowning.

Her friends tried so hard to help her—especially Keefe. He was constantly teasing and pushing her, trying to drag out the slightest hint of a real emotion. But she didn't have the energy. It took every ounce of her strength to pull herself out of bed every day, to eat whatever food was placed in front of her, to answer questions when people asked her, and not constantly obsess about how many days were slipping away—or what that meant.

And then somehow it was finals, and she fumbled through her exams, not caring if she passed or failed. What did any of it matter, when the Neverseen were winning—and would keep winning until they unleashed their next horrible plan?

Her friends tried to draw her into the celebrations afterward—tried to show her all the finals traditions she'd missed the year before because of her kidnapping. But she couldn't pay attention to any of it. There seemed to be games and prizes. She definitely felt lots of laughter tickling her ears. And there were piles and piles of presents.

Grady and Edaline found her in the cafeteria, staring at her unopened gifts, and wrapped her in a crushing hug to congratulate her on moving to Level Four. Their smiles were wide and proud—begging her to be excited.

"Can we go home now?" Sophie asked instead.

Their smiles fell.

She'd been trying not to notice how shadowed their eyes had become—trying not to admit that this time she was the source of that grief and worry.

"Never mind," she said. "We can stay a little longer."

"No, kiddo." Grady kissed the top of her head. "We can go home. Need help packing up your presents?"

"And don't forget to clean out your locker," Edaline added.

The halls were empty when Sandor led her back to the Level Three atrium—everyone too busy celebrating to gather used notebooks and scattered pens. She shoved whatever she could fit into her satchel and tossed the rest before handing the heavy bag over to Sandor.

"You look terrible," an oily voice said behind her.

Sophie glanced over her shoulder and found Keefe's father standing there in an extravagant silver cloak.

"Mind you, my son doesn't look much better," Lord Cassius added, stepping to the side to reveal a slump-shouldered Keefe. "If Foxfire didn't require a parent or guardian to collect exam grades, I doubt he would've acknowledged my existence at all."

"I wouldn't have," Keefe mumbled.

"Ooh, fun! Is it time to dredge up the daddy issues?" Ro

asked, striding out of the shadows. "Why do I never have snacks when I need them?"

Lord Cassius clicked his tongue, smoothing his always immaculate blond hair. "If my son has any issues, they're entirely his own. I'm simply waiting for him to realize he's pushing the wrong parent away."

"And I'm waiting for him to realize that neither of his parents deserve him!" Sophie snapped, slamming her locker shut.

The clang of metal tingled through her.

Anger.

The feeling was a revelation—and not just for her.

"*There's* the Foster we all know and love," Keefe said, offering a grin that had a whole lot of relief mixed in. "Come on, let's get out of here."

"Are you sure that's wise?" Lord Cassius called after them. "You need my help."

"Ignore him," Keefe whispered.

"I wouldn't if I were you," his father warned. "Because I know what you're looking for in Atlantis, Sophie. And I know where you can find it."

SEVENTY

HY SHOULD I BELIEVE YOU?"
Sophie asked, refusing to turn back.
She wouldn't let Keefe's father see
how much his words had affected her.

But then he told her, "Because I brought this."

She stole a glance over her shoulder and found Lord Cassius
holding a small handmade sketch of the Nightfall symbol.

"That's all I'll say for now," he said, grinning as Keefe
wrapped an arm around Sophie to keep her steady. "This is not
the place for this conversation. But if you'd like to know where
to find that signature in Atlantis, you'll come with me—now."

"You know it's a signature?" Sophie whispered.

"I know everything." He reached under his jerkin and

grabbed the glinting chain of a simple pendant. A home crystal. "Answers are this way."

Sophie glanced at Keefe. "Is it a trick?"

He stalked closer and snatched his dad's hand, brushing a finger across his skin. "It . . . doesn't feel like he's lying."

"Your parents are waiting for you back in the cafeteria," Sandor reminded her.

"Limited time offer," Keefe's father warned.

Sandor wheeled on him. "Sophie's not going anywhere unless you tell me where that crystal leads!"

Lord Cassius's smirk looked uncannily like his son's. "Bodyguards are welcome, if it helps. Even the princess."

"That doesn't answer where we're going," Ro noted.

"Just think of it as my beach house," Lord Cassius told her.

Something sparked in Keefe's eyes—a seething kind of fury—but it was gone by the time he turned to Sophie. "I'll go, and I'll let you know what he says—"

"Not an option," his father interrupted. "I'll talk to both of you or none of you. And the time to decide is almost up."

He held the crystal to the light, creating a shimmering path.

Sophie tugged out an eyelash. "I could leave my parents a note on my locker. That way they'll know where I am."

Sandor sighed, seeming to know there was no point arguing as he handed Sophie a notebook so she could scribble a vague message:

Gone to a beach house with Keefe and his father.

Be home soon—and don't worry, I have Sandor.

"Grady is going to strangle me," Sandor said as he tucked the note into the seam of her locker door.

"Glad to see you've made the right choice," Lord Cassius said when Sophie grabbed Keefe's hand. Sandor took her other hand, and Ro completed the chain.

"Don't make us regret it," Sophie warned.

Lord Cassius made no promises as he reached for his son and dragged their group into the light, letting the warmth whisk them away.

"I take it this isn't what you were expecting?" Lord Cassius asked, leaning against the wall as they surveyed their surroundings.

"It's not nearly as pathetic as your desperate-for-attention tower," Ro told him. "Less sparkly, too—I approve."

So did Sophie—not that she'd admit it. Lord Cassius had kept his son away from this strange sliver of his life for some reason, and he certainly didn't deserve praise for it.

But the house *was* beautiful. A single, sprawling level with mother-of-pearl walls and massive windows overlooking the turquoise ocean. The scattered rooms were connected by vine-wrapped arches and broken up with sun-baked inner courtyards. Everything was bright and airy. Elegant, but comfortable. Decorated in dove grays and soothing shades of blue.

He led them to the back patio, made of swirled abalone shell, and motioned for them to sit in the huge cushioned porch swings rocking back and forth in the crisp breeze. The beach itself spread before them, a shimmering cove of smooth black sand. Gulls cried overhead, mixed with the deeper, much more exotic song of some bird Sophie couldn't see.

"Can I get anyone anything to drink?" Lord Cassius offered, lingering in the archway to the main house. "I think I have a few bottles of lushberry juice."

Keefe snorted, kicking his legs to make his swing rock harder. "Can we stop pretending this is a dinner party and get back to why you have a drawing of the Nightfall symbol?"

"It's a drawing of Vespera's *signature*," Lord Cassius corrected, pulling the sketch from his pocket to study it again.

"How do you know about her?" Sophie asked.

"The Black Swan told me." He smiled when her eyebrows shot up. "I don't know why that surprises you. You both know I've offered to swear fealty several times."

"I still don't understand why," Sophie admitted.

He crossed to the railing, watching the orangey orb of sun slowly slipping beneath the horizon. "Our world is fracturing. And I'd like to be on the right side of the divide."

"Pretty sure you just want revenge on Mom," Keefe said, kicking his swing even harder.

"I won't deny that'd be a welcome bonus. But believe it or not, I do respect much of the Black Swan's cause. And I could be a valuable asset for them—and they know it. But for *some* reason"—he turned to face his son—"my admission continues to be denied. Which has cost you dearly. All these days you've wasted wandering aimlessly around Atlantis—"

"Were you following us?" Keefe interrupted.

"Shockingly, Keefe, I have far better ways to use my time. But I have been staying in my apartment in the city—"

"Why?" Sophie asked.

Lord Cassius's eyes darkened. "I'm not a fan of living in the house where my wife lied to me. My marriage was far from perfect—my need for other residences is proof enough of that. But since I had these built-in escapes, I figured, why not put them to use? And when I saw you two in Atlantis, despite how casual you pretended to be, I knew you had to be looking for something—and since very few know the city as intimately as I do, I reached out to the Black Swan and offered my assistance. But my offer was refused. And your search was far too aimless for me to figure out what you were looking for. So I put it out of my mind—let it be your problem—until the Black Swan came crawling back. Apparently, they've grown quite concerned about the mental state of their moonlark, and now that I've seen you, Sophie, I can't say I blame them."

Sophie shrank back into the cushions of her swing, pulling her hair around her cheeks to hide.

"They finally told me what they were looking for," he

continued, "and it really is a pity they didn't let me start sooner. It only took me a week to find it."

Sophie refused to think about how much time that could've saved—refused to ask him where he found it.

This was a game for him. And she wasn't going to play— even if it was killing her.

"So stubborn," he murmured. "I can't decide if that makes you two perfect for each other or heading for utter disaster."

"Just tell us where it is," Keefe snapped.

"I'd be happy to. But my help comes with conditions."

"Of *course* it does," Keefe muttered. "Just like Mom."

"Yes. We were matched for a reason. But unlike your mother, my demands are *fair*. Honestly, they're things I shouldn't even *have* to demand. But since you insist on shoving me out of your life, I have two simple conditions. First, you go to the Collective and tell them to admit me to the order. And second, you move in here. With me."

Keefe dropped his legs to stop the motion of his swing. "You want *me* to live in your precious secret beach house?"

"Unless you'd rather we live in my apartment in Atlantis," Lord Cassius told him. "It's far less convenient to access, so I'm assuming you'd prefer the ease of here. But if you're looking for somewhere more luxurious, we can go there."

Sophie rarely saw Keefe at a loss for words.

"Don't look at me like that," Lord Cassius grumbled. "It's bad enough that I have to deal with constant slander because of your mother. I'm sick of the additional gossip about my runaway son."

"Awww, *there's* the father I remember."

There was a smirk on Keefe's lips as he went back to swinging, but Sophie could see the lie behind it—see the way his shoulders drooped and his chin tucked tight, as if he was shrinking away.

"Forget it," she told Lord Cassius. "You can't force Keefe to live with you."

"Do you even know where he's staying right now?" Lord Cassius countered. "Because I do."

"So you *were* following me," Keefe noted.

"Forgive me for wanting to make sure my son wasn't squatting in the street—not that you've chosen much better."

"Where *are* you staying?" Sophie asked Keefe.

He cleared his throat. "Don't freak out."

"Not the best way to start it off," Ro warned him.

Keefe rolled his eyes. "It sounds bad when I say it—but it's fine. I'm . . . staying at Alvar's old place—and I know what you're going to say. But it's actually really smart if you think about it. Alvar was always grumbling about how he could never go back because the Council had to be watching the place. *And* it gave me a chance to snoop around. That's how I found all those updates on the ogres that he intercepted from Lady Cadence."

"That feeling you have right now?" Lord Cassius said to

Sophie. "I've lived with it every time I've had to watch him jump from one poor decision to the next."

"Whatever," Keefe muttered, kicking his swing higher again. "It's been fine."

"Just because you didn't face any consequences doesn't mean you made the right decision," his father argued. "I know you love to think you're so brilliantly independent, but you're only fourteen years old—"

"Fifteen," Keefe corrected. "But you were close. They both start with *f*."

Lord Cassius sighed. "You know, if you were capable of having a snark-free conversation, we might actually get along."

"Maybe," Keefe said. "But that's always been the problem, isn't it? I'm not some boring mini-*you*—and you can't stand it."

"What I can't stand is watching my son throw away his life. Especially when you have so much potential. You're made for greatness, Keefe. But you always settle for 'good enough.' I'm trying to help you be more."

"Yeah, well, sorry—the role of 'manipulative parent' has already been filled by Mom. And if you have some sort of grand plan for me, the word 'legacy' is also taken."

Lord Cassius pinched the bridge of his nose. "The only *plan* I have is to push you to *try*—and to keep you safe."

"Safe is *my* job," Ro told him, grabbing the chain of Keefe's swing and jerking it to a halt. "But I'm all for moving here. I can watch you guys fight all day!"

"Does that mean we have a deal?" Lord Cassius asked.

"No," Sophie said, standing to face him fully. "I'm done with bargains. If you want your son to live with you, try begging for his forgiveness. And if you want to join the Black Swan, maybe you shouldn't hold vital information hostage—especially after they came to you for help."

"And here I thought you were desperate to find Nightfall."

"I am. And I can drag anything I need out of your mind."

"I'd like to see you try," Lord Cassius told her. "I have rather creative ways of keeping my thoughts to myself."

"I'll get past them," Sophie promised.

"After how long?" Lord Cassius countered. "Do you really want to waste *more* time?"

"Hey," Keefe said, jumping off his swing and wheeling Sophie around by her shoulders. "Much as I'm enjoying this sudden overflow of adorable Foster-rage—it's not worth it. He's *good* at dodging Telepaths—and this is way too important." He turned to his dad. "I'll tell Forkle I don't care if you swear fealty, as long as he keeps you on different assignments from me. And I'll move here—but I won't be following your rules. Plan on some epic pranking, too."

"Keefe," Sophie warned.

"It's going to be fine, Foster. I know you probably think I'm trying to take over again—"

"It's not that," she interrupted. "It's . . . can you really handle this? I see what he does to you."

"I don't *do* anything," Lord Cassius snapped.

"The fact that you can't even see it is the worst part," Sophie told him.

Keefe leaned closer to her. "I can handle him. What I *can't* handle is any more of the Sophie Shell who's been wandering around for the last few weeks, scaring the snot out of all of us. I need my Foster back—the real one, who bosses me around and is way too much fun to tease."

"Awwwwww, is anyone else chanting *Kiss! Kiss! Kiss!* in their heads right now?" Ro asked.

"Just you," Sandor said through a sigh.

Keefe stepped back, scowling at both bodyguards before telling his dad. "Deal. Now spill it. Where's Nightfall?"

Lord Cassius's lips twitched. "Right where it's been for thousands of years. You've probably walked by it a hundred times without realizing. And I'll give Vespera credit, it took some major audacity to hide it where she did."

"Which is where?" Sophie asked.

"Right in the heart of Atlantis. In the Unity Fountain. On the statue of the human."

SEVENTY-ONE

THERE WAS A TREMENDOUS DEBATE that night over who would go to Atlantis with Lord Cassius in the morning to try to figure out how the fountain actually led into Nightfall. And in the end, they chose Linh, Tam, Fitz, and Grizel.

Linh, because water would likely play a role. Tam, because he refused to let his sister go under the ocean without him—and because he promised to find creative new ways to annoy Keefe's father. And Fitz, so it wouldn't seem suspicious for Grizel to be there for protection.

Everyone else was stuck at Havenfield, pacing and waiting—waiting and pacing—until Sophie decided she owed everyone an apology for her zombie-girl days.

"You have nothing to apologize for," Mr. Forkle told her. *"Nothing."*

"Well . . . you *did* ditch us yesterday," Grady corrected, pulling Sophie into a hug. "But we're letting you off the hook this time, because it's way too good to see you smile."

"It really is," Edaline whispered, wiping her misty eyes.

All of her friends nodded.

So did the Collective.

And Alden and Della.

Even Ro and the goblins.

"Hang on—does anyone else think Foster should have to apologize for ignoring her finals presents?" Keefe asked. "I'm pretty sure I saw half the school crying about it."

"No one was crying," Edaline said, snapping her fingers and conjuring up the hefty stack of packages Sophie had left behind when she went to pack up her locker. "But it's not too late to open them."

"But . . . I didn't get you guys anything," Sophie mumbled.

Biana shrugged. "Just promise you won't try to stop us from going with you to Nightfall, and we're good."

"Hey, speak for yourself," Keefe told her. "I also demand a hug! And public declaration that my gift wins for Best Gift in the History of the Universe!"

"Uh, Fitz showed me what he got her, and it's pretty hard to top," Biana warned him.

"Please," Keefe scoffed, grabbing a flat package from the

pile—wrapped in blue paper covered in tiny green gulons. "Go on, Foster. Show them who's the Gift Master."

"It's not a competition," she told him as she tore through the thin paper, peeled it back, and . . .

"Told you," Keefe said when she sucked in a breath.

"I . . ."

He smirked. "Look at that. The Mysterious Miss F. is speechless."

She was.

She'd known he was an incredible artist—had often marveled at the detail in his sketches.

But these?

The first painting was a close-up of her with Grady and Edaline, the three of them leaning on each other and looking so . . . natural. As if they'd always been together.

The other was a wider scene—Sophie with all of her friends, standing near Calla's Panakes tree. It was the kind of incredible group Sophie had never dreamed she'd someday be a part of. But there she was. Right in the center.

"Smooth move painting yourself next to her," Ro told Keefe, peeking over Sophie's shoulder.

"Uh, we all know Foster can't bear to be away from me—and art is about honesty. That's why I made sure I have the best hair."

"I don't know," Biana argued, "you made mine pretty awesome. I should braid my hair more often."

Granite looked anything but thrilled with the possibility. "Do we even have the resources to stage a simultaneous raid into Nightfall *and* provide proper security for Wylie?" he asked.

"It would be a challenge," Mr. Forkle admitted.

"My queen would probably be willing to send additional soldiers," Sandor offered.

"And I bet my dad would send a couple of extra warriors," Ro added. "But your Councillors would have to be cool with having ogres stalking around Atlantis, making fun of all the sparkles."

"I don't think that would be wise," Mr. Forkle told her, "mostly because the Neverseen won't go near Wylie if he's surrounded by armed guards. Any security we provide would have to be discreet."

"Like this?" Della asked, vanishing and reappearing a second later with a goblin throwing star pressed against Lord Cassius's throat.

"That yelp you just let out totally made my day," Keefe told him.

"Mine too," Ro said. "But anyone can scare Lord Fancy-clothes," she told Della.

Della vanished again, reappearing across the room as she unsheathed Grizel's sword and pointed it at Sandor's chest.

Ro shrugged. "Those guys are too busy making sappy eyes at each other."

Della vanished again—and Ro anticipated the attack. Her sword was drawn and ready, slashing the air.

in the History of the Universe! And feel free to add that it's way better than anything the Fitzster has given you."

It was, actually—but saying that didn't seem fair to all the awesome things Fitz had done. So she went with a simple "thank you."

Keefe pulled her a little closer. "Anytime, Foster."

It was probably her cue to let go, but . . . she couldn't seem to do it.

Someone cleared his throat, and Sophie leaned back, prepared to give Grady a death glare—but the sound had come from the doorway, where Lord Cassius now stood, along with Tam, Linh, Fitz, and Grizel.

"Looks like we missed something," Fitz said, his eyes darting between the paintings and where Keefe's arms were wrapped around Sophie's waist.

Sophie pulled away. "So . . . how'd it go?"

"A mix of good news and bad news," Lord Cassius told her.

She didn't breathe until Fitz told her, "The good news is: The symbol is definitely there. It's on the scepter the human statue is holding."

Sophie's knees nearly gave out with relief.

"I could feel the currents in the fountain brushing the seam of a door under the statue's pedestal," Linh added. "One that should be easy to access once I part the water."

"If the door's underwater, how do the Neverseen get in and out?" Biana asked.

"Gusters can part water with their winds," Alden reminded her.

"So . . . we definitely found Nightfall," Sophie said, needing to feel the words on her lips to truly believe them.

Fitz closed the distance between them to take her hand. "We did."

She twined her fingers with his, taking all the support she could get in order to ask, "What's the bad news?"

"The bad news is: Linh made us buy *this* as our cover for being in the city," Tam grumbled, holding up a small clear bag with a tiny creature floating in water. It looked like a mini-kitten covered in purple-blue scales. "Of *all* the pets she could've made me get for her, she had to pick one with venomous fangs."

"Hey, murcats are sweet once you train them," Linh insisted.

"Uh-huh. Don't blame me if you lose a couple of fingers," Tam warned.

"Questionable pet choices aside," Granite said, not looking thrilled at the newest addition to his household, "is that the only bad news?"

"No," Fitz admitted. "Linh said the door feels locked."

"I tried sweeping waves against the handle," Linh explained, "but I couldn't budge it."

"No big deal," Dex assured them. "I've never met a lock I can't pick."

"What about the cache I hear you've been trying to open for months?" Lord Cassius countered.

"Isn't my dad fun?" Keefe asked. "Aren't you glad we're working with him?"

"Am I wrong?" Lord Cassius countered.

Dex scowled. "The cache isn't *locked*. It's *guarded*—which is way more complicated."

"We'll make sure you have enough time," Mr. Forkle told him. "In case there's also an alarm to deal with. And we'll need to stage the raid at night, to ensure that no one's around to see us enter the fountain. The Council has made it clear that none of the citizens in Atlantis can see what we're doing."

"Are they really going to keep Nightfall a secret?" Sophie asked.

He nodded. "At least while any of the Neverseen remain at large."

"That's the other bad news," Fitz jumped in. "I don't think there's a way to sneak in without the Neverseen knowing we're coming."

Keefe shrugged. "So? I'm sure they're already expecting us. Vespera left her signature on Alvar's foot."

"I agree," Grady said. "But it also means they'll likely have plenty of security ready—and this time we don't have any idea how to prepare for it."

"It can't be worse than giant mutant beast things," Tam argued.

"I wouldn't be so sure," Mr. Forkle told him. "Vespera has had a long, long time to plan for this. Fortunately, the same strategy we used to rescue Miss Foster and Mr. Dizznee should work for this as well."

"You mean a diversion?" Squall clarified.

Mr. Forkle nodded. "To draw them out of the facility. I'm sure they have eyes on that courtyard. So all we have to do is show them something they can't resist."

"Like what?" Della asked, beating Sophie to the question.

"It has to be something shocking," Granite mused. "Something like . . ."

"Me," Mr. Forkle finished. "If the Neverseen see me, they'd have to investigate."

"Why?" Lord Cassius asked.

"Because they think I'm dead."

Lord Cassius's eyes widened.

"Wouldn't that be too suspicious, though?" Tam asked. "I feel like the Neverseen would expect a trick the second they see you. They might even think it's not really you—just someone we fed a bunch of ruckleberries and elixirs."

"Tam's right," Blur said. "They know we're coming—and they know we've lured them out of their hideout before. The only way this is going to work is if we show them something they're so desperate for—"

"Or some*one,*" Linh interrupted. The pink faded from her cheeks as she turned to Granite. "I know who they wouldn't be able to resist. But . . . I hate to ask him."

Sophie guessed who Linh meant at the same time as Mr. Forkle.

And with equal dread—they both mumbled, "Wylie."

SEVENTY-TWO

E CAN'T ASK WYLIE TO DO
that."

Sophie must've said the words
three times, trying to silence the
desperate, selfish part of herself that kept thinking it was an
awesome solution.

It wouldn't be fair to ask Wylie to take that risk. He'd *barely*
escaped his abduction—and she didn't want to imagine what
Fintan would do if he captured Wylie again.

"I actually think we should ask him," Linh told her—which
Sophie definitely hadn't been expecting. "He'll tell us if he
doesn't feel comfortable doing it. And after everything the
Neverseen have done to him, he might want to help."

Granite looked anything but thrilled with the possibility. "Do we even have the resources to stage a simultaneous raid into Nightfall *and* provide proper security for Wylie?" he asked.

"It would be a challenge," Mr. Forkle admitted.

"My queen would probably be willing to send additional soldiers," Sandor offered.

"And I bet my dad would send a couple of extra warriors," Ro added. "But your Councillors would have to be cool with having ogres stalking around Atlantis, making fun of all the sparkles."

"I don't think that would be wise," Mr. Forkle told her, "mostly because the Neverseen won't go near Wylie if he's surrounded by armed guards. Any security we provide would have to be discreet."

"Like this?" Della asked, vanishing and reappearing a second later with a goblin throwing-star pressed against Lord Cassius's throat.

"That yelp you just let out totally made my day," Keefe told him.

"Mine too," Ro said. "But anyone can scare Lord Fancyclothes," she told Della.

Della vanished again, reappearing across the room as she unsheathed Grizel's sword and pointed it at Sandor's chest.

Ro shrugged. "Those guys are too busy making sappy eyes at each other."

Della vanished again—and Ro anticipated the attack. Her sword was drawn and ready, slashing the air.

But Della appeared behind her, snatched the dagger from Ro's breastplate and pressed the point against Ro's spine.

"Huh. I think I finally get how elf-y abilities could be an advantage in battle," Ro admitted. "Too bad most of you don't show this kind of flare."

"You'd be surprised," Della told her, handing Ro back her dagger.

"Your skills are highly impressive," Mr. Forkle told Della as she smoothed her dark silky hair and adjusted the skirt of her gown. "But a single Vanisher against the Neverseen won't be enough."

"Then let me help," Edaline said, snapping her fingers and making a melder appear in her palm. She snapped again and swapped the gadget for a tightly coiled lasso—which she swung in a fluid motion, looping the rope around Ro and cinching tight. "I have access to an entire arsenal of weapons," she told them. "And I can restrain a woolly mammoth with one hand."

Ro grabbed the rope and pulled, but Edaline easily kept her balance.

"I can help too," Squall offered, curling her ice-crusted fingers into a fist and making frozen cuffs bind Ro's hands.

Ro fought to break free, but every time the ice cracked, a new layer formed.

"Okay, you guys are my new favorites," Ro told them.

"And I doubt the Neverseen would suspect them either," Blur noted. "Since Vanishers, Conjurers, and Frosters are rarely seen as threats."

"I would be there as well," Granite added. "*If* Wylie agreed—though, I have to say, I think we might be overestimating how the Neverseen would react to seeing him. The idea that they'd immediately abandon their facility in an attempt to recapture him seems far too impulsive."

"Okay, so what if we give them time to plan?" Fitz suggested. "What if Wylie requests a meeting—and we plan our raid for the same time?"

"Do you really think they'd fall for that?" Tam asked.

"They might," Mr. Forkle said slowly. "If his offer was tempting enough."

"Couldn't Wylie offer to give them the answers they wanted about his mom—and maybe even say he'll give them the missing starstone?" Fitz asked. "I bet they wouldn't be able to resist that."

"But Wylie would have to ask for something in return to make it believable," Sophie reminded him. "And I don't know what that would be."

"How about revenge?" Keefe suggested.

"Uh, pretty sure the Neverseen aren't going to volunteer to let him punish them for kidnapping him," Tam told him.

"*Not* the revenge I meant, Bangs Boy," Keefe said with an enormous eye roll. "I meant revenge for what happened to his mom. Wylie could act like he thinks my mom killed Cyrah—it's not like it's a stretch, since I'm still not convinced she didn't do it. And he could say he went to the Black Swan for help and we refused, because we're working with her. So now he's going to the other side to see if *they'll* take her down for him, and offering the secrets as a trade."

"I actually could see them believing that," Mr. Forkle admitted.

"So could I," Granite mumbled. "Though I'm sure they'd still be suspicious."

"Suspicious is fine," Blur reminded him. "As long as they leave the facility to go to the meeting."

"Okay but . . . did I miss something?" Dex asked. "How is Wylie supposed to tell them any of this? We don't have a way to hail the Neverseen."

"Could we leave a note?" Sophie said. "I know this is probably going to sound cheesy, but . . . the Neverseen must have a way of monitoring the Unity Fountain. So couldn't Wylie write up a message, slip it in a bottle, seal it with their symbol, and leave it floating in there?"

Mr. Forkle stroked his chin. "I suppose we've left notes in stranger places."

"And at least we'd know if they got it, if the bottle disappears," Alden added.

"It sounds like we're settled on this," Granite said through a sigh. "I guess that means I'd better talk to Wylie, but if he says no—"

"We'll come up with something else," Sophie promised.

"Hail us as soon as you have his decision," Mr. Forkle added as Granite leaped away.

Blur, Wraith, and Alden left soon after, to scout possible meeting places. And Della, Edaline, and Squall went to check Havenfield's weapons stash to see what other items they might want to bring with them.

"We should figure out our strategy for Nightfall while we wait," Grady said, turning to Sophie. "And I'll make you a deal. I won't argue about you or any of your friends going—if you don't fight having me join you."

"And your bodyguard," Sandor added.

"That may not be possible," Mr. Forkle warned the goblins. "Nightfall isn't a place that should be seen by other species. It's . . . not a proud moment in our history."

"You'd really leave Sophie unprotected to hide something that happened thousands of years ago?" Grizel asked.

A long second passed before Mr. Forkle sighed. "I suppose . . . whatever's down there . . . we'll have to own up to it eventually. But—"

"Don't," Ro warned when he turned to her. "Don't even think about telling me I'm not going. There's no way I'm letting Scrawny Boy go in there without me. Some of my father's traitors could be serving as guards."

"Scrawny Boy?" Keefe asked. "Did I, or did I not beat you at arm wrestling?"

"*One* time!" Ro argued. "And only because you tickled me!"

"Ogres are ticklish?" Tam asked.

"Apparently," Sophie said, not sure how to picture that. She stopped trying when Ro shot her a glare, instead turning back to Mr. Forkle. "It probably would be good to have Ro with us."

"I guess I'll be facing plenty of heat from the Council anyway—why not add a little more?" Mr. Forkle told her. "But I'm trusting all of you to keep whatever you see in there to yourselves until we've decided what to do about it."

When everyone nodded, he asked, "So how many does that put us at?"

Sophie took a quick count. "Thirteen, including all of our bodyguards and Ro. Though I wasn't sure if I was supposed to count you."

He grimaced. "Much as it pains me to say this, I think keeping the fact that I'm alive a secret might hold more value than whatever I could contribute to this mission—especially since the group is already so large. In fact, how about we limit it to only two goblins? I'll let you decide which—though I'm sure I can guess."

Sandor and Grizel pulled rank immediately.

"Okay, so now we're down to eleven," Sophie said.

"Twelve," Mr. Forkle corrected. "Miss Redek should go too."

"Marella Redek is part of the Black Swan?" Lord Cassius asked.

Sophie cringed.

She'd forgotten he was there. And given the way he'd tucked himself into a shadowy corner, she suspected that had been his goal.

"Think of her more like a consultant," Mr. Forkle told him. "And do not ask any more questions. In fact, you've done all we need from you at the moment."

"Am I to assume I'm dismissed?" Lord Cassius asked.

"For now."

Lord Cassius's eyes narrowed, and Sophie waited for him to argue. But he said, "Fine. If you want me to prove I'll respect your authority, I can do that."

He pulled out his home crystal and lifted the chain up over his head, handing the necklace to Keefe. "When you're finished here, come *home*."

Keefe stared and stared at that crystal, long after Lord Cassius left. And he didn't put it around his neck—but he did tuck it into his cape pocket.

"Okay," Mr. Forkle said, clapping his hands, "that leaves us with a group of two goblins, an ogre, a Telepath, an Empath, a Vanisher, a Shade, a Hydrokinetic, a Technopath, a Mesmer, and a Pyrokinetic—and of course Miss Foster's Telepath-Polyglot-Teleporter-Inflictor-Enhancer combination."

Ro blinked. "Wow. Now I get why everyone's always trying to kill her."

"Indeed. But what I meant was, I think this group should sufficiently cover any challenging situation—assuming Miss Redek is willing."

"Shouldn't we wait until we hear what Wylie decides?" Biana asked. "In case that changes anything?"

They didn't have to wait long.

When Granite returned to Havenfield, he didn't come alone.

"Hey," Wylie said, stealing a glance at Linh before he turned to Sophie. "I hear you have a job for me."

SEVENTY-THREE

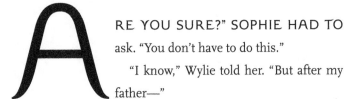RE YOU SURE?" SOPHIE HAD TO ask. "You don't have to do this."

"I know," Wylie told her. "But after my father—"

"You don't owe me anything," Sophie interrupted. "I healed Prentice because I wanted to. And because it was the right thing to do."

"So is this. Your parents don't deserve whatever's happening to them." His bright blue eyes dimmed, and Sophie wondered if he was remembering the horrors he'd endured during his interrogation.

She didn't let herself think about it—didn't want to sink back into that numb panic.

But she had to ask him one more time, "You're sure?"

He was.

So was Marella—though she looked a whole lot happier with her decision once Sophie had clarified that there would be no gorgodons or cold, sticky ash.

And even though it earned Sophie lots and lots of eye rolls, she asked each of her friends if they were sure too. And Della. And Grady. And Edaline. And Sandor and Grizel. And Ro.

Each time, they promised that they were certain.

Even the Collective wasn't safe from the question—though for them she was mostly trying to make sure that there wasn't some better, safer, plan they should be focusing on.

"We're sure," Mr. Forkle told her. Over and over and over. Until he turned the question back on her.

"Are *you* sure?" he asked, removing a black bottle from his cape pocket. The note Wylie had written—following their explicit instructions—was already sealed inside, with white wax in the shape of the Neverseen's eye. "Once Wylie leaves this in the Unity Fountain, the plan will be in motion. You'll have less than twenty-four hours before you head into Nightfall. Are you ready for that?"

"I have to be."

"That's not the same as a yes," he noted. "And as someone who's faced far too many moments like this, can I share something I've had to learn the hard way?"

She nodded.

He stumbled closer, lowering his ruckleberry-swollen body onto the couch beside her. "You can't control everything that's going to happen, Sophie. I know on some level you know that—but I still see you trying. And I understand that instinct. But the real secret to facing these kinds of challenges is to go in knowing that something *will* go wrong. Many things, most likely. It's not about perfect plans. It's about believing you can handle whatever happens."

"But what if I can't?" she whispered. "I couldn't handle Lumenaria. And this time we're even more unprepared. We don't know what kinds of security we'll be facing. We don't know anything about Vespera. We don't know if the soporidine plays into any of this, or if that's a separate thing we're going to regret ignoring. Or if Keefe's mom has left out anything important because she has her own plans."

"Is that why you haven't told your sister about any of this?"

Her heart stumbled. "How do you know I haven't?"

"Because as much as you hate to be coddled and sheltered, you do exactly that to others."

"So you think I should tell her?"

"That's up to you. But let the choice come from love. Not fear."

She nodded, sitting on her hands so she couldn't tug on her eyelashes.

"You're more afraid this time," he guessed. "Is it because of your family?"

"That's part of it." She could've left it there, but she went ahead and admitted, "After Lumenaria, it's . . . different. All the jokes about 'almost dying'—they're not jokes anymore. It could happen. It *did* happen."

"I know." He reached for her gloved hand, his fingers tracing over the spot where her scar was hidden. "When I joined the Black Swan, I knew I'd be facing risks and danger. But I don't think I'll ever get used to how hard it is to watch others do the same. Especially now, when I should be going with you, and instead I'm stuck hiding away, trying to convince myself that my new limited situation isn't letting everyone down."

It was probably the most open he'd ever been with her.

And that trust—that honesty—made something shift inside her. As if a torch had been passed—and instead of feeling terrified, she felt proud. Strong.

Wraith, Wylie, and Tiergan arrived then, to take the bottle to Atlantis, and she didn't feel like asking them if they were sure.

"Be careful tomorrow," she said instead.

Wylie nodded. "You too."

Barely an hour later, Wraith hailed Mr. Forkle to let him know the bottle had vanished from the Unity Fountain. And the countdown to Nightfall had officially begun.

SEVENTY-FOUR

LOOKS LIKE *SOMEONE* DIDN'T SLEEP,"
Keefe said, following Sandor into Sophie's room
the next morning.

"Are you really surprised?" she asked, pulling
her hair closer to her face to hide her puffy, shadowed eyes.

"Of course not. But was it nightmares? Or were you lying
there overthinking everything? Or were you up late talking to
your sister?"

"About all of the above," Sophie admitted, sitting on the
edge of her bed.

He plopped down next to her. "How much did you decide
to tell Amy?"

"I told her we found the other Nightfall, and that we're

going in tonight. Mostly I tried to assure her we have everything under control, but I don't think she believed me."

"I'm sure she didn't. *This*"—he traced a finger over the crease between her eyebrows—"doesn't make you very convincing."

Their eyes locked and it was suddenly much harder than it should have been to come up with a response.

Iggy saved her from having to by jumping around, demanding attention.

"How come you're here already?" she asked as she headed to her desk to scratch the tiny green imp through the bars of his cage.

They weren't supposed to meet until closer to midnight, once they were all dressed and ready to head to Nightfall. They'd be wearing Neverseen cloaks this time, hoping it might help them blend in. But the gnomes were still scrambling to make enough cloaks—especially ones large enough for Sandor, Grizel, and Ro.

Keefe moved to her side. "I figured if someone didn't come over to distract you, you'd have no eyelashes left by tonight."

She dropped her hand, not realizing she'd been tugging.

"Besides," he added, reaching into the pocket of his burgundy tunic, "I realized there's one thing we forgot to do. And I figured you'd strangle me if I did it without you, so . . ."

He pulled out his old Imparter.

Sandor glowered.

"Hey—don't blame me, Gigantor. You never asked for it back. I bet you didn't even notice it was missing until right now."

"Of course I did!"

"Nice try," Ro said, peeking into the room. "We all know you would've been pounding on the door to the Shores of Solace if you'd realized."

"The Shores of Solace?" Sophie asked.

"Apparently that's what my dad calls his beach house," Keefe told her. "And yes, he says it with a straight face."

"Meanwhile, I keep calling it the Waves of Wimpiness," Ro said proudly. "Lord Pretentious is *not* a fan."

Sophie had to smile at both nicknames, but it faded when she asked Keefe, "How's it going, living there?"

He shrugged. "It smells better than Alvar's house."

"But . . . is your father being nice?"

"Oh yeah, it's a big cuddle fest. And then we sit down and make lists of all the reasons we love each other."

She crossed her arms. "I mean it. Are you really okay?"

"It is what it is. And focus, Foster—wrong awful parent! Right now, it's all about Mommy Dearest." He pointed to the Imparter. "I swear I don't have any crazy plans. I just know my mom loves to hold something back to see if someone calls her on it."

"Plus, I get to stab him again!" Ro said, unsheathing her dagger and jabbing the tip of his finger.

Keefe didn't even flinch.

"Hopefully this is the last time you'll have to do that," Sophie said as they both sat on the edge of the bed again and he smeared his blood across the sensor.

"Pretty sure we're never going to be free of her," he mumbled.

"If you were *free of me*," Lady Gisela sniped through the blank screen, "you never would've gotten this close to finding Sophie's parents. And yet, I don't hear a thank-you."

"You're not helping us. You're helping yourself," Sophie told her.

"Why can't I do both? And let's see . . . I'm guessing this is the part where you accuse me of hiding something to sabotage the mission, and I have to remind you that we're on the same side—*and* that I need you to recover my Archetype. It's a thick black volume—in case you were wondering—secured with a latch made of bands of silver and gold. You'll most likely find it near your parents, but if not, *don't* leave the facility without it."

"Yeah, sorry, we're not risking our lives to get your book back," Keefe told her.

"It's more than a book. It's *my* vision—and it's a thousand times more elegant than Fintan and his criterion. I know you're still refusing to see me as anything more than a villain in this conflict, but like it or not, I'm the only one trying to build a *solution*."

"To what?" Sophie asked.

"Problems you're still not ready to face. So let me give

you some advice before you head into that facility. Remember who your enemy is—*really* remember. Because it'll be easy to lose sight of everything once you're in there. Think about who brought down Lumenaria, and burned Eternalia, and unleashed the gnomish plague, and stole the lives of the people you love."

"Translation," Keefe said, "you want us to take out Fintan instead of Vespera."

"You also agreed to wipe out the facility," Lady Gisela reminded Sophie.

"Technically, I didn't," Sophie argued. "You told me I'd want to once I saw it, and I didn't correct you. But I didn't agree, either."

"So you would allow it to remain, even knowing what goes on there?" Lady Gisela countered.

Unease bloomed in Sophie's gut. But she kept her voice steady as she said, "I won't destroy it unless I know I can get everyone out of there safely—and that I won't somehow damage the city."

"Ah, the Black Swan's philosophy—overthink, overplan, stall, stall, stall. Haven't you seen how quickly that fails you? I'm only going to say this once. You will regret it if you don't destroy that facility, Sophie. Just as you will regret it if you allow Fintan to remain breathing. So if you get your chance, do whatever it takes to wipe them out of existence, regardless of the cost."

"Why not Vespera?" Sophie asked.

"Because I'm inclined to believe there's more subtlety to her—and her research—than her journals imply. She's an Empath, after all. And Empaths feel every hurt they trigger."

"Not all of them," Keefe muttered, and Sophie's heart ached, knowing he had to mean his dad.

"How do you know she's an Empath?" Sophie asked.

"I just do. It's actually why I chose Keefe's father from my match lists. I knew if I wanted to build my own Nightfall someday, I was going to need an Empath to help me run it. But he turned out to be . . . incompatible. Fortunately, he gave me a son who manifested with far more power than he ever had. *That's* your legacy, Keefe. But we'll talk more about that later. For now, go get me my Archetype. And try not to die."

The Imparter went silent, and Sophie and Keefe just stared at it.

Eventually Keefe mumbled, "So . . . all of that's getting shoved into a really dark corner of my head—and we're not going to talk about it, okay? At least not until we get through tonight."

Sophie nodded. "Well . . . at least we know Vespera's ability isn't something scary."

"Don't be so sure. My mom's never trained as an Empath, so she doesn't get it."

He stood, moving to Sophie's bookshelf, where she'd displayed the paintings he'd given her around her old human scrapbook. "My empathy mentor warned me when she saw how strong my ability was—that there's a risk that comes with feeling too much and not having the right training. Our mind's natural reaction is to shut down when things get too intense—but *everything* is intense for an Empath. So if you're not careful, you can end up going . . . numb. You'll still feel what *others* feel. But you won't feel anything yourself. And it can mess you up, since emotions overlap when you don't know all the thoughts and memories that triggered them. So, like, the rush that comes with anger? It's not actually all that different from what I feel when someone's super giddy—in its basest essence, at least. They both give a burst of adrenaline. They both make the heart race and cause a surge of shivers. You only notice the bigger differences when you take the time to figure out *why* you're feeling it."

"Not sure I get what that means," Sophie admitted.

"I don't totally either. But my mentor said if I don't watch myself, I could get to a point where I'd feel the same thing if I hugged somebody or punched them in the face. And if Vespera let that happen to her, well . . . it would explain how she was able to do such horrible, creepy research and write about it like it was no big deal."

Goose bumps erupted across Sophie's arms and she rubbed them to calm the chill.

Keefe did the same, which made her realize . . .

"Is it harder to be around me?" she asked. "Since my emotions are stronger?"

His lips tugged into a smile. "Don't worry, you're worth it."

"Ugh—why didn't you tell me?" She stood, moving toward the door, trying to put as much space between them as she could.

He laughed. "Trust me, a few feet doesn't make a difference."

"Then you should stay away from me," she told him.

"Now you're being ridiculous."

He strode over to her, and she tried to back away but crashed into the wall.

"I'm serious, Keefe."

"Oh, I know. But you're forgetting something, Foster."

He was close enough to reach out and gently tuck her hair behind her ear as he leaned in to whisper, "I like a challenge."

His breath tickled her skin, and her stomach filled with fluttery things.

"Speechless again?" he asked, grinning as he leaned in to whisper, "You know, there's—"

A loud slam had them both scrambling back, and before they could blink, Sandor and Ro were jumping in front of them, both drawing their weapons as heavy footsteps thundered up the stairs.

"Good—you're together." Mr. Forkle gasped between heaving breaths as he stumbled into the room, with Grady and Edaline right behind him. "That saves me one trip."

"What's going on?" Sophie asked.

"Change of plans. You need to go—all of you."

"Where?" Grady demanded as Mr. Forkle dug through the pockets of his cape.

"We've had Wraith keeping watch over the Unity Fountain. And this morning he found a new bottle floating near the base of the statues—with the Endal Crest for the seal. Wylie rushed to Atlantis to retrieve it, and apparently the Neverseen have named their own terms for the meeting—new time, new place. *No* negotiation. But it's fine. We just have to hurry. Squall's already at the new location, and she seems to think it's safe. It's public, at least. But Wylie should be joining her any minute, so the sooner you can get there the better." He handed Edaline a pathfinder. "I already have the crystal set to the facet you need."

"Wait—now?" Edaline asked.

"Unfortunately. Blur went to warn the Vackers while I came here, so Della should be on her way—if she's not there already. And Tiergan will be there as soon as he gets Tam and Linh what they need. So you five have to hurry," he told Sophie, Keefe, Grady, Sandor, and Ro. "I'll go get Miss Redek and have her meet you there."

He handed Grady a pale glowing bottle—light from Candesia—and a small piece of magsidian.

"That will take you to the heart of the city," he explained. "The Unity Fountain is only two blocks over. Stay in the southern alley until everyone's gathered."

Sophie blinked. "We're going to Atlantis *now*?"

"Not just Atlantis," he told her. "You're going into Nightfall."

SEVENTY-FIVE

I WISH I COULD'VE CHANGED," SOPHIE
mumbled, fussing with the sleeves of her long white tunic.

She'd been planning to wear the green Neverseen-style
vest she'd used for the mission to Ravagog a few months
earlier—but there hadn't been time to change. So now she was
stuck in ruffles and frills, trying to be grateful that her low
boots at least had soft soles, and didn't make a *clack, clack, clack*
as she paced the narrow alley.

"Tell me about it," Fitz said, fanning the front of his red
bramble jersey. "I was halfway through my morning run when
Blur showed up—so now I'm all sweaty."

"And smelling *awesome*," Keefe added with a choked cough.

Fitz, Biana, and Grizel had already been waiting for them

when Sophie's group had arrived in the city. Marella showed up a couple of minutes later, followed by Dex and his father.

"I'm a slight amendment to the plan," Kesler explained, "to clear the crowd out of the courtyard, since we're having to do this during a busy time."

He patted the worn satchel slung around his shoulder, and Sophie could hear the *clink* of glass vials knocking into each other.

"Stink bombs?" Keefe guessed.

"Some of my finest," Kesler agreed.

"Ohhhh, can I set one off?" Ro asked.

Kesler laughed. "Pretty sure that would cause an interspeciesial incident."

"Which is why it'd be so much fun!" Ro countered.

Sophie tried to smile, but she couldn't take her eyes off the courtyard, where tiny shops and cafés surrounded the fountain in the center. The golden figures gleamed among the streams of colorful water that blasted around them in neat arcs before splashing into the swimming pool–size basin. She was too far back to see where Vespera's signature lay hidden on the top of the human statue's scepter—but she could feel it there. Waiting for her. Promising answers.

"So when do we unleash the stink?" Keefe asked.

"As soon as I get the signal," Kesler told him. "I guess Alden's setting up something in another part of the city, to try to draw everyone's attention over there."

"And we have this to keep us hidden in the meantime," Dex said, pulling an obscurer from his pocket. "I made some tweaks to it last night, so it should even cover some of what Linh does to the fountain—at least for a while."

"Where *is* Linh?" Fitz asked.

"And Tam?" Biana added.

"Sorry," the twins said a couple of minutes later, plodding into the alley carrying thick stacks of black fabric.

"Tiergan made us wait for these," Tam explained, pointing to the white eye symbol on the sleeves.

Sophie's stomach filled with all kinds of squirmy things.

The wriggling grew stronger when Linh passed out their disguises and Sophie found herself surrounded by the black-cloaked figures of her nightmares—and dressed as one too.

"Right there with you, Foster," Keefe mumbled. "I'd kinda been hoping I'd never have to wear one of these again. Even a fake one."

"Does anyone else think it's a bad sign that the Neverseen are rushing us?" Marella asked, her petite frame hidden completely by the dark fabric. "Or are we all going to pretend we're not freaking out?"

"I'm *not* freaking out," Grady promised, pulling his hood over his head. "Let them think they're calling the shots. Nothing's going to stop us from getting Sophie's parents back today."

"Agreed," Fitz said, resting a hand on Sophie's shoulder.

"Okay, but what's our *actual* plan?" Tam asked. "Do we

know where we're going once Linh and Dex get the door open?"

"Grizel and I will go first, to scout for guards," Sandor said, strapping his sword outside of his cloak. "We'll use our senses to find a path to where Sophie's parents are being kept."

"And *I'll* make sure they don't mess that up," Ro added. "But just so we're clear, if I see any of my father's traitors, I'll be killing them on sight. If you want me to leave the Neverseen breathing, that's your call. But any ogres are going to die."

"I have no problem with that," Sandor told her. "I'll happily help you strike them down."

"I doubt I'll need your help," Ro said. "But . . . I guess it's good to have backup."

Sandor nodded and Sophie wondered if this would be the first time an ogre and goblins had fought together.

"The rest of us will follow," Grady told everyone. "Try not to be noticed—and stay behind me. If I tell you to do something—do it."

"*Now* who's taking over everything?" Keefe muttered. "And I bet *he* won't get cut off for a week."

"Uh, you're not helping yourself in the father-approval department right now," Ro whispered.

Keefe shrugged.

"Okay," Sophie said, before an argument started. "We're going to do this like we always do—listening to each other, and counting on the fact that our plans are going to change about a million times as soon as we get in there. No one goes off alone. No one single-handedly tries to be the hero. If we see the Archetype—grab it. Otherwise the goal is finding my parents and getting out as fast as we can."

"Am I turning anyone else invisible?" Biana asked.

Sophie shook her head. "If we can't hide the whole group, it doesn't make sense. Especially since I should probably save my mental energy in case I have to enhance Grady."

Everyone shuddered at that.

"I'll cover us with as many shadows as I can," Tam said.

"And I'll have flames ready," Marella added.

Sophie rubbed the knotted emotions in her chest. "I'll inflict if I have to—but it'll be less painful for you guys if I don't. And if anyone needs me to enhance them, let me know."

"Same goes for needing a mental boost," Fitz told her.

"And calming any panic," Keefe added.

A distant chime rang through the city, and strange music followed—a series of soft, lovely sounds woven into something peaceful and melodic.

"That's one of my mom's compositions," Linh whispered, glancing at her brother. "She . . . she must be here."

Tam whipped around, as if he'd be able to see his mom performing. But the rows of silver-blue towers blocked everything.

"I think that's also my cue," Kesler said, pulling Dex into a strangle-hug before he headed out of the alley. "And I'd plug my nose and cover my mouth if I were you guys."

He waited until he'd entered the courtyard before he subtly poured one of his vials on the ground.

"Dude, what's *in* that?" Keefe asked, looking both queasy and impressed as he tried to fan the stench away. "It smells like a hundred gulon farts baking in the sun."

The crowd had noticed the odor as well, and there was a whole lot of coughing and gagging and sputtering—which turned into full-fledged stampeding as Kesler poured out a couple more vials.

"We should move," Grady said, and they pushed into the fleeing masses, dodging elbows and trampling feet as they fought their way to the fountain.

"Should I part the water yet?" Linh asked as Dex tossed the obscurer into the center of the basin.

"Give it another minute," Fitz said. "There are still a lot of people here."

Sophie used the time to study the gleaming golden figures. The elvin statue looked especially regal in an elegant cape and circlet, with part of his hair braided back and the rest hanging gracefully past his shoulders. His hand held a scroll, which he seemed to be offering to the human statue, whose head was bowed with gratitude. The human had rougher features and seemed to be wearing some sort of armor, but instead of a sword, he clutched a long, etched scepter. And carved onto the orb at the end was the symbol that turned the whole image into a mockery.

"I think we're clear," Grady said as the final few stragglers dissipated. "And if there *is* anyone in Nightfall, I'm sure they know we're here. So we should head in before we give them time to prepare."

Sophie nodded and Linh climbed onto the rim of the fountain's basin, her brow furrowing while she raised her hands and flicked her wrists. The ebb and flow of the fountain halted, and the colorful streams of water stilled. And when the surface of the pool was smooth as glass, Linh swept her arms in opposite directions.

The water followed her silent command, rippling down the middle and rising on either side—so much more water than Sophie had expected. The fountain sloped sharply toward the center, the pool so deep that they would've been in way over their heads. But Linh kept drawing the water higher and higher, until she'd formed two gurgling walls with a space in the center—a narrow, puddled path that cut straight to the human figure's pedestal.

Even with the distance, Sophie could see the outline of a door—marked once again with Vespera's signature.

"You okay?" Tam asked as sweat trickled down Linh's temples.

She nodded. "The other water just keeps calling to me now that I've opened my senses."

She tilted her head to the dome covering Atlantis, and a smile stretched across her rosy cheeks.

"We'd better hurry," Tam warned. "The last time she got that look, she flooded the city."

"I can resist it," Linh promised.

But Dex had already hurdled over the edge of the fountain and sprinted for the door.

"This lock isn't too bad!" he said, placing his hands on the metal and tracing his fingers in circles. "Just give me a second."

Tam climbed up next to Linh and wrapped an arm around her shoulders.

"I'm fine," she assured him.

But she didn't take her dreamy eyes off the dark depths beyond the dome.

"Almost there," Dex called. "I'm just trying to feel for any alarms."

An agonizing minute passed.

Then the door slid silently open.

No sirens blared.

No guards rushed out to attack.

Only a blast of cold misty air swirled out of the shadowed space beyond.

Sandor and Grizel raised their swords and charged down the slippery path in the fountain, disappearing without a word.

"Give us two minutes," Ro told Keefe. "Then follow—unless you hear a whole lot of screaming."

Sophie choked down her nerves as she darted toward the door. She couldn't see much of the facility—just a hall of ancient silver and gold stones that wound down, down, down and vanished into dark mist below.

"How did she keep this place from crumbling when they sank the city?" Biana whispered.

"Most likely it was already buried," Grady murmured. "I wouldn't be surprised if this hall was actually much longer originally, and sinking the city brought Nightfall closer."

He traced his hand over the doorframe—over the ancient runes that proved how long this lie had existed.

"I need to get Linh away from all of this water," Tam called, pulling his sister into the fountain.

Linh let the path close behind them, leaving their group in a bubble of air nestled against the entrance.

They lingered there, in that last safe space, locking hands and giving themselves a second to prepare. Then together, they stepped onto that dark, impossible path, to find Sophie's parents and chase down truths their world might not be ready for.

SEVENTY-SIX

THIS IS TOO EASY."

Marella was the first to breathe the words, but Sophie was pretty sure they'd all been thinking them with every step they'd taken down that long, winding passage.

They'd detected no one. Seen nothing but the silent silver and gold stones and the flickering balefire sconces that bathed everything in soft blue light. Eventually, they reached what seemed to be the hub of Nightfall's only level, centered around an opulent, round foyer. Vaulted ceilings, sweeping balefire chandeliers, gilded pillars, mosaic floors, and walls inlaid with gold filigree were the only things that greeted them, along with an array of quiet, shadowed corridors—seven in all.

It was far more palace than prison.

And totally empty.

No sign of the brutal experiments Sophie had been mentally preparing for.

"I should double back," Ro whispered, halting their group at the edge of the foyer. "They could be planning to ambush us from behind."

Sandor went with her, while Grizel stayed to keep guard. But when they returned, neither had anything to report.

"Well . . . maybe they *all* went to meet with Wylie," Biana suggested.

"If they did, can Tiergan and our moms handle that?" Fitz asked.

"Of course," Grady promised. "But I can't imagine the Neverseen would be so single-minded."

"Then why isn't there *any* security?" Dex pressed his hands against the gleaming walls. "I keep searching for surveillance tech or alarms—but all I feel is solid stone."

"The door's underwater," Linh reminded them, her silvery eyes focused on the ceiling, as if her mind was still on the pool far above—or the ocean beyond. "Maybe they think no one will find them."

Tam reached for her hand, giving her arm a gentle shake until she pulled her gaze away. "We left a note floating in their fountain. They know we're onto them."

"Technically, Wylie pretended to be working against the

Black Swan," Fitz told him. "But I know what you mean."

"And your senses aren't picking up anyone down those corridors?" Grady asked the bodyguards.

Sandor and Grizel shook their heads.

"All I'm getting is dust and ash," Ro added.

"Ash?" Marella said. "Could they be using the same trick we used last time?"

"That wouldn't work on me," Ro assured her.

"So wait," Tam said, pressing his lips together like he wished he didn't have to ask his next question. "If no one's sensing anything . . . does that mean Sophie's parents aren't here?"

Sophie sagged against the wall. "If this is another dead end . . ."

"No way," Keefe told her. "All the clues led here. We just have to figure out what the trick is." When she didn't nod, he reached for her gloved hand. "Need me to calm the panic?"

She took a shaky breath, blinking hard. "No, it's fine. We should save our energy."

"Or put it to better use," Biana told her. "Can't you track their thoughts like we did in the other Nightfall?"

Sophie straightened. "I don't know why I keep forgetting about that."

Biana smiled. "That's what I'm here for."

"Need a boost?" Fitz asked, nudging Keefe aside to offer Sophie his hand.

"Actually, I need Tam. Last time, he slipped a shadow into

my mind, and it made it so I was able to sense through a force field."

"Hmm," Keefe said as Tam nudged both him and Fitz aside. "On the one hand, the look on Fitz's face is pretty priceless right now, and I know it's killing him not to say, 'But we're Cognates!' But on the other hand . . . don't go thinking this lets you into the Foster Fan Club, Bangs Boy!"

Tam rolled his eyes. "Ready?" he asked Sophie.

She nodded, and his shadow slowly crawled into her head, the dark energy mixing with her own mental reserves before she flung her consciousness down each of the seven corridors.

A headache rewarded her for the effort, but it was nothing compared to the ache in her chest when all she sensed was cold, empty nothing. The hole inside her stirred—still healing from her zombie days—and she could feel the despair reach out to drag her down into that dark pit of hopelessness. But she pushed those feelings away and shoved her thoughts farther, draining every bit of power she could muster. She didn't know the layout of the facility, so she couldn't tell if the turns and twists her mind made were real or imagined, but she followed them anyway, stretching herself thinner and thinner, until it felt like her brain was going to shred.

The pain was worth it when the softest whisper of life skated along the edge of her consciousness. "I feel someone down there." She pointed toward one of the shadowy corridors. "There's a flicker of warmth—but that's all I can tell."

"That has to be your parents," Biana told her.

"Only one way to know for sure," Sandor said, stalking toward the dark hall.

"Stay here," Grizel told them as she and Ro followed.

"Yeah, like that's going to happen," Keefe said, glancing at Sophie. "Unless you want to wait."

"Are you kidding?" She charged forward.

Sandor sighed. "Fine. But stay behind us—and if we tell you to run, *run*."

No one breathed a word as they tiptoed across the foyer and headed down the sloped hall. The walls turned smooth, covered in intricate whorls of gold, and gleaming orbs dangled from the arched ceiling, flickering with balefire.

"Does it seem like it's getting hotter?" Marella whispered.

Sophie nodded. "And brighter."

The hall was curved, so they could only see a few feet ahead—until they made the final turn. A closed door waited for them, with a glaring glow seeping through the seams.

Grizel motioned for everyone to be quiet as she reached for the handle, slowly testing the knob—and finding it unlocked. She and Sandor shared a look, and he tucked himself out of sight on one side of the door while Ro mirrored him on the other, their swords raised over their heads. When they were each in position, Grizel inched the door open and crept into the room.

Her gasp sent everyone rushing in after her, their bodies

crashing into each other as the bright light bleached their vision.

Sophie blinked hard, forcing her eyes to adjust to . . .

"Breathe, Foster," Keefe said, catching her as her legs gave out.

She could feel him reaching for her glove—and yanked her hand away. She didn't want to be calm as she sprinted toward the glaring white force field that split the enormous room in two. A towering cage of blue balefire burned on the other side, and between the dancing flames she caught a glimpse of two unconscious figures chained to the floor.

Their faces were swollen, their bodies pale and bruised and burned.

But she could still recognize her parents.

She hugged her chest, certain that every part of her was about to crumble. Which was why it took her a second to notice the slitted yellow eyes watching her from the shadows near the balefire.

The beast raised its massive head, revealing long, curved fangs jutting from its pointed, reptilian snout. Its talons scraped the floor as it stood, stretching its lionlike body, which was covered in silver feathers that trailed up to an enormous pair of sharply angled wings.

When it curled its armored tail like a scorpion, Sophie finally understood what she was seeing.

One of Lady Gisela's gorgodons must have survived.

SEVENTY-SEVEN

ON'T WAKE UP.

Sophie repeated the plea over and over, begging her parents not to stir.

Don't notice the chains—the fire—the huge, horrifying beast—the injuries . . .

She was trying *so* hard not to think about the injuries.

Sleep. Sleep. Sleep.

And they did.

They didn't even stir when the gorgodon let out a screechy roar and lunged against the force field, sending lightning sparking across the invisible barrier.

"That thing *definitely* wants to eat us," Tam mumbled.

Marella nodded. "I liked it way better when we thought the gorgodons were dead."

So did Sophie. Especially with the way the beast kept holding her stare. As if it knew she was the most desperate to get past its guard.

"Those taller flames must be the decoy Lady Gisela told us about," she whispered, pointing to one of the corners of the balefire cage, where a clump of flames flared higher than the others. "That's where we can slip through to pull my parents free."

"Awesome," Keefe said. "So how do we get there without becoming a gorgodon snack?"

Dex turned to Tam and Biana. "Think either of you guys can sneak past?"

"Probably not without ash," Biana admitted.

"But, uh, there's a bigger problem," Tam said. "I can only take down the *whole* force field—and none of us can rebuild it. So once I do, there'll be nothing to stop the gorgodon from coming after us—unless Marella thinks she can cage it in."

Marella frowned as she studied the huge empty room. "I don't know if I can make a barrier that big and not lose control."

"Is there a way to restrain the gorgodon?" Sophie asked Grady.

He shook his head. "That beast is pure muscle—and it's angry. Even with a fleet of gnomes, I doubt we'd be able to get it under control. Especially without any rope."

"Could we let it chase us out and then double back and lock it out?" Linh asked.

"Depends on how fast it is," Tam told her. "Plus, then we'd be trapped in here, so . . ."

"And that's if the door can even stop it," Marella added. "Remember the damage we saw at the other Nightfall?"

Biana chewed her lip. "How do you think the Neverseen even got it here?"

"There must be a tunnel somewhere," Dex said. "I wonder if we can find it and lure it back there."

"That sounds time consuming," Grady warned.

"We need to burn it," Marella said, making everyone flinch. "I know, it'll be ugly. But . . . if we don't kill it, it *will* kill us."

"Can you do that without burning my parents?" Sophie asked.

Marella tugged on her braids. "I want to say yes, but . . . the ability is still so new."

"Then we can't risk it," Sophie decided.

"I suppose . . . I could put a bubble around your parents and drown the gorgodon," Linh suggested with a shudder.

"Lady Gisela said it can breathe underwater," Sophie reminded her.

"Of course it can," Keefe grumbled.

"So we'll kill it the old fashioned way," Sandor said, slashing his sword.

"Can't be done," Ro warned. "Not without long-range weapons strong enough to pierce that super-thick skin. If we try to get in close with blades, that tail will take us out, and I'm pretty sure the barb on the end is dripping venom."

"Then we'll have to be fast," Grizel said, stalking closer to the gorgodon.

She'd barely closed half the distance when its tail slammed into the force field, flashing sparks and lightning everywhere.

"That would've been a direct hit," Ro told her. "But if you don't believe me, you can go for it and I can say 'I told you so' while your insides liquefy from the venom."

"No one's going for anything," Sophie jumped in. "Not until we come up with a plan that won't get anyone killed."

She stopped herself from taking another look at her parents.

She needed to stay calm. Needed to find a different angle. Needed to—

"The answer you seek does not exist," a female with an especially sharp accent said from . . . somewhere—everywhere. Her voice echoed all around them.

Sandor grabbed Sophie, hauling her against his side as Ro and Grizel shifted to shield the others.

"Such noble grace," the voice said, still bouncing off the walls and leading to nothing. "And yet . . . it is a pity. All this time—thousands upon thousands of years—and still we remain reliant on simpler species for our defense."

"Pretty sure that's the cue for you elves to use your fancy abilities to drop this creepy mystery lady," Ro told them.

"They will try," the voice said, and indeed, Grady's eyebrows were squeezed together, as if he was fighting to grab control of her mind. "But they will find that I am well prepared. It is all I have been able to do these long years."

The last words left a trail, and Sophie followed the sound to a balcony hidden high in one of the corners, where a shockingly pale female in a stiff burgundy gown gazed down at them like a queen studying her court. She'd even crowned herself with an arched piece of jeweled fabric, similar to the Tudor headdresses Sophie had seen in her human history books. And her features were gorgeously dramatic—thick, arched eyebrows, wide-set azure eyes, angled cheekbones, and long pointed ears. But there was an unnatural stillness to her face. As if she wasn't used to moving or speaking. Or feeling . . .

"Vespera," Sophie whispered.

"*Lady* Vespera," she corrected, smoothing the bodice of her dress. The gown was probably supposed to be fitted, but her shoulders were so frail that it gaped in places, and one of the silken sleeves kept sliding down her shoulder.

"This is far prettier than a thinking cap, is it not?" she asked, tracing her finger over the chains of rubies that draped off her headdress and were woven into an intricate net over the tight coil of her ebony hair. "And it provides far superior protection—even from the moonlark's mind tricks. There is nothing any of you can do that will harm me."

"Nothing?" Ro asked, whipping a dagger out of her cloak and launching it toward the balcony.

The blade spun in a smooth arc and slammed into Vespera's stomach with a strange crash that splintered her gown—because it wasn't a gown. And she wasn't actually there.

A mirror.

"I told you," Vespera said, and they whipped toward the sound to find her perched on another balcony on their opposite side. "I have had plenty of time to prepare."

"And I have plenty of weapons," Ro said, hurling another dagger—harder that time, aiming for Vespera's head.

The blade punched through the pane of glass, sending shards raining down, only to reveal another image of Vespera standing behind it.

"It is always so tiring, being underestimated," Vespera said as a dozen versions of herself flashed along the walls. "Everyone has grown so accustomed to mediocrity that when they find themselves faced with true greatness, they fail to appreciate it."

"Appreciate this," Ro said, whipping three knives in rapid succession—and shattering three more mirrors.

But there were more mirrors behind them, already displaying Vespera's reflection.

"Might want to save your knives," Tam warned. "She's probably not actually here. That would explain why no one could sense her."

"But she'd have to be close—and above us, somehow," Biana said, mostly to herself. "There must be stairs . . ."

"You will not find them," Vespera promised. "And I see you testing me," she told Dex, who'd pressed his hands against one of the mirrors. "Your talent will not help. When I built this facility, we did not rely on technology. Light creates the strongest illusions. Even for the mind."

Dex ignored her, closing his eyes and tapping different portions of the mirror.

Vespera shook her head. "If you had done your research, you would know that I designed many of the tricks that keep our cities hidden. Even all this time later, my methods hold."

"Uh, there's nothing to research," Fitz told her. "You've been erased."

Vespera's chin dipped—the closest they'd gotten to a show of actual emotion—and all but one reflection faded away. It seemed to darken as she said, "The world I knew was a small-minded, ungrateful place that was not worthy of the help I gave it."

"The *help*," Sophie repeated, unable to stop herself from stealing a glance at her parents. "That's what you call this?"

"Yes." Vespera slipped her fallen sleeve back onto her shoulder. "And I suppose we should focus on why we find ourselves here today. Fintan told me the moonlark would be unable to resist coming after us. I did not believe you would be so careless, but here you are, risking so much for so little—and still not risking enough."

She pointed to where the gorgodon promised a swift death to anyone who dared enter its cage—then to the two helpless figures sleeping among the flames.

"An elegant dilemma, is it not?" Vespera asked. "Seemed a decent means to get your measure."

"So this is a test," Sophie said.

"You have set yourself up as my opponent. Do you blame me for longing to discover what I might be up against?"

"I blame you for torturing innocent people!" Sophie's mind flashed to the wounds she'd seen on her parents, wondering how many more Elwin would find once she got them out of there.

"Torture is about pain and control," Vespera told her, moving her reflection again, to the closest wall, down at Sophie's eye level. "This was research. First about them. Now about you. We shall see how you think. How you fight. Where you draw your lines."

Sophie's knees wanted to buckle—but she stepped closer, moving away from her friends. "Let. My. Parents. Go."

"Or?"

"Or . . . we'll destroy this facility."

Vespera inclined her head. "I do not believe you."

"You think we can't?" Tam asked, pointing to where Linh had gathered a giant orb of water.

"No, I suspect many of you are capable," Vespera said. "Just as I suspect the moonlark could tear these halls down stone by stone if she truly unleashed herself. But she won't. None of you will."

"I don't know," Ro said. "They wiped out half my city. You just haven't gotten them angry enough."

"Is that the trick?" Vespera's eyes glinted as they bored into Sophie's. "If I describe your parents' screams, would it change anything? Or if I tell you that their minds will never escape their nightmares? Or maybe I should share how they pleaded for me to spare them because of their daughter? Or how I told them their daughter is to blame for their current predicament?"

Sophie clenched her jaw to hold in her rage—but red still curled around her vision, and acid boiled in her core, and everything was shaking shaking shaking. The wrath clawed at her—ate at her—but she shoved it deep, saving it for when Vespera would feel every horrifying drop.

"Close," Vespera said. "But still you hold back. I wonder if it would change anything if you knew that I can lower the flames protecting them? If I let you watch as the gorgodon feasts on their weary flesh?"

"Don't!"

Sophie couldn't tell who shouted it. It might have been her.

Her ears were roaring too loud, head pounding too hard—and sour revulsion coated her tongue as she forced herself to say, "Please let them go. They're not a part of this."

"A simple plea? That's all you'll give?" Vespera folded her

hands. "What if I told you I would release them right now if you swore to leave this facility and never return? Would you take what you want and go, knowing I would continue my research on others?"

"Yes," Sophie admitted, hating the selfish answer.

"And what if the two prisoners were strangers?" Vespera asked. "Would you strike the same bargain?"

"Yes," Sophie said again, that time with a tinge of relief.

"Why does that make you feel better?" Vespera wondered. "Stranger or friend, you still endanger many to spare the few."

"I spare the people who need it," Sophie argued. "Because I can come after you again once they're safe."

"And what of the people who suffer in the meantime?" Vespera asked. "Do you think I will not ensure that *many* pay the price for every life you spare?"

Sophie didn't have an answer.

Disappointment puckered Vespera's features. "Fintan was so certain that your parents had been chosen because they were ideal specimens. But I knew even before I tested them that they lacked the necessary gifts. Which is a tragedy, really. The Black Swan was wise to have you learn from humans. But they chose the *wrong* humans, and now they have a powerful little girl who will always make the wrong decisions."

"Says the person who spent thousands of years in prison," Keefe said, wrapping an arm around Sophie's waist to calm her shaking. "Not exactly a model of awesome choices."

Vespera's brow lowered as she studied Keefe. "You must be the one Fintan called 'the disappointment.'"

Keefe flushed at the too-familiar insult. But all he said was, "Some people aren't worth impressing."

"I suppose. But looking at you now, I do not understand how you could fit into your mother's plan."

Keefe snorted. "That makes two of us."

"Do you even *know* her plan?" Vespera asked. "Did she tell you why she was so obsessed with my research? Why she burned the world to make her precious soporidine?"

"Yeah . . . Mom wasn't a big fan of sharing secrets. But hey, if you feel like showing her up, why don't you tell us what you know?"

"Because it does not matter. We have new plans now—ones that do not waste time on sorting and gathering. I am, however, curious."

Vespera disappeared—then reappeared across the room, clutching a black book wrapped in bands of gold and silver.

"Have you read this?" she asked, holding up the Archetype.

"Have *you*?" Sophie countered.

"It is locked."

"Yup," Keefe agreed. "And I have the key. Care to make a trade?"

Bad idea, Sophie transmitted.

Not if we give it to her in pieces—and only include three of them.

But we don't even have it with us, Sophie reminded him. *And—*

"I have no need," Vespera said, interrupting their silent conversation. "I saw enough of her vain attempt at my facility to know she has missed the point entirely. A few ideas could be salvaged—but most had to be let go."

"Is that why you left my brother there?" Fitz asked.

"Your brother has found himself in his current state because *I* do not hold back from making the hard choices. And that is why I will win."

"Keep telling yourself that," Keefe told her.

"I do not need to. I can show you. It is time for your first lesson."

"In what?" Grady demanded.

Fintan's deep voice bounced all around them as he said, "Ruthlessness."

SEVENTY-EIGHT

THE DOOR SLAMMED SHUT BEFORE Fintan finished the final syllable, and Sophie knew it would be locked long before Fitz tried—and failed—to wrench it back open.

Dex rushed over to help, pressing his hands against the metal, pushing his ability as hard as he could. But he wouldn't be fast enough—not if Fintan was there.

Sophie peeled off her gloves, bracing for searing heat and choking smoke as she shouted for Linh to get close, hoping that enhancing Linh's ability might be enough to douse any blazes Fintan would ignite. She also transmitted to Marella, warning her not to reveal her own flames until the last possible second.

But when Fintan appeared next to Vespera on the far wall—with a floppy white thinking cap for mental protection—he simply flicked a speck of lint off his black cloak and told them, "There's no reason to burn you in your present predicament. In fact, by the end of this you'll be begging me to."

Ro's blade smashed the mirror, right between his sky-blue eyes.

"Good to see you too, Princess," he said as he reappeared with Vespera on a different wall. "And I must say, our uniform looks good on you."

Ro held his gaze as she shredded the robe with her claws, leaving curls of black fabric at her feet.

Sophie yanked off hers as well, as did everyone else—except Biana, who must've turned herself invisible.

Sophie was trying to figure out where Biana was hiding when Fintan told Ro, "It seems rather ill advised to side with those who took so much pleasure in flooding your homeland. Or is there some betrayal in the works?"

Ro gritted her teeth. "The flood only happened because you dragged my father into your stupid plan."

"Then you should blame Gisela as well," he told her. "And yet I hear she's behind your current assignment. I'm surprised you didn't find that more . . . concerning."

"I'm assuming you know this because another fool betrayed my father since I left?" Ro asked. "Any of the traitors around? I'd *love* to say hi."

"Sadly, they're off handling other matters. You know how it goes." Fintan's eyes drifted from Sophie to Fitz to Dex. "By the way, your mothers say hello."

"Do they?" Grady asked, sounding far calmer than Sophie felt. "I wouldn't have thought you'd have time for much conversation given how quickly you finished your meeting."

"The meeting's still going. I left Gethen and Ruy to handle our plans there. I couldn't miss my special guests—especially when they've gone to so much trouble to avoid me." His eyes shifted to Marella. "And I get to meet the new recruit—a Redek, no less. I'm assuming your mother doesn't know about this new hobby, given how much she sacrificed to keep you away."

"What's that supposed to mean?" Marella snapped.

Fintan smiled. "Nothing you should concern yourself with anymore. By the time we're done here, I doubt you'll even remember her."

Careful. Sophie transmitted the reminder when Marella's hands flashed with a single spark—hopefully too quick for anyone else to notice. *If he sees your flames, he'll ignite his own.*

Sounds like we're in for worse than that, Marella noted.

I know. We need to get out of here.

And how are we going to do that?

Still working on it. For now—stall. Every minute we keep him talking is another minute he isn't trying to kill us.

I'm pretty sure he's smart enough to multitask, Marella warned.

"Communicating telepathically, are we?" Fintan's eyes locked on to Sophie's. "Think you're going to find some brilliant plan for escape?"

"There is a way," Vespera told them, adjusting her sleeve again. "But you will never see it, because you are still trying to save everyone. It is why you will always lose—time and time again. You will always delay. Always try for the impossible while ignoring the most logical options—"

"And what exactly are these 'logical options'?" Keefe interrupted. "Why don't you tell us what we're missing? Show us how much smarter you are."

"Do you think I will not answer?" Vespera asked. "As if the options are such a closely guarded secret that you have to trick and flatter them out of me?" Her focus shifted back to Sophie. "Your parents would already be free if you'd been willing to sacrifice part of your group to the gorgodon. Or you could have fled the moment you understood the gravity of my challenge and dropped any foolish notions of sparing the humans. Even now, there is a way to free yourself, if you abandon the others. But you do not see it. And if you did, you would not take it. You would rather remain trapped—facing my tests along with your friends—because you refuse to accept that it takes ruthlessness to win in this world. There is no room to be noble. No reward for heroes. No space for sentiment or camaraderie. If you want to succeed, you should be severing ties, limiting your connections, viewing anyone around you as expendable. Because every time you allow yourself to care, every friend you surround yourself with, will only make you weak and vulnerable."

"Are you sure about that?" Biana asked, flashing into sight between Fintan and Vespera.

Somehow, she was part of the projection, and when she lunged for Fintan's thinking cap, she was able to yank it off his head. She leaped for Vespera's headpiece next, but Vespera managed to shove Biana back, both of them toppling out of the mirror's range as Fintan raised his hands, shouting for flames and . . .

. . . his body stilled, eyes widening.

Grady smiled. "If you wanted a lesson in ruthlessness, all you had to do was ask."

Bone crunched as Fintan punched himself in the face.

Then again.

Then in the stomach.

Again.

Again.

Sophie watched in dazed horror, until Biana's scream snapped her out of it, followed by several thumps and crashes.

"She needs help," Fitz said, cupping his hands around his mouth and shouting, "HOW DO WE GET UP THERE?"

Another scream was Biana's only answer.

Fitz grabbed Sophie's arm. "Please tell me you can track her."

"I'm trying," she promised. "But I think I need help."

She took his hand to enhance him and Fitz squeezed his eyes shut.

His whole body shook as he told her, "She's somewhere above us."

"I know—but I can't tell how she got up there. Can you?" Sophie asked.

Sweat streamed down Fitz's face as he shook his head.

"Scour the room for a staircase," Grizel ordered when glass shattered and Biana screamed again.

"It's not in here," Ro warned. "Biana's scent leads out the door. She must've slipped free before they locked us in."

"Then, how's it going on that lock, Dex?" Fitz shouted.

Dex rattled the door. "I'm trying everything I can think of. But Vespera wasn't lying about how this place doesn't use technology."

"Does this help?" Sophie asked, grabbing his hand.

He shook his head. "It's not a gadget. I can't talk to it—I don't know what to do."

"Stand back!" Ro commanded, shoving Dex aside and slamming her body against the door.

Sandor and Grizel joined her, but even with their combined strength, they only managed to warp the metal.

"I'll make Fintan open it," Grady said, gritting his teeth. Veins bulged across his forehead and Fintan turned, eyes full of pure, black hate as he stumbled out of sight, heading their way.

The small victory only lasted until Biana shouted, "RUN!" followed by an agonized scream and a whole lot of shattering glass.

Vespera's voice hissed around the room. "You want to see ruthless?"

The air sizzled and popped as the force field unraveled—and the gorgodon bared its fangs and leaped for their throats.

SEVENTY-NINE

NOW WOULD BE A *REALLY* GOOD time for us to figure out how to get that door open," Keefe yelled as they all tucked and rolled out of the gorgodon's path.

The beast slammed into the wall, crashing through layers of glass and sending jagged shards flying as it scrambled to its feet and roared.

"On it," Dex called back, pulling a melder out of his cloak and popping off the back. "I'm going to blast through the whole stupid door."

"We'll keep the gorgodon away while you work," Sophie told him. "Everyone spread out and try to distract it."

Her friends obeyed—though Fitz kept screaming Biana's name, asking if she was okay.

"She's probably hiding," Grady told him, glass crunching under his feet as he stumbled to the nearest wall. "And you'd better work fast, Dex. I'm no longer controlling Fintan."

"Does that mean he can torch this place?" Tam asked as he blanketed Dex in shadows.

"No. I could feel my hold slipping, so I made Fintan knock himself out. But I don't know how long the unconsciousness will last." Grady slumped against the wall, his face sweaty and gray.

"Are you okay?" Sophie asked.

He closed his eyes and nodded. "Fintan fought me pretty hard."

"I'll cover you," Marella offered, gathering flames as she ran to Grady's side and held them in front of her like a weapon.

"Uh, I think that's making the gorgodon angrier," Tam warned. He pointed to the snarling beast, which had crouched into a pounce stance, its yellow gaze locked on Marella.

Marella snuffed out her flames, but the gorgodon still leaped—and it would've been a perfect strike, if a wave of water hadn't slammed it into the far wall, shattering more mirrors.

The gorgodon was back on its feet immediately—shaking its feathers dry and raising its wings as it launched off the floor and circled above them.

"Oh good, now it's airborne!" Keefe said as Linh gathered

water for another attack. "Any chance you feel like manifesting as a Psionipath, Foster? Because a new force field would really come in handy right now."

"I wish," she mumbled.

But maybe she could control the beast a different way. . . .

She closed her eyes, stretching out her mind the way she'd done with Verdi and Iggy and Silveny, hoping she could convince the gorgodon that they should be friends.

But the gorgodon's mind was a swirling pool of nothing. No sounds. No images. Only shadows of what used to be—as if everything had been blotted out by its cavernous grief.

The bleakness made Sophie's eyes water—made her want to help the tortured creature. Maybe if she—

"WATCH OUT!" Sandor screamed, dragging Sophie behind him.

He raised his sword at the gorgodon, which was diving straight for them.

Fitz threw out his arms, whipping dozens of fallen shards toward the beast with telekinesis. But nothing slowed the gorgodon's plummet—until Linh knocked it back with a massive geyser.

Glass rained down as it slammed into the ceiling, and Tam shrouded Linh in shadows while the beast scanned the room for its attacker.

"Anyone have a plan yet?" Tam shouted.

"Besides 'don't die'?" Keefe asked, leaping over rubble as

he sprinted across the room. "How about you guys keep that thing away from me so I can get Foster's parents and we can flee this death trap the second Dex gets that door open."

"Do you need help?" Sophie called as Sandor struggled to keep her shielded.

"Nope, I got this. Just keep the gorgodon distracted."

"Done!" Ro hurled a dagger at the beast's flank.

The knife bounced off the gorgodon's thick skin—but definitely got the creature's attention.

Grizel tackled Ro to save her from a tail-sting to the face, and Linh knocked the beast back with another wave.

Sophie tried to think of a way to help, but she couldn't take her eyes off Keefe as he charged straight into the tallest section of flames.

"Made it!" he shouted. "Good thing my mom wasn't lying about that!"

"And my parents are really there?" Sophie asked, not sure what she'd do if they'd fallen for another of Vespera's illusions.

"They are!" Keefe promised. "And they're breathing!"

Hope bloomed in Sophie's heart—but it was quickly choked out by thorns of dread as her mind dredged up the glimpses she'd caught of her parents' wounds.

"What's taking so long?" Ro shouted as she and Grizel dove to avoid the gorgodon's talons.

"Just trying to break these chains," Keefe told them.

Lots of metal clanking followed.

"Keefe's going to need help," Sophie realized. "Even if he can break them out, he won't be able to carry both of them."

Sandor's nod looked grim. "I'll go—but I want you to stay over there."

He pointed to where Marella was guarding a slumped Grady while Fitz covered Dex a few feet away, as Dex screwed some sort of contraption onto the end of the melder.

"Deal," Sophie said, darting for her friends.

Sandor dashed into the fray, dodging the water balls Linh was hurling at the gorgodon to keep its focus away from Keefe. Tam had covered Ro and Grizel with shadows, helping them sneak up on the beast's sides—but as they got close, the gorgodon flapped its wings, knocking them over.

"You okay?" Grady asked when Sophie made it to his side.

"I think so—you?"

"Yeah, I'm just trying to figure out where Fintan is. I can't feel his mind anymore, and I'm not sure if that's because he's still unconscious, or if my brain is too tired, or if he's woken up and moved beyond my range. Any progress on the door, Dex?"

"Actually, yeah." Dex showed off his melder, which now looked like some sort of alien ray gun. "Just making sure this thing won't blow off my hand."

"What about you?" Sophie asked Fitz, noticing how pale and sweaty he looked.

He shook his head, eyes on the ceiling. "Biana's still up

there. And I haven't heard her scream since she told us to run. Have you?"

Shame heated Sophie's cheeks when she admitted she hadn't.

She hadn't even been listening—or thinking about Biana at all.

And when she stretched out her consciousness . . .

Silence.

Which made her wonder if Vespera was right.

What if there wasn't a way to get *all* of her friends out of this safely?

And not just that day—but the next? And the next?

"We can't keep this up," she whispered.

"Yes we can," Grady promised. "When Dex gets the door open, we're going to find Biana and Fintan—maybe Vespera too—and get your parents out of this miserable place."

"It won't be that simple," Sophie told him. "The gorgodon is going to chase us. And I doubt the door will hold it back—*if* we can still close it after Dex blasts though."

"Then I'll burn the beast," Marella told her. "Or put up a wall of flame in the hall."

"You really think you can do that without burning this whole place down?" Sophie asked.

"Are you *sure* about any of the dangerous things you do?" Marella countered. "Besides, why bring me along if you're not going to let me use my power?"

"Or . . . maybe we *should* let the fire get out of hand," Fitz suggested. "I know destroying this place is what Keefe's mom wants, but it's pretty creepy here."

He wasn't wrong.

But the facility was also the only evidence of what had really happened to the humans in Atlantis.

And what if the fire got out of hand and spread to another part of the city?

Even the idea of killing the gorgodon felt wrong—especially after feeling how much it had already suffered.

"I don't think we should turn to fire just yet," Grady said, sitting up and rubbing the spot between his eyes. "Not until we've exhausted all other options."

"Haven't we?" Marella asked.

"No," Grady insisted. "Sophie hasn't tried enhancing me. Maybe I can control the gorgodon—"

"Uh, shouldn't you have done that a *while* ago?" Fitz snapped.

"I wanted to. But controlling Fintan drained me too much." He struggled to his feet and held out his hand.

"You're sure you're not going to freak out and start controlling all of us?" Sophie had to ask.

He smiled. "Let's hope not."

"That's not actually 'no,'" she reminded him. But her reluctance faded when she spotted Sandor and Keefe cornered by the gorgodon.

They each held a limp figure wrapped in discarded Never-seen cloaks, which was making it nearly impossible for them to duck around the venomous tail.

She grabbed Grady's hand—then yelped from the jolt of heat that zapped between them.

"Is this how it always feels?" Grady asked through gritted teeth.

Sophie shook her head. "It's never this intense. Want me to let go?"

"No. Just . . . give me a second." An eerie sort of stillness settled over him as sweat beaded on his upper lip.

He turned toward the gorgodon—and the second his brow scrunched, the beast plummeted to the floor, rolling onto its side with wide, glassy eyes and stiff limbs.

"You didn't kill it, did you?" Sophie asked.

"No!" The word was both a shout and a snarl as Grady's eyes glazed over.

"Do I want to know what just happened?" Keefe called.

"Just hurry!" Sophie shouted, trying to pull her hand free—but Grady held on.

"Are you okay?" she asked him.

His attention slid to her, brow furrowing again as he studied her with that vacant stare.

"Grady," she said, tugging harder on her hand. "Dad!"

The second word did the trick, crashing through the haze enough for him to let go and stumble back.

"Are you okay?" Sophie repeated.

He covered his face. "Never let me do that again."

She nodded. "What happened?"

"I—"

His answer vanished when Linh, Ro, and Grizel sprinted over—followed by Keefe and Sandor.

Sophie stared at the limp bodies in their arms, telling herself not to look at her parents' swollen cuts and bruises and blisters.

All that mattered was that it was *them*.

And they were still breathing—still sleeping.

She had to let that be enough.

Tears streamed down her face, pouring even faster when Dex blasted the door handle and shouted, "Okay, let's go!"

EIGHTY

INEED YOU TO GET MY PARENTS OUT OF here," Sophie said to Sandor and Grizel as Dex used his modified melder to seal the door to the gorgodon's chamber. Grady had warned them that the beast wouldn't stay stunned for long.

Later, she would ask Grady why he kept mumbling "never again, never again, never again" and glancing at Sophie's hands—but at the moment . . .

"I know what you're going to say," she told Sandor, "but we have to find Biana—and my parents need to get to a Physician—and you and Grizel can carry them back to city level way faster than any of us can."

"How will they get out of here?" Tam asked. "Isn't the door blocked by water?"

"The fountain is dry," Linh corrected. "I called every drop to fight the gorgodon."

"Okay," Sophie said, glad she had friends to help her think all of this through. "Once you're back in the city, find Wraith or Kesler or Alden and tell them to leap you with this."

She held out her hand and mumbled, "Two twenty-one B Baker Street," to call the vial of Candesia's light that Mr. Forkle had given her from the void. A magsidian black swan charm was tied around the top, and she showed Sandor the facet that would take them straight to Foxfire.

"Fintan and Vespera might still be here," Sandor argued, "hiding near Biana."

"If they are, I'll handle them," Ro assured him. "I know trusting me goes against those stubborn goblin instincts, but you have my word that I'll defend everyone with my life."

"If it helps," Grady added, "I can't feel Fintan. Either he's still unconscious, or he left."

"Or he put on that nullifying cap again," Sandor reminded him.

"Please," Sophie begged. "We can't waste time arguing."

Dex and Fitz were already running their hands over walls, desperately trying to find whatever door Biana had used to get upstairs.

"My parents need protection way more than I do," she added. "Please—if you really want to help me, get them somewhere safe so I can concentrate."

Sandor gritted his teeth, looking ready for a long fight. But he told her, "*Don't* make me regret this."

He adjusted his hold on her father as Keefe handed Sophie's mother to Grizel, and both bodyguards ordered everyone to leave Atlantis the second they found Biana. Sophie promised they would, barely managing to add a hushed "thank you" before the goblins turned and sprinted for the exit.

"They're going to be okay," Keefe whispered, reaching for Sophie's still-gloveless hand and sending one of his calming mental breezes.

She clung to the blue rush, reminding herself that Sandor and Grizel could handle anyone they ran into on their way out. And Elwin had saved her from fading—saved Sandor after he'd been hurled off a cliff—saved Keefe after he'd been gutted by King Dimitar. And the Washers would take care of the rest.

Then she forced herself to turn back to her friends.

Tam and Linh had joined Fitz and Dex in scouring the halls, and Sophie closed her eyes and stretched out her consciousness.

"I can feel Biana up there," she told them. "Her thoughts are weak—but it's definitely her. So once we find the stairs I should be able to track her."

"Her scent is strongest over here," Ro called, waving them over to where the hall curved.

Linh was the one who spotted the thin palm-length slit tucked among the gold filigree painted on the wall, and when she slipped her fingers in, the wall tilted ever so slightly.

The light shifted, revealing an arched opening behind them. And through the gap was a winding staircase.

"I don't understand these illusions," Keefe mumbled, shoving his arm through the archway, even though the wall had been solid a few seconds earlier.

"Who cares?" Fitz snapped. "What are we waiting for?"

Ro grabbed Fitz's shirt to stop him from heading up the stairs. "I'm going first—and none of you are going to follow me until I give the all clear. Got it?"

She didn't let go until Fitz nodded.

Then she was gone, squeezing her muscled body into the narrow stairway and winding up and up and up.

"Biana has to be hurt," Fitz said, tearing his fingers through his hair. "Otherwise she would've come back by now. Or she's a prisoner."

"We'll get her back," Sophie promised, wishing she could reach for his hand. But she had to save her enhancing energy for when they might actually need it.

"We got Foster's parents back, didn't we?" Keefe added.

No one wanted to mention how injured they'd been.

"Okay," Ro whispered down. "Head on up—and get ready for some serious weirdness."

"Weirdness" didn't begin to cover it.

The attic-style space was part theater catwalk, part funhouse maze—a tangle of wooden walkways and dangling lights and silks, lined with mirrors in every shape and size. Everything was attached by gossamer threads to an elaborate system of pulleys and hooks that dangled from the sloped ceiling. It was like stepping into a magician's workshop.

"There's no motor for any of this," Dex mumbled, crouching to examine one of the larger mirrors. "I wonder if they . . ."

His question trailed off when he spotted a splash of red near his foot.

Ro nodded and pointed ahead to another splatter. And another. A gruesome trail leading into the shadows.

"It's not just Biana's," Ro whispered as Sophie clung to a nearby railing, trying to clear her spinning head. "I'm picking up Vespera's scent too, so Biana must have given as good as she got."

None of them found that comforting.

"Does that mean Vespera's still here?" Tam asked, keeping his voice as low as possible. "And what about Fintan?"

"I'm not feeling either of them," Grady murmured.

Sophie stretched out her consciousness again. "Neither am I."

"But that could be a trick," Dex reminded them.

"I think I smell Fintan," Ro said, pulling herself up to a higher catwalk and sucking in several deep breaths. "I can't tell how fresh the trail is. But he went that way."

The narrow ledge she pointed to went the opposite way from Biana's red-stained trail—disappearing around a sharp curve.

"You're sure?" Grady asked, lowering himself onto the rickety walkway.

Sophie grabbed his sleeve. "What are you doing?"

He leaned closer. "If Fintan's still here, he's either knocked out, or planning something. Either way, someone needs to check."

"You can't go alone," she whispered.

He brushed a strand of her hair off her forehead. "I'll be fine. It's you I'm worried about. Stay behind Ro, do everything she tells you, and get out of here as soon as you find Biana."

"You can't handle Fintan by yourself," Sophie argued. "Look how much he wiped you out last time."

"I'll go with him," Marella offered. "Seeing me spark a few flames might distract Fintan enough for Grady to get control of his mind."

"I'm not putting you in that kind of danger," Grady told her.

"Uh, it's not like the other path is any safer." Marella pointed to the red splatters around their feet.

"The girl has a point," Ro admitted as Marella hopped down onto the same platform as Grady.

Sophie hated this new plan with every fiber of her being. But . . . if they had a chance to find Fintan, they had to take it.

"Be careful," she begged both of them.

"Right back at you," Grady told her, kissing her cheek before leading Marella down the creaky path.

Sophie's group went the opposite way—and with every step she expected to hear Grady's scream or Fintan's taunts or the crackle of flames. But the only sounds were from their feet scraping along the splintered floor as they struggled to follow Biana's bloody trail through a maze of mirrors and ledges and sharp curves they couldn't see until they'd nearly fallen off an invisible edge.

And then—in the middle of a wide platform, with a steep drop on one side and mirrors lining the other—the trail just . . . ended.

"You don't think she . . . ?" Tam didn't finish the question. But the way he peered over the edge said enough.

"Easy there," Ro said as Fitz sank to his knees. "I can still smell her."

"I can feel her too," Sophie added. "Her thoughts are blurred— but they're close."

"Then where is she?" Fitz snapped.

"There must be another trick," Linh assured him, reaching for his hand.

"The illusions seem to be about the angle of the light," Dex said slowly. "So I wonder . . ."

He studied one of the mirrors hanging from a gossamer thread and tilted the glass enough to send the light bouncing toward a different mirror. "Can someone tilt that one down a little?"

Keefe did as he asked, and the light refracted toward the edge of a new mirror, then bounced to another and another and . . .

One of the mirrors seemed to vanish, revealing a cramped cubby of space.

And tucked into the shadows was Biana. Passed out in a pool of blood.

EIGHTY-ONE

GLASS CRUNCHED UNDER FITZ'S knees as he knelt next to Biana. "Biana? Can you hear me?"

He shook her shoulders and her head lolled to the side, giving them a better glimpse of the spiderweb of red gashes covering the left half of her face. Thick shards of glass jutted out of her arm, hip, and leg along that same side of her body, as if she'd been slammed into a mirror and shredded as it shattered.

"Biana?" Fitz tried again, choking on the word. "Do you think they drugged her?"

Sophie couldn't tell. But judging by how much red was splashed around them . . . "I think she might've passed out from the blood loss."

"She's breathing," Keefe added, placing a hand on Fitz's shoulder. "As long as she's hanging on, Elwin can fix the rest."

"How are we supposed to get her to him?" Fitz asked.

The guilt nearly knocked Sophie over when she realized she'd given Sandor and Grizel their only quick path to Foxfire. Now they'd be stuck dragging Biana through the whole stupid city to get to the stupid bubble wand statue to use the stupid geyser to finally leap her home.

"I'm sorry," she whispered, rubbing her knotted emotions to hold them together. "I shouldn't have let Sandor and Grizel leave until we found her."

"Yes, you should have," Keefe told her. "Seriously, Foster. You had to get your parents out of here—we all know that. Don't we?" He nudged Fitz until Fitz nodded. "We'll figure something out."

"Like what?" Fitz wanted to know.

"What about Livvy?" Linh suggested—and the name felt like a lifeline, dragging Sophie out of her panic.

"You're right!" she breathed. "We just need to get Biana to Quinlin's apartment."

"Do we even know how to get there?" Fitz asked.

Sophie hated having to tell him, "No." Especially when Fitz's features tightened into grim lines.

"But Alden knows," Keefe reminded them. "And he's probably still in Atlantis. Or if not, we'll hail him and ask for directions."

Fitz sucked in a shaky breath. "We'll have to make it work."

"We should bind her wounds before we move her," Ro said,

already slashing thick strips off the bottom of Biana's Never-seen cloak to use for bandages.

"Do we really have time for that?" Tam asked, squinting at the shadows. "Vespera could still be here."

"Her scent is fading," Ro told him. "I think she's gone. Besides, we need to stop this girl from losing any more blood."

"I have these," Sophie added, pulling a handful of Panakes blossoms out of her pocket. The flowers were shriveled and crushed, but she still placed a few petals on Biana's tongue and pressed the rest into the worst of her wounds as Ro made quick work of wrapping Biana's injuries.

"I guess that'll have to be good enough," Ro said, scooping Biana up, careful not to press on any of the glass sticking out of her as they slowly backtracked toward the entrance. "Can some-one use their fancy powers to get a message to Grady? He should know we're heading out so he doesn't count on us for help."

Sophie did as Ro asked, but couldn't help admitting, "I hate leaving him and Marella here alone."

"I don't like it either," Ro told her. "But—"

Biana's moan cut her off.

Fitz grabbed his sister's hand, tears streaming down his cheeks as Biana's eyes fluttered open.

"Fitz?" Biana's voice was thin as paper—and her lips twisted as she scraped her tongue against her teeth.

"You're feeling the Panakes petals," Sophie explained. "Try to swallow them—I think they're helping."

"Of course. I go down there, wave my sword around to herd everyone somewhere I can defend them—like maybe I get them all to the other side of the canal. While I'm doing that, I can lure her out by shouting about how creepy she is, and how she has a secret lair underneath the city, and how she's going to drag you into war with humans—"

"You think that's her plan?" Sophie interrupted.

"Seems pretty obvious after that long, boring speech about ruthlessness," Ro said. "Sounds like she's been studying humans to figure out how to make you guys into elf-y killing machines, and she's probably teamed up with the traitors who fled Ravagog, to learn some proper battle tactics. I bet she'll use the soporidine to drug your enemies, so all you have to do is slaughter them while they sleep—which actually isn't a horrible strategy. It's brutal—and kinda cheating. But she doesn't seem like she'd be too broken up about that."

Dozens of new worries squeezed Sophie's heart from all sides. "If you're right, we need to get her back in custody—now."

"Does that mean we're going with my plan?" Ro asked.

"Uh, if you go down there covered in Biana's blood, waving a sword, everyone will run from the scary ogre," Tam told her. "And not in the direction you want them to run. I also didn't actually hear any explanation for how you're going to restrain her."

Ro glanced down at her breastplate, which was smeared with red. "Fine—amended plan. We send in the moonlark.

"They would've noticed if two of us went missing." She glared at Fitz. "Stop looking at me like that—we *all* take risks."

"You took on two of the leaders of the Neverseen *by yourself*!" he growled back.

"Yeah, well, I'm fine." She reached for his other hand, turning green when she saw the shards sticking out of her arm. She looked away. "Where are Grady and Marella? Did they go after Vespera?"

"They went after Fintan," Sophie told her. "Ro could smell him somewhere in the halls."

"So no one went after Vespera?" Biana asked.

Ro shook her head. "Pretty sure she's long gone, judging by her scent."

Biana struggled to sit taller in Ro's arms. "But I know where she went! I heard her hail Ruy after she lost track of me in the mirrors. She told him she'd be waiting for him in the promenade— and she seemed frustrated when he said it was going to take him a little while to get there."

"The promenade?" Dex asked. "The one by the main canal?"

"That's what I'm assuming," Biana said. "It sounded like she was going to walk there."

"But why?" Tam wondered. "That's one of the busiest spots in Atlantis."

"Maybe *that's* why," Linh suggested. "Maybe she's trying to hide in the crowd."

"Why wouldn't she leave the city?" Sophie asked.

"She might not be able to," Dex reminded her. "The geyser is triggered by registry pendants. And maybe she doesn't have any light from the unmapped stars to use instead."

Ro groaned. "I know those looks—and you can all forget it. We're getting this girl medical help, not going to some sparkly promenade to hunt down Lady Creeperton!"

"That's not a seven-person job," Biana argued.

"It is as long as *I'm* the one carrying you," Ro told her. "No one's going after Vespera without me."

"Then have someone else carry me," Biana insisted. "Or leave me here."

Fitz snorted. "Yeah, that's not happening."

"Why not? I'm fine!"

"Fine?" he repeated. "Half your face is shredded!"

Biana winced.

"I know," she whispered. "All I'm saying is . . . let's make it worth it, okay? Don't waste everything I did by giving up now—not when we have a real chance to stop her."

"I could carry you to Livvy," Dex offered in the silence that followed. "That way Ro could go with everyone else. I doubt they're going to need a Technopath."

"It's a good plan," Keefe jumped in. "But you should stay with them too, Fitz. You guys will move faster if you carry Biana together—and you'll have twice the backup if you run into any problems. Maybe Bangs Boy should stay with you too."

"You're going to need my shadows to slip through the city

unnoticed," Tam argued. "Plus, Ruy's going to be there, so there could be a force field. And I'm not leaving Linh alone in Atlantis—and don't roll your eyes," he told his sister. "I know—you have amazing control now. But I'm your brother. It's my job to have your back, even if you think you don't need it."

"I love how you're all talking about this like it's a done deal," Ro said. "I swore to Sandor that I'd protect *all* of you."

"Eh, as long as you stay with Foster you won't have to face the wrath of Gigantor," Keefe argued. "And if there's a chance we can grab Vespera, we have to try."

Ro sighed, shifting to study Biana. "Are you really okay with this?"

"I'll be in good hands," Biana said, offering a weak smile at Dex and her brother.

"Then I'm going to leave it up to the moonlark," Ro decided, turning to Sophie. "That way you get to take the heat if things turn ugly—and keep in mind that they probably will."

Sophie tugged hard on her eyelashes.

Dividing their group *again* probably wasn't a smart idea—and taking on Vespera in a public place definitely wasn't.

But she kept thinking about what Vespera had said about the innocent people she'd make suffer to punish Sophie for saving her friends and family.

"Let's go get her."

EIGHTY-TWO

I DON'T SEE HER," SOPHIE MUMBLED, KNOW-
ing she'd said the words twice already, but needing something to fill the agonizing silence.

Tam had shielded them with shadows their entire
trek to the promenade, and shrouded their hiding place
under the arch of one of the gleaming silver skyscrapers so
they could study the crowd bustling along the canal without
anyone noticing.

"Do you think she's already gone?" Linh whispered, voicing
the question Sophie hadn't wanted to touch. "It did take us a
while to stop the gorgodon and find Biana and head here."

"Or she's hiding," Tam countered. "She's an escaped prisoner. She can't just wander the city. And if she could build an

entire underground facility, it seems like she could easily have a few spots where no one can see her unless she wants them to. Especially since we know she's good with optical illusions."

"And I'm guessing you can't feel her thoughts?" Keefe asked Sophie.

She shook her head. "But that could just mean she still has her headdress on."

"So then, what's our plan?" Ro asked. "Stand here until our feet go numb and hope she comes out of hiding? Boooooooooooooooring. And how are you going to capture her, by the way? I'm guessing you don't want a massive tackle-brawl in the street. Want me to pelt her with daggers? That could be fun!"

"And dangerous," Sophie reminded her. "You could accidentally hit the wrong person. Plus, we need to bring her in alive."

"Oh, I can keep her alive," Ro promised. "Though, are you *sure* that's a good idea? She already escaped once."

"After thousands of years," Tam argued.

"Still seems like a problem Future You isn't going to want to deal with," Ro noted. "But I get it—you want a chance to poke around her head without that ugly hat blocking you. Fair enough. You need to figure out how you're going to restrain her, though. Because she *will* put up a fight. And this place is super crowded—and she totally seems like the type who'd grab a couple of hostages to force you to back off."

"Okay, got any ideas?" Keefe asked.

"Of course. I go down there, wave my sword around to herd everyone somewhere I can defend them—like maybe I get them all to the other side of the canal. While I'm doing that, I can lure her out by shouting about how creepy she is, and how she has a secret lair underneath the city, and how she's going to drag you into war with humans—"

"You think that's her plan?" Sophie interrupted.

"Seems pretty obvious after that long, boring speech about ruthlessness," Ro said. "Sounds like she's been studying humans to figure out how to make you guys info elf-y killing machines, and she's probably teamed up with the traitors who fled Ravagog, to learn some proper battle tactics. I bet she'll use the soporidine to drug your enemies, so all you have to do is slaughter them while they sleep—which actually isn't a horrible strategy. It's brutal—and kinda cheating. But she doesn't seem like she'd be too broken up about that."

Dozens of new worries squeezed Sophie's heart from all sides. "If you're right, we need to get her back in custody—now."

"Does that mean we're going with my plan?" Ro asked.

"Uh, if you go down there covered in Biana's blood, waving a sword, everyone will run from the scary ogre," Tam told her. "And not in the direction you want them to run. I also didn't actually hear any explanation for how you're going to restrain her."

Ro glanced down at her breastplate, which was smeared with red. "Fine—amended plan. We send in the moonlark.

Let her bat those big brown eyes and give everyone a nice, pretty speech about your world's tainted history, full of enough insults that Vespera won't be able to resist showing herself—and then I jump in and shove this in her mouth."

She opened a tiny compartment at the edge of her breastplate and pulled out something that looked like a slimy ball of tapioca and smelled like a rusted-out septic tank.

"Ugh, what is that?" Keefe asked, plugging his nose.

"A handy colony of a bacteria we grow to make you elves violently ill. Aren't you glad none of you have made me angry enough to use it?"

Sophie's mouth went dry. "Do all ogres carry that?"

"Oh, don't look so freaked. You already know I'm carrying dozens of blades. At least this won't kill you."

"I guess," Tam mumbled.

"Any chance I can get a dose of that for my dad?" Keefe asked.

"Not until I'm not stuck living with him. Even *I* can't take the smell of what comes out of you when you take this stuff."

"Uh, guys?" Linh whispered. "Look."

She pointed to the eastern end of the promenade, where a figure in a long black cloak with the hood raised was descending the steps from one of the bridges arching over the canal.

"Good old Ruy," Keefe grumbled, white showing on his knuckles. "Looks like he's heading for that curve in the embankment."

Sophie nodded.

It was the spot she'd focused on the most when she'd listened for Vespera's thoughts, thinking the gleaming silver lanterns lining the railing might help shape an illusion.

Ruy skirted the edge of the crowd, managing to avoid their notice as he took up a position in the center of the curve.

One second he stood alone, his cloaked form facing toward the water. And the next second Vespera stood beside him.

"I'll give her this—she's got the dramatic-entrance thing mastered," Ro said under her breath. "But her clothes need work."

Vespera had added a hooded cloak to her outfit, and the thick golden fabric cascaded over her in layered ruffles, hiding any hint of her figure—and disguising any injuries she might have sustained in her scuffle with Biana.

"Okay, you guys have five seconds to tell me your plan," Ro warned, "or I'm charging in for an epic slashfest."

Before any of them could respond, a flash of white light triggered a wave of gasps and screams through the promenade.

"I don't understand," Sophie whispered, blinking hard to make sure she really was seeing what she thought she was seeing.

Ruy had trapped Vespera under a dome of white pulsing energy.

"This isn't going to be good," Keefe said, pointing to a

second black-cloaked figure carving a bold path through the scrambling masses.

The newest member of the Neverseen kept their face covered as they headed straight for Ruy, and Sophie assumed it had to be Gethen—until the figure raised their arms and shouted, "You're welcome!"

The voice was Lady Gisela's.

EIGHTY-THREE

OU CAN COME OUT NOW, KEEFE!"
Lady Gisela called as Ruy encased her and
himself inside a wider force field, then
formed another glowing white dome around
the entire promenade. "You too, Sophie! I know you're both
here. You'd never give up while Vespera was still in the city. It's
time for all of us to stop hiding."

"Don't you dare," Ro told Keefe, grabbing his sleeve as he
took a step forward. "She's already blocked my weapons with
that energy thing. I'm not letting you give away our location."

"Ro's right," Sophie whispered as Lady Gisela silenced the
terrified crowd. "We need to figure out what game she's playing before we do anything."

"Are you sure she's playing one?" Linh asked, keeping her voice low. "She just captured Vespera."

"With my mom, it's *always* a game," Keefe mumbled. "Besides, she's like, Vespera's number one fangirl."

"Then this seems like a strange way to meet her hero," Tam noted. "And why is Ruy helping her?"

"She told us Ruy and Fintan don't get along," Sophie whispered. "Maybe she used that to recruit him to her side."

Keefe gritted his teeth. "I should've expected that."

"It's not your fault," Sophie told him. "I didn't catch it either."

Her mind raced through every conversation she'd had with Lady Gisela, trying to spot any other clues they might've missed, since she was sure they were about to come back to haunt them.

"Clearly you're still refusing to trust me," Lady Gisela called from the promenade. "Do you really not see how much I'm trying to help?"

"What I *see*," Keefe snapped, earning a groan from Ro as all heads whipped toward where they were hiding, "is you dressed up like the Neverseen."

"It's called taking back what's mine," Lady Gisela told him. "You have no idea how many strings I've had to pull—how many plans I've had to weave together—to clean up Fintan's mess and get us to this moment. But here we finally are."

"We're not a *we*," Sophie shouted to remind her.

"That's what you keep saying. And I've been waiting for you to realize your mistake. But this one"—she pointed to Vespera, who stood with folded hands, studying her—"has accelerated the timeline. So it seems I need to give you both a nudge."

"Is that supposed to scare us?" Keefe asked, yanking free from Ro's grasp and stepping out of Tam's shadows. He crossed his arms and gave his mom his coldest smirk. "Because it doesn't. And what's with the hood? If you're done hiding, why don't you let everyone see how shredded your face is?"

"Oh boy, this is *not* going to end well," Ro muttered as she drew her sword and stalked toward Keefe.

"Hello, Princess," Lady Gisela practically purred. "So glad you could make it. Though it doesn't look like this crowd feels the same."

Ro's appearance had caused even more screaming and scrambling than Ruy and Lady Gisela's arrival had.

"It's not *my* fault elves are skittish," Ro told her. "And obviously you are too, otherwise you wouldn't be hiding behind your little force field."

"A simple precaution," Lady Gisela promised. "I assure you, I'm *very* happy to see you."

"I'm going out there," Sophie whispered to Tam and Linh. "But I think you guys should stay hidden until we figure out what she's planning. And don't break down her force field yet, Tam. Save that for when we can make it count."

They both nodded.

"Ah, here's our fearless moonlark!" Lady Gisela said as Sophie marched toward Keefe and Ro. "I assume the Vacker boy is nearby, along with the rest of your ever-loyal friends. And your inseparable bodyguards, of course. Perhaps we could speed these reveals along? One at a time is going to be tedious."

"No one else is here," Sophie told her. "We split up. Aren't you the one who's always going on about delegating?"

She could hear the smile in Lady Gisela's voice when she said, "I suppose. Though judging by the amount of blood I'm seeing on the princess, I'm guessing some of that delegating wasn't necessarily by choice."

"It was not," Vespera agreed, smoothing a ruffle on her cape. "I made sure their Vanisher will never be the same."

Sophie's hands shook, and when she noticed Keefe's doing the same, she hooked her arm through his.

She was grateful for that bit of support when Vespera added, "I could have finished her. But she showed such promise that I decided to give her a chance at becoming useful someday."

"See, now *that's* why I'm looking forward to working with you," Lady Gisela said. "Finally, an Empath I can count on to make the right decisions."

"Is that what this whole thing was about?" Sophie asked, choking back a swell of nausea. "You needed us to get to *her*?"

"I wouldn't say *needed*. But you definitely made it convenient. I knew Fintan would sequester her away and I'd have to flush her out. And he'd already gone to so much trouble to make this personal for you, I figured, why not take advantage?"

"To what end?" Vespera asked as Keefe's arm shook harder. "Do you truly expect me to form an alliance with my captor?"

"I expect us to have an important discussion without either of us trying to kill the other," Lady Gisela told her. "And hope you see wisdom."

"See, and I think that's a missed opportunity," Ro said. "A deathmatch would be way more entertaining—who's with me?"

She turned to the crowd, but everyone shrank back another step.

"If conversation was your aim, I cannot fathom why you chose to hold it with an audience watching," Vespera wondered.

"Because it's high time for our world to be properly educated," Lady Gisela said. "Now that I'm taking back control, I want people to see the *real* Neverseen. Not the imprudent, vengeful fools Fintan painted us to be."

No one looked impressed. But some were whispering into their Imparters, calling for help.

"Am I to assume that Fintan is no longer part of the order?" Vespera asked.

"He may not even be among the living," Lady Gisela said, "but that's up to Sophie's father. I knew Grady wouldn't be able to resist targeting Fintan today—after all, Fintan trained his daughter's murderer."

Sophie sucked in a breath.

She should've realized that would be part of Grady's motivation—maybe even why he looked so exhausted after controlling Fintan.

"But who'll emerge from the facility alive is up to them," Lady Gisela added.

"My money's on Grady," Ro jumped in.

"So is mine," Lady Gisela agreed. "He's the most ruthless elf I've ever met."

"I noticed that as well," Vespera said. "It is a pity he stands on the wrong side."

Lady Gisela nodded. "Believe me, I'm working on that."

Keefe snorted. "You seriously think Grady's going to join the Neverseen?"

"People aren't hard to predict when you understand what drives them," she told him. "It's how I knew we'd all end up in this promenade today. And how I know there's no way you and Sophie limited your group to the two of you and the princess. So how about whoever's hiding in those shadows stops pretending we don't realize they're there? Or, if you'd rather, I can have Ruy cut you off from the rest of your friends. I'll give you three seconds to make your decision."

Lady Gisela made it to "two" before Tam emerged from the archway.

Linh didn't follow.

"Only *one* of the twins?" Lady Gisela noted. "You expect me to believe that?"

"Believe what you want," Tam told her. His voice was as steady as the arm he stretched behind him, drawing the shadows away from where he'd been hiding—and revealing an empty alley. "Linh can't be underwater for very long. So she left with the others."

"I didn't realize the Girl of Many Floods had learned such restraint. Interesting." Lady Gisela dragged out the word. "Once again, your group proves to be full of surprises. Thankfully, this one works in my favor."

"I know what you're doing," Ruy snarled at Tam as swirls of shadow crawled through all of the force fields. "Do you really think I can't block you?"

Light flared, beating back the black swirls.

"Impressive," Lady Gisela said, tilting her head to study Tam. "But before we get to *that*"—she turned to the crowd—"I see you sneering at me. I even understand why. The change our world needs comes with a cost. One many of you are afraid to pay. But we must, if we want to save what matters most. That's the truth the Black Swan refuses to accept. And it's why they'll fail. Both of our orders are fighting the same problems—but mine is the only one willing to make the necessary sacrifices."

"You mean murdering people, and burning down cities, and threatening an entire species, and collapsing a castle full of people, and torturing humans for *research*?" Sophie asked. The last accusation earned a wave of gasps.

Lady Gisela shrugged. "I already told you I'm here to clean

up Fintan's mess. But sometimes we *do* have to tear down what isn't working in order to have enough space to rebuild something stronger. That's what she taught me." She pointed to Vespera. "Her teachings have guided every plan I've built. And now we'll finally have a chance to combine our visions."

"They cannot be combined," Vespera informed her. "Our philosophies are opposite."

"They aren't as different as you think. Once you read my Archetype—"

Keefe laughed. "Soooooooooooo, is this the part where I tell you I didn't bother getting your stupid book back? Or the part where I promise you'll never get the key, either?"

Lady Gisela drew out her sigh. "You get your photographic memory from me, Keefe. I only asked for the Archetype as a test. Which is the same reason I asked you to destroy the facility. And clearly you're still not ready."

"He never will be," Vespera warned. "None of them will. And the fact that you haven't accepted that does not bode well for our alliance."

"Does that mean you're rejecting my offer?" Lady Gisela asked. "I'd think carefully before you answer. I *will* leave you trapped until the Council locks you away for the rest of eternity. But I'd much rather we tear down the world and rebuild it together."

"Yeah, like that's *ever* going to happen," Keefe snapped as Ro tightened her grip on her sword.

Vespera tilted her head toward Lady Gisela. "Even if I were to agree, you realize the second you lower this force field, the ogre is going to attack."

"Of course," Lady Gisela said. "That's why I brought this."

She pulled something from her cloak the same moment a searing flash whited out the world, and even Vespera screamed as the promenade erupted into chaos—everyone tripping over each other as they fought to back away.

Sophie clung to Keefe as she rubbed her eyes. And when the world snapped into focus, the force field that had been around Lady Gisela and Ruy was gone, and Keefe's mom was clutching some sort of silver-nozzled weapon, now pointed at her son.

Ro was slumped at his feet, her chest splattered with a slimy purple glob that looked like a splotcher. Black veins were already spreading from the center, spiraling across Ro's sweat-slicked skin as her limbs started convulsing.

"What did you do to her?" Sophie shouted.

"You really can't guess?" Lady Gisela shook her head. "This is my present to Dimitar for what he put me through in his prison. His princess just got a lethal dose of soporidine."

EIGHTY-FOUR

ON'T EVEN THINK ABOUT IT!" Lady Gisela warned, aiming her weapon at Sophie's trembling chest—the gadget already loaded with another purple sphere of soporidine. "If I feel the slightest hint of your inflicting, I'll dose you as well. And then you'll lose any hope of saving the princess."

"Breathe, Foster," Keefe told her, his voice choked as he grabbed Sophie's hand and flooded her mind with blue and white breezes.

"I thought you said the dose was lethal," Sophie managed to spit out as her rage ebbed.

"It doesn't have to be," Lady Gisela told them. "I have an

antidote. The same antidote your parents are going to need if you want any chance of them waking up again. Remember when I told you that you'd need me to restore their sanity?"

"Prove it!" Tam, Keefe, and Sophie all demanded together.

"So little trust," Lady Gisela said, reaching into her pocket and holding out a clear vial with a slimy green ball inside.

"CATCH!" Linh shouted, leaping out of the shadows and charging toward Keefe's mom as she threw out her arms.

A wave surged out of the canal, slamming into Lady Gisela and Ruy, and the antidote went flying out of Lady Gisela's hand.

Linh blasted the vial as far as she could, and Tam leaped after it, flying so high he must've levitated—and even then, his fingers barely managed to curl around the vial before he landed.

"So the Hydrokinetic *is* here," Lady Gisela said, waving her arms to silence the crowd as Ruy secured both her and himself inside another force field. Her drenched cloak clung to her frail figure, and her hood was plastered to her head. "I love when you manage to surprise me—especially with the way you all lied so smoothly. And that shadow trick you used to hide your sister was *very* impressive, Tam."

"You want to see impressive?" Tam sent shadows tearing through Ruy's new force field.

Ruy managed to halt the darkness, but sparks flew everywhere, landing in the puddles at Lady Gisela's feet and making a hissing sort of steam.

"You may very well be a greater asset than my son," Lady Gisela told Tam.

"Aww, my mommy likes you," Keefe muttered. "Isn't that just the best news *ever*?"

Tam rolled his eyes.

Linh, meanwhile, had grabbed the antidote from him and knelt over Ro, carefully scraping what remained of the purple poison off the ogre-princess's chest with the edge of Ro's sword.

"Are you sure you want to do that?" Lady Gisela asked, before Linh could press the green blob onto fresh, unexposed skin. "Since you've taken it upon yourself to steal from me, I'm no longer feeling generous. So you can either use that on the princess, or save it for Sophie's family. But you won't be able to do both."

Sophie closed her eyes, giving herself one second to sink into dread and anguish. Then she told Linh, "Do it. Ro needs it more than they do."

She tried to convince herself that Elwin and Livvy and Lady Cadence and the ogre scientists and the Washers would be enough to help her parents. But even if they weren't . . . she couldn't live with herself if she let Ro die.

"Fascinating," Lady Gisela said as Linh pressed the green blob onto Ro's chest. "I wonder if this is proof that you're finally learning. I guess we'll see soon enough."

Sophie tuned her out, her knees nearly collapsing with

relief when the black veining on Ro's skin started to recede. She'd also saved one Panakes blossom when she treated Biana—in case they ran into any other catastrophes—and she begged its healing power to speed Ro's recovery as she slipped the wrinkled petals between Ro's cold lips.

She couldn't help wondering what Calla would say if she knew one of her flowers was being given to the ogre princess.

Dimitar didn't deserve Calla's help—not after the plague.

But Ro did.

And Sophie had to believe the kindhearted gnome would agree with her on that. Maybe she'd even be glad to build that small bridge between their species.

"That still won't be enough," Lady Gisela told them. "And do you really think the princess is the only piece of my plan? Revenge is fun—but if this were just about her, I wouldn't have gone to so much effort to bring all of us together here today. Mostly I needed the princess out of commission so I could teach you some proper priorities. I must get both of you ready for everything ahead."

"They never will be," Vespera warned, still trapped in Ruy's force field.

"We'll see soon enough," Lady Gisela told her. "I'll win either way—I made sure of it. But I'm hoping to see some *growth*. Before we start the new game, though, I need your answer. Ready to work together? Or ready to go back to prison?"

"You're not giving me much of a choice," Vespera noted.

"No," Lady Gisela agreed.

Vespera nodded. "I suppose I can respect that. Very well. Consider me your reluctant new ally."

"Uh, do you really think we're letting either of you walk away from here?" Sophie asked.

"Yes," Lady Gisela said. "Because there's another reason I recruited a Psionipath."

White light flashed again, and Ruy shouted something Sophie couldn't hear over the screams as he raised his arms and pulled them back down in a strange twisting motion.

Thunder boomed, shaking the city hard enough to crack some of the crystal towers, sending shards raining down on the fleeing crowd. All of Ruy's force fields vanished as he stretched out his arms again, sending bolts of lightning blasting into the dome.

Linh shrieked and stumbled backward as darkness poured into the city through a jagged, inky splotch. It took Sophie a second to realize the falling streaks weren't made of shadows.

The air turned thick, filled with a strange salty wetness that shifted from mist to full-fledged rain.

Emergency sirens blared, matching the wails of panic as people poured from the buildings to stare at the sky in horror.

Because Atlantis's force field had been breached.

EIGHTY-FIVE

OU NOW HAVE TWO CHOICES," Lady Gisela shouted over the roar of the rain, which was falling hard enough to rock the buildings. All around them people were splashing through the flooding streets, following a trail of glowing blue flares that seemed to be guiding them toward an evacuation point that looked much too far away.

Keefe lunged for his mom and she pointed her weapon at his chest.

"Don't tempt me, Keefe. Same goes for you, Sophie. Keep your inflicting under control, or count on losing a friend." Lady Gisela shifted her aim from Keefe to Tam, then to Linh—who was trying to keep the rising water away from Ro—then back to Keefe. "Now that everyone's listening, you should know that the princess is still dying. The remedy I gave you isn't enough to save her—did you really think I'd make it that easy?"

Nausea poured through Sophie, faster and colder than the rain. "What do you want?"

"I want to see that you're capable of making the right decision. So I'll make this simple." She used her free hand to pull a vial of Candesia's pale light from her cloak, along with a small crystal that looked like it had been shattered and glued back together. "You can take this light and this crystal and use both to bring Ro to Foxfire."

She squeezed both so tightly that there was no way to grab either with telekinesis—and Ruy looked ready to form another force field the second Linh tried anything with water.

"Hopefully you'll make it to the Healing Center in time for Elwin to melt off any skin that was exposed to the soporidine," Lady Gisela added.

"And let me guess—you'll only give those to us if we let you go?" Keefe asked.

"Do you really think I need *your* help to escape? Trust me, Keefe, the second Ruy, Vespera, and I decide to leave—we will. This isn't a bargain. It's a test. To see if you're beginning to understand the losses and gains we're going to face in the times ahead. Which is why your other option is to stay. Ignore my help. Do what you always do—try to have it all, try to be the hero—and *fail*. You may even drown, depending on how long it takes for you to accept that there's nothing you can do to stop this—even with your Hydrokinetic friend. And by then, it will be too late for the princess."

She pointed above them, to where the hole Ruy had punched through the force field was already twice as wide as it started. Then to Linh, who was leaning on Tam, veins bulging in her forehead as she strained to keep the water away from Ro. She finished by pointing to the rising water, which was now past their ankles—and the canals were already spilling over their banks.

"You're destroying an entire city—to test us," Keefe said.

Each word had shockingly little bite. And there was no fury in his voice. No rage.

Only bleak resignation, as if Keefe had stared into the monster's eyes and realized it was far too wicked to face.

"We should've let go of this city long ago," Lady Gisela told him. "Atlantis is our past—not our future—and the more we cling to it, the more impossible it is for us to move forward."

"It's also filled with thousands of innocent people," Sophie snapped.

Including her sister. And Quinlin and Livvy. And Biana, Fitz, and Dex. Maybe even Grady and Marella.

Each new name felt colder than the freezing water crashing around them.

"Yes, and the strongest and smartest of them will manage to

evacuate," Lady Gisela told her. "The rest aren't worth saving. And let's also not forget that many, many more will be in danger if King Dimitar declares war—which he absolutely would do if he found out you had a chance to spare his only daughter and ignored it. The right choice sometimes isn't easy, Sophie. But that doesn't mean it's not *right*. I need you to show me you understand that."

Sophie closed her eyes, trying to think past the pounding in her brain.

Maybe they couldn't save the city from flooding. But Linh could still clear paths through the water to give everyone time to evacuate—especially if she let Sophie enhance her. They might even be able to buy enough time for the Council to send a Psionipath to repair the breach. Someone must have already hailed them and explained what was happening.

And maybe the Panakes blossom she'd given Ro would help the ogre princess hold on long enough for them to clear the city before they leaped her to safety. Already most of the black veining was gone, and her breathing looked slow and steady, as if Ro was simply sleeping.

Besides, for all they knew, the crystal Lady Gisela was offering wouldn't even take them where she claimed.

"Time's almost up, Sophie," Lady Gisela warned. "Thirty seconds."

"You show more ruthlessness than I expected," Vespera told Lady Gisela. "But you are giving her the wrong options. A real test would be to see if the moonlark takes her chance to capture us."

"She doesn't need to sink to that level to be useful," Lady Gisela argued.

"Is that what you tell yourself?" Vespera asked. "How you justify the slight shake in your hand whenever you point that weapon toward your son? Would you be willing to pull the trigger if they forced your hand?"

"My son is important," Lady Gisela argued.

"He is not. You need to see that. Otherwise, you're just as useless as him."

Keefe glared at his mom. "Sounds like your creepy new alliance is off to a great start."

"She will learn," Vespera told him. "Look how far she has already come. But you will not do the same. And neither will she." She turned to Sophie. "You could have stopped this flood before it happened if you had been willing to sacrifice yourself— or your friends. It is not your fault. You were made that way. But you will always make the wrong choices."

"WHO CARES?" Keefe screamed, tearing his hands through his hair. "WHO CARES ABOUT CHOICES?"

"Our choices define us," Vespera informed him.

"Wrong," Keefe argued. "Choice is only a tiny part of it. You're an Empath—you're supposed to know that."

He reached for Sophie's hand. "Don't let them get into your head. You know what we need to do."

"And what is that?" Lady Gisela asked.

Sophie watched the waves in the flooded canal wash away a chunk of a nearby bridge, then turned to her friends—and she didn't need to read their thoughts to know what they were trying to say.

"We're staying here," she decided. "Until everyone is safe."

"And you're staying with us," Linh added, sending a wave crashing toward Gisela. But before the water hit, Keefe's mom grabbed Vespera and Ruy and the three of them leaped away.

The last thing Sophie saw was Vespera's cold smile—a promise of all the havoc she planned to wreak with her freedom.

"Still the right choice," Linh said, reaching for Sophie's hand.

"I don't have my gloves on," Sophie warned. "Can you handle being enhanced?"

Linh nodded, her eyes shifting to the breach in the force field, which was still growing wider by the second. "I think it's time to see what the water and I can truly do."

"I guess it's not like we have to worry about you flooding the place," Tam added.

"Here," Keefe said, offering a hand to both Sophie and Linh. "I can make sure you guys stay calm and don't lose focus."

"And I'll get Ro to higher ground," Tam told them, using telekinesis to float the ogre princess safely out of the rising water.

Everyone nodded, each of them taking a long breath as the plan settled.

"Ready?" Keefe asked.

"Ready," Sophie and Linh said.

Together, the three friends reached for one another's hands, forming a small, brave circle—that trembled slightly as their palms connected.

Linh gasped at the heat that shot between her and Sophie.

"You okay?" Tam called to her.

"Better than okay," Linh promised, a dreamy smile stretching across her face. "I was wrong to fear this. The water doesn't get to command me anymore. Only I command it. And I think I can save the city."

EIGHTY-SIX

ARE WE SUPPOSED TO BE LEVI-tating?" Keefe shouted as Linh propelled him and Sophie out of the rising flood-waters, leaving their feet dangling above the churning waves.

"I need to get closer to the breach," Linh explained. "But first . . ."

The rain halted around them, forming a strange pocket of silence as all the water that had been drenching their skin and clothes separated into tiny drops and drifted toward Linh. They hovered like stars for a second, then merged into a clear, swirling orb, leaving the three of them warm and dry again. Keefe's hair even bounced back to its tousled style, and Linh's silver-tipped strands drifted gracefully around her face.

Sophie couldn't decide if it was the glint in Linh's silver-blue eyes, or the determination etched across her brow, but as she studied her friend, she didn't have the slightest doubt that Linh truly would find a way to save the city. And the more her hope swelled, the more the energy crackled between their clasped hands—a pulse now living and breathing between them.

"So what's the plan?" she asked when Linh called a stream of gurgling droplets up through the center of their circled arms, adding it to the watery orb she'd made.

The glassy, rippling sphere grew bigger and bigger and bigger with each bubble she added, until it hovered over them like a watery moon.

"I'm going to plug the hole," Linh said simply. "Until the Psionipaths get here."

Keefe's eyebrows shot up. "Will that really hold back the ocean?"

"It will if I tell it to."

Linh added more water to the orb, tightening her grip on Sophie's hand with each addition. Tingles crept up Sophie's arm and spread down her torso, until her whole body hummed with buzzing energy.

"You okay, Foster?" Keefe asked, sending her mind a steadying blue breeze. "You look a little freaked."

"I'm fine. I just . . ." She swallowed. "I can feel the pull of the water now. I don't know why. But it's like it's crawling into my veins, digging into every cell—taking over everything. Is that how you always feel, Linh?"

Linh nodded. "It's incredible. And overwhelming."

"Yeah," Sophie mumbled, staring at the water rising toward her boots. Each ripple seemed to speak its own language, begging for her attention—and she wanted to listen, wanted to pull every drop closer, wrap them around her.

"Easy now," Keefe said, his lips curling with a faint grin as he sent another mental breeze. "We're supposed to be stopping the downpour, not adding to it—though it'd be fun to call you the Foster of Many Floods."

"I need to take us up now," Linh warned, erasing their smiles. She kicked her legs and raised their arms, launching them toward the breach so fast their ears popped and the city blurred to a silver streak.

"I think I left my stomach back there," Keefe groaned when they finally halted.

Sophie nodded, fighting off a shiver. "I never realized the dome was this high."

She tried not to look down at the gleaming spires that were far, far below—tried to focus on the dark rain roaring all around them, even as Linh kept them dry and safe, parting the waterfalls like curtains.

"You're starting to feel drained," Keefe warned Linh when her hands began shaking. "I'm going to try something."

Linh let out a squeak. "Oh wow—that's . . . that's like a summer breeze inside my head."

"Is it helping?" Keefe asked.

"It's amazing." A blissful peace settled into her features—but it faded when she studied the damage Ruy had caused. The shadowy tear in the energy field had now stretched halfway across the city, and churning water poured through every inch, so relentless and powerful that it was battering the buildings.

"Can you really hold all of that back?" Keefe asked.

Linh's jaw set. "I have to."

"I'll help any way I can," Sophie promised, twining their fingers together and sending a fresh rush of tingly heat through her skin.

"Same," Keefe promised. "Whatever it takes."

This wasn't just about saving Atlantis. Or the innocent lives at stake.

They needed to prove to Gisela that she'd underestimated them. And that they would *never* let her win.

"Okay," Linh said, taking a deep breath. "Here goes nothing."

She shoved the watery orb into the center of the tear, making it swallow up the downpour—but the sphere strained as it expanded, and Sophie could feel the rippling bubble wanting to burst. Linh refused to let it, and a loud grunt slipped from her lips as Linh twisted the form to her command, molding and stretching it to match the shape of the breach, until every drop of the cold, salty water was sealed away, leaving them floating in a cloud of salty mist.

Silence followed.

Then the city erupted with cheers and whistles and chants that might've been their names. It was hard to tell—hard to think with the way the ocean was slamming against Linh's rippling barrier, determined to break through again.

Linh closed her eyes, sweat trickling down her face as she fought back the water's furious currents. Her grip on Sophie's hand was so brutal, her bones ached.

Sophie gritted her teeth through the pain, channeling every drop of her mental energy to her hands and letting Linh take it all as Keefe sent a deep green breeze through her mind that somehow helped dull the strain.

"Hold on," Sophie whispered, closing her eyes as the water turned heavier and heavier.

It became their group chant: "Hold on. Hold on. Hold on."

And they did.

Together.

Minute by minute.

Breath by breath.

Until there was nothing but the ringing in Sophie's ears and the tingle in her hands, and the pressure in her head.

But a low rumble like thunder dragged her out of her daze, and her vision focused as white lightning flickered across the dome.

"The Psionipaths must be here," Linh whispered, tears streaming down her pale face.

The three weary friends stared in awe as the torn edges of the breach slowly knitted back together. And when the last stitch was in place, the entire dome glowed like morning sunlight.

Cheers erupted again, and Sophie's cheeks turned wet with her own tears as the crowd's roar turned to a command.

"Come down!"

She decided they were her new favorite words, and Linh and Keefe looked just as relieved, clinging to each other as the world smudged and blurred and they drifted down, down, down toward the city streets.

Sophie could feel her consciousness draining away—feel her mind reaching for that dreamless oblivion—but she managed to dredge up a final burst of strength to slow their descent until she felt the thud of stone against her feet.

Strong arms saved her from collapse, and a voice that sounded familiar—but she couldn't place it—whispered in her ear.

"Atlantis is safe now, Sophie."

She let the words echo in her mind as she surrendered to her weariness, letting the sleepy darkness carry her away.

EIGHTY-SEVEN

SOPHIE WOKE UP IN HER BEDROOM IN Havenfield, with no memory of how she'd gotten there, or who'd helped her into pajamas and slipped silky gloves onto her hands. But warm arms were wrapped around her, and when she rolled over . . .

"Edaline?"

Her adoptive mother gave her a relieved smile.

Grady wasn't there.

Neither was Sandor.

"It's okay," Edaline promised, tightening her hug to stop Sophie from bolting out of bed. "They're safe. Everyone's safe."

"Everyone?" Sophie asked as Edaline's soft fingers trailed up and down her back. "Even . . . Ro?"

She barely managed to choke out the name—too terrified she was going to learn that she'd overestimated the Panakes blossom's healing power.

But Edaline nodded, and Sophie felt tears leak down her cheeks.

She sent a silent thank-you to Calla's tree for keeping Ro safe, vowing to make a batch of starkflower stew as soon as she had a chance and pour it into the ground, right near the roots.

"Ro's currently enduring a week of bed rest—and *not* happy about it," Edaline added, still rubbing Sophie's back. "But Elwin expects her to make a full recovery. And King Dimitar has issued death orders for Gisela and Vespera, but thankfully he didn't hold the attack against anyone else. In fact, he agreed to allow Ro to remain as Keefe's bodyguard once she recovers. I guess she's particularly looking forward to watching Keefe dance around in a yeti costume at the Opening Ceremonies."

Sophie had to smile at that, even if internally she was cringing at the reminder of the humiliating Foxfire tradition she'd also be forced to participate in.

But she had so many bigger problems.

"What about Biana?"

"Doing well," Edaline assured her. "She's already back home at Everglen. And Kesler and Dex are over at Slurps and Burps, working on some new elixirs to help with the scars."

"Scars?" The word tasted of bile and rage.

"Not as bad as you're thinking," Edaline promised. "I went

to check on her yesterday and I could barely see them."

The "barely" part was really hard to get past. Which was why it took Sophie a second to realize . . .

"*Yesterday?* How long did Elwin sedate me for?"

"He didn't. Your body pretty much shut down the second you hit the ground in Atlantis. Same thing happened with Keefe and Linh. Tam had to carry all three of you—and Ro—out of there. His telekinesis really is extraordinary."

It was. Sophie made a note to thank him later. "So how long have I been asleep?"

"Only a little more than a day."

"A DAY?" Sophie managed to drag herself to her feet—then immediately regretted it when the head rush hit and her knees collapsed. She would've crashed face-first onto her flowered carpet if Edaline hadn't guided her back to the bed.

"It's fine, Sophie. We've been handling everything. You needed the rest."

"But what about . . . ?" She didn't know where to begin.

Or maybe she did. "Any sign of Vespera or Gisela?"

"None."

The news wasn't surprising. But Sophie was sure they were planning something. Hopefully their rocky alliance would at least slow them down. "And what happened with Wylie?" she asked. "Fintan made it sound like they had some big plan for you guys."

"If they did, it must've fallen apart when Ruy left—which

was only a few minutes after Fintan. All Gethen did was ask Wylie a few questions about Prentice."

Sophie frowned. "Not about Cyrah?"

"No. Somehow he knew that Prentice had been healed, and wanted to know how much Prentice remembered—and Wylie did a brilliant job of making it sound like Gethen should be worried. Wylie's now back at the cabin with his dad, and *lots* of guards—though I think he's planning to help with the cleanup efforts in Atlantis today."

Sophie's heart paused. "How bad is the damage?"

"Not as bad as you might imagine. Some buildings will need remodeling, and a few people got banged up in the scramble to evacuate. But Livvy set up a temporary triage center in one of the squares. And Quinlin is with your sister, in case you're wondering."

She had been—but she also hadn't been brave enough to ask. And she couldn't find the voice to raise the most logical follow-up question.

"They're going to tear out the unity fountain," Edaline said, breaking the awkward silence. "And believe it or not, they're talking about putting a statue of you, Linh, and Keefe there. I'm sure Keefe will have a *lot* of fun with that."

He definitely would. But the idea made Sophie's insides feel slimy. She wasn't sure she wanted a statue in her honor on top of such a cruel, hateful place.

"Does that mean the Council is still planning to cover up Nightfall?" she had to ask.

"'Cover up' isn't the right way to describe it," Edaline told her. "But revealing the truth is going to take some time. First, they need to secure the facility, which means moving the gorgodon out of there."

Sophie's eyes widened. "Where are they planning to move it to?"

"Here." Edaline smiled. "I know—it's going to be a challenge. But it doesn't seem right to destroy an innocent creature, at least not without trying to tame it. The gnomes are already redesigning one of the pastures into an enclosure that can keep it contained."

"I might be able to communicate with it once it's here," Sophie offered, remembering the grief she'd felt haunting the poor beast.

"I'm sure we'll take you up on that. We're going to need all the help we can get. And once the gorgodon is out of the facility, the Council is planning to scour every inch to find any secrets Vespera might have hidden. And at some point after that, they'll reveal the truth to our world. They want to wait until people aren't feeling so scared. What happened in Atlantis has definitely shaken everyone."

Sophie nodded, reaching for Ella and holding on tight, even though the treasured blue elephant was a painful reminder of the question she'd been carefully avoiding.

"We don't have to talk about them if you're not ready," Edaline told her, guessing why her hands were shaking.

"I know." Still, Sophie took a slow breath and forced herself to ask, "How bad are they?"

"They're . . . what we expected."

The careful answer only added to Sophie's queasiness.

"You've seen them?" she whispered.

Edaline let out a breath. "I have—but only briefly. I didn't want to be away too long in case you woke up. And physically, they're fine. Most of their injuries only went skin deep, and Elwin and Livvy have already treated everything."

"And . . . mentally?" Sophie asked, strangling poor Ella.

"Unfortunately, it's really hard to know," Edaline admitted, reaching up to tuck a strand of Sophie's sleep-rumpled hair behind her ear. "Mr. Forkle has tried searching their minds, but your parents each bear the same brand on their feet as Alvar."

"Soporidine," Sophie mumbled, refusing to think about the green antidote she'd told Linh to use on Ro. She would never let herself regret that decision. "I take it that means no one knows when they're going to wake up?"

If *they wake up.* . . .

"That's . . . the part I'm not sure how you're going to react to," Edaline warned her. She leaned back, fussing with the trim on her burgundy cape. "Haven't you been wondering where Grady and Sandor are?"

Sophie had—and a thousand horrible theories sprouted in her mind at the suggestion.

But none of them prepared her to hear, "They're with Fintan."

EIGHTY-EIGHT

INTAN?" SOPHIE WHISPERED, NOT sure how to force the idea into her head.

Edaline nodded, explaining that Grady and Marella had found Fintan unconscious in Nightfall. They'd been dragging him out of the facility when the flood sirens started blaring—and by the time they got Fintan to city level, Sophie, Linh, and Keefe were already working on the breach. Apparently, Grady nearly had a heart attack when he saw them hovering up there.

"Where's Fintan now?" Sophie asked.

"That's . . . where it gets tricky," Edaline admitted. "Fintan has made a number of demands. He doesn't want any Telepaths coming near him—especially you. And he wants to be kept in a private prison, like where we're keeping Alvar, instead of a cell in Exile. He also wants a guarantee from the Council that no memory break will be ordered, and that no harm will be brought upon him. And—"

"Why would we agree to any of that?" Sophie interrupted.

Edaline reached for her hand. "Because he has a small stockpile of the antidote to soporidine."

Everything inside Sophie stilled.

"The Council made a demand of their own," Edaline added. "Fintan will have to work with Bronte to help him gain access to the secrets in his old cache."

"Does that mean they're going to agree?"

"They already have. Oralie is livid, of course—and Grady's not much happier. But the hard truth is, if Fintan's willing to cooperate, it's our best chance of learning at least a few of the secrets we need from him. We didn't recover anything useful during his previous memory break. And given what happened to Kenric, it's not worth attempting another—especially since Fintan's demands aren't *that* unreasonable."

"I'm sure he's planning something," Sophie argued.

"So am I. So is everyone. That's why the Council is working with the Black Swan to build something to hold Fintan that will ensure he can't escape again."

Sophie wasn't sure a place like that would ever exist. But she focused on the more immediate problem.

"How do we know this isn't a trick? Or that Lady Gisela hasn't moved the antidote somewhere else?"

"Grady retrieved the stash this morning. It only had a dozen vials, but Elwin confirmed that the ointment matches the traces he found on Ro's skin. And Lady Cadence and her team of ogres are already working to replicate it."

She paused there, twining her fingers with Sophie's. "Livvy took two of the doses for your parents."

A lump lodged in Sophie's throat. "Did it work?"

"I'm sure it will. But Livvy doesn't think it would be wise to have them regain any form of consciousness until a Washer is there to erase their memories. Alden's been working to make all the arrangements. He wants to use one of the same Washers he used before, to make their new identities as seamless as possible with their old."

Sophie looked away, pressing a hand to her chest, as if she could feel that lingering void beginning to widen again.

She'd known all of this was coming. And she'd seen enough of her parents' wounds—and heard enough of Vespera's horrifying philosophies—to understand why.

But none of that eased the ache in her heart, or dulled the burning in her eyes.

"So when is Livvy going to do it?" she whispered.

"That's up to you. Their vitals are stable, so they can definitely wait a little longer if you want some time to say goodbye."

Sophie frowned. "I thought we had to erase their memories the second they wake up."

"We do." Edaline wrapped an arm around her shoulders. "I was talking about your sister."

"Oh."

A headache flared to match the pain already in her chest. "Does Amy know her memories will have to be erased?"

"Yes. Livvy explained everything when they brought her to see her parents. She . . . struggled a bit."

The words felt like another blow. "She's seen them?"

"She insisted. And don't worry, Livvy waited until their wounds were completely healed. Amy wanted to see you, too, by the way. But you were still too out of it. So if you'd like to spend some time with her—"

"What's the point?" Sophie interrupted, the question sharper than she intended. "It's just another memory for the Washer to erase, right?"

"He won't be erasing *your* memories," Edaline gently reminded her. "I know all of this is going to be so, so hard for you. But . . . I think it might help if you have that small bit of closure."

The words echoed around the room, sounding as hollow as Sophie felt.

"I'm sorry," Edaline said, reaching up to brush away Sophie's tears. "I wish it didn't have to be like this."

"Me too."

And maybe it was selfishness, or recklessness, or pure desperation, but she found her mind circling back to that first conversation she'd had with Alden in Atlantis, when she'd reminded him that if her family had known the truth about the danger they were in, that they might've been able to prevent themselves from being taken.

If Nightfall and Vespera had proven anything, it was that buried secrets had a way of coming back to haunt them.

So she let herself ask, "Why can't Amy keep her memories? She hasn't been through any major trauma. And then she'd be prepared if the Neverseen came after them again."

"If only it were that simple," Mr. Forkle said from the doorway.

Sophie whipped around, flinching when she found him standing with Grady and Sandor—and Councillor Bronte.

"I understand where you're coming from," Mr. Forkle added. "But think of what you're suggesting. Your sister would be forced to lie to her parents every minute of every day."

"Sounds a lot like how I had to hide my telepathy," Sophie reminded him. "And I was only five years old."

"I remember," Mr. Forkle agreed. "I also remember exactly how great that struggle was for you."

"Maybe Amy wouldn't care," Sophie argued. "Shouldn't it be her choice? Alden promised it would be."

Mr. Forkle sighed. "Your sister has shown a tremendous amount of resilience these long weeks. But she's still a child, and cannot possibly fathom the magnitude of this responsibility."

"I'm sure she's also freaked out about having someone poke around her memories," Grady added. "And that's not a good reason to choose a life of constant deception."

"I agree," Mr. Forkle said. "And I say that as someone who understands the complexities of duplicity better than anyone."

Sophie looked away. "I know. I just . . . hate this."

"So do I."

Surprisingly, the words came from Bronte.

He crossed her room, the soft petals in the carpet shifting under his feet as he moved toward the windows and stared out at the sea.

"All my life, some small, secret part of me has wished the divide between humans and elves could be bridged," he whispered. "I never fought for change, because I believed the lies that had been fed to me. But now that the deeper truths have been revealed . . ."

Several seconds dragged by before he turned back to Sophie. "Do you truly believe your sister could hide our existence?"

She forced herself to think it through before she said, "Yes."

Amy had always been a good liar—and when she wanted something, she never gave up.

"There's more at stake than the secrecy of our world," Mr. Forkle reminded them. "All it would take is one slip around your parents—one wrong word—and the trauma of what they've endured could be triggered."

Sophie shivered. "Will they really be that vulnerable?"

"Not in the way you're thinking," Mr. Forkle assured her. "It would take *very* specific triggers. The kind your sister would *only* know if her mind wasn't cleared."

"So tell Amy that," Sophie told him. "If she knows the risks, she'll be careful. Especially if you come up with a really good cover story for her."

If Mr. Forkle could keep his identical twin hidden—and maintain multiple identities—surely he could guide Amy through the process.

"It seems at least worth *considering*," Bronte said, mostly to himself. "I suspect I could convince the rest of the Council to agree with me—or at least the majority I'd need."

A tingle hummed in Sophie's heart and she tried to ignore it, because it felt way too much like hope—and she was sure a "but" was coming.

"*But,*" Bronte said, right on cue. His sharp eyes locked with Sophie's. "Before I do anything, I would need to explain the options to your sister—and I would need to make the risks *painfully* clear."

"You mean you'd need to scare her," Sophie said.

Memories of their early inflicting sessions flashed through her head—but she had no doubt her sister could face down anything. Even Bronte in stern mode.

"And if Amy decides she wants to keep her memories?" she asked.

He turned back to the windows. "Then I would head straight to Eternalia and make the arrangements. Assuming I could count on the Black Swan for help."

Mr. Forkle nodded, and the room went silent as everyone processed the gravity of what they were suggesting.

A human knowing the secret of the Lost Cities. Maybe even having some contact with their world.

It would be messy and complicated—but that was the Black Swan's specialty. And if her sister understood the stakes, she'd find a way to make it work.

"Talk to her," Sophie told him. "I bet I know what she'll say."

EIGHTY-NINE

KAY, FOSTER," KEEFE SAID, GUID-
ing her to one of his dad's porch swings and
forcing her to take a seat. "We need to get
your mind to a happier place. Want me to
sing? Or how about I bust out more of my incredible dancing?"

He folded his arms behind his head, shaking his hips and
flapping his elbows like wings.

Of *all* the places the Black Swan could've hidden her human
parents, Sophie never, *never* would've expected they'd ask Lord
Cassius to keep them at the Shores of Solace.

They'd had their reasons, of course. Something to do with
security and the overall tranquility of the surroundings—not
to mention Keefe's dad *was* part of the Black Swan now.

Thankfully, they'd asked Lord Cassius to leave for the afternoon, to give Sophie privacy.

But it still felt wrong.

Then again, everything felt wrong. Probably because everything *was* wrong.

Sophie had been so sure her sister would be excited to keep her memories that it had felt like a double sucker punch when Amy chose to have her mind erased. She *did* understand why Amy had been afraid after Bronte's warnings. And she couldn't fault her sister for choosing what she felt would be safest for her parents. Plus . . . it wasn't like they were close. They'd barely seen each other while Amy had been in the Lost Cities. They weren't friends. And they weren't *actually* sisters.

They were just two girls from two different worlds.

It was time for them to go their separate ways.

And yet . . . it hurt, more than Sophie was willing to admit, knowing Amy was *choosing* to erase her. So she'd made an important decision too.

A choice to protect her parents' sanity—and her own.

Closure.

"You're sure you don't want your adoptive family to be here for this?" Mr. Forkle asked.

He stood with Sandor near the porch railing, and Sandor side-eyed Keefe's wiggly dance as he added, "Or any of your other friends?"

"Are you implying that I'm not good enough, Gigantor?"

Keefe asked, wiggling harder and kicking his legs. "Or are you just jealous of my moves?"

"I'm implying that today will be difficult for Sophie, and she might want to surround herself with as much moral support as possible," Sandor informed him.

"I'll be fine," Sophie promised. If she'd had it her way, she'd be alone. She'd even tried asking Keefe to leave, but there was no getting rid of him.

That actually turned out to be a good thing, though, when Physic and Amy arrived a few minutes later, dragging a storm of awkwardness in with them. Amy wouldn't look at Sophie, and Sophie was happy to return the favor, pretending to be fascinated by the jewels on Physic's mask. So Keefe jumped in to fill the silence.

He'd just agreed to tell Amy all about the Great Gulon Incident when a loud knock halted the conversation. Sophie was too nauseous to care that she'd lost another chance to hear about Keefe's epic prank—especially when Mr. Forkle shuffled back into the room, followed by a tall elf in a long gray cloak.

He tossed back his hood, revealing dark skin, buzzed dark hair, and shockingly handsome features—though most of the shock came from how young he looked. Sophie wouldn't have guessed him a day past sixteen.

"Everyone, meet Mr. Kafuta," Mr. Forkle told them.

"*You're* a Washer?" Amy asked, clearly as surprised by his obvious youth as Sophie was.

He flashed a bright white smile. "I am, and you're welcome to call me Damel, if it's easier. Oh, and yeah, I know I have a baby face. Don't worry, I've been doing this for years."

"Since he was a Level Four, I believe," Mr. Forkle agreed.

"And next year you'll be . . ." Keefe prompted.

"A Level Eight," Damel told him.

Which didn't actually sound like a whole lot of experience— but Sophie reminded herself that in a little over two years she'd faced fires and floods and plagues and beasts and tribunals and banishments and far too many Healing Center visits.

And if she'd survived all of that, surely she could survive this.

Damel frowned at Amy. "Is this the girl I'll be . . . ?"

"I'll sedate her when it's her turn," Physic promised, squeezing Amy's shaky hand. "But she wanted to see that her parents were safely through their wash before we started on hers. And I can't blame her with how tricky this one's going to be."

"That's what I hear." Damel turned to Sophie. "I was told you want to be in the room with me. Planning on assisting?"

"In a way." Sophie held up her right hand and peeled off her lacy glove. "I'm going to enhance you."

Damel's eyebrows shot up. "I'd heard your powers were legendary, but . . ."

His voice trailed off as Keefe tried to cover his choked laugh with a cough.

"This particular ability of Miss Foster's is not public knowledge," Mr. Forkle explained.

"Gotcha," Damel said, rubbing his chin as he studied Sophie. "I've never been enhanced before. What should I expect?"

"I'm not sure," Sophie admitted. "But I'm hoping you'll be able to get everything that could be triggering completely out of their heads. Especially all their memories of me."

"What?" Amy and Keefe asked at the same time.

"Will that work?" Amy added.

"I don't know," Sophie said, turning back to Damel. "But we have to try. *I'm* the reason my parents were captured. So if something ever made them remember me, it could trigger all of their other horrifying memories. The only way to keep them safe is to try to wipe myself totally out of their heads, and maybe if I enhance you, your instincts will tell you how to do it."

Damel whistled. "Alden said this one would be intense, but this is a whole other level."

"It is," Physic agreed. "And there's one other variable. The sedative they're under—let's just say you've never seen it before. So I'll have to administer a special antidote to wake them up. And I'll be honest, I have no idea how that's going to affect what you're here to do—especially since I don't feel comfortable sedating them again."

"I've done one other wash with someone awake," Damel told her. "It's weird that way, but I should be good."

"Then shall we?" Physic asked, adjusting her mask as she headed down a dove-gray hall.

Keefe hooked his arm through Sophie's. "Don't argue, Foster. You're going to need me."

"He's right," Mr. Forkle told her. "And we'll wait here," he added, placing a hand on Amy's shoulder to stop her from following.

Sophie didn't look at her sister as she walked away. And she tried not to think about what was happening—tried to focus on one foot in front of the other.

But as they entered the dimly lit bedroom, she realized . . . this was it.

The last time she'd ever see her human parents.

The last time she'd have a connection to the people who'd tucked her in every night, and read her bedtime stories about fairies and hobbits, and taught her to ride a bike, and let her cry on their shoulders when she skinned her knees.

She gave herself one minute to study their familiar faces, memorizing every line and shadow. They looked like themselves again.

Peaceful.

Happy.

She hoped they would be.

"Ready?" Physic asked, removing two small green vials from her cloak.

The antidote hadn't been shaped into spheres like the one they'd used on Ro, but the thick green sludge looked familiar as Physic smeared it on Sophie's father's foot.

Within seconds he began to stir—limbs thrashing, eyelids fluttering. And Sophie held her breath as his eyes opened and slowly seemed to focus.

For one moment his gaze met hers, and she could've sworn a hint of recognition flickered.

"Bye, Dad," she whispered. "I love you."

Damel took her shaky hand. "Wow. That's, that's . . . different."

"You okay?" Physic asked him.

"Yeah. Just trying to settle my head for a second."

His forehead creased, and he took a long, slow breath before he reached for Sophie's father's temple and pressed his fingers against the pale skin.

Sophie let her mind go blank, not wanting to see any of the horrible things Damel had to be witnessing. Whatever they were, they had him quivering and moaning.

"It's okay," Keefe whispered, pulling off Sophie's other glove and sending her a blue mental breeze.

He had to send two more before Damel stumbled and fell back, bending to rest his head near his knees.

"Need a break?" Physic asked.

"No, I think . . . I think I just want to get this over with." He rubbed his temples. "It's a lot to process."

Two more breaths and he straightened, glancing at Sophie. "Ready?"

She really wasn't. But she nodded, and Physic smeared the antidote on her mother's foot.

It took longer for her mom to stir, and her eyes were cloudy when they opened. But when Sophie whispered, "Bye, Mom," they seemed to clear.

"I'll always love you," Sophie added, choking back a small sob.

Her mom blinked hard and looked away.

But right as Damel pressed his hand against her temple, she rasped, "I'll always love you too, Sophie." Then her eyes rolled back and Damel washed her memories away.

NINETY

I'M FINE," SOPHIE TOLD KEEFE.

She'd already said it a dozen times. But he kept his grip on her hand and sent another soft breeze rushing through her head.

It helped, a little. But the numbness was fighting hard to take over. Which was probably why Keefe wouldn't let go.

They'd moved back out to the porch—Sophie, Keefe, and Damel—craving air and sunlight after that suffocating room. It was Mr. Forkle's turn at the moment, and he was busy flooding her parents' minds with the new backstories he'd meticulously crafted to fill the gaps in their memories and prepare them for their new lives. Shaping them into people Sophie would never know.

"She remembered me," she whispered.

Damel nodded. "I'm sorry she won't anymore."

Sophie shook her head. "It's fine. It's how it has to be. But were you really able to erase everything we needed?"

"Everything," he agreed. "As far as they'll know, you never existed."

"And nothing can change that?" Amy asked from the far end of the porch.

Sophie hadn't noticed her hiding over there, tucked into the shadows next to Sandor.

"Nope," Damel promised. "With the enhancing . . . I don't know how to describe it. But every memory I washed didn't just get buried—it's gone. And it was super easy to find them. The second I thought Sophie's name, it dragged every thought they'd ever had about her right to me, and all I had to do was wash them away. Same thing worked with anything about elves."

Amy's sob rang out over the crashing waves, and a tiny, bitter part of Sophie was tempted to let her cry alone.

But she got up to be the big sister one last time. "It's going to be okay," she promised, resting her hand on Amy's shoulder. "You won't even remember any of this in a couple of hours."

"NO!" her sister shouted, nearly knocking them both over as she threw her arms around her. "I've changed my mind. I don't want anyone taking my memories."

Sophie twisted in the stranglehold, trying to breathe. "I know how scary this all seems—"

"That's not it!" Amy insisted. She leaned back, waiting for Sophie to meet her eyes—which were so much like her mom's eyes that Sophie's chest tightened. "I'm not scared. I just . . . I don't want to forget anything. I only said I did because I didn't want to put Mom and Dad in any danger. But I can't now, right?"

"You shouldn't be able to," Damel agreed.

"Then, please," Amy begged him. "Don't erase my memories. I want to remember Havenfield and Atlantis, and Quinlin and Livvy, and Silveny and Greyfell and everyone else, and—"

"Especially me?" Keefe couldn't resist jumping in.

"Yes." Amy sniffled. "I want to know that elves are real—and so much cooler than all the stories people tell about them. I want to remember what mallowmelt tastes like, and what it feels like to ride on a beam of light. But mostly . . . I want to know that I have a super-amazing sister out there who's way too cool for me, but . . . I love her."

Tears blurred Sophie's eyes. "I love you too."

Amy hugged her tighter. "Does that mean I can keep you?"

"Only if I can keep you."

"Awwwwwwwww, you guys are going to make me cry too!" Keefe said, wrapping his arms around them and turning it into a group hug.

Sandor joined in too—much to everyone's surprise. And Sophie had no idea how long they stood like that, or what Damel must've thought of them.

But eventually Mr. Forkle cleared his throat and said, "Looks like I need to hail Bronte."

"You can never visit here," Bronte told Sophie as he led her and Amy up the stone path to a fancy Tudor-style house with cut-glass windows glinting in the pale dawn light. It was slightly bigger than her family's last house, and nestled closer to the neighbors. But Mr. Forkle had done a good job of finding a place that would feel familiar.

"I know," Sophie growled at Bronte. "I've sat through *all* your lectures."

Amy had spent the last two days at Havenfield, while Bronte went over all of her new *rules*. The basic gist was: Amy wouldn't tell anyone anything. And Sophie would stay far away. Not because they were worried about triggering her parents' memories, but because they didn't want to draw the attention of the Neverseen.

The Council would also be keeping a close watch on Amy and her family—as would the Black Swan. And Amy had an Imparter for *extreme* emergencies.

Someday, they hoped things would calm down and Amy could visit the Lost Cities.

In the meantime, she'd have to settle for keeping her memories.

"So . . . I guess this is it, then, huh?" Amy said when they reached the front door. Watson was inside barking and scratching at the wood.

"You're sure you're ready for this?" Sophie asked.

Amy nodded. "It'll be . . . an adventure."

Her parents had been brought in the night before—and were currently sleeping off a mild sedative. Once they woke up, Amy would feed them the final details of the cover story Mr. Forkle had perfected, and life would hopefully settle into some sort of new normal.

"We need to hurry," Bronte said, glancing over his shoulder at the empty street. "We are far too conspicuous."

Sophie could've pointed out that if he wanted to blend in he should've removed his cape and circlet—and put a hat over his ears.

But that would've cost precious seconds she refused to use for anything other than pulling her sister into a strangle-hug.

"Take care of yourself, okay?" Sophie whispered.

Her sister nodded. "And you keep . . . saving the world."

Sophie smiled through her tears. "I'll try."

Neither of them said goodbye.

But they let go, and Bronte immediately dragged Sophie toward a small cluster of trees where they'd have enough privacy to leap away.

She stole one final glimpse over her shoulder as Bronte adjusted his pathfinder, and spotted Amy still standing in the doorway, half in and half out of her new life.

She used her foot to block Marty and Watson from sprinting into the street and gave a small wave, shouting, "See you later, Sophie."

NINETY-ONE

KEEFE WAS WAITING UNDER Calla's Panakes when Sophie leaped back to Havenfield after a final lecture from Bronte. And Sandor stood beside him, for once not looking annoyed by Keefe's existence.

"I figured you were having a rough morning," Keefe said, patting a spot on the grass beside him. "And since I still have a few more days without Ro driving me crazy, I thought I'd bring you a cheer-up present, since apparently that's a *thing*."

He held out his arms.

"Um . . ." Sophie didn't see a gift.

Keefe smirked. "Foster, Foster, Foster—always so adorably oblivious. *I'm* the gift. I'm all yours today—though I might be willing to extend my servitude if you call me the Gift Master."

Sophie rolled her eyes as she smiled. "You're ridiculous, you know that?"

"And you love it." His grin shifted into something softer, something that made her stomach tighten. "So what do you need, Foster? A shoulder to cry on? A good old-fashioned cuddle? Or should we go back to brainstorming my favor?"

Sophie tugged an itchy eyelash. "Actually, Fitz will be here any minute."

"Oh? And why is the Fitzster coming over? Hot date?"

"He didn't tell you?"

"Can't say that he did." He frowned when she reached for her eyelashes again, and his eyes dropped to his hands. "Why so nervous, Foster? *Are* you guys finally making Fitzphie official? Because if you are—"

"We're not," Sophie interrupted, not sure she wanted to know how that sentence ended. "If you *must* know, we're going to see Alvar. Mr. Forkle is going to use some of the antidote on him to see if we can get some answers."

Keefe was immediately on his feet. "Any chance I can be part of the big awakening? And maybe borrow your Sucker Punch while I'm there?"

"Only after I get the first shot," Fitz said behind her.

Sophie spun around and found him standing between Alden and Grizel. It was hard to decide who looked most exhausted among them.

"You guys going to be okay with this?" Sophie asked.

Fitz's nod looked grim. "I should be asking you the same thing. How'd it go with your sister?" He'd been reaching out telepathically every night to check on her, even though she'd told him to focus on helping Biana with her recovery.

Sophie shrugged. "Not as sad as I thought. Just . . . weird."

"I bet."

Neither of them seemed to know what to say after that.

"It's okay if I crash your Alvar party, right?" Keefe jumped in, draping an arm around Sophie's shoulders. "Foster made it sound super fun."

"Sure," Fitz said slowly. "I guess I should've known you'd be here."

There was a strange edge to the words, and Keefe was quick to change the subject.

"Della and Biana aren't coming?"

Alden shook his head. "Biana's not feeling up to leaving the house yet, and Della didn't want to leave her alone. Especially since Dex and Kesler are supposed to stop by with their next round of elixirs. We're hoping this might be the last batch she needs."

Sophie opened her mouth to ask for more details about Biana's recovery, but Mr. Forkle glittered into the pastures and appeared to be in quite the hurry.

"I need to get back to being Magnate Leto by this evening," he explained as he dug a magsidian ring out of his pocket, "and we still have a long walk ahead."

"Of *course* we do," Keefe grumbled. But it didn't stop him from joining hands with the others and stepping into the path Mr. Forkle created—though he probably regretted it when they reappeared in the middle of a sweaty, putrid bog filled with sticky vines and an abundance of skittering things.

"Any chance I can convince either of you goblins to carry me?" Keefe asked, the third time he ended up knee-deep in sludge.

"No, but I'd be happy to carry Sophie," Sandor offered.

Keefe clutched his heart. "That hurts, Gigantor. I bet Ro would carry me."

"And probably bang your head into all the trees," Grizel added.

"No one needs to carry anyone," Mr. Forkle told them. "We're here."

He kicked aside the long grass, revealing a metal hatch sunken into the muck.

"Please tell me it smells better down there," Keefe begged.

It didn't.

A slippery ladder brought them down into a tiny round room that was so humid and foul it felt like crawling inside someone's snotty nose. But maybe that was deserved, since the only occupant was a violent traitor.

And yet, Alvar didn't look much like a monster when Sophie spotted him strapped to a cot in the center. He looked . . . defeated. His frail body was covered in angry red scars, and he was strapped to the bed with thick metal bands across his chest, knees, and ankles.

"Where are the guards?" Sandor asked, his muscled hand hovering near his sword.

"It's the dwarves' shift," Mr. Forkle reminded him.

"You okay?" Sophie asked, noticing the death glare Fitz was giving his brother.

His nod was far from convincing, so she reached for his hand—but he scooted closer, wrapping an arm around her shoulders and holding on like she was the only thing keeping him steady. And maybe she was. He was shaking almost as hard as his father, who'd leaned on the room's only table to keep his balance.

"I'll talk first," Mr. Forkle told them as he held up a vial of the green antidote. "Then his father should have a turn. And his brother. Miss Foster can go next—"

"So I'm *last*?" Keefe interrupted. "That stings, Forkle. And shouldn't a Physician be here, by the way?"

"I've had plenty of medical training," Mr. Forkle reminded him. "Everyone ready?"

They each held their breath as he spread the green slime over Alvar's heel.

The antidote took longer to set in than it had with Sophie's parents—long enough that Sophie was wishing the cramped room had an extra chair.

Keefe looked ready to go back to whining when Alvar finally stirred. His eyelids peeled open, revealing pale blue eyes just like his mother's—though at the moment they were bloodshot, and stretched wide with terror.

"Easy," Mr. Forkle told him as Alvar strained against his bonds, screaming and kicking and flailing. "You're going to hurt yourself."

That only made Alvar thrash harder.

He tried to say something, but his voice was like shredded sandpaper.

"Here," Sophie said, grabbing a bottle of Youth off the tiny table. "Try drinking this."

He flinched when she stepped closer, but let her press the bottle against his lips, greedily guzzling down the cool liquid.

"Not too much," Mr. Forkle warned. "His stomach has been empty for a long time."

Sophie gave him one more second, then pulled the bottle away.

Alvar cleared his throat and managed to rasp, "Where am I?"

"Somewhere you cannot escape," Mr. Forkle told him. "So do not try. Once we see how that water settles, I'll bring you some broth. And in the meantime, you can tell us why the Neverseen wanted to get rid of you, and what they're planning next."

"I don't know what you're talking about!" Alvar snapped.

"Right," Fitz snorted. "You're seriously going to cover for them? After they cut you up and left you to die?"

Alvar thrashed against his bonds again.

"You're going to hurt yourself," Alden warned.

"Then let me go!" Alvar shouted. "Please, I don't know any-thing."

He turned his desperate gaze to Sophie. "Please help me."

"None of us are buying this, Alvar," Fitz snapped. "Just stop."

"Alvar?" he repeated, every line on his face twisting with confusion.

His eyes darted between them, studying their expressions. Then to his bonds. Then back to Sophie.

He huffed out a shaky breath. "Who's Alvar?"

Acknowledgments

Yeah . . . that really was the end. (And, yes, I realize you're all probably glaring at me right now.) But don't worry, it's not the end of the series! I still have more story ahead! I just have to, you know, write it—which I promise I'm doing as fast as I can!

In the meantime, I hope you know how much I adore each and every one of you. You're worth the sleepless nights and stressful days spent yelling at characters who refuse to cooperate. Thank you for going with Sophie (and me) on this journey. I say this every year, but it never stops being true: I really do have the most amazing readers ever.

I also would not have survived the chaotic deadline schedule if it weren't for the patience, support, and enthusiasm of an incredible team of people. You each deserve your own paragraph, but since this book ended up an *epic* length, I have to lump you all together:

My brilliant agent, Laura Rennert (and everyone else at Andrea Brown Literary, as well as Taryn Fagerness). My tireless and inspiring editor, Liesa Abrams Mignogna, and everyone else at Simon & Schuster, especially Jon Anderson, Mara Anastas, Katherine Devendorf, Adam Smith, Rebecca Vitkus, Jodie Hockensmith, Lauren Hoffman, Catherine Hayden, Anna Jarzab, Nicole Russo, Jessica Smith, Tricia Lin, Karin Paprocki, Bernadette Flinn, Steve Scott, Michelle Fadlalla, Anthony Parisi, Mike Rosamilia, Jenn Rothkin, Ian Reilly, Christina Pecorale,

Victor Iannone, and the entire sales team. Cécile Pournin, Mathilde Tamae-bouhon, and everyone at Lumen Editions also deserve my eternal gratitude for the hectic scramble they endured to get this book translated for my wonderful French readers. And Jason Chan has once again topped himself with a stunningly gorgeous cover.

I'd also be lost without Amie Kauffman, Lisa Mantchev, Victoria Morris, Kari Olson, Cindy Pon, CJ Redwine, James Riley, J. Scott Savage, Amy Tintera, Kasie West, and Natalie Whipple. And this series never would've found its way into readers' hands if it weren't for the efforts of booksellers, librarians, and educators, especially Mel Barnes, Katie Bartow, Lynette Dodds, Jo Gray, Maryelizabeth Hart, Faith Hochhalter, Heather Laird, Katie Laird, Kim Laird, Angela Mann, Barbara Mena, Brandi Stewart, and so many others I'm probably forgetting (SORRY). And special thanks to the California Young Reader Medal for giving me my first "win."

Last, but absolutely not least, I have to thank my family. Mom and Dad, I don't have enough space to list all the things you do for me and this series—but I hope you know how much I appreciate you. And Miles . . . I could ramble endlessly about how happy I am to be married to you, but I think what we both want to hear more than anything is: I AM DEADLINE FREE!

(You know, for a couple of weeks. Then it's on to book seven! Aren't you glad you married a writer?)

Read on for a peek at Sophie's next adventure in
Keeper of the Lost Cities, Book Seven: **FLASHBACK**

O IS IT STRANGE COMING HERE AND
not being the one on trial?" Keefe asked, checking
his expertly styled blond hair in a shiny facet on
one of the jeweled walls before he followed Sophie
into Tribunal Hall. "Because I'd be happy to help you break a
few laws if you're feeling left out."

"Me too!" Ro—Keefe's bodyguard—jumped in. Her pierced
nose crinkled as she surveyed the empty auditorium, which
was built entirely out of emeralds. "Ugh, you guys have really
out-sparkled yourselves with this place. It's basically begging
me to smash something."

"No one will be smashing anything," Sandor—Sophie's
bodyguard—warned. "Or causing any other problems!"

The threat didn't sound all that terrifying, thanks to Sandor's squeaky voice. But he backed it up by flexing some seriously impressive goblin muscles.

Ro flashed a pointy-toothed smile and patted the rows of daggers strapped to her toned thighs—a recent addition to her ogre battle armor. "I'd like to see you try to stop us."

"Believe me, I'd enjoy every second," Sandor growled, gripping the hilt of his giant black sword. "I still can't believe the Council is allowing you into these proceedings."

Neither could Sophie.

Then again, she hadn't expected to be invited either.

The Tribunal was supposed to be restricted to members of the Vacker family, since it was only a sentencing hearing—and mostly a formality. Alvar was already being held in the secret prison the Black Swan had designed specifically for him. The Council was simply deciding how many years he'd have to stay there.

But Alden had stopped by Havenfield that morning and explained that he'd gotten permission for Sophie to attend. And when she'd light leaped to Eternalia, she'd found Keefe and Ro already waiting.

Keefe looked dressier than usual, in a starched white shirt with a fitted black jerkin and an embroidered gray cape—and Sophie was relieved to see it, since she'd decided to show her support with a dusty-rose gown that was much more Biana's fancy style than hers. She'd also used the gold-flecked eyeliner

Biana had been telling her would bring out the glints in her brown eyes—even though she hated drawing more attention to their unique-for-an-elf color.

"What?" Sophie asked, wiping under her lashes when she noticed Keefe staring. "Did I smudge it?"

"No, Foster. You look . . . perfect."

She blushed at the slight catch in his voice—and then wished she hadn't when he flashed his trademark smirk.

"Did Alden tell you he wanted you to be here for moral support too?" she asked, stopping in the center of the hall as she realized she didn't know which of the hundreds of seats were theirs.

His smile faded. "Yeah. He said Fitz was going to need a friend today."

"He said a lot more than that," Ro mumbled.

"Relax, Foster," Keefe said, shooting Ro a glare before he pointed to the crease that had formed between Sophie's eyebrows. "No need to get all crinkly on me. Nothing's going on. Alden's just . . . worried about how Fitz is going to handle this."

"So am I," Sophie admitted.

Anger was often Fitz's crutch in emotionally fraught situations—and nothing brought out his fury more than his traitorous older brother.

"Yeah, well, now I'm stuck listening to a bunch of stuffy, know-it-all elves arguing with each other," Ro groused as she twisted one of her choppy pigtails, which she'd recently dyed the same vivid pink she'd painted her claws. "It almost makes me wish I was still bedridden. Seriously, who thought having *twelve* Councillors was a good idea?"

Sophie was tempted to point out that the system was much more balanced than having a single power-hungry king. But since Ro was the daughter of the ogres' fear-inspiring leader—and the elves' alliance with King Dimitar was especially shaky—she decided it was smart to avoid that particular conversation. Especially since the elvin Council was far from perfect.

She turned toward the twelve jeweled thrones that filled a large platform at the front of the glinting green room. Each had been ornamented to reflect the style and taste of the Councillor whose name was displayed along the top: Clarette, Velia, Alina, Terik, Liora, Emery, Oralie, Ramira, Darek, Noland, Zarina, and Bronte.

Sophie knew some of them better than others, and there were a couple she'd even grown to trust. But she would never stop wishing that there was still a simple, sturdy throne for Councillor Kenric.

Kenric had been kind. And funny. And one of Sophie's most loyal supporters.

And he'd still be alive if it weren't for her.

She tried not to let herself think about it, because the guilt might shatter her sanity. But she could still feel the stinging heat of the flames—still hear the crunches and crackles and screams as the jeweled tower melted all around them. And she'd never forget Fintan's taunt as he'd ignited the Everblaze to prevent her from retrieving his memories.

Sophie had only been in Oblivimyre that night because of a direct order from the Council. But if she'd been stronger, faster, smarter than Fintan . . .

"You okay?" Keefe asked, flicking a strand of her blond hair to get her attention. "And before you answer, remember: You're talking to an Empath. Plus, you've already pulled out two eyelashes since we got here, and I can tell you're dying to go for a third."

She was.

Her eyelashes itched whenever she felt anxious, and tugging on them was *such* a relief. But she kept trying to break the habit, so she held her hands at her sides and forced herself to meet Keefe's sky blue eyes. "I'm fine."

When he raised one eyebrow, she added, "I'm just frustrated. I wish the Council was holding a Tribunal for Fintan, not Alvar."

Keefe leaned slightly closer. "I wouldn't let the Fitzster hear you say that."

"I know. Or Biana."

The younger Vacker siblings had been counting down the days to Alvar's sentencing, and Sophie didn't blame them for wanting everything settled with their older brother.

But . . .

She glanced over her shoulder, grateful the auditorium was

still empty, so she could ask the question she'd been trying not to say.

"Doesn't this feel like a waste of time?"

"Because Alvar can't remember anything?" Keefe asked.

Sophie nodded.

Alvar had been involved in many of the Neverseen's cruelest schemes before Sophie and her friends found him drugged, bleeding, and trapped in a cell in an abandoned hideout. And when he'd finally regained consciousness, he couldn't even remember his own name.

He didn't seem to be faking, either. Sophie had checked. So had Fitz. And Alden. And Mr. Forkle. And Quinlin. And Councillor Emery—along with every other Telepath the Council trusted. None of them could find a single memory in Alvar's head, no matter how deeply they'd searched. The Black Swan had even brought in Damel—a trained Washer—who'd told them that Alvar's past had been scrubbed cleaner than he'd realized was possible. And Sophie had tried using her unique telepathic abilities to perform a mental healing, but it hadn't made a difference. Neither had any of the elixirs a team of physicians had given him.

Alvar's mind wasn't broken or damaged.

It was . . . blank.

Sophie had never felt anything like it—and she'd experienced some pretty bizarre mental landscapes. There was no cold, suffocating darkness. No sharp, fragmented images. Just soft, fuzzy gray space.

"I don't understand why the Council is focusing on someone with amnesia," she whispered to Keefe, "when they have Fintan in custody and they're doing *nothing*."

The former leader of the Neverseen was currently being held in a cushy prison, in exchange for sharing the location of a small supply of the antidote to soporidine. He'd also demanded that all Telepaths be kept far away, and while the Council did at least make him agree to help them gain access to his old cache—either Fintan was sabotaging the process, or caches were flawed inventions, because weeks had passed and they hadn't recovered a single piece of information.

"You think he's planning something," Keefe guessed.

"Don't you?"

Fintan had already proven that he was the master of long, intricate schemes, and Sophie knew she could find out what he was up to if the Council would just let her meet with him. But all of her requests for a visit had been denied. And when she'd asked the Black Swan's Collective for help, they'd told her the Council wasn't giving them access either.

"Why is Fintan still calling the shots?" she murmured. "He already gave us the antidote."

"I don't know." Keefe seemed to debate with himself before he added, "But he's never going to cooperate. So do you *really* want to do another memory break on him? After what happened with Alden—and Kenric . . ."

Sophie stared at her hands, tracing her finger along one

of the Cognate rings peeking through her lacy gloves—a reminder that she and Fitz shared a rare telepathic connection that made them far more powerful together than they'd been the last time they'd taken on Fintan. She'd also manifested as an Enhancer, which meant she could boost Fitz's mental strength with a single touch of her fingertips. So she had no doubt that they *would* get past Fintan's blocking and find whatever he was hiding.

But . . . memory breaks were horrible, brutal things—even when they were necessary.

"I don't see any other choice," she admitted. "Even if he's not part of some bigger scheme, Fintan has to at least know what Vespera's planning."

"But he won't know what my mom's up to," Keefe reminded her. "And she's the one running things now."

Sophie wasn't entirely convinced that was true.

Lady Gisela *had* seized control of the Neverseen. But Vespera only allied with her because Keefe's mom forced her to. And Vespera didn't seem like the type who'd cooperate for long.

"We have too many villains," Sophie said through a sigh.

Keefe snorted. "You're not wrong."

She wasn't even counting the other members of the Neverseen. Or the ogres who'd defected from King Dimitar. Or the dwarves who'd disappeared months ago, presumably to join the rebellion. Or—

"Hey," Keefe said, fanning the air the way he always did

when her emotions started to spiral. "We've got this, okay? I know it doesn't feel like it—"

"It doesn't," Sophie agreed.

They'd been trying to come up with a plan for weeks and still had nothing. And whenever the Neverseen kept them stumped like that, people got hurt. Sophie had even risked using Keefe's old Imparter, but Lady Gisela was either ignoring them, or she'd severed the connection. And the Black Swan had confiscated the gadget in case anyone could use it to monitor them.

Keefe grinned. "You're so adorable when you worry. I've told you that, right?"

Sophie gave him her best glare, and his smile only widened.

He stepped closer, reaching for her hands. "Let's just get through today, okay? Then no one will be distracted by Alvar anymore, and we'll be able to focus."

"Yeah. I guess."

"Hmm." He traced his thumb over the sliver of skin between her glove and the edge of her beaded sleeve. "There's something you're not saying right now. I can feel it."

There was.

The *other* question she'd been trying not to ask, because she was pretty sure she knew what her friends would say.

"Come on, Foster. It's me. You know you can trust me. And you already know all of my worst secrets, so . . ."

It was the sincerity in his eyes that made her glance over her shoulder again, making sure the room was still empty before she whispered, "Do you think it's weird to punish someone for crimes they don't remember committing?"

"Weird?" Keefe asked. "Or *wrong*?"

"Both, I guess."

He nodded and stepped back, running a hand down his face. "Well . . . everything about this is weird. But, just because Alvar doesn't remember the creepy things he did, it doesn't mean they didn't happen."

"True."

Sophie knew better than anyone what Alvar was capable of. And yet . . . the few times she'd seen him since he lost his memory, he'd seemed *different*.

He wasn't slick, or arrogant, or angry.

He was terrified. And desperate. And he'd spent the whole time begging everyone to realize he wasn't the person they thought he was.

"He could still get his memories back," Keefe reminded her. "Just because we haven't found the right trigger yet doesn't mean the Neverseen didn't plan for one."

That was another reason Sophie wanted a chance to poke around Fintan's head. They'd recovered Alvar months before Fintan was arrested, so he had to know why Alvar ended up in that cell.

But since the Council wasn't cooperating, Sophie had convinced Mr. Forkle to bring Alvar to places from his past, like the apartment he'd been living in and the destroyed Neverseen hideouts they'd found. They'd also spent days exposing Alvar to random images and sounds and smells—even tastes—trying to trigger a hint of familiarity.

None of it had caused even the tiniest flashback.

And she was starting to think that nothing ever would.

"I'm not saying I trust Alvar," she said, turning to stare at the hundreds of empty seats. "But I also know how terrifying it is to stand in this room and face the Council, and I can't imagine going through it without even remembering why I'm on trial. I mean . . . Alvar's future is being decided by a past he doesn't believe is his."

"But it *is* his," Keefe argued. "It's not like we're making this up. He helped kidnap you and Dex, and he helped them grab Wylie and torture him, and he helped abduct your human family—and that's only the stuff we know about. I saw what he was like when I was pretending to join the Neverseen. He was *all in*. One-hundred-percent committed to their cause, no matter what they asked him to do. And he'd still be just as dedicated if they hadn't gotten rid of him—if that's really what happened. Do you want to let him off the hook just because they wiped his mind to keep him from telling us their secrets?"

"No. But keeping him locked up in that miserable cell still feels . . . unfair, somehow."

"Ugh, you elves overthink everything," Ro grumbled. "It's simple: A traitor's a traitor, and they need to be punished so everyone understands there are consequences for treason. If you're not willing to end him, lock him up and destroy the key. Or better yet, leave it hanging in his line of sight so he has to stare at it forever, knowing he'll never be able to reach it."

"For once the ogre princess and I agree," Sandor added.

Sophie sighed. "Well, I guess it's a good thing I don't have to make the decision."

"It is," Keefe agreed. "'Cause I'm pretty sure Fitz is going to have a meltdown if the Council gives Alvar anything less than a life sentence."

The idea made Sophie cringe.

The elves called their life span "indefinite," because so far no one had ever died of old age. So if Fitz got his wish, Alvar would be spending thousands of years locked in his stuffy, miserable cell—maybe even millions.

Keefe moved back to her side, leaning in to whisper. "I do get what you're saying, Foster. Punishing the bad guys is supposed to be easier than this—and way more fun."

"Yeah," Sophie said quietly. "I've been angry at Alvar for so long, I never thought I'd end up feeling sorry for him."

"Aaaaaaaaaaaaaaaaand this is why we're going to be stuck here for hours," Ro whined.

"Nah, I'm sure the Council already made their decision," Keefe told her. "They're just putting on a good show for the Vackers."

"Wanna bet?" Ro's grin looked dangerous when she added, "I say we'll be here until sunset—and if I'm right, you have to wear ogre armor to school, instead of your uniform."

Keefe smirked. "No big deal. I would rock that metal diaper. But *I* say that this hearing will be done in an hour—and if I'm right, you have to call me Lord Hunkyhair from now on."

Sophie shook her head. "You guys are terrible."

"That's why you love us!" Keefe draped his arm around her shoulders. "You should get in on this, Foster. I'm sure that devious mind of yours can come up with some particularly humiliating ways to punish us if we're wrong."

She probably could. But no way was she risking having to wear a metal breastplate to Foxfire. Ro's looked like a medieval corset paired with spiked metal bikini bottoms.

"Hard pass," she told him.

Keefe heaved a dramatic sigh. "Fiiiiiiiiiine. I guess I can't blame you, since I already owe you a favor. Any thoughts on what my penance is going to be, by the way? Don't think I haven't noticed how long you've been stalling."

"I'm not *stalling*," Sophie insisted. "I just . . . haven't figured out what I want."

"Yeah, I know." The teasing tone faded from his voice, replaced with something that made Sophie very aware of how close they were standing. "Take your time," he told her, the words mostly a whisper. "Just . . . let me know when you figure it out. Because I—"

The doors to the hall burst open, cutting off whatever else he was going to say.

"Oh good. Here comes the elf parade," Ro muttered.

"The *Vacker* parade," Keefe corrected. "And get ready for it. They're the sparkliest of us all."

They really were.

Sophie's jaw even dropped a little as she watched the legendary family filing into the hall in their elaborate gowns and perfectly tailored jerkins and jeweled capes. She'd thought she was used to the extreme wealth and ageless beauty of the elves. But the Vackers *demanded* attention in a way she didn't know how to explain. There was something striking about each and every one of them—which was extra impressive considering how different they all looked from each other. She spotted every hair color, skin color, feature shape, and body type. It probably shouldn't have caught her by surprise—the family line went back thousands of years, and elves didn't separate themselves by appearance the way humans often did. But she was so used to how closely Fitz, Biana, and Alvar resembled their parents that she'd foolishly imagined all their relatives with similar dark hair and pale coloring.

She studied everyone as they passed, hoping she'd catch a glimpse of Fallon Vacker—Fitz and Biana's great-great-great-great-great-great-great-great-great-great-great-great-great-great-great-great-great-great-grandfather. She'd been trying to meet with him for months, hoping he could tell her more about why he'd sentenced Vespera to the Lumenaria dungeon. But he'd been annoyingly uncooperative.

There were quite a few males with pointy ears, but Sophie

didn't know any other details about Fallon's appearance to help her narrow it down. And she couldn't ask Keefe—the hall was *way* too quiet. No one said a word as they climbed the auditorium's stairs and took their seats.

And yet, somehow, the silence grew thicker when the doors opened again and Alden and Della strode into the hall, followed by Fitz and Biana and their goblin bodyguards—Grizel and Woltzer.

Sophie had seen her friends shattered by grief, shaking with anger, sobbing with hysterics—even battered and bloody and half-dead. But she'd never seen them looking so . . . timid. Their clothes were dark and boring, and they kept their teal eyes focused on the floor. Biana even disappeared for longer between her steps than her vanishing ability usually caused.

So did Della, who'd worn her long hair pulled back into a simple knot, along with a gown and cape that were dull gray, without any frills.

Alden's cape and jerkin were equally plain.

Not that any of it helped them draw less attention.

The air in the room shifted, turning hotter and heavier with each stare sent their way—a blast of searing judgment aimed at the family of Vackers who'd brought scorn upon the name. And Fitz and Biana seemed to shrink under the weight of it, ducking their chins and picking up their pace as angry murmurs echoed all around them.

Sophie tried to think of something to say as they drew closer, but her mind wasn't cooperating—and for once Keefe didn't seem to have a joke ready to go. So she was forced to go with the less-than-inspiring, "Hey."

Biana's head snapped up. "Whoa, what are you guys doing here?"

"Your dad didn't tell you he got us in?" Keefe asked, dropping his arm from Sophie's shoulders when he noticed Fitz frowning at them.

"I wanted it to be a surprise," Alden explained. "I hope that's okay."

"Of course it is!" Biana practically tackled Sophie with her hug—but Sophie hugged her back as gently as she could.

Biana kept claiming that she'd recovered from the brutal injuries she'd suffered in Nightfall, but Sophie had noticed that Biana always wore long sleeves now and chose gowns and tunics that covered her neck and shoulders.

"By the way, you look awesome," Biana said, pulling away to admire Sophie's dress. "Now I'm wishing I braided my hair or something."

"Oh please, you look amazing," Sophie assured her. "Like always."

It wasn't a lie.

Even in a hall full of Vackers, Biana managed to shine.

So did Fitz—though Sophie was trying not to notice.

"Hey, Fitzy," Keefe said, elbowing Fitz's side. "Wanna join our bet on how long this Tribunal is going to last? You get to name your terms—oh, but if you lose, you'll have to wear a metal diaper to school and call me Lord Hunkyhair from now on."

"Uh . . . yeah, *no*," Fitz said as Biana asked, "Hunkyhair?"

"*Lord* Hunkyhair," Keefe corrected. "What? It's accurate." He tossed his head like he was in a shampoo commercial. "I think we need to make it a thing either way—don't you, Foster?"

"I think you're ridiculous," Sophie told him.

Then again, Biana was giggling. And Fitz's lips were twitching with the beginning of a smile. Even Alden and Della had relaxed a little.

But everyone turned serious as Alden motioned for them to follow him toward a narrow silver staircase that led up to a platform with a row of chairs facing the Councillors' thrones.

Fitz offered Sophie his arm, and she tried to ignore the way her insides fluttered at the gesture. He was probably only doing it because everyone knew that climbing things without tripping wasn't one of her strengths—particularly when she was wearing heels. But her face still grew warm as she hooked her elbow around his.

It got even warmer when he told her, "I'm glad you're here."

"So am I."

She meant it, even though the buzz in the room was shifting—and she caught enough scattered words to know they were now talking about her.

"*. . . raised by humans . . .*"

"*. . . genetically altered . . .*"

"... *Project Moonlark* ..."

There were also a few mentions of "matchmaking" in the mix, and Sophie decided she did *not* want to know what they were saying. Especially when she noticed Keefe's smirk.

Fitz guided her to a chair on the far left of the platform and took the seat next to her, with Keefe sitting on his other side, followed by Biana, then Della, and Alden on the end. All the bodyguards took up positions behind them.

"Where's Alvar going to be?" Sophie whispered, noticing that there were no empty seats.

Alden pointed to a portion of the floor that had a square pattern. "That platform will rise once he's standing on it."

"He has to face the Council alone," Della added quietly.

"And it looks like our time starts *now*," Keefe told Ro as two dozen heavily armed goblins marched into the hall and took up positions around the Councillors' thrones.

"They call *that* security," Ro huffed. "I could take them down without even drawing a dagger."

Fanfare drowned out Sandor's reply—which was probably for the best. And Sophie's insides squished together as all twelve Councillors shimmered onto the platform in their gleaming silver cloaks and twinkling circlets.

Ro snorted. "Wow. Do the jewels in their crowns *seriously* match their thrones?"

"I suppose you'd rather we ink our adornments to our skin?" Councillor Emery called back.

His deep, velvety voice bounced off the emerald walls—but Ro didn't look the least bit intimidated as she reached up and traced one of her pink claws over the tattoos swirling across her forehead.

"I doubt you guys could handle the pain," she told him.

"I think you'd be surprised what we can bear," Councillor Emery responded.

His skin was usually a shade similar to his long dark hair—but whatever memories inspired his statement had turned him slightly ashen.

"But that's not what we're here to discuss," he added, taking a seat in his sapphire-encrusted throne, which matched both his circlet and his eyes. "I know many in this hall have important assignments to return to. So let's not waste time."

"Did you hear that?" Keefe asked Ro as the other Councillors sat in their respective thrones. "They're *not* going to waste time."

"Psh—like that's going to last," Ro told him.

"Bring in the accused!" Emery commanded, and four additional goblin warriors marched into the hall, flanking a hooded figure who blinked in and out of sight with every step, just like his mother and sister.

Alvar had never been as effortlessly attractive as his younger siblings, but he'd always made up for it with immaculate clothes, perfectly gelled hair, and a build that looked like he'd spent hours working out every day. He would've been horrified by the scrawny, battered person he'd become. His loose gray cloak seemed to swallow him, and greasy strands of his dark hair hung in his pale blue eyes.

But worst of all were the curved red scars marring his gaunt face.

"The Council better get this right," Fitz whispered as the platform raised Alvar to the Councillors' height.

"State your name for the record," Councillor Emery ordered.

Alvar gave a wobbly bow and drew back his hood. "I'm told it's Alvar Soren Vacker."

"You sound as if you don't believe that to be the case," Emery noted.

"I don't know what I believe," Alvar told him. "Like I keep telling you, I have no memory of my past."

Fitz reached for Sophie's hand when Councillor Emery closed his eyes. As spokesperson for the Council, Emery's job was to telepathically mediate all arguments, to ensure the Councillors presented a unified front for the audience.

Several long seconds passed—and Ro's grin widened with each one—before Emery asked Alvar, "Do you understand why we've brought you before us today?"

Alvar bowed again. "I understand that certain charges have been raised against me. But I have no way to verify them."

"Are you implying that we're liars?" a sharp voice barked.

All eyes shifted to Councillor Bronte, the oldest member of the Council—with the pointy ears to prove it, along with the piercing stare of an elf who could inflict pain on anyone he wished with a simple glance.

Alvar shrank back a step. "Of course not. I'm just . . . emphasizing my predicament. You keep outlining my crimes, but I feel no connection to any of it. Just like I feel no connection to anyone in this room, even though I'm told you're my family." He glanced behind him, studying the intimidating crowd before his eyes settled on Alden and Della. "I wish I could remember you. I wish I could remember *anything*. But since I can't, all I'll say is . . . whoever did these horrible things that you've accused me of—that's not me. Maybe it used to be. And if that's the case, I'm truly sorry. But I promise I'm not that person anymore."

"Right," Fitz muttered, loud enough for the word to echo off the walls.

"I understand your skepticism," Councillor Emery told him. "We have doubts as well."

"Then let me prove myself!" Alvar begged. "I realize the chance of regaining my freedom is slim. But if you *did* decide to grant it—"

"We'd be endangering the lives of everyone in the Lost Cities," Councillor Emery finished for him. "Whether you remember your past or not, your connection to the Neverseen poses a threat we cannot ignore."

Alvar's shoulders slumped.

"But," Emery added, and the whole room seemed to suck

in a breath, "your current imprisonment also creates quite the conundrum."

Fitz's hand shook and Sophie tightened her hold, twining her gloved fingers with his as Councillor Emery closed his eyes and rubbed his temples.

Ro leaned down and whispered to Keefe, "Settle in for a long debate, Betting Boy. And get ready to prance around school in our tiniest armor."

Keefe shrugged.

But Emery stood, pacing twice along the platform before pausing to face Alvar. "I'll admit, none of us are entirely comfortable with what I'm about to say—but we're also not willing to issue a sentence while there are so many uncertain variables."

"WHAT?" Fitz blurted, jumping to his feet.

"We understand that this is an emotionally challenging situation for you," Emery told Fitz. "That's why I'm tolerating your interruptions. But surely you can agree that the primary goal of any punishment must be to prevent further crimes from being committed. And we cannot determine what's necessary for your brother in that regard until we discover who he is *now*. We need to witness how he interacts with others and study how he behaves in ordinary situations—which cannot happen in his isolated cell. But since we can't trust him either, we must move him to an environment where we can keep him constantly monitored and separated from our larger world while still providing ample opportunities for us to take his measure."

Sophie noticed the total lack of surprise on Alden's and Della's faces the same moment she realized that *this* was why she'd been invited for moral support.

A quick glance at Keefe told her he'd come to the same conclusion.

So neither of them gasped with the rest of the crowd when Emery announced the Council's decision. But she still felt a sour wave of dread wash through her when he said, "For the next six months, Alvar will be returning to Everglen."

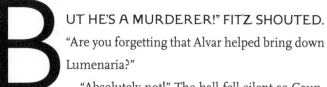

BUT HE'S A MURDERER!" FITZ SHOUTED. "Are you forgetting that Alvar helped bring down Lumenaria?"

"Absolutely not!" The hall fell silent as Councillor Terik rose from his emerald-encrusted throne.

Sophie hadn't seen him since the devastating Peace Summit, when the majestic castle had crumbled around them, and he actually looked better than she'd been imagining, given his injuries. His pale skin showed no sign of any scars, and his cobalt blue eyes were bright and clear. But when he stepped forward . . .

His right leg moved smoothly, but his left leg was much stiffer and slower. If it weren't for the silver cane he pulled from the folds of his cloak, he would've toppled over.

"As you can see, I'm still adjusting." He tapped his left leg with his cane, filling the hall with a soft clanking that confirmed what was hidden underneath the thick fabric of his clothes.

Elvin physicians were light-years ahead of human medicine, but even they couldn't regrow a severed limb. Instead, a team of Technopaths had built Terik a custom prosthesis.

But metal would never work exactly the same as muscle and bone.

In fact, when Terik took another wobbly step, he couldn't hide his grimace—which was probably why he told Fitz, "I understand your fury better than anyone. But . . . we must not let our anger make us overlook potential."

The last word rippled through the room as his meaning sank in.

"Yes," he said, tucking a loose piece of his wavy brown hair back under his emerald circlet. "I performed a new reading on Alvar."

Terik was the Lost Cities' only Descryer, which meant he could sense the potential of anyone he tested. But he rarely put the ability to use, claiming it caused too many problems.

He turned to study Alvar. "I told myself that if the results were the same as my prior reading, I'd push for a life sentence. But something's changed."

Alvar sucked in a breath. "What does that mean?"

"Truthfully? I have no idea," Terik admitted. "Readings can be difficult to interpret."

"Then how do you know he's not worse?" Fitz countered.

"I don't. Potential is a tricky thing. We have to live up to it in order for it to matter. But it shouldn't be ignored either—especially in a situation like this. We're all born with certain qualities. Certain limitations and abilities. But our experiences are what truly shape us. Everything we see and learn and do makes us who we are. And in Alvar's case, all of that has been wiped away. So we can't presume to know anything about him. Nor can we assume that he'll make the same choices he once did."

"Which is why we're giving you these six months," Emery told Alvar. "Prove yourself worthy, and we'll take it into consideration during your final sentencing. Fail to impress, and we'll make sure you never see daylight again."

"And don't expect any leniency," Councillor Alina—Sophie's least favorite Councillor—added. She tossed her dark hair, which gleamed with caramel-colored highlights as she rose from her peridot-covered throne. "The smallest mistake will end your trial period immediately. And you'll be sharing your apartment with two of our most trusted goblin warriors, who'll make sure we know everything you do."

Biana frowned. "What apartment?"

"A team of gnomes is building a separate residence for Alvar on our property," Alden explained. "Your mother and I figured that would be easier than having him in the main house."

Fitz whipped around. "So then you guys knew this was happening."

"Fitz," Della tried.

He shook his head, turning to Sophie and Keefe. "Did you know too? Is that why you're here?"

"They're here because I asked them to come," Alden jumped in. "I didn't tell them why. But yes, your mother and I found out this morning, when Councillor Terik stopped by to make sure the Council had our permission to move Alvar to our private property."

"And you gave it?" Biana asked, moving to Fitz's side, as if an invisible line had just been drawn between them and their parents.

Della sighed. "I know this isn't what either of you want to hear. But Alvar's our son—and your brother. We owe it to him to—"

"We don't owe him *anything*!" Fitz interrupted. "He betrayed us! And if you think he won't do it again, you're—"

"I'd think twice before resorting to insults," Councillor Emery warned. "This is the *Council's* decision."

Fitz clenched his jaw so tight, a muscle twitched along his chin.

Alden cleared his throat. "I know you're angry, Fitz. And I won't tell you not to be. But try not to make this a bigger deal than it is. It's six months of your life."

"A lot can happen in six months," a voice called from the

hall's entrance, with the same crisp accent that Fitz, Biana, and Alden all shared.

Whispers rustled through the crowd as a blond male wearing a pristine white cloak stepped the rest of the way through the doors. His face was all lines and angles, and his ears had the highest points Sophie had ever seen, so she wasn't completely surprised when Bronte said, "It's good to see you, Fallon. I wasn't expecting you to join us today."

"I wasn't expecting to be here," Fallon admitted, glancing behind him, like he was tempted to turn and flee.

Sophie craned her neck to get a better view of the notoriously reclusive Vacker—and for the first time, she understood why people often paired the word "handsome" with "devastating." His white-blond hair grew to a dramatic widow's peak, adding a severity to his perfectly chiseled features. But it was his eyes that demanded the most attention. Dark as a midnight sky and shining with an intensity that could only come from millennia of wisdom.

"Well . . . we're glad you could make it," Emery said as all twelve Councillors gave a slight dip of their heads. The gesture wasn't a bow, but Sophie suspected it was meant to acknowledge the fact that Fallon wasn't just a former Councillor. He'd been one of the three founding members, serving for nearly a thousand years before he resigned to marry Fitz and Biana's great-great-great-great-great-great-great-great-great-great-great-great-great-great-great-great-great-great-great-grandmother.

Councillors weren't allowed to have husbands or wives or children in case it biased their decisions.

Fallon wrung his hands as he gazed around the room. "Forgive my tardiness. I prefer the solace of home. It's the only place where my mind doesn't struggle to separate what *is* from what used to be. I don't know how you bear it, Bronte."

"It helps to stay immersed," Bronte told him. "Keep myself fully in the present."

"I suppose." Fallon's eyes glazed over as he stared at some distant point. "But the world has grown . . . exhausting."

Silence followed, until Emery said—with the slightest hint of irritation—"I assume you have a reason for interrupting our proceedings."

Fallon blinked hard, dropping his hands back to his sides. "I do. Or . . . I did. I think I lost track of it. What did I say again?"

"This guy's my new favorite," Ro whispered as she grabbed Keefe's shoulders and gave him a rough shake. "Get ready to show off those skinny legs at school."

"They're not skinny," Keefe muttered before he called to Fallon, "You said, 'A lot can happen in six months.'"

"Ah. Yes. That does sound familiar. And a lot *can* happen." Fallon stared at his fingers, twisting them around each other. "But there was something else I was going to add . . . and I seem to have lost my hold on it."

Ro snickered through another long stretch of silence, and Sophie tried not to smile at the way Keefe squirmed.

Eventually Emery said, "Well, you're welcome to visit our offices whenever you remember. But for now, we must get back to the matter at hand." He turned to Alvar. "We'll move you to Everglen as soon as—"

"Everglen!" Fallon repeated. "That's what it was!" He stepped closer, into the shadow of the Council's thrones. "You don't think it's imprudent to send him home?"

"Why would it be?" Emery asked.

"I can think of two reasons," Fallon told him. "For one, Everglen is an Ancient property. In fact, I believe some of the original structure still stands."

"One room does, yes," Alden agreed. "The space I use for my personal office has been there since the beginning. Why does that matter?"

"I can't say for certain." Fallon's eyes shifted to Bronte. "But things from our past are often more than they seem."

Sophie's heart paused at that, and her mind ran through a list of the lies she'd already helped uncover.

The Four Seasons Tree. Nightfall. Even the reason the elves sank Atlantis and severed all ties with humans.

All of those had turned out to be very different from what their Mentors taught in elvin history—if the stories had been mentioned at all.

The Lost Cities wasn't a bad place. But it wasn't the ideal world everyone wanted it to be either. And it had a *lot* of buried secrets.

CPSIA information can be obtained
at www.ICGtesting.com
Printed in the USA
LVHW091027110520
655304LV00005BB/1423

9 781481 497411